1979

Harry Ka

University of St. Francis
GEN 813 F251r
Fast

S0-BQX-753

The Howard Fast Reader

By Howard Fast

The Howard Fast Reader

A COLLECTION OF STORIES AND NOVELS

BY HOWARD FAST

CROWN PUBLISHERS, INC., NEW YORK

LIBRARY
College of St. Francis
JOLIET, ILL.

© 1960 by Howard Fast

Copyright © 1938, 1941, 1942, 1944, 1945, 1946,
1947, 1948, 1949, 1950, 1955, 1959
by Howard Fast

Library of Congress Catalog Card Number: 60-8629

Printed in the United States of America

Contents

813
F251r

12-18-79 Edition $6.01

88324

The Howard Fast Reader

The Man
Who Looked
Like Jesus

O~N A COOL~, clear summer morning, as my wife and I were walking down Dwight Morrow Street in Cuernavaca, down from the hilltop toward the old market, we saw a man riding on a little donkey—or burro, as they call them there—and he looked like Jesus Christ. You might observe that no one knows just what Christ looked like, but there is a face that has formed with time and taken shape in ten thousand paintings and sculptures, and this was the face of that man.

He was Indian. He wore an old poncho and a flat-brimmed hat, and his long hair hung down under the hat on either side of his sensitive face. His face was filled with sorrow, as so many faces in Mexico are, and his dark, beautiful eyes reflected a burden as large as a heavy wooden cross. His saddle was a homemade, hand-carved and crude wooden affair, and the two small milk cans slung on either side of the pommel and the thong sandals on his feet showed that he was a peasant who had come into the city to sell the milk of his few goats. He rode slowly, and his thoughts as well as his sight must have been turned inward, for he seemed to see nothing at all but his own cares and memories.

We stared at him directly and impolitely, for we could not help but stare at him, and after he had passed by, we looked at each other in wonder; for it is not a very common experience for anyone to see the living image of Christ riding on a donkey.

We talked about it as we did our shopping, and then we took our basket of food to the plaza, the village square, so that we might sit and drink a cup of the wonderful Mexican coffee and enjoy the morning sunlight before we walked home.

When we reached the plaza, we saw sitting alone at a little table in front of the cafe, the man whom we always thought of as "the exile," and because he was witty and charming and gentle, we were delighted to join him and have our coffee with him.

Of course, there are many exiles of one sort and another in

1

Cuernavaca, as there have been for years and years, the Spanish Republican exiles and before that the German exiles, and before that exiles from all over Latin America; for if one has to be an exile, where is there a town as beautiful, as gentle and mellow as Cuernavaca? At one time, not so long ago, there was a considerable colony of exiles, but that colony had dwindled, as one by one the refugees either moved to the urban satisfactions of Mexico City or gave way to homesickness and the pressures of poverty, and returned to face whatever awaited them in their own land.

Symbolically, only "the exile" remained that summer when we were there. For the moment, he was the last in Cuernavaca. He was filled with sadness and grief because he had burned so many bridges between himself and his home and because the path was so tangled and impossible now, but he covered his grief and depression with wry humor and ironic commentary. He knew that he evoked pity, but he resented such a role, and he greeted us impishly and caustically.

After we had ordered coffee, my wife told him, "We saw Christ riding on a donkey to the market place."

"Ah?"

I explained, sipping my coffee and looking out at the green and white sun-drenched square, the old Palace of Cortez, and the bowl of incredible mountains all around us.

"I am not surprised," he said. "In Mexico, anything can happen. Consider, four hundred years ago, this country was nailed to a cross by the Christian Spaniards. The national anthem became the song of the whip. Why does it surprise you to meet Christ on Dwight Morrow Street? This is a most likely place for him."

"You're not impressed?"

"Fewer and fewer things impress me. Being an exile breeds an inevitable cynicism. Anyway, I find this a curious reaction on the part of two people who consider themselves materialists."

"What we saw was quite material," my wife said. "It was an Indian man on a donkey."

"That is what was there, no doubt," "the exile" pointed out. "What you saw, as you have been telling me, is Christ."

We talked a while longer, "the exile" gently prodding us and making us feel increasingly credulous, and finally, with a little less than an apology, we were ready to admit that it was a trick of our imagination; and over the next several days, the matter faded from our minds. Then, one day, we met Dr. Arno Serente on the street, and I happened to mention to him that I was troubled with a large and painful boil, and he suggested that I drop by at his office and allow him to lance it. I didn't think the boil was that important, but Dr. Serente loved to talk about things in America and in other places of the world, and he was also a very interesting and colorful talker, so I agreed to stop by that afternoon.

He too had been an exile once, but for so long, so very long that he appeared to have forgotten, and he was a part of Cuernavaca, his longing to return to his own beloved Spain put away, compartmentalized, deep down inside him, and his life full of his little black bag, his rushing to and fro, and poor Mexican patients who could never afford the money to pay him, and rich American alcoholics whom he overcharged and from whom he made his living.

He had been a captain in the Spanish Republican Army, and finally had been driven across the Pyrenees with thousands more and his wife too, and the end of his long odyssey was Mexico, with the clothes on his back and not a penny or a franc or a centavo in his pockets. But that was fifteen long years ago, and even long ago were the days when he had practiced in little Indian villages where you go in on muleback because there are no roads, no dirt roads or wagon tracks even; and now he was successful, as such things go, with a pleasant house and an office and a nurse, eating three meals a day and with the feel of good money in his pockets. Spain lingered on the way a dream does, but also like a dream, it blurred over the edges, until bit by bit, Serente faced and accepted resignation and the permanence of his existence here. "I will return someday," remained locked away in a precious part of his soul, but that day had no place on the calendar.

His office was in a little brick and plaster building past the market, and you went into a brown, dirty, ancient hallway and up a flight of stairs to a landing where a long bench and two chairs represented his waiting room and where a pile of ragged magazines in English or Spanish gave you temporary companionship with your misery. There I went at about three o'clock in the afternoon; and sitting sadly in the waiting room was the man of the donkey, the Indian who looked like Jesus Christ.

This time I was able to take a long, full look at him, without any of the magic of morning sunlight to confuse me, and I discovered that my wife and I had been right in our first reaction, that this man looked like Jesus Christ in the flesh, in old, work-worn Indian clothes.

When one is for any time in Mexico, one comes to accept the sorrow in a Mexican face, even as the face itself accepts the sorrow; but some hold that no faces on earth are so beautiful as the dark, lined Indian faces of that unhappy land, and therefore the sorrow is never a commonplace. It is an intrusion, a deformity, for here are a people made for the sunlight of happiness—and always there is the mystery of how sorrow can be etched so deeply. Thus it was etched here, and I had to know something of it and, in my very bad Spanish, I asked the man whether he was waiting for the doctor.

"No, for my daughter," he said, and then he went on to explain that she was in there with her mother, and that she was very sick. He had the incredible forbearance of most plain Mexicans and when you spoke his language, even so badly, he unlocked some of his heart. He had a rich, pleasant voice, a tender voice, and even before he told me that his little girl was everything in the world to him, it was obvious that he was a man concerned for children. He explained that his daughter was twelve years old, and that it was both their fortune and misfortune to have no other children. Their misfortune because a man with no son looks forward to a tired old age, especially a small farmer like himself, with only a hut and a little plot of land and a few goats, all of which give sparingly and with only the most sedulous care; yet it was also their fortune to have a child like this one and to be able to lavish all their love upon her, for—as he pointed out to me—a child who gets a full measure of love grows like a single plant in a rich, loamy river valley, waxing both strong and beautiful.

Not all of this did I understand, missing a word here and there; but I understood all when the mother and child came out of Serente's consulting room, for the child was beautiful enough to take my breath away, and the mother still retained a similar beauty from her youth and happiness. Though they were frightened by the consultation and doctors' offices in general, and though the mother's eyes were full of the moist focus of grief, it did not lessen their beauty but rather increased and accentuated it. They sat down to wait while Serente called in the man as the father and head of the family. I could not talk to them. I only sat and looked at them sometimes, and then the father came out, and managed, before he left with his terror, to fulfill the requirements of courtesy with, "A good afternoon, Señor, and goodbye."

Then they went down the stairs and Serente called me into his consulting room.

The boil was soon done with. "That man who was outside," I said. "Have you ever thought, Arno, of whom he resembles?"

"He looks like any other Indian, I suppose."

I told him about the morning on Dwight Morrow Street and what our reaction had been.

"It is wonderful to be a writer, because then you see nothing just as it really is, and I suppose that is necessary."

"No more necessary to a writer than it is to a physician."

"Then it was the burro."

"The trouble with so many people and a lot of writers too is that they stop seeing anything."

"Perhaps it is your business to see as much as you can and our peace of mind to see as little. And that's as it may be. My wife wants to know whether you can join us at dinner tomorrow, where we are having a young and honest and very brave labor leader from Mexico City, and he also wants to meet you."

"Why do you Mexicans always use *brave* the way it is not meant to be used at all?" I asked rather peevishly.

"In the first place, and regretfully, I am not a Mexican but a Spaniard, and in the second place, the word is quite correctly used in our language. It is only when I translate it into English that it becomes incongruous, and that is either because you have no word of your own to match it properly or because the whole concept of bravery is distasteful to the North American."

"I don't want to engage in a discussion of semantics. We will be happy to come for dinner because you have a charming wife, a beautiful garden, and good food."

"The difference between you and most North Americans," he smiled, "is that you are consciously insulting, and they quite unconsciously achieve the same effect. At seven o'clock then."

I promised to come, and then as I turned to leave, I asked him about the little girl who was the patient before me, expressing the hope that she was not very sick and would soon be well.

"I'm afraid she's very sick," Serente said.

"Oh? But surely she can be cured?"

"I'm afraid not," he differed calmly.

"You mean she has a fatal illness? My God, man, how can you stand there and talk about it that way?"

"How else shall I talk about it? I am a doctor, and my concern is with sick people, not now and then, but twelve and fifteen hours a day. And many of them die. Here in Mexico more seem to die than in other places."

"Do you mean that she's going to die?"

"I'm afraid so."

"No—no, that's impossible. It's not possible that a child as young and beautiful as that should be condemned to death."

"My dear North American friend," he said patiently, "what have youth and beauty to do with it? The child is very sick."

"Granted that she is—this is not the Middle Ages. We live in a time of antibiotics, of all sorts of miracle drugs and miracle surgery. Surely you can do something—"

"I can do nothing," he said sourly, turning to put his instruments back in the sterilizer. "Where you live, it may be an age of antibiotics and so forth. Here it is still a good deal of the Middle Ages. Furthermore, you are being sentimental, and I wonder whether you are sincere."

"Now it's your turn to be insulting."

"Not at all. The fact of the matter is that I live and work here. But because you have been emotionally moved by the sight of an Indian peon on a donkey and the fact that his little girl is beautiful —not an unusual thing with the Mexicans, you will admit—you have raised the issue of this child's sickness as if I could save her but will not."

"And can you?" I insisted.

"I can not. First of all, she is suffering from a severe kidney ailment. One of her kidneys must be removed, and even then it is anyone's guess whether the other could heal to any extent to take over the burden."

"But there is a chance. You have just said so."

"I have said nothing of the sort. Do not turn your thoughts into my words, please. How are her parents to pay for an operation— they have not even money to pay for their calls here? My fee from you is fifty pesos; if they can pay one, it is a lot, and an operation must cost two thousand pesos, that is, without the cost of a trip to Mexico City, and living there and extras like hospital and anesthesia and drugs and heaven knows what. That is, considering that they would consent to an operation, and a very dangerous operation, you must know."

"How could they not consent to something that might save the child's life? Surely it's plain that they love her. The father told me that she is their only child."

"Surely it is not plain. Everything that might be plain to normal people," Serente said bitterly, "is turned on its head for a *gringo*. Please, I'm not being insulting and only angry at myself and the world I live in. I like you and admire you, but you share the worst characteristics of your countrymen, not the least of which is to endow the entire world with your mental processes. For fifty years, your people have been educated to the fact that operations are beneficial, even when they are not necessary. But to plain, poor people who have never seen a hospital, an operation is a terrible and frightening thing. And if the patient dies in spite of the operation, they conclude that it is murder. Anyway, it is out of the question. There is no money."

"I can spare the money—"

"Can you? Name of God, will you spare the money to operate on a hundred patients of mine who need operations just so urgently? Will you declare yourself God to decide who shall live and who shall perish? Or perhaps this will become a new game for the North Americans—an amusing lottery to see which Mexican deserves life—"

"Really, Serente, that's not called for."

"No, I suppose not. I'm sorry. But don't you think I have any feelings? Don't you suppose I saw the mother and the father and the child? Now why did I choose you for this scene? I don't know. This is every day for me, day in and day out, every day for every Mexican doctor. But why should I torture you, when you are already tortured enough?"

"You are not torturing me at all. I understand."

"How can you understand? I have been here fifteen years, and I still do not understand, and still I do the wrong thing because I have never been a peasant who in all his life never knew what it is not to be hungry, not to be cold, not to be sick. Yesterday morning a peon came in, with his wife and his son and daughter. Both children had been having bloody stools for months, but what a decision it was for them to pack up their household and journey thirty miles to the frightening city! Finally, they are here. They tell me and I examine the children, and to do anything for them I must know what organism it is. So I give the father two cardboard cartons with the children's names on them and tell him to have the children defecate in the boxes and then bring the stools back to me. He looks at me like a hurt animal, but after fifteen years I do not understand. I am too busy. I have too many other patients and I am insensitive. But of course he never returns. Why? Because to him, I am like a God, and when I tell him to bring me boxes of stools, it is some dreadful joke I am making on him, or an insult, or just horror. Does he know there are organisms that cause disease? Has he ever seen a microscope? So now, probably, the two children are dead, and it is my fault because I have forgotten the terrors and suffering of plain people. Well, enough. Come to dinner, and when I am your host, I will have to talk gently."

"Talk the way you want to talk," I said. "We will be there."

As I walked home from his office, I remembered that I had to stop by at the carpentry shop. It had long been a dream of my wife to use this vacation to do some sculpture, and a few days ago I had stopped at a little carpentry shop and had asked them to make an armature for me. I had wanted a very simple thing, a block of wood with a wooden upright about which the clay would be moulded. The carpenter understood immediately, and said he would have it in a day or two.

When I came into his carpentry shop now, the armature was ready. The carpentry shop itself brought me back to my earlier mood, for it was a place that reached back to the oldest memories of man's work with tools, bent-bow rawhide drills, the same drills one sees painted on Egyptian tombs, hand-made planes and hand-made saws, yes, even the adz unchanged from the Spanish adz that the conquistidores had brought to the land four centuries ago, and even the nails they used were four-sided and hand-hammered. Sleepy, with its white front, the shop lay in the afternoon sunlight like a painted picture of some long, long ago, the two carpenters, in their leather aprons, with their work-hardened hands and their fine brown faces, in the picture and of the picture, yet possessed of that particular and peculiar quality which the carpenter, of all workers, has—a singular relationship to tools and wood and people, a gentleness of visage, a certain contemplation of life, a particular warmth and oneness with the world around him and its people. This is not my imagination; I have worked with carpenters and seen them in many places and situations, in Europe and Asia, in Maine and Vermont and California, in my home, on a job, and as prisoners working in prison, and always the quality is there.

"Here is your armature, Señor," the older of the two carpenters said to me, holding it out to me, a marvel of beauty and workmanship which made me gasp with astonishment, a base of polished mahogany, the upright jointed into it, the whole finished and polished like a piece of precious furniture. "It must cost four pesos," which is thirty-two cents in American money. And then, seeing my face, he asked whether that was too much money. I answered, no, that it was very little money, too little money for the work he had done and the beautiful wood he had used. No, I said, my astonishment was due to the fact he had taken such pains to make it beautiful.

"And why should it not be beautiful, Señor?"

The question posed itself with no answer, for behind the meaning of beauty to this man lay a thousand years of culture and experience of which I knew all too little, and could comprehend even less. It brought to mind the unending stream of peasants and workers who travel far in Mexico to look at the paintings that bedeck their walls and buildings as no other buildings in all the world are bedecked. I took the armature from him, paid him, and went home. . . .

I saw the priest the next day. It came about quite by accident, for my wife and I and the children had wandered into the great cathedral with no other thought than to see what the old rock and mountain of a place contained, but soon the cold gloom of the church drove the children back into the sunlight and my wife went after them, leaving me to contemplate alone the mass of jewel-laden images, the ancient murals, the gold and silver candlesticks, the silks and tapestries and precious stones—all of it gathered here in the wet twilight, shut off by wall and darkness from the bright Mexican sunlight and the heartbreaking Mexican poverty. I must have been entirely lost in contemplation when the priest addressed me, for I was entirely unconscious of his approach and rather startled when he said, "You like our cathedral, Señor?"

"I don't know that I have thought about liking or disliking it. I am impressed by it."

"Then Señor is not a Catholic," which was more a statement of fact than a question. His English was excellent, and I remarked upon that. "Yes, I studied English in Spain."

"But you are not Spanish, you are Mexican." He was obviously Mexican, a heavy-set, fleshy man of about fifty, with the round, healthy look that some priests have. I told him briefly the story of the man on the donkey who looked like Jesus Christ and of his daughter and her sickness. Was there nothing he could do, I wanted to know?

"And why do you ask a priest?" he said.

"I think because there is no one else to turn to."

"But this man—he is a Mexican, and he will turn to God."

"Perhaps, but that will not cure his daughter."

"Are you so sure, Señor? If it is God's will that his daughter should live she will live, and if it is God's will that she shall die, then she will die. Such things are ordained and not for you or me to decide."

"But isn't such an attitude old-fashioned, to say the least?" I asked carefully, considering each phrase before I spoke it. "There is a science of medicine and there are hospitals and surgeons and antibiotics, and surely you would not deny that people are helped by these things?"

"We talk at cross purposes, Señor," the priest smiled. "Do you believe in God?"

"That's somewhat of a personal question, isn't it?"

"And do you talk less personally, Señor? You see a man, who to you looks like our Savior. Would that occur to a Christian? You do not think twice before you pronounce your thoughts to me, blasphemous though it may be. And then when I ask you whether you believe in God, you feel I am asking a personal question. No, it is not antibiotics the Mexican needs, but faith."

"In other words," I said, no longer attempting to conceal my annoyance, "you remain unmoved by this story and have no intentions of doing anything about it."

"Quite the contrary; I am deeply moved, and I shall do something about it, more than you, I believe."

"May I ask what?"

"I shall pray," the priest said.

Dinner at Dr. Serente's was always a special treat. Not only was his lovely Spanish wife a charming and thoughtful hostess, not only were the people one met there always interesting and very often amusing, but the food was good, and when Mexican food is good, it is better than any in this hemisphere.

The Serente house was an old one, in the old Mexican style. The living quarters lay in one row, presenting a flat, characterless front to the street, the few windows barred, and the entrance through an arched carriage-way. But once inside, inside the walled quadrangle that contained house and garden, a veritable fairyland opened to one's view. A long veranda stretched the full length of the living-quarters, each room opening onto it, a veranda upon which the Serentes lived, entertained and ate, all the while facing the lovely garden. Like most of the best Mexican gardens, it was not very large, and owed its beauty to the intensity of its tropical green and to the variety of its trees and shrubs and the surprising velvet quality of its grass. In the twilight, as now, it became a place of utter enchantment, connected with our world only through the play-cries of the doctor's son, who was about ten years old, and his friends.

When my wife and I arrived, the labor leader was already present, a man of about thirty, heavy-set, broad-shouldered with a broad and warm Indian face. A few minutes later, "the exile" and his wife arrived, his wife a thin, weary woman with fine dark eyes and an air of incredible loneliness. A Chilean, a member of the Chilean Senate, completed the party. After we were all introduced, we sat around and sipped the excellent drinks the doctor served and talked, the conversation half in Spanish, half in English, flowing from one language into the other, the stiffness of the English soothed and modulated by the melodious lilt of the Spanish. The Chilean had been in Spain during the Civil War, and he and Serente's wife—whom he had known as a nurse then—recalled old memories, most of them tortured by time, defeat and resignation. The Mexican labor leader, whose name was Diego Gomez, was too young to recall those times, and Serente, to whom talk of Spain always brought sorrow, changed the subject by telling the story of how I had seen Christ riding down Dwight Morrow Street. He told it mockingly, watching my reaction, and then "the exile" pointed out what a charming title for a story it made, "Christ on

Dwight Morrow Street." What in the whole world could be as incongruous?

"Just Dwight Morrow Street," Mrs. Serente said. "Each time I hear it, I find it as unbelievable."

"Christ in Cuernavaca," Gomez said in Spanish. "There is the best title. Only I am dubious. Of all the places on earth, I feel that Cuernavaca will be the last for Christ to visit if He returns."

"And why?"

"Isn't it obvious?" Gomez said. "The sorrows of Mexico are doubly visited here. My people, who have an affection for pungent phrases, explain all that afflicts them by pointing out that Mexico is too far from God and too close to North America. You have peopled our plain Mexican saloons with your rich alcoholics, our dancehalls with your homosexuals and our lovely plazas and streets with your lean and ravenous and sexless women. You have built your great mansions all over our hills, and you dazzle us with your wealth. My sister-in-law's cousin, a plain peasant woman, works as a domestic for the Thompsons here, the one who used to be ambassador to the Argentine. She is paid one hundred and fifty pesos a month and she works seven days a week. Last week a Texas oil-man was visiting the Thompsons. He had too much to drink and he was courting Thompson's wife. As a gesture, he lit her cigarette with a twenty-dollar bill. Yes, each time she asked for a cigarette, he lit it with a twenty-dollar bill, four times—one thousand pesos—and only last year this woman, the domestic, this woman's child died because 250 milligrams of terramycin costs two pesos—"

"I know," my wife broke in, "that happens. But it isn't all of us. You don't judge a hundred and sixty million people by the Thompsons."

"Who am I to judge?" Gomez smiled. "We are talking of Christ in Cuernavaca."

"You see, the Mexican is always the center of the earth," the Chilean said gently. "Oh, what a people!"

"With good reason," Gomez said.

"Any Mexican reason is a good reason. Their ego would even include a monopoly of the world's suffering—a monopoly of all afflictions, including the United States."

"You are too kind to us."

"The trouble is," "the exile" said, "that no European can even begin to understand Mexico."

"With the possible exception of yourself," Serente put in.

"Possibly. I think I understand Mexico—in part, at least."

"I don't," the Chilean said comfortably. "Nor will I ever. I have even decided to stop trying. I have been here only three weeks, but I have decided that it is easier to love Mexico than to try to understand her."

"We are very easy to understand," Gomez said slowly. "We are plain people and very poor and our backs are bent because always upon them there has been either a Spaniard, or a North American. Why is that so hard to understand? Why does everyone complicate it so?"

"And when your backs are no longer bent?"

"You will see Mexico then," Gomez nodded. "It will be like this garden—all of it."

"But we have all forgotten the little girl," said my wife. "What will happen to her?"

"She will die," said Gomez flatly.

"And we must accept that?"

"I have never really understood," observed Serente, "why people come to Mexico to vacation."

"To see our cathedrals," said Gomez, and then I observed that we had seen one of them today, and that I had told my story to a priest.

"In your Spanish?" Serente snorted.

"He spoke English excellently."

"And did he listen attentively to your story?"

"Very attentively."

"And what did he say?"

"He said that the life or death of the little girl is up to God, and he resented my interference."

"The exile" smiled bitterly.

"Once together," nodded Gomez appreciatively. "A simple act that often takes many centuries to perfect."

"I don't like your smile," Serente's wife commented. "It's rather nasty."

"But homely. Don't you think we often confuse the two?"

Then the Chilean asked me, "But what made you think that the man's face was the face of Christ? How could you know?" He

used a Spanish idiom that confused me, and Serente had to translate the question.

"Well, there is a face. It's the face that reoccurs in most of the
paintings and sculptures."

"I wonder," the Chilean reflected. "There is so much speculation.
Rembrandt painted Jewish faces, if there is such a thing. When
the Spaniards came to our land, the Christ they brought had a
Spanish face, but little by little, our own painters and sculptures
made it a Chilean face, the patient, tired face of the Chilean miner
or the Chilean peasant. I don't understand why you felt so strongly
that this was the face and figure of Christ."

"Neither do I," said Serente. "The man has been a patient of
mine, and it never occurred to me."

His wife said, "Things occur to writers that would never occur
to you. That is why they are writers. But really we must come to
dinner. It's an interesting dinner, but it will spoil if it waits too
long."

More than that, it was a very good dinner, a wonderful dinner,
with hot *tortillas,* veal with *mole* over it, that ancient, incredible
chocolate sauce that the Aztecs perfected a thousand years ago,
frijoles, hot and whole in their own sauce, *arroz,* the good Mexican
rice, with chicken and shrimps to go with it, and *calavo,* mashed
with onions and garlic, fresh tomatoes and cucumbers, and cold
Mexican beer, which is as good as any beer in the world and better
than most.

The talk at dinner turned to other things—with a consequent
sense of relief to my wife and myself—and they talked of Mexican
art and of Chile, and then the difference between Mexican dances
and Spanish dances, and why so many Spaniards in Mexico owned
grocery stores, and how the super-highway between Mexico City
and Cuernavaca had been built by peons who were paid six pesos
a day. Then "the exile" spoke of University City, and the wonders in mosaic that Diego Rivera had wrought there, and the
Chilean asked whether it was not true that because the new university had been built so far from the city, the students lacked
bus fare to get there? It was true, Gomez admitted, admitting that
Mexico had the most magnificent university and possibly the poorest—in pesos—student body in the whole world.

So the evening went, a good evening, with warm people and good
talk and good food. None of these was a person who lived by the

secure retreat of talk and speculation; all of them had ventured
their bodies and souls in what they believed, and they knew the
winnings and the losses in the life they lived. And finally it was
over and time to go, the moon high in the sky which the brief
evening rain had washed so clean and pure, and we began to say
our goodbyes. Dr. Serente offered to drive us home, but Gomez,
who was staying with an uncle who lived near our hotel, said he
thought he would like to walk home because the night was so
fine, and we decided to walk with him. We said little as we walked
through the darkened streets, for when an evening such as this is
finished, it is hard to pick up new threads, and as a matter of fact
the silence was restful and comfortable. Because it was the shortest
direct way, we turned into Dwight Morrow Street after we had
crossed the empty plaza, and in the last block before we reached
Morales, we saw a man standing under the street light.

He was a telephone cable repair man, out on a late call, and he
had just climbed down from the cable pole. The light lit him and
magnified him as he stood there, legs spread, arms akimbo, a coil
of wire over one shoulder, a climbing rope slung over the other,
his tools in his leather belt and his feet in heavy leather climbing
boots. He stood there like a rock, his muscular body and his fine
chiseled Indian face of one piece and part, his cotton shirt open
at the neck, his lips parted in the slight smile of recognition that
honest folk have for one another so late at night. Gomez greeted
him softly and with dignity, and he in turn returned the greeting
with the same calm dignity. There was no comment made, and
Gomez needed to make none. We said goodnight to Gomez, and
we went home. . . .

A day or so later, my wife, not willing to let the matter rest as
it was, went to see Serente and begged him to take money from
us to go through with the operation on the little girl; but as in
my own case, he was able to convince her that it was impossible.
He pointed out to her that he did not even know where these
people lived; he had no address for them; they had a few acres of
land, somewhere out in the hills; and unless they came to his office
again, he could not reach them. Better than I was able to, he
pointed out the overwhelming difficulties in what had seemed to
us to be a very simple matter. He also stressed that there was no
proof at all that the operation would be successful. "You offer

charity," he said to her. "You do it because you are kind and good. But I think you know what charity is. Charity is like facing a thousand hungry people with a crumb of food."

To us, our frustration was a lash on pity and sentimentality. In Mexico, where the dollar can buy twelve and a half pesos, the poorest American tourist is overcome with delusions of grandeur until the moment when he looks at himself. It is true that many never look at themselves, but some do—and for those there is at least a flash of insight in which they see themselves as others see them. . . .

About ten days more passed before we saw Serente again. His practice was an uneven one. If somewhere in the hills there was a sudden sweep of dysentery, of virus or of one of many other diseases, a flood of patients would overwhelm his office. The poor Mexicans knew he was Spanish—and Spaniards are not liked by Mexicans, whose memory is a long one—but they also knew that he never turned patients away, and there was many another doctor who would not look at a patient unless the pesos laid on his palm first, so his practice slackened only rarely. But then, one day, he turned up at our apartment at about two o'clock, haggard with the pressure of work, and said to me, "Either I get away for a few hours, or I go out of my mind. What do you have for this afternoon?"

"Like all afternoons here, I work hard at resting."

"Oh. Why can't I be a tourist?"

"You don't have the personality for it. Where do you want to go?"

"To a strange, wonderful place called Xocalco, an ancient city on top of a mountain. It is about thirty kilometers from here, and it will do us good to spend an hour there. It is very restful. Will your wife release you?"

"I think so. But I'm told I'm a sick man, so I wonder about climbing mountains."

"This one we can climb most of the way in my car. It will do you good, believe me, as a doctor." My wife agreed with him, and in a little while, Serente and I were in his car, speeding through the green, gleaming rice fields and then climbing into the great wall of mountains that lies south and west of Cuernavaca. Then we turned off the main highway onto a small side road through a broad, beautiful, but strangely uninhabited valley. Even the grass

huts and little patch fields of the peasants were missing here, nor
was there a burro to be seen munching the grass or a bullock
pulling a wooden plow against the horizon.

We drove on until Serente pointed to a hulking purple mass.
"There it is," he said, and I commented that it was very high and
that it hardly seemed possible that a car could climb it. "Perhaps,
but the old Mexicans built a stone roadway up to the place, and
much of it still remains and the rest is dirt fill. They were mighty
workers in stone, and a very great people, and their works dwarf
the antiquities that we Europeans admire so. Mexicans are very
proud, and one of the reasons is that they have not forgotten the
old times."

"Others have."

"Yes, others have."

Serente was an excellent driver. We turned off the road onto what
seemed to be only a dirt cow track, but after we had crossed several
fields, it emerged as a fairly good dirt road. It wound up the side
of the mountain, with ancient stonework buttressing the hillside
above it as well as the road below, and it went on and on, in endless
curves and convolutions, and as it mounted, the hills around us
rolled back and the whole broad vista of the valley below spread
out before us. Finally, we came to a place where the car could go
no further, and Serente parked in a small clearing, and from there
we went on by foot over the four or five hundred feet that remained
to the summit.

From Serente's description, I had anticipated an unusual sight,
but my thinking was shaped by the other ruins I had seen near
Mexico City and in the south. Those ruins represented years of
archaeological work, and this place had hardly been touched—only
a single pyramid excavated—yet in its vastness, in the grand purpose of the concept that had made it, in the immensity of its ruins,
it dwarfed anything I had seen before. It took my breath away.
It left me awe-stricken and speechless, and full of a sense of the
awfulness of time.

We had emerged on the top of a long, rolling plateau, and for
a mile of its length in front of us, and half a mile behind us, an
enormous dead stone city lay, dead and clothed all over with
verdure, but with here and there an outcropping of stone, a ledge,
a wall, a sill; and under the green cloak, the shapes remained,
mighty buildings, tall pyramids, sunken courts, giant columns with

only the base left, formal gardens where brightly dressed people had once walked, and fountains which had once picked the Mexican sunlight into all of its bright colors. We walked through its lonely emptiness, interlopers in time, and examined the single pyramid that had been uncovered. It was strange, different from any pyramid I had ever seen before, but precise and handsome in its workmanship. I asked Serente whether he knew what manner of people had once lived in this city. "They don't know yet," he replied, "but whatever they called themselves, we know that they were the same people as the peasants who live in the neighborhood now. The people who are fastened to the earth never change. They endure everything and survive everything—" But did they, I wondered? Serente had told me that at one time, it was estimated, ten thousand people lived in this city on a mountaintop, and how many tens of thousands had lived in the valley below to grow the food to feed these? But now the valley was silent and empty. I asked Serente.

"It is not empty. A few people still live there. They are the remnant of agony. Possibly at one time, a hundred thousand people lived in that valley below, and someday a hundred thousand people will live there again. Now only a handful are left. But they have not gone—no, they have not gone. Their children will plow the land, and the land will bloom."

We walked down the slope of the plateau to a ceremonial ballpark, looking up at the stands where the dukes and knights of the old Indian civilization had sat, and our thoughts filled in the panorama of bright color, of painted walls and painted gods, of banners flying and gold glittering. A little Indian boy joined us there, his flock of goats scattered behind him, munching among the ruins. "If the señores desire," he said, "I will show you where the priests of old lived." We said yes and gave him a peso, and his beautiful dark face lit momentarily with a smile of appreciation, and then he and his goats led us down a winding path to a broad ledge where a long row of houses had been partly excavated. They were invisible from above. "Who told you they are the houses of priests?" Serente asked him, and he replied, "When the curator comes from Mexico City, he instructs me carefully. He tells me that my own people built these houses, and that I must remember all I can, for someday we will rebuild them. When I am older, I will go to the university and study such things and be an archaeologist myself.

See, already I think about it. Look on that hillside there." He pointed to a mountainside toward the end of the plateau. "Do you see the even space between the trees—like a storm cut a swathe there? Well, I have decided that no trees grow there because a stone road lies beneath the grass, and even the curator did not know that until I pointed it out to him. Next week he will make what we call a *sinking* there. Do you know what a sinking is?" We said we did, and we followed him to other places and listened to more of his chattering and his uncanny childish wisdom.

When we said goodbye to him, he bowed formally with that courtly grace which so many Mexicans have and which no Mexican needs to be taught, and as a host, he invited us to come again and to bring our friends. "Because people do not know what lies on this mountaintop. You must tell them."

We returned to the car in silence, and in silence we drove down the mountain to the road below. Only when we were well on our way back did I ask Serente, "Is there any news of the little girl?"

"She died two days ago," Serente said evenly. "Yesterday, I went to the church where her body lay." I learned afterward that he had provided the money for the funeral, but he said nothing about that. "She was a beautiful child," Serente continued. "I wanted to weep. I am afraid I am becoming sentimental, like a North American, and with a few exceptions, I dislike North Americans as much as I hate sentimentality. You are one of the exceptions, my friend, and I am sure you have learned to forgive me for the things I say. Anyway, it will comfort you a little to know that in my opinion, she could not have been saved."

"It doesn't comfort me, and anyway, I think you are lying."

"Perhaps I am lying. What difference does it make? All children are beautiful, whether in Mexico or in North America."

The clouds were gathering as we entered Cuernavaca. Serente dropped me at the hotel, shook my hand warmly, and begged forgiveness. But no one could be angry at him, and therefore no one ever had any need to forgive him. I went upstairs to our apartment and told my wife about the afternoon. The children were still playing in the garden, and she suggested that we go out onto the terrace and smoke a cigarette, and then there would still be time before dinner for a drink in the restaurant downstairs. The terrace was a favorite place of ours at this time of the day, for during the rainy season, each evening presented a breathtaking and impressive spectacle. Most often, the clouds would begin to gather at about five o'clock, and from our terrace, one had a clear view of a mighty gorge in the mountains, down which a wild river ran. As the rain approached, this gorge would fill with dark green and purple clouds, and the clouds would appear to tumble down through the ravine, even as the river did. The whole vista then became unearthly, full of fright and grandeur and shot through with wild beams of sunlight, so much like an El Greco but so much more real and colorful.

As this took place, I told my wife what Serente had said about the little girl, and she nodded silently and woefully. Then the rain started, and we went down to the restaurant.

We ordered whiskey—and I proposed a toast. My wife nodded.

We drank to Mexico—to Mexico, the mother, who shelters the oppressed, the driven, the hungry, not to poor, bleeding Mexico, but to Mexico angry and proud.

We went back to our apartment, and our children were there, where they had fled from the rain, playing games of fear and defiance to the mighty peals of thunder, the savage arrows of lightning; and they saw our faces and asked what was wrong. We embraced them and held life in our arms, assuring them that nothing was wrong—only live and grow valiant and proud and strong!

About a week later, walking on Guerrero, the narrow, crowded market street of Cuernavaca, the street with the savage and defiant name, we saw him again, riding on his little donkey. "There he is!" my wife said to me, and as if in answer to her words, he raised his head. Oh, how his face had changed! The repose was gone; the peace was gone. We no longer saw Christ as one sees him in the thousand paintings and sculptures; we saw a Mexican peon, whose heart had filled to overflowing and had broken with the weight of sorrow.

Rachel

Pa sat on a stump with his elbows on his knees and his face in his hands, for the Lord only knows how long. Just like that, without moving and without eating. I cooked a piece of meat for dinner and offered him some, but he shook his head, and when I cooked a piece of meat for supper, he did the same. He just wouldn't eat and wouldn't move and wouldn't talk. So I went to sleep, and when I got up in the morning he was still sitting there.

I said, "Pa, how long you going to carry on this way?"

Then he looked over to the edge of his cleared land where there was some fresh dirt and a cross, and then he looked at me as if he had seen me for the first time in maybe six months.

I told him, "Pa, it's two days since Ma died, and you ain't moved from that stump. Sure, you'll starve to death."

Then he grinned a little and got down off the stump.

"Get out the skillet, Dave," he said. "We'll fry up some smoky."

So we sat inside the cabin with the pan of smoky between us, eating and looking at each other. I could see that Pa wanted to talk to me, but figured I was too young to be talked to. Instead, he smoked his pipe after he had finished eating. Then he got down Ma's old Bible, opened it, and set himself for writing with a piece of charcoal stick.

On the front inside cover of the Bible, which was the only book we had in the house, there were a lot of dates and places and names. Pa held the book a long way off, squinting at the writing. He was all right when it came to slow reading of block print, but not so good with writing.

"Births and deaths," he said slowly. "Back East, when kin passes, all the kinfolk gather for funeral doings. You wouldn't know, Davey, but it makes the heart easy. Here—well, here there ain't nothing but this Bible."

"It's a mighty pretty good book," I said.

"Sure it is, Davey, sure. But it ain't like kinfolk. A man can't rightly live and be human without kinfolk. How old are you, Davey?"

I figured awhile and then said, "Ten years, two months and maybe a for'night."

Pa figured and summed on his hands. "You were born third day of March, 1778, Davey. So this is the seventeenth day of May, 1788."

I nodded.

Pa fiddled for a while with the charcoal stick, then gave it to me. "You write it in, careful like, Davey."

I wrote out, "Susan Harvey died on the fifteen day of May, year of our Lord, 1788, of fever."

"Age twenty-nine," Pa said, his voice kind of hoarse. When I put that in, Pa read what I had written. "Put in Northwest Territory, Davey." Then he closed the Bible and put it back on its shelf.

He went outside, and I was afraid that maybe he had gone back to sitting on the stump with his face in his hands. But when I came out, he was harnessing the horse for plowing.

It was a week later when Pa made up his mind to go into the stockade. The stockade was called Murry's Fort, and it was the nearest place where there were folks and a store to buy and sell. It was thirty miles odd if you used the ford, and nearer forty if you took the ferry, and it was a mighty big place, with eighty-seven people living inside the walls and in the neighborhood. Mostly, I was shy of so many folks, but it was a wonder to see what they had to sell in that store.

Pa said that morning, "Dave, a boy like you can't run wild like a critter."

"Why not?" I demanded.

"Well, it ain't right. We ain't woodsy folk; we're proper farmers, and a man goes bad if he can't have bread with his meals and a stitched garment for his back. Your Ma had reading and writing, and I got a little, and it ain't proper you should go wild."

"I'm going to be a hunter," I said. "Just as soon as I can tote a rifle, I'm going off to hunt and trade with the Indians."

With that, Pa fetched me a smack across the head, the first since Ma had died.

"Davey, don't say that again," he whispered.

"Why?"

"You'll learn why. Maybe out here's the deep wilderness where you forget the word of God, but I ain't forgot. Menfolk in our family and in your ma's were farmers and smiths and maybe a doctor or a law man. But not no-account." And with that he went to saddling up the horse.

"We're going in to the stockade," he said.

"Why?"

"To get me a wife and you a ma."

"I won't have no other ma!" I yelled. "I'll be damned if I will!"

"Dave," he said quietly, "you put on your shoes and shut your mouth. You swear again and I'll tan your hide right off you. See if I don't."

I could tell that something came over Pa. He didn't seem easy, all the way in to the stockade. He kept muttering to himself, and he rode stiff in his black Sunday britches. We rode together, me behind him and holding onto his waist, and he held his gun away from his white Sunday shirt, so that he shouldn't dirty it.

The stockade sits across the river on a little hill; if you use the ford in dry season, the water runs under the horse's belly. The stockade isn't much for looks or size, and most folks live outside.

Pa and me, we forded the river with the low evening sun at our backs, with the water running like fat oil. We came up on out and Pa switched north, and for a moment I was glad, thinking maybe he had changed his mind. But he stopped in front of Parson Jackson's house, dismounted and lifted me down. The parson came around the house from the back, where he had been washing his face and hands in a bucket of water. The parson's wife poked her head out of the door, and the parson's four kids held back and stared at our horse. The parson's kids were townfolks, not woodsy but soft and small, and I didn't pay much attention to them.

"Good evening, Brother Harvey," the parson said. . . . " 'Evening, David. . . . It's a long time since you came in out of the woods."

"A long time," Pa agreed. "A man gets wanting for the sight of folks."

"Sometimes when preaching, Brother Harvey, I feel that my flock is scattered beyond call. With you out in the deep woods, with the Grants forty mile down the river, with the Sutters north in the wilderness—well, a man's voice carries just so far."

"I know," Pa said.

"And Mrs. Harvey?"

Then I began to whimper; what with riding the great distance to the stockade, with this and that, I had almost forgotten. I had hoped that Pa would forget too.

"Stop that, Davey," Pa said. Then he told the parson what had happened.

The parson's wife came out to listen and click with her tongue. The parson folded his hands and looked grave and sympathetic.

"And that's how it was," Pa said.

"The will of the Lord," the parson nodded.

"First I thought I would go crazy," Pa said. "Couldn't eat, couldn't sleep, couldn't think. Wanted to take my gun and go off into the deep woods. A man in the deep woods goes like an animal, and it's easy forgetting. Then I told myself, 'You got to raise up the boy, like she wanted. Raise him up proper, with Bible reading and writing.' But a man can't be alone with thirty acres cleared, a hundred more to clear, crops going in and meat to be hunted, and expect to raise a boy proper."

"What you need is a wife," Mrs. Jackson said.

"Ah," the parson nodded.

"I been fighting it," Pa said.

The parson nodded and looked thoughtful. The parson's wife looked even more thoughtful.

I said, "Damn it, no! We can get along, Pa and me!"

"Shut up, Dave!" Pa snapped.

So I went off toward the river, crying awhile in the grass with my face in my hands and hating Pa. Then I felt better and went back. They were in the house now, drinking tea; it wasn't much better than our house, just one room, with a loft for the kids, squared logs and paper in the windows.

Pa was saying, "I don't know. It ain't fitting a man with thirty acres clear should marry a bondwoman."

" 'Tain't what's fitting but what's practical," Mrs. Jackson said.

"Unless you wait for new womenfolk from back East," the parson said. "And there might be none coming this year."

"Or wait for Millie Flann to grow up," Mrs. Jackson nodded. "Fifteen's a mite too young to take on a widower's responsibilities."

"But a bondwoman—"

"Put pride behind thee, Brother Harvey. It ain't for love you're wedding, but to have a woman on the farm."

"True," Pa agreed.

"You got the twenty dollars to buy out her year's service?"

Pa went through his pocket, sorting out money. In his wallet, he had an English pound and six old shillings. His other pockets gave out silver dollars and old notes. I never knew Pa was that wealthy. He and the parson counted it over three times.

"Nineteen dollars, sixpence," the parson said finally. "A dollar's for the ceremony and sixpence for the church leaves eighteen. You ain't got other money, Brother Harvey?"

"None outside my britches," Pa replied.

The parson rose and put on his coat. He gathered the money into his pocket and said, "I'll go to Brother Green and make the bargain."

"The two dollars?"

"I'll make the bargain, brother. Come along."

I went, too; nobody told me not to—in fact, I think Pa was kind of glad to have me along with him.

Pa kept glancing at the bondwoman while the parson argued the price of her indenture with Mr. Green. Folks said there weren't so many bond persons around as before the war, and other folks said that back East laws were being passed to keep persons from being bound into service. Being bound was the same as being a slave; a father could sell his daughter for ten years' service, and people in debt could be bound in by their creditor. Or if a man died in debt, his children could be bound into service by his creditors.

As near as I could make out, that was the case with this bond-woman. Back East, her folks had died, and she had been bound in for the debt. Mr. Green had got her from some river traders for a thousand pounds of parched corn, and I didn't think much of the bargain. But there wasn't but one woman in the house then, and Mrs. Green needed a hand to help with the cooking and the baking and the washing and the putting by. Since then, Mr. Green's son had married, and that's why Parson Jackson considered that maybe he could pick up this bondwoman for Pa at a bargain price.

The bondwoman sat in a corner, on a stool by the hearth, while Pa and the parson and Mr. Green argued about the price. The bondwoman wasn't much to look at; just a little thing with a white face and dark hair. She watched them, and sometimes she glanced at me.

"I ought to be making a profit, not selling at a loss," Mr. Green said. He was a down-East Yankee, and I could see that neither Pa nor the parson thought a lot of him.

8 8 3 2 4

College of St. Francis Library
Joliet, Illinois

"When there ain't none to buy, the seller can't be choosy," the parson said.

"There's one to buy, all right."

"She's a bondwoman, and Brother Harvey here, he's buying her out of bondage. It's a Christian thing to do."

"I paid out in good corn for her."

Pa sighed and said, "Look a here. Suppose I pay that two dollars out this fall."

"Won't be no profit," Mr. Green protested.

The bondwoman looked down; then she put her face in her hands.

"I'll make it three dollars," Pa said.

"My wife stitched her three calico dresses."

"It ain't like she's a good woman," Pa said. "I'm taking her to wife because a man can't keep a place out in the forest alone without he goes woodsy or mad entire. I got thirty acres clear and a hundred more to take the wood off. The boy needs a rod taken to him, and mine ain't the hand can do it."

"Damn it, I don't!" I yelled.

Pa fetched me one and said, "Four dollars."

The bondwoman looked up and murmured, "Please—"

Mr. Green glanced at her, then said, "I'll take it."

"Done," the parson said.

"How old is she?" Pa wanted to know.

"Four and twenty, and good health."

I ran outside; I heard Pa calling for me, but I didn't come back. I wondered how he could forget so soon, after all the years with my mother.

It took us two full days to get back to our cabin from the stockade. That was because the horse couldn't carry all three of us; so Pa and I rode and the bondwoman walked behind. Her name was Rachel.

Pa insisted on having the marriage ceremony performed that night. He said that the stock wanted feeding; anyway, he had spent all his money and might as well get back as soon as he could. I was brokenhearted about the money; I thought maybe he would buy me some sugar hards at the store.

So I stood there and saw him married to the bondwoman. I suppose, if she wanted to, she could have protested that being a bondwoman didn't mean she had to marry her new owner, but the parson had spoken to her about bettering her place in life, I guess. She didn't have a lot of spirit; she just stood there with her head down and became a wedded woman.

And the next morning, Pa woke me before sunrise. The horse was saddled up, and the bondwoman was there, looking pale and tired, her two calico dresses in a bundle under her arm. The bondwoman came toward me, as if to say something, but I shied away; I didn't want any truck with her.

I said, "Pa, let's be getting back." And Pa nodded and climbed onto his horse. He reached down an arm and swung me up behind him.

"Come along," he told the bondwoman.

I was glad it was that way; it made me see that she was still a bondwoman, and that Pa hadn't married her out of wanting someone to take Ma's place, but because he needed a woman to work out at the cabin.

At the river, Pa set me down on the other side and then went back for the bondwoman; and I could understand that, him not wanting her to spoil her dress when she had only three calicoes. We didn't go very fast, because the bondwoman had to rest every now and then.

We had smoky for noontime meal, and Pa let the bondwoman cook it. Pa and I ate first, but he didn't stint on how much smoky she ate; Pa wasn't the kind to stint on food. But a few slices were enough to satisfy her. While Pa was smoking his pipe, I took a good look at her, for the first time, really. She wasn't bad looking; not comely and big and strong, but white-faced, though not so bad looking. I saw that her eyes were blue and light; something I hadn't noticed before, since most of the time she kept her eyes cast down.

After Pa had smoked a while and figured it was time to start again, he rubbed his mustache and cleared his throat.

"Rachel," he said, "my boy here, Davey, he's ten years old and growing like ragweed. I guess you'll cotton to him." Then he knocked out his pipe and said, "You ain't much of a walker?"

"No," Rachel answered.

"Don't talk much either."

"No." She never looked at him.

"Well, I'd just as soon let you ride, only it ain't fitting a bondwoman should ride and her master walks, even if she is wedded wife to him. Also, it ain't fitting a woman in calico should ride astraddle."

"I think I understand," she whispered.

Pa nodded and rose; he mounted his horse, and Rachel picked up her bundle and followed him.

That night, Rachel made her bed aside from us. Pa looked at her strangely and then said, "You'll be cold, away off from the fire."

"I'll be all right," she said.

"Good and tired, I reckon," Pa remarked.

"No, I'm not tired," she answered slowly. "A bondwoman can't know how it is to be tired."

Pa shot a deer on the way home; he told Rachel she could start it salting and smoking the next day. The first thing he did when we reached the clearing was to point out Ma's grave.

"A good woman," he told Rachel.

"Not like you," I muttered.

It was fine, clear weather, the end of that May and into June. Pa said that if things held out that way, settlers would be flocking in thicker than bees. Pa cleared two more acres.

Rachel kept the house; one thing about her I couldn't deny, she kept things neat and spick-and-span. She made bread every other day, and she cooked growing things, like parsnip and redtop. And I'd see her washing out one of her calico dresses each day; evenings, she'd sit with her needle and mend.

But it wasn't enough for Pa, and I made sure it wasn't enough for me either. Pa was always finding fault with one thing and another; the meat wasn't smoked right or the cow wasn't milked right; the food wasn't cooked right. Not like Ma had done it; he kept reminding her about that, day after day, week after week. He wouldn't let her forget her place as a bondwoman. But that was before the hunter came.

Rachel was supposed to school me for an hour each morning. Even if she was a bondwoman, she had plenty of schooling, reading and writing and sums and subtraction, and history and even geography. That was another thing I held against her; Lord, I hated that schooling.

Well, one morning I heard her calling me. I came slow and easy, for all her calling, "Davey, Davey, where are you?"

"What is it, Rachel?" I asked her.

"Learning, Davey."

"Well, damn it, why don't you leave me alone?"

"Please don't swear, Davey," she said.

I said, "Rachel, I'll swear like I want to."

She stared at me with those wide blue eyes of hers, and then she said, "Why do you call me that, Davey?"

"What?"

"Rachel."

"That's your name, ain't it?" I demanded.

"Yes, but I'm your mother."

"You're a bondwoman," I said. "I seen my Pa pay out your price —eighteen dolars cash and four dollars owing."

She reached out a hand as if to find something, but found nothing and stood there with that arm outstretched, trembling. I was frightened, thinking that she would fall, but then she seemed to get hold of herself, moved over to a bench and sat down. All that time her eyes never left my face.

"How about the schooling?" I asked her.

She said, very slowly, "You can go out today, Davey—without schooling, please."

I didn't wait to hear any more; I ran outside, whooping and yelling.

But that night Pa put it to her. I was up in the loft, supposed to be sleeping, but through the open hatch I could see Pa sitting at the table with his pipe in his hand.

"Rachel," he said.

I could hardly make out her voice. "What is it?"

"Davey tells me you didn't give him schooling today."

"No, I didn't."

"Why not?"

There was a long silence then, and finally Rachel said, "He called me a bondwoman."

"And was the hurt of that so that you couldn't school him?"

"There was no hurt," Rachel said; "only shame."

"How?"

"You wouldn't know!" she cried. "You wouldn't know!"

Well, it was fine weather all along, and Pa turned the black earth like it was cheese and rooted out stumps and put in his crops.

The hunting was good, too, and as much work as he did, Rachel matched him. He never let up on her for work, making sure, I guess, that she would pay out the eighteen dollars and the four owing. She salted meat and smoked meat, mended britches and sewed shirts, and did the cooking and the putting by. Her skin turned brown, and her eyes seemed to be lighter and lighter blue. She wore her hair in two long braids down her back.

And then the hunter came.

Out in the deep woods, paying a call wasn't a measure of distance. Hunters came by and paid their respects after they walked a thousand miles down from Canada country, and then, maybe, a walking man would range down to Kentuck or off to French Orleans. Packmen, mostly Scots and Jews, would come by with their two mules loaded up with trade trinkets. "Hello," they'd say, and then be off for the land of the Ojibway; and then pay their respects five months later back to New York and Boston to sell their furs.

The hunter's name was Jim Fairway, and he was a walker, all right, a woodsy man who never had homespun on his back, nothing but buckskin and fancy Indian beadwork. A thousand miles was grass under his feet. A big man with long yellow hair.

He came into the clearing one day, walking soft and easy, and twirling his long rifle over his head. "Hullo, there!" he yelled. "Hullo, there, you Sam Harvey! . . . Hullo, there, Davey!" He seemed sure glad to have listening folk to hear the sound of his voice.

I came running, and Pa laid down his work to grin at Jim. He liked Jim, even if Jim was no-account and woodsy.

"Where you from, Jim?" Pa called.

"Canady."

"Walk it?" Pa asked.

"You don't sight no horse," Jim grinned, swinging me up to his shoulder. I sure liked Jim.

"Well, set and rest," Pa said. "Set and rest."

"Pleased to."

"Seen Injun sign?" Pa asked.

"Some."

We were all walking toward the cabin now. Pa said, "This is been a mighty fine year, without no trouble."

"You get trouble when you don't the least expect it," Jim said, and Pa crossed his fingers. I knocked wood on the stock of Jim's rifle.

"Where's Susan?" Jim asked.

Pa sobered and pointed to the grave. "Two months now," he said.

Jim shook his head and squeezed my arm. We walked on a while, and then Jim said, "Must be mighty lonely out in the deep woods with no womenfolk."

"Well, it is and it ain't."

"Can't raise a boy proper without womenfolk," Jim said.

"No."

"Can't a man live without them either, less'n he goes wild or woodsy," Jim said. "This time I figure to get me a wife and a piece of land to plow and break wood out of."

"Why, that's fine," Pa said.

We were at the cabin now. Jim put me down and laid his rifle against the wall. Pa led the way inside; Jim came in last.

"Well, it's mighty nice feeling, inside of four walls," Jim remarked.

"Set yourself," Pa nodded, pointing to the table. "Fried pone and smoky ought to—" But Pa didn't finish what he was saying; he saw that Jim wasn't listening to him at all but staring at Rachel. She stood by the hearth, her face flushed and bright from the heat of the fire.

"Who's that?" Jim asked softly.

"That?"

"Her name's Rachel," I said.

"Rachel," Jim nodded.

Pa said hurriedly, "She's a bondwoman I bought from Matt Green. Had to have a woman round the place."

"Sure."

"Can't raise a boy—"

"Sure," Jim said. "She a serving girl?"

"No."

Jim never took his eyes from her face. "Kinfolk?" Jim asked.

"No."

"Just a bondwoman?"

Pa stuttered, "Sure, Jim, bondwoman or no, Christian folk can't live together, man and woman, without taking in marriage."

Jim smiled. "How y'do, Mrs. Harvey," he said.

Rachel said, "It's the first time a—man called me that."

I could see that Pa was worried about something; I could see it by the way he growled at me and by the way he set to working twice as hard as any man should work. It got worse and worse, until a week had gone by and Jim was still staying on.

Rachel had changed in that week. She seemed to get taller and straighter and prettier, and she laughed a lot. She never used to laugh before Jim came.

She fussed with things, too, setting fresh flowers around the house, and sometimes wearing a flower in her hair. Once Pa came in all hot and sweating with his work and saw Rachel standing in front of the cabin with a red flower in her hair.

"You look mighty pretty, Rachel," Pa said curiously, looking at her the way he'd look at a stranger.

"Thank you, Mr. Harvey," she said.

But Jim had more time for Rachel than Pa did, and it seemed to me that Pa was purposely staying away from the cabin more than he had to. Jim was always there, except when he went out to hunt; and Jim was a mighty fine and easy hunter, bringing in so much meat that Pa couldn't rightly complain about him staying on. When Jim wasn't hunting, he was hanging around the cabin, talking with Rachel and admiring her cooking and telling her his adventures way out in the deep woods. Even when Rachel gave me schooling, Jim hung around, explaining that he was sure in need of a little schooling.

Well, one day Pa came into the cabin when Jim and I were there by ourselves, Rachel having gone down to the spring for water.

It was a hot day, and after Pa had hemmed and hawed about not having cold water to douse his head with, he said to Jim, "This is a mighty nice long visit you paid us."

"Sure is," Jim nodded.

"Mighty long for a walking man with a itch to his heels," Pa said.

"Oh, I got rid a' that itch," Jim grinned.

"Never knew a walking man who could stop walking and root in one place."

"Some can," Jim said.

Pa scratched his head. "Yup," he admitted, "I remember you saying how you were prepared to settle down. Well, Jim, wives don't
grow on trees. You got to get out and go a hunting."

"Don't reckon I got to do much hunting," Jim said.

"How's that?"

Jim turned and nodded to where Rachel was coming up the hill
with the buckets of fresh, cold spring water. "There's Rachel."

"Rachel?" Pa said.

"She's a mighty fine, fair woman," Jim drawled.

"How?" Pa said.

"Well, you bought her out for eighteen dollars cash and four
owing. I got silver money in my pockets, and I'm prepared to pay
you out thirty dollars cash."

"Hell," Pa grinned, "you're joking."

"I ain't."

Pa said, softlike, "She's my wife, Jim."

"Is she? You don't treat her like men treat a wife; you treat her
like a bondwoman."

Still softly, Pa said, "Better be walking, Jim. I been ten years in
the deep woods and I got thirty-five acres clear, but I ain't yet
ordered folk off my place."

"You ain't ordering me," Jim said. "Leastways, not without
Rachel. I offered to buy you out, fair and—"

I never saw Pa's face like that before. He muttered something
under his breath, and then he let go at Jim like a wildcat springing. Jim was taller than Pa, but Pa was broad and hard.

Jim went down with Pa on top of him, and then they raised dust
like two panthers, hitting and gouging and swearing.

I whooped it for Pa, but they were tangling so hard I couldn't
rightly tell which was which. And inside of a minute from the time
Pa had jumped Jim, Rachel was there, dragging them apart.

"Stop it, stop it!" she cried.

Somehow, with all their tangling, they heard her. She pulled
them apart and to their feet, almost by main strength. Pa and Jim
were both bruised and bleeding, their faces splotched and their
clothes torn. Rachel stood between them, glaring first at one and
then at the other.

"Men!" she said. "Oh, you fools!"

Pa and Jim Fairway just stood there, staring down at the
ground.

"Making out a fine picture for Davey," Rachel said. "Two grown men fighting like a couple of wild Indians. Why?"

Pa kept his eyes on the ground; so did Jim. Rachel turned to me and demanded, "Why were they fighting, Davey?"

"You shut, Davey," Pa said.

"You speak up, Davey," Rachel said, her voice very cold and even. The way she said it and the way she looked at me, I couldn't help telling her.

"Jim wanted to buy you with eight dollars' profit for Pa, and Pa told him to go to—"

"You shut, Davey!" Pa roared.

"He'll speak," Rachel said, her voice trembling a little. "He'll speak all he wants to. And so will I."

I never saw her like that before, her eyes blazing, her whole body tight with anger.

"Maybe that's best," Jim said. "Tell him you're going along with me, Rachel."

"Going with you!" Rachel cried scornfully. "So you can buy me and sell me, just as you please! So you could have a wife and a slave at the same time, just as he had!"

"Now, Rachel—" Pa said.

"You shut!" Rachel snapped, and Pa kind of folded back and stared at the ground again.

"I'll tell you where I'm going," Rachel said. "I'm going back to the stockade. And if you think the work I've done here for you and for Davey and for that lazy, no-account hunter isn't worth eighteen dollars cash and four owing, you can warrant me with Judge Lang when he makes circuit. Only I wouldn't, if I were you. He's like to put the whole lot of you in jail."

Rachel came out of the cabin with her two calicoes under her arm and a bag of smoky and bread. Without a glance at Pa or Jim, she strode off down the hill in the direction of the stockade. Pa and Jim watched her go into the woods.

Jim scratched his head.

Pa said, "Well, I'll be damned."

Jim said, "Lazy, no-account hunter."

Pa said, "Feels kind of strange with Rachel gone off."

I felt that way too. For all that I had plagued Rachel, I felt that everything was kind of empty and to no purpose with her gone off.

Pa went out to the fields and came back, leading the horse. Then he went into the house and got his gun and pouch and horn.

He mounted and said, "Come on up, Davey."

"Where you going?" Jim demanded.

"After her."

"Can't see that you can do much without waiting for the circuit court and putting a warrant to her," Jim said. "Unless you lay hands on her."

"Never laid hands on a woman in my life," Pa growled.

Jim shrugged.

Pa said, "I ain't bringing her back. If a woman's ungrateful enough to turn on a man who's bought out her indenture and married her legal, then I don't want her."

"You don't?"

"Nope. Only I wouldn't let no woman walk in the dark woods without menfolk to see that harm didn't fall."

"That's so," Jim admitted.

"She might get lost."

"I guess I'll come along," Jim said.

Pa growled and spurred the horse, but when I looked back, I saw that Jim was running after us.

We rode hard for about three or four minutes, until we were well into the forest, and then Pa pulled up the horse and said, "Get down, Davey."

"Why?"

"I told you to get down."

We walked on, leading the horse, and in about ten minutes more, we saw Rachel in the woods ahead of us. Pa quickened his pace, so that I almost had to run to keep up with him. When we got to Rachel, she was standing still and facing us.

"What do you want?" she demanded.

"Nothing; nothing, Rachel. Only I reckoned you might as leave ride, it's that long a distance to the stockade."

"I walked it once before," Rachel said.

"Here's the horse," Pa muttered.

"Then ride him back and leave me alone." And she turned and walked on.

Pa tagged after her. "I can't leave you walking alone in the deep woods," he said.

Then Jim caught up with us, toting his long rifle and panting

from his run. Rachel turned and faced them, her head caught in
a long ray of sunlight, her eyes blazing.

"Leave me alone!" she cried.

But Pa and Jim kept following her, Pa leading the horse.

That night there wasn't enough that Pa and Jim could do for
Rachel. They made a big, roaring fire for her, but Rachel would
have none of it and built her own fire about ten yards away. She set
the smoky to cooking and the bread to warming. Pa and Jim had
come away too quickly to think of bringing food, and they just sat
in front of their fire, wrinkling their noses and sniffing the smoky.

When the smoky was done, Rachel said, "Davey, would you like
something to eat?"

"I ain't very hungry," I muttered.

"Just a little?" she said.

That smoky smelled terribly good. Pa and Jim were just staring
into their fire as if nothing else interested them. So I went over to
Rachel's fire.

I ate smoky and hot bread until I felt good and warm and comfortable. "Thankee," I told Rachel.

"That's all right, Davey."

I felt mean and small, thinking of the way I had acted toward
Rachel. She put her arm around me, and soon I fell asleep.

When I woke up in the morning, Rachel was still sleeping, but
Pa and Jim were sitting in front of the dead embers of their fire,
just as they were the night before.

I called, "Pa, ain't you slept at all?"

He shushed me, pointing to Rachel. She woke up, stretching and
yawning, smiled at me, and then let the smile go as she saw Jim
and Pa. She cut cold smoky and bread for our breakfast.

"I guess they're mighty hungry," I said.

"I guess they are."

We set off again, only this time I walked along with Rachel. She
was so nice to me, I couldn't lift up and light back to Pa. Jim and
Pa followed along with the horse, about ten yards behind us.

Once, Rachel said, "Your ma must have been nice, Davey."

"She was—but so are you."

"I reckon you favor her," Rachel said; "not your Pa."

Noontime, we finished the smoky and bread. Jim and Pa built a
fire again, but I helped Rachel make her own. They must have

been awful hungry, because all morning they walked with their guns ready, like men hunting; only never a sign of a creature crossed our path, and I guess neither would go off to hunt and leave the other alone.

Noontime, Jim did say, "My, that smoky smells awful fine."

But Pa never said a word.

It was some hours after noon, when we were walking along and getting near to the stockade, that I heard a turkey gobbler calling behind us.

"That's a turkey gobbler," I told Rachel. "It would make mighty nice eating if Jim or Pa would go off and hunt it."

"I don't think they will," Rachel said.

The gobbler called again, and I looked back to see what Jim and Pa would do. For some reason, they had stopped and were facing the other direction.

Suddenly, Pa threw up his rifle and fired. There was a long scream, not the scream a gobbler makes.

Rachel put her arm around me.

Pa and Jim ran toward us, and without saying a word, Pa lifted Rachel and swung her onto the horse.

"Shawnees," Jim said.

Pa threw me onto the horse. "Tell them at the stockade!" he cried, and slapped the horse across the rump. The old horse clattered through the woods, and when I glanced back, Pa and Jim were crouched down behind a fallen tree.

I guess we had gone a few hundred yards or so when Rachel seemed to come out of her trance. She pulled the horse up sharp and slipped down from it.

"Davey," she whispered, "can you find the stockade?"

"Sure."

"Then go there and bring them. Davey, I have to go back—I have to." And she began to run toward where Pa and Jim were.

Well, it wasn't much to ride the five or six miles to the stockade and come back with Parson Jackson, Matt Green, Lem Thurley and four or five others.

Lem said he didn't believe the Shawnee story because there hadn't been Shawnees within a hundred miles for God knows how long. Sure enough, we weren't more than three quarters way back when we met Jim Fairway, walking along with his long rifle over his shoulder and whistling like there wasn't a Shawnee in the country.

"Hey, you, Jim Fairway!" Lem Thurley yelled.

Jim grinned and waved, and we rode up to him.

"How about the Shawnees?" Parson Jackson said.

"Lord, I feel free," Jim said. "I'm a walking man and a hunting man. I got an itch to my heels and a load in my gun, and I ain't touched food in two days."

"How about the Shawnees?"

"They was two, and they're dead," Jim told us.

"Well, that's that," Lem Thurley said. "I might 'a' known."

"I guess I'll go along back to Pa," I said. I felt petered out.

Matt Green said, "Hold on. How about the four dollars your pappy owes me?"

Jim grinned and fetched silver from his pockets. "I'm paying," he said. "I'm sure happy to. I got silver money to spend." And he paid Matt Green out the four dollars.

They went back, Jim with them, and I rode on. I got to the fallen log, and there were Pa and Rachel, just sitting and looking at each other. When Rachel saw me, she jumped up with a little cry of relief.

I slid off the horse and began to whimper.

Pa said, "Davey, stop that bawling!"

"Let him if he wants to," Rachel said.

I looked at Pa, and he said, "Davey, do like your Ma says."

Onion Soup

WHEN THE PURSER, a tall, heavy-set Italian, entered the galley at seven o'clock in the morning, the gray ship was prowling through a fog off the Newfoundland Banks; but there was no sea to speak of, just a gentle swell, and in spite of the stoves the galley was cold and wet.

The purser looked first at the stock, which had been simmering in a ten-gallon kettle these twenty-four hours past. "How does she ride?" the baker asked. He was a small man with a pocked face, and the purser nodded at him. Six years ago, in the prehistoric past of peace, the purser had been second cook on a fruit boat to the Islands.

"If I was Bill," the baker said, I would take that little sonova-bitch who threw away the carrots and I would put a knowledge of God into him, so help me, I would."

"He didn't mean anything," the purser said, recalling the wrath of the steward when he discovered that the carrots had gone overboard. For weeks and weeks, ever since Sydney, Australia, where he bought them, the steward had husbanded a crate of carrots. Together with two pounds of raisins and a jar of Miracle Whip, they were to make a salad for the steward's dinner. Sometimes, it was hard for the purser to understand how a department, like the steward's, could look forward so long and consistently to one dinner.

He thought about that as he watched Bill, the steward, curse out the messboy. Here they were, so long out from the States that even the memory of the beginning was blurred. From San Pedro on the coast they had gone out to the Hawaiian Islands, from there to Fiji, to New Zealand, to the Solomons, to Iwo, to Australia, and then up the circle to Calcutta; to Ceylon, to Yemen, to Suez—to how many other places? Day in, day out, the stewards put the meals on the table, until, the last day before making port in the States, the order was reversed, and the cooks, bakers, messboys and the others sat down at the table, to be waited on and served and fed. The purser had volunteered to do the cooking, and the carpenter had come on as his second, and a fool of a messboy had thrown out a crate of carrots.

"It is not," the steward said, speaking his slow Texas drawl, "that we can't put on a meal for them. I got three hundred and fifty pounds of *filet mignon* in the box and there's plenty of potatoes to fry. But I was counting on the carrots."

The purser agreed that a salad was nice.

"It's not only that. Sure they can sit down to steak and potatoes. But you eat one meal out of a thousand and you want something special."

"Like what?"

"God knows," the steward said. "But not Jello and not canned peaches. Last week we had apples—fried apple rings. But the apples are gone. The eggs are gone."

"How about onions?" the purser asked. "Because once I ate a Normandy onion soup that was something to dream about."

"Plenty of onions," the steward said without excitement.

He didn't particularly like onion soup.

"This isn't like what you ate. This is out of the world. I only ate it once."

"How do you know you can make it?"

"I like to cook," the purser smiled. "I got a feeling for it. As long as you have plenty of onions."

But actually, it was a long shot, and he didn't know whether he could make the onion soup or not. He had a crate of onions out, and he was peeling them when the carpenter came in, put on an apron, and went at the potatoes.

"Onion soup," the carpenter said, "is bad gravy with onions floating in it."

The purser shook his head. "I come from a people who know food and like food."

"How's that?"

"You know what my mother, she used to tell me when I was a kid? Eat your vegetables, she used to say, because when you grow up and marry an American girl, you'll eat boiled vegetables."

"What's wrong with boiled vegetables?" the carpenter wanted to know.

"Nothing. But food is a mark of civilization. This onion soup is a mark of civilization. In all my life, I ate it only once. That makes me sad."

"It wouldn't make me sad," the carpenter said.

When he had finished peeling the onions, the purser went out on deck. They were not doing more than six or seven knots, and the wind was off shore, and the purser wondered whether he could smell home in it. Yet he was still three thousand miles and more from home and a wife and two children, who were in the San Fernando Valley; it was what would happen to him, he thought, to go out of the West Coast and into the East. For a while, he watched the sluggish gray water, until the third engineer came along and said:

"I hear you're making an onion soup for the stewards."

"So?"

"I ate good onion soup in France but no place else," said the third, a small, dry and melancholy man in his late forties, but only to make conversation, leaning on the rail alongside of the purser. In the purser's home, food was life and life was food, with avocado trees in the front yard and the best paste in all of California, or so he thought and his four brothers and his three sisters and his wife and their wives. The white bread was home-baked and the *manicotti* had once made a poet sing of it. You sat at a table and life rewarded you for having the temerity to live.

"This is a Normandy onion soup," the purser said slowly, apart from the third, born and brought up in the States, but always a stranger to these folk who had no food, only quantity, no love for food, no understanding of food, no relationship to food.

The third shrugged and spat onto the rush of wind, and the purser went back into the galley. "I only ate it once," he said to the carpenter, "and it was golden brown, creamy, and the essence of onions came from it; but never a taste or touch of onions. You get to figure you can make a food, if you know how to cook, even if you don't know just what goes into it."

"I was a short-order cook in a diner in Omaha once," the carpenter said. "I was also cook in a lumber camp for Toohey Brothers back in the old Wobbly days, but what they ate shouldn't happen to a dog. Where did you learn to cook?"

The purser sliced onions and remembered that he was second in the huge galley of the old *America*, and way back in forty, before it properly began, he had shipped on an oiler that later went down on the Murmansk Run. He was first cook, but where had he learned to cook? In a hot, sunny California memory, he watched his mother cook, but the nostalgia of the memory was apart from any curriculum. The onion juice ran over his hands as he brought back the wonder of childhood, adding to it the strange fact of his own children.

"Slice me about five pounds of bacon, thin," he said. And then added, "You don't learn to cook."

The cook and the second cook joined the carpenter and the purser. The ship was a condition of perpetual hunger, and even if this was the day of the steward's department, three meals had to be cooked and served. But a lunch of potato salad and cold cuts and a supper of baked macaroni with cheese and ham was recognized and admitted as a bow to the special nature of the day. The top of the long galley stove belonged to the purser and the carpenter, and the cook, a fat, pock-marked mountain of a Greek, and the second cook, yellow-haired and skinny, from southern Oklahoma, both recognized this fact, adopting a deliberate and somewhat mawkish dilettantism. It pleased them that they were strangers in the galley on this day, and having little enough work, what with the cold cuts and the one huge casserole, they snooped around like tourists.

"Onion soup?" the cook asked.

"With *filet mignon* and fried potatoes," the carpenter added. "You won't starve."

"I don't see a potato again in this life, I won't shed no tears," the second cook said.

"But onion soup—" the cook said, and then, fearful that he had hurt the purser's feelings, added, "I got some gallon cans of bouillon if you need it."

"Bouillon," the purser said softly. "Mother of God, bouillon!"

"You leave him alone," the carpenter said. "What in hell are you guys doing here anyway? Take your stinking cold cuts into the pantry. Take them to the head. Here we are slaving away over a hot stove and you got no appreciation, only an interest like a couple of marks in a summer carnival."

He shouldered them out, and the purser selected a frying pan thirty inches in diameter, laid out the bacon on it, and set it to fry. As the bacon began to sizzle and blister, he mentioned to the carpenter:

"Why do you suppose he ships out as cook?"

"It's a living," the carpenter said. "I'm an old man, but if I was a young feller, I'd learn me to cook. I wouldn't be no deck hand."

The purser hung over the frying pan, guiding the strips of

bacon, lifting out each piece as it browned and laying it on a big sheet of Manila he had spread on the table. As the fat in the pan increased, the remaining strips of bacon danced merrily. It was a long and tedious process, but he carried it through until he had a pan of fresh, bubbling lard, not burned and not smoking, and all of the bacon crisp and browned evenly.

"You going to eat lunch?" the carpenter wanted to know.

The purser shook his head. For the first time in months, the loneliness, the awful combination of space and time, was falling away. Standing in his shorts, his big, brown, hairy body warmed to the heat of the stove and swayed to the gentle roll of the ship. The onion soup became more than a soup, more and beyond his explaining to anyone.

When the last of the bacon was finished, the purser added salt to the fat and ground down peppercorns, which he spread through it evenly. He set it on a low light and tried to think of spice. After he had eaten the Normandy onion soup, that single time, he had gone in to the cook and asked her. She was a wizened shred of a woman, with blue eyes as pale as the winter sky.

"You make it," she said.

"But how—how do you spice it?"

She put her hands on her flat dugs and rocked back and forth, gurgling with laughter. "You go to hell, huh?" she laughed, and then added, *"Tu peux m'embrasser quelque part."*

He went out and told his wife. "That's a nasty old woman," his wife had said. "It's good soup, but I don't see why you make such a fuss about it."

"It's the most wonderful soup a man ever ate."

Now he brooded over the matter, tossed a mental coin finally, took a small sifter, and put a heaping tablespoon of curry powder through it, spreading it evenly over the fat. Then he separated the onions into rings and added them. The mountain of onions fried slowly, the purser perched on a stool and poking at it now and then with a long fork. While he sat there, the carpenter brought him a sandwich, which he munched thoughtfully. He had been sailing for five years now; suppose he came home and found that the war was over? Would he go on sailing? Where do old sailors go? He looked at the carpenter.

An A.B. came in, a lad of twenty-eight or so, nodded at them and then studied the onions. "You got a lot a fat," he said appraisingly.

"I drain it off after a while," the purser said, "and I let it dry out on the pan."

"I hear you're making onion soup," the A.B. remarked.

The purser grinned. "It gets around."

The A.B. stayed until the fat was drained off and the onions nursed back on the pan. "I'll need some bread," the purser said to the carpenter. "About thirty slices. Cut them about half an inch thick, shape them round with a cake cutter or something, and then sprinkle them over with garlic salt. Pack them up like six-decker sandwiches and let them sit." The onions were finished now, and the purser let them simmer on a very low flame. Then he crushed the dry bacon with a pestle and put it in with the onions, mixing it slowly.

"It don't make sense about the bread," the carpenter said. "What in hell's name will you do with it?" Scrunching through the great icebox, he had found two shriveled survivors of the apples they had taken on at Sydney. They hitched up on the table and chewed the apples.

"That's the one thing I know," the purser answered. "There was a slice of toasted bread on the soup, and it was done with the garlic salt, packing it, and letting it soak through. It does it, if the bread is fresh."

"A guy as crazy about food as you," the carpenter said, "he ought to be pretty fat. You're not fat."

"I like good food," said the purser, "but it doesn't depend on how much I eat."

"If a guy likes dames—"

"I got to put that mess through a sieve," the purser sighed. "A ricer wouldn't be any good." The steward came in while they were searching through the cupboards and he found them a huge iron cone, threaded through with holes, like a helm out of the Middle Ages, and he stayed to hold it as the purser pounded through the onions and bacon, which emerged as a purée. Two oilers who had heard about the soup joined the carpenter.

To the purser, one of the oilers said, "I been in Normandy. I never ate onion soup there."

The other had an ache behind his left ear that had been bothering him all day, and since the ship carried no pharmacist's mate, the purser dispensed medicine and sometimes surgery out of three large books. He went to the cabin with the oiler, looked into his ear, looked into the book, and then gave him two aspirin and some sulfa gum to chew. With afternoon, the sun had emerged, and the purser stood on the boat deck for a while, craning his neck to watch them paint and bed down the twenty-millimeter guns. The steward was waiting for him when he returned to the galley. They put the purée into an eight-quart pot and then drew the stock, while the whole galley steamed with the strong smell of twenty pounds of meat, bones and gristle that had thirty hours of cooking behind it.

When the stock was drawn, the purser mixed it slowly and gently. The second mate joined the oiler, and the carpenter, who was opening cans of peaches for dessert, said, "Why don't you taste it?"

"First, the *roux*."

It had become ritualized. A wiper and the first mate added themselves to the crowd, and the steward went to the box and returned with two pounds of butter. Putting it in a pan to melt, the purser began to sift his flour. There was an easiness about them, they had been together so long, but also a tenseness, and the steward could only think, "What a damnfool thing over a pot of soup." But the wiper said stolidly, "I'd use arrowroot."

Nobody laughed. The purser stared at him for a long moment, and the wiper, a dark little man, nodded back solemnly.

"You got arrowroot?" the purser asked the steward.

The steward went for the arrowroot. The purser let the butter brown delicately, and then turned it with the arrowroot, bit by bit, using a big wire whip and thickening the *roux* as he worked. They were silent while the roux cooked, and then, when it was ready, they watched him blend it into the soup. There it was, golden brown, almost eight quarts of it.

"Taste it," the steward said.

"It looks right," the purser murmured, a curious expression on his face.

"Go ahead and taste," someone else said.

The purser tasted it, and it wasn't right, and he thought of the little, dried-up Normandy woman laughing in his face. The others watched him but didn't ask to taste it themselves. He added pepper and salt and tasted it again. The steward raised his brows inquiringly.

"Something's missing," the purser said slowly. They all felt what he felt now.

"You'll get it," the wiper said. "You only ate it once. You want to remember what it tasted like. Maybe that was a long time ago. Just think about the taste."

Now they felt worse than he felt, and there was an element of love as well as sadness as they watched him walk out of the galley onto the deck. "To hell with it, it's just soup," the carpenter thought, but he was sad too.

The purser walked to the after hatch and sat down next to the cook, and for a while the two of them sat silent, watching an ordinary paint over the rust where shrapnel had scored and punctured the rail.

"The son of a bitch," the cook said finally, but the purser said nothing at all, and the Greek guessed what it was. "They can somehow pull through on steak," the cook said. "It will be tough, but they'll pull through."

"It's not that. I feel like I'm coming home empty. It's a crazy way to feel, but that's what I feel."

"I was on a C3," the cook said, "and I had a second who was a Swiss, and he put nutmeg into every soup he made."

"Nutmeg?"

"Nutmeg," the cook said. "Me, I make an onion soup from old gravy. I fry some onions and let them swim. To hell with it—it's onion soup."

"You ever put nutmeg in soup?" the purser asked.

"I beat the ass off that damnfool Swiss once I found out."

"You got any nutmeg?" the purser asked.

"I got a bag of nuts somewhere."

"Let's try it," the purser said.

They went inside, and the cook found the nutmegs. The purser took half a ladle of soup, and the cook scraped the nutmeg into it. Then the purser tasted it. "A little more," he said. He tasted it again, and it was right, like no other soup the world had seen, and then he let the carpenter and the cook taste it, while he thought about the way the old Normandy woman had laughed. The steward wanted to taste it, and so did the wiper and some of the others, but the purser shook his head.

"If any's left over," he told them. "I got to get supper." And he put the garlic bread into the oven to dry out slowly.

That night, the purser stood on deck, arms on the rail, and watched a lighthouse blinking, on and off, on and off. He felt warm and close to a lot of people, and he wanted to cry because he was home and he'd say good-by to them and never see them again. There were twenty-two people in the steward's department, and when the meal was over, one by one they came into the galley where he was washing dishes, and they shook his hand and each of them said something about the soup.

Then the old man sent down for a plate of the soup. The old man was a Dane and fussy about his food and always cursing out the cook, but he sent back for a second plate of soup. He wanted to know how it was made.

"Tell him to go jump in the drink," the carpenter had said.

It was funny, the purser thought, because they were as hard-bitten a group of men on the ship as he had ever known, hard men who were all knotted up with work and too many long trips and too many torpedoes and too many dive bombers and the closeness of a piece of iron where they had been living almost forever. It was funny, he thought.

And he thought of how he would tell his wife about it, and she would not see anything in a pot of onion soup to make all this fuss about. He thought about his wife easily and pleasantly now, and he kept on thinking about her as the blinking light faded into the distance.

Three
Beautiful
Things

Mark traven, the writer, entered the Waldorf, looked around for a while, because he was five minutes early, and then went to the express elevators that go up to the tower apartments. He was wearing his best tweed, which meant the best of two, and he was a little excited at seeing Mr. Calwell, but not too excited, since he had no real hopes of anything lasting coming from it. Still, you could never tell, and it was with not a little pleasure that he told the elevator boy to take him up to the twenty-ninth floor.

"It's a nice day," said the elevator boy.

"It's a real fine day," said Traven. That was the way he felt. When the door of Mr. Calwell's suite opened, Traven entered with what he considered a fair mixture of humility and self-assurance. Miss Deale ushered him into the room. Miss Deale was about thirty, brunette, and very pretty; but with her good looks went an uncertainty that told people it was no picnic to work for Mr. Calwell. She and Traven had lunched the day before. Now she introduced Traven to Mr. Calwell, who waved the writer to a seat without rising.

Mr. Calwell sat with his back to the windows, and he motioned Traven to a deep chair facing him. He wore a dressing gown of green and red plaid and an ascot of the same material; slacks, also of the same material, were matched by slippers of green and red plaid. On his fingers were a wedding ring and a signet ring with a large diamond. He was older than Traven had expected, at least sixty.

"This is Mark Traven, the writer," Miss Deale said.

"It is always a pleasure to meet talent," said Mr. Calwell.

Traven, who was rehearsing in his mind those of Mr. Calwell's pictures he had seen, so he could talk intelligently about them, nodded and said that he was very pleased to be here. It was his first interview with an important Hollywood producer, and it had so turned out that he was talking to just about the most important of the lot. He felt honored and said so.

"It is I who am honored," said Mr. Calwell. "Even if I am not always and continuously honored by talent—and for a man who don't respect talent I have no respect—I am honored by Thomas Jefferson."

"Thomas Jefferson?" Traven inquired.

"Thomas Jefferson," Mr. Calwell repeated, treating the name with both love and respect. "Of course, for Thomas Jefferson, you are younger than you should be."

"For Thomas Jefferson?" Traven said.

"But he himself was young, wasn't he?"

"Who?"

"Thomas Jefferson," Mr. Calwell smiled.

"I suppose so," Traven agreed, looking desperately at Miss Deale. But Miss Deale, who sat over on the other side of the enormous room, preserved a poker face.

"Of all the people in the world, you might say," Mr. Calwell explained, "who was there greater in the whole world than Thomas Jefferson?"

Traven shook his head, sparring for time.

"Washington? Lincoln? Theodore Roosevelt—not FDR, you don't see FDR on a mountain in stone—but you don't compare them to Jefferson."

"No, I guess not," Traven said.

"If I was talent and I had a choice, I would say to myself, go on writing about Jefferson."

Traven swallowed and said, "I did a book about Paine, Mr. Calwell, my last book."

"Who?"

"Tom Paine," Traven whispered. "Citizen Paine—"

"With Orson Welles," Mr. Calwell smiled. Then the smile vanished and he said, "That too is talent. Welles is talent if he doesn't break you. But he shouldn't mix in politics. That's the kiss of death, to mix in politics. That's why you're smart with Thomas Jefferson. Jefferson is not politics, he is immortality. You take a newspaper publisher and make a picture about him, that's politics. Orson Welles is talent; I admit that, and talent you got to respect. So I respect Welles."

Traven nodded.

"Not like I respect Jefferson," Mr. Calwell added.

"No," Traven said. "Of course not."

"But is there a place in Hollywood for Jefferson?" Mr. Calwell questioned seriously.

"I had hopes about Paine—" Traven began.

"You got a deal with Orson Welles?"

Traven shook his head, feeling like a blind man at the edge of a precipice.

"Then don't discuss him," Mr. Calwell said. "Even at Jefferson in short pants, people could laugh."

"Sir?"

"With Bing Crosby, a costume piece is something else. I am not against laughter."

"No, sir."

"The world should be filled with laughter. But they shouldn't laugh at Thomas Jefferson."

"Yes, sir," Traven said. "But I'm afraid you have confused Jefferson with Paine."

"Welles confused him. Welles is talent, but if Welles comes to me and wants to work for nothing, I don't have him."

"That's Citizen Kane, sir," Traven said softly.

"But it's not Jefferson. First, I said to myself, if it's the last thing I do, if I lose a million dollars, I will make Thomas Jefferson. That's a public service; the whole world can look at America with Thomas Jefferson. But maybe the time isn't ripe. When I doubt a thing, even a little bit, I say to myself, the time isn't ripe."

"Yes, sir."

"Of course," Mr. Calwell added, 'if it has three beautiful things, it will make money."

"Sir?"

"Mr. Traven, in all the world there are three beautiful things. Three beautiful things are immortality. You have three beautiful things and you will make money, even out of a public service."

"Yes, sir."

"Suppose I asked you to name three beautiful things?"

"Any three beautiful things?" Traven inquired uncertainly.

"No—no. You see, a talent is something. You got a talent for Thomas Jefferson. You should go on writing about Jefferson. That's a service. Can you write too much about Jefferson?"

"I don't know—"

"Your play is a service. Your play is something everyone in America should see."

"My play?" Traven asked.

"About Jefferson. Jefferson is immortality. But there are three beautiful things that are immortality in the box office. There is beautiful love. There is beautiful music. There is beautiful laughter. Those are three beautiful things. Those are sweetness. If you make a picture without them, even about Thomas Jefferson, what have you got?"

Traven shook his head.

"You got a public service, but not in the box office," Mr. Calwell said. He rose to indicate that the interview was over. "I'm happy to see you. Talent, I'm always happy to see. Talent is the most precious thing on earth. You shouldn't go to Hollywood and destroy your talent, Mr. Traven. You should go on writing about Jefferson."

When Mr. Calwell closed the door of his tower suite on Mark Traven, the writer, he turned to Miss Deale.

"I pay you three hundred a week to bring me lunatics," he said. "I pay you to waste my time."

"I'm sorry, Mr. Calwell," Miss Deale said. "I think you mixed him up with Sidney Kingsley."

"Who?"

"The man who wrote *The Patriots*, the play about Jefferson. Mr. Traven wrote about Tom Paine."

"I need Orson Welles like I need the measles. If you got to bring me talent, Miss Deale, you should only not bring me lunatics. Without that, I can live."

The
First Rose
of Summer

I WAS FOURTEEN when first love came to me, which was older than some yet younger than others. A round and appropriate age, you might say, and I was ignorant of ductless glands and such things, but knew only the blaze of glory that poets have always sung about.

At that time, my brother and I had a newspaper route, which netted us fifteen dollars on good weeks and which we both conducted after school. Before we were finished on this particular day, my brother knew that childish things were behind me and that there were more than material reasons for the deep and saintly sadness in which I had wrapped myself.

"What's eating you?" he asked me, and I told him about it. It had been a gentle day, a sweet day. We delivered our papers for the most part in five-story tenement houses, and my brother's idea of equity was for me to take the top three floors while he took the bottom two; being a year and a half older than I and some sixty pounds heavier, he could enforce this edict, but out of a basic concept of equal rights, I fought him on every house. Today, however, I accepted. There was a flavor to suffering; my whole heart was filled with music.

"I'm in love," I said.

"What?"

"In love," I said. "In love with a woman."

"No?"

"Yes," I said, with dignity that couldn't fail to impress him. "Deeply in love."

"When did this happen?" His respectful curiosity combined interest and a touch of admiration.

"Today."

"All at once?"

"Yes," I said. "I saw her in my English class, and I knew it."

"How could you know it?"

"The way I feel."

"You mean like taking the top three floors?" my brother asked hopefully.

"That's only a part of it. My own suffering is of no consequence any longer, because now I'm consecrated to something bigger than I am."

My brother nodded and watched me intently. "How *do* you feel?" he asked.

"Noble."

"Not sick?"

"Not with physical sickness. It isn't something I can explain to you."

"I guess not," he agreed. "What's her name?"

"Thelma Naille."

"Thelma?"

"Thelma," I repeated, savoring the sound of it, the joy of it, the inflection of it.

"You're sure?"

"Of course I'm sure."

"That's a strange name," my brother said. "She doesn't lisp or anything?"

"She has a voice like music."

"Oh. Does she know about this?"

"Naturally not," I said—almost sorry that I had taken him into my confidence at all. However, it was necessary. Being in love was going to complicate my life; that I realized from the very beginning, and I couldn't have become a cross-country runner without my brother knowing what the motivating forces were.

At that time, we both went to George Washington High School, which is at the upper end of Manhattan Island. School let out at three; we finished our newspaper route at six, and then, since we had no mother, we prepared supper, ate it with my father, who came home from work about seven, did our homework and turned in. Love alone threw new drains on my energy. With the cross-country running, only a holy devotion permitted me to operate . . .

My brother was waiting for me when I came out of the English class the next day.

"Which one?" he wanted to know, and I pointed her out.

"The tall one?"

"She's not so tall."

"She's five feet nine inches if she's an inch."

"Oh, no. No. Never. Anyway, I'm five feet eight myself."

"Five six," my brother said coldly.

"Not with heels. Anyway, the rate of growth is different in different people. I'm just hitting my stride. She's all finished. Growing, I mean."

"How do you know?"

"Well, how tall can a girl get?"

"If you can keep on growing, so can she. That's logical."

I conquered the chill of fear that stole over my heart. He was understandably bitter; I held no resentment against him; I was filled with an inner purity and I let some of it shine through.

"You look sick," my brother said. "I hope you're all right. She didn't even look at you."

"She doesn't know me."

"Well, why don't you introduce yourself?"

"I can't until I have some achievement to lay at her feet. I'm no one. Did you see how beautiful she is? Anyone would be in love with her. That's natural."

"I'm not in love with her," my brother said.

"Anyway—"

"What do you mean by laying an achievement at her feet?" my brother asked. "Are you going to buy something for her?"

I walked away. It was no use talking to him about this; it was no use talking to anyone. It was something I had to contain within me until I had won my struggle to make myself worthy. For a week I brooded about that. The football season was too far gone, and anyway I weighed only one fourteen, and football was a long-term project with all sorts of special skills required. Love, I was beginning to discover, was not something that stood still; it was a dynamic force that moved a person to immediate action, and when the week was over, I turned out for the track squad. After all, how many football players ever made an Olympic?

"Your feet are too big," the coach told me.

"For what?" I had gotten along very well with them until then.

"For sprinting."

"I don't suppose my feet will grow much more, and I intend to."

"We can't wait," the coach said.

"Don't you want to try me?" I pleaded.

"It's no use," the coach said patiently. "You can't sprint with such feet."

"Well, isn't there something where you don't have to sprint?"

"Your feet are against you. If you jumped, it would be just the same. Also, you're small and light—and that's bad for discus or shot. If you want to try for cross-country, you can."

"Cross-country?"

"That's right. You spend a year at that, and then maybe the rest of you will catch up with your feet. It's good training, if your heart is all right."

My heart was all right, and at three o'clock I was shivering in my underclothes in Van Cortlandt Park. It was a cold, bleak fall day, and a hundred other boys shivered with me. Then we started out, and for the next half hour, over hill and dale, we ran a course of two and a half miles. It may be that education, in probing the bypaths of knowledge, has discovered something crueler and more senseless than a cross-country run; if so, I missed it. I don't know what upheld the rest of the squad, but love carried me through pantingly to the end. I showered and joined my brother on the route, an hour and a half late.

This time I couldn't make the top three floors, and I told him why.

"You mean you're going up there and run two and a half miles every afternoon?" he demanded.

"Yes."

"But why?"

"For her."

"You mean she asked you to do this?"

"How could she ask me when I've never spoken to her?"

"Who asked you then?"

"No one."

"You're crazy," my brother said, which was what I might have expected, his mind being capable of rising no higher above the dirt. For the rest of that week, there was a certain bitterness of feeling between us, something I sensed only vaguely, since all my acute perceptions were blurred by a fog of constant weariness. If ever in the history of western romance love was stretched to a breaking point, that was it, and it seems to me that it is a real tribute to the gentle passion that both my devotion and I survived. However, my survival was a touch-and-go business; if I did not walk in darkness, I certainly walked in a gray haze, and my classroom response became, if not downright idiotic, at least far from alert. More than before, I realized that I would have to become the best cross-country runner America had ever produced to redeem a faltering, tired, incoherent young man in the eyes of the woman I loved.

Somehow, the five weekdays passed, and without a complete loss of the saintly gentleness that was the most manifest outward indication of my passion. The cross I bore was made no lighter by my brother's grim curiosity; in a completely scientific manner, he experimented with my new tolerance. I came late to work, but I certainly did my share.

The paper we delivered was an afternoon paper, except on Sundays, when it came out in the morning. That meant we had to dig ourselves out of bed at 3 A.M., stagger over to the assembly room, and collate mountains of newsprint. By seven or seven-thirty in the morning, we were through with the delivery and could go home and catch a nap. Ordinarily, I would be tired enough, but the cross-country team—and whoever was the diabolical brain behind it—decided to hold a conditioning run on Saturday, five miles instead of two and a half; and when Sunday morning finally rolled around my accumulated fatigue was something to see. My brother's respect was tinged with awe by now, and there was almost a quality of gentleness in his suggestion that I go home and sleep most of the day.

"No," I said wistfully. "It would be nice, but I can't. I'm going to her house."

"You mean you've met her, you've talked to her? She invited you over?"

"Not exactly."

"You mean you're just going over and introduce yourself," my brother nodded admiringly.

"Not exactly that either. I'm just going to stand outside her house."

"Until she comes out?"

"Yes—yes, that's it," I agreed.

"Don't you think you ought to get some sleep first?" my brother suggested.

"I can't take the chance."

"What chance?"

I didn't try to explain, because there are some things you can't explain. Her house was a fourteen-story building on Riverside Drive. It awed me and overwhelmed me; it widened the gap; it made me search my memory for any evidence that America was a country where cross-country running was even nominally honored. And to make things more difficult, the house had two entrances, one on the Drive and one on the side street. There was no bench from which I could observe both entrances, so I had to take up my vigil on a windy street corner, reflecting morosely on the fact that even if the rest of me grew, I was not treating my feet in a manner calculated either to keep them at their present size or preserve them for sprinting.

There are cold places on earth; there are places that have a whole literature of coldness woven around them; they do not compare with a street corner on Riverside Drive on a cloudy November morning. That is a special cold; a nice, wet, penetrating cold that increases slowly enough for you to perish with a minimum of pain. By twelve o'clock I had finished with my consecration to life and had newly consecrated myself to death. There was a new poignancy to the realization that I would die here like this, on her very doorstep—a communal one, true enough, but hers too—and that she would not know. Yet wouldn't she have to know? When she looked at my pale white face, the ice rimming my lashes, wouldn't something tell her, and wouldn't she regret that never by word or sign had she indicated anything to me?

It was about that time my brother appeared. He had a brown bag under his arm. "I brought you some lunch," he said.

"Thank you," I murmured. "It was sweet of you and good of you to think of me, but food doesn't matter."

"What?"

"I didn't mean to hurt your feelings," I said gently.

"That's all right," my brother nodded. He was beginning to realize that with love, you felt your way with an open mind. "Try a salami sandwich. Suppose we go over to a bench and sit down."

"No—we can't."

"Why not?"

"I have to watch both entrances, and you have to stand here to see them."

"Won't she look for you when she comes out?"

I shook my head. "She doesn't know I'm here."

"What?"

"You keep saying *what*. I think you don't understand what this means to me."

"No. I guess I don't."

"How could she know I'm here," I asked my brother, "when I never spoke to her?"

"Then what are you waiting here for?"

"For her to come out," I answered simply, eating the sandwich.

"And then?"

"Then I see her."

"But you see her every day, don't you?"

"Yes."

My brother looked at me searchingly. "Oh," he said.

"What do you mean by that?"

"Nothing. But suppose she doesn't come out?"

"She has to come out sooner or later."

"Why?" my brother demanded, parading the cold vista of logic. "On a day like this, she would be very smart to stay at home. She could stay at home and read the funnies. Maybe she's even got a party up there and all kinds of people are coming in to visit her."

"Stop that."

"I'm only trying to be logical," my brother said.

"You don't know how you're hurting me. If you knew, you wouldn't talk like that."

Indicating that if I thought so little of his advice, I could maintain my vigil alone, he left me to my meditations and to the incredible combination of damp wind that blew in two directions at the same time. The top of me wasn't so bad; I had a woolen cap and a short coat we used to call a Mackinaw; but my feet suffered. It was ironical to consider that it might be *her* fault that I would never be a sprinter; even the question of plain and simple walking began to raise doubts in my mind.

The sun had set behind the Palisades and the policeman on the beat was beginning to eye me uncertainly when my brother appeared again.

"Still no sign of her?" he said.

"I'm above anything you can say."

"All right. But Pop thinks you ought to come home."

"You didn't tell him?"

"Not exactly."

"How could you?"

"It's all right," my brother reassured me.

"How could it be all right? How could a man Pop's age know what I'm going through? Even you can't understand it."

"I try to," my brother said. "Don't think I don't want you to be a great cross-country runner, because that wouldn't be true."

"You don't even understand that my only interest in this damned cross-country running is because I want to lay something at her feet."

"I just feel you ought to introduce yourself. Then if she were to come out while you're standing here, she'd know you. You got to admit that would be an advantage."

It was true; I had to. I turned it over in my mind until Wednesday of the following week, and then because it looked like rain practice in Van Cortlandt Park was canceled. I took my heart in my hands and I stopped Thelma Naille when the dismissal bell rang. As I looked up at her, she was more than ever the Greek Goddess. I asked her how she went home.

"By bus."

"Do you go alone?"

"Sometimes," she said.

"Do you like to sit on the top—where it's open?"

"Sometimes," she said.

"Could I go home with you today?" I managed.

"If you want to," she said.

I walked on air. My heart beat like a trip hammer. Once, her hand even touched mine for just a moment. Outside, a northeaster blew, and I found a bus with an open top.

"It's cold up here," she said, when we sat down on the top of the bus. We had it to ourselves, the two of us alone with the whole world beneath us.

"You get used to it."

"And I think it's going to rain," she said.

"Maybe it won't, and anyway that's lucky for me because there's no cross-country practice."

"Oh," she said.

"That's like sprinting, only it goes on for two and a half miles."

"Oh," she said.

"I made the team," I said.

"Yes? Don't you think we ought to go downstairs?"

"You'll get used to it in no time. There are seventy men on the team, but that's the kind of a sport it is."

"Oh," she said. She turned up the collar of her coat and wrapped it more tightly around her. She stared straight ahead of her.

I made small talk to the best of my ability, but she didn't unbend, except to shiver occasionally. I even made one or two excursions into the matter of my feelings, and that was just as nonproductive of reaction. Then the sleet started, not much at first, actually not enough for you to really notice.

"I think we should go downstairs," she said.

"Oh, no. No. It's nice up here. Up here, you can see everything."

"Well, you did pay the fare," she said.

"That doesn't matter. I always pay the fare when I take someone on a bus."

"Aren't you cold?" she wanted to know.

"No. No—"

The sleet increased and then it turned to rain. For a minute or two more, she sat huddled against the rail. Then she stood up and walked to the back of the bus and down to the lower deck. I followed her, but I couldn't think of anything else to say until we came to her house.

"I'm soaked," she said. "I'm soaked through and through. And it's your fault."

"Just a little wet."

"No, I'm soaked," she said. "I'm good and soaked. Thank you for taking me home."

I told my brother about it later and he observed. "There you are. You can't tell."

"I love her more than ever," I said.

"Well—"

"What do you mean, well?"

"Nothing. Only tall girls don't like short men. That's something to think about too."

"I think it was mostly the rain. I guess she's delicate."

"She's awful big to be delicate."

"But she's sensitive," I said. "You wouldn't understand that."

She wasn't in school the next day, and I went through the tortures of the damned. "Call her up," my brother said.

"Call her?"

"Sure. Phone her. You know her address. Look up her number in the phone book and call her. She'll think it thoughtful of you."

I did as he said. A lady's voice answered. "Thelma is sick," the voice said coldly.

"Can I speak to her?"

"You can't," the voice said, and hung up.

I wouldn't want anyone to suffer the way I suffered those next few days. Penance was all I could think of. I had read in books about how people spent whole lifetimes atoning for some awful wrong they had done. I saw myself walking in her funeral. No one knew me, but no grief was like mine, because when all was said and done, I had slain her. I and no other. A lifetime would be hardly long enough to atone for that. I decided that I would do good things. My love would never change, never slacken; people would think of me as a saint, not knowing that in all truth I was a murderer. Even my cross-country running suffered. Instead of leading the pace, I lagged. The coach called me up for it, but what did cross-country mean now?

And then Monday came, and she appeared in school, and my heart sang again. She was paler—that was true—but it only increased her beauty. I went up to her and said:

"You were ill, and I'm sorry. If it was my fault—" I had thought the speech out very carefully, but she didn't permit me to complete it. Instead she broke in:

"You are a horrible, nasty little boy. Please don't speak to me again."

I skipped cross-country that day. I turned up for work at three and my brother shook his head somberly when he saw my face.

"What happened?" he demanded.

"The world ends, and you want to know what happened!"

"You'll still take the top floors, won't you?"

"Yes," I said sadly. "It doesn't matter. I still love her. I will always love her, I guess." I saw the future then, a grim and bitter man who turned his face from all women. They wouldn't know and neither would she.

Where Are
Your Guns?

In the land of the Goyim, my father traded with the Indians. We traded for beaver, and my father's word was as good as his bond, and we never carried a weapon except for our knives. From the lakes in the north to the canebrake in the south and as far west as the great river—there we traded and we never carried a weapon, never a musket or a rifle or a pistol, for these are weapons of death; and if you deal with death, what else can you expect in return? Is it not said in the Book, "Thou shalt not hate thy brother in thy heart"? And is it not also said, "I will also give thee for a light to the Gentiles"?

Among the Mingoes, we dwelt and traded, and among the Delawares, too, and among the Wyandottes and the Shawnees and the Eries and the Miamis and the Kickapoos, and even among the Menomini, where only the French have been, and never did we carry a weapon. "Men do not kill for the sake of killing," my father answered once to a hunter who could not understand why we didn't walk in fear of the red savage. "My people walked in fear for too long," my father said. "I don't fear what is different."

The hunter was one who slew his meat and ate it, even as the red men do, but our law is different. We kept the Law. Would you understand if I told you how we suffered to keep the Law? The Law says that when a beast is slain, it must be with the hand of a holy man, so that the lifeblood will run out as an offering to God rather than as a wanton slaughter of one of His creatures— with God's will and God's blessing.

Long, long ago, when I was only nine, my father said, "The high holy days are coming, and we have not sat down with our own people since your mother's death three years ago," speaking in the old tongue, which he taught me so carefully, being a man of learning. "I would have you pray for your mother's soul, and I would be with my own people for a little while, there is such a hunger in me." So we saddled our horses and made the long journey eastward to Philadelphia, where were a handful of our own people. Not that they welcomed us so well, we were two such wild buckskin folk, my father's great black beard falling to his waist; but we prayed with them and we ate meat with them.

You would have thought that we were unclean, they were such fine people there in Philadelphia, and when they talked about certain things, politics and who ruled over whom, indeed we sat as silent as the red men in their own woods. What does a man who trades with the Indians know of politics, my father thought? And what is it to a Jew who rules over a land? A Jew is a Jew, whether it be the old world or this new world, where the forest rolls like the sea. But when they talked of the Law and of holy things, then it was different, for my father was a man of learning, and when he lifted the meat to his mouth, he pointed out that this was the first meat he or I had eaten in years—and even after that day in Philadelphia, no unclean meat passed our lips.

I speak of this because I must make you understand my father, the man who traded with the Indians, so you will not judge me too harshly. I am not my father. My father fared forth to a wild land from far-off Poland, and of Poland I know no more than a dream and a legend, nor do I care. With his own hands he buried his wife in the wilderness, and he was mother and father to me, even though he left me with the Indians when I was small, and I lived in their lodges and learned their tongue. I am not like my father. He had a dream, which was to trade with the Indians until there was enough money to buy freedom, peace, security—all those things which, so it goes, only money can buy for a Jew; and because he had that dream, he never knew any comfort and the taste of meat was a strange thing to him. A stream of beaver skins went back to the Company on the donkeys and the flatboats that were owned by the Company, and all of it went to a place called London, and in this place there was a thing called an *account*.

Those were names and words and without meaning to me. I cared nothing of the beaver skins and nothing of the account, but if my father said that these things were of such importance, then indeed they were, even as the Law was. I knew other things; I knew the talk of the Shawnees and Algonquin talk, and I could make palaver with the men of the Six Nations too, if need be. I knew Yankee talk, the talk of those long-boned hunters of the East, and I knew the French talk and the high-pitched nasal talk of the British, who claimed to own the land, but knew nothing of it and stayed huddled in their outposts and stockades. I spoke the old language of the Book and I knew the Law, and I could catch trout with my bare hands and steal the eggs from under the nesting bird never disturbing it. I knew the step and the stride of nineteen moccasins, and where the wild parsnip grows and the wild turnip too, and with only a knife I could live the year round in the dark woods, where never the sky is seen. By heart in the old Hebrew, I knew the Song of Songs, which is Solomon's, and I knew forty psalms. And from the time I was thirteen, I prayed twice a day.

I also knew what it is to be a Jew.

But not like my father, whom you would have remembered, had you seen him come into Fort Pitt on that day. My father was six feet and two inches tall; fifteen stone he scaled, and never an ounce of fat, but hard as rock, with a black beard that fell to his waist. All through the woods, in those times, which are the old times now, the half-forgotten times, were Jews who traded with the Indians and went where no other white man had ever trod, but there was no one like my father, you may believe me. No one so tall or so wide or so heavy—or so sweet of speech and gentle of mien, yet I remember so well a cart and horse mired belly-deep, and my father heaved the horse out and the cart too. Or the time a year before at the company post of Elizabeth, where two Delawares were crazed with drink; they would have been slain, for what is better sport for a redcoat than to slay a drunken Indian? But my father lifted them from the ground like puppies and shook them until the drink went out of them, and instead of going to their deaths they went home to their lodges and were grateful.

I am not like my father, believe me. No man touches my forehead, unless he kill me first; but when a hunter met my father and saw that he was a Jew and begged to feel for the two horns nestling in his hair, my father would smile and agree, and then kindly commiserate with the man when he discovered that the old wives' tale was no more than that. Nor did my father sign for surety—ever, be it old MacTavish, who fended for the company in the north, or Ben Zion, who provided trade goods in Philadelphia, or Pontiac, whom my father told me to look at and heed, so I would know what was best in my own people in the ancient time when they followed the way of war and not of peace.

That was my father, who bound the phylacteries on his head faithfully every morning, and kept the Law and did justice to all who knew him. That was my father, who came into Fort Pitt with me on this day. We drove seven donkeys and they carried eleven hundred skins, and for a month I had listened to my father plan how now we would go to New York and demand an accounting from the Company, and there we would live with our own people and roam the woods no more. He was filled with it. A mile from the fort, we had stopped to drink water at the outhouse and mill of MacIntyre, and my father told him.

"No more this way, Angus," my father said, "but eastward and the boy will wear woven cloth on his back."

"Ye been a woodsy man these twenty year," MacIntyre said somberly.

"I'll be woodsy no more. And young Reuben here will make a company of his own, the good Lord willing."

"Heed the new commandant. He has no love for Jews, or for Scots either. I am glad to see you safe, because there is war with the Mingoes."

My father laughed because we had bought two hundred skins from the Mingoes, and there was no war talk in their cities. But when we came to the fort, there was a new guard at the gate. The doors were closed, and the men on the walls wore yellow facings and shakos I had not seen before. It was a new regiment for the woods.

"Who goes there?" a sergeant called.

"Two traders with skins."

"And where are your guns?"

"We bear no guns," my father said. "We are Jews who trade with the Indians."

Then the doors opened, and we entered with our donkeys, but there was never a smile or a nod. I looked at my father and he looked at me, but there was nothing to make out of his face; and when we looked around us, we saw that these were new men. Their cloth clothes were still fresh with the East, and they stared at us as if we were creatures; were we not Jews, they would have stared at us too, but there was that in their eyes that was singular for Jews.

Where, I wondered, were the Yankee folk, Benson, the smith, Bryan, the cooper, Wheelbury the harness maker? Where were the Indians, who were always a crowd in the fort? Where were the woodsy folk, the hunters, the French, in their green buckskin and red hats? Where were Stuart and Stevenson, the storekeepers? That too was in my father's mind, as I could see, but his broad face was calm, and he smiled at me as we prodded our donkeys into the low town. As if this were the first time we had come to old Duquesne, soldiers barred our way and a British subaltern demanded of us:

"Who are you and what are your names?"

"We are Jews who trade with the Indians," my father said. "My name is David, and this is my son, Reuben. Twelve years I have been in and out of this place, even when it was Duquesne, and I am known in the forest country."

"I don't know you," the young man said, as if we were dirt and less than dirt.

"Then I be sorry," my father said. "Stevenson knows me, for I have always traded with him and paid my loanings. Benson knows me, for he shod my beasts, and Bryan knows me, for he boxed my goods. I am not a stranger here."

"You are a Jew and damned insolent," the young man replied. "As for the scum of this place, they know the dregs of the woods. Where are your arms?"

"We bear no arms but our knives."

"And how did you come through the Mingoes? There is war with the Mingoes."

A mass of soldiers were around us now, and now I could see Benson and some of the others, but keeping off. I am not like my father. I would have made a story then, but it was not in him to speak anything but the truth. He was going to New York, but I knew of a sudden that he would be lonely and forsaken in such a place. The green woods was his home, and it was not in him to speak anything but the truth.

"There is no war with the Mingoes," he said slowly. "I traded two hundred skins with the Mingoes, and I lay in their lodges this fortnight past. There is no war with the Mingoes."

The young officer said, "You're a damned liar, a filthy Jew, and a spy as well."

My father's face was sad and hard and woeful. I moved, but he moved quicker, and he struck the officer a blow that would have felled an ox. Then we fought a little, but there were too many of them.

They put us in a cell and they gave us no food and no water. We were bleeding and bruised, but it was not hard to go without food. It was hard for my father to go without his phylacteries, but after the second day I didn't care. They came every few hours and asked us to tell what we knew of the Mingoes, but what we knew was of no interest to them.

The colonel came finally. It is so different now that you cannot know what a colonel was in those days in a place like Fort Pitt. He was an English gentleman and he was God too, and he prodded us with his stick.

"How old are you?" he asked me.

"I am fifteen," I croaked.

"You are large for fifteen," he lisped, holding a lace handkerchief over his nose. "The Yankees come large, but I should not think it would be so with a Jew. I shall hang your father tomorrow, but if you will tell me what you know of the Mingoes, you may go free and take your seven beasts with the skins."

"I know nothing of the Mingoes."

"And how do you travel in the woods without guns? I am very curious."

"That you could never know," my father said, almost sadly.

Even these days you will hear things said of Jews; it is that way; but once my father found a robin with a broken wing, and made splints for the wing and a sling, so that we could carry the bird with us, and he nursed it until it flew away. So I will remember until I die how the British drums rolled as they hanged my father, who traded with the Indians in the land of the goyim, and whose word was as good as his bond. And then they gave me thirty lashes until I bled like a pig, and drove me from the fort to die in the forest.

A Jew dies hard, they say. I crawled a mile to Angus MacIntyre's mill, and he washed my back and cared for me until I returned to my senses and could walk again.

"Weep for your father," he said, "for you are only a laddie, and he was much of a man."

"I weep no more and pray no more. My father is dead, and I am not like him."

"You will be like him, lad."

"I will never be like him, Angus, but I will make my word like my bond. I give you my word I will bring you forty beaver skins if you give me a musket and powder and shot."

A long time the old Scot looked at me, measuring me and weighing me. "Go to the land of the Yankees, lad," he said, "and wear woven clothes on your back."

"The Yankees stood by while my father was hanged. When that redcoat filth drove the Mingoes from the fort, the Yankees stood by. When two Mingoes came back for the little they left behind and were slain at the gate, the Yankees said nothing."

"How many of them were there?" the Scot said quietly. "They are a strange folk, dirty and bragging and mean and sometimes, in a most curious way, a little noble. Will they be silent forever?"

"Will you give me the gun?"

"You are one of them," the Scot said.

"When they are no longer silent—I will be one of them. When they strike, I will strike with them."

"And your father traded in the woods with never more than a knife. For the Company. Are you for the Company?"

"I am against any man in a uniform."

"I will give you the gun, lad," the Scot said sadly, "and you will slay your meat and eat it."

"And other things."

"Then put no price on it, for what you seek has no price but a man's blood. You are one of them."

He gave me the gun, and I left him and walked eastward.

The Gentle
Virtue

THE SERIES of lectures which Carrol presented during his two-week stay at the University were more of a success than he had anticipated, considering that the subject was "The Inner Ethic of Herman Melville," and at the final convocation he drew a crowd of more than seven hundred, a very singular and unprecedented occurrence.

He had to admit to himself that he had not done badly; four years in the service might have cut him entirely adrift, or it might have had the opposite effect of driving him to the close security of an assistant professorship, both shelter and retreat and a certain amount of dignity too; but he had resisted more successfully than some of his colleagues. He had written and published a book, and he was well on his way with the second one now. To go it alone required more courage than anything he had faced during the war, but he had managed and he would manage, and there was not only relief but a wonderful sense of freedom in the thought that tomorrow he would be returning to New York, to the complicated and variegated world where anything could and did happen. The sense of excitement he experienced whenever he undertook even a minor variation in the course of his life was something he would not willingly surrender; and all things taken together he was, he felt, about as happy as a man could be in these troubled and perturbed United States.

The talk to the convocation was delivered freely and wittily, in a fashion that prompted Madelin Burroughs to tell him, afterwards, that he had a voice that could lull children to sleep, and when he had finished, he managed very well with the few words he had to say to each of the many people, students and faculty and some townspeople, who came crowding around him. A year ago, he would have been terrified and embarrassed by their approach, but he had achieved what he liked to think of as a sort of maturity in that time, and it gave him real pleasure to know that there were many people who thought well and warmly of Brighton Carrol.

He was the middle of a small circle; some people came up and introduced themselves and plunged directly into what was on their minds; others held back and waited, and some stood there and smiled at him because they liked him and what he said and the way he looked; and there was one young girl who stood on the edge of the circle watching him, and he could hardly help noticing her, she was so lovely and clean looking. When Professor Andrews drew him away to take him to the reception the English faculty was giving him on this, his last night, he felt a sense of regret that he had not had a chance to talk to the pretty girl. That made it all the better when she was there, getting into Andrews's car with him. They squeezed in with a young instructor, and both were introduced casually by Andrews, who, after he had told Carrol that the girl's name was Lucy Reed, bubbled with praise for the convocation.

"You think," Andrews said; "and you will never know, Brighton, God willing, how rare a quality thought is on a campus."

"Isn't it a new campus though?" Carrol wanted to know. "Practically everyone I met is a vet."

"That makes a difference," Andrews admitted, and the girl, Lucy Reed, said:

"You haven't met any women, have you?"

Carrol began to apologize, but she took his hand, laughing at him, and then he sat there, uncertain and uneasy about the way she held his hand, uncomfortable too at the overtness of her approach. Yet he couldn't help but feel her assurance, and the almost aggressive approach at him held in it an assured warmth, as if she were an old friend and not someone he had only met this evening. But as they drove along he realized that he had seen her before, at least once, with Andrews, but not noticed her as he was noticing her tonight. He felt, tonight, that fine alertness and sensitivity to life that comes even to the happiest of human beings only once in a while, and then more than makes up for dull days, boredom and frustration. The reception, which would include all of the English faculty, their wives, their petty lusts, jealousies and discontents, he somehow looked forward to with pleasant excitement, as if the evening were bound to promise something.

He was not listening to Andrews denying the universality of Melville. "To me, he is a uniquely American product, and it is precisely on that point I'd take issue with you, Brighton." The girl next to him and holding his hand, he discovered, was more than handsome and quite beautiful, pale. but with fine, clean-cut features and a long-limbed body. His own reserve, he finally decided, qualified everything; that was one of the reasons he remained unmarried at thirty-five; that was why, if the evening were not otherwise so pleasant, he would have resented fiercely Andrews, whom he hardly knew, a professor in Elizabethan Poetry, calling him by his first name and plunging on with an obviously ridiculous criticism. Andrews didn't know what he was talking about, but that he dismissed with an offhand remark and spoke to the girl, but only a few words. Then they were there, looking for a parking place outside of the department head's house.

"You will be lionized tonight," the girl said.

Andrews told him, as they got out of the car, "We can get away at twelve, if you just want to sit down at my place and relax, my wife and perhaps one or two others."

He answered noncommittally, more annoyed with Andrews because the girl had slipped away and gone into the house than because Andrews's invitation was not in the best of taste. However, he liked Andrews's wife, whom he remembered as a pleasant, healthy-looking woman who had sat through one of his seminars, and he substituted "I'll see" for a straight refusal.

Inside, everyone had liked his talk at the convocation and told him so, and he reflected again that this was a department in which he would work very comfortably and perhaps with a good deal of satisfaction. There was something large and straightforward about Carrol, and he had that easy youthfulness which is characteristic of many American men, and which, when combined with any degree of intelligence, can be immensely charming. Also, early in his stay at the University, he had endeared himself to the English faculty.

The head of the department had a pleading, Middle Western passion for Wordsworth, which he indulged to the extent of spending all of the department's museum money on first editions of the British bard. Aside from resentment on national grounds, there were other poets who ranked higher in the estimation of various members of the department, and their joy knew no bounds when Carrol said to the head, at lunch one day:

"I should think it would be Riley."

"Who?"

"Instead of Wordsworth, I mean."

"Did you say Riley?"

Innocently enough and without smiling, Carrol managed, "Yes, James Whitcomb Riley. I mean, he trod this very soil—"

The head of the department never quite made up his mind whether Carrol was a Philistine or a boor, but the story was told around, and everyone else loved him for it. Now, tonight, they were genuinely sorry that he was going away, and the group of animated men and women, drinking sherry and brandy, almost took on that warm and wise and balanced combination of wit and civilization that had become so foreign to America, but still lurked on a campus. Or it may have been that Carrol wanted to see it that way and did. In any case, he was at his best, and they talked of what he felt were better things than war and the threat of war, the ugly, crouching monster which implied that this was the end of all things for all time.

Lucy Reed sat near him, but not obtrusively. She would move away and then be back again, watching him. When he had a minute alone with Eve Andrews, he asked her, "How old is the Reed girl?"

"Why?"

"I thought I'd like to know something about her—what she does. Is she on the staff?"

"She's twenty-nine. She was after her doctorate, but gave it up."

And he was moved to say lamely that he thought she looked younger. It was the way Mrs. Andrews regarded him that thrust him away, and he found himself listening to the conversation instead of being a part of it, and thereby it became commonplace, a good deal of it rather stupid. He listened to people saying things to him, and he answered them too, but an insatiable loneliness had suddenly taken hold of him; and he wondered whether in a foolish, adolescent way, he was forming a crush for Lucy Reed. It would be ironic, indeed, he told himself, if after waiting as long as he had— incapable for some reason that had never troubled him overmuch of forming a permanent alliance or relationship with any woman— he were to form what he liked to think of as a fixation on a girl in a provincial Middle Western college town.

But he forgot that when he found a few minutes alone with her and they were able to talk. She was quite tall, a strong, long-limbed girl, and in the way she stood, her actions, her speech—in everything about her, actually—was that quality he envied so much, a fierce devotion to life, a love of life, a consuming interest in the very essence of living. There was no cynicism in her, yet obtuseness was not there as a substitute. She seemed to be better read and better informed than most of the people he had met on the campus, and she looked at him with the kind of alert delight that he had not found in the eyes of any woman in a long, long time.

"I like you," she said to him. "I do wish I had met you when you first came."

"Would it make much difference?"

"Of course it would," she said. "In a world as rotten and as beautiful as this one, you are a rare, good person."

"How do you know?"

"What did you do in the war?" she asked him.

"I was an infantryman."

"And it didn't affect you, and you came back to Herman Melville. Now I've hurt you."

"You haven't hurt me," he said, enormously contained.

"Only I wish I could have seen what you saw and been through what you were through."

"Why?"

"You don't know why, do you?" she asked him curiously.

"Couldn't we get away from here?" he wanted to know. "Couldn't I buy you a beer and couldn't we sit down and talk?"

"Why?" she smiled.

"This is not getting us anywhere, is it?" Carrol said. "I have my ticket on the nine o'clock plane in the morning. I would like to spend an hour with you."

"That's flattering."

"No—you know what I mean to say."

"I don't, really, but I'll see you at the Andrewses' later, won't I?"

"Will you be there?"

"Of course I will. I live there."

"You live there?"

"I'm the professor's adopted daughter—didn't you know?"

She said it seriously, yet he took it as an awkward jest, and reinforced himself, as he always had, with the failings of others. She was not as bright as he had thought, and having already projected, in an indulgent and inward way, as he had with so many other women—projected but never consummated—a situation in which he followed his fancy, fell completely in love, married, lived his life, he found it neither attractive nor hopeful. And as if she had read his mind, she looked at him almost pityingly before she turned away.

He wanted to speak to her again, but did not have a chance to until much later. Instead, his eyes followed her, wherever she was in the room, picking her up again and again and sometimes meeting her eyes and sometimes finding her smiling at him. Only a part of his mind was in the conversations he fell into here and there. The most of him was with her now in a warm, petulant desire; and while he talked about literature, campus gossip, and the war too, he was erecting in his mind the mechanism whereby he might find time alone with her that evening to at least have a stab at making love. He forced the substitution of a night with her for that endless span which a man had to consider once he admitted to himself that he could love a woman and that perhaps she could love him. Yet he couldn't help wondering what that remark about being the adopted daughter of Andrews meant, feeling at the same time a wave of resentment against Andrews for the fact that she lived with him. His own casualness in terms of any man-woman relationship had long ago convinced him that cohabitation inevitably followed proximity, and the possibility of some sordid triangle within Andrews's home sickened him. More curiously than before, he studied Andrews, a matter-of-fact academic type, in his late thirties, sandy-haired, spectacled, civilized to the high impotence of those few cloistered and cultured beings America boasts, and vegetating quietly in a Middle Western university.

At about eleven o'clock, when the reception showed signs of breaking up, Carrol sought out Lucy Reed and reminded her. "I have my car outside," she said, "and if you can manage to slip away, I'll take you home with me—if you want to come?"

"To Andrews's place?"

"Yes. Won't you come? After two hours of talking to fifty people, I should imagine you'd like to sit down and talk with two or three."

"Or one," said Carrol.

She shook her head, and Carrol said, all right, he'd find some way to get out.

"The car is a little, beat-up Ford coupé," she said. "I left it at the corner under the lamppost before the convocation, and it's probably still there."

"In ten minutes," Carrol said optimistically.

He saw no reason to be secretive about it, and he told Eve

Andrews that Lucy was driving him over to their place. "All right," she said. "It's nice that you can come." Then he made his excuses, said his good-bys, and got out into the cool spring air. That finished it, and he was glad to be away. It had taken something to get out of there alone, and they would talk about it, but he didn't much care. He found the car, with Lucy already in it, and there was almost a note of casual old acquaintanceship in the way they nodded at each other. She drove to the Andrewses' place in a roundabout route that took them past the edge of an old limestone quarry, filled with a placid pool of water that shimmered gently in the fine moonlight. Feeling that he was expected to kiss her, Carrol tried; she didn't resist, and then he couldn't do anything more than sit beside her lonely and quiet and disturbed until they reached the Andrewses', thinking of what she would say if he blundered out that he loved her, even though he knew nothing more about her or who she was or where she came from or where she thought she was going.

At the Andrewses', aside from the professor and his wife, there was just an amiable young instructor from the law school. There was a good fire in the old-fashioned living room, and they all sat in front of it, drinking bourbon and soda, and talking that kind of literary talk Carrol loved better than anything else. When Carrol remarked, "I'm afraid I took the edge off the reception, bolting out like that," Andrews observed that the host and hostess were probably everlastingly indebted to him for ending it so early. They made no further reference to his impending departure, but Carrol was conscious by now of their liking for him, a strange liking that was tinged, at least on the part of Eve Andrews, with a curiosity he hardly understood. If it had not been for the very naturalness and warmth of this late evening gathering, he might have sensed something terrible and impending; but how could he when the conversation flowed so normally and well?

They talked about the ten best tales that men had written, and then, enthralled, as people whose work is literature will be, by the process of storytelling and storymaking, they traced the lines of development through many lands and cultures. That kind of talk, Carrol reflected, can be in this world a sort of wine, gentle and civilized, heart-warming and soul-comforting, reclaiming as it does what man has achieved and not what he has destroyed. At first Carrol had to fight down a sort of childish resentment against the young law school instructor, but everything he said and did made it self-evident that he was no more than a good friend to Lucy Reed, while everything Lucy Reed did and said made it plainly apparent to Carrol, if not to everyone else there, that he was a special quality with her. With no self-consciousness, innocently as a small girl, she gave her heart to him, and he would have had to be insensitive indeed not to feel it and respond to it. Withal, she was so easily a part of the group that Carrol found himself completely unable to fathom what relationship she bore to the others.

That they loved her was obvious, but the quality and nature of the love only puzzled Carrol. He habitually made the mistake of so many intellectuals, that of oversimplifying people whom he considered of lesser capacity, and he found himself revising his estimate of Professor Andrews and his wife—and his estimate of Lucy Reed too. Watching her pale, clean-cut, lovely face in the shadows of the firelight, he became more and more convinced that the seemingly aimless flow of events had paused meaningfully as it brought them together, and as the early morning began, he no longer denied to himself that he was completely and wonderfully in love.

During the decade past, he would have strongly and reasonably denied the spirituality of love, the selflessness and wonder of it, and now he accepted it wholly and felt as so many others have felt, that he suddenly was different from and beyond all other human beings. The imminence of age, which only lately had come to prey upon him and bedevil him, turned into a flower of youth, and the youthfulness became a bond between them. His whole future suddenly had turned and fixed upon a woman, and between fragments of conversation, he made plans. He would go to New York, even as he was scheduled to, but in a week at the most he would be back here. He might live and work here for a while; the place would not only be bearable, but charming. After all, he told himself, the attitude which led him to reject this place was a manufactured sophistication; had he not told himself a hundred times, during the war, that any corner of America could be wonderful?

That way, his thoughts roved along, and suddenly it was past one in the morning. Lucy Reed rose and said abruptly:

"I'm very tired. Will you excuse me?"

Carrol got up and took her warm hand in his. "Good night," she said. She left then and Carrol heard her going upstairs. The evening was over now, and Eve Andrews, catching his eye, said, "I'll drive you home whenever you're ready to go, Brighton."

"What about a nightcap?" the professor asked. "One more small one."

The law school instructor stretched his arms and yawned, and at that moment, while Eve Andrews emptied an ash tray into a silent butler, Carrol heard the noise—a harsh, grating human noise. Someone was moaning or calling aloud in pain, he thought, but no one else appeared to notice it. The noise came again, and he started and demanded:

"Didn't you hear it? What was that?"

"Lucy," Eve Andrews said shortly. Suddenly the professor and the law school instructor were contemplatively silent, absorbed in their drinks.

After a long moment, Carrol said, "What do you mean, Lucy?"

"She's ill. She has difficulty keeping anything on her stomach."

"She doesn't look sick," Carrol said. "What is it—an ulcer?"

"It's worse than an ulcer," Eve Andrews said quietly. "It's a kind of cancer called 'Hodgkin's disease.' "

"Is it bad?"

The professor asked shortly, almost angrily, "How bad can cancer be?"

Driving Carrol back to the Grand Union, where he had boarded during his stay at the University, Eve Andrews was strangely unresponsive to Carrol's horror. "It happens," she said, almost coldly. "And her family couldn't face it. They couldn't deal with it. Every night the girl went to bed with mortal fear that she wouldn't wake in the morning. She's better since she came to live with us."

"When—" Carrol began.

"Six months ago was the date they set."

"But she doesn't look sick or act sick."

"That's right."

"And isn't there anything to hope for?" Carrol pleaded.

"A miracle—if you believe in them."

"No cure, no method . . . ?"

"No cure, that's right."

"No, it can't be," Carrol said. "Not that beautiful, wonderful girl. It can't be."

Eve Andrews shrugged, and Carrol turned on her fiercely and demanded, "How in hell can you be so cold about it?"

"Do you think I'm cold about it?" she said tiredly. "I grew up with Lucy. I'm a year older than she. We played together as kids and then we had dates together. Now we try to make the little bit left normal and worth while. You don't want to face that, do you? Were you falling in love with her before you found this out?"

When he didn't answer, she went on, "What have you ever faced? You saw no death in the war, did you? You don't live in a world where people are born and where they die."

"That's a hell of a thing to say."

"What do you want me to say? Did you see her eyes tonight? Suppose you had a day or three days or three weeks to live? There's a good deal of nonsense talked about love, but there's something else about love too—or maybe you don't know?"

They had drawn up before the Grand Union now, and for a minute or two, they sat there in silence. Then Eve Andrews said, "Good night, Brighton."

"Good night," Carrol said.

Carrol spent a sleepless night. It was not until sunrise that he understood how foolish a quixotic action can be. It was not until sunrise that he could blend peace and pity with a calm understanding that grown men did not fall in love in that fashion. He told himself that he would always remember Lucy Reed with pity and affection; and he also told himself that the quick image he had conceived the night before of marrying a girl in such a position was hardly sensible and beneficial surely to neither.

A few hours later he was boarding his plane, reflecting, as he so often did, on the virtues of a civilized man in a basically uncivilized world.

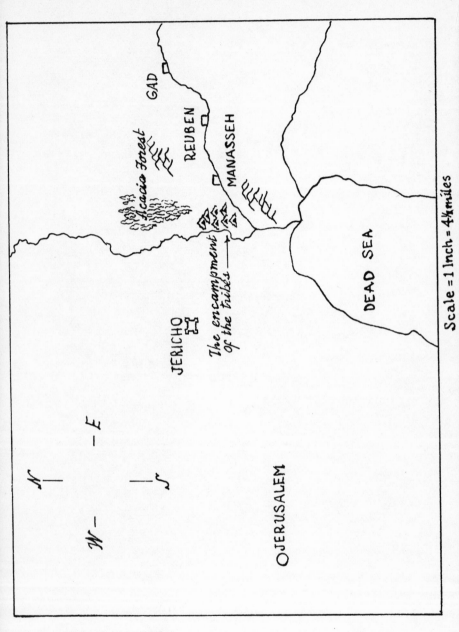

Scale = 1 Inch = 4¼ miles

The Golden River

THIS STORY WAS conceived not as an attempt at historical investigation or as an interpretation of Scripture. It is an entertainment, in which some readers may, if they so desire, seek a parable.

However, some understanding of ancient Hebrew terminology may put the reader more at ease with the setting.

Mother god is used as a generic term for the numerous deities of the matriarchal and fertility cults of the ancient New East.

Lord is the accepted translation of the Hebrew word *adon*, a general title of respect, distinction and nobility; and, as in English, applied both to man and God.

Priest is the literal translation of the Hebrew word *kohan*. In the Mediterranean cultures of the same period, the equivalent word is more often translated as *king*, and for that time, when speaking of tribal cultures, the words are interchangeable.

Horeb is most often translated as *The Mountain of God*, and is frequently explained as another name for Sinai. However, most modern scholars doubt that these two places are the same. A rabbinical source holds that *Horeb* means *Mountain of the Sword*, but many scholars today believe that *Mountain of the Sun* offers a better explanation of the origin of the name. Some scholars are of the opinion that *Horeb* is a now-extinct volcano in the Sinai Desert. There is no evidence to show exactly where *Horeb* was located, although the fact of its literal existence is accepted by almost all authorities.

Nebo means *Mountain of the Far View*; from its peak, most of Israel can be seen.

The characters of this book, and the tribes of Israel to which they belonged:

THE TRIBE OF LEVI

Moses
Nun
Joshua (the son of Nun)
Eleazar (the son of Moses)
Joash (the son of Joshua)

The Half-Tribe of Manasseh

Gamaliel (war chief of Manasseh)
Deborah (his wife)

The Tribe of Reuben

Nohab (war chief of Reuben)
Sarah (Nohab's sister, the wife of Joshua)

The Tribe of Gad

Jephta (war chief of Gad)

The Tribe of Judah

Caleb (war chief of Judah, one of the four war lords of the confederation)

The Tribe of Simon

Gath (war chief of Simon, one of the four war lords of the confederation)

The Tribe of Kenn

Gershom (son of Moses, war chief of Kenn and one of the four war lords of the confederation)

The Tribe of Ephraim

Joel (war chief of Ephraim)

NOTE: The *Joseph Tribes* were Manasseh and Ephraim, the two tribes of the Israel confederation who claimed their descent from the sons of Joseph. Half of the tribe of Manasseh lived east of the Jordan, and were known as the Gileadites.

PART ONE. DEBORAH

I

At sunset, but at dawn too, there are days when the river appears to be flowing gold, and especially is this the case where it flows through the plain, with the City of Jericho on one side and the acacia woods and the high hills of Gilead on the other.

This is the River Jordan, but in the old, old times, to the people who came across the dry, sere plains and the burning desert and saw the river for the first time through the dark green of the acacia, it was a miracle of life and sustenance beyond the simple fact of water. In their tongue, as it had to be, it was *Nahar Zahav*, the golden river, even as the acacia woods became for them the holy wood of *Shittem*.

When they came to the bank of this golden river for the first time, they brought with them a legend of an ancestor who had once lived in the land across the river. They also brought with them the dry dust and the burning memory of the desert, a memory of Bedouin wandering without end, of hunger unsatisfied and of thirst unslaked. And with this memory so deep and dry inside of them, they gazed across the river at the green hills and pastures of the Land of Canaan.

Across the river were other things too, walled cities so incredible to the wanderers and tent people of the desert—and men of war in shining armor who rode in high-wheeled chariots.

The tent people of the desert were not afraid of the men in shining armor. Many things they feared, but not men with weapons, for among the tent people a weapon was given to a boy almost when the nipple was taken from his mouth. But when the tent people first came to the riverbank, they were only a handful, a family, a clan. Yet they crossed over, drawn by the green fields the way an iron splinter is drawn to the magnet, and when they were driven back, they fought for their foothold with a fury beyond the experience of the Canaanite defenders.

But the Canaanites had never known what it is to look at green fields from the hot desert sand, and therefore the Canaanites never understood why the tent people fought with such awful fury. Again and again, the tent people recrossed the river, and again and again, they were driven back. But in the course of years, a name for these tent people found its way into the language of the Canaanites. They were called, "Those from across the river," in the language of Canaan, *Ivri*, containing the meaning and the threat in a single word. And in time, the word became *Hebrew*.

II

On this night—which was the night before the morning of which the tale is told—there was no sleep for Deborah, the wife of Gamaliel. He, Gamaliel, was war chief of the half-tribe of Manasseh, and because the three clans that constituted this half-tribe had built for themselves a walled city on the southernmost edge of the land of Gilead, the men of Manasseh spoke of Deborah as the princess of their house.

The title was a little presumptuous, not only because the City of Manasseh was small, but because the Land of Gilead, stretching eastward from the bank of the River Jordan, was the ancient preserve of the warlike Ammonites and Amorites. Over the past hundred years, two tribes of the dry and bitter desert Bedouins who styled themselves, along with so many other tribes and clans, the Children of Israel, had found a foothold in Gilead. They had made an alliance with the Ammonites against the Amorites and thereby they had been given land in the valleys on the east bank of the Jordan, pasture for their cattle and fertile bottoms for wheat and barley.

But because they lived in mortal fear of the vengeance of the Amorites, they had hired stoneworkers from the Land of Canaan to build them walls around their tents. And, in further time, they learned to put away their tents and build houses.

So it came to be that of all the fierce and thirsty clans and tribes who called themselves the Children of Israel, and who grazed their herds over hundreds of miles of sere badlands, from the Red Sea to the Plains of Bashan, from the Sinai Peninsula to the Syrian Desert, only the tribes of Gad and Reuben, and the half-tribe of Manasseh lived in walled cities and tilled the soil with plough and hoe.

The city of Manasseh, however, was less old than the cities of Reuben and Gad; for the building of their city had happened in the time of Deborah's father. The three clans that made up the half-tribe were camped on the bank of the Jordan when the Amorites came down on the city of Reuben. The people of Manasseh left their tents then and fled to the city, pleading for shelter; and when the Reubenites took them in, they fought alongside the Reubenites against the Amorites. They were fierce and effective fighters, as desert people always are, compared with city people. And because the Reubenites valued them, they were given land and the knowledge of stone-building and tillage.

The tent of Manasseh became the House of Manasseh, and when Gamaliel took Deborah as his bride, she was hailed as a princess; but the title was as empty as her marriage and as joyless.

In her mind, the word for it was "mockery," and she whispered the word to herself early on this night of sleeplessness, lying still and rigid with her eyes closed, as the Lord Gamaliel opened the door of her chamber and took three long steps toward her bed.

Then she prayed to the mother, "God who is our mother, let him believe that I am asleep."

"So you sleep, my lovely Deborah," said Gamaliel, and closed though her eyes were, she saw him clearly and in detail, the curled black hair, the arched brows, the small, deep-set eyes, the long, thin nose, and under his beard and mustache, the lips curling contemptuously. As she had come to hate him, slowly, over weeks and months, her hatred had to focus on something physical—and of all of him, she hated most his sardonic smile. The smile was in his voice; she did not have to open her eyes.

"Let him go away," she prayed.

"You sleep as poorly as you lie," he said. "Is that to be said in your favor? I don't think so, Deborah. You are not clever. Only clever people are capable of deception. It is true that I was willing to endure having a fool for a wife, particularly one so beautiful; but I don't enjoy being made a fool of."

She lay motionless.

"What you do, I can endure," he said. "I take some comfort in thinking that we have become more civilized than the tent people. I find it less easy to endure what is said behind my back. As a matter of fact, there is a simple and direct virtue in the thinking of the tent people. They would stone you to death."

Now she opened her eyes and faced him, sitting up in her bed. He carried a lamp in his hand, and he wore a long red robe in the manner of the Canaanites.

"What do you want of me?" she asked.

"At this point—nothing."

"Then go away and leave me alone."

"Yes. You satisfy no thirst. I find you empty."

"Go away," Deborah whispered.

"I leave you with one thought," Gamaliel smiled. "Joshua, the son of Nun, is a bull, a steaming, stinking red bull. When the bull sees what he wants, he moves toward it. He drops his head and begins a motion, and unless you kill the bull, that motion can't be changed."

His words came to Deborah without meaning; but her husband was also without meaning, and as she looked at him, she felt spread and hollow with emptiness.

"One more thought," Gamaliel said. "If you go to him tonight, you will pay a price tomorrow. Do you understand?" Then he added, "No matter." And turned on his heel and walked out.

Again, after he had gone, Deborah closed her eyes and tried to sleep. But her mind was in a turmoil now, and she felt her heart racing and pounding. An image caught her fancy, and she saw a great, red giant of a man, who was like a bull. In her thoughts, she told him what Gamaliel had said, and he laughed and moved one hand to brush Gamaliel away as one brushes an insect aside.

III

When he left his wife, Gamaliel, the war chief of Manasseh, went to the wall of his city, where the war chiefs of Reuben and Gad awaited him. Gamaliel was conscious and proud of his city; it was still building when he was a child, and his father, like Deborah's, had been born in the black felt tent of a Bedouin. Perhaps for this reason, he had told Nohab and Jephta of the tribes of Reuben and Gad, that he would meet them later upon the city wall.

Now, as he walked through the sleeping city, his pride dwindled and his boastfulness reproached him. He imagined Nohab and Jephta discussing his tiny city, the walls only thirty feet high and more than half the houses flimsy huts of acacia wood. They would probably discuss other things too.

His attitude toward these two men was compounded out of respect and envy. So long ago had they put aside their tents that the culture and manners of Canaan were second nature to them, and he had no doubt that when the time came, they would name themselves kings. His own half-tribe of Manasseh consisted of less than two thousand souls, but they ruled over their tens of thousands, and their cities were teeming hives of wealth, trade and—as Gamaliel saw it—culture.

Culture was the nature of cities; culture was the softness of fabric, the richness of gold and the savor of food; culture was a way of making love to a woman that exposed the crudity of those who leaped on women like bulls in heat. Culture was wealth and substance and stability and the sense of belonging to a place. Culture was also power, for that completed Gamaliel's definition.

He belonged. He came to the stone stairs that led to the top of the wall, and as he climbed them, each step brought him the gratification of power and substance. On the wall itself, Nohab and Jephta, the lords of Reuben and Gad, awaited him.

They looked like brothers, both of them broadshouldered and of middle height, black-bearded and with the tense muscularity of the athlete, as those who live for war must need be. They were hard men and they were also crafty men; and they greeted Gamaliel as a valued friend.

"Welcome, Prince of Manasseh."

A diplomatic, thoughtful greeting; also barbed, if one read it so, for who were they to welcome him to his own walls? The nature of a war chief is not simple, Gamaliel told himself. In the old Bedouin times, the patriarch led the tribe; but when the business of the tribe changed from cattle-grazing to war, the need was for another kind of man.

"It is a cool and a very pleasant night," Gamaliel said, "especially here on the battlements. I try to plant fragrant blossoms in my gardens. The fragrance comes out at night and the whole air is perfumed. I trust you were not bored."

They both smiled, and Gamaliel had the sudden feeling that he had made a fool of himself, telling them of the nature of jasmine. What could they be thinking? That this was a fool and an upstart, this son of Joseph who had built his shabby little city by their leave and will. But they said, "No fear of that, Gamaliel, when one can look down at that sight." Nohab pointed to the valley below, where the Jordan flowed silver and black in the moonlight. On the east bank of the Jordan, stretching fully two miles, there was a great pattern of twinkling lights.

"You see it only tonight," Gamaliel said bitterly. "Night after night, I see it, and day after day, I look at their black tents. Their cattle have eaten my grass to the roots, and their screaming and wailing make peace a memory."

"You have reason not to like them," Jephta nodded, making no point of his statement.

"I have reason."

"You know how many of them there are now?" Nohab asked him.

"Over a hundred thousand, I have heard."

"Well over."

"The cursed red bull boasts that he can put thirty thousand men into the field."

"As he can, make no mistake."

"Who would have believed it?" Jephta, the war chief of Gad, wondered. "Who would have believed that any man could bring them together like this, camp them alongside the river and hold them in peace under his hard hand—and make a day for the crossing too?" His voice carried the muted eloquence which admits an impossible fact, but his broad, black-bearded face was filled with hatred and resentment. Almost with astonishment, Gamaliel realized that these two chiefs of Reuben and Gad were not the kind of city men he liked to think of them as being; they were no smooth-faced, painted Canaanites. They were as cold and desperate as any of the desert chieftains in the mighty encampment alongside the river.

"Tomorrow," Nohab said.

"Oh?" Gamaliel looked at him.

"I said, he will take them across the river tomorrow. And what then, my friends?"

"Tomorrow. Yes, tomorrow." It was worse for Gamaliel than for the others. His shabby little city was infinitely precious. "And you think," Gamaliel said, "that he will go through with it, that he will demand the last letter of the pledge—that we leave the cities, burn them, and that we go across the river with him?"

"I didn't say quite that," Nohab replied.

"Then let me tell you something," said Jephta, "if you think that any force we know, god or man—I say that, god or man—can turn Joshua ben Nun from what he plans to do tomorrow, then you are fools! Lying to yourselves! I tell you, he will do it tomorrow. What else has he lived for? And what else would he die for?"

"Men die," Gamaliel said.

"Oh, yes—yes, men die," Jephta smiled. "What are you thinking of, Gamaliel? Do you know how he sleeps?—"

There it was. Gamaliel cringed, and his skin became wet and cold; but Jephta went on, "—The Levite guards stand around his black tent, a spear's length apart. Have you ever seen his Levites in battle? Not men, these—but like the wild scream of the fight itself. No. Forget that. Not a mouse could enter that tent where Joshua sleeps—"

Nohab stopped him with a look, and then there was an uncomfortable silence among the three men. Then Nohab spoke softly and thoughtfully. He was the oldest of the three, and different from the other two.

"It had to be," Nohab said. "If it were not Joshua, it would be someone else, because a time is ripe, and when a time is ripe it moves. Can you stop the river from flowing?

"Your blood is too hot against him," he said to Gamaliel. "I know what you feel. His wife, Sarah, is my own sister, remember that. We all have pride. But even if we killed Joshua, those tent people would not turn away from the river and go back to the desert. They are too many now. It began when Moses put an end to the fighting and blood-letting among them, when he brought them together at the mountain of the God, at Horeb. That was when it began."

"And we must bow our heads and accept it?" Gamaliel cried. "And I must watch him make a whore of my wife and a mockery of your sister? And we must burn our houses and abandon our gods? All this?"

"Not so angry—not so quick," Nohab smiled. "There is still to-morrow."

Jephta said, "Trust Nohab, Gamaliel."

"Whatever Joshua wants," Nohab nodded, "he wants Canaan more."

IV

Sarah, the sister of Nohab, was tall and strong, as so many of the Reubenite women were, but under her dark brows, her eyes were bright blue, the inheritance of a Philistine concubine that her grandfather had taken to bed with him. The effect of these piercing blue eyes was electrifying and exciting to many men; in her youth, it enhanced the tall strength of her figure, and it gave people a sense of regal power. But as she became older, the light in the blue eyes faded. They became cold and dead, and especially among the tent people, they were a reminder of something alien and distasteful.

More and more, as she lived among the tent people, did she feel alien. At first, when the red giant of a man led the desert people into Gilead and up to the gates of her brother's city, naming the ancient kinship of Israel as a claim upon the loyalty of the Reuben-ites, she had felt all the excitement and wonder of young love—

wild, heady passion that could face the war lord, Joshua ben Nun, of all Israel open-eyed and unafraid. Then, what other woman could? It was she who pacified her brother Nohab's rage and fear when Joshua led his barbaric desert spearmen against both the Amorites and the Ammonites, destroying the one and breaking the power of the other.

"Be happy! Be grateful!" she had told her brother.

"For what? I had a man for a master. Now I have changed him for a beast."

"Joshua is no beast. He is a Bedouin, as our own father was once."

"Not your father or mine. A hundred years have passed since we left the desert. Would you go back now? Are you in love with that animal?"

"Animals have been tamed," she smiled.

"How little you know!" Nohab had said, then. "How very little! You see a man with red hair and an iron sword, and you think you know his heart."

"But I do."

"No. You know nothing. You are headstrong and willful and you will do as you wish, but you know nothing. I tell you, this man Joshua is like a fire that is burning us. Nothing is the same. Nothing will be the same."

She remembered that now, on this night, and she remembered how she had soothed Nohab's fears and pacified him; but Nohab had been right. He had been right from the very beginning. He had been right, she told herself, recalling it and wrapping herself tightly in her bitterness. She stood in her black tent, recalling it, and out of the darkness of the tent, the voice of her son, Joash, came to her.

"Where is my father?" He was a timid boy. It took courage to ask, yet he had to ask. She knew that.

"Where is he?" the boy asked plaintively. "Where is he?"

What was it, she wondered, that a boy could love and need so in a man who had as little use for him as for herself? A boy needs a man. The boy had not yet turned thirteen, and he was small for his age. Was it gall and wormwood to the red giant that he had seeded a boy so small and puny? When the father, Joshua, the son of Nun, strode through the camp, his harness blazing in the sunlight, his high spear-point dipping and gleaming, the boy followed behind but at a distance, the way an uncertain puppy runs after a grown dog.

"Why don't you answer me?" the boy begged her.

"Then what should I answer you?" she said sharply. "The war lord sleeps in the war tent. What else?"

"Other boys—" he began, but she cut him off and said, "You had better go to sleep and stop thinking about other boys. You are not like other boys. I have told you that so many times! Can't you understand?"

"I do, I do," he muttered defensively.

"No, you don't. Who is your father? Your father is Joshua, who is judge and war lord over all the hosts of Israel. He is not anyone. He is not this one or that one. He is Joshua of Levi, and Levi are the holy ones who serve the God. And when the old man, Moses— when he dies, the God will call Joshua, your father, and talk to him face to face—"

"No, don't scold me, please," he begged her.

"Then go to sleep. Don't you know how much there will be to do tomorrow? Tomorrow, we fold the tents and we go across the river into the Land of Canaan. There will be no rest for any of us tomorrow—" Then she heard him sobbing, and she stopped and softened. She went over to her son and knelt to where he lay on his pallet and kissed him. The talk of the God had frightened him. She had been too harsh; she never meant to be harsh; it happened, and then her whole heart contracted with the pain of love for this son.

"Sleep, sleep, my beloved," she told him. "Why are you afraid of the God of Horeb? He will not harm you."

"Would my father let him?"

"Let him?" Sarah asked.

"Harm me? Kill me?"

"No, no. The gods are not interested in little boys or girls. Be a man first before you worry about the gods. When I was a little girl in Reuben, we worshipped the mother god. That was before Moses brought the God of Horeb into Gilead. But that was a long time ago. It doesn't matter."

"The mother god was kind to you," the boy said.

"How do I know, it was so long ago? And what do you know of the mother god? Her temples are smashed, and she is gone away forever."

"Where? Where has she gone?"

"What questions you ask? How do I know? Who knows where the gods go when they have no worship or sacrifice or temple? Perhaps they wander on earth, like poor and homeless people. Now go to sleep. Already, it is late. You'll see your father tomorrow—" In spite of herself, her voice took on an edge of bitterness. "Yes, you'll see him tomorrow—"

At the door of the tent, she softened again and told her son, "Sleep well, my child."

Who would tell *her* to sleep well, she wondered? Do we ever stop being children? Was she less afraid, less lonely than her son? And where do the gods go when their worship is over and their temples destroyed?

She stood there at the door of the tent, looking at the sea of black tents that populated the plain. People thought her cold and withdrawn—but it was a shell of fear she had built for herself, knowing herself as she was in the center of this great host of wild desert folk. How else could she survive? From all the deserts and rocky tablelands and parched valleys, they had come, at the will of an old man named Moses, a grim warrior named Joshua and an angry and terrible God named Jehovah. Now they were camped here, in their tens of thousands. Tomorrow, they would cross the river and go into the Land of Canaan, which they would take for themselves.

As Sarah stood there, the first edge of the moon rose above the desert mountains. The moon was sacred to the mother, and she felt a strange flush of knowledge and purpose. With long strides, she walked through the darkened camp. Some saw her, for it was a restless night, and they whispered about the Reubenite princess who walked alone at night, and slept alone too, as they well knew.

She saw the war tent of her husband, but avoided it. She knew how the Levite guards would sneer at her, and how easily she could lose her temper and rage at them; and this was not anything she desired now. For the moment, she was cool and composed within herself, and she could look at the Levite spearmen, ghostly and silvery in the nightlight, and have pity for the barren savagery of their lives. It occurred to her that their manhood must flow into the great nine-foot spears they carried; and as terrible as they were in battle, so were they foolish and impotent in the plain way of living, although, she mused, it was questionable whether any other way of living than by war and conquest could be endured by these restless and barbaric tent people.

So she thought as she walked through the great, sprawling encampment, a gathering of desert tribes greater than any other in man's memory. Her desire was to be outside the camp and apart from it, and without thinking of where she was going or planning her path, she passed through the groves of acacia to the rocky shelf of roadway that led to the city of her people. There, where she could look over the whole dark plain of black tents to the quicksilver of the River Jordan, she paused. She remembered.

She remembered the first coming of the Children of Israel, only a handful; they came out of the desert, and the old man led them, the old man whose name was Moses, already frail, already white of hair and beyond the call or knowledge of passion. Was it from this very spot that she had first seen them, and had seen him stop and look across the golden river into the green and lovely land?

Her thoughts were interrupted by the beat of horses' hoofs and the clatter of chariot wheels over the rocky roadway. This much could be said—that no one she need fear would dare approach the sleeping camp, and she stood and waited. The chariot drove out of the moonlit haze and the driver reined in the horses when he saw her. She recognized him before he knew her, and called out to him, "Nohab! My brother!"

Then he left his chariot with the reins on the ground and walked over to her, his brow furrowed and his face troubled.

"What are you doing here, alone in the night?" he asked her.

"I am alone in the daytime, too, my brother."

"Have you no shame, to walk about like this at night?"

"No more shame than I have when I walk in sunlight, if you must know," she replied.

"You made this particular bed for yourself," he said tightly.

"Do I plead for your pity, Nohab?"

"Arrogant and willful!"

"Don't pity me. Don't curse me."

"One would think that I sold you to him for peace gold, for pride gold, for ransom gold."

"Who would think so, my brother? Everyone knows all there is to know about me. I flung myself at him. I forced myself upon him. He never loved me."

"Whether he loved you or not, you are a princess of the House of Reuben and you are my sister. For you, remember that, if you please. For him—I swear by the God of Horeb that he will pay!"

"Why him? I know Joshua better than you—strong and witless and wild. But the evil is not in him. If anyone must pay, let it be she. Let it be that whore of Manasseh who pays."

"They will both pay," Nohab nodded.

"Why are you laughing?"

"I am not laughing," Nohab said. "I was only thinking how strange it is that as much as you love Joshua, so does he hate her—Deborah."

"Who?"

"Gamaliel, her husband. In the end, he will exact the price. Rest easy about that."

But as Sarah walked back to the camp, she felt that rest and peace were gone from her forever. What was love and what was hate? Who would say?

V

Deborah, the wife of Gamaliel of Manasseh, and she who was called—not alone by Sarah—the whore of Manasseh, had also asked herself the meaning of love and hate. The priests said that the moon was love and the sun was hate, but no wheat grew in the moonlight and no flowers bloomed in the moonlight.

In the temple of the mother, before the grim Levites smashed the images, had been a full-bellied and heavy-breasted god with two fronts and two faces; she smiled on one face and scowled on the other. The priestesses would explain that both were one, but such an explanation had all the misty uncertainty of temple lore; and to Deborah the fire that heated love and hatred was not one but two flames. When Gamaliel left her, she lay in the darkness of her bedroom with fear pressing on her like a weight; and the fear was mixed with hatred. The two interacted; as the fear grew, hatred waned, and at last, unable to sleep or relax, she dressed herself and fled from Gamaliel's house.

The gates of the city were open. That was Joshua's doing. "How can I come to you?" Deborah begged him. "The gates are closed. I am penned in, like a beast in a corral." And he had replied, "You will be penned no longer." Then he had said to Gamaliel, "Why do you lock your gates by night, my brother?"

"To keep out my enemies," Gamaliel had answered.

Deborah could remember how Joshua smiled at the lean, dark war chief of Manasseh. It was not simply with words but with his whole great red vastness that Joshua despised him; and Deborah remembered feeling that if she had been a man, she would have died before she bore that look of Joshua's. But Gamaliel did not die, as he would have had he drawn his sword against Joshua, and Joshua said to him mockingly, "You have grown soft and fretful behind your city walls, my brother. Come out on the desert sand and look at the sky above you. You have sucked the milk of the mother god too long. We who sacrifice to the God of Horeb carry our own walls with us."

Still, Gamaliel said nothing.

"Then who are your enemies? Tell me, my brother," Joshua prodded him.

"We built our walls against the Amorites," Gamaliel answered sullenly.

"Oh? Then you close your gates against the dead," Joshua taunted him. And when he still remained silent, "Even their gods are dead, Gamaliel. For a hundred years Reuben and Gad cringed under their blows, but when I came here to Gilead with my Levites and Caleb with his Judites and Gath with his Simonites and Gershom with his Kennites, we made a sweet sacrifice of Amor to the Lord God Jehovah? Am I right, my brother? A smell of burning such as your acacia groves have not known in the past. Am I right, my brother?"

"You are right," Gamaliel muttered.

"And the cities of Amor are no more—only ashheaps. Am I right?"

"Yes—"

"And when the Ammonites came to take tribute, we let them feel what our spears weigh, a just weight for which we took a just measure. And you pay no more tribute to the King of Ammon? Am I right, my brother, or do I lie to you?"

Gamaliel had nodded, bleakly and wordlessly.

"And we followed Ammon into the hills and burned his city and taught him that our god is an angry god—so that the Ammonites tread softly in the sight of the Children of Israel. Then against whom do you close your gates, my brother? Against your own blood and kin? Then close them no more, or I and the other war lords will be angry!"

This Deborah remembered very well indeed, and after that, the gates of the city of Manasseh remained open by night, even as they were open now.

But as she walked through the gates into the night, Deborah remembered her husband's face when Joshua spoke to him so mockingly and so contemptuously. It was the face of a man who decides to wait. She shivered, wrapped her cloak tightly about her, and climbed into the hills. The moon rose, and on an outcropping of rock, Deborah paused and looked down upon the encampment of the tribes of Israel, just as Sarah was looking down upon the same scene a mile to the south.

Then Deborah went on. She came to a narrow wadi, half of it in shadow, half in moonlight, and she clambered into it and went along it. Narrower and narrower it became as it twisted up the hillside; then a cleft intersected it, and into this cleft Deborah turned. She walked about two hundred paces, feeling her way in the darkness, for no moonlight penetrated here, and then suddenly the cleft opened into a round bowl of rock, perhaps fifty paces across. There, in a tangle of thorny cactus and withered acacia, were the broken remains of a small temple. Slowly, Deborah approached it, filled with a sense of the sadness and desolation of the scene, filled with a sense of nameless loss and emptiness.

The tall, fluted pillars which had once supported the crown of the temple were overthrown and broken, the bright gilt and color worn by the weather and muted by the moonlight. Time had embraced it. In a thousand years, it would appear no older, no more broken. As Deborah stood in what had once been a flagstone courtyard, once gay with bright flowers and sparkling fountains, a scorpion ran in front of her. She bowed her head but did not flinch. Let it bite me, she thought, let it make a final and irrevocable decision for me.

But the scorpion ran on, and from inside the ruined temple came a cackle of senile laughter, and an old woman's voice called out, "Who are you, beautiful one, that you have no fear of a scorpion?"

Then it was true, what she had heard, that the five old sisters who were the last priestesses of the mother god still crawled among the ruins of the temples! Or at least one of them. Who else would be here in the dark hours of the night?

"I am Deborah of the House of Manasseh," she replied.

"And you are not afraid? Here, at night?"

"Why should I be afraid at the temple of the mother?"

Another's voice, also the voice of an old woman, shrilled at her, "The mother is dead, the mother is dead! Look at these ruins! What kind of a fool are you to come here, Deborah of Manasseh?"

Still another voice, "Leave her alone! Why do you scold her? She is troubled. She is young, and more beautiful than any woman in all the tribes of Israel, but her grief is all over her. We are sisters in grief. Leave the child alone!" Two thin hands pushed aside the withered acacia leaves, and an old woman hobbled out of the ruins up to Deborah, peering at her curiously.

"I am Milcah," the old woman said. "I am of the old holy blood of Joseph, of Manasseh and Ephraim. I was first daughter to the mother. I was priestess of this temple. The brightest and comeliest men of Gilead came here to embrace me and do honor to the mother through me. But that was long, long ago, Deborah."

"I have nowhere to turn," Deborah said, speaking like a child and strangely childlike in appearance as she stood in the silver moonlight, and to the old woman, she seemed for a moment to be the very incarnation of Astarte. "I came here to find the mother."

Hidden in the ruins, the other old voices cackled with senseless laughter, and Deborah felt a tight prickle of fear all over her skin. But Milcah screamed at them to be quiet, and then said to Deborah, with strange compassion, "The mother is dead, my child. We are just foolish old women, hiding in the ruins of the old temple."

"How can the god be dead?" Deborah pleaded.

"Are the gods immortal? Perhaps. Who knows? But when their images are broken and their altars smashed, they are no better off than the mortal dead. How can they remain where they have no worship? Perhaps they go across the River Jordan, where there are many temples to the mother, who is called Rahab in the Land of Canaan, and if she is the same mother we call Astarte, then why should she remain here and pit herself against the hate and curses of Jehovah, the angry God of Horeb?"

"What should I tell the God of Horeb?" Deborah said miserably. "Would he listen to me, old woman?"

"He will listen to Joshua."

"What do you know of Joshua, old crone?"

"Who doesn't know? Why do you sneer at me, Deborah of Manasseh? Do you think that you will be young and beautiful forever? Don't you think we were young and beautiful once? Don't you think the young men came to us here at the temple and lay with us, because our bodies were soft and sweet? They did. They did—yes, just as you lay with that great red bull, Joshua—"

"No! No!"

"Why do you deny it to me? Who is here to listen to us? But why do you come seeking the mother for sympathy? Joshua serves Jehovah. Will he tell Jehovah to have pity on you? Or will the God of Horeb tell Joshua, 'Kill her! Kill her because she is a whore!' "

"Enough, old woman!" Deborah cried out.

"What did Jehovah say? Cursed be the man who whores after the mother! And it was your Joshua who smashed our temples and broke our images—"

From inside the ruins came wild, cackling laughter of appreciation. Deborah fled. Sobbing, she fled from the broken temple of Astarte.

VI

Not as a lover goes with joy and anticipation—but frightened and driven by the tearing forces within her, Deborah came into the camp of the war tribes of Israel. By now, half of the hours of darkness had passed away and the moon was high in the heavens, and this woman of the House of Manasseh was weary and full of grief and pity for herself.

As with so many beautiful women who are unhappy and tortured of themselves and within themselves, Deborah of Manasseh had a different picture of herself than those who looked at her. In her own mind, her beauty was fraudulent; by some mystical means, some spell, some device of witchcraft, she was able to induce otherwise rational and clear-eyed people to see her as a person of great beauty. But she was also convinced that this fraud, this hoax which she perpetrated was supported by a tissue-frail structure which could at any moment collapse; and she also felt that beyond this fraudulent beauty, there was nothing in her character or being of worth or value. This heritage of forgotten childhood hurts and blows and rejection lay upon her like a pattern of destiny. People like herself move toward a destiny of their own making, yet they are powerless to turn aside or to unmake what they have made.

When she was wed to Gamaliel, she was conscious of a union with a man she could not love, and conscious too of his dark and passionate pride of possession. In her very act of marriage, she revenged herself upon his lust for a beauty she believed fraudulent. Thus, by a double deception, she was able and willing to accept a man she despised.

When no children came from the union and Gamaliel's frustration increased to the point of open anger, she went into the hills of Ammon to a temple of Astarte, and there sharpened her self-contempt by serving through the night as a temple harlot, giving herself to each and every Ammonite who came with a sacrifice to the mother god. In the light of that dawn, the priestess of Astarte said to her, "Until you yourself want life inside of you, my child, no seed will bring it. You are too beautiful to be afraid of men. Men are like children, no wiser and no more dangerous, if you handle them properly. Remember that."

But she could not remember or act upon something she neither understood nor accepted, and from a dark and petty and selfish man, she turned to a somber red warrior who called himself the war lord of the God of Hosts, and who had in ten years united all the wandering tribes of the desert and brought them together under his iron hand to invade and conquer the Land of Canaan.

All this she thought of as she went into the camp of Israel, but her thoughts were powerless to turn her steps away. She thought of the great red-bearded, red-haired man whose name was Joshua, and who was so feared by all other men, excepting his own tribe of wild and blood-hungry and terrible men, who were called Levites. She remembered hearing Nohab of Reuben say to her husband, so long ago, when asked why the Levites bore the russet tint in their hair and beards, "As a warning to other men, so stained with blood are they."

She remembered the first time Joshua of Levi had looked at her, the way his gray eyes had fixed on her in a crowd of the people of Manasseh, caught her, singled her out and then cut into her very soul, so that every voice of her own sanity begged her to turn away, run away, hide herself from him.

She remembered the first time he held her in his arms and kissed her, and then, even in her plunge toward whatever destiny had been prepared, how she had to know, "Who are you, whom they call Joshua, the son of Nun? Who are you Levites?"

"Like yourself,"—and the answer was rote, not thought or explanation—"we are the children of the same Father Abraham."

"And who is not from the seed of Abraham? You are not like any Bedouin people we ever knew."

"We are out of the Land of Egypt, just as your own tribe of Manasseh came out of Egypt once, long ago."

"But there are no such wild red people as you in the Land of Egypt."

"Not now, for we went out and away from them," Joshua had answered, putting the questions aside, making it plain that he found no pleasure from her asking questions or from his having to answer them. "We were a thorn in their side, and we gave them an end to their pain when we left them. We went away."

"And is it true that your god walks with you, and that he is an old man whose name is Moses?"

"There is an old man whose name is Moses," Joshua said strangely, "but he is not our god. Our god is the God of Horeb. The old man, Moses—it was he who led us out of the Land of Egypt."

"And he is alive?"

"Yes, he is alive."

"Why have I never seen him then?" she had asked.

"Why do you ask so many questions? You will see him someday. He sits in the holy tent, which we call the Tabernacle. He sits there with the God of Horeb. Now ask me no more questions. Is that how the women of Manasseh make love, with questions?"

She remembered so many things now, as she walked into the great encampment, but she remembered nothing that had the power to turn her away.

She remembered nothing that could help her, nothing that could turn her away from what she was building with her own hands. She remembered the moods of Joshua ben Nun, the times when he looked at her as if he had never seen her before, his eyes blank and empty, his thoughts far away. She remembered times when he seemed to hear the harsh, angry voice of the God of Horeb, when his face would twist with the pain of guilt and remorse, and when he would tell her to get away from him and leave him. She remembered his times of frustration, when he dropped his cover of being a fierce

and terrible man, cut out of red stone, and wept with the hopelessness of his task, cried like a child because his own Levites numbered less than a thousand fighting men, and who could conquer a
land of fifty walled cities and eighteen kings with less than a thousand men? He wept because the tribes and clans of Israel were
greedy, self-centered, afraid, disunited and given to constant bickering with each other, to petty jealousies and to a lack of constancy.

She remembered that somehow she had found virtue and splendor
in his demonic single-mindedness of purpose, his lust to cross the
river and conquer the green land there—a lust much deeper and
more fiery than any lust of the flesh.

Yet it must be said that she also remembered the times of his
love for her, the uncanny wonder of this great wild man turned
tender and gentle, his hands as light as feathers, his voice soft and
sweet for her ears, his kisses of insatiable hunger and need—who
else had made her feel that her beauty was more than a fraud?
Who else had given her such a sense of value and power—to tame
and control and see the sweetness and the whispering softness of
such a man as Joshua ben Nun?

So even if she could not help herself, she could find strength and
purpose in her memories, for the camp of Israel by night was not
such a place where a woman like Deborah could come without
many fears and misgivings. Even by daylight, the sight of ten thousand and more black tents filled her with deep trepidation; by
night, it was worse. In such a tent dwelt Jehovah, the God of
Horeb; they were the tent people. No mother god had ever been
among them, to listen to the sweet music of pipes and to taste the
fruits of the warm earth. A somber, harsh people, who fed hot
blood to their god and who lived by the beast of the range and the
sword of tempered iron. She passed by some of the thorn and
acacia corrals, into which their beasts had been driven this past
week, and she cringed from the strong smell of their droppings. The
cows and bulls lowed at her.

Not all of the people slept. The thought of tomorrow had made
some of them too tense and excited to sleep. She passed young
couples sitting together in the warm moonlight, warriors brooding
over their weapons, putting an edge on sword and axe with whet-
stones, greasing bronze arrowheads, weaving clan feathers and colors
into their brass helmets. They looked after Deborah curiously, but

she had hooded her face with her cloak. She was a small figure, like a boy going quickly past them.

But the tall Levites who stood guard with their heavy bronze shields and nine-foot spears around the war tent of Levi—they knew her, but they said nothing to her and made no move. In the other tribes, there were herdsmen who were eager and awful in war; but the Levites were not herdsmen. They lived only for war; they were soldiers of their god, and him they feared and they also feared Joshua ben Nun, but nothing else that walked or breathed on earth. They were well-disciplined and obedient, and they stroked their long spears and crooned over them.

She walked past them and between them slowly, her heart pounding, her whole body trembling, but determined that they should never know how much she was afraid of them. She went into the black tent and stood just inside, trying to force her eyes to pierce the darkness.

She could feel him there, hear his breathing. The warm scent of his body went into her; the tension disappeared. Whatever price she paid, whatever the cost, she found herself here as a woman; and in the darkness was a great, red-bearded man who loved her. Strangely and ironically, it was only at moments like this, in the war tent of the People of Horeb, under the long and angry hand of the God of Horeb, that she fully understood what the worship of the forbidden mother god meant.

But her mind did not move in ways philosophical or theological; she approached the gods with the same needful simplicity that a child knows, when he approaches bread and meat. She had never known the peace or repose that makes for clear and direct thought; she moved as her pleading, throbbing heart directed.

She moved toward the couch of Joshua ben Nun. In his sleep, he heard her, for he who lives by the sword never sleeps as other men sleep; and she heard him stir, and then the rasp as he clutched the pommel of his iron Hittite sword, half drawing it from the scabbard.

"Who is there?"

Before she answered, he knew. She heard the sword slide back in its scabbard. He was sitting up in his bed, the light cover falling away from his naked body. Her own cloak dropped as she went to him, and then she lay in his arms, with all that she ever desired fulfilled—for this moment at least.

She tangled one hand in his curling beard and drew his face down to hers, then running her fingers against his broad full mouth, his shaggy mustache, his big, jutting nose and wide cheekbones.

"My lord Joshua," she whispered, "I love you as no woman ever loved a man before in all the time since Father Adam and Mother Eve first looked at each other in their garden of desire. Now the whole world is a garden for me."

"I love you the way a man should love a woman," he said simply. "That's enough, I think. And tomorrow I'll find you a garden across the River Jordan and make you a gift of the heads of eighteen kings. Do you want more?"

"I only want Joshua, the son of Nun."

PART TWO. ELEAZAR

I

In many of the tribes and clans of the kindred but far-ranging desert herdsmen who spoke the same language and claimed descent from an ancient patriarch called Israel and a still more ancient ancestor called Abraham, there were people who had never laid eyes upon the prophet Moses—and there were others who hardly knew whether he existed in the flesh, or whether he was of the same fearful but unknown substance as the angry God of Horeb, whose will they did and whose Law they obeyed.

In the Law, it was not differentiated; there was the Law of Moses and there was the Law of Jehovah, they were one and the same.

Especially was this uncertainty concerning the man Moses true among the young, the young men who were a generation of war and conquest and the young women who decked themselves with the spoil of walled cities. For fifteen years, Joshua had led the young men from one conquest to another. Joshua, they knew, and his tall Levite spearmen, and his old father, Nun; but even those who had seen Moses knew only the confused and contradictory legends that were told about him, the wonder stories of magic and miracles.

Himself, he neither denied nor confirmed stories told about him, and many felt that he was too old to know the difference between invention and truth. It was told how once he had been a young and splendid prince of Egypt and had lived in the great house of

Rameses, in the old city of Tanis. Again, it was told that the House of Levi, which was his blood, was one of the old houses of the Egyptian god-kings, and that the men of Levi were his personal retainers in olden times. It was also said that under the God-King Rameses, Moses had been a mighty captain of chariots and had led the hosts of Egypt to victory against the Kushites, the black ones who lived near the headwaters of the Nile.

So many things were said—it was told that he had carried his own new-born son in his arms up the black-ash slopes of Horeb as a sacrifice to Jehovah, and that there he had wrestled with the God, face to face, and won his son's life in exchange for the infant's fore-skin—and that was said to explain, why in the old times the fearful Levites slew so many who would not submit to the rite of circum-cision. But who knew what was true and what was false? For years now, as Joshua became more and more firmly the war lord of the confederation, Moses emerged less and less frequently from the Tabernacle, where he stayed by the side of the God of Horeb. Who could question him? Who would dare?

Even Gershom of Kenn, who was said to be the son of Moses, almost never made any reference to that fact; and whether the priest Eleazar was truly the son of Aaron, or, as some held, the son of Moses and brother to Gershom, was also a matter of heresay and dispute.

To the young men and women of the tribes, it had always been Eleazar who was the son of Aaron, the brother of Moses; but these were questions of the far past. Eleazar was a man of middle years, and Aaron, the brother of Moses, was dead. The old tales grew thick and heavy with time. Once, Moses had been married to a woman of the tribe of Kenn, who had borne him two children, Gershom and Eliezer. Gershom, a dark and dour man, whose blood was a mixture of the red fury of Levi and the age-old curse of Cain, or Kenn, as the Children of Cain called themselves, because the war chief of Kenn and was now one of the five war lords of the con-federation. Of Eliezer, nothing was said, and the old man Moses sat alone with his God, wifeless and childless in the evening of all his days.

But the old men could remember a time when Eliezer was known as the son of Moses; Joshua too could remember such a time.

"How are the names different?" the old men would nod somberly. "Eleazar, the son of Aaron—Eliezer, the son of Moses?"

Moses had called his son Eliezer, which means, *my God has helped.*

Aaron had two sons, and with Caleb, the Judite and Joshua, the Levite, they had led two hundred men across the Golden River and raided deep into the Land of Canaan. Each of the four leaders led a fifty of men. When the Canaanites in their chariots attacked them, Joshua and Caleb stood fast with their fifties of spearmen, but the sons of Aaron fled with their fifties. They fled to the banks of the River Jordan and waited there, ashamed to cross over alone; there they were found by Caleb and Joshua and those men of their fifties who had survived.

Perhaps the sons of Aaron knew what would come, for they were Levites. Joshua reminded them. "You are out of Levi," he said, as he drew his iron sword, "and you have shamed my God and cursed my blood."

Then he killed one son of Aaron and Caleb killed the other, and they dragged the bodies through the ford of the river and flung them on the bank, where the birds and jackals tore the flesh until Aaron came with his servants and buried the remains.

That was when Moses had gone into the Tabernacle and remained there a full twenty days. When he emerged, he embraced his brother Aaron. They tore their garments and rubbed ashes on their faces, and they wept together. Then Moses had relinquished his son Eliezer forever. His name was changed to Eleazar, which means, *God has helped,* and he became the son of Aaron. But why Moses made this slight and subtle change in his son's name, no one ever knew.

Only Nun, the servant and companion of Moses, heard what Moses said to Aaron when he gave his son to his brother. These were his words: "I cannot give you your sons, my brother. What is done is done. No one can raise the dead. But let my son be a servant to you in these tired years, because you are even older than I am, and often enough I feel that I am too old to go on. Eliezer will help you and be a crutch to you, for he defied the habit of Levi by being gentle and understanding. In the olden days, I would have fought the God and berated him for what He has done. I would have taunted him with how He will be remembered as a cruel and angry God. Now I no longer berate the God. Let Him berate me. When I came to these people, their backs were bowed with the lash and with suffering, but I made them drunk with the power of the God. So I have failed, I think, not the God. One son I had, Gershom, and he became a man of war, hard and dry and bitter, with his iron sword for his companion. Let people forget that Gershom was ever my son, and the children of Gershom are not my children. The other son shall also be forgotten. Call him Eleazar instead of Eliezer, and if his seed shall survive, let it be remembered as the seed of Aaron, not the seed of Moses. For myself, I am alone, and that is best. Wifeless and childless, I want no one to weep for me. I smashed too many images. I wanted a God of whom no image could be fashioned, a God both just and righteous. I found him, and I gave him my own people of Levi to be his servants. But they became righteous. A God can be righteous, but not a people, and for this I am cursed forever."

Aaron did not understand what his brother meant, but Eliezer, the son of Moses, did understand. He cut his arm and mixed his blood with the blood of Aaron, and he became Aaron's blood and seed and changed his name to Eleazar.

Nun also understood, for he was the father of Joshua, who was judge and war lord over all of Israel. Nun also rent his garments, put ashes upon his head and for five days took no food or water.

II

On the day of which this tale tells, which was the last day in the life of the sage and prophet of all the Jews, the man Moses, Eleazar the Levite woke in the early morning hours, and went through the camp of the tribes to the Tabernacle.

His awakening was in that time which all the people of old called the holy hour, the hour when there is neither day nor night but a gray and cloudy blending of both. In this hour, they held, night and day, which had been sundered and set apart by the original force of the Creator, merged so that he who walked abroad at this time actually breathed the formless substance of the beginning.

So it was that Eleazar walked slowly and thoughtfully, contemplating the curious and so often unfathomable mysteries which appear always to be associated with the beginning and end of all things. Never before in all his life had he realized how totally the beginning of something must involve the ending of other things; but he realized it now.

Like so many in the sprawling city of the tent people, he had slept only intermittently and poorly. They were all of them on the edge of a day which partook of the inevitable, and when that conviction fastens upon human beings, many of them seek not to avoid it but to embrace it. This was the case with Eleazar. Let the day come, he said to himself. Whatever it might bring, let it come.

He was a tall man, as most of the Levites were, but like his brother Gershom, he wore the dark cast of his mother, who had been Zipporah of Kenn, with dark hair and dark beard. Because he was a sworn and chattel servant of Jehovah, the God of Horeb, and of the Tabernacle, he carried neither spear, nor shield nor armor, but only the breastplate of the magical Urim and Thummim, hanging from his neck, the sign and symbol of Levi, and the blazon on their war banner as well. The two layers of the breastplate were square, and the inner one was set with the holy jewels, red rubies, black bits of basalt and white pearls. His sacred girdle, which bound in the white linen kilt, almost like the holy kilt of the Egyptians, took up the red, white and black, which were the ancient clan colors of Levi. From the girdle, there hung a long bronze dagger, his only weapon; for in battle the bond-servant of the Tabernacle fought with the armor of the God of Horeb all over him.

Slowly and thoughtfully, Eleazar walked past the endless clusters of black tents toward the Tabernacle. The black tents stood like rocks about the low-lying morning mist, like the false rocks of Mardok, which lured travelers into the Sea of Temptations. Presently, he came to one black tent that was high as a pavilion, and all around it stood sleepless Levite spearmen—the war tent of Joshua—and over it waved the black and red and white tricolor of Levi. The spearmen watched him as he came toward them, but they were forbidden to address him unless he spoke first to them; and as he passed, Deborah of Manasseh emerged from the tent, small, wrapped in her cloak against the morning chill, bent over with the guilt and shame that sent her forth like this to return to her own place and house.

She came face to face with Eleazar, who stopped to look at her; but he said nothing nor did he look back as she hurried on. Eleazar then went to the Tabernacle. It was still an hour before the sun would appear above the hills of Gilead.

As with the war tent, Levite spearmen stood guard around the Tabernacle. The old man, Nun, the father of Joshua, had just awakened from where he slept on his pallet to one side of the entrance to the tent. He was not a bond-servant of the Tabernacle, the old man, nor was he pledged to the God; but among all the stories told, there was one which held that in the old, old days Moses, Prince of Egypt, had bought Nun from the slave block in Egyptian Tanis and that afterward, they had mixed their blood in eternal brotherhood. Whether or not that was true, the old man lay each night like a dog at his master's feet, and not a harmless dog either, for Nun had been a great warrior in his day and had himself trained the spearmen of Levi.

Now this old man sat up and looked inquiringly at Eleazar.

"Does my master sleep?" Eleazar asked him.

"It's not day yet."

"Soon enough."

"It was dark when I awakened and looked into the holy place. He sits with the God. No, he does not sleep."

"Shall I enter?"

"But if he does sleep, don't waken him," Nun said.

"But I must."

"Why? Why is this place so full of haste and restlessness?"

"Don't you know that we fold the tents now, old man?"

"I know that. And we have folded our tents before."

"Not like this."

Nun shivered suddenly. The faces of the Levite spearmen, watching and listening, were inscrutable. Eleazar entered the Tabernacle.

The Tabernacle was full of dusk and full of mystery, and, as always, it had a deep effect upon Eleazar. In the Tabernacle, in his Ark of acacia wood, the God of Horeb lived, far from his black volcanic mountain of smoke and fire and soot. He lived there by virtue of Moses the sage, who now sat in the shadows of the outer part of the Tabernacle—who sat with the God and lived with the God and talked with the God, too, it was said. Now this old man Moses turned his head to the sound of someone entering the high tent, and asked, "Who comes to me now, before the day?"

"Eleazar, your servant." Had the old man looked for someone else, Eleazar wondered?

"Come in, my son," Moses nodded. Eleazar saw him in blurred silhouette, the once mighty figure bowed and frail, bent over upon the little wooden stool where he sat.

"I must speak with you," Eleazar explained.

"Of course. I understand that."

"Because this is the last day," Eleazar said slowly.

"I know, I know. I am old but not senile. To people like yourself
—younger people, I mean—it doesn't seem possible that an old
man can be in full command of his senses. And I suppose it is very
strange that the mind remains after all else has failed. You continue
to think. For most of the night, I have sat here, thinking."

"Have you decided?"

"Do you mean have I decided what I will do if Joshua comes
here with his sword naked? What can I decide? I am an old man,
and Joshua is young and strong. In the olden times it was always
thus—the new priest slew the old priest."

"I have no blood anger or enmity for Joshua," Eleazar said. "But
you are my father and the voice of the God."

"Aaron is your father," Moses sighed. "And another will be the
voice of the God when I am gone."

"If Joshua does this, the whole people will curse him."

Eleazar could not see, but he fancied Moses smiled as he answered,
"The whole people hardly know that I exist, hidden away here in
the Tabernacle."

"Then go to them!"

"No—no, Eleazar! I am too tired for any more battles. I am too
old to cry out that this or that is the truth—and I am not sure I
know. If Joshua comes to the people today and tells them that
Moses is dead and that he, Joshua, is the priest of the God of Horeb,
they will sing hosannas and praise Joshua too. There will be enough
bloodshed today. But tell me, does your brother Gershom of Kenn
know of this?"

"I think not."

"I want no bad blood between him and Joshua, or between them
and Caleb."

"Yet there will be," Eleazar sighed. "They are filled with pride
and righteousness, and they are men of war, not of peace."

"Yes—angry men. I gave them an angry God. Now they are
angry men."

"And this time Joshua has sworn that we will never come back
across the Jordan. The land is promised and they will take it and
divide it among the tribes. Who will be satisfied?"

"I watched it happen," Moses sighed. "I watched it happen, but
I could do nothing to stop it."

"The God willed it."

"Yes, I suppose so. A long, long time ago, my son, before you were born, I wandered in search of a God who would answer the riddle of mankind. Did I find him?"

"I don't understand," Eleazar said slowly. "I don't know what the riddle of mankind is."

"Man is here and he asks why? It is as simple as that."

"I don't understand."

"No, I don't suppose you do. Jehovah is a just God—terrible and angry, but also just in the end. I must believe that because I am so old. Do you believe it?"

"I do," answered Eleazar, the question, as he felt, came out of the wandering of an old man's fancies. Who could ask such a question? Then Eleazar said, "But still Joshua is war lord and judge. He told me to tear down the altar of God this morning, and to cast the stones into the fields."

"Do as he says," Moses whispered.

"Then you will not oppose him in any way, my father?"

"Only in one way. He will never be priest over Israel. For if the God is a just God, his justice is not simple."

"What are you telling me?"

"Have you the courage to be priest, as Aaron was, and as your seed must be?" he demanded, rising and moving toward his son.

"Are you asking me whether I am afraid of Joshua?" Eleazar said evenly. "I can't lie to you. I am."

"I know you are. But are you more afraid of the God of Horeb?"

"Yes."

"Then come with me to the Ark, and I will make you priest." And then Moses lifted the folds of the Sanctuary, and led Eleazar into the Holy of Holies itself. There a lamp burned fitfully on the polished table of acacia wood, and beside the table, the Ark, also of acacia wood, hung from its carrying poles, which rested upon stone stilts. The Ark was inlaid with gold and precious stones, and the carrying rings it hung from were also of gold. Eleazar stood to one side of it, Moses on the other; and now Eleazar saw how old and thin and tired and used up his father was. So much did his heart go out to this trembling old man that he forgot to be afraid of the awful presence of the God.

"Do you know what the Ark contains?" Moses asked him.

"The presence of the God—"

"No—oh, no. We are just a poor, wandering desert people, for all our boasting and pride. But even our own poor notion of the Lord God of Hosts could not sit in a wooden box all gaudy with gold and jewels, and made of the wood that grows here in the Forest of Shittem. Not even of cedar wood or ebony wood, but the only wood we had here. Any workman in his little shop in the old City of Tanis in the Delta of Egypt could turn out a better box than this, for they are skilled in such things and we are not. But it was always in a box that the Bedouin folk carried their god, whatever the god was. And how else would the people believe that the god was with them, unless we made an Ark?"

"What are you saying?" Eleazar asked hoarsely. "That the God is not with us?"

"If He stretched out his hand, He would be with us," Moses answered gently. "Do you understand?"

"No. No—then what *is* in the box?"

"A little dust, for man is dust, and he must remember that and be humble. A little soil, for it nourishes what man is. And also a black stone, for what the God touches can also be eternal. Just that —no more."

"Then where is the God of Horeb?" Eleazar pleaded.

"That you will have to discover for yourself," Moses said sadly. "It will not be easy. Perhaps if you hunger enough, he will speak to you. Be firm, but not proud. The God is something strange and splendid, but man is also splendid. Be proud but not righteous. Remember that you are man, and never be shamed. When you demand of Him, be compassionate, for even if man is cruel, he is also compassionate, and it is hard for the gods to understand that, just as it is always so hard for the father to comprehend his son. Now he is your God, and jealous and demanding. Worship no other gods."

The tears were running down Eleazar's cheeks, and he nodded wordlessly.

"Bend over the Ark, my son," Moses said.

Eleazar bent his body forward, and Moses took from the table a little vial of oil and poured it over Eleazar's head. "Thus I anoint you. Be faithful to Jehovah and serve Him well, and when evil tidings come, accept them. The God remembers what will be, but we only remember what has already been. Joshua is judge over all the tribes and clans of Israel. Be his right arm, and plead for the

God to speak through your lips. Now go to the altar and leave me, because I am very tired."

Weeping, Eleazar left him, and Moses, swaying over the Ark, whispered, "My God, my God, where are you? Alone, I came to this world and alone I am leaving it. Why? Why?"

PART THREE. JOSHUA

1

In the tent. The tent is a symbol and a horizon for his life. There he slept restlessly, turning from side to side. The heat was on the land, pouring down out of the sky, baking the sand and baking the warmth in the hearts of men until it became fire.

He had closed the side flaps of the tent to keep out the heat of morning, but when the sun rose above the edge of the earth, the black goat-hair felting of the tent sucked in the heat until the tent was full of it.

Then, before waking, he dreamed. He dreamed of the golden land of Egypt, which he had never seen, the monkey-land of abominations that was so beautiful that a man's heart broke just to walk through its painted gardens, the cat-land that was a stink and a stench unto the nostrils of the Lord God Jehovah; and who is mightier than the God, more jealous or more bitter in his anger?

He dreamed that he was a slave in Egypt, as his father had been; but the whip that curled across his back in such mighty strokes bespoke a mighty strength. He twisted and turned with the agony of the whip, and each blow of the whip left a livid welt an inch high, standing up from the skin of his back. For in the sense of his dream—as so often happens in dreams—he was both himself and an observer, and not only did he feel the lash and hurt of the whip, but he also stood apart and saw it descend and sear his own back.

He would not cry out. Thirst had kindled a fire in his mouth. The pain of the whip went away, so that all his facilities might center on the fire in his mouth.

He would not plead for mercy.

"Proud—you are too proud, Joshua ben Nun," a voice said in his dream.

He twisted and turned and tried to find the voice, and face it, and explain that the pride was like the blood in his body; and can a man cut his veins and let the blood run out and still live?

"You squeeze pride too tightly, you whose father was a slave in the cat-land of Egypt. You are too proud, war lord."

"Give me to drink," he whispered, and thereby his pride was broken.

As he wept, the second part of him looked at the weeping with contempt and anger. An Egyptian woman brought him water.

Dressed as Egyptian women dress, the linen that covered her was thin as gossamer, and through it he could see all the parts and places and curves of her body, the roundness of her breasts, the rose-dark flower in the center of each breast, the pink nipples, the wondrous beautiful valleys and hills of her belly, the dark loins and the long slim legs.

A voice said, "Cursed be the daughters of Egypt, the whores of Rameses, the harlots of Isis! They shall be wed with the cat and they shall lie with the swine! Their wombs shall turn into hot fires, and their comeliness shall wither the way a flower withers when the desert rains are over!"

Like a child scolded and threatened, this Egyptian woman stood shivering before the curse. He looked up to see her face, and as he had somehow known, she was more beautiful than words could describe. And then he lowered his gaze and saw with horror that as her hands trembled the water in the cup poured over onto the sand.

The voicelessness of his dream was interrupted by a supreme effort to produce sound through the fire in his mouth, to tell her and beg her not to waste the water when he lay there dying of thirst.

His effort was convulsive. The tears poured from his eyes and the sweat fell on his neck like rain. Then he awakened.

II

Hot and choking, he awakened, and he reached out with his right arm for the earthenware flask of water that always stood at his bedside for the morning. Sitting up, he drained the water without ever removing the flask from his lips.

Inside the tent, the darkness was latticed with streaks of light from the morning sun. Joshua sighed wearily; it was morning, but he was not rested. He let drop one naked, muscular leg over the side of his couch, and as he did so, a flap was thrown back and a soldier stood in the golden blaze of sunshine; silhouetted, he stood there, trying to determine whether Joshua slept or not.

"I am awake," Joshua grunted, knowing that the other was blind in the black sheeting of the tent.

"Caleb sends his greetings."

"Thank Caleb for me," Joshua replied sourly. "I could not have awakened without his greetings."

"And he wants to know," the soldier continued, "should he come to you, or will you come to him?"

"I will come to him. It is early morning, man."

"Today is the appointed day."

"I know that. I don't need reminding, soldier. My memory isn't failing me. Get out of here and leave me alone. Tell Caleb that I will come to him."

The tent flap fell back; Joshua heard her interrogate the soldier. The soldier was of Levi, and more arrogant and pushing than any soldier had any right to be; but Joshua had to tell himself, "I am also of Levi, with more arrogance and more pride than that soldier; and even the way I pay my price, so will he."

She must have stopped the soldier as he left the tent.

"Is he awake?"

"He was awake and sitting up on his couch."

"Naked?"

"It's hot. The tent is like a furnace. So he sleeps naked."

"Do you sleep naked, soldier?"

"That's neither here nor there."

And Joshua thought, "Who is she to ask him? What kind of wanton chatter is that for a woman? What kind of a bitch have I nested here?"

"Answer me, soldier."

"I sleep in the long tents with the men of war. We lie with a sword and a spear, not with a woman. Shall I uncover my parts for the sake of my shield? What do you want of me, woman?"

"What should I want of you?" she snapped. "Are you different from the other holy stallions of Levi? I want nothing of you. Only get out of my sight!"

"Gladly, lady."

"I spit on the ground you walk on."

"Yes, my lady," the soldier flung over his back, "so is the measure of a Reubenite princess cast. The wombs of the wives of Reuben drop precious things."

She brought her frustration and rage into the tent with her. She flung open the door flap and it remained up, the golden sunlight racing into the tent before her. Sarah was a strong, dark, handsome woman, as so many of the Reubenites were, but it had been long months since Joshua had seen beauty in her. And now, as she strode into the tent, he took up the corner of a cloak and pulled it across his loins. The gesture was without thought or plan, and the gesture was defensive. When the will to cut and lash and hurt is in two people, attack and defense follows without thought. An action begets action.

"Cover yourself," she said. "Hide your parts from me—it is too sacred for my eyes. Not for the eyes of harlots."

"I just awakened," he replied sullenly. "You wake up and your heart doesn't know what your hands do."

He sat like a bear, a giant of a man and bearlike. His breadth of shoulder and heaviness of arm was of his father, Nun the Levite, but from his Kennite mother, he had come by the great height and the long stride of the Bedouin. He was not a city man or a farm man, but a man of the tents and the sea of sand and the wilderness. But whereas most of the desert men were black of hair and eye, his eyes were gray and his hair was orange-red with the bloodstain of the house of Levi. And this made him ugly to some and beautiful to others.

"The nighttime is the time to sleep."

"I dreamt of whips on my back. Was it your voice I dreamt of?"

"Who are you to talk to me like that? And who am I? Am I some slut—some whore who creeps in to you? Like your whores of Egypt?"

"I have never been to Egypt, so I know nothing of the whores of Egypt," he answered tiredly.

"You heard how that soldier spoke to me!"

"You meant me to hear, so I heard."

"He ought to be stoned." And when he said nothing, only staring at his naked feet, she cried out, "Stoned, I say!"

"I heard you. Would you stone every man who looks sidewise at you? Let it be. He's a soldier. He'll get a spear in his belly soon enough, and then you'll have your hurt-money."

"And if Jehovah is a just God, it will be you with the spear in your belly."

"Thank you. But you get what you ask for, my dear Sarah. When you discuss my nakedness with a soldier, he will spit to windward of you, make no mistake."

"And whom shall I discuss it with?" she demanded hoarsely, coming close to him. "I sleep alone. Shall I put it to myself—how is it that Joshua sleeps alone in his black tent, apart from his wedded wife? How is it that the soldiers stand guard around his black tent? How is it that he turns his back on the House of Reuben and finds his contentment in the sand and filth of a Bedouin tent?"

"Because I am a Bedouin," biting the words.

"Better that I enjoy my sleeplessness without the pleasure of conversation—or should I step outside and tell any soldier to answer me, or any wife, or any child? Who is there in Israel who doesn't know the whore of Joseph who crawls into your bed each night?"

Joshua raised his eyes to stare at her bleakly.

Almost in a whimper now, she said to him, "You loved me once. You looked upon me with fire in your eyes, and your heart pounded when you held me. Did I come empty-handed when I came to you? Or did I bring you the fair cities and the lush fields of Reuben, the gold and the jewels and the fighting men of Reuben? And what does she bring you, this whore of Joseph? Who were you when you came here—you and your ragged lot of desert savages? Did you know a ploughshare from a flail? Did you know to sit at a table or lie in a bed? What else did you know but how to kill—and then cry out with joy to your war god, Jehovah, that you had killed in his name? But we took you in, and we gave you land and cattle, and we taught you to break bread under a roof-tree—and when your Levites set up the altar of Jehovah, we cut down our sacred groves and sacrificed to your gods—"

"We have one God," Joshua said, as if there was nothing more that he could find to say.

"And why did we do it? Because we were all the Children of Israel—or was it because I pleaded and begged—"

"What we took from Reuben, we gave twice over. What we borrowed we returned, and with more spoil than the treasure-chests of Reuben could hold—"

"That's all you have to say?"

"Leave me alone. Go out of here and leave me alone."

He avoided looking after her as she left the tent, and when she had gone, he pulled down the door flap and dressed himself in the semidarkness. He tied on a loincloth, belted a kilt over it, and slung a sword from his shoulder: There was some bread and a basket of dried figs in one corner of the tent, but as he raised the fruit to his lips, he stopped. Without tasting the food, he left the tent.

III

Outside, the sunlight blinded him. He stood with shaded eyes until he could face it. Meanwhile, the soldiers standing guard by his tent had saluted him, clashing their spears against their brazen shields.

This they had learned from Reuben and Gad, and other fine tricks as well; for in the desert, when your skin dries out like parchment and when your belly squeezes dry like a clenched fist and when your tongue is as thick and swollen as black goat felt, there is no saluting of captains or princes; what a man is, he is.

It must be said that what Joshua, the son of Nun, was, he was; and as he strode away, one soldier said to the next, "The serpents eat him. They eat his liver. I look at his face and I can feel the fire in his belly."

"That's what happens when you are a great captain. You serve Jehovah, but Nehushtan the snake settles in your bowels."

"I remember him when he was a young man."

"He was not a great captain then."

"No, he was not. In those days, he wore his red hair long and fastened it behind him with a golden clasp. It fell to his kilt."

"I wouldn't think he would wear his hair like a woman."

"Oh? Tell him that. But wipe the snot from your child's nose first. You're good enough with the women, but you have something to learn about men. I'll tell you something. When the sun caught that red hair of his, he seemed to be robed in fire. Then they began to say that if Moses saw the flame of Jehovah in a bush, Joshua carried it with him, all over his body."

"Esau was red. Since you know everything else, was his mother of the blood of Esau?"

"You talk too much."

"And who doesn't? Are there any secrets from us? When that

whore of Manasseh came here last night, who held the tent flap open for her? Who let her in to the great captain, Joshua ben Nun?"

"A fool forgets nothing," the other soldier answered with contempt.

IV

For three days now, the boys under thirteen years of age—who had not yet come to any of man's estate and who took no part in battle, not even to shout and bring water for the parched throats of the spearmen, not even to clash the cymbals or run with fresh arrows for the archers—these boys had been rounding up the livestock and bringing it in. While they were so engaged, the women cut thorn bush and laid it down for temporary corrals.

The Reubenites and the Gadites notched the ears of their cattle for identification; and there was agreement between them and the heathen Ammonites that at roundup time each would respect the stock of the others; for the hilly rangeland in the north was free and unfenced. But the Benjaminites and the Judites and the Simonites and the Levites and the other tribes of Israel would not mark or brand their stock, for Moses had taught them that a sacrifice to the Lord God of Hosts must come unblemished and unmarred; even as they themselves were cursed and thrice cursed if they tattooed their faces like the Amalekites, or pierced their ears for earrings like the Edomites or raised welts with ashes like the Ammonites.

After the first day of the roundup, Joshua went among the cattle and saw that they were unblemished. He called his son, Joash, to him.

"Where are the cattle of Reuben and Gad?" Joshua demanded.

It was no easy thing to be the son of Joshua. There were some men who whipped and caned obedience into their children, but no son of Joshua had ever felt his hand; for all of that, they sometimes envied children who were caned and whipped. You had to be Joshua's son to understand why.

Twelve years old, soft-spoken and gentle, Joash averted his eyes and said, "The children of Reuben and Gad have trouble finding their cattle."

"Why?"

"They say that their cattle are used to ranging north into the valleys of the Ammonites."

"Cattle are used to nothing. They are beasts, and Jehovah gave them no knowledge of where the range is good or bad. If they are in the valleys of the north, they are driven there."

"Yes, my father," Joash agreed, his eyes still averted.

"Yet Jehovah gave his own children eyes and sense. Is it so?"

"Yes, my father."

"And you saw no cattle with notched ears?"

"I saw cattle with notched ears," Joash admitted.

"Then you are telling me that the children of Reuben and Gad are blind?"

"No, they are not blind."

"Yet they couldn't see what you saw?"

"I don't know, my father."

Joash sensed how tense and angry his father became when subjected to this kind of submission; yet he could not do otherwise. The more afraid he became, the more abject he became. Now he bit his lips and fought to hold back his tears, while there came into his mind a picture of what might have been, of Joshua swinging him up into his great arms, as sometimes other fathers did with their sons, of Joshua embracing him, Joshua smiling at him with love and kindness.

But the plain fact was that Joshua spoke to him very quietly and evenly, "When you go out to bring in cattle tomorrow, my son, make no difference between the cattle of Reuben and Gad and the unblemished cattle of Jehovah's people. Tell that to the other boys, as something that I have said."

"Is it right?" Joash found the courage to whisper, and he was amazed when his father smiled and said, "Should it not be right for a brother to help a brother? If they have no eyes to see with, we will be their eyes, and we will help them. We are all the Children of Israel, and blood runs thicker than water."

It was the fact that his father had smiled at him. For that smile, he would do anything. To the boy, it seemed to light up the whole world, and he felt such a sense of love and adoration of the brass-clad giant that Joshua could not help but notice and be moved.

It was at such times that Joshua wanted desperately to break through the wall that separated him from his son. He knew of its existence, but he was rigid within it, and trapped and bound, not only barred from the boy, his son, but from every human being in the great encampment except only the frail and beautiful woman whom he had taken from Gamaliel of Manasseh. Perhaps the boy Joash sensed this, for as Joshua bent on one knee beside him, Joash was bold enough to reach out and touch the thick, heavy forearm of his father. The boy was trembling a little out of the plain joy of standing there, his great father down on one knee beside him, his own small fingers moving across the curling red hair.

"I want you to try to understand me," Joshua said as tenderly as he could. "I am not asking you and the other boys to steal the cattle of Manasseh and Reuben and Gad, but only to bring them into the corrals—so that when we cross the river, we can drive the cattle with us and have to eat and to drink. That is why I say, whether or not the cattle have notched ears, whether it is their cattle or our cattle, drive it into the camp."

Still Joash was confused. "Don't the boys of Reuben and Gad know that? Won't they cross the river?"

"They will tell me that their cattle are in the mountains," Joshua said with sudden harshness. "They will lie and whimper and plead. They will close the gates of their cities against us and cower behind their stone walls and try to find the guts to fight us."

"Why? Isn't the land promised to all of us?"

"Nothing is promised," Joshua said, his voice dry. "Nothing is promised and nothing is given. You take it. That's the bitter fruit for you to chew on when you become a man."

"But the land was promised to Moses our father," the boy pleaded.

"Ah, yes—yes. Now, listen to me, Joash, my son. I promised you once that when you were thirteen years of age and had come into the man's estate, I would give you an iron Hittite sword to hang by your side, a sword so hard and keen that it would cut through a bronze buckler as if the shield were made of cheese. That is the nature of iron. So it is promised. And how shall I come by it, tell me?"

"You promised me, and you will come by it," the boy said, looking into the red-bearded face beside him.

"So I will, but I must pay the price. Perhaps I will strike down some painted Canaanite lord and find that he wears an iron sword by his side. Or perhaps I will have to buy it from the Hittite merchants when they come to the markets in the cities. Either way, I must pay a price, for the great captains of Canaan do not give up their lives or their swords at my asking, and as for the Hittite merchants, they will have the last piece of gold in my pouch. Either way. Do you understand? Tell me, what would you be when you become a man?"

"A war lord," the boy answered. "Like my father."

"And why?"

"So that all would know me," the boy smiled. "I would wear a brass helmet, as you do, with the black and red and white plumes of Levi."

"I thought so once," Joshua nodded. "And then the clan chiefs made me war lord over all the host. How can I tell you what the price is? I don't know—" He looked down at the small hand resting on his arm. "I don't know. You asked me before why the people of Gad and Reuben and Manasseh don't want to cross the river with us. How can I explain. The whole thing is my life. My life is not like yours, Joash. You lived your life here with the river beside you, but I was fourteen years old when I saw the river for the first time. It was a dry year. There were no rains in the desert that spring, and the wells and watering places dried up. Then our cattle died. We had no beefs then, only sheep and goats, no horses, only donkeys, no chariots—only the donkeys to bear burdens. They all died. We tried to carry the tents, but then we began to die, and we abandoned the tents first and then our weapons and then the food that remained. The water was gone. We were a people dying when we crawled over that ridge to the east of here and saw the river below in the valley past the acacia woods, lying there like a ribbon of gold—"

He paused and rubbed his brow and then shook his shaggy head. Silent and entranced, the boy listened. Never before had his father spoken to him like this.

"—and the green land across the river," Joshua went on, his voice dropping to a whisper. "We rested, and then we went across the river and took the stock of the men of Jericho, because our own stock was dead. But we were only a handful, and the Canaanites drove us away. But our brothers, the Reubenites and Gadites, they closed their gates and watched us with scorn and contempt. We were their own blood, but we were dirty savages—and they neither sheltered us nor fed us, nor offered us a single beast to sacrifice to our God because we were saved. I swore then that one day I would come to the river with a mighty host and go across it and take that green land and hold for myself and for my children, so that never would they know how it feels to be dying of thirst in the desert—"

The boy's eyes were full of wonder and devotion, and fear too. "Do you understand?" Joshua demanded, almost fiercely, gripping the boy by the shoulders as he flinched away. "Do you understand? Thirteen years ago, I came back, and this time with Caleb and his Judites and Gershom and his Kennites and Gath and his Simonites, and we were five thousand fighting men, with brass armor and iron swords. Then Caleb and Gershom wanted to break into the cities of Reuben and Gad and Manasseh and put them to fire and sword, but still I thought of that green land across the river. So instead, we fought Ammon and Amor and broke their power in the Land of Gilead, and in return, the war chiefs of Gad and Reuben and Manasseh swore a sacred oath that when we had forged a confederation of all the desert tribes—to go over the river and take the Land of Canaan for ourselves for all time—then, they swore, they would leave their cities behind them and go with us, with all their fighting men and their women and children."

The boy looked at his father newly, with wonder and fear, but newly also; and Joshua, as if the telling were too much, suddenly rose and stalked away.

V

As he stood in front of his tent on this morning, Joshua remembered and nodded to himself. Blood runs thicker than water, blood pacifies and seals and binds. He recalled the story his father had told him of the great battle where Nun and Moses had gone up with the hosts of Egypt against the black men of Kush. Then they made a covenant of brotherhood, Nun and Moses, signed with their own blood. Iron chains can be split apart, but a bondage in blood is forever.

His eyes swept over the encampment, the forest of black tents that filled the whole belly of the valley, the high, rocky, scrub-clad mountains, the corrals with the thousands of cattle, the sweet morning smell of their droppings, the turbulent, restless motion of the people as they began this day which was like no other day he could remember, the drifting tails of smoke from a thousand cook-fires and the pungent smell of burning chips.

The sight and scent squeezed his heart and made his pulse pound faster. He was alone; no one knew him and no one penetrated him.

How could he tell anyone what he felt now, the bursting mixture
of joy and frustration as he saw this scene, so familiar to him and
so much a part of him? It would sour in him as the day wore on;
already he felt the skin of dullness being pulled over it. Why was
he as he was? Other men laughed their easy way through life; why
was he like this?

He shook the thoughts away, and went to do what he must do.
When Joshua the son of Nun walked as he walked now, no one
halted him, no one interfered with him. He walked to a corral
where beefs were, and he pushed his way among the horned cattle.
There were the horned beasts of Bashan, who would battle a lion
for their young and toss a wolf as a child tosses a ball; but they
sensed the mood of the red man among them, and because he was
without fear, they feared him and backed away from him, snorting
and pawing the ground with their forefeet. He came to a cow with
calf, and with a single motion of his arm, he flung the calf to the
ground, gripped its forefeet in one hand, its hocks in the other, and
flung it over his shoulders.

The cow lowed pleadingly and the calf bawled with fear, urinat-
ing across Joshua's neck and back, but without breaking his pace,
Joshua strode through the cattle and out of the corral. As his long
stride took him through the camp among the tents, people looked
at him and whispered to each other, but no one approached him
or spoke to him.

Two men who were strapping each other into leather greaves and
plated jerkins eyed him keenly, and one said to the other, "I have
been near him in battle, and he moves like that and he looks like
that."

The other nodded. "I have heard it said that he is a berserk."

"Well, you're wrong."

"No need to get provoked over it. Isn't that what you said?"

"No. I said the way he is. Is he berserk? Don't be a fool."

"He's possessed."

"That's a damned foolish thing to say. Would you want to bear
witness on that?"

"I just said it. What's wrong with you?"

"I hate the way people talk about him. They don't know him.
They have no right to talk about him like that. The talk runs
through the camp like a sickness."

"Then why does he walk like that?"

"Because he's turned inward on himself. He's of the same blood as Aaron, isn't he. Maybe he listens to the voice of Jehovah, the way the old man used to."

"So they say."

"Well, you grow old and a god doesn't want that. An old man is no use to anyone. Among the Ammonites, when a man is too old to lie with a whore in the temple, they cut his wrists and leave him in the mountains to bleed to death."

"I can believe that. There's nothing I'd put past the Ammonites. If it weren't for Reuben and Gad, we would have settled with the Ammonites, believe me. And there's good land to the north of here. The Ammonites are rich. They have five times the cattle we have, and they have gold and silver. They say the roofs of their temples are of pure silver."

"There is better land to the west of here, and the Canaanites are richer."

As he went through the camp, others watched Joshua and discussed him. There were two young women of a Jashubite petty chief named Ura, the one a concubine and the other a wife but both of them as thick as peas in a pod. They kept nothing from each other but a great deal from their husband; and as Joshua passed, with the bleating calf slung over his shoulders, the wife said to the concubine, "There goes a bull, my sister."

"You wet your lips when you say that, sister."

"Are yours dry, my sister?"

"I have more sense than to go a-whoring after Joshua ben Nun."

"Then you have more sense than Deborah of Manasseh."

"Or more fear, if the truth be told, sister. We make a great to-do about a man lying with a woman, but Manasseh has the habits of Reuben and Gad. If a woman is dry or barren, she doesn't weep and tear her hair. She creeps away to the temple in the hills of Ammon, and she goes a-whoring there with the first worshipper."

"Cursed be all they who go a-whoring after strange gods."

"I'm glad you said that, but all the same—"

They were packing away their household goods, the pots and the water-flasks and the grinding stones and all the rest of it, even as people all around them were packing and preparing to take down their black tents.

"—one thinks of a cow under a bull like that. One can't help thinking, can one, my sister?"

"I suppose not."

"One thinks about the Canaanites, and when their enemies go down in battle before them, they don't kill the women, saving only the virgins, the way we do. They bring them to the mother-god instead, and then they sit in the temple and do no work at all, waiting for men to come to worship—"

"Oh?"

"And what can one do, my sister, if the Lord God Jehovah is overthrown, being in such a strange land and so far away from his own mountain of fire?"

VI

Thirteen years ago, before the Tabernacle in all of its wild beauty had been woven and sewn together by the women of Judah and Levi, before the Ark had been fashioned out of polished acacia wood, Moses had built an altar to the God of Horeb. This altar was perhaps two hundred feet above the valley-bottom, on the first slope of the Mountains of Gilead, and with an unobstructed view across the River Jordan. The altar was of plain fieldstone, untouched by tools and unshaped, even as the Law said in those times, before there was a Tabernacle and a holy place of sacrifice.

Although the altar in the fields was rarely used after the construction of the Tabernacle, it could not remain there now and become a place of sacrifice for any wandering herdsmen who came by. Eleazar, assisted by three of the older Levites who were chattel to the God and to the Tabernacle, were taking it apart, laying the stones back on the earth, here and there, in a random manner. Eleazar had not yet told these bond-Levites, or indeed anyone at all, that he had been anointed as priest by Moses; it was still a strange and upsetting thing that had to become much more a part of himself before he could share it with another. But for all that, there was a look about him that spelled out change and difference, a look that kept the other Levites silent at their work until they saw Joshua mounting the slope with long strides.

"Look there, my lord Eleazar," one of them said.

They paused in their work, and their eyes followed his pointing hand.

"What is he doing with a beef calf on his neck?" another Levite asked.

"The calf is alive," said the third.

But Eleazar said nothing, only watched Joshua who, without pausing for breath or rest, strode up to what remained of the altar and flung the calf to the ground. For a moment, the animal lay still; then it struggled to rise. It had gained its feet when Joshua struck it with his fist on the side of the head. Its legs crumpled and it lay at Joshua's feet, bleating feebly.

"Levites," he said to them, "I have brought a sacrifice to the Lord God of Hosts." And then he stood and looked at Eleazar, who met his eyes and held his gaze. A long moment went by before Eleazar said, "This old altar is broken down, Lord Joshua. If you have a beast for sacrifice, take it to the Tabernacle and let the Lord Moses bleed it."

"Enough of the altar is left," Joshua replied stolidly.

"A poor sacrifice on a broken altar."

"I haven't come here to bandy words, Eleazar. Take a knife and cut the beast's throat. He is a good beast, a male, and without blemish or hurt. We will bleed him and burn the soft shoulder meat. It will make a sweet smell for the God's pleasure."

Eleazar took a deep breath and shook his head slowly. "This is no place for a sacrifice, Joshua ben Nun, as you well know—and who am I to make one? Go to Moses with your beast."

"And by whose order are you dismantling the altar?" Joshua cried in sudden fury.

"Your order, Joshua."

"Then why must I hear the name of Moses every time I move? Every time I breathe, every time I take a step! I am sick and tired of that. Where is he now?"

"In the Tabernacle with the God," Eleazar said evenly.

"So the old man still sits in his tent! Now let me tell you something, Levites! The God of Horeb is a God of war! My right arm is the sword of my fury—this says Jehovah! Why must I hear nothing but the name of Moses? What are you? Are you Levites?"

"We are Levites, my Lord Joshua."

"Then give me the name of the God! What has the Lord God Jehovah to do with an old man who sits in his tent and babbles of the past, of what is dead and gone!"

The blood drained from Eleazar's face, but he held himself rigid and never raised his voice as he said, "Let it be, Joshua ben Nun. You are highly strung today, and that is understandable. You have waited a long time for this day, as we all have. I beg you not to do anything that would bring the anger of Jehovah down upon us."

"I will do what must be done. If you are afraid to make the sacrifice, I will. Give me the knife!"

"I have no knife," Eleazar said, more with pity than with anger or contempt. "The sacred knives are in the Tabernacle—as you should know."

"Then I'll use my sword." And to suit his words, he drew the blade halfway out of the scabbard.

"In God's name—no! You are unclean!"

"Who are you to say?"

"I say it! Listen to me, Joshua! I say it!"

"Why? Why am I unclean? I have not broken my fast. No bread crossed my lips this morning. Who calls me unclean?"

"I do," a voice cried out behind him. "I call you unclean! You stink with the beast's piss, and your heart is dirty with passion and fear! I say that! Unclean!"

Joshua turned around and saw his father, and the old man said, "Take your hand off your sword. You face me, not the Levite on the other side of you. Take your hand off your sword, Joshua ben Nun, before the wrath of the Lord God strikes you dead as you stand!"

Joshua let his hand drop. The old man, Nun, was panting a little from his climb up the slope; but his voice was level. A head shorter than his son, his strength was with him in his years, the great shoulders and arms veined and knotted, but still with their strength. How old can he be, Joshua found himself wondering. Seventy-five, eighty years? How long can a man live and have the strength of a bull and the step of a tiger?

Nun said, "Fear—it's a sickness in you."

How had he known? What devil's knowledge lay behind his ragged beard?

"What do you want of me, old man?" Joshua demanded. "Haven't I enough to do and enough weight of responsibility on my shoulders without being hounded by you? Accused by you? I didn't draw my sword against you."

"Against whom did you draw it? Against God?"

"I began to draw it to make a sacrifice to Jehovah. I brought him a fatted calf to sacrifice. Is that such an evil thing? Today is my day. Would you have me go into it without his help?"

"Who gave you the right to sacrifice? Who made you a priest?"

"Why do you bait me so, old man?" Joshua cried angrily. "Moses made me judge over all the people. He put his trust in me? Why must you doubt me?"

"And how well have you judged?"

"As well as I might!"

"And now you come here stinking of the beast's piss, to make a sacrifice to the Lord God! It will be a stench in his nostrils!"

"Why do you bear down on me? What have I done to you, my father? Why do you hate me?"

"I don't hate you. The hate is inside of you. You make yourself hateful."

Joshua shook his head dumbly. The Levites, watching and listening, for they had no other choice, felt a sudden wave of pity for this great red man who stood before his father like a hurt and frightened child. Now the calf, still bleating, stumbled to its feet and ran off, its clumsy gait like that of a drunken man. But no one moved to halt it.

"The men of Israel are fruitful," Nun said, "but I had only one son—not even a daughter, but only one son."

"Have I been such an evil son to you?"

"Not to me—but to this host that is spread out there in the valley."

"Why? Why do you curse me? Have I betrayed Israel? Have I led them into battle where they failed? Or have I made a blood offering to Jehovah out of their enemies? Who has slain more? Who has glorified his holy name more? Who has brought more spoil to the Tabernacle? Why don't you weigh my sins against the offerings I laid before the Ark?"

"I am not a merchant to weigh this against that," Nun answered coldly.

"Look at their numbers!" Joshua cried, throwing his arm out in a gesture across the valley. "Have they fared so poorly? Have they hungered? Count their cattle! Is there a nation in this land that doesn't answer with fear when they hear the name of Israel?"

"You measure all things by fear."

"I am a soldier."

"Once I was a soldier, as was Moses, my master."

"And what am I supposed to understand from that?" Joshua demanded. "Have I said otherwise? Have I tried to lessen your glory or the glory of the old man?"

"Why do you call him *the old man*? Call me the old man? Am I more than he is? Or am I younger than he is? We are of an age, and for three generations, as Jehovah bears witness, I have served him and he has been my master, and I his blood brother."

"I meant nothing by it. He is old, so I called him an old man."

"I am old too."

"And I called you old man before. Will you curse me for that? What have I done to you, my father? Just tell me that. The Law says to honor thy father and mother—"

"That thy years may be long in the land."

"In the land that Jehovah promised us."

"You know the Law well," Nun nodded. "And what else does the Law say, Joshua, my son?"

"A great deal."

"What?" Nun demanded fiercely.

"Are you playing games with me?" Joshua pleaded.

"No. You play the games, Joshua."

"What are you asking me? Come to my tent—or I will go to yours. Must you shame me here?"

"What shame? To talk in front of Levites of something all the people know? They are your kin and blood. Tell me what the Law says, my son—or does it say nothing of those who lie with the wives of other men? Or is it silent on wives who lie with the husbands of other women? Or does the Law say, surely she shall be driven forth and stoned to death? Or does Gamaliel of Manasseh read the Law differently? Is he a companion in this?"

"Leave off me!" Joshua cried wildly.

"Then answer me! Is Gamaliel of Manasseh your companion in this? Is it not said of Manasseh, as it is of Reuben and Gad, that they go up into the hills of Ammon, where the temple whores await them and lay with them? Or does the Law say nothing about whoring after strange gods? Answer me!"

"In God's name—stop it!"

"Who are you to call God's name to you? Who are you, Joshua ben Nun, the son of a slave? It was Moses who bought me out of bondage, Moses who freed us from the curse of Nehushtan, the snake-god of fear and ignorance, and Moses who brought us to the

Holy of Holies! What stink and abomination arises from you,
Joshua? What ways have you found that you join with Gamaliel to
make a whore of a woman of Israel?"

Joshua tore himself away. Like a man taken leave of his sense, he
plunged down the hillside, like a great, craggy tree uprooted, like
a rock toppling and toppling without ever falling.

Nun stood where he had been, breathing heavily. Then he bowed
his head and smashed his fist into his open palm again and again.
Silent, frightened at the storm they had witnessed, the Levites
waited for a calm that did not come. Then Eleazar said, "Nun?"

The old man lifted his head and looked at Eleazar with the
confused hurt of an animal. His anger, so full of pride and righteousness, wilted and left him under the searching gaze of Eleazar.

"What do you want?" Nun asked.

"I honor your years and your knowledge. You are old and full
of things that we have not seen or dreamed of."

"I am old and full of pain and weariness."

"No. Memories and the glory of the God. But do your years make
Joshua a child, that you spoke to him the way you did?"

"I spoke to the sinner. His soul is black!"

"Nun—if you are father to Joshua, are you less of a father to
me? Who held me in his arms when my memory began? Who sheltered me against the demanding fury of my own father? Who?"

Nun nodded, slowly, sadly.

"I talk to you with love and respect. Will you listen?"

"I hear you," Nun muttered.

"Let the God of Horeb curse Joshua—not you, but the God.
Joshua is your son. Who are you to curse him?"

"He has cursed himself."

"Let another decide. Whatever else Joshua is, he is war lord and
judge over Israel, and all of his life, he has waited for today. Go
back to Moses, Nun, and stay beside him."

VII

These were a tent people, and when they raised a temple for
their jealous war god, this too was a tent, which they called the
Tabernacle. At that time, Moses was already *full of his years*, as
they put it in their speech; the memory of the temples of old Egypt

was clouded and indistinct, but the colors, the clear blues and whites and scarlets, were clear and fresh.

But Jehovah was a God robed in fire, and they would have it no other way than that the great tent of the tabernacle should be burning red. The young men then, Joshua and Caleb and Gershom, the strong young men, the proud young men who married their swords before they ever knew a woman's touch—these young men wanted it so.

"Let the Edomites stand on the mountains and see the fire of Jehovah's Tabernacle burning," Caleb said.

"Let Amalek see it," Joshua smiled. "It will burn his eyes, so that he will not feel strange when the sword burns his heart."

"My sword will be red when I make my first sacrifice," Gershom agreed.

The young men were what they were; they were children of a God of war and fire who hated all other gods, and their growth and life and thoughts had shaped their hands for a javelin and a brazen shield, not for a plough or shepherd's crook. They were quick to love and quick to hate, wild and lustful and cruel and quick; and in all the world, they feared only the old man Moses and the terrible, angry God of Horeb whom he served, the jealous God of fire and war, whose name was Jehovah.

But if their fear of the God was a fear of his fire and quick anger and unbridled fury, their fear of the old man, his servant, was another thing entirely, for the old man was without anger now. They feared him because he was Moses.

Yet they had their way with the covering of the Tabernacle, which was made of close-cropped rams' skins, dyed blood red, like the fire of the God, and topped with a black hood of badger-skin to symbolize the cloud of smoke that hovered over Horeb, the cone-shaped, ash-covered Mountain of God.

But the old man had his way with the inner part, even to the extent of sending men all the long distance to Ashkelon, that they might buy flax and purple dyes and blue dyes; and he himself supervised the spinning and weaving of linen as fine and light and soft as the holy fabric of Egypt—and then the dyeing of it into lengths of sky blue, Sidonian purple, and the joyful scarlet-vermilion that the women of Egypt wear at the Assembly of the Sun God. There was a good deal of muttering and resentment among the people, especially among the Judites and the Simonites, who were closest to the Mountain of Jehovah, and who from time beyond memory had journeyed to the burning cone of Horeb to seek Jehovah's blessing before they took up their arms in war; but the muttering remained muted, for had not the fire of Horeb died away in their time, and had not the living God taken his place among the people, unseen and pervasive?

Who else but Moses knew His will? "We will make him a Tent and an Ark, in which He will dwell among us," Moses had said to them, "and He will be with us until we find the land which He has promised us—and there the new mountain of God will make itself known to us, and there we will build a new Tabernacle, where He can live among us in his goodness."

The old man spoke that way, in rambling and clouded terms, but he was still the Moses who had brought out the captive people who had been slaves so long in Egypt. To the young men, it seemed that he had been forever and lived forever; they were afraid of him. And when the curtains were raised across the Tent of God, which they called the Tabernacle, the people exclaimed with delight at the bright, shining colors, at the feel of the sheer linen. For that was still in a time when they were a desert folk, with the few pleasures and sophistications of desert people. Though Moses was old, Joshua and the other war lords were young. But now Moses was older, and Joshua was young no longer.

VIII

From the Holy Place, where the Levites were taking apart the Altar of God and returning the stones to the sloping fields from which they had first been moved, Nun went to the Tabernacle, which had been raised in the center of the encampment.

All around the Tabernacle, the people were preparing for the departure, since this was the appointed time. It was thirteen years, almost to a day, since the first tribes had pitched their black tents in the long valley of Nebo, and the place was as much of a home to them as any place had ever been. Just to the north and east of the valley, at the entrance to the green pasture lands of Ammon, were the walled cities of the Reubenites and the Gadites, and there too was Hesh, the city of the half-tribe of Manasseh, who had become spoiled for living in the black tents and had raised wooden roofs against the sky.

"Cursed are they," the people said, "for they have taken a field and they are satisfied when Jehovah promised them a land!"

But the curses were whispered, and if hatred began between this half-tribe of Manasseh and the other tribes, the hard hand of Joshua kept it from being any more than hot words. "What do you expect," the whispers said, "when he lies with that whore of Manasseh?"

But today the people laughed with contempt at the Manassites, the contempt of tent people for city folk who cower in their houses and raise up stone walls for defense. "Jehovah is my wall!" the Judite and the Simonite cried, and today the men whetted the edges of their weapons and the women took down the black tents.

The sprawling tent city, with its thousands of people, was melting away from the Tabernacle when Nun approached, his heart swelling with a mixture of many emotions. The quarrel with his son had sickened him and exhausted him, and he felt empty of all but bitterness and resentment. Thereby, he was a stranger in a strange place, and as he cast his burning black eyes here and there, the people cringed from him and touched wood and stone and spit the curse back into the air. In spite of the storm he had been through, the sight of the Tabernacle, standing there in its barbaric color and splendor, eased his heart and cooled the fury of his emotion.

It would have been hard for him to say who was more godlike in his mind, Jehovah of Horeb or Moses of Egypt; both were of the Tabernacle, and for the full twelve years since this mighty tent had first been raised, it had given Nun a focus of worship and comfort too. He moved toward it and worshipped as he did so; he bowed his head; the tears stung his old eyes.

"Comfort for all your days, servant of Moses," the Levites on guard around the Tabernacle saluted him.

"Well—I thank you," said Nun. "All my days are not so many."

"Jehovah will lead you into the land he promised us."

"Oh? He'll lead Joshua there anyway," Nun muttered. "Where is Moses, my master?"

"In the Tabernacle."

"Has he given orders to take it down and fold it for the journey?" The Levites shook their heads.

"Will he be disturbed?"

"He waits for his servant."

They drew back the striped hangings for Nun to enter. Moses

was there. He stood in one corner of what was called the "Outer Place," in contrast to the Holy of Holies which housed the Ark.

He wore a long, white linen robe, which covered him from neck to ankle, and the sunlight fell upon him in bands of scarlet and blue. He smiled as Nun entered.

"Old friend, welcome," he said.

Other men bent with age; Moses stood straight and tall; his beard lay full and white upon his breast. But his height and breadth were deceptive; the strength had gone out of him. It was only two days since Nun had last spoken with him, but in those two days, some awful change had taken place. To Nun, it seemed that Moses' flesh had fallen away; and he had the sudden thought that the God had turned from him, leaving him alone in the Tabernacle. Thought was speech with Nun, and he blurted out, "Where is the God Jehovah?"

"Where?"

"No. Forgive me, my master."

Moses sighed. "Do we go on forever without change? It is more than half a century since I gave you your freedom and we sealed the bond with blood. Still—you call me master."

"I am a fool," Nun muttered, shaking his head.

Then Moses walked to him and saw the tears in his eyes. "Oh, what is it, old friend?" Moses asked, taking him by the shoulders. "For whom do you weep? We are old men who have lived past our time, and all those who were our comrades are dead. There is nothing left for us to weep over."

"I suppose I weep for myself," Nun said. "I saw Joshua, and there were hot words between us."

"Why?"

"Why are there ever harsh words between us? Because he thought evil and did evil."

"What evil? Why is your hand so heavy on him, Nun?"

"What evil, you say? He took a calf on his back and went up to the Altar of God, which the Levites were dismantling, as he had told them to. He flung the calf down there and told them he had a sacrifice for the God. They begged him not to, for there were no priests, and then he began to draw his sword to sacrifice the beast himself. The Levites cried out that he was unclean."

"Was he?" Moses asked, his voice quiet and distant and thoughtful.

"The calf had pissed on him. He was unwashed and unclean. He had come from his bed, and his hair was tangled from sleep, and the perfume and paint of that whore of Manasseh was on his body."

"He's your son," Moses said.

"My son is cursed and evil."

"You say that," Moses said sadly. "So much—and you tell me of Joshua ben Nun. No. You don't understand, Nun."

"What don't I understand?"

"He has to make the sacrifice today. Otherwise, there will be no priest to Jehovah."

"What?" He shook his head angrily. "Don't talk like that. You are Jehovah's priest."

"No longer. Why did you look around when you came in here? Do I seem alone? You asked me where is the God? They cannot leave here and go across the river to conquer the land without the God? All of Canaan trembles at the mention of Israel, who comes with a sword in one hand and a torch in the other. Who can stand before them? But we have seen soldiers in our time, old friend, and they were brave because they were soldiers and Rameses gave them gold. But these are brave because the spirit of God is with them, and Jehovah is a God of war and fire and vengeance. Will they cross the river without the God?"

"No," Nun whispered. "But you said you will not cross the river."

"So Joshua must sacrifice and make himself a priest and give a burnt offering to the God. And before the sun sets, he must kill me, too, in the old way, as the old priest was always slain at the hand of the new one."

"No—no!" Nun cried out. "You have been alone too long. Never have I gone against you, Moses, my master, but you say against my own blood and seed!"

"I say what must be."

"Why? Are we in the old times? Have these people learned nothing from you? As long as any of them live, you have been over them, and the God has been with you!"

"They learn a little, Nun—a little."

"And will my son go against my curse? My body will be a shield to you. Will he cut down his father?"

"We are so old, Nun—old and used up and tired. What are you clinging to?"

Trembling, Nun pleaded, "I cling to our dreams. You didn't dream alone, Moses, my master. You dreamed your dreams with me. I cling to them."

"Give them up," Moses said shortly.

"No."

"I tell you, give them up!"

Nun rent his cloak; the motion was without effort or thought; he took hold of the striped wool that covered him and tore it apart. "This way?" he cried painfully, with an animal voice, the voice of a wounded beast. "Shall I mourn them as I mourn the dead? Then I curse the day you gave me my freedom! I curse what you made of an ignorant Bedouin! I curse it!"

Moses took his old friend by the shoulders and shook him gently. "Nun—my dear Nun. Never did I want to cause you pain and sorrow."

"Then put a knife in my heart and have done with it. Let the blood run. Let it be the way it was in the old days, when they took the first-born and offered him up to the God. I am old, but I was first-born. Make an offering of me. Then they can raise temples to the whore-gods and the snake-gods."

"Stop it, Nun," Moses said coldly. "That's enough."

"Enough?"

"Enough, I say. Enough."

"Enough," Nun said stupidly. The last flame had burned away.

"Sit down and rest yourself." Then Moses led him to a bench, and Nun sat down, all of him trembling. Moses gave him wine to drink, and as he drank it, some spilled and ran down over his beard.

"Rest—rest, old friend."

"Yes, my master."

"The God is with us. You thought it was empty in here, but the emptiness was with you. Let it fill."

"Yes."

"The God is with us. Here is his Tabernacle."

"Speak his name," Nun whispered, looking into the eyes of Moses.

"Jehovah is mighty! Who is like Jehovah!"

"Call upon Him!"

"No."

"Moses, call upon Him!"

"No."

"Moses, plead with Him, plead with Him! Call out His name! This place is filled with the stink of iniquity! Call Him!"

"No," Moses answered sadly. "No."

IX

Deborah came to the Tabernacle while Nun was inside with Moses. She had to pass through the encampment among the people, so she threw a cloak over her head. Yet they knew her. She could not cringe; she had never carried a burden and she was erect and straight, the way a princess is. So every head turned as she passed, and they whispered her name. "There goes the whore of Manasseh," they said. "See how the harlot walks!"

The Levites on guard at the Tabernacle also saw her, and one of them said, "Joshua is no fool. There is a woman!"

"There's trouble," a second said.

And a third, "The whore is cursed! Would you stand outside the Tent of God and admire her?"

"And does the Law say you can't admire a whore?"

"The Law is Levite Law. We are sworn to an angry God."

"The Law doesn't make a Levite or any of us a eunuch. I'd be a rich man if I had a piece of gold for every soldier who crawled through the night into the hills one time or another these ten years past to whore after the mother gods of Reuben and Gad."

By now, Deborah was close to them. The Levites crossed their staves and one of them said, "Stand back, woman—or the God's curse will strike you. This is holy ground."

She halted, hesitated a moment and then threw back her cloak, revealing the proud and lovely face that was the envy and bitterness of every woman in the encampment. The Levites had never seen her so close before, and her beauty stunned them into silence. Men dream of beauty like that, and the Levites were men; and they stared at her, at the perfect mouth, the planes of her face, the arched brows, the thin, straight nose and the flood of black hair over her shoulders. They stared at her and removed their judgment from Joshua the son of Nun.

"I am Deborah of the house of Manasseh," she said simply.

"We know who you are."

"I must talk with Moses the Levite."

"Not here."

"I must talk with him."

"Not here. The ground is holy. The air is holy. No woman enters the Tabernacle."

"I beg you—"

"Go away and stop tempting us, woman of Manasseh. Go to your walled city. You are unclean—as all of you are. Go back before you profane this place."

She was distraught and pale with fear and excitement, but her voice was like music, and she pleaded with them, "Levites—listen to me, listen to me and have mercy. I am pleading with you. Do I look like a woman who pleads easily?"

Then the curtain of the Tabernacle was drawn aside, and Moses stood there and said, "No one pleads poorly or well, easily or un-easily, woman of Manasseh. We plead with fear as we do most other things in life. Do you have the courage to walk into this sacred place and try the temper of the God?"

"Yes, I do," she answered him.

"Then come with me," Moses said, and he led her into the Tabernacle, leaving the Levites speechless and afraid.

X

In the Tabernacle, Moses was silent. Who had not seen him—but always from a distance! It was said that once it had been dif-ferent and he had moved among the people and with them, and he was a part of them; but that was a long time ago, before he was this old and skinny man. From a distance, he stood like a white tower, and if the children were told that the God Jehovah was a jealous God and an angry God, it was not the flames of Horeb that they saw but the white beard and the white hair of Moses. He was carved from the white rock of the mountains, high above the place where the goats grazed. Let the wildest winds blow and let the thunder rock the whole earth, this man would not be shaken.

Deborah, close to him, saw that he was thin and frail, old and very tired. He tried to wear his weariness as he wore his white robes, but it was too heavy for him. His hands were thin, the skin wrinkled and blue, every vein showing. Deborah remembered the songs she had heard of his great strength, of his prowess in battle, of how he had broken the huge tablets of the Law in his two hands and smashed the rock to powder, of how he had climbed the Mountain of God and stood face to face with Jehovah, of how when Jehovah, in his godly anger, had moved to destroy the Children of Israel, Moses had interposed his own body and wrestled hand to hand with the God, even as the Patriarch Israel had once done, of how he had stood among the belching flames of Horeb and made a covenant with Jehovah—all this and much more, Deborah had heard, and now she saw the man who was Moses.

The man who was Moses pointed to Nun and said, not unkindly, "Do you know who this is, my child?"

She shook her head.

"And what does a woman do in God's Tabernacle?" Nun growled.

"If the God wants her dead, she will die here," Moses said.

"Aren't you afraid to die, whore of Manasseh?"

"Yes, I am afraid," Deborah whispered.

"Suck on your fear," Nun said. "Suck on it the way you suck the nipple of the mother god, the whore of whores!"

"Who are you? Why do you hate me, old man?"

"Joshua is my son. My first-born and my last-born. Motherless, I brought him to the wet nurse and took him away. A father and a mother I was to my son, Joshua. Shall I love you?"

"I love Joshua. Don't you understand that I love him? For what other reason do I walk through the encampment like someone accursed."

"And now she talks of love," Nun said to Moses.

"Have we taken away her right to love?" Moses asked.

"Let her love God and fear him too! What is love to this slut?"

"*What* is it to you, my child?" Moses asked.

"To want someone and need someone. Without him I am incomplete. I am half a woman. I am empty."

"Is that such a bitter feeling?"

"Yes—yes, it is. It is full of death."

"Life is full of death," Moses said.

"You're old, both of you—you're so old. I didn't believe that you could be so old. You have forgotten."

"I suppose I have," Moses nodded.

"I thought you were like a God."

"Men are only men."

"You have other gods in Manasseh," Nun spat at her.

"Why do you hate the mother so?" she cried desperately. "Why do you curse us and call us harlots and sluts? What have we done to you?"

"You are an abomination!"

She turned suddenly to Moses, tall in her posture and pride, her face hot with a flush of anger. "And you too?" she demanded of him. "Are we an abomination to you? You had a sister, Miriam, who was a priestess, and when she danced with the joy of freedom and the eyes of the men glowed with her beauty, you hated her and feared her, and you put her to death—"

"That's a lie," Moses answered.

"The people say—"

"Harlot, be quiet!" Nun cried.

"Let her speak," Moses said. He shed his age. The voice was vibrant, and Deborah knew now what it meant to people to hear that voice long ago. "Do you think only we lie of what goes on in Gad and Reuben? Do they speak no lies of us? My sister Miriam was an old slave woman, worn out with work and sorrow."

Speechless now, she stared at him.

"Why did you come here, my child?" he asked her, almost tenderly.

"Don't you know?"

"No—I don't know."

"For sanctuary."

"There is no sanctuary here."

"This is the God's place! This is the Tabernacle!"

"There is no sanctuary here. It is too late."

She knelt down before him, clinging to the hem of his white robe. "Let me stay—please." She took up the hem of his robe and kissed it; and Nun, looking at Moses, saw the tears in the old, sunken eyes of his master.

"There is no sanctuary here, my child," Moses said.

Part Four. CALEB

I

At the other end of the encampment from where the Tabernacle was pitched stood the black tent of Caleb the Judite, and pricked out in felting and golden thread on the tall flaps of his tent, in the same burning red that was the color of the Tabernacle, were the lions of the Tribe of Judah.

The Levites were annoyed when the red lions first appeared. "Who is this barbarian of Judah," they said, "that he uses this color of the God without so much as by your leave?"

Caleb laughed when he heard what they were saying. "Tell the Levites," he said to Joshua at the time, "that when their ancestors were crawling in the black muck of the River Nile, making obeisance to Nehushtan the snake, who looks for the womb of the mother god—may she be always accursed—my own father brought the sacrifice to Horeb. Or tell them nothing. If the Levites don't like the color of the Lions of Judah, let them come to the tents of Judah and tear the lions off."

This did not make Joshua, who was a Levite himself, love Caleb any better, but neither did it provoke him to quarrel. Secretly, he envied Caleb of Judah and Gath, the Simonite; theirs was the heritage of war from their fathers' fathers' time; they were born to war and bred to war. If Joshua's sword was quick and if the swords of the five hundred Levites who stood behind him were also quick, it was something they had learned with Judah on one side of them and Simon on the other. It was of their heads and not of their hearts; and Jehovah of Moses, of the Ark and the Tabernacle, had already become something else than Jehovah of Horeb.

Caleb was whole with his sword; himself and his sword were one, and he loved battle. Joshua hated battle; he was full of fear, and for every cut of his sword outside, it left a scar inside; and because he was so much afraid, he was even more terrible in battle than Caleb or Gath or Gershom, the son of Moses, who led the Kennites.

The Judites disliked and respected the Levites, who were hard in peace and awful in war; the Simonites feared the Levites; and th Levites smiled knowingly at Benjamin and Simon and Judah, and made ambiguous remarks about men who would rather bury their spear in a man's body than their manhood in a woman's loins. And the dark, small Kennites and Danites mistrusted and feared all of these wild marauders who crooned lovesongs to their weapons, even as other men do to maidens. So it was not for Joshua to take hurt or umbrage. He was war lord over them the way a lion-trainer is master of his half-tamed lions. Let Caleb embroider a whole wilderness of animals on the doors of his tent, for all of him; he cared only that the alliance should be kept, and that the tribes of Joseph and the Children of Israel should fight with the people across the river, and not with each other. And when tempers boiled and knives were drawn, Joshua would roar at them, "A curse upon all of your tribes and clans and blood debts and blood feuds! When our swords are drawn and our shields cover us, we are Hebrews!" meaning simply, all of those from the East, across the River Jordan.

So the lions remained on the flaps of Caleb's tent, and when people called it "the lion tent" a chord in Caleb was touched. He liked the sound of that. He was a burly, ugly man, with a shaggy black beard and a great mane of hair. It pleased him to think of himself as the Lion of Judah. And whenever the war lords pitched their standards in front of his tent, the mandrake of Reuben, the snake of Dan, the horned bull of the Joseph tribes, the wolf of Benjamin, the jackal of Kenn, the doe of Naphtali—Caleb would acknowledge them derisively and condescendingly.

The war lords were there today, and the twenty-two banners of the tribes and clans of the tent people who acknowledged the God of Horeb flew in the morning breeze; but many of the chieftains had discussed what there was to discuss with Caleb and Gath and Gershom, and had then gone back to see to the arming and placement of their own hundreds for the crossing of the river.

The great war lords remained. Caleb of Judah, Gath of Simon and Gershom of Kenn waited for Joshua of Levi, who was war lord and judge over the confederation of Horeb. There were things to be settled that could not be settled without him, nor could the river be forded until these things were settled.

The men with whom Caleb and Gath and Gershom and Joshua must deal stood apart from the war lords, in a little group, Nohab of Reuben, Jephta of Gad, Joel of Ephraim and Gamaliel of Manasseh. These were the war chiefs of Gilead, and they whispered among themselves.

Thus, while on every hand, the tents of the encampment melted away, the tent of Caleb, with the battle standards of Israel flying in the wind in front of it, stood and waited for a settlement of things that had to be settled.

II

"They whisper too much," Gath said to Caleb. "I don't like men who put their heads together and whisper. Honest men talk up."

"Where is Joshua?" Gershom demanded. "With Joshua here, we can settle this, once and for all."

"We can settle it without Joshua," Gath said. "We are Judah and Simon, and we can spit with the wind without Levi."

"Why don't you show that you can think without Levi?" Caleb observed dryly.

"I can think without Levi! And without Judah!"

"We're all on edge," Gershom said soothingly. "We're tired, and our tempers are short. We've waited too long for today to fight over it. For ten years, we have worked to bring all the people together for this."

"You're right. It will be better when we fight," Caleb agreed. He saw it simply. A man became sick with peace; he healed in battle.

"Then get them away. I am sick and tired of looking at them." He pointed to five old women who crouched mutely under the raised flap at the edge of the tent. They crouched pleadingly and patiently. They were old, old women and withered.

"They do no harm," Gershom said.

"They are witches. What does the Law say of the witches—you shall not endure them. They shall be put to death."

"We have no time for that," Caleb said with annoyance. "Let the Levites take care of the Law."

"They are not witches, they are priestesses," Gershom said.

"Are they? What else is a witch? The woman who worships at the womb is a witch. The woman who whores for the Mother is a witch. Do we endure a woman for a priest? Did not Moses strike down his own sister?"

"He did not," Gershom answered, trying to contain his anger. He was an older man than Gath, but tall and lean and powerful, as once his father, Moses, had been. "A lie has a life of its own. It grows with filth, like an infected wound. Those are old women, not witches. They are the daughters of Zelophehad, who was the grandson of Gilead, who fled here to this land out of Egypt a hundred years ago. Even now the Gaddites call the land Gilead, and they say that he was grandson to Manasseh, which makes them blood-kin with the Joseph tribes."

"I am sick to death of the Joseph tribes, and their claiming and pleading and whining," the Simonite said.

"Then bite your tongue," Caleb snapped, "for they can bring twelve hundred spearmen into battle, and I am not interested in whether or not you are sick of them."

"And one day you will go too far, Caleb, I tell you that."

"And let me tell you something," Caleb answered coldly. "If you have such a taste for blood that you grow impatient and would like to try the edge of your blade on those women, then think of it. For as surely as Jehovah is God over Horeb, I will kill you if you do."

"What are we to talk like this?" Gershom cried. "What kind of fools are we?"

"All kinds—every kind," Gath muttered.

"Talk to them, Caleb," Gershom said.

The three war lords walked over to the old women, who knelt and fell on their faces. Provoked and annoyed with them, Gershom demanded, "Are we gods that you worship us?"

"Great captains, listen to us, but don't kill us, for we are old and without the will or strength to do harm to anyone," one of them said.

"Get up, old women," Caleb ordered them. "We have business here today. Tell us who you are and what you want."

"We are the daughters of Zelophehad," whined the old crone who had spoken before. "My name is Hoglah, and her name is Noah and hers is Tirzah and hers is Mahlah and hers is Milcah," pointing to each of her sisters in turn. "We are the daughters of Zelophehad, who was the son of Hepher, who was the son of Gilead, and Gilead was born of Machir, and is it not said that Machir was the son of Manasseh, the child of Joseph, and Joseph—"

"We'll take your word for your genealogy, old woman," Caleb interrupted impatiently. "What do you want of us?"

"Great war lord and chieftains, take pity on us."

"Old woman, old woman, don't you know what day this is?" Gershom said. "Try to come to the point."

"The appointed day," the old crone nodded.

"Yes, and this is the war tent. What business have you in the war tent?"

"Our portion, gracious master," she pleaded. "The young men will take up their shields and spears and march away. A land of milk and honey will be theirs when they cross the river. But what is our portion? Dry sand and hot rock is our portion."

"You have no clans," Gershom said, trying to be both patient and kind. "What need have you for a portion?"

"You are Gershom of Kenn. You are a good man. Moses is your father, and your mother was Zipporah of Kenn."

"Go to Reuben and Gad, old women," Gath told them, his impatience and annoyance increasing. "Go to their temples, where they whore after the mother god."

Tirzah spoke up shrilly. "They drive us from the temples. The young women laugh at us and spit at us. We had our own temples once, but when you wild young ones came into this land where we lived so long, you threw down our temples and you stoned our priestesses to death, and then you took your iron hammers and beat the mother god until she was dust, dust, dust. We ate the dust. But now you go into Canaan, and the mother god is everywhere in Canaan. Do you think that Jehovah of Horeb will be as mighty as she is in Canaan? Who will turn her curses from you? Jehovah? I laugh at that." She began to cackle with senile laughter, and one by one, her sisters joined in.

Then Hoglah said shrilly, "And what if the God of Horeb cannot go across the river? How do you know he can go across the river? Can the gods of Canaan come to Gilead or the gods of Egypt to Canaan?"

They rocked with their cackling laughter.

"And who is priest to Jehovah?" Milcah grinned toothlessly. "Aaron is dead, and will Moses go across the river? No, no, no. You see, he is afraid—you are all afraid, you great war lords."

"Give us our portion," Tirzah shrilled, "and we will go with you across the river and we will sacrifice to the mother god, so that she will turn her curses away from you."

"Let me kill them," Gath said.

Caleb gripped his shoulder. "Wait now. You are too old, old women. If you have your portion, who will defend it for you?"

"Our sons will come back to us if we find favor with the mother god. They went to the Joseph tribes and became soldiers, but they

will come back to us if we find favor. They will plant their seed, and
our clans will live with them."

"Drive them away!" Gershom cried out.

"We will have young women, clean and fresh and beautiful—"

The chieftains of Reuben and Gad and Manasseh and Ephraim
had been listening. They drew closer as the old women pleaded.
Then, quickly and without warning, Joel of Ephraim struck. He
was a tall, dour and powerful man, judge over all of Joseph, bitter
in intercourse among the people and awful in war. He drew his
sword and struck a terrible blow at Tirzah. Her body remained
kneeling, but her head rolled in the dust.

"Enough!" Caleb roared.

The other four sisters wept and shook with fear.

"You will have your portion when the portions are allotted,"
Caleb said grimly, "but if ever your clans live again, there must be
no blood debt from Ephraim. Now speak no more of your whore-
gods, but take your sister's body and get out of our sight."

Toothless delight penetrated their fear. Laughing and weeping
at the same time, they took their sister's body, trunk and head, and
went away. When they had gone, Caleb turned to Joel, who still
held the bloody sword in his hand, and said, "That was no good
thing you did, brother."

"When I want the Law read for good or evil, I will go to the
Levites," Joel said slowly, unshaken and unmoved. "My arm was
the arm of Jehovah. My sword was the sword of an angry God."

III

When Joshua, the judge and war lord, fled from his father's
curse, he felt the tempests and furies beating about his head and
tearing at his soul; and through his agony, he said to himself, "It
is in the hands of the war lord of Horeb now! I no longer care. A
man's will is nothing. Was it the will of Moses to go to Horeb and
talk with the God? Was it the will of Egypt's king to visit such
grief on his people? No, it was the God who willed it. Let the God
do what he desires with me now."

Then he felt better, and he walked to his tent. Few enough tents
were standing now. But as with the war tent of Judah, the tent of
Joshua the chieftain of Levi stood, the red, white and black stand-
ard of Levi flying from its peak-pole, the blazoned Urim and Thum-

mim rippling in the sunlight. The bodyguards still stood in their places, and the soldier at the doorflap said to Joshua, "Caleb the Judite is impatient, Lord Joshua. His messengers come and say that he rages like a lion."

"Let him rage then. Smell me. Do I stink? Do I stink with the unclean and the piss of the calf and the night dirt?"

"You are unclean," the soldier nodded. "A strong, sour smell."

"Then bring me water to lave myself and then you will help me arm. Don't worry. I will go to Caleb. I have quieted the Lion of Judah before," he said wryly, "and I can quiet him again. Get me water now."

Joshua went into the tent, unslung his great iron Hittite sword, tore off his kilt and loincloth, and stood naked on his long, almost slender legs, the massive, powerful barrel of his body seeming to balance precariously and uneasily. When the soldiers came with skins and buckets, he commanded them to pour the water over his head and neck, and he quivered and sighed with pleasure and relief as the cold water cascaded down his body. They gave him towels, and he walked over to another part of the tent to dry himself. He took a fresh loincloth, tied it around him, and then pulled a linen shirt over his head.

Then the soldiers lifted the mighty brass breastplate which had once belonged to Uraush, the war chief of Ura, a clan of the Moabites, and which Joshua had taken from Uraush's body when he killed him in hand-to-hand combat. But before they could strap it onto Joshua's shoulders, a voice interrupted them, "Put it down!"

They hesitated. Nun came across the tent to Joshua.

"I have your curse," Joshua said bitterly. "Have you come to give me your blessing, my father?"

"Send them out!" pointing to the soldiers.

"Wait outside," Joshua said.

The soldiers left.

"Are you my first-born?" Nun demanded.

"Your last-born as well."

"My only-born."

"You say it, sir. It is told that men love their only-born."

"I hear too much of love today," Nun growled. "You left it in the past, like a milestone on the king's road. The God of Horeb loves Moses, my master. Will he love you?"

"Not if my own father hates me."

"Am I still your father?"

"Have I denied you?" Joshua asked hopelessly.

"With words—no."

"Then what do you want with me?"

"You are my first-born. What did our father, Abraham, want of Isaac when the God of Horeb called him to the altar?"

"A blood sacrifice," Joshua answered steadily.

Nun took a curved bronze knife from under his robe. "I brought this from the holy Tabernacle."

"And through whom did the God order the sacrifice?" Joshua demanded, almost contemptuously.

"I don't speak with the God. I am Nun, who is servant and slave and brother to Moses. His life is my life. I was mother and father to him, as he was mother and father to me. Are you my son?"

"I am."

"Are you afraid?"

"Do whatever you must do, my father."

Nun flung the knife from him, shouting, "Cursed animal that you are, you and your bloody comrades!"

Without emotion, Joshua picked up the knife and held it out, haft-forward, to Nun. "Do what you must do."

"And were I you and you me, I could! I curse the day you were conceived! I curse the day you were born!"

"I'd rather you'd kill me than let me live with the burden of those curses."

"Do you say so? And what keeps your hand from me, when your heart is full of murder for Moses? Do you deny it?"

"No. I don't deny it. But you are my father."

"And Moses? What is Moses to you? Is he just an old man? Will his body welcome that iron sword you carry? Will the ages shout the praise of Joshua, for he slew the prophet Moses? He was a great war lord over all the confederation, and he vanquished an old man! And why not? Who is this old man to you, with his Law, and his foolish ways of peace and reason, and his command to all Israel— thou shalt not kill!"

"Why do you bait me?"

"Do I bait you, my son?"

"You know why I must do it! Will the God go with us if we have no priest? And wasn't it always this way in the old times, that when the priest had seen his day, the new priest slew him?"

"And nothing changes?"

"If I do it, it means the God wills it."

"And are you the creature of the God's will, as I was once the pawn of the will of Nehushtan the snake? Is the God all and man nothing? Is that what the Covenant means? Or do we stand side by side with the God of Horeb, proud that we are men even if he is a God?"

"We have no other gods. Will you send me into Canaan naked? Do you know how long I have worked and planned for this day and dreamed of this day? Do you know what it means to bring together twenty-two tribes and clans—and hold them together? For as long as any living man can remember, the land was promised, but I was not content with promises, and I said to the people, 'The land will be yours!' It is eleven years since Moses made me judge over the tribes. I am forty-five years old. How long shall I wait? Shall I go back into the desert and suck the hot rock and the dry sand?"

"When the God of Horeb tired of these people," Nun said, "and He told Moses, 'I am sick of these people and they are an abomination to me,' did Moses cringe because he was a man?"

"Men are not gods."

"Moses is a man. Did he ever claim to be a god? Yet he placed his body between the terrible anger of the God and ourselves. He stood face to face with Jehovah, and said to the God, 'Why will you do this to my people? Because they are weak? Foolish? Vain? Cruel? Ignorant? Blind? Selfish? But what they are, I also am, because I am of them, so if you destroy them you must destroy me as well.' And Jehovah held back, for though He knew a great deal, there was much that He did not know, and never had He known the worship of a man like Moses before." Nun's voice had fallen into the tempo of exposition; it softened. He held out one trembling hand to Joshua. "Is it an accident that we are chosen of the God? He is a cruel God and a jealous God, but even as we cannot live without Him, so He cannot live without us."

Joshua bowed his head. Nun said softly, "He will not remain behind when you cross the river. Cleanse yourself. Put wickedness out of your heart. Put aside that whore of Manasseh. You go into a strange land where every man's hand will be raised against you. How long will Israel survive if Joshua is cursed and corrupt?"

"I will not go without the Tabernacle and the Ark," Joshua said stolidly.

"Give me the life of Moses, my master, and I will promise you the Tabernacle and the Ark and the blessing of priesthood."

"A promise made must be a promise kept. This is the appointed day. I will not wait for the old man's moods."

"I swear it in the holy name of the God! Jehovah, hear me!"

"And what do you ask in return?"

"Only that you put aside that woman. Destroy her, or she will destroy you."

Joshua raised his head and stared long and thoughtfully at his father. Then he said, "No man will raise a hand to Moses the prophet. When noon breaks, I will come to the Tabernacle for his blessing"

"Come without your sword."

"I am a soldier. While I live, my sword hangs by my side."

IV

Clad in the full panoply of war, Joshua stepped out of his tent; and Deborah was there. He loomed over her, not a man, but a giant of brass and iron, his great round shield slung from one shoulder, his iron sword from the other, his crested helm, black- and red- and white-feathered with the colors of Levi, adding a full foot to his height, his nine-foot, bronze-shod war spear tipped back over his right shoulder, even as his shield lay upon his left.

"My lord," Deborah whispered.

The nighttime was buried in his mind; he was consecrated to war. His Levite soldiers were grinning with anticipation, and their war cries rumbled in their throats. Let the barbarians of Simon and Judah boast of their kills; when had the war god of Horeb sanctified another like the son of Nun? They saluted him with a crash of their spears upon their brazen shields, and the sound echoed and re-echoed across the encampment.

"What are you doing here?" Joshua demanded. "You should be with women's work. The whole host marches in a matter of hours. We will go into the river, and the God willing, we will fight our way across it. You know that."

"I know it, my lord."

"Then what are you doing here? Is it to shame me in the bright daylight, now that I have put on my shield and offered myself to the God?"

"Am I without shame, my lord?"

"I have no time for riddles. I am sorry that I spoke roughly."

"How else should my lord speak when he stands in the panoply of war?"

"Well, I have a lot on my mind. Do you think that there is nothing to be done today?"

"I know that my lord is the war chief and judge over Israel. I am proud and happy that my lord is so honored."

"Then go to the house of Gamaliel."

"I was cast out of the house of Gamaliel. My lord Gamaliel cursed me and made the sign of death over my head. He waits now to cast the first stone, and then I will die."

Joshua's face darkened. "He will not dare! Who is that running dog of Joseph that he presumes so much? He will not dare!"

"Where will I find sanctuary, my lord?"

"Go into my tent and wait for me there," Joshua said, and turning to two of his soldiers, he cried out, "Johab and you, Phineas, stand guard at the door of my tent. I don't care who comes. Whoever it is, whether of the Joseph people or of Simon or of Benjamin or of Judah—or any other, whoever it is, turn him away or drive your spear into his breast. And no man touches this woman, unless I send my own Levites for her myself. Do you understand?"

"We understand, Lord Joshua."

She knelt down before him and pressed her lips to the instep of his brass greave. He raised her up. "No, Deborah. It's a poor way, when all is said and done, to prove my love for you."

"Your love is great, my Lord Joshua," she whispered to him. "I was full of fear, but now I am not afraid. I was afraid of the Law, but Joshua the son of Nun is higher than the Law. I was afraid of the God of Horeb, but you will stand between me and the God."

"Don't talk like that," Joshua said hoarsely. "We are Levites here all around you. Go into the tent and wait for me."

V

"Well, sir," Caleb said angrily, as Joshua strode into the high-roofed, open-sided pavilion that was the war tent of Judah, "I thought not to see you until the sun set. You take things lightly, if I may say so."

"Today you may. I will not quarrel with you today, Caleb of Judah. Anyway, it is still morning."

"There are many ways to put a knife into a man's pride, Joshua. You hold us in contempt too easily."

"I will not debate that now." He lowered his voice and nodded toward the other group of men. "Those lords of Reuben and Gad and the Joseph people would like nothing better than to have us fall out among ourselves."

"Joshua talks sense," Gath said. "What of the Tabernacle and the Ark?"

"They go with us."

"My way?" Caleb asked. Gershom listened and watched Caleb thoughtfully.

"Moses will give me his blessing and make me priest."

"Have you his word for that?"

"I have my father's word, and he swore by the God's name."

"We hear too many things," Gershom said, his words for the three men, but his eyes fixed narrowly on Caleb. "I too have waited a long time for this day, and I will make no move to hinder it. But so help me, if one hair of Moses' head is harmed—"

"Has he loved you and cherished you so well that you must repay him in kind?" Caleb asked softly.

"What is between us is for us and no others. His ways are his ways and mine are mine, and to him, my way is the way of iniquity. But he remains my father," Gershom said calmly.

"You take it easily enough."

"How else? And what of you, Joshua? Is this a place for your weapons? When I come to council, I leave shield and spear and helm outside."

"When I wake to a day of war, I dress for war," Joshua answered shortly, "and I say enough of this bickering. Moses will be no blood offering to the God, whatever the whispers were. He will give us the Tabernacle and the Ark, and his blessing too."

"I hope so, Caleb said. "By all that is holy, I hope so—"

The men of Joseph and Reuben and Gad approached them now, and Nohab of Reuben said, "Let us get down to cases, Joshua, now that you are here."

"I am glad to see you this morning, Nohab of Reuben."

"I said I would be here. Here I am. I said that Jephta would be here, and he is here. And I said that Gamaliel of Manasseh would be here, and he too is here."

"Gamaliel of Manasseh," Joshua nodded, and said tightly, "I bid you welcome, Gamaliel."

"Your fortune is my fortune, Joshua of Levi."

"We are both of us too formal." Joshua's smile was as cold as his gray eyes. "Will we give each other titles when we clamber over the dead and slip in their blood? Not I, Gamaliel. I will thank the God of Horeb that the Children of Joseph raise their shields alongside me. And he will smile on the Children of Joseph who are loyal to him—as they are."

"I'll talk for myself when the time comes, Joshua."

"And for himself only," Joel of Ephraim put in. "Leave me out of their quarrel, Joshua. I have seven hundred spearmen, and they stand in their armor now. We are people of Joseph, and you are too quick with your sneers for the Children of Joseph, I think. But if there is no portion to be allotted to us, I will take my seven hundred spearmen and carve out my own. I fear the Lord God Jehovah, but not you or your Levites or the men of Simon and Judah either. The land is promised. We will not go back to the fleshpots of Egypt or the hot sand of the desert either."

"Oh, well said, well said!" Caleb cried, and Gath slapped his thighs and laughed deeply. But the faces of the war chiefs of Reuben and Gad only darkened.

"We have no quarrel, Joel," Joshua said. "I treasure your spearmen more than my own blood. Your portion will be a fair portion, I swear it. So go back to your men and tell them we march when the noonlight breaks shadow."

Joel nodded shortly and went to join his bodyguard, who waited for him outside of the tent. They clashed their arms in salute.

"He is a hard man, that Joel," Gershom said.

"But when he crosses the river, he will find harder men."

"And still I am here, Joshua of Levi," Nohab said.

"Yes. Yes. And let me tell you this, my friend," Joshua said thinly, "better here than behind the walls of your cities."

"Our men still man the walls of our cities," Jephta said.

"So long as they bear their arms, I care little where they stand now. But I tell you this and understand me, Manasseh and Gad and Reuben, when we blow the rams' horns for the crossing of the river, you will open the gates of your cities and your spearmen and your bowmen and your slingers will march out and join us."

"Do you plead or do you threaten?" Nohab asked.

"Neither. I state a fact."

"And if we refuse? A walled city is also a fact."

Joshua's glance flickered toward Caleb, who was smiling thinly— and then it went back to the faces of Nohab and Jephta and Gamaliel.

"It would be foolish of you to refuse," Joshua smiled. His voice became soft and winning. They had only known why men feared Joshua; now they had their first hint of why men loved him. "You would not refuse. When the land was promised, you put your hands on ours and swore an oath that if the tribes could be gathered together, you would join us."

"Yes, we swore such an oath. But that was many years ago, and things change."

Caleb, speaking without heat, said, "Don't press Joshua to it. He is judge, not over this tribe or that tribe but over the whole confederation. I think, though, that if you were to play us false now, we would turn aside from the river and tear down your cities stone by stone and do away with, once and for all, the curse of your mother god and the whores who serve her. I think the God of Horeb would want it that way. But who knows? I am not a priest— not even a Levite—and why do I presume to talk for Joshua?"

"Neither is Joshua priest to the God," Gamaliel said sullenly.

"Yet he will be; before we march, the prophet Moses will bless him."

"Is that true?" Nohab demanded.

"It is true," Joshua nodded.

"I don't like to be threatened."

"None of us likes threats."

"Yet you would make a slaughterhouse of your brother's house?"

"Caleb's thoughts—not mine."

"Deny him!"

"You are my friend; Caleb is my friend," Joshua said placatingly. "Shall I deny either of you? Or shall I take the words from whence they come? The men of Judah are hot and flame up quickly. It passes away. We are all of us who sacrifice to the God of Horeb like that—and He is a God for us—full of anger and passion, and very jealous indeed."

"What are you getting at, Joshua?"

"Where were my thoughts leading me? Moses will bless me, and I will be the priest of the God. I will go into the Ark and I will open my heart to the God. He is an angry God."

"Still you threaten us!" Jephta cried.

"You read your own fear into my words," Joshua said sternly. his smile gone now.

"Joshua, son of Nun, tell me something," Nohab said now. "We are people who talk the same tongue. We are all the children of Father Abraham, who sits with the gods—even the angry one of Horeb. Gamaliel here is of the blood of Joseph and Manasseh, and thereby blood-kin to you of Levi. We all make homage and sacrifice to the thunderer, the angry God of Horeb. If you have contempt and hatred for our household gods, who live quietly and gently under our rooftrees, we accept the fact that this is because you are tent people and the ashes of your fires are too transitory for gods to find peace there."

Nohab drew a long breath and looked at the faces of the four war lords of Israel, the moody, troubled red countenance of Joshua, the dark, ugly haughtiness of Caleb, the hawklike, barbaric features of Gath, with his curled beard and braided hair, and the thin, joyless, almost ascetic mask that covered the thoughts and the past of Gershom, the son of Moses. How could he reach them, Nohab wondered? How could he bridge the gap between his own background and life and way—and the way of these wild and headstrong tent people, who considered themselves born for war and bred for war, and dedicated to war and the fiery war god they worshipped? Where could he touch them? He was playing for a high stake, for the cities of his fathers and for the lives of his people.

He went on, "Yet when the Levites wrote down the Law, we held our gods as little worth after the God Jehovah, nor do we mock at the beast gods who have watched over your clans from the olden times, the lion of Judah and the snake of Benjamin and the others. It is said that once, long ago, even the Levites sacrificed to Nehushtan, the serpent, who had intercourse with Eve, the mother—"

"Much is said," Joshua interrupted, "much of filth and much of scorn. A thoughtful man lets what is said go in one ear and out of the other."

"I mean no insult—no implications, even, Joshua of Levi. I only try to point out that different tribes have different ways. But when you came into our land, we did not look at your different ways and therefore turn our backs to you. No—not at all. We opened our grain-bins and fed you. We gave you cattle, so that you could make a burnt offering of horned beasts. And we sent you craftsmen to forge cunning rings and hooks of gold and silver for the Tabernacle. Is it right that you should threaten us now, when your strength is so much greater than ours, and talk to us as if we were strangers to you, blood enemies instead of blood kin? Is it right, my lords? Or does the Law say to give a just measure and a just weight? I ask you that, my Lord Joshua and my Lord Caleb and my Lord Gath and my Lord Gershom."

"There are two sides to that story," Caleb nodded. "The sword of the Amorites was over you. They stole your cattle and your women. They stood outside the walls of your cities and taunted you and mocked you. And each night the people of Reuben and Gad cowered behind their locked gates for fear that Amor would come in the darkness with fire and sword. What then? Do I speak the truth or not?"

"What we are, life made us," Gershom said. "In the olden times there were few of us, and we could find life and food in the desert. But when our numbers swelled and we became a people, the swords and shields were raised wherever we turned. What were we to do? Lie down and die of hunger and thirst in the desert sand? Our God is a just God. We served him well, and he promised us the land."

"Did we take your land?" Joshua asked. "Or did we harness our horses to our chariots and go up with you against the Ammonites?"

Abruptly, he flung down his shield and held out his left arm, revealing a crisscross of welted scars. "This is the mark of Ammon, Nohab of Reuben, and for this your children sleep in peace today, and if a boy drives cattle into the Ammonite hills, no man will raise a hand against him. So the scales balance, I think, and it's measure for measure. Now we go across the river into the Land of Canaan, which is promised to us. Would you have us go alone? When you went up against Ammon, we went with you. Do you cast us away like a broken sword? We are not a broken sword—not by any means."

"It is easy for you to talk, Joshua of Levi," Gamaliel put in. "We are Manassites, and in my father's time, we were tent people. But now we have built our city here, and we have married the women of Reuben and Gad. It is easy to fold your tents and march. The

God of Horeb will follow his Ark and the smell of burnt offerings, but what of our gods, who are household gods?"

"I only know," Joshua said slowly and emphatically, "that there are five thousand fighting men of Reuben and Gad and Manasseh. Either they will fight with us, or they will fight against us."

"If our portion is here," Nohab argued, "then there is less land and less spoil to be divided in Canaan."

"Canaan is a broad and fruitful land. There is enough for all."

But Caleb and Gath and Gershom looked at each other thoughtfully.

"You would give up your portion?" Caleb wanted to know.

"Our portion is here."

"And what of the spoil?"

Manasseh was poor; there were only three clans in the half-tribe. Gad and Reuben were rich in sheep and oxen, but they had little of gold and silver and precious stones. Nohab, who played the game carefully and cautiously, had sent a secret delegation to Balmelech, the King of Ammon, to inquire whether an alliance might possibly be constituted against the Children of Israel; but the King of Ammon, still smarting over his defeat at the hands of the desert tribes and seeing no fruits of land or spoil in a war against a people both landless and poor, had indicated a willingness to supply ten thousand fighting men, but at the price of a golden shekel a man. Come what might, Nohab had no intention of paying such a price, but the lesson was driven home to him, that when a land is small and its fighting men few, gold will buy an army. So he was not quick to give up the spoil.

"When we took the cattle of Ammon, we gave you the lion's share of it," he reminded them. "Will you bar us from the spoil of Canaan?"

Joshua stared at him incredulously. Caleb roared with laughter. Jephta tried to look innocent and noncommittal. Joshua's face hardened. "Don't trifle with me," he said.

"I think this is no trifle," Caleb put in. "They will give up the land but not the gold."

Joshua cared nothing for gold. Let there only be land, green land and blue water! In his own memory, the whole people had thirsted. As a child, he had wept for water and made himself poorly content with a wet cloth pressed to his broken lips. He had no love for the Reubenites, the Gadites or the Manassites. He had the tent-dweller's scorn of and contempt for their household gods—even as he despised the beast gods of the desert tribes.

The morning sun was no longer in the tent. Through the open side-flaps, Joshua could see column after column of spearmen shaping up in their tens and in their hundreds; and in the distance, he heard the drumming of hoofs as the horses were driven in from the range to be harnessed to the chariots. The rams' horns blew their hoarse and savage signal for the boys still on the fields to come in with the last of the stock. The black tents had vanished, and where once a great encampment had been were only thousands of people and thousands of donkeys and oxen being loaded.

He was afraid to delay. All the emotion and desire and dreams and battle-thirst of these people had been keyed to this day. Let another day pass and the camp might turn into a snarling fratricide. His own life had been entirely for this moment; and not as a figure of thought or speech, but as a cold fact, he would cut off his own right hand now for the five thousand fighting men of Reuben and Gad and Manasseh.

Caleb studied Joshua curiously, for while he knew something of what he was thinking he also knew Gamaliel of Manasseh, for whom Joshua had only hatred and contempt. He looked at Gamaliel. The man licked his lips. There were beads of sweat on his brow, and his fists clenched and unclenched. Then, when Joshua turned to Caleb and met his black eyes, Caleb nodded slightly.

"Keep your cities and your portion," Joshua said at last. "Give me the five thousand fighting men, and when we have taken the Land of Canaan, we will give them the full share of their spoil and send them home to the Land of Gilead. This I swear in the name of the Lord God Jehovah!"

"Will you swear it in blood?" Nohab demanded.

In reply, Joshua handed his spear to Caleb, drew his iron sword from his scabbard and passed the keen edge lightly across the back of his arm above his wrist. He sheathed his sword, held out his left hand with the blood welling from the cut and with the forefinger of his right hand traced out the holy name.

"I swear it in blood," he said.

"Oh, not so fast—not so fast at all," Gamaliel said. "It's not that easily done."

"I thought you spoke for the people of Gilead," Joshua said to Nohab.

"The tribe of Manasseh are our brothers."

"I could choose better kin," Caleb smiled.

Nohab was a large man, large and slow of motion and speech. But now he turned to Caleb and said, "Someday, Caleb of Judah, we will see whether a Reubenite or a Judite is better kin for a fighting man."

"Any day or now. My sword is dry. My sword is thirsty. I promised it would drink deep of blood at Jericho, but it mocks me for promises broken—"

"You make me sick, all of you," Joshua cried.

"Someday—not now," Nohab said.

"I promised you spoil. I swore it to you. What else?"

"You ask us to leave our own gods behind," Jephta said. "We go with the God of Horeb and make our burnt offerings to him. Then shall we put aside his Law and risk his anger? You are a Levite, Joshua. Tell us."

"You will keep his Law when you come into the host of Israel. He is a bitter God, and no man shall break his Law and live."

"Well spoken," said Jephta, and then Nohab said, "I am no Levite, but I know the Law. It was a matter of study, and the profit I had from the civilizing force of Simon and Judah and Levi. I took the task and I learned it, for you put your God over me and over my people—"

"I said, what else?" Joshua interrupted. "Are we here for idle chatter? I am content with the history of Reuben that I already know."

"I will get to the point," Nohab said stolidly. "I only desired to remind you that our gods are simple gods, our law a simple law."

"As simple as the harlots who serve your mother god," Gershom snapped.

"We have no mother god," Nohab went on placidly. "When the God of Horeb came into our land, we tore down the temple and smashed the image of the mother, as you desired and instructed us. As you instructed us in the Law. And what is the Law of Horeb? It says, plainly and simply that if a woman is an adulteress, she shall be cast out and stoned to death. She is an abomination to the God Jehovah. So says your Law. Am I right?"

He was not answered. No one looked at him; they looked at Joshua, the son of Nun; and the silence in the tent was so thick and heavy, so hot and hateful that the guards outside turned to see what had happened among the tight group of metal-clad war lords.

In the mind of Joshua, thought rolled on thought, until he felt that he would plunge mindless into some bottomless deep. His heart tightened, and his great bulk swayed slightly. The pulse in his neck beat like a hammer.

Caleb put a tight hand on his right arm, which was bent to the iron sword, and Gath and Gershom moved close to him and beside him, the long, brown face of Gershom was tight with rage and disgust.

"Oh, excellent—excellent indeed," Gershom spat out. "I thank you, Nohab. I am a poor, foolish barbarian, desert born and bred, and I thank you for your lesson in civilization. My sword is also thirsty. The iron grows hot in the desert, and the sword reminds a man that blood is cooling. I am half a Levite, but it remained for Joel of Ephraim and Gamaliel of Manasseh to teach me how the Law should be interpreted. Neither am I a prophet, but I tell you this: Cursed be the Children of Joseph, and may the names of Ephraim and Manasseh stink through the ages! With Reuben and Gad, a time will come when you come on bended knees to plead for us—like dogs on your knees, and like dogs, we will kick you away!"

"You are very moving in what you say, Gershom of Kenn," Jephta smiled, "but we are not greatly concerned with what the future may bring. The question is, what do you intend to do now?"

Trancelike, Joshua pointed to the flag of the Joseph tribes, waving among the battle standards in front of the war tent. "I always wondered why the flag of the Joseph people was black. Is their heart blood red, I wonder?"

"Let us put this away," said Caleb, controlling himself with effort. "Let us have it as if it had never been said. We are men and warriors here, and we go out of here, not for a day of battle, but for many years of battle, for all we know. We have given you what you wanted, Nohab, your share of the gold and silver spoil and your cities in Gilead as well. Joshua has sworn in the God's name. Let this end!"

"It will end when it is properly ended," Gamaliel put in. "You would not dare to kill us here in the war tent. If you did, there would be no promised land but a river of blood out there in the camp. And you know that as well as I do. And what will the people

say when we tell them that we have named a whore, and the Levites
and the Judites come between her and the Law?"

His whole body trembling, Joshua whispered, "What manner of
man are you that you call your wife a whore?"

"What manner of man are you, Joshua of Levi? Tell me that?"

"He calls her what she is," Nohab said. "Already a year ago, she
would go into the hills to serve the Ammonite mother."

"How do you know?" Caleb growled.

"How does a man know?"

Joshua moved then, animal noises coming out of his throat, but
Caleb hung on one arm, Gath on the other; yet he dragged them
and flung them as if they were weightless. It was Gershom, facing
him and pleading with him who stopped him.

"For today, Joshua, for all the dry and bitter years we talked
about this, for all that my father and your father bore and suffered
—Joshua, listen to me!"

Joshua listened and they spoke to him. Caleb said to Nohab and
Jephta and Gamaliel, "Get out of the tent and let us talk of this
among ourselves."

"We will get out of the tent, but we will wait," Nohab answered
stolidly.

VI

"Joshua?"

Large and red he stood. Who was Levi, in a place where others
were brown and burned like the desert rock? Who was Levi that so
many of him were red? Who was Levi, so wild and terrible, and
drunk with fear and adoration of the jealous God of Horeb?

"Joshua?"

The tricolor crest on his brass helm swayed as he looked at them,
Caleb and Gath and Gershom. Caleb still held Joshua's war spear.
Twenty pounds it weighed, three feet of it shod in bronze and
brass, the rest of the same polished wood of Shittem that the Ark
was fashioned from. He was the first of Levi in battle, and it was
his chariot that rode out for the challenge, making the offer of
single combat between two men that could decide the fate of the
battle. Caleb could close his eyes and see Joshua leap from his
chariot, war spear in one hand, shield on his left arm—and then
the convulsive cast that drove the great barb home at a distance
where the enemy was supposedly safe. Then it was Joshua for Israel,

and the roar that went up from the host would be heard miles away.

Caleb said, "Joshua, I was thinking of battle. It flushed my heart's eyes. I was thinking of how the war chiefs cast their spears, and then how the whole host gives voice to the glory of the great one."

"The Law is like the God," Gershom said, "hard and terrible. What joins us but the God of Horeb? And we are also like Him, hard and fierce. Who lives by the sword dies by the sword. So it is. Why do we hate the mother god so? She has no law. The Law is ours and the God's. And love? Is love for us? The women of Canaan are whores for the mother god. They serve her with love, and the men come to them in the temples and worship with love. Is that for us? Shall we go whoring after the strange gods of Canaan and become servants to the fat, belly-soft lords of their stone cities? Shall we deck ourselves with every manner of soft cloth and wear golden rings in our ears and shave our beards and pluck our brows and paint our faces, and shall we make our wives a gift to the stranger who comes into our house? Is that for us, Joshua? Is Jehovah a brothel-keeper or is He a man of war? I spit on Manasseh and Reuben and Gad for the robes they wear, for their gardens and their soft hangings and their painted women! Give me my war cry and my iron sword in my hand, and I will die as I lived!"

He gripped Joshua's arm and said softly, "Have you ever wondered what came between my father and me? Moses, my father, is soft and gentle and meek—not cowardly but meek—it was no coward that faced the God of Horeb. But Moses is a man, and the God is a God. What is a man to try to turn the God into his own image? Our God is a God of battles, and Moses would make Him a God of love. Can that be? I tell you, that is why Moses hides his face in the Tabernacle, and that is why the God will go away from him and leave him. My father was of Egypt, the cat-land, the monkey-land of harlot gods and whore-masters, but he seeded me in Kenn, where I spit the desert sand with my first breath. 'You live to kill!' he charged me once. I said to him, 'No—no, my father, I kill to live.' 'And who lives by the sword will die by it,' he said to me, but if I could not choose the manner of my birthing, I choose the manner of my dying, and gladly. I will give my sons a heritage of a land where the air is sweet and clean, where the green wheat grows and where the grapes hang heavy on the vines; but as for myself, I am sworn to the war god, and my sword will drink enough to take away my thirst. I ask no more than to die that way, with my sword in my hand and with the scream of battle all around me."

Gath said, "Joshua, son of Nun, you are Levi and I am Simon, so we are not made for sweet words together. A hundred times we have looked at each other in anger and reached for our swords. But anger is not hate. We make burnt offerings to an angry God, but He does not hate us. And I tell you, Joshua of Levi, that if it is the God's will that you and I find ourselves in a cul-de-sac of battle, I will lay down my life for you and gladly. I tell you, son of Nun, we were born for today, born for this bloody promise of ours, and all the thousands of burnt offerings we made were only one end— that the four war lords of Israel would go across the Jordan River with their swords naked in their hands."

"That is what we are," Caleb said. "Let the whoremasters of Gilead count their spoil. I lay my own spoil in the Tabernacle at your feet, for you are war lord and judge over all of Israel. Let all the other nations of the world have their strange gods. My God is my own, and as hard and purposeful as He has made me, and jealous, and quick to taste the burnt offering torn from the living heart. His Law is just and His measure is just."

Words came from Joshua like a whimper torn from a tortured child. "You condemn me!"

"No, no, son of Nun," said Caleb. "What alternative is there? Shall we go without the five thousand of Gilead? My right arm is cut off then, for no matter what hosts we gather, the Canaanites will have ten fighting men to one of ours. But even if we were to give up the spearmen of Gilead, do you think that those swine would let it rest there? Oh, no—no, never. They have feared and hated us from the day we set foot in their land, sneering at us for desert barbarians, and from day to day, they have waited to be revenged upon us. No, they would never let it rest, Joshua. They would go through the camp whispering that Joshua gave up five thousand spearmen and the heritage of our father, Abraham, and the promise too, all for a whore of Manasseh. Yes, they would do that. I saw it in their eyes."

Joshua bent his head, his clenched fist beating his clutched palm, his great body shivering. He walked away from them, swaying, his steps uncertain, until he came to the opposite edge of the tent, where Joel of Ephraim had cut down the old woman. Then he stopped, his eyes fixed on the pool of fresh blood.

"What is this?" he asked, pointing.

"There was an old woman, a priestess of the mother god, and she came with her four sisters asking a portion of the promised land."

"What is the blood?"

"Joel cut her down."

"Joel murdered her?"

"She was an abomination."

"And what am I but an abomination?"

"Joshua, she worshipped the mother god in the old way."

"And her sisters?"

"They left in peace. We promised them a portion."

"Why? Why should there be pity or regret? Did the God ask it? Joel acted better. Joel is a pious man."

"Joshua—"

He swung around to them and cried out, "All is as it must be! I tried to tell my father that! And Moses sits in the Tabernacle and weeps! God of Horeb, spare me the blessing of years! Only let me never sit as Moses sits!" And then he said to Caleb, harshly, "Give me my war spear."

Caleb hesitated.

"Don't be a fool. I am naked without it."

Caleb gave him the great spear, and then Joshua picked up his shield from the floor of the tent and slung it upon his shoulder.

"Now," he said, "call in the filth of Gilead and tell them that the Law will be kept."

VII

The Levites of Joshua's guard were glum and silent. The march should have begun an hour past. They told the two men at Joshua's tent, "The Lord Joshua commands her."

Deborah came to the door of the tent, and looked at them strangely. "He told me to remain here."

"Now he commands you, lady."

"Do you know why?"

"We know only that he commands you, lady."

"And where is he?"

"At the war tent of the Lord of Judah."

"Very well."

She put her hood over her face to hide it, but the people recog-

nized her, and the idle and curious, now with no more to do than
wait, followed after her until they were halted by the columns of
soldiers who made a square around the war-tent. The Levites took
her through the soldiers to a space outside the tent. Gamaliel and
Nohab and Jephta stood there.

Cold as ice, it struck to her heart. She was enveloped with fear,
suffused with it; it was like a shriek inside her, swelling the confines
of her body.

"Where is Joshua?" she asked.

Gamaliel pointed to the war tent, and under its shade, darkly
held against the burning sunlight of the outside, she saw the figures
of the four war chiefs, the figure of Joshua like a somber giant in
his brazen armor. She ran toward the tent, then stopped. Beyond
the soldiers, the people were coming up, hundreds and hundreds
more.

She walked on into the shade of the tent.

"Joshua?" she said.

In the full noontide heat, she was as cold as ice. Joshua had
departed from her. Only death was in the brass-girt war chief with
the tricolor plums of Levi nodding above his head.

Caleb walked toward her. "Call him no more, lady."

"Why did he summon me?"

"Your fate is outside this tent, where your husband stands, lady."

"Joshua summoned me."

"He had to, lady. Such is the Law. What the God wills, men do.
It can be no other way."

"Let me speak to him."

"Can you speak to him, lady? Look at him."

"He summoned me."

"As he had to, lady. As he had to."

"In God's name, do you know what I am to him?"

"I know, lady."

"Only last night—"

"It will do no good to talk of those things, lady. No good at all.
Put them away."

"What are you saying?"

"Lady, I say what I must. I think you know what I mean."

"Only let me go to him once."

"I will not stand in your way or lay my hands upon you, lady.
There he stands. You are free to go to him."

She took two steps, then stopped. The tears were running down her face. She wiped them away with the cowl of her cloak—and then shook off the cloak entirely, standing in a linen dress of red and black stripes. For him, she had woven and worn the colors of Levi.

"I will not go to him," she said to Caleb.

"That is best and wisest, lady."

"Am I to plead with my husband for my life, Caleb of Judah? Or has my fate been decided beyond any plea?"

"What am I to say, lady? Your husband is the man you married. Some day, perhaps, I will sit in judgment over the Children of Joseph. Not now."

"What is my fate?" she asked softly.

"You know that."

"Let me hear it from you, Caleb of Judah. Let me hear it from a war-girt man who worships the jealous God of Horeb. I am a woman, which is less than nothing, and I make my offerings to the old gods."

"I am sorry, lady. I can do nothing."

"I want no pity, not from you and not from the war lords who hide their faces in the shadow. I was afraid before, but that was because I was full of love. Now I am empty and without fear."

"I see that. I don't know what I can do for you, lady."

"You can tell me what my fate is."

"What the Law says it must be."

"The Law of Horeb."

"Yes—the Law of Horeb."

"The Law of the war god. And the war lords wait to carry it out."

"No, lady, that is for your husband to say. He is your husband, as I said. If it is any comfort to you, I will kill him one day."

"And that is all the comfort you offer me, Lord of Judah?"

"All I can offer."

"Then may your poor angry God pity you—you and those who stand with you. And tell Joshua, the son of Nun, not to feel guilt or remorse. Tell him that I did not want to live. There is no world for me to live in."

With that, she turned on her heel and walked away from him and past the three men of Gilead, never looking at them, standing finally alone and in an open, sun-drenched place. She stood there

plainly and simply, and to the columns of soldiers who were staring
at her, she was more beautiful than words can say.

That, perhaps, is why the soldiers never moved when the stones
came. Others threw the stones, and at last she lay with her face in
the sand, with the rubble of stones all around her.

Part Five. MOSES

I

Iron-girt and bronze-girt, Joshua went to the Tabernacle to claim
the God and the blessing of the God's priest.

The tents were folded and the beasts of burden were laden. The
two-wheel carts were piled high with the food and goods and wealth
of the tribes. Six oxen drew each cart, and each of the thick wooden
wheels was five feet high.

The war chariots were harnessed, and the high-spirited horses
champed nervously, with their cloudy memories of the scream and
chaos of battle. The drivers, who would live or die within the
chariots they drove, were already pricking their forearms with their
daggers, drawing blood and outlining the holy tetragram above
their brows, the *Yud* and the *Heh* and the *Vav* and the *Heh*. Not
so with the war chiefs, for they would leap from their chariots,
spears raised, to find a blood covenant on the field of battle.

The cattle were in motion, their motion slow as they filled the
hot noonday air with their mooing and baaing; and the women and
children drove them toward the river.

The soldiers stood in their tens and hundreds, hot and dry; but
in the river they would wet themselves and drink before the blood
ran. They stood by clan and tribe, their war standards waving
above them, and their close-crowded helm-crests made wild and
barbaric splashes of color, the tricolor of Levi, the sky blue of
Judah, the pink-pearl white of Asher, the somber black of the
Joseph people, the green of Simon, the snow-white of Zebulun, the
dark maroon of Naphtali, the ultramarine of Dan, and the rainbow
helms of Benjamin, whose shields were painted with the red-
tongued open-jawed head of the wolf.

In the ranks of Judah, the captains of hundreds wore the lion-
skin, the head cresting their helms, the long yellow and black fur
falling behind them to their heels. Neither they nor Simon nor

Levi nor Kenn wore armor on their backs. "Who turns his back is twice cursed if he hides it with metal," was said among them. It was burning hot under the sun, but the captains of Judah felt no heat under their lion-skins. Already and lightly, they had begun to beat the battle rhythm upon their brazen shields, chanting:

> "Who among all the gods is like you, oh, God of Horeb,
> What God can stand before you, oh, Jehovah?
> With your anger you will strike our enemies,
> And your fire will sear them!
> Like the harvest in a hailstorm, they will fall before you,
> Like the wheat under the sickle, they will go down!
> Judah, your son, will shout your name,
> Judah will glorify you—"

The other tribes picked it up; and as Joshua walked past toward the Tabernacle, his face set and frightening to behold, he heard the tribes and clans declare themselves:

> "Simon will be your shield,
> Simon will glorify you!"

One, two, three, four—one, two, one, two—went the beat of hard palms upon the warshields.

> "Dan will be your war spear, even as a javelin flung,
> And the sword of Dan will exalt you!"

The constant beat, the thrum, the pervading vibration that flowed like hot wine over the entire encampment drove stabbing needles of pain into Joshua's aching head. He had to firm himself not to stagger, not to reel, not to cry out to them, "Stop it! Stop it! Enough!"

His own Levite spearmen marched behind him. They knew. They had seen. They hated as he hated, but their pain was not his pain. In a rank of them, one whispered, "As it is written, the God is a jealous God."

"He reaches out with a heavy hand," another said.

And a third observed, "He looks to the captains of the hundreds and the thousands. They stand too high for a jealous God."

"No—the red of him marks him with the God's blood. My mother was red. It's a cursed blessing."

"Too much. When has Israel seen one like Joshua?"

"Still too much. Greatness is a curse. The gods are jealous of a man that stands too high."

II

Nun sat in the Tabernacle, where the gossamer striped curtain broke the sunlight into many colors, and he waited for his son. He was very old. Joshua was the child of his years. He had taken only one wife, and again and again, she aborted and cast out the stillborn child. Only Joshua lived, for the curse was upon his head and the mother died in the making of him.

Like many old men, he dozed easily, for the line drawn between sleeping and walking became thinner and thinner, and the present was intermixed more and more with his memories of the past. He had a great many memories, some good, some bad, some brighter and more vivid than yesterday and some so clouded that they were hard to separate from his dreams.

Now he dozed a little and saw some of his memories. These were of his son, and he came awake with that fullness of love and wanting and compassion that only a man with a single son can wholly experience. He came awake as Joshua parted the curtains and entered the tent, and said, in a dry and lifeless voice, "I greet you, Nun, my father."

"And I you, Joshua, my son. May your days be long in the land that Jehovah has promised you."

"I thank you, but with bitter breath, my father."

"I heard what took place."

"So quickly does such news fly. The birds bear it on wings, don't they, my father?"

"The evil word runs like the spring rivers in the wadis."

"Evil?" The war lord's voice was like dry desert branches breaking. "What the Law specifies was done. Is that evil?"

"No—not if it was done for the Law. For what the God has written is food of our lives, for better or for worse; and who am I, the lowest of Levi, to sit as a judge over the Law? But if it was done for the five thousand spearmen of Reuben and Gad and Manasseh, then by all that is holy, it was evil!"

"Oh, no," Joshua said, "it is not for you to judge the Law. But to judge your son, yes—and what a quick judge you are there!"

"Who else is my son, Joshua?"

"I did what I did for the God."

Nun nodded.

"For the God of Horeb!"

"Yes—"

"And if I am evil," Joshua said, "and if this holy tetragram and this blood oath here on my arms brands me for the whole world to see—then for me better that than the comfort of the righteous man who sits in judgment over me!"

"Only the God will judge you, Joshua."

"Then let Him judge me!" Joshua cried wildly. "Let Him judge me! Hear you, Jehovah, God of Horeb—here I am, I, Joshua the son of Nun, and I stand before you in my own priestly vestments which are my girt armor and my war spear and my shield! I am faithful and holy, and I will make you burnt offerings of all the noble cities of Canaan!"

"Joshua—Joshua, my son," Nun said pleadingly, the old man, the old man of Levi, the Levite.

"Listen to the battle chants," Joshua sobbed. "Listen how they praise the name of the jealous God!' the tears running down his face. "Listen how the young men praise His name—like this," letting his war spear crash to the ground and picking up the rhythm of the soldiers with the heel of his palm against his brazen shield.

"Joshua, my son, we stand here in the Holy of Holies."

As if sleeping before and somnambulating before, he awakened now and picked up his heavy spear from the ground. He shook his great, crested helm, the tricolor waving from side to side, and then he faced Nun and told him, "I did what had to be done, that's all," His voice was controlled again, hard and cold. "I was born naked and not with the war spear in my hand. We become men, but our fathers remember us as children. If you had wisdom, old man, why didn't you nourish me with it?"

"The wisdom of the old has no nourishment," Nun answered bleakly.

"No? Well, that may be. I will not grow old, for I have made a pact with the God of Horeb and with my war spear. When the gods promise, they exact a just measure in return, and when they weigh you in the balance, they keep a heavy hand on the scale. The land was promised to Moses, your master, but a god's promise is an easy thing. It fell to your son, Joshua, to lead the people across the river."

"Yes, it fell to you," Nun said.

"So if a blood price was paid for that poor, frightened girl who

loved me, let us count it exactly. And don't teach me righteousness
—it is too late. Her world is her world, mine is mine. The piece of
Hittite iron that hangs by my side was burned and hammered out
for a sword, and it was not for love or pity or joy either that
Joshua the Levite lived his years until now. No—oh, no, my father.
It was to lead his people across the river Jordan. And right now,
let the truth be naked! The God is jealous and angry and willful,
but He is a truthful God and most terrible in that way. So I tell
you this, my father, without those five thousand spearmen of
Reuben and Gad and Manasseh, I would have had to turn away
from here and go back to the desert. And this, I would not do."

"Always, it is too late," Nun whispered.

"I don't know about that, and I don't care any more. For us, the
battle has already begun. It is one hour's march from the river to
Jericho, and as we stand here talking, the princes of Jericho say to
each other, 'The host of the God of Horeb is chanting His name.
Let us prepare ourselves, for soon they will be upon us!' The only
food my belly craves is waiting for me, and I am full of hunger and
lust. My chariot is harnessed, and my Levites stand outside, waiting
to pick up the Tabernacle of the God and bear it with us."

Nun pleaded, "Joshua, be kind to an old man. I have put away
my pride."

"What have I to do with kindness, sir?"

"You are my son."

"What the God gives, he also takes. Does he ask us to be merci-
ful? When our rams hammer down the walls of Jericho, there will
be pleading for mercy, but in the streets the blood will run like
water after the spring rain. As you said before, it is too late, so
call Moses to me, and let him give me his blessing."

"Moses has gone away. You will see him no more."

"You mean he is dead?"

"I don't know," Nun answered slowly.

"Then what do you mean?"

"When he heard what had happened at the war tent of Judah,
he told me farewell and went away."

"Where did he go?"

"I saw him climbing the hillside, toward where the altar had
stood. So my word is broken and the oath I swore is nothing."

"No matter," Joshua shrugged. "We will take up the Ark, and the
God will be with us. We will give him spoil and gold and silver,

and we will make a burnt offering of the place called Jericho. We
have kept our part of the covenant, and the God will keep his
part."

"I am the servant of Moses," Nun said desperately. "Ask me for
my blessing. I am your father, and you are Joshua, the son of Nun.
Ask me for it!"

For a long moment, Joshua stared at the little old man, his
father. His face was full of pain, fixed, saturated with a grief that
would mask him for a long, long time; and this moment and that
time merged, leaving Nun bereft and poor.

"No, I will not ask you," Joshua said. "You told me to rid myself
of the whore of Manasseh, but if I did not do it for the Law,
neither did I do it because my father bade me do it."

"Are we so far from each other?" Nun pleaded.

"Yes. For it seems to me, my father, that you will not go with
me, but where Moses went, you will follow."

Then Nun bowed his head and put his cloak over it, for he was
ashamed of his tears and his grief-stricken face.

III

Nun did not even pause or turn around to see the Levites fold
up the bright cloth of the Tabernacle or raise the shining glory of
the Ark. As he climbed the hillside, the Ark was borne among the
people, and the mighty, swelling chorus of hosanna followed him
and enveloped him.

When he came to the place where the altar had stood, he paused
to rest. How tired he was! Only six or seven hours had passed since
he climbed this same hillside earlier this same day, early among the
morning mists; but in that time, his life-strength had poured out of
him. His years lay on his back like a burden.

He climbed higher. The scrub pine and the wind-twisted cedar
gave way to sparse tuft grass. He climbed on and on, and where the
first rock outcroppings were, he rested again. The rams' horns were
sounding now. Out of a thousand curving horns came the deep and
somber sound of the God of Horeb. The sound was heard in
Jericho, too.

Nun bent back to look up at the top of the mountain. It was high
and steep and rocky. How could his master have gone to such a
place? Yet if he had not gone there, where else?

As Nun climbed on and on, each step more effort and pain than the step before, his hope waned; but when at last he dragged himself onto the flat rock outcropping of the top, he saw him. He sat upon a shoulder of the rock, his white and pale blue robes of priesthood torn and dirt-stained and blood-stained, his white head bent and resting upon his hand. And through all his tiredness and grief, Nun cried out joyfully, "Moses, my master."

Moses rose and turned to him, and they embraced there.

"Are you weary? Sit beside me, Nun, my brother," Moses said. But his thin form trembled and shivered in the cool wind that blew across the bare mountaintop. Nun took off his own cloak and laid it upon Moses' back.

"Then I will be warm and you will be cold."

"I am younger—"

"Oh?" Moses smiled. "Is it a year that you are younger? Yes, I remember. And all my life, you watched over me, like father and mother both."

"I am childless. Whom else have I but you, my master?"

"We are too old to weep as you have been weeping," Moses said. "I think tears can be only a promise. We are past promises."

"Yes, I know, my master."

"I heard the hosanna before."

"Joshua brought the Ark to the people."

"And the rams' horns."

"The march began and the horns were sounded."

"They are chanting now," Moses said. "Can you make out what they are chanting?"

"Praise be unto the Lord God of Hosts,
Praise be unto the angry God of Horeb!"

Moses leaned forward, shading his eyes with his hand. "No use," he sighed. "My eyes see almost nothing now. Can you see them, Nun?"

"I see them, master."

"Tell me."

"The vanguard has reached the river, and the chariots are driving across the ford. The river foams up from their wheels and the sun catches it, so it is hard for me to see."

"Look for your son, Joshua, who is judge over Israel."

"No, not my son and not I his father. He turned his back on me, his face full of anger and bitterness."

"Look for him."

"I see his brass shining like gold."

"And the men of Jericho? Do they wait on the other bank?"

"No, they have gone behind their walls," Nun said. "The promised land is open."

"How long we dreamed of a promised land," Moses said. "The dream is a signpost down all the roads of our memory. We hung it as a sign across our hearts and etched it with the whiplashes that scarred us. We framed it with the dry and fruitless grit of the desert."

"The spearmen are crossing the river, my master," Nun said. "Levi is first. They have reached the other bank and planted their star cards of black and white and red, and it is as if the lord God had commanded into being a field of waving, colored grain."

"We would have planted other grain," Moses nodded. "It was a place without hunger or want that our hearts made, a land of equity and justice, a land of peace promised to us, a cool and gentle land—"

"And Judah and Simon have planted their standards. The war spears are as thick as the corn in a river-bottom valley. A host is already pitched there on the holy soil."

"And how will they sanctify it? We promised ourselves a land where a little child could walk unafraid. Love would make it holy. When we cut the foreskin from Gershom, my son, and laid it upon the Altar of God, I said, 'Here is the redemption and blood of my first-born. And may it be your will that never again in all the time left to man on this earth does he make a living man a sacrifice on the Altar of God.' I was not afraid of the God, was I, Nun?"

"No, my master—you were not afraid."

"And I walked into the hot ashes of Horeb, where no other dared to go."

"You walked there, my master. I remember well."

"And I said to the God, 'Will you be less than your servant, Moses?'"

"Yes, you said that, my master."

"And the God was shamed," Moses said. "For he saw that he was jealous and cruel and without love or mercy or forbearance. And he saw that his servant, Moses, the least of his people, was not without love or mercy or forbearance; and he was shamed. For he saw that the gods were less than the men who worshipped them and gave them burnt offerings. He stood naked in his own sight, and he cried out, 'Who are the immortals that mortal man, whose years are as a moment and whose soft bodies are food for the worms and the grubs, shall stand up to them without fear!' He called upon me to be afraid, and I would not be afraid, for if he had a pride of godhood, I had a greater pride of manhood. Who was he in his agelessness to know the meaning of man's life and the holy sacredness of man's life?"

"Oh, my master, what are you saying?" Nun moaned.

"That what was written on the stone, I wrote, I, Moses the Levite, and I wrote it there plainly and simply, so that the God could read it and the man could read it—" He stood up, stretching out his right arm to the valley where the people were crossing the river. "—plainly, I wrote it—THOU SHALT NOT KILL!"

Then he sat down on the rock again, shivering and trembling, used up with his effort. Nun sheltered him and soothed him.

"No, master, do not be afraid."

"I am not afraid," Moses said. "I am old and tired and used up, and my life is ebbing away, but I am not afraid."

"The God of Horeb," Nun began, but Moses interrupted him sharply with the voice of long ago, the full, vibrant voice that had preached to the people once from the black-ash slopes of Horeb itself, "The God of man is more than the God of Horeb!"

"Thou shalt have no other gods before me," Nun pleaded.

"There are no other gods! The Ark is an empty shell! The God of man is full and indivisible, and mankind is his voice and his work, and he is worshipped only with love and forbearance."

"Master, you are tired. What do such things mean when you say them?"

"I am tired, Nun—very tired."

"The God will forgive you. He will look at you and say, 'My servant, Moses, served me well and faithfully, and I will not turn my anger against him.' And then, Moses, my beloved Master, I will make a fire here. Not too far below there is wood, and I will go and fetch some. It will give up warmth against the cold of night, and perhaps with a stone I can kill a hare or bird. We will not bring it alive to the fire, yet we can make a burnt offering and a sweet smell to blunt the anger of the God—"

"No, my good Nun," the old man replied. "Make no burnt offerings for me. I know the God of Horeb of old. I do not fear his anger."

"I only wanted—"

"I know what you wanted, Nun," he said gently. "But I will have no need of a fire tonight, and you must not stay in this cold and lonely place, but go down to the valley—"

"Don't talk like that!"

"I say what I must here and today, Nun. If it will be said that I served the God of Horeb well and faithfully, then let it also be said, if only in your own heart, that I also served the truth as well as I might. I am so tired of the ghosts and demons men fear! I have lived and I will die, which is all that any man can say. It doesn't seem that my life has mattered a great deal or changed anything very much."

To which Nun could say nothing, nor think of any answer. Silent, he sat beside Moses, now and again lifting back his cloak when it slipped from the sagging shoulders of the old priest.

"Is it evening?" Moses asked after a while.

"No, my dear master," Nun said with alarm. "The sun is still high in the heavens."

"Don't be apprehensive about me, dear friend," Moses said. "My eyes are bad, and I have so little sight left that even the sunlight is dulled to the color of evening."

But Nun knew.

Presently, Moses said, "Tell me where they are now, Nun, my blood brother? Have they all crossed over?"

"No, master—they are too great a host. The battle will be joined at Jericho before they are all across the river. The spearmen of Reuben and Gad and Manasseh are only now crossing. The cattle are being herded to the banks. There are thousands of cattle."

"So many—so many," Moses sighed. "And when we led Levi out of Egypt, we were only a handful, and the dry air of the desert purified us. You remember when I said to you, 'These people are chosen, for the hand of mercy and fortune hovered over them, and they lived and flourished where another people so broken would have been destroyed. Now I will teach them, and they will become priests and teachers for others.'"

"I remember, master."

"And what were we chosen for?"

"They are only people, my master. Only men and women."

"Only people, Nun? More than people, the world knows not."

"The gods will hear you, master—yes, and even the God of Horeb."

"Then he has heard me speak worse blasphemy, and to his face."

"Never could I tell what you would think of or say next," Nun said with resignation. "I used to ask myself, 'Why must he always war with the gods—why does he hate them so?' First it was Egypt and Egypt's gods whom you mocked and derided. Then the gods of Kush, whom you mocked and pitied. Then it was Nehushtan, the serpent, and when he bit you nigh to death, you laughed in his face—"

"No, my brother, it was you who saved me from Nehushtan."

"But I cannot save you from the God of Horeb," Nun begged him.

"He will not harm me," Moses smiled. "I am too tired and too weak to arouse any anger in him. I want to sleep, Nun. Surely it is nighttime."

"No, master—no it is not nighttime. And here on the mountain it will be cold and bitter. You can't sleep here."

"Look down, Nun, and tell me what happens now."

"They are beginning to drive the stock into the river. All of the soldiers have crossed over, and by now the chariots must be on the plain in front of Jericho's walls. I know how it will be," Nun nodded. "It will be Joshua and Caleb racing across the plain, their horses thundering, their battle cries shaking the walls. Do you remember, master, so long ago, when we stood in the chariot, I the driver and you the captain in the host of the mighty king, Rameses of Egypt?"

"I remember," Moses whispered. "My eyes are dead already, but with my mind's eye, I see it."

"I know how it will be. Their horses race in, driven by the bold young ones, so honored to share a chariot with the war lords, and all the frustration and hatred of those two hard and bitter men will be flung at the walls of Jericho, at the painted dukes of Jericho. Joshua, my son, my only son, will taunt them and mock them and curse them; and those smooth-faced, painted and perfumed ones will go pale and shake at the sight of the red giant of Levi. 'Who is this man,' they will say, 'whose thunder voice shakes our walls? Who is he and whence comes he?' For they know not Levi and the ways of Levi, as they know not Judah the lion. But Joshua, my son, will disdain them, and even under their arrows, he will leap from the chariot, clad in all his metal gear. Then his arm goes back—back to very ground, and he hurls his great war spear like a javelin of cedar wood. Oh, was there ever such a throw, Moses, my master! For the mighty spear goes up, up, up until it hangs on the face of the sky—up further and over the wall of Jericho! And then from the host of Israel, there rises a cry, such a hosanna as the world has never heard before—"

"Ah, stop! Stop, my brother, enough!"

Nun turned to Moses. The old man was weeping.

"No. No, master. Don't weep."

"Why do I love them so?" Moses cried, the words coming with ache and pain. "Why do they wring my old, dying heart? Why do they make an exultation within me? I know them. Half a century, I was a father to them, and who knows them better? They are wicked and cruel, without mercy or pity. They live only for war and the war cry, and wherever they walk, the soil is soaked with blood. Thou shalt not kill, I raged at them, yet they killed and made themselves wild war songs to celebrate their blood lust. I went to their God, their dark and vengeful war god of Horeb, and I became his prophet, yet I could not change him to my image. They had already made him in theirs. I know them. I know them! Even at the end, when I pleaded with them not to go into the Land of Canaan, not to go into that rich and fruitful land and make a waste of it, a place of grieving widows and orphaned children, and they looked at me, stony-faced and pledged to their own wild destiny—even then, I could not hate them. Tell me why?"

"Master, I don't know," Nun said miserably.

But the old priest was used up. The last outburst burned away whatever small strength remained.

"Nun," he whispered, "Nun, my servant and brother?"

"I am here—here beside you."

"Dear brother, help me to lie down. I am very tired."

"Yes—yes, surely, master. Here on this flat rock, which is warm, and the sun is warm too."

"I am cold, Nun."

"Let me wrap you tighter." Nun knelt beside him, pulling the cloaks about him. "Are you warmer now?"

"A little warmer, yes."

Nun had to bend close to him to hear his words.

"Nun?"

"Yes, I am here."

He lay for a while with his eyes closed.

"Nun?"

"Good master?"

"How is it, Nun, that my life is like an empty, broken cup? I dreamed of a chosen people, good and righteous and loving of heart, but my chosen people were wicked and full of iniquity. I dreamed of a promised land where a god of loving-kindness and mercy and justice would rule a golden way of life; but the promised land is a lie, Nun. It is full of tears and sorrow, and a fierce and angry God has entered it. And my whole life is nothing, for nameless and out of nothing was my beginning and nameless and out of nothing is my end. All my hopes and all my dreams lie in ashes around me, and all the gods I have known are drunk with contempt and hatred for mankind. And mankind himself is a wayfarer in darkness with no one to lead him to light."

"When we were hungry and thirsty and lost and afraid, you led us—even you, Moses, my master," Nun said, the tears rolling down his cheeks and onto his ragged beard.

"Did the blind lead the blind? I don't remember any more. It is all going away, even Moses, who was once a prince of Egypt and once a servant of the God of Horeb—all going and fading. Who will even remember my name, as lost as the nameless grave where you must lay me and let me rest—"

Kneeling beside him, Nun wept. He wept and rocked back and forth with his heartbreaking and wordless grief, even as his seed and blood would weep for their grief for untold generations to come. He lifted Moses' head and shoulders, holding him in his arms to warm him and cherish him, but no warmth could quicken him now.

Then Nun lifted his master in his arms. He was so frail, so thin, so light that though Nun was an old man, his burden seemed no burden.

Nun carried him to a cleft in the rock on the top of that high mountain, and there in the cleft, he laid the old priest to rest. He straightened his limbs and closed his eyes. He combed out the long white beard and thin white hair. And then he kissed him on his pale lips as tenderly as a mother kisses her child.

He covered his face and his hands and his feet, so that the flesh might not be bruised. Then he brought stones and bits of rock, putting each one in place gently and firmly, stone after stone, until the whole cleft was filled. Then, with a supreme effort of will and strength, he lifted a great slab of rock on end and let it fall across the cleft, covering it and hiding it.

Then he said, "Sleep well, dear master and teacher. Here is a place where no one will disturb your rest, and in all the years to come, no one shall know your sepulchre. That is the way you wanted it, and that is the way it shall be. I was with you at the beginning, and I am glad it was I who was with you at the end. If the world forgets you, I will not, for of all the men I have ever known, you were the gentlest, the wisest and the best. I too am old and weary, and if my time comes soon and I am laid in the earth, I want them to mark me and note me with only one line, only these words: 'Nun, the servant of Moses.' "

Then Nun turned away from the grave. Far in the west, the sun had begun to set, its afterglow flooding the plains of Jericho with golden light. Shading his eyes, Nun thought that he could see in the distance the walls and towers of Jericho with a great mass of people all around it.

But he was not sure.

Then he looked at the River Jordan, golden-red in the sunset. As he started to climb down the mountain, he thought to himself, "I will sleep in the old encampment tonight, and tomorrow I will make my way across the river into the Land of Canaan. What was done is done. I am of Levi, and where else can I go but where they go?"

Neighbor
Sam

THE TROUBLE started the day that young lawyer showed up. First it rained and then it cleared, and then it rained and then it cleared, all in four days, and nobody ever knew any good to come of something like that. And then Pa shot a wolf not more than two hundred paces from the house, when there hadn't been a wolf in the neighborhood in maybe two years. And, as if that wasn't enough, the well went dry.

"I never seen to beat that," Pa said. "I never seen a well go dry in such even weather, first rain, then shine, then rain."

"Either coax water out of it or dig a new well," Ma said.

"Not just a scratch well," Pa said. "Twenty feet deep, and I rocked up the sides."

Ma and Jenny and me, we got a rope and lowered Pa into the well. He mucked around in there for two or three hours, and when we pulled him up he was black from head to foot. But he hadn't coaxed out a drop of water.

"I got dishes to wash and greens to cook," Ma said, her eyes narrowing. Pa nodded, and wiped some of the mud from his face; I guess he could see that Ma was already looking around and picking a spot for the new well.

Well, Pa was standing like that, full of mud and peevishness, when Matt Stevens rode up on his old mouse-colored mare. Pa and Matt had never got along since Pa decided against him last spring and awarded four sows in question to Jim Hogan. At that time, Matt called Pa an old idiot and said there wasn't much hope for a country that put the law into such hands as his. And ever since then he called Pa "Sam," instead of "Squire," like everyone else. Pa said Matt came from no-account folk who didn't know the meaning of respect.

"Now he ain't here for no good," Pa muttered.

Stevens leaned over his mare and grinned at Pa. He said, "Lord, that's a lot of mud, Neighbor Sam."

"Honest mud."

"Maybe so," Stevens nodded, still grinning.

"What's on your mind, Neighbor Stevens?" Ma asked. She knew that Pa and he had been spoiling for a fight ever since last spring, and now, the way Pa felt, she was anxious to be rid of Stevens quickly.

"Nothing—nothing. Just thought I'd stop by and pass the time of day."

Pa grunted.

"Thought you might not know about the new lawyer-man, being as how you're off the beaten track here."

Pa stared. There was no trouble now knowing why Matt Stevens had come by to pay a call.

"We ain't heard of any lawyer-man excepting the Squire, here," Ma said slowly.

"I reckoned you hadn't," Matt grinned. "Of course, this feller's a mite different from the Squire, here. Just come into the village day before yesterday and took the old log house Frank Fellows built. Got it fixed up already and shingle hung out. Elmer Green, Counselor at Law. Parson Jackson been in to see him, and says he's a right smart young feller. Graduated out of Harvard. Got his degree framed up, and folks been going in and out all day to have a look at it. Got a desk and pen and ink and pile of paper that high. Got a row of law books that long." He spread his arms as far apart as they would go.

Pa stared at his hands, rubbing the mud down the length of his fingers. Ma said, "Can't see that it matters to us how many lawmen set up hereabouts." But I could see that Pa was worried. Twelve years now, since two months after I was born, Pa was the only lawman in this part of the country.

Not that Pa was a real lawman with a framed degree; but he was the sort of man other men looked up to. Twelve years past, when the Shawnees came down and burned out Zeke Cooly's farm and Aunt Elsie Hack's chicken run, Pa organized the defense at the fort. After that it wasn't any trouble for him to get the nomination for district judge, and every two years since then Pa was re-elected. In fact, the voting was just a formality; nobody had ever presumed to run against Pa.

But now I could see that Pa was hard hit, and you can be sure that what hit him hardest was Matt's description of a row of books about six feet long. Pa had a book; after he had been district judge four years, what with all sorts of fancy bits of law coming up, Pa decided that he didn't have enough law inside of his own head to handle everything. So, whenever anybody took a trip back East, Pa would say, "Pick me up a lawbook somewheres, if you see one handy." There probably weren't many lawbooks handy, because it took nearly a year for one to come. But that was a fine book, all bound out in red leather with leafwork in real gold just covering it. People came in from all around to look at that lawbook for months on.

The only thing Pa had against that lawbook was the name on it. On the cover it said, "English Common Law." Pa didn't hold against the "common law" part, since he considered common law good enough for himself and his neighbors; but the "English" part was a bone in his throat. The war of the colonies against England had been going on for five years then, and Pa didn't consider it right to deal law out of an English book. But since there wasn't any other lawbook within two hundred miles, Pa just scratched out the English part on the cover. The law inside suited folks fine.

Pa stood there rubbing the mud off his hands, and Matt Stevens sat on his old gray mare, grinning.

Finally, Pa said, "Now, maybe I ought to go in and make a calling visit with that new lawyer. He and I ought to get together on common law and such, if he's planning to try cases in my court."

"I don't reckon he plans to," Matt said comfortably.

"How?"

"I don't reckon he plans to," Matt repeated, "seeing as how the election comes up soon, and how certain citizens of the community have asked him to run for district judge. They figure it ain't proper, calling an election without no contest. Also, they figure they might get a mite more law out of a Eastern lawman, with a degree all framed and hung." He kicked at his mare, and called back, "Good luck, Neighbor Sam!"

"Good luck," Pa muttered.

"I never did see no good come out of Matt Stevens," Ma said.

"Rains one day, shines the next, kill a wolf on my own land, well goes dry, and now this."

"Pa," Jenny said, "Pa, don't go to worrying. Folks hereabouts aren't going to shuffle you out for any eastern lawman."

"That's gospel," Ma nodded.

But Pa shook his head. His beard hung down against his chest, and he seemed old all of a sudden. He shuffled into the house.

I followed him and left Ma talking with Jenny. When I got into the house Pa was standing there with his book of common law, turning the pages slowly.

I sat down and waited for him to notice me. Finally, he said, "Hello, Jess."

"Lord, I don't know whether I hate Matt Stevens more than that new lawman," I said.

"Don't take the Name in vain," Pa said, "and shut about hating. It ain't Christian, Jess. I ought to tan your hide."

"Some day I'll get big enough to take a gun to Matt Stevens—"

But Pa didn't even hear me. He was staring at the lawbook. . . .

Pa had almost finished digging the new well, when he decided he was going to stump for the election. Out here, on our side of the mountains, you didn't find much argument for elections; if you reckoned a man was good for something, you voted him in, and there were hardly ever two men good for the same thing. But back East stumping for votes was becoming popular, and Pa had read about it in newspapers, usually a month or two old.

But what really decided him to go stumping was Jenny. My sister Jenny had turned eighteen then, and both Ma and Pa were after her to find a man who would make a good provider. She was a catch, all right, even though I didn't think so; people said Squire Burton's daughter would know how to run a home and a man. But, every time a boy was calling, Jenny had this or that to say about him. Even though Ma told her that in no time at all she would be an old maid.

Well, Pa began to have his doubts when more and more people turned off to our house to speak about the new law-man. They were so full of bits of law he had let drop about that Pa got good and nervous, so nervous that even his gathering good, clear water in the new well didn't cheer him any. And then, when the well was almost finished, the lawman himself came calling.

He rode up one day on a sleek brown horse, with fat saddlebags, such as any proper lawman might carry. Pa was working on the well, but when he heard the hoofs he h'isted himself up. Then he saw the strange face, knew right off it was the lawman, and dropped back. Pa didn't want any truck with him.

The lawman dismounted and called to me, "Sonny, what's your name?"

I didn't answer, but spat over my shoulder. If Pa had been there he would have whacked me; but Pa was down the well.

The lawman smiled. "Squire Burton around?" he inquired.

"I don't see him," I said.

"He lives here, doesn't he?"

"Times when he does," I said. It was hard to stand up against that lawman. He had a nice, square face and blue eyes that sparkled with interest as they looked at you; but I had made up my mind not to like him, and Pa had always said I would grow up into a stubborn man.

Just then Jenny saw us from the house, and she came running out.

The lawman said, "How do you do, miss? My name's Elmer Green. I rode up here to pay my respects to Squire Burton. He lives here, doesn't he?"

"He lives here," Jenny nodded; but her eyes narrowed when she heard his name.

"Is he here?"

"He was a moment ago. Jess, you seen your Pa?"

"Not lately," I said.

"Then he isn't here, and you needn't wait," Jenny snapped.

The lawman turned his hat over and over in his hands. "Miss, I'm sorry if I offended you in any way. I aim to make friends here, not enemies."

"We don't need new friends. My father had enough friends until you came. It's people like you who ruin this land, coming here where my father worked all his life, to tear down what he built."

"That was not my intention, miss," the lawman said softly. "This is a democracy we live in. And the great and necessary thing to any democracy is free election with more than one candidate."

"My father judged this district well enough."

"Well enough, I agree with you," the lawman said. "And he'll continue to, probably. Only, this time people will choose between two of us—" They began to walk away from me, slowly. I stayed by the well.

Pa whispered, "Jess, did that lawyer go yet?"

"Not yet, Pa."

"Well, keep an eye peeled."

Pa stayed down that well at least an hour and a half. And it was drawing water, mind you. And all the time Jenny and the lawman sat in the shade of the house, talking. Jenny brought out some cold milk and some cake. Then the lawman mounted his horse.

"Tell Squire Burton I'll be around again," he called.

After he had got out of sight in the woods I said to Pa, "You can come up now."

Pa crawled up out of the well, muddy and soaking wet. Jenny came over and said, "My goodness, Pa, what were you doing down there all this time?"

"Looking for lizards," Pa snapped.

"I was talking with Elmer Green," Jenny said. "I like him."

Well, it was then and there that Pa made up his mind to stump for the election.

Pa put off the stumping until just two or three days before the election. That was because Ma put her foot down and said that he'd look like an awful fool, going around and asking friends to vote for him.

"Maybe they're friends," Pa said, "but there's that lawyer-man with six feet of lawbooks, and folks are already saying that what they've had six years now ain't American law, but English law. Matt Stevens, he's put it around everywhere that there's a heap more law comes out of six feet of books than out of one book."

"And maybe they're right," Ma pointed out.

"What! By all that's mighty, my own wife's against me!"

"I ain't against you," Ma said calmly. "Only, one thing you got to remember—that for every case you tried there was a plaintiff and a defendant, and if you gave the case to the defendant, then the plaintiff went away stamping mad. And the other way round."

"A woman I been married and bedded with twenty-two years come June," Pa muttered.

"Well, it seems to me you ought to be satisfied with twelve years of lawgiving," Ma said.

Pa didn't speak to Ma about the election again, but I could see that he had taken what she said awful hard. Instead of going out to stump raring mad, he put it off from day to day. And all the while the lawman was stumping up and down the river. Twice, he came to the house to see Pa, but the only one he saw was Jenny. The first time, Pa went out to the stable and fed the stock two hours straight; the second time, he sat up in my attic room until I gave him word to come down. He sure was doubting what he might do to that lawman if they ever met.

And then, two or three days before election, Pa made up his mind to go out and stump. By that time I was the only one around the place who had any truck with him, he was so eaten up and burning about the lawman.

"Jess," he said, "saddle up the filly and the big white. We're going to take this election in hand."

When I had the horses ready I went into the house. Ma's lips were tight and she wasn't speaking. She was putting together a bag of food for Pa to take with him.

"After all, I been judging this district twelve years," Pa said.

"And long enough. . . . Jess, you catch cold and I'll tan your hide good and lasting. . . . Don't know why you need the boy with you, anyway," she said to Pa.

"Don't know that I got anyone else," Pa snapped.

The first place we went was to the Joneses' farm, up the creek. Pa and Lancy Jones, they came out to this country together, fifteen years back.

Lancy was rooting stumps in a patch he was clearing when Pa hailed him. Lancy walked over and said, " 'Evening, Squire."

" 'Evening, Lancy," Pa said.

"Good weather," Lancy said.

"My well went dry," Pa told him. "Couldn't figure it nohow."

"Plenty of rain," Lancy said.

"Crop weather," Pa agreed.

"I already seen a well to go dry just out of pure contrariness," Lancy Jones said.

"No telling at all."

"But that was a fine well."

"Mighty nice well," Pa said. "Twenty foot deep."

"Going hunting?" Lancy asked Pa.

Pa hesitated, glanced at me, and then tugged at his beard. "Deer," Pa said.

"I seen deer sign over at Lasting Hollow."

"Come on, Jess," Pa said. "Good day, Lancy."

"Good day."

When we were out of sight of Lancy's place I said to Pa, "That was a mighty queer way to stump for votes."

"That's the way it's done back East," Pa muttered.

"I'd have asked him straight."

"Jess, you shut up and don't be prying into affairs of your elders," Pa snapped.

We went on down the valley to where the Humphrieses had their place. It was ten miles, and by the time we got there night had settled down. Rand Humphries was an old river keel boatman, and he and his wife had built themselves a little cabin to spend the last of their days.

At the Humphrieses' it wasn't much different. Rand's wife made a bed for us in the attic, and Pa and Rand spent most of the evening talking about how much better it was in the old days. But if there was one thing Pa and Rand didn't talk about, it was the election.

We were up and off early the next morning. Pa said he kind of took to this stumping business and that he was just beginning to warm up to it. He said you just can't go to old friends and ask them to vote for you out and out; a man's pride wouldn't let him do that. You had to work around the subject, this way and that way.

Well, Pa sure had a lot of pride. We rode the horses most to death paying calls, and Pa talked with a lot of people about 'most everything under the sun, about taxes and land speculation, and corn against oats as a crop, and the price of calico and lots more. But not about the election and not about votes.

"That's that," Pa said as we turned home. "I feel better now that I been out stumping."

"You ain't worried about the election now, Pa?" I asked him.

"Not a bit, Jess," Pa smiled. "You see, all them folks, well, they're old friends."

"That lawman, though, he's canny. You remember about that shelf of books."

"I ain't worried about them books, Jess. I reckon now that the war's over, folks won't mind a few more years of English common law."

We were near home when we met Matt Stevens. I was afraid that might mean trouble out here, but Pa was feeling so good he just grinned.

" 'Evening, Matt," Pa said.

" 'Evening, Sam."

"I guess you're riding into the village to do your voting," Pa said.

"I am. Heard you were out stumping, Sam?"

"Right up and down the valley," Pa said.

"You don't reckon you're late?" Matt grinned. "Elmer Green, he finished his stumping last week. Today and yesterday and the day before he's been out at your place courting Jenny."

"What!" Pa roared.

Matt rode off, still grinning.

Pa turned to me and said, "Jess, what do you figure he meant by that?"

"I guess that lawman's sweet on Jenny. I guess a blind man could have seen that. . . ."

Ma didn't give Pa any satisfaction. When he stamped around the house, roaring, combing his beard with both hands, she just turned her back on him. When he tried to take it out of Jenny, Ma told him, "That's about enough and too much, Sam Burton. Leave the girl alone. If you were home here, minding your business instead of traipsing around the country pestering your friends, you wouldn't have reason to complain."

"Since that lawman came," Pa moaned, "one thing and another, and now my wife and daughter."

All that next day, which was Election Day, Pa mooned around, his face so black that nobody dared speak to him. But toward evening he cheered up a little. He said to me, "Jess, even if everyhing else has gone wong, tonight I'll put that no-account young buck in his place. He'll see that he can't just walk in with his framed degree and take a district away from a man with friends."

The next morning Pa was up with the sun, intending to ride in and get the tally on the votes. He hadn't voted, himself, because he didn't consider it sporting to put down a vote for himself. Besides, he was so sure of the election that one vote didn't mean anything, one way or another.

Pa had saddled the horse, and he was having breakfast, when through the window we saw Lancy Jones ride up and dismount. Lancy came in and stood in the doorway, seeming nervous and ill at ease.

" 'Morning, Lancy," Pa called. Pa was mighty cheerful today.

" 'Morning, Squire."

"Going down to get the tally on the vote?" Pa asked him.

"Seems folks voted early," Lancy said. "Vote was all counted yesterday."

"Yesterday?" Pa paused, with a piece of hot bread halfway to his mouth.

"It kind of hurts for me to have to bring the news," Lancy said. "But twelve years is a long time to serve. This young Elmer feller, why, he's got a fine stock of good law sense. Got a framed degree from one of them Eastern colleges, too. Not that we weren't satisfied with your way of doing things, Squire—"

Pa just shook his head; he shook it back and forth, like it was stuck on a spring.

"Now, Sam, don't excite yourself," Ma warned him.

"Lancy, who won the vote?" Pa whispered.

"Elmer Green, Squire."

"What count?" Pa whispered.

"Hundred ninety-seven to eight-two."

Suddenly Pa sprang to his feet, knocking over his chair and pushing the table away from him. "You're a liar, Lancy!" he roared.

Lancy didn't move, but his face tightened. Quietly, he said, "Sam Burton, you know me twenty-four year, and you know I never took words like that from any man."

But Ma pushed Lancy through the door. "Go on now," she said. "Go on. The Squire ain't in any state fit to argue with." But after Lancy had left she turned to Pa and shook her head. "To say that to a friend," she murmured.

Pa sat down by the fireplace and put his face in his hands.

"Jess, go out and unsaddle the horse," Ma told me.

Pa sat like that by the hearth without moving until midday. Jenny and Ma and I went around him on tiptoe; we knew that after what Pa had said to Lancy there was no meddling with him or talking with him.

Well, it was about midday when we heard the sound of a horse outside. Ma went to the window, and I saw a funny expression fix on her face. She grabbed Jenny and pushed her through the door. I followed. Ma called, "Jess, you come back!" But I ran on after Jenny.

It was the lawman, calm as day, smiling, and dismounting right in front of our house.

"Elmer," Jenny cried, "you were crazy to come here today! Don't you understand how he feels?"

"He'll feel different after I speak to him," Elmer said.

"But you can't speak to him. Go away, please. In a week, or a fortnight, he'll feel different."

"And you'd want me to go away—for a fortnight?"

"No, no. Why are you twisting my words?"

"It's all right," the lawman smiled. "The only decent thing for me to do is to go in and speak with him, tell him. From what I've heard of him, that's what he'd want." And, with that, the lawman pushed past Jenny into the house.

I crowded after him. I didn't want to miss whatever happened. I saw Ma standing with one hand over her breast. Pa was still where he had been sitting before. Jenny stood by the doorway, trembling.

"Squire Burton," Elmer said.

Pa looked up. He saw the lawman, but I don't think he knew him from Adam right then. He just stared at him.

"Squire Burton," Elmer went on, "I'm truly damned sorry it had to happen this way. All I can say is that it was a free election. All I hope is that I'll be as worthy of the position as you were. Yet it isn't as if the judgeship were gone from the family—but shifted—" He paused and swallowed. "You see, I want to marry your daughter. I love her. She loves me—"

Slowly, Pa came to his feet. He shook his head several times and combed through his beard. I could almost see how the words were tumbling over and over in his head.

Ma must have seen it too, because she cried, "Pa, don't aggravate yourself!"

Pa exploded. A bearlike growl rumbled from deep in his stomach, and then he leaped for his long rifle, hanging over the fireplace. He tore it down. "Get out!" he told the lawman.

Elmer hadn't moved. He was watching Pa coolly, and now he said, "I would have given you my hand if I had lost."

"Get out!" Pa yelled.

The lawman moved quickly. I saw his hand dart out for the gun, and then the long rifle went off. The room was suddenly full of smoke and noise and flame. Jenny screamed.

I guess the lawman had been in the war back East, because now the gun was in his hands. Pa stood with his arms hanging loose, staring at Elmer. Jenny sobbed. Ma put her arms around Jenny.

"We'll go now," Ma said. "This ain't a fit place for decent folk."

Pa just stood there without stirring.

The lawman said, "Wait a minute, Mrs. Burton. Don't you think—?"

"I know what I'm doing, young man," Ma said. "He's gone from bad to worse. From just plain ranting, he's turned to murder. Come along, Jess, and you, Jenny."

Pa sank down by the hearth and put his head in his hands. Ma went around the house picking up all Pa's firearms, two pistols, a fowling piece, and a musket—that besides the long rifle. "Can't trust him with these," she said. Pa didn't move. Elmer tried to speak, but Ma shooed him out of the house. Then she called me. Jenny followed.

But Pa didn't move. . . .

We had gone perhaps a mile or two toward the village when I decided to slip back. Ma and Jenny were going to put up with Parson Jackson, and Elmer kept trying to talk them out of it and into going back. But Ma was stubborn as a long night, and she said there'd be no going back, leastways not until Pa came to his senses which she reckoned would be some time.

I felt it was bad enough, with all that had happened to Pa, without me leaving him, along with the others. So, without saying anything, I turned and started to run back.

Ma called after me, "Jess, where you going?"

But I think I heard Jenny say, "Let him go, Ma."

When I got back to the house, Pa was still sitting on a little stool by the hearth. He glanced up as I came in. "Hello, Jess," he said.

"Hello, Pa."

"They didn't send you back?" Pa asked me.

"No—I just come."

"Uh, huh," Pa nodded. "Just look how it is, Jess. A man should be humble toward life. There I was, Squire Burton, judging a district twelve years. Then it rains, shines, rains. Then I shoot a wolf, right on my own land. Then the well goes dry. Then there's election, and I ain't a judge, just because a young buck comes into the country with six foot of law books. Then I lose my wife. Then

I lose my daughter. Didn't mean to shoot that young no-account, either. But he grabs the gun and it goes off, and there I am. Jess, know what I aim to do?"

"What, Pa?"

"Jess, I aim to get drunk—rolling, snorting drunk. Jess, I been a family man twenty-two year. Ain't tasted hard liquor in twelve, since they gave me the judgeship. But, Jess, I ain't a judge no more, and I aim to get rolling, wild drunk. I always been a good family man, a good provider, but now I aim to get rolling drunk."

"I reckon it helps," I said.

"It's a sinful thing for you to see, Jess," Pa said. "But it seems to me I'm down and along the road to becoming a sinful man. It'll be a thing to remember and make you humble."

Pa had a jug of corn standing down the cellar for as long as I remember. When someone came who liked corn, Pa would pour out a glass or two, but it was a big jug, and there was plenty left. Now he fetched it up and set himself to drinking.

"Pa," I warned him, "better take it slow. Old Casper always said that, and he ought to know. I reckon Casper put away more corn than anyone hereabouts."

"I reckon he did," Pa said. "I reckon to overshoot his mark."

It was late afternoon now. Pa was tilting the jug on his shoulder and beginning to feel pretty good. He was singing, "Little brown jug, how I love thee—"

I went to the door and saw something, and slammed the door and barred it. I ran around the house, flinging the window shutters to and barring them.

"What's that, Jess?" Pa demanded.

I pointed toward a loophole in one of the shuttered windows. Pa rose, stumbled over, and looked. Then he staggered back, rubbing his face and pulling at his beard. Then he grabbed the jug of corn and shattered it against the hearth floor.

"The punishment of a sinful man! Mark me, Jess; sinful eyes seeing what ain't there."

"There's Shawnees there, all right," I said. I was beginning to feel good and scared now.

"Jess, I drank the corn, and you, in your innocence, smelled the vapors. There ain't been Shawnees in this part of the country for twelve years." He went to the window, looked, rubbed his eyes, and stared again. Then he came back slowly and sat down.

"Shawnees," he said. "Shawnees in war paint, Jess. And there ain't a firearm here—" He shook his head.

There was a hammering on the door. I began to sniffle, but Pa said, "Stop that, Jess."

One of them poked a musket into a loophole and fired; smoke and flame darted into the room, but we were out of the line. Another fired through a loophole. Both the rooms of the house were laced with smoke and pungent with the smell of gunpowder.

"Your ma, she always knew best," Pa said. "Twenty-two years she was always right, Jess, but this time she had no call taking away the guns."

They were hammering on the door again. The shutters were thick, of oak; and the door was thicker.

The room got heavier with smoke, hotter, closer. Then I heard a crackling, like a heavy man walking on dry brush in the forest.

"Jess," Pa said uncertainly, "Jess, they're burning down the house. We'd better go down in the cellar and pray to God he sent us Injuns so damn' ignorant they don't know what a cellar is."

The cellar was not built under the house, but off to one side. You went in a trap in the floor and then through a slanting shaft. It was unusually cold and wet, because a spring oozed up out of it and ran off through a wooden drain. Most everyone had a cold cellar like that to keep roots and milk in, but it was hot in that cellar then. It had always been the coolest place in the world, but now it was as hot as if the devil were sitting in there with Pa and me.

Pa sat with his arm around me, muttering to himself. Like this: "First that crazy weather, rain, shine, rain, then the wolf, then the well goes dry, then I ain't a judge, then my wife and daughter, and now—now they burn down the house over my head."

I don't know how long we stayed in that cellar, but Pa wanted to give the house plenty of time to burn out and the Shawnees plenty of time to go away. Finally, when it got so we could barely breathe, Pa pushed up the trap and we came out.

The house was down, and we hopped over the black, smoldering logs. It was night, and the Shawnees had gone.

Pa looked at what had been his house, and then at what had been the barn. Then he looked at me and shook his head. "Jess,

Parson Jackson would say I ought to give thanks, but I'm afraid I'm turning into a mean man, a mean man."

I said, "Pa, what about other folks hereabouts?"

Pa jumped like he had been hit. "Jess, I'm a fool. I got a lot to hold against Lancy Jones, but I won't see his house burn over his head."

It was eight miles to Lancy Jones's place, but we made it in less than two hours, on foot. I could see that Pa was steamed up, and when Lancy put an old musket into his hands, Pa seemed to have forgotten all about the house burning down.

From Lancy's place we went down the valley, pulling in men left and right. I don't know what had happened to the Shawnees, but Pa said that after all the work of burning down a house, they were like to throw themselves into the grass and sleep it off, like some men do a corn-whisky jag.

Pa took charge of everything, and in no time at all he had it in hand. Women and children in carts and wagons and headed down to the village, which was no more than a blockhouse and half a dozen shacks, men to guard them, men to ride up and down the valley and warn outlying farms.

I guess it was the same as it had been twelve years past, when the Shawnees came the first time. Everybody "Squired" Pa to death, and nobody seemed willing to do anything without asking him first. And by midnight he had them all down in the village. And nobody ever said a word about the lawman. . . .

Pa and I were among the last to get into the village. Pa kept pestering me to go, but I stuck by him, both of us riding Lancy's big, white work horse. And when we got into the village Ma and Jenny were almost frantic. I guess Ma had repented plenty about walking off with all the firearms.

Ma tried to get around Pa and kiss him and hug him, so she could show him how sorry she felt; but Pa was busy and he couldn't have any truck with women.

Then Ma and Jenny took to kissing me, but Pa said, "The place for women and kids is over there in church, singing hymns with Parson Jackson."

Ma was close to tears, but she nodded and started to walk away. Jenny said, "Come along, Jess."

"The devil I will," I said.

Pa fetched me a wallop. "Jess," he said, "for a boy who's seen the rewards of sin, you sure talk awful loud."

Ma came back. "Sam Burton," she snorted, "that's a fine way— to hit a boy who's been through all he's been through."

"I might have known," Pa said. "Everything else, and now Jess."

"Don't you talk like the fool you are, Sam Burton," Ma cried. Then she bent her head, so that he wouldn't see her tears.

"Sarah," Pa said, "you ain't never been in tears before—and we been married twenty-two years, come summer."

"There's a start for everything."

"I had justice on my side," Pa said.

"Maybe you did. But I had the same kind of justice on mine."

Then they stood there, just looking at each other. Then, who should come walking up but the lawman. Pa saw him, out of the corner of his eye, and I looked for fireworks to start. But Pa never moved, and Ma never took her eyes off his face.

"Squire Burton," the lawman said, like he had practiced the speech over and over, "I feel there's a lot to explain and a lot to apologize for."

"Ain't nothing to explain," Pa said, "except why you're here instead of up there in the blockhouse, sitting over your gun. For a man who's done fighting back East, you're sure mighty slow in covering orders."

And Jenny said, "Elmer, you do what Pa says. . . ."

Well, the Shawnees didn't come that night. I went to the church to do hymn singing, but I didn't sing much. I fell asleep, and slept right through until almost noon the next day. Then I learned that Pa and Lancy and others had been back to our place, picked up the Shawnee track, discovered there weren't more than five or six of them. They had gone back across the river.

Pa said he reckoned it was safe enough now, and folks were beginning to load up to go back to their farms. But before any of them left they gathered around Pa to shake his hand and show him how sorry they were for voting against him.

"Well," Pa said, "it looks like I got to go back and build up again, and that's a tiresome thing for a man at my age."

Everyone nodded, but Lancy said, "Listen here, Squire; we been talking things over last night about how you served the public twelve years. Young Elmer here, he said as how they're going to make a state out of the section hereabouts and up and down two, three hundred miles. Well, when you got a state, you got to have a man to send to Congress, and it seemed to us there wasn't no better man to have sitting in Congress for us than Squire Sam Burton."

Pa stared at them, then looked all around the crowd, from face to face. Everyone was nodding.

"Never had but one lawbook," Pa mumbled. "Up there in Congress—"

"A man who could read law to a whole district out of one book wouldn't have any trouble in Congress," Parson Jackson said.

Ma was wiping her eyes. She went over to Pa and put her head against his shoulder. He ran his hands through his beard.

"You'll have to stump the district," Elmer said.

Pa grinned and put an arm tight around Ma. "Don't you worry about that, youngster. I'm an old hand at stumping."

Departure

IN A WAY, it was like I had become old overnight, and I woke up heavy; I woke up like a man suddenly with a family, two kids and a wife, and rent to pay, but I had none of those things, only a feeling that this, for me, was the end of a lot of things, crazy drinking sprees and whoring and foolish bats of one kind or another, all the things that made them grin at me and put up with it, too, whatever it was, the way you put up with a clown. "Clowning," they would say, "that sonovabitch is always clowning." But they didn't mind.

I shaved carefully and thoroughly, and Laurencon, who had a four-year-old girl at home, made some crack about how she did as well but without a blade, just a timeworn inept crack, but an indication that it was nobody's lark, nobody's day of grace. "Go to hell," I told him.

"No offense, Sonny."

"To hell with you, Pop. You can't offend me. My mind to me a kingdom is. Age is no achievement; it's just a passage of time."

The trucks were waiting, but I still dressed slowly and deliberately. For some reason I didn't fully understand, I had a relationship with my clothes, the boots I had won at the bandage raffle, the heavy brown pants, the blue ski jacket, the black beret. I had never liked my clothes before, but I liked them now; they seemed to be unusual clothes, and I felt foolish and sticky and sentimental toward them. I even borrowed a clothesbrush from Cohen and brushed them off. It was good for a laugh from everyone who saw me, but I didn't do it for a laugh.

The whole battery was like that. To see them offhand, you wouldn't have known, but as I was with my clothes, so each of them was with one thing or another; and in the thick soup of dawn, they moved with measure and deliberation, as if they were counting out steps to a prearranged dance. I try to think of some of the things that were said, but it was so long ago and I was young. Words don't stick as well as the scent of the damp earth, the sound of the truck motors idling, the pale flash of a spotlight that had overstayed the darkness. These things made a pattern for memory; I suppose Lossowski was telling us to step lively and get moving, but I don't remember for sure. I do remember that the truck we got into was already half-full of Croats, big, sleepy-eyed, blond men, who grinned at us and pushed together to give us plenty of room.

Our truck roared into life, and we drove out of the hospital compound.

"Good-by, Denia," Mac Goldstein said thoughtfully and respectfully. Then he handed me one across the behind, and told me, "Nice to go home, huh, kid?"

"Home is where you make it." Parker, an Englishman, used to say that, and I picked it up. I would pick up a lot of words and phrases then; maybe that's the way speech grows when you're a kid. Sometimes, I used them right, but mostly wrong, I suppose, and it may be that they stand out across all that bridge of time for that reason. A word, a phrase, or a sentence is flung away, and how are you supposed to remember, even if you have taken an oath and are up before a formal court of the law? If I were under oath and answering, I don't know but that I'd perjure myself anyway.

How old were you?

I don't know—twenty or twenty-one.

You don't know? Surely you know. Surely you can think back and calculate. You are an intelligent and thoughtful human being.

Am I?

What date was it?

It was the fourteenth of January, or the fifteenth, or the sixteenth. They don't figure a date by a date, you know; the way they figure —when my first-born saw the light, or when I threw a fistful of dirt on the grave of my blessed mother, or when the cow calved, only there were no more cows then, or when the shadow of the church was ragged instead of straight and heat lightning of four colors flashed in the east; but not by a calendar. So I can remember that before we went into the barracks at Valencia, where they all were, the men of all nations, French and Slavs and Croats and Serbs and Germans and yellow-haired Northmen and dark-haired men of the South, the Italians and the Greeks and the Crete men—before we went into the great barracks there, I saw a Spanish girl who was more beautiful than any other girl that lived, slim and with a lissome stride, and she walked past and was gone, but I remember her and that was the day it was, and I have been in love with her ever since but never saw her again.

I remember too the color of the Mediterranean sky that evening when we went down to the boats.

It was the same day?

Well, I think so. It seems to me that it was the same day. You see, I was in love with the girl, and thinking about her, and it seems that I was only in the barracks for a while, because all I remember, aside from the fact that there were many thousands of men there, was that the Greeks were singing a song. I remember that because I always thought what strange people the Greeks are, not like us or the British or the Germans, either, more like the Spaniards, maybe, and they never seemed to grow tired; it was always beginning for them; wherever they were, it was beginning, a very hopeful people. I remember the song because it was a song of love, and I was in love, in a way of speaking, and the sky over the harbor was like that, pink that turned violet and made me want to cry. You know the way guys are; they kept ribbing me because I had stopped clowning; it wasn't fair to them, I should have kept on clowning, but I couldn't; and then when we marched onto the boat, I began to cry; but it was almost dark and nobody noticed.

It was an excellent operation, smooth and without a hitch, just the way the League of Nations and the Congress of the United States and the Reichstag wanted it to be, except that the boats were old and dirty and rusty and nobody was very sure about what kept them afloat. We marched onto our boat and down the steps into the hold. Before we went down into the hold, I looked back at the beautiful city, Valencia, the jewel, the ancient one. How do I recall what I thought then? I was a kid, a tough, hard-boiled, wisecracking kid who would live forever, but I was tenderly in love and my face was wet with tears, and I must have thought profoundly and deeply. Or perhaps I thought of nothing but good-by.

If I thought good-by, it was the way you do when you are very young, and every place you are you will be back again, so dry your tears of sorrow. The French have a good word for it, but there is no word in English that is just right. There was a Welsh miner there from Pittsburgh, who was a captain with the 129th Brigade, who were Yugoslavs, and a hand grenade had torn open his loin, his testicles, his stomach and his legs, yet he was able to walk; and he stood at the edge of the hold, watching the darkening city, the jewel city, the bereaved one, but said nothing. I don't know what his good-by was. There were thirty-five or forty of us who were Americans, and we went down into the cargo hold, a big, empty place at the bottom of the ship, and all around us there was warmth and odor from the men of many nations, the sick, the wounded, the stretcher cases too, and they clamped on the hatches so that not an ounce of light shone through, and the ship put out to sea.

I can tell it as a dream, but not really as a memory. When I lie at night and I am afraid to die, as all men are, except now and then when there is a thing worth dying for, I think of it, and it's like a balm for a troubled soul. But what is memory as against the facts? And, believe it or not, there is no memory for terror, for there in that hold men couldn't breathe or sleep or move, but I do not remember that anyone was afraid. But maybe my memory is poor and because I was a kid, they were good to me, asking me:

"How's it going, kid?"

"Good enough."

"Well, take it easy. Easy does it."

"Look, lay off me. I'm all right."

"Sure, you're all right, kid, you're all right."

But where do you stow your thoughts when your thoughts tell you that the fascists must know, and they will come out in a fat-bellied German battleship and pick off the old tubs like a hunter picks off ducks? The Slavs made a song; they are the loneliest people in the world, and yet they are never lonely the way we are lonely, and when they sing a song there is a memory of all the hurts they knew and their fathers and their grandfathers. I like our songs better. We sang "Digging Our Way to China." Then we sang "There's a Long, Long Trail a-Winding," which is the most beautiful song in the world, and the saddest, too, as I remember, for someone in love and lost of his love. I don't remember anything else of particular importance, and I suppose we slept.

It was seven o'clock in the sunny morning when we arrived at Barcelona, and for some strange reason our arrival there is confused in my mind with all the old newsreel pictures I have seen before then and since of troops coming home by ship and departing too; but really I don't suppose it was too much like that. But there were people on the dock, and I heard afterwards that Negrin was there. I don't remember him, but I remember André Marty; it was the first time I had seen him, and the guys pointed him out.

They had let us up on deck with the sunrise. A submarine was escorting us, and after I saw it, I felt a lot better. I don't remember us talking about anything else but the submarine, even when we entered the bomb-wracked harbor and saw the sunken ships. And the bigness of Barcelona was different from the loveliness of Valencia. We hold Barcelona, so I told it to the nameless girl who had walked past me with such a lissome stride. We hold Barcelona, and, by God, we will hurl the fascist back into the hills of Portugal, and there will be a victory parade in Madrid, and as I march down the Avenue, I will see her and she will recognize me.

You remember well, and you remember badly?

It's that way, I'm sorry, some little things you remember and some big things you forget. I remember a melon rind floating in the water.

By eight o'clock we were all of us disembarked. The trucks for us were drawn right up to the docks, and we climbed into them. They took us to the barracks, which were on top of a hill outside of Barcelona. I don't know what the hill was called, or what was the name of the barracks, but it was a barracks in the old Spanish style, foursquare, with a compound in the center, and there were balconies all around four or five stories high, a place big enough to hold all of us, and we were thousands. There were all the Internationals who were left; there were the men of the nations. Someone —I don't know who it was—but someone said to me:

"Put it in your memory, kid, put it in your heart."

"My heart is full," I said, speaking in Spanish. "My heart is full and flowing over. I don't want to go home. I have no home, I am the homeless one." You say things in another tongue, and they do not sound foolish, as they would in English. Whoever he was, he answered so softly, *"Vamos juntos, vamos juntos—"* And I thought of the thousand and one times I had wanted to go home, whimpered to go home, pleaded to go home, wept to go home, a frightened kid and no soldier, but now I was a soldier and no land to fight for, no people to give me arms and say: Stand here, stand and no further.

They called us out and we filled the balconies and listened to Marty speak. Then Negrin spoke. Then the whole place broke into the "Internationale," in fifteen tongues, and that is a memory, for when had it happened before and when would it happen again? And we were going away; we were leaving Spain, who is like a beautiful woman you love, and we were going away.

It could have only been a day or two later when the thing happened. The fascists had reached Barcelona, you understand, and we had moved up to a place called Casa d'la Selva. It was the way out; it was the end already, and there were only the Cubans and the Mexicans with us, and we had stayed too long; we were guests departed but lingering, and we had given away to the Spaniards left behind our guns, our leather belts, our boots, and whatever else was of value. We ate and we slept and we waited, and rumors filled the air; but the strongest of all the rumors was to the effect of Barcelona being handed over to the enemy, the pig with a voice, the dog without even a dog's soul, the fascist; given up and no struggle; handed over and no struggle; a gift for the devil. I lay in the sun, and my love lay beside me. I told someone then that I was in love. With whom? With a Spanish girl whose eyes are like black olives and whose lips are like poppies. They would have been fools to believe me, but we believed anything then. It was my first love and my last.

You remember what you want to remember; a man's past is part of all the past, and everywhere little gates are carefully closed. Only when it is all finished, our way, will we open all the gates. It was two or three or four days after we were there that the big meeting was called in the one theater the town boasted. Seven or eight hundred of us crowded in there, full and overfilled and cloudy with the smoke of our brown-paper cigarettes.

This is it, kid, someone who knew and was on the inside.

He spoke in Spanish, "You men of the Internationals, *amigo de corazon*, you men of the Internationals who are my comrades, my brothers-in-arms, listen to me! We will defend Barcelona to the death! We go back!'

That is also a memory. I cried again; I put my hands over my face and wept, but I haven't wept since then. Through all the rest, I was dry-eyed. No more clowning, and the kid was not a kid any more. Sitting and listening to the speakers, one after another, telling how Barcelona could be held and made a bridgehead for all free men, I made a disposition of myself. Then we went outside into the dry sunlight of Spain.

The people from our land, America of the lovely name, the free land over the mountains and over the sea, went to a carpentry shop, and there some volunteered and others said they would go home. The volunteers would not go home any more. They stayed

together, talking and making arrangements for the battery; I didn't
have anything to say, and someone asked me:

"What is it, kid, worried?"

"No."

"Take it easy, kid. Nobody is brave."

"I'm not brave," I said. My childhood was over, youth and
adolescence and the sprouting of the weed as juices run through
its stem, and the wonderful, beautiful conviction that you will live
forever while all other mortals die; manhod is a benediction as well
as a curse, and the calm inside of me was life's repayment. It was
a fair exchange. "I'm not brave," I said. "I want to stay here."

You see, it was to defend Barcelona to the death, if necessary, and
most likely necessary, and you made your own choice. The great
bulk of the Internationals were gone, but you had stayed with the
leave-taking. You had overstayed; then sleep, and tomorrow we
will break bread again.

What else do you remember?

Well, then, I also remember these things: the children who
played in the streets, they the inheritors, and I was grown now
and saw them as children. The fresh-baked bread we had for our
dinner—oh, honored guests. We shared our bread with the children,
who made us at home as you do when a guest is no longer a
stranger. There were also things to be done, arrangements for the
new guns, which were coming down from France, arrangements
for officers and for a table of organization, arrangements into the
sunset, the sweet, cool night. I was bedded with a cobbler's family,
and we sat before bed with a glass of wine and a piece of sausage.

Partake, oh cousin, and tell us about how it goes in the South.
Is there death in the South? Will there be victory or defeat? Will
the fascists be driven back?

A su tiempo.

Cunning words from an old fighter. You are one of the new
ones, a machine gunner?

An artilleryman.

Drink the wine and don't spare the sausage. When will Spain
see better men? A glass of wine makes the couch easy.

And then I slept until a whistle wakened me, and this was it,
was it not? We formed into ranks and then onto the train, and
nobody really knew except—rumors; but after a while we understood. The train was going north, not south. Barcelona would not

be held; the last of the Internationals were going away. This was a night train for the border, salute and farewell. Somewhere, men were afraid; somewhere men lost heart and hope, and they had opened the doors and said: Take this maiden for yourself, she with the lips as red as poppies and the lissome stride. I had only hatred and contempt for those whose eyes were wet now.

"What is it, kid?"

"To hell with you! To hell with you!"

And when the train stopped in the morning, we were in France.

The
Gray Ship

WITH WORK WELL done, the gray ship lay in the eastern sunshine and slept. Moored to the dockside with heavy hawsers, fore and aft, she was as immobile as part of the earth, the dock, the rusty, war-weary storage sheds. She had come halfway around the world, her holds stuffed with the food and the teeth of war, her deck piled; she had threaded her way through the islands and atolls of the Pacific, crawled around the belly of Australia, crept lightless and soundless through the tropical night. She was sufficient to herself; when her engines broke down, she hove to and repaired them; when danger threatened, she manned her guns and slewed them belligerently to the part of the horizon which menaced her. She had been a living, vibrating world, rusty and hard; now she was painted over from head to foot, and she lay in the sunshine and slept.

The purser was nervous; big, heavy, his usual smile gone, he stood by the rail, drummed his fingers on the hot metal, and wanted to be away. That nervousness had communicated itself to the whole crew; longing for port, talking port, dreaming it, when it came it was always less than it should have been, and when port time ran over schedule they became restless and uneasy. And this they tried to cover over by pointing out that their pay went on, good pay in this, a danger zone.

"It stinks," the purser said. He meant it literally; in the basin, the garbage could not be thrown overside; it littered the aft deck, mixed indiscriminately with the dunnage. A ship in port, loading or unloading, isn't clean. Crows screamed and cawed and swooped over the garbage. Flies made a netting over it.

"A dead ship," the purser said. "She sleeps, she lays on her belly like a whore. I don't like a ship that way." He began to hum, "Don't fence me in—give me land." The chief came up and joined his music; the chief's eyes wandered from the burnished metal skies to the ship, to the crows. Of the crows, he asked, "What are they?" "Crows." "I don't like crows," the chief said. "I don't like crows by the hundreds. I liked to hear them way off across the meadows at home, but not like this. What's new?"

The purser said he didn't know what was new, and anyway, what should be new? The chief thought that maybe he had some news on where they were going, but the purser only grunted. But inside, momentarily, he had a quick, wide thought: fifteen thousand miles from stateside, the whole world was theirs, its waters washing motes of land, unimportant land, wretched, hot land; he had a sudden sense of freedom, and he pitied the army guards, seeking shade under the rusty shed, he pitied the natives of the land who were like the trees, rooted to the land.

"I want to hear the turbines," he said.

"You want to hear the turbines," the chief muttered. "The rotten noisiest can I ever been on, and you want to hear it. You got bugs in your head."

"When the engines turn over, she's alive; now she's dead. A ship without power, she's dead."

"We ought to have a funeral service," the chief said; but the purser, pouring ample quantities of sweat, drummed with his fingers on the rail and wanted to be away.

The gray ship was a Victory, which meant that whatever her given name, it would be followed by the word "Victory," as, for instance, the *Arkansas Victory* or the *Burnside Victory*. It also meant that, in a very limited sense, she belonged to an aristocracy; she was meant to survive for the postwar period, provided that no torpedoes ripped out her guts, that no mines caved in her plates, that no shells or bombs smashed her superstructure into scrap; provided all that, she was a little less expendable than the bathtub hulls of the Liberties, a little more expendable than the C1s, the C2s and the C3s.

Her displacement was about ten thousand tons, her length something over four hundred feet. She had a forecastle deck, which gave her a graceful swoop up to the bow, and differentiated her immediately from the unbroken deck line of the Liberty. Amidships, she had a deck housing. Square, ugly, undifferentiated from the gray-painted metal of the rest of the ship, it climbed from the main deck in this fashion: boat deck, which housed the four lifeboats and gave the ship's officers a limited promenade; quarter-deck, bridge, topside and flag deck. One fat sack poked out of the housing, and four king posts surrounded it.

The gray ship was built for the belly of cargo she could carry, and every detail of her was a concession to cargo—no more. Five huge hatches opened to reveal that she was no more than a shell. The seven masts and king posts swung booms to load and unload her, and her own forest of booms, cable and rope made her capable of eating and then disgorging her own diet. Whatever comfort she held existed because cargo could not be disassociated from men, and her guns watched over that same cargo.

Her guns gave her a will of her own; expendable she was, but not defenseless. She had the power to strike, and to strike hard. Fore and aft were two gun tubs, raised platforms sheathed in half-inch steel plate. The forward gun was a seventy-millimeter, quick, agile, able to swivel and snap like a swan's neck; aft, long, ugly, was a five-incher, able to fight a surfaced sub on equal terms, able to fling its shell six thousand feet into the air. Amidships, in six smaller tubs, were the twenty-millimeter machine guns, good for a curtain of lead when the dive bombers came in. She was not quarrelsome, the gray ship, but she could hit back if someone struck at her, and she could make her blow felt.

The guns were a navy affair, and under the five-incher was the gunners' forecastle, where eighteen navy men slept. Six more navy men slept forward.

As the purser said, the life of the gray ship was in her engines, oil-burning turbines which, when put to it, could turn over one hundred and five revolutions per minute and drive her at seventeen and a half knots. Turbines, boilers, fires and generators were housed amidships, heart and guts, the bull's-eye for torpedoes, for shells and bombs.

Such was the gray ship, unlovely, stubby, confident, long of range, ready to go where orders took her.

About two hours after the purser's impatience, the gray ship cast off, and from slumber she came alive. From the midship housing aft, she trembled and purred; her plates vibrated; her propeller washed the dirty water, and the basin water washed back. The master, his patience tried the limit, demanded the pilot. In all his years, he'd never known a pilot to be on time, never; but the first officer, easy now, said, "He's on board, sir." "Then, mister, where is he? Is he drinking his tea? Is he sitting on the head? Or is he blowing his nose over the rail?" But at that moment the pilot came

up the companionway, natty in his white suit, white shorts, white
socks and shoes. . .

Below, on the gray ship, those who slept felt the change, the
slight movement, the vibration, the waking up and the coming
alive, and they turned in their sleep, more easily than uneasily; in
their sleep too they heard the hiss of the tugs, the chugging, the
shouted orders, the second officer's repeat of the pilot's command,
"Wheel amidships—" the blast of the whistle, the swirl of water,
brown water which would presently become green and then blue
water. The purser went back to his books, his nervousness gone.
Two short whistles warned the change of watch, and the men coming off duty leaned on the rail and watched the harbor swing as they
warped toward the canal. All over the basin, packed ships, mer-
chantmen of all nations, patrol craft, destroyers, and menacing
ships of war watched them. There were around the harbor the
regrets men feel when they see another ship putting out to sea,
the envy and the nostalgia. The gray ships, in time of war, have
no proclaimed destination; somewhere, men wait for a ship; somewhere else a man knows where all ships are going and from whence
they come; but he who sees the ship passing by knows only that it's
outward bound . . .

The English pilot stood on the bridge and called his orders.
London was in his voice, but he had been out here twenty-five
years now. He went nowhere; for twenty-five years he had taken the
ships in and out of the complex channel, released them from their
brief, fretful imprisonment, and given them leeway for the ports
of the world—San Francisco, Rio, New York, Antwerp, Saipan,
Said—and then himself gone back; no ship liked his port, and
sometimes it occurred to him, though he was not an imaginative
man, that no ship liked any port. By now he went through his
movements mechanically; you could roll back the water of the river,
and it would not make much difference to him; he knew every
mud hummock, every bar and channel. Always ahead of him was
the thought, somewhat unclear, like the muddied waters of the
channel, that he would take ship one of these days and go home;
but he stayed on and the gray ships came and went.

Some of the men on the ship wrote letters, because the restless
wonder of open sea again had to be expressed, and they would say
things like ". . . my darling, we are going through the channel,

and finally will be out to sea. So we should be home soon . . ." Or
". . . it was so hot here that it is good to be away . . ." But it could
have been too cold as well as too hot; the core of the matter, on
the gray ships, was movement. Logistics, the military called it, and
on the gray ships movement expressed their purpose and their
reason. Indeed there were a few men on the ship who never went
ashore, in any port, as if the covenant to them was so dear that it
couldn't be violated.

So the gray ship, which had slumbered, which had been dead to
the purser, stinking dirty to the engineer, shirking to one, whorelike
to another, came to life again and sailed out to the open sea. The
gray ship was a stitch in a broad-woven pattern which had only
slight variations in the whole of the warp and the woof. It sought
little credit and found less. Though there was glory enough to go
around, the gray ships did their job without glory; as their men
wore no uniforms, so did they wear no medals.

They put out to sea again, and in a way that was its own reward.
The brown water turned to green and the green water turned
blue. The time-old phrase went the rounds of many lips, blue
water, blue water, no bottom and a deep swell. The pilot shook
hands all around, wished them good voyage, and climbed overside
to his bobbing boat. On shore the blinker gave them clearance and
wished them good voyage too. The captain, relaxed for the first
time in many days, took his sharp turn on the quarter-deck, six
paces port, six paces starboard, six paces port again. The messmen
dumped the garbage overside, and the crows flew back to their
own hot land. Full speed ahead came down to the engine room from
the bridge, and given a lasting course finally, the helmsman fixed
his eyes on the compass. Night fell and land dropped away, and in
the brief, tropical twilight the gunners stood to general quarters.
With darkness the ship blacked out and faded into the inky sea,
and in the crew's mess three sweating A.B.s sat down for their evening of euchre.

The
Suckling Pig

He CALLED Marcus and said, "I just heard about it. Jack Brady passed away this morning."

"No!"

"Got up, took a shower, began to dress, and then keeled right over."

"No! Heart?"

"That's right. It makes you stop to think. We're none of us as young as we used to be."

"That's the God's honest truth. But a guy like Brady, you'd think he had twenty good years ahead of him."

"Never had a sick day in his life. It makes you stop to think."

"That's the truth. How's his wife taking it?"

"She's making a big thing. But I got my own ideas on that subject."

"I got mine," Marcus said. "I guess I'll see you at the wake."

"I guess so."

After he called one or two more of the boys, he told his girl to get Rialto Liquor to send a case up to Brady's, half Scotch and half bourbon, and to have a big wreath made up out of red and yellow roses.

"I wouldn't think red and yellow roses for a wreath," the girl said.

"What in hell's the difference? Jack Brady liked red and yellow roses."

The rest of the afternoon dragged slowly, interrupted only by phone calls to tell him what he already knew, that Jack Brady had passed away. Thoughts of death, more and more frequent lately, clouded his mind, and he half regretted that he was not a Catholic, like Brady, so he could let others do the worrying for him. At five, he canceled the tickets for that evening, and went over to Toots's for a drink.

A half a dozen of the boys were there at the bar, and he killed four Scotches with them, and then felt better. They were all men in their middle fifties about the same age Jack Brady had been, and they thought of themselves as well as Brady.

"Anyway, it's a nice, clean exit," someone said.

"Clean or not, it ain't nice."

"I had dinner with Jack at the Hickory House last night. He didn't have a thing on his mind, except he thought he'd go down to Florida a little early."

"That's the way it is."

"How is Sue taking it?"

"Breaking her heart."

Some of them grinned, and someone said, "It's a god-damned dirty shame, because there never was a finer guy than Jack Brady."

"You can say that again."

It was after seven before they sat down to eat and almost nine before they had finished. He had clams, roast beef, and finished up with a piece of blueberry pie and coffee. He felt full and comfortable and resentful against the wake, and chastised himself with the thought of how it must have seemed to Brady, just keeling over at the last minute, the way he did.

They ordered a round of brandy, and over it one asked, "Did anyone call the Mayor?"

"Frankie did. Frankie's taking care of the arrangements."

"He would. What about a drink up there?"

Glad he had remembered, he told about the Scotch and bourbon he had ordered—"Not that Jack didn't always have a little on hand."

On their way out, they picked up two sports writers from the *Journal* and Gibbon, from the *Telly*.

"I wrote the obit myself," Gibbon said. "Did you know he was with the old 77th?"

Some did and some didn't.

"He was worth five punks from this fracas. That was a war."

They got into three cabs and rode over to the Park Avenue address. The Garden crowd were just entering the building when they arrived, and everybody paused in front to exchange hellos and introductions in a subdued tone of voice. Then Dan Raye arrived and said that he had canceled his performance for tonight. They crowded into the elevator.

He felt a little funny about all the big wheels, and began to wonder if he had ever been really close to a big-time operator like Jack Brady. He had thought of the liquor and he had thought of the wreath and he had rushed over before noon to see what he could do, but Brady moved in the top crowd, and it made him question whether he wasn't walking into Brady's death the same way he had walked into his life.

"The hell with it," he told himself. "I had some damn good times with Jack Brady."

Toots had made up a big basket of food, which Joe Schree was carrying, and he wondered now why he had not thought of that himself. But when they got upstairs, there already was a table loaded down with sandwiches, plates of cold cuts, and a suckling pig, half-carved, looking like a monster embryo. At least thirty people had already arrived, and the bar was set up in one corner, with everybody making his own drinks. Helen Canyon was acting as hostess and when he had a moment, he drew her aside and asked about the body.

"It's in the funeral parlor," she said. "It's no use making it worse for Sue than it is."

"Sure," he said, thinking that after all it would be easier for everyone present without Brady also being present. "How is Sue?"

"She's a soldier, all right. She's in the bedroom."

Almost all of the few women there were in the bedroom with Sue. He went in and said a few words to her, and in spite of himself he couldn't help but imagine himself crawling in with her. She was a big, handsome blonde with a good figure, and he said to himself:

"What a lousy, cheap line of thought for Brady's wake!"

He went back to the living room and passed an hour or so just milling around and saying hello to various people and being introduced to others as a good old friend of Jack Brady's. It was after ten o'clock now, and some of the people were leaving. He and four or five of the others, all boys who had been pretty close to Jack Brady, stood in the pantry and swapped memories about one thing and another that they had shared with the dead man. A lot of the stories concerned the time Brady was in Chicago, and he felt somewhat left out of them, but when the stories shifted to the close past, he felt more at home, and he told about how he and Brady had shacked up with the Deleharty sisters in Philadelphia.

It was almost eleven when Father Costello came in. Most of the men still left were pretty drunk by then, but if Father Costello noticed it, he didn't remark on it. Father Costello was an old friend of his, and that made him feel better, especially the way Father Costello sat down next to him and said:

"Well, man comes and man goes, even the best."

"Even the best, Father."

"And somewhere in it there's reason and justice and a supreme guiding intelligence. That's what's important to remember."

"I try to remember that, Father. I sure as hell do."

At a quarter to twelve, he called Alice, who should have just been finishing with a hot glass of milk at home, after the show, but no one answered the phone, and he said "The bitch!" sourly, the drinks wearing onto the bottom of his stomach by now.

A kind of sallow joylessness had settled over the apartment by one-thirty in the morning, and some of the boys agreed with him that it did no one any good, least of all Jack Brady, to spend the night here. Sue had gone to bed and Father Costello had gone home, so they made a few calls and arranged to go over to the Cub Room. He tried Alice again and told her to meet him there.

"You sound lit," she said.

"I had a couple of drinks. Jack Brady was maybe the best friend I had in the world."

They went downstairs and got cabs and went over to the Stork Club. He felt sick and low and suddenly hungry, and he kept remembering the roast suckling pig and wishing he had made a sandwich of it. He asked Alice if she liked roast suckling pig.

"What a question!"

"Well do you or don't you?"

"I don't. It tastes like baby would taste roasted."

"How in hell do you know what baby would taste like?"

"That's what it would taste like," Alice said stubbornly.

"I ought to kick her in the teeth, the big blond bitch," he said to himself.

"Why don't you order some caviar and toast?" she asked him.

"Because I don't want caviar and toast. Let's go over to Reuben's and have a steak."

"If you want a steak," she said.

But when they got to Reuben's he changed his mind and had scrambled eggs and Nova Scotia salmon. It was four o'clock in the morning when they had finished, and only Ed Hartly of the boys was left. They dropped him off at his place and then rode over to her apartment.

He sat down in the bedroom, and as she began to undress he thought to himself, "If she's got one of those wire brassières on, I'm

going to spit right in her face." She had a wire brassière on. He got
up and started out of the room.

"What is it now?" she demanded.

"Nothing. Nothing. I'm going home."

"What did I do now?"

"Nothing. You don't expect me to come out of Jack Brady's wake
and crawl into bed?"

"Why not?"

"The hell with you," he said, slamming the door into the face of
what she said, something about a suckling pig. As he waited for the
elevator, he tried to remember Father Costello's words about reason,
justice and something else.

Old
Sam Adams

(THREE TALES)

JOURNEY TO BOSTON

From the journal of Reuben Joshua Dover, it will be noted that even after he had well passed the allotted three score years and ten, he wrote with a firm, round hand. Therefore, it is not surprising that at the age of only sixty-six, he was a sound, dry and healthy man, able to do his day's work if it was necessary for him to do it; the trouble was that it was not wholly necessary, since he had four strong sons and two buxom daughters—and they were good children, which is not so often the case.

Like an old nut, Reuben Dover rattled a little, but he was sound, drying slowly like an apple that begins just bulging with juice and never has a bad spot on it. Of Puritan stock, he was city born, town born—he never forgot that and wore it like a badge—until the big layoff on the rope walk pushed him out to the stony fields of Middlesex where he hired on and learned what a damned crofter does. He was a man for a working wage, and he liked the feel of a wage and the companionship and good feeling that goes with a social way of work; and if left to himself he probably would have gone on that way, with occasional shipping out to see all the various Christian and heathen places of the world, the way a Boston boy does, until he ended deep in Davey Jones locker or on a board in the poorhouse; that's the way it probably would have been if left to himself, but he married Annie Cartwheel, an ambitious girl, and then he was not left to himself again, but had to go out after the war to the Mohawk bottoms and till the land and build a hard stone house. But prosperity never brought him the gladness of a glass of rum with the hard-headed boys on the waterfront. He had eighty-three milch cows, but he could climb his peaked barn roof and never see a ship or something that resembled one, and he could walk all over his acres and never see the pretty little whores that walked on King Street or the wonderful sights of the yellow Chinese or the great black men from the warm places. At night, there was the chirping of the crickets everywhere, but nowhere the soft sweet singing of the Portugee fishers who sailed their boats across from the Azores and often enough bedded down with and even married some Yankee lassie, and nowhere the gentle crooning of the Kanaka harpoon men, so strong and graceful.

There was work and prosperity and a lumber mill and the six children, and suddenly he was old but not too old and what his sons couldn't take care of were just odds and ends of nothing at all, just miserable chores and not for a man who had worked a lifetime.

Thus, when it came out of the east, riding and sighing on the wind, brought by the fast post and by word of mouth too that the man Samuel Adams, old Sam Adams, seldom Sam Adams, had passed away and gone to rest with the best and the least of them, laid down his tired old body for ever and ever, Reuben Dover an-nounced to his wife and children and grandchildren: "Now I think I'll go and walk in the procession and pay my respects, you know."

"As if they intended to put him on ice and just keep the corpse awaiting you," his wife commented sourly.

"Now maybe they would, knowing how folks will come from here and there as the news spreads."

"He's buried deep under right now," the son Joshua said.

"And if that's the case, I'll have me a glass of rum on his grave and toast him good, God bless him."

"Good riddance to a trouble maker," his wife said, and he told her sharp:

"You shut your mouth, Annie. I never took a hand to you, but sure as there's a God in heaven I will, talking that way."

"A sudden belief in God?" the son Adam said.

"I never had no trouble with God, you young fool—just never stood in no awe of Him nor no other, I tell you that! And how would you know today when there ain't men left! And how would you know about old Samuel either?" thinking to himself, by all that was holy, he wouldn't come back, but go and pay his respects and then ship onto some four-master out for nowhere, even if he went as a cook's helper.

"Wouldn't know a thing about him," the son Adam agreed.

"Still I'm going, and that's that, so we don't need to hash it over and over. I'm going, do you hear me? And I'm going on my best mare with my best suit and my best hat, and I'm going to pay my respects regular, deep and regular and sorrowful. Do you hear?"

But he thought to himself, there will be no one to weep, no one to know the truth of it, no one to remember, when it was all so long ago and like a dream that it had ever happened at all. And that very morning, he saddled up the mare and left for Boston.

It was a two hundred mile trip to Boston, and no more Indians along the way to threaten your scalp and no more danger of British patrols, as there was once a quarter of a century past, but everywhere the mushroom growth of town and city and mill and farm, with the Yankees out to make a dollar where a dollar was to be made. The copper smelter smoked and the iron works glowed red by night; the gathered corn stood in the fields. The geese honked south in mighty flocks, for the Yankees had not yet figured out a way to get rid of the geese as expeditiously as they had gotten rid of the deer, that had once been as thick as flies over this land.

But for all of that, the land was still beautiful, with the lovely Mohawk wending its way toward the lovely Hudson, and with the shadow of the pretty Berkshire hills on the eastern horizon. It was autumn time, the maples already red, the birch yellow, the dead leaves rustling as they fell, and the wonderful clean smell of coming winter on the air; and as old Reuben Dover rode along, he felt that his youth was flowing back into his veins. He felt free and footloose and full of good memories, and sitting bolt upright in his saddle, he put back his head and sang:

> *"Oh, pretty are the riggers as they sail across the sea,*
> *But prettier is the lassie who waits at home for me,*
> *With her sewing and her spinning and her weaving and her*
> *   song,*
> *May the best winds only grant it that she never waits too*
> *   long,*
> *That she never waits too long,*
> *That she never waits too long,*
> *For when I up and left her, I did mighty wrong."*

The better he felt, the younger he felt, the more certain Reuben Dover became that he would not go back to the farm, to his family, to his pinch-faced, carping wife. And when round about sundown, he saw a little stone Dutch inn, nestling in the shade of two giant maples and two giant oaks, with all the wood trim painted a neat white, he made up his mind to spend the night here. Most prob-

ably it was true that Sam Adams had already been taken into the
earth, and a body in a grave will keep for more than a day or two,
and it was seven years now since he had gone anywhere at all. He
was in no hurry, and the dead were not impatient.

The boy who took his horse had been a crawling babe the last
time he came this way, and that gave him additional thought about
what happens when a man beds down in just one place. The innkeeper had a new wife, and sitting before the strong red fire in
the tap-room were two of the new men, the selling men or salesmen
as they were occasionally called, who took merchandise made in
the Boston and Albany mills and drummed it to the farmers through
the valleys. In the old days, Reuben recalled, you could always find
at one of these wayside inns a Jew or a Scotsman with his pack of
trinkets, cheap jewelry and piece goods, going out with a couple
of pack animals to trade with the Indians for furs; but such men
did a barter business pure and simple, while these new ones
drummed for cash sale and nothing else. The wandering Jews and
Scotsmen of the old times went out with never a thought for the
time it took and were always ready to pass the time of the day over
a cup of coffee, but these new ones were sharp and brisk with no
time for anything that stood in the way of business.

There was also a neighborhood farmer, Fromm Vanjoorden by
name, who had come in for a glass of hot rum and butter, and there
was the post rider from Albany, a tall and sallow man in his middle
thirties. The merchandise men were stout and neatly put together,
intent on the fat barmaid, but Reuben, full of the juices of youth,
set himself on the innkeeper's wife, a fine-looking woman of fifty or
so; and when the innkeeper himself failed to appear, he began to
think of the coming night just like some hot lad of twenty. He
pinched her behind and shouldered her thigh and put away a pint
of hot rum before his dinner.

She, on the other hand, looked sidewise at him, her blue eyes
sparkling; for he was lean and hard and healthy-looking, for all of
his years, and her husband was off to the market in Albany.

Talk was on, and Reuben listened before he put his oar into it.
He himself was a Democrat and a strong one, but the two drummers seemed to talk Federalist talk; and whenever Reuben heard
Federalist talk, he began to think of himself not so much as a Democrat as a Jacobin. He kept eyeing the Dutch farmer, speculating

on whether he might not be a Jacobin too, which would make the
odds better if he had to put the two damned fat fools in their
places. But you could never tell about a Dutchman; they were as
unpredictable in politics as in anything else; and Reuben bided his
time until one of the salesmen called Tom Jefferson a "scut" and
a "canting liar."

"I didn't hear you," Reuben said.

"I said, liar."

Then the lady of the house said, "Not in my house. No such talk
in my house—or out you go."

"It's a free country, ain't it?"

"And no great credit to you," the Dutch farmer drawled. "No
sir, mister."

Reuben was bulwarked. When the older of the two drummers
said, just as he had expected, "What is this, Jacobinism?" he rose
to his feet and answered: "God damned right!"

"There are ladies present."

"My apologies," Reuben said to the lady gallantly. And to the
salesmen, "Did you call me a Jacobin?"

"If the name fits."

"It fits," Reuben said shortly. "And better than that, I'm on my
way to pay my respects to the best of them all, old Sam Adams. I'll
drink to him." He raised his glass.

"Not me, sir."

A long-limbed, red-faced man came in then, sleeves rolled and
his leather apron of trade on him. "Did I hear that name?" he
demanded. "Who's talking about Sam Adams?"

"I am, sir," Reuben said aggressively.

"For him or against him?"

"For him. If you'd a come a moment sooner, you would a heard
me called a Jacobin too."

"Are you one?"

"I am." And then he added, "What in hell are you?"

"A bottle blower," the man in the apron answered.

"Politically?"

"A Democrat to my friends, and to them—" Nodding at the drummers, "Jacobin."

"Let me buy you a drink," Reuben said. . . .

By nine o'clock, he was comfortably, homely drunk as he hadn't
been in fifteen years, and he had kissed the landlady in the pantry

and given her his gold watch fob to remember him by, not ten years from now, but around midnight, when he said he might just happen along to her room; and she called him a dirty old goat, which made him feel prouder than he had felt in a long time.

The two salesmen went to bed, and Reuben, the Dutch farmer, and the glass blower held down the fireside, with the boy fetching wood to keep it blazing and port wine to be mulled and keep them burning at least to a degree.

Like most of the Dutchmen, the farmer had served in and out of the New Jersey line, and the glass blower had been on the long hike north to Canada with Arnold, whom he hated with a just and ripening hatred, not a quiet resentment at all. But neither of them had known Sam Adams, whom they toasted again and again.

"God bless him," they said.

"He never had a bad moment with God," Reuben pointed out. "A most religious man, orthodox, if you understand, but it never interfered with his tactics. Now Joe Warren never believed in God; came from cutting up too many bodies and seeing what was underneath, but Samuel respected the quality of disbelief. Could he have built a movement of Puritans—now answer me that?"

"That's granted," the glass blower said.

"So when Reverend Sutter came to him and demanded that Warren go out for being a damned atheist, Samuel asked him, Now what is most necessary for belief—mind, heart or body? Sutter thought to outsmart him, and knowing that Sam was one for tactics, answered—mind, just like that. Not at all, said Samuel, for I believe with the heart and Joe Warren—before Sutter could get a word in —believes with the body. There he was. A man who never had a mite of trouble with God."

"And I wonder how he died?" the Dutch farmer speculated.

"You can be just as sure that he died confident—and with everyone in that cursed city hating him," Reuben said.

"There should be a delegation," the glass blower nodded.

"With Yankees?" the farmer asked scornfully.

"Now wait a minute. There are good ones and bad ones. What did we build a movement out of, but the Yankees?"

"The quality of him was Yankee," Reuben agreed. "My own folks came from Plymouth, and that's nothing to be ashamed of, but he was not limited. Not narrow. Let me point this out to you—what

did they fix on when they wanted to put a noose around his neck
and squeeze the character from him: that he was a thief, and I tell
you this, what honesty was to him is something different than what
it is to you and me. With him it was the way of life, that no man
should be ground down under another man. All right, they still
grind them down, don't they, but it's a little different and it will be
more different, mark my word. Well, what for did they make out
of him a tax collector? That was the mad thing to do, and did they
expect him to collect from poor people who could not pay? But
mark this, there was a man who went out of the world with as little
as he came into it, never a penny—and never a penny did he have
but the little bit he needed to eat and feed his children."

"Amen," the farmer said.

"Now you ask them that go on the road to drum business. They
won't say many amens."

"That's the truth."

A little drunk now, for he had more this evening than any evening in a long while, and that on top of the wonderful sensation
of freedom, Reuben's thoughts wandered idly through the past,
with now and then just a flicker of anticipation toward the immediate future and the landlady. When men sit for hours looking at
a roaring fire, and getting a little drunk in the bargain, they will
see in the flames what they want to see, and sometimes very clearly
indeed. Into life in Reuben Joshua Dover's memories came the
Boston of long, long ago, when it was Sam Adam's town, when the
carpenters and rope-makers felt for the first time on the continent
the inevitable and irresistible strength of men who work together,
and when they formed their revolutionary committees and lit a
spark that burned for quite a while.

In his mind's eye, he breasted the hills to the west, and saw the
whole pretty little town standing on its neck of land, and then he
went walking on, through the gates and along Orange Street, but
he was young and hale and bold, and the palms of his hands—from
walking the ropes—were hard enough to drive tenpenny spikes
with, as the saying went. As he walked on, he saw the Boston that
would not be again, that strange, unruly, stiff-necked, puritanical
yet worldly, narrow yet cosmopolitan town that had already sent its
ships to every corner of the civilized and the uncivilized world too.
He saw the pigtailed sailors, parrots and monkeys riding their
shoulders, and he recalled how carefully the commission merchants

and the prim bankers avoided them. He saw the fat, respectable, matronly housewives shudder aside as the tarts passed, for that was a time when for every two honest women in the town there was one that was a little less than honest. He saw the swaggering students from Cambridge, arm in arm, blasphemously singing, "Study is the most original sin!" And of course, he saw Sam Adams. You could not take a walk through Boston along Orange, up Newbury, through Marlbrough, then around past King's Chapel and over to Hannover along the neck without running into the old man and having him buttonhole you and say, in that close, inviting, confidential way of his:

"Now what do you hear, Reuben?"

"A ruddy sunset," if you were one of them, and Reuben Dover was from the beginning. Then the old man roared with laughter and squeezed your arm in a way that made you want to do anything for him.

"Working?"

"On and off, Sam. If the ships don't sail, you don't need rope, and that's the mighty hell of it."

"Sure, Reuben." It wasn't just that he seemed to feel for you, he did feel for you. "Who takes the ships from the port—they or us? But I tell you, there are other uses for a prime piece of cordage. A mill turns on rope, and you can pull a cannon with a rope harness —and, do you know, I have even heard it said that a man can hang on the end of a rope?" It came as a question, and questioningly the pale gray eyes regarded you, the big, square face gently curious, the big square nose inquiring rather than aggressive. Only the mouth was round and full and sensitive as well as sensuous, and knowing. . . .

Then in his mind's eyes, Reuben Dover saw more, for he passed the day with Sam Adams and walked on to the Old Wharf, where the ships lay in every stage of construction, some with just ribs and keel, like herrings picked clean, some with flesh over the ribs, and some all decked and ready for the launching. One year merged with another, and as he dreamed, looking into the flames, he put the years together haphazardly, the good ones with the bad ones, taking from them what he wanted. So it was that when he came to the shipyards, they hummed with work, and men put down their hammers, saws and planes to wave to him and ask him how it went in the walks.

Rope to rig them, cloth to sail them, food to stock them and men
to man them. Then they would dance over the waves like girls to
their lovers and across the whole world the yellow folk and the
brown folk and the black folk would see the colors of the Massachusetts Bay Colony.

He shook himself awake, wiping the moisture from his eyes, and
muttering, "He should a perished then, and what good was it for
him to go on living, when I met up with one who had seen him
in Boston, sitting by the window of his house, his spittle dripping
and his hands so palsy they couldn't hold—and never a word of
sense out of him, except when you called him a Jacobin, and then
the old pride flowed back into him for a minute, God granting him
that—"

"Who?" the glass blower asked.

"Why the old man, Sam, who else? He lived a proper life," Reuben said. "He did what he had to do and what he intended to do.
And what he had finished, he had finished, that's all."

"And when was that?" came gently.

"To put your finger on it? As a moment? You know, I think I
could do it—and I'll tell you of it, too, word by word. It was in
'seventy-five, and he was already by then fifty-three years old—or
was it fifty-four? Well, I don't know and it don't matter, does it?
There he was, anyway, riding his horse across the ploughed fields
of Andy Simmons—"

"When was that, Reuben?" the glass blower inquired, for Reuben
Dover was nodding over his rum as he spoke, tending to wander
and live through the scene himself, without much thought for the
others.

"I told you in 'seventy-five."

"But when? On what side of the year?'"

"I told you in April!" Reuben shouted, sitting bolt upright, but
the Dutch farmer wagged an uncertain finger at him and said:
"Now you did not—not at all."

"And when would it be but in April?" He looked from face to
face, and then he smiled, the wrinkles spreading all over his dry,
leathery features. The landlady came up then, pulling a stool alongside his chair, and once again Reuben noticed what a fine figure of
a woman she was, a ripe plum with clothes like the peel, for all of
her years.

"Shouting," she said. Her voice was deep and filled with honey, but maybe Reuben was drunk and a woman's voice would be like that the way he felt now.

"In April, I told them," he said.

"Yes—and look at the time." She pointed to the tall clock in the corner, and the hands were coming together for midnight. "Would you burn every stick of wood I have?" she wanted to know.

"And how would you have us keep out the chill, woman?" the glass blower wanted to know.

"There are other ways," she answered, smiling at Reuben, who smiled back at her, just as graciously.

"Time enough," he said. The clock began to strike, and he cocked his head, and then they all listened until the twelve chimes had sounded out. "I'll cut you wood in the morning. I'll cut you a cord and stack it up as high as your nose. Now have a drink with us and I'll tell you about that April."

She poured rum from a pitcher, a tot for herself too, and sat on the stool, stroking a cat that cuddled in her lap. She hummed a little, the soft sound of a country dance, which Reuben didn't mind at all. It made a sound together with the roar of the blaze, and he wet his throat and told about that sweet April morning, with the sun coming up all red and clean in the east, and the crows flying and cawing, and the beads of dew all over the fields.

"It could have been yesterday," he said, and they nodded, all of them being old enough to know how time makes its way. "It could have been yesterday, and I had a place three miles from Lexington, south over east, where there used to be a stone mealy mill—" But they didn't know the land, being New York bred, and he said, "Well, there it was anyway, and I had a rotten few acres where you broke your plough on the rocks, so when I heard that shooting begin, like frozen twigs snapping, I say to myself, there it is, Reuben, and time enough too. Here's up and off and something doing, and I'll leave ploughing to them as wants it. That's what I said to myself, and I pulled on my britches. What are you up to? my wife says. What am I up to? My land, I'm up to making something and making it prime. Prime. So I took down my gun, a handsome musket of the French make, and I filled my pockets with ball and I took me a bottle of powder, and out I went—with her shouting after me that I hadn't heard the end of it yet—" He chuckled to himself over the memory. "Hadn't heard the end of it yet—"

"Where you at now, Reuben?" the glass blower demanded. "You started out with Samuel."

"And I'll be at him. He comes along. He comes along with that son of a bitch, John Hancock, the two of them riding hell for leather until Samuel sees me."

"What?"

"Why don't you keep your ears cocked? I told you before he came across the fresh ploughed field of Andy Simmons. Never was much of a rider, either, if the truth be told, just hanging onto the saddle and glad enough to pull up when he sees me. Come along, Hancock says to him, and Samuel answers, What do you mean, come along? This here's an old friend of mine, Reuben Dover. Then he says to me, a good day to you, Reuben; and I say, Good morning to you, Samuel, and what was all that commotion I heard?"

"Just like that?" the Dutch farmer grinned, slapping his knee.

"Just like that."

The landlady smiled her warm smile and remarked, "I never known one yet connected with that war that wasn't the biggest liar in the nation."

"All right now," Reuben answered her patiently. "What is a lie and what ain't a lie? Twenty-eight years ago, that was, and the man who says he remembers this and that was said, literal, why he just talks big. Nobody remembers that way, and also it's proper a thing should ripen a little, the way a good wine does, and while it's a ripening, you want a little coloring, the way a painter does, and that's proper—wholly proper."

"Wholly proper," the glass blower agreed. "What I seen, with summer marches and winter camps, and suffering until you wouldn't know blood from tears, my children won't never see—and for their kids, by God, maybe they won't never hear of it even; for what are they saying already of old Samuel but that he was just a dirty and cantankerous old man? What we seen, it was just normal for then, but it ain't normal for now, and you got to dress it a little."

"Just a little," Reuben defended himself. "But I tell you I remember that morning just like yesterday, and when I ask what it is with all that snapping and crackling, the old man says, gunfire, lad, gunfire. It's gone and happened, he says, and the dead are stretched out on the green grass in the most unholy way, and there's going to be a terrible anger all over the land. That's what he says, him who brewed the anger himself for fifteen years—. And I brewed a little of it too," Reuben nodded.

"But he was going the other way," the landlady reminded him.

"Sure, and I said to him, How is it, Samuel? Well, he said, I made it, and I'm off to tell the Congress a little about it. So I asked him, You going to miss the fighting? Miss it, he says, why there's going to be a bellyful for everyone, and I won't miss none of it! It ain't finishing, it's starting. So I waved him goodby, him and Hancock— who I never liked—and I ran North and found them at the bridge. . . ."

"Was you at the bridge?" the Dutch farmer asked.

"I was. I was that," Reuben whispered. "In at the first, and in at the last."

"Time for bed," the landlady said.

"You seen him again?" the glass blower wanted to know.

"I never seen him again, may he rest in peace. That's why I say, he could have died then. A man should know the proper time for packing his things and going off."

"A fine way to talk!" the landlady snorted. "Such a lot of talk, and where does it get to? A fine thing. Now go home—go home now," she said to the glass blower and the Dutch farmer. She bustled around them like a big hen and then she let them out of the door. Only Reuben Dover was left, he and the cat; the cat had curled up on a warm stone of the hearth, and Reuben Dover sat with his elbows on his knees, and his chin in his palms, looking at the fire. Perhaps ten minutes went by while the landlady made things fast for the night, and during that time, Reuben examined the past in the flames with a growing sadness. It was true, he reflected, that life was a moment; it came and it went, and the great treasure of youth was gone from you even before you made a full acquaintance of it. Then you filled yourself full of rum to loosen the strings that tied up your memory, but you never talked what you thought, and the rare goodness and courage of those you had known defied you. You babbled and that was all.

By the time Reuben Dover reached Albany, he had already come to the realization that he would not continue on to Boston, that he would not stand over Samuel Adam's grave and pay his respects, that he would not ship out in a square rigger for all the youthful and wonderful places of the world—but that he would go back to his farm and accept the scolding of his wife and the pitying looks of his children, and that he would go to church and listen to the pastor's sermons on the Godless, and he himself would lock his own godlessness within him. He realized that youth is for the young and that youth is a land no one ever revisits. He realized that this journey upon which he had embarked so lightheartedly was a strange contradiction in itself, for more than a journey to do homage to anyone, it was a desperate and rather pathetic search for those things which had animated him so long ago; and he also realized that an old man could not solve the essence of a betrayal so enormous.

A number of things brought him to these realizations. Only the two men he had spent that first night talking to were interested in either him or Samuel Adams. In places where he stopped to eat or sleep thereafter, he was a bore, a tiresome old man. Twice he was roundly insulted, and at Cohoes, where he announced himself a Jacobin, a glass of beer was flung in his face, and when he fought back, a blow in the head laid him out flat. At Cohoes, too, the Merchant's Association had a Jacobin hanging in permanent effigy and now a card was put on his neck naming him Sam Adams; and after his beating, Reuben lacked the courage to tear it down and despised himself for that lack of courage. At Albany, a newspaper carried a story entitled: "An Intimate Exposure of the Frauds and Thieveries of the Late but Not Lamented Samuel Adams." And these were just a sampling of many small but telling incidents. Yet even all of these together did not explain the bitter sadness of Reuben Dover, which he later entered in his journal in this fashion:

"I take this opportunity (he wrote) having taken no other, of paying my own tribute to my olden Comrade, Samuel Adams, may he rest in peace and without disturbance. For I have set out on a long journey to make some gesture to him, yet never completed that journey at all. My intent was to go to Boston, but no farther came I than Albany. Never finding along the way respect or consideration for the virtues I knew and labored for, I have no heart to continue more but will return now to my home.

"I must take note of the way this nation has changed, so that the Young are not brought up with honor for those who took the situation as it was and made from it a Revolution. Nor do citizens in the fullness of their life recall the splendid trials we endured. Rather do they embrace what was mean and narrow in the Yankee than the shining things that seem now so seldom. The honor of men who worked with their hands and their tools is now turned into dishonor, and to ask a wage for wife and child is to be called a Jacobin. To speak a good word for old Samuel Adams, that too is termed Jacobin, and it would seem that the brave People we knew are lost to us. I do not hold that way, for many of them must be in the towns and the countryside, and I think they will rally again as they did once. But who is to call them when those of us who remember are so old? I saw in Albany the new Smelting Mill, and the men who went in there to work took their children with them, holding them by the hand. No head, it seemed, was lifted with pride. The little children walked in shame and the grown ones too. And at a Goodsmill at Shineyside, I saw the same. I saw beggars in the streets and I was stopped by hale and hearty men who whimpered that they had no work.

"I can do honor, but what is the use if not to the living! I turned home because my part is finished and this land does not greet old men."

THE ANCESTOR

You would have to understand the word *Puritan* to comprehend the ancestor. Later the word came to mean something else, something more specific, and in this land of ours something rigid and hard, shaped by the very stones that appeared to obscure the earth. But it had no defined and exact meaning at this time, which was in the fourth decade of the seventeenth century. It did not mean particularly a church or a sect—or even yet the rolling, indomitable ranks of Cromwell's men; it did not mean that you were either in or out of the established Church of England; it was a way of life being defined, a manner, a curse to some, a liberation to others.

It was the way young Henry Adams was, who held about seven acres of land from the Manor of Baarton St. David under its lord, George Alvin, to begin his seven names, who was a fop and a fool, even in circles that were noted for neither morality nor brains. It was in the manner of Henry Adam's stance, which was erect, tight, and even arrogant, but in a new way to the Lord who, observing him once, asked of his overseer,

"Who is that who stands like that?"

"Adams who holds the Coldhill cottage."

"Is he a king that he stands like a king?"

"He's no king, my lord, unless the devil crowns kings."

"Which he does, I have no doubt. What is he then?"

"One of them."

One of them was something in England beginning, growing, spreading, shaking everything that had established castles and manor houses to be the way of life forever and forever. It wanted a new way, and it was ugly, threatening and inevitable.

"Is he? Then fetch him here," the Lord said, and then watched the way Henry Adams came, the slow, reluctant spring of his steps, the back that stood like a ramrod held it, the dark, broad, sullen face, the close-cropped hair, banged at the top of the forehead. The sun shone over the wooded and lovely park and over the treeless hills beyond, but the Lord shivered as if he was cold. The Lord tried to recall how he had not noticed this man before, being that he was born and brought up on the place, and then the Lord realized that there was much he had not noticed before this chill wind began to blow through England.

Then the man stood before him, and the Lord said,

"What do you do?"

"I plough the land," was the slow, high-pitched nasal response.

"With no more courtesy than that?"

The man's dark eyes probed with neither courtesy nor fear.

"Have you no other address for your Lord?"

"I know of one Lord," the farmer answered stolidly, unemotionally, "and he walketh by mine side."

"What?"

"He walketh by mine side in everlasting glory," the farmer repeated stolidly, the words contrasting oddly with his stone-like attitude.

"What does the clod mean?" the Lord addressed the overseer.

"He denies you and quotes book."

"He denies me?"

"That is what he means, my Lord."

"You deny me?" the Lord asked. "Am I not your liege?"

"Nay," the farmer said simply.

"And how many lashes to make you say yea instead of nay?"

"I'll take no lashes unless they are ordered me in court," the farmer answered, unperturbed.

"You are a proud man, and maybe too proud for a sod."

"I am a humble man," the farmer countered, "and I will bear no lashes unless they are ordered me in court."

"They will be ordered you," the Lord replied.

Twelve days later, he sat as magistrate and summoned Henry Adams before him. As a justice of the peace, the Lord felt inspired by the notion that a simple sequence of punishment would not only silence this stiff-necked man but might very well put down the whole curse of Puritanism that was sweeping the countryside, and might particularly influence a nearby squire, another of "God's chosen people," who affected homespun dress, close-cropped hair, and a constant castigation of the Lord's morals and way of life. Whereby, the ruler of St. David heard three witnesses against Adams:

"I saw him poach."

"He cut a hare and I found the entrails."

"His wife cooked up the stew, which I heard from Miller, which he heard from Cooper."

It was flimsy evidence at best, and the dark face of Henry Adams clouded over with rage. "What have you to say?" the Justice asked him, and he answered, "They lie."

"I think you be too stiff-necked in your words and too imprudent," the Lord said. "You and your kind have a new way of making the lie out of anything that does not come from you. Soon you will want the whole of England."

"I have done nothing in crime," Henry Adams said. "I am a God-fearing man and keep God's law. I do not poach; am I some dirty thief that you tell me I poach with the testimony of pimps and hirelings?"

"They only do their tithing," the Lord said patiently, since he could well afford to be patient.

"Their cursed tithing," Henry Adams said, "that has made out of all our folk a community of informers and Iscariots. What kind of fires do you stoke?" he cried, raising his voice.

"Enough," the Lord said. "I have been patient enough." He prided himself as a lawyer, which he was not, even to the extent of the ordinary squire. "I could put distraint or escheat upon you, but I give you lashes instead. I give you thirty lashes to make you humble. Then thank God your ears remain."

So the ancestor was given thirty lashes, and with a bleeding,

lacerated back returned to his stone cottage, his wife, his nine
children and his worldly goods. But from that day on he was
different, and it got about that he had met with a number of other
yeomen and even a squire—all of them of that peculiar persuasion
that was yet neither church nor movement, but a way of life and a
hatred, *puritanism*, that took fire as its weapon and the Lord God
as its ally. They had no secrets because the system of *tithing* or in-
forming, long established, brought all news to whoever was master.
But they had something that was more potent than secrets; they
had a fierce and righteous conviction that the old way was over and
done with and that the future belonged to them. And slowly but
insistently they were gathering their forces to take hold of the
future.

The ancestor was a stubborn, stiff-necked man who was driven
by what some would call perverseness and others a fanatical in-
ability to compromise with the principles he had come to live with.
The Lord God had put weapons in his hands with which to defy
authority, level aristocracy and drive out whatever devils Rome
might send. That his whole world was changing, that a new era of
commerce and industry was being born, and that the forces within
this new way were powerful beyond resistance the ancestor did not
know. He was a vessel in which the wrath of God dwelled, and he
was not minded to inquire as to how he had become that vessel.
What he was, he was; what would come would come.

His wife might have suffered, his children too; be that as it may
be. We don't know what his wife, Edith, suffered or if she did, but
only that she was the daughter of another farmer, dead by this time,
whose name was Squire, and that he had given her away without the
maritagium. That was a marriage fee that was already archaic, a
purchase price to the liege instead of the right of the first night,
which had been fought down long past. But when the ruler of St.
David heard that meetings were being held by those whose close-
cropped hair was already giving them the name of Roundheads, he
called before him once again the stiff-necked farmer Henry Adams.
By now, it was a vendetta which he was compelled to pursue, and
by now, in the mind of the ancestor, who read one book over and
over until he knew almost every word of it by heart, this Lord of
the Manor was indeed and literally Pharaoh. As Moses had come
before Pharaoh, so did he come before the Lord's court.

"Pay me the *maritagium*, which is long overdue," the Lord said.

"It is not mine to pay or any man's to pay. What manner of free men are we to pay a fee to take a lass to wife. She has born me nine children and now you come to me for the fee."

"I am not disposed to argue that point. Is your back healed?"

"It will never heal," Henry Adams answered.

"All flesh heals," the Lord smiled.

"It was not the flesh that was seared but my immortal soul."

"And how would your immortal soul feel about distraint?"

The farmer said nothing but his black eyes never wavered from their keen, unblinking scrutiny of this man who was persecuting him. To repeated demands that he pay a fee long outlawed, he kept silence, and then he went home. But that same evening, the Lord's men came, and they picked the farm clean. This was distraint. They took his stock and his feed and his crop and his tools and even his dogs. They took the furniture from his home and the clothes from his small wardrobe. They took the pewter dishes and the copper pots. In other words, they took everything except the clothes off the backs of the man, the woman and the nine children; and they left behind them varying degrees of grief except in the man Henry Adams.

So does Pharaoh serve those who are stiff-necked, but God has his own way of serving Pharaoh. Adams called his family around him and said to them.

"We will go away out of this place, but first there is something I must do. All of you set out *now* for Squire Aldrich's place, and he will shelter you until I join you, and that will be before morning." It was ten miles across the moors to the farm of this squire, who was a leader of the Puritan people thereabouts; but the family knew better than to argue with the father when he spoke like that, and they did as he told them to do.

They went in tears and sorrow, weeping as the children of Israel had once wept when they left behind them the fair and goodly land of Goshen and fared forth into the wilderness to face they knew not what; but the man who was left behind moved through his empty house with dry eyes. What the Lord of the manor had taken away in distraint were but things, and what were things for a man to weep over? Aloud he said, as he stalked through the empty house and the lifeless barnyard,

"The Lord God is my rock and my salvation, and I shall not be afraid. I shall not fear. Naked and with only my two hands I came into this world, and naked I am now, with only my two hands, yet they serve the Lord God of hosts, in his righteous anger."

And indeed he felt such cold and righteous anger as would not be unbecoming the fierce and just God he served. He looked at a pigpen from which the pigs were gone, at a chicken coop from which the chickens were taken. Contemplatively, he examined a sheep fold that was bare of sheep, a stall bare of horse. All was gone; all was bare by distraint. Well, he had his own manner of distraint, and he thought of it aloud, since at this moment he felt compelled to share his bitter reflections with the only being he acknowledged as his superior.

"I will wipe this land like dirt from my feet," he said, "for it is a cursed and lousy land. I will go away to the wilderness where others went before. Better in the wilderness with the savages than in this cursed land."

But first there was that which the distraint had failed to unearth, and from the corner of the barnyard, Henry Adams dug up a clay pot which contained forty golden crowns. Protest and prudence went hand in hand; lightning will strike from the heavens, but only a fool expects gold from the same source.

Then, with the money tucked securely away under his belt, Henry Adams set about to do that which had to be done, and by the time he was high on the moor, cutting over to Squire Aldrich's place, all of the sky behind him in the direction of the great manor house was lit with a ruddy glow. Thus, his heart eased by justice, his soul lightened by a fair vengeance, he trudged along to reclaim his flesh and blood.

Even from the Aldrich place, the great fire at St. David's was visible. Not the manor house, but all of the barns, cotes, bins, silos, pens and stacks were a burnt offering; and the Squire said, with a grave face,

"I know not what devil you have raised, Henry, but you go away and I am left here to put it down."

"I do not go from fear but from hatred of this place and this land."

"Then go tonight," the Squire said, "before the chase starts. I hate this Lord of St. David as much as you do, but I have no stomach for burning and destroying."

"Was I to bear what he did in silence?"

"There are other ways," the Squire muttered.

"I knew of no other ways," said the ancestor, "but if you want me to go, I will go."

"I will give you a wagon and a driver to bear you and your family to the sea, and I will lend you money."

"I want no money," Henry Adams said stiffly, with little enough grace. "I thank you for your hospitality and for the wagon, I will pay. I will take me and mine and go to a seacoast town—and then to a place where things are different from here."

And that night the ancestor went, with his wife and his nine children—on the long, long journey to the place called America.

THE CHILD AND THE SHIP

The child was then eleven years old, and if you must have a time, it was the year 1733, in the town of Boston in Massachusetts Bay Colony. The ship came from the West Indies, to where she came from the old country, a dirty old bark that still could make enough money for the owners, and she came sailing into the harbor like a monster from hell.

A bark is a three-masted sailing ship. Foremast and mainmast are square-rigged, and the mizzenmast, which is the shortest mast, at the stern of the ship, is rigged fore and aft—in other words, two booms carry a sail slung between them, and this can be swung and set any place in a full arc of a hundred and eighty degrees. This was the kind of a ship which sailed slowly and not too well into Boston harbor, and the boy saw it. Who would not see it? The boy was on Union Street, and the ship pointed north around the Long Wharf, and people ran from everywhere like crows flapping down on a cornfield. An old sailorman, Jack McKinney, an Irishman and therefore scum and dregs and dirt in that town at that time, called out to the boy: "Hey there, Sam'l, and what in hell's name do you suppose they are running for, what they got nothing better to do, them fine folk!"

They were fine folk too, as well as others, the merchants out of their shops in their velvet caps, and the fat ladies of quality in their little lace aprons, and the old deacons and the young apprentices. The ropewalkers and carpenters and wrights came more slowly, with a different kind of dignity.

"There's a vessel, there is," young Samuel answered, proud to be singled out for an inquiry by a man as unrespectable and exciting as wicked Jack McKinney, whom he had seen at other times lying dead drunk in the gutter and again with one of the fat, toothless prostitutes who were such a disgrace and plague to the town. Now they stood where there was a break in the houses and a narrow run of vision down to the bay, and the boy saw the ship framed there an instant. He had grown up on terms with ships of every sort. "Stinking old bark, she is," he said. They were already part of the drift to the waterfront. "Bad language makes for a bad one, now, young Sam'l. It ain't fitting." Samuel said, "No, sir, Mr. McKinney, but there is something funny about her." Then, when they came past the hogpens where Faneuil Hall would be raised up seven years later, the child saw what was funny about her. They crossed Merchant's Row, and there was the bark standing in drunkenly, with the fore and aft booms swinging loose and crazy, and with a little boy—and no older than this child, Samuel Adams—hanging from the upper one. And from the yardarms of the two forward masts, four other men hung, their bodies swollen and ugly and torn where the birds had fed upon them.

Boston of that time was a hard city, and in her there were some hard men, and what else would you expect from a place that had scrabbled its own bed out of the wilderness only a century before, with no guarantee to anyone except the odds that he would die under thirty? But if she was hard, she wasn't hard enough to see this unmoved, and there was a lot of vomit cast up by people who saw that child's body swinging back and forth like the pendulum of a clock. The child Samuel Adams pressed close to the sailorman Jack McKinney, who folded his big horny hand around the boy's little one, holding the lad close beside him and protectively, but not sufficiently the master of his own curiosity to turn away—as was no one else either.

And the bark moved in as the crowd of people gathered on the dockside to watch her. Many a small boat pushed toward her, but you could see that these bumboat peddlers and bottom fishermen had no urgent desire to get onto that dirty old ship, so reeking with death, even though there were those on board who were alive. Now the people on shoreside could see them, the helmsman on the stern deck, the captain beside him, the sailors sullenly—and that was plain from every movement they made—and poorly working the

ropes and canvas, some passengers in their shore clothes close together on top the midship housing.

"Why that's the *Larkspur*," someone said, and everyone agreed
and wondered why they had not recognized her before.

"And that's old Ebnezer Saxon," someone else said, pointing to
the captain, "by God, it is, the wicked old sinner." "And more to
answer for too, and many a day to spend in church before he makes
God or the citizens forgive this," another said. But still another
said, "What happens on the high seas is not what happens on the
hard earth, before you make judgment." But many made their
judgment just looking at the child's form.

His Majesty's customs palavers with ghosts, if the need warrants,
and they ran out and stood under her side. Captain Hixby went up
and spoke to Captain Saxon of the *Larkspur*, and those with good
eyes—and young Samuel's were very good indeed—could see the
vigor with which Captain Saxon pounded one fist into the other
palm, and they could also see the obedient nods of Hixby. The
Larkspur had no motion now, just lying broadside to the shore and
not too far off, making for Samuel and everyone else a convenient
stage for drama. Thus Samuel, all sick and shaky and terrified and
excited, saw how the customs man pointed at the little boy's body,
and how Captain Hixby pointed at it too, nodded his head and then
pointing from one to another of the sullen seamen, and then calling
to one of the passengers who came down from the housing and
joined them. Then the three spoke, Hixby pounding palm with fist
again and the customs man uneasily pulling at his lower lip and
scraping wax from his ear, and the passenger judicial and sober.

Then young Samuel began to cry, and McKinney, moved by a
sudden tenderness, gathered the boy up in his arms and carried him
away to a little inn by the Old South Church, where he bought him
a small beer and talked to him soothingly. For McKinney did not
have to see any more. He knew the story, all of it, and what detail
he was not aware of would be supplied him a hundred times over
for many weeks to come. And anyway it was a commonplace story,
and some sense, some strange intuition, told the Irishman that this
was no commonplace boy at all.

"But why did they want to kill the lad?" Samuel asked him.
"Will they kill me?" he added anxiously.

"If you did what the lad did, Sammy, why sure and make no
mistake."

"What did he do?"

"Ah now—and that's still a matter of conjecture." The Irishman had a large, long, bony face. Samuel could see how tight the skin stretched over the bones, weatherbeaten skin that was traced over with the red finery of broken capillaries and made a nest of wrinkles for each of the little pale blue eyes, a hard, savage face he had always thought when he was somewhat afraid of Jack McKinney; which he was not now, but rather warm inside with the small beer which he had never tasted before. Perhaps a little drunk too, which was the sin of the old sailorman. Now Jack McKinney stroked his head and answered gently, "But I conjecture pretty good, huh, Sammy, I tell you, Sam'l, you ask a pretty deep question, all right, when you ask what he did. He did wrong, Sammy. Wrong for you? Now what is right and what is wrong for you, just a shaver and never out of Boston, which is just a bit of a town and would never be noticed even a mite in one of the old countries. Wrong for me? Well, now, I'm an old evil one, and going to burn my fill too, Sammy, for what there ain't no redemption, none at all, considering the sin I sinned. But, you know, Sammy, sometimes I say to myself, maybe I never sinned no sin what I would call it. But I don't know, Sam'l, and that's the round world of it. And how shall I say that the little lad, God rest his soul, did wrong. I ain't no preacher, am I, Sammy? Come along—let me see a smile out of you."

"You ain't no preacher, no," Samuel said, smiling.

"And don't you go home and tell your bonny mother I fed you small beer, or every cursed Christian in this town will have the whipping of me, and me in the stocks soon after too."

"Are you no Christian then?" Samuel asked.

"Hah!" The Irishman drank deeply of his beer, smacked his lips, and wiped his mouth on the sleeve of his shirt. "Tastes good, Sammy, and calls to mind too the hot days I spent in the stocks of this same cursed town. For what? For not being no Christian, so they give me Christian treatment, thirty or fifty hours in the stocks with never a spot of water, never saying beer, to wet my poor cracked lips and my poor swollen tongue. Ah, it is a hell of a life that a sailing man lives, Sam'l, with a dry mouth on shore and a dry mouth on sea, too, where all is water. Now what is a Christian, Sammy?"

"Don't you know?"

"Do I know? That ain't the point, Sammy. Do you know? A good

Christian, I tell you, is Captain Saxon of the *Larkspur*, him that hanged a little lad from the boom for the birds to eat! In this town, it is a blue-nosed Puritan what's a Christian, 'begging your pardon, Sammy. So I ain't no Christian, am I? Only fit to put away in stock if I have a wee little bit too much. But the mother and father of me was Roman, Sammy, which even I ain't, since I was never confessed or given the Sacrament these twenty years. No. I am no Christian, Sammy, and I don't lose no sleep over it. I will burn in hell properly, and maybe a fine, good lad like you will say a prayer for me, a candle being not permitted in that dry barn you call a church. But I tell you this, Sammy, there will be some fine folk burning with me. . . ."

He cocked his head at the boy, who looked back at him with wide, terror-stricken eyes. So would the lightning, proper partner for the hellish thing he had just witnessed, fork down from heaven and consume this iniquity! But instead, the sun shone.

"And the *Larkspur* was a proper Christian ship," the sailorman went on. "Proper, Sammy. You asked me how I knew what had betaken her. I conjectured from out of experience, laddie, and don't you never go to sea. Mother of God, I could take off my shirt and show you, in the many raised welts on my poor aching back, a history all right. The dirty miserable food, the lashes, the work, the freezing cold, the dry time when she's blown off course and no water no more, no more, the scurvy with the teeth a-dropping out, the wet that goes into your bones when she storms—and work, Sammy, such work from the poor body of a man. Sometimes you vomit it up, like they musta done on the *Larkspur*, and that is mutiny, and the punishment is death. But if you want to make a mutiny, Sammy, out of your terrible misery and despair, you will want a gun, won't you? And where are the guns, Sammy, but in the captain's cabin and in his fowling chest? And who can get to it but the cabin lad? So he must be one of you, the poor motherless, lost lad who has no childhood but only the bitter years at sea. So you entice him, Sammy—God forgive you, you entice him—and his tender little heart bleeds for you, and he does your will. And then, when the mutiny is put down, like always the revolting and striking of scum like me is put down, you got to pay the price. That's right, Sammy—that's proper. He who dances must fair enough pay the pipers, and every one of them, Sammy. So that is why you see the little lad hanging from the boom, hanging out there in the hot sunshine, while his soul races off to hell for the terrible wrong he done."

Only then did the Irishman realize that the white face of Samuel Adams was covered with tears. In a fumbling and awkward way, he took the boy's small hand between his big, coarse ones and fondled it, and remembered a lad of his own who had died of the pox, and said, "Bide your own way, Sammy, in quiet and peace. Don't take heed of what is said of adventure and far places, for it is all a rotten curse. Stay at home, Sammy, and make no revolts—for when you strike out against what makes you less than a man, there is always a lash for the back and a rope for the neck. Now heed me, Sam'l."

It was wrong to say that all and anything that happens to a child is of great consequence—and as wrong to say that nothing that happens to a child is of great consequence; and this was a child who lived in a world of ships, where the land was only shelf for the ship to nuzzle to, but who did not take ship? There began somewhere at some time in this child, in his mind, in his blood, in his heart, in the whole of him, a series of less than thoughts and more than thoughts, patterns perhaps, for there is no precise way of describing the formation and growth of what is sometimes called personality and sometimes character and sometimes other names as foolish—but is actually a fire the world stokes and then sometimes in return sets the world on fire. You will have to look hard to find the *Larkspur*, and it doesn't matter; for once the boy saw a carriage roll over a mouse, just seeming to touch it but killing, even though the mouse was able to kick and squirm and make tiny mouse cries of terror and anguish and pain, and the boy, picking the mouse up in his two hands and holding it close to his face, thought that in all his life he had never heard anything so heartrending, and as the life went out of the mouse, he pressed it against his cheek, filled with the sense of suffering and hurt that he shared with the world, not in equal guilt but in equal sufferance.

The child sat at home at table with his mother and his father and his sister and his brothers, and each and all knew that a ship terrible and horrible had come into Boston Harbor, but to each it was different and to none as it was to him. "Blessed art thou, oh Lord our God, King of the universe," said his father, in a rough and

homely grace, stripped, as he so often put it, of the swinish filth
of that iniquity of iniquities, the High Church of England, "who
layeth our board and giveth us bread to grace it." They said,
"Amen," and one of them then said, "Who saw the ship?" knowing
they all had seen it.

"There will be no talk of that," said Samuel Adams, the father,
and the son, Samuel Adams, said, "I saw it."

"With the black, heathen Irishman McKinney," said his brother,
with malice; and in the child there were the unspoken words,
"Damn you, curse you." His eyes probed at his brother who was
soon to die, in a time when few enough grew to manhood; the
memory of sickness goes, but the memory of hatred festers and
lingers; and while the two children stared at each other, the father
said stolidly, "This is a house where God is not unwelcome and we
do not talk of godless things. No ship came into Boston harbor
today. A ship of inequity is no ship."

Large jawed, big-boned and righteous was the father, Samuel
Adams; he was a fierce and God-fearing man and he had done well
in the world—justice of the peace, deacon, selectman, representative
of the people on one hand and the Almighty God on the other, a
merchant of means, a man who conducted his business with a word
bonded by the sword of the angel Gabriel, a man of substance and
property, he could be understood better by what he hated than by
what he loved. What he loved was unspoken and often unrealized
in the conscious parts of his mind, but what he hated he catalogued
day in and day out; English he hated, the sound of the London
language, the men who used it, and the high Church they worshipped in; he hated Rome a little less, and he hated the Irish
who deserted ship and profaned the Boston streets and worshipped
images, even as the Children of Israel did when they heeded not
Moses who led them, and of all folk in all the past, he loved Moses
best. He hated the whores who multiplied in the streets day by
day, and he hated the red Indians, the black-eyed somber men who
wandered in from the wilderness like a conscience in motion; he
hated the West Indian rum that cursed his land, and he hated all
men who wore the uniform of His Majesty's regiments, even as he
hated His Majesty and all the crowned "scum," as he put it, of all
time back. These and much more he hated, but what he loved he
had never formulated; he was not a sensitive man, and when his
children spoke, he often as not hardly listened. So the name of the

Irishman McKinney echoed in his mind for a time before he reacted to it, slowly then, fixing his pale eyes on the child who bore his own name.

"Samuel," he said.

"Yes?"

"You were with the Irishman McKinney?"

"Yes," said the child.

"Can we not eat in peace?" the mother asked, a thin and ailing and tired woman.

"There will be peace," the father said. "Peace, Mary, comes with the truth. And what is the truth, Samuel?"

"I went with him to look at the ship," the child said.

"Through the public street?"

"Yes."

"And you knew that you walked with a handman of the devil?"

"Yes," Samuel whispered.

"But it was not the child's doing," Mary Adams pleaded, "and if the child didn't know, it was not the child's sin."

There was a frozen, timeless silence at the table, and even the brother who had betrayed him was awed and crushed by what he had done. Calvin and Wesley stood one on either side of Samuel Adams, the father—who stared so somberly and thoughtfully at Samuel Adams, the child, and to the mother there came a phrase from the book that was so knit with their lives, *and he hardened his heart against him.*

"And he hardened his heart," she said to herself over and over.

The father then said, "And this is a just household, Samuel— heed ye, we walk in justice and in righteousness. Perhaps he enticed you?"

The child could not speak; but he moved his head from side to side, just a fraction, just a trifle.

"Cozened you? Wheedled you?"

"No," the child whispered.

"Threatened you?"

No answer.

"Dragged you?"

"No," the child managed to say again.

"Then you walked with him of your own free will, through the public streets."

"Yes," the child admitted, with no sorrow, no regrets, no resentment, but only a projection of himself into the image of the lad who swung and swayed from the yardarm. And also no sorrow and no fear when the father rose and motioned. In the midst of the meal, the two departed, so that justice might be done according to the lights of the elder, but for the younger justice was a thing forming in a riot of troubled impressions and doubts and wonders.

The town was already old, a century old in this new land, and the men of the Massachusetts Bay Company who had put it there were all of them dead and gone and many of them forgotten too. The town had the aspect of something old and established, perhaps more so than would ever again be the case in the future. Only an occasional citizen whose imagination was a little more vivid and active than most would pause to think of how the great and endless wilderness swept away westward from this town, a green sea, unknown, untouched, unexplored, unchanged, crossed only by the narrow, moccasin-beaten trails of the red men and filled with all manner of wild beasts. If you looked at the town with that in mind, you would have realized that it was just a scratch on the shore; but that was not the point of view of the child, born and raised in the town. For him it had always been here, since he could not accept emotionally what he knew intellectually—that a group of men had come from a share-holding company in an old country called Britain, and that they had planted the few shacks with which the town began. His sense of time was not yet developed to a point where he could wholly accept such a thing; he saw the town as it was in the moment of its being.

He had crept out of the house, and the town lay there in the spring moonlight, in the gentle, sweet New England evening, all black and all over with a ripe velvety sheen. The great silver-blue moon sailed in the heavens and its trail coursed across the bay. The town was old and homely and lovely in that moonlight, with all the hard edges softened away and ancient too, and for the first time in his life, the child was able to make a conscious appraisal of the relationship between himself and his city. His heart filled with wonder and love and awe, and he was able to put into words a feeling that this was his place and he was able to realize himself as a plant that had sprung out of this cobbled earth. The sense of identity flowed through him like heady wine, and he felt like he walked on air as he moved down toward the waterfront. He felt that he would like to touch every piece of wood in every house in this town, and the sleeping folk in the houses communicated to him. He felt a song in his heart that was nameless and wordless but which he knew very well indeed and would never forget, and now, in this moment, the future was assured and resilient and ready to be kneaded, like a wet lump of clay. He remembered the Irishman McKinney, and he felt a great pride in his ability to know people and like them and understand them—and no fear for the sin he had sinned. Sin would not trouble him again.

So he thought as he came onto the dock and curled up against a tangle of rope and looked out over the bay to where that awful ship floated. Still, the bodies hung, and the boy looked without fear at the obscene thing that had been done to the living.

But horror, already muted, was less horrible in this caressing moonlight, and the child who had paid with his life for acting in the mutiny was familiar by now. From the child on the dock, there went out a current of love and sympathy to the child on the yard-arm, and sitting there, Samuel Adams wept softly and without fear or pain for what the other had suffered.

The
Vision of
Henry J. Baxter

There's no doubt about it," Mr. Baxter said to his wife, Clarise, at dinner that night, "the Russians have the H bomb."

"I don't believe a word of it," his wife answered calmly, raising her voice just a little to span the expanse of mahogany table that lay between them.

"I'm afraid you have to believe it, my dear," Mr. Baxter said gravely. "I was talking to Somerville out at the plant—he's heading up that new atomic project we've undertaken for Washington, and there's a cool ten million in it if there's a penny—anyway, I was talking to him, and he says there's no doubt about it, they have it, and he should know, my dear."

"But it's impossible, Henry," his wife smiled, helping herself to the buttered peas that the butler was holding at her side. "I do like buttered peas. I think there's no vegetable quite so delicious. Do you know that the Thompsons have a new West Indian houseman. They brought him back from Kingston. They're right when they say you can't find help in this country any longer. Not competent help. He has the most charming accent. It's impossible, Henry."

"What is impossible?" Mr. Baxter frowned.

"That the Russians should have the H bomb. They're just savages. It's like saying that those blacks who have been causing such trouble for the planters in that place—oh, what is that place I mean, Henry?"

"Kenya?"

"Yes, Kenya. It's like saying that those awful people have the H bomb. Only last week Mr. Eugene Lyons lectured about Russia at the women's club—really, Henry, it would do you good to listen to our lectures once in a while—and he certainly did not paint a picture of a place where they would have the H bomb. Why they don't even have shoes, and the whole nation walks around practically barefoot, and Mr. Lyons should know, since he's spent his whole life studying what's wrong with Russia."

"Nevertheless," Mr. Baxter said doggedly, "they have the damned H bomb."

"Then they must have stolen it. It shows what comes of having atom spies all over the place, even in the White House when that Mr. Truman was there."

"Clarise," Mr. Baxter said grimly, "people like you and I are going to have to re-think this business from beginning to end. They didn't steal it. They had the damned bomb first."

Usually, Mr. Baxter had no trouble sleeping, but this night he rested poorly. He had a dream about being atomized, and it hurt even after he had dissolved into the constituent energies of his being. He became a pain-filled cluster of neutrons, and he awakened with a film of sweat all over him. Mr. Baxter was only fifty-three years old, and not long ago his doctor had gone over him from head to toes, and had informed him that all things considered, there was no reason why he didn't have thirty good years head of him. "And I'm damned well going to," Mr. Baxter announced aggressively into the dark silence of his bedroom.

Mr. Baxter liked to think of himself as an active captain of industry, and he had nothing but contempt for rentiers, dilettantes and playboys who were content to bounce or wobble through life while they lived on their incomes. It was his pride that he went to his plant five days a week except for two months of vacation each year, and that he had gone to it five days a week for some twenty years now; and he could point with the same pride to results. His father had left him an ancient, dilapidated plant which employed some five hundred men and existed with a profit that never passed a million a year and often enough shrunk to almost nothing. The plant he drove to this morning covered twenty-six acres and employed seven thousand men, and for the year 1954, each share had paid eleven dollars and twenty-two cents. Let General Motors match that.

Mr. Baxter sat down at his desk, glanced at his mail, flicked the switch that opened the intercom to his secretary, and told her to send Mr. Somerville to him as soon as Mr. Somerville could come, which meant immediately.

Mr. Somerville was a ten thousand dollar a year man with three children, and he wore loose tweeds, black horn-rimmed glasses and a worried look. If he weren't a scientist, he would be earning twenty-five thousand a year in his managerial capacity, but Bob

Herman, Mr. Baxter's personnel director, did not believe in spoiling scientists and was of the opinion that even at ten thousand a year they got out of hand, and since Mr. Baxter shared his deep distrust of intellectuals and since Somerville was constitutionally unable to assert himself—the more so now that the word scientist had become practically synonymous with subversive—his wages remained stationary, regardless of his position. He entered Mr. Baxter's sumptuous office with a look of apology, and at Mr. Baxter's nod, seated himself in front of the desk, facing Mr. Baxter.

"Had a bad night, Somerville," Mr. Baxter began, "thinking about the damn bomb. It's Mrs. Baxter's opinion that they haven't got it. Shrewd woman, Mrs. Baxter. Not on the surface, but women have an instinct about things."

"Not about this, I'm afraid," Mr. Somerville said apologetically.

"What?"

"I mean, sir, that there's no doubt about them having a hydrogen bomb." From the expression on Mr. Somerville's face, one would think that he had personally handed the bomb over to the Russians. "I mean, sir, that there's no room for doubt in these matters. You see, Mr. Baxter, it's not a question of information or intelligence or spies or anything of that sort. We derive our information from instruments. The instruments can't lie."

"But Senator Howland says the whole thing's commie propaganda and that the Russians couldn't make the bomb in fifty years."

Mr. Somerville sat silent; he didn't want to put his disagreement with Senator Howland on the record.

"But you're convinced?"

"I'm afraid every scientist working in atomics is convinced, Mr. Baxter. Even the president is convinced, I hear."

"I wonder what it does to his game?"

"Sir?"

"His golf game, Somerville. Old Harrison at Consolidated lives for golf. Plays almost every day, and plays a pretty good game too. He tells me he picked up eleven strokes since this H bomb business started."

"It's quite provoking, sir."

"Provoking puts it mildly. It's a god-damned blunder that someone ought to pay for. Well, what's done is done. Is this bomb all they say it is, Somerville?"

"I'm afraid so," Mr. Somerville admitted sadly. "If one were dropped properly in Connecticut, let us say, it's fallout would destroy every living thing in the entire state."

"The devil with Connecticut. What would it do here in Ohio?"

"Well, Mr. Baxter, that depends. Suppose a little cobalt was added to one of them and it was dropped here in the lakeside vicinity. If there were prevailing north winds, it would have just about the same effect."

"You mean one bomb would kill everyone in Ohio?"

"Yes, sir, and the cows and the ducks and the pigs, too. And the wheat and the corn," Mr. Somerville added, unable to contain his bent for precision.

"I'll be damned."

"It's a remarkable weapon," Mr. Somerville said with a note of enthusiasm.

"I'll be damned. Do they know all this in Washington?"

"Oh, yes, Mr. Baxter. They've published some very fine material on the subject—scholarly material."

"Well, why in hell's name don't they do something about it?"

Mr. Somerville reflected that perhaps there was nothing they could do about it, but he did not voice that opinion, knowing full well that as a scientist it was not his place to meddle in politics.

"Of course, we could do the same to Moscow," Mr. Baxter added as an afterthought.

"Yes, sir—indeed we could."

Mr. Baxter knitted his brows and stared at Mr. Somerville. For almost a minute, he sat like that, staring silently at the scientist. Then he burst out, "Damn it all, you'd think those fools in Washington would drop everything else and set about building shelters. What about that, Somerville?"

"It's not quite as easy as it sounds, Mr. Baxter. An ordinary air raid shelter, such as they used in the last war, would be worthless. Even deep subways are quite useless."

"I don't mean a direct hit, Somerville."

"We can no longer even think in such terms as a direct hit," Somerville said, inspired as he always was when it came to expounding a scientific point to Mr. Baxter, and even more delighted that Mr. Baxter was willing to listen. Usually, Mr. Baxter's reaction would be not to bother him with the damn details, but to go ahead and get the thing into production. But this time, it seemed, Mr. Baxter wanted details. "You see, a hit is direct enough within a ten mile radius, and atmospheric poisoning may extend to a hundred or two hundred mile radius, depending upon the constituent factors of the bomb. Theoretically, it is possible for a single cobalt bomb, with proper wind currents, to destroy every human being within the continental United States—theoretically, of course, but not very likely. Still in all, we can't think in terms of direct hits and avoiding them. That's probably what has Washington so baffled."

"And how long does this atmospheric poisoning last?"

"We really don't know, never having faced such a situation before, but guesses vary anywhere from a few days to a few centuries."

"A few centuries?" Mr. Baxter gasped.

"Oh, yes, sir—yes, indeed. Of course, surface life of any kind might not survive, but life would go on in the depths of the sea, and eventually the normal course of evolution would resume, and it's even conceivable that one day, billions of years from now, man would appear again."

"That's damn comforting," said Mr. Baxter.

"Of course," Somerville added thoughtfully, "a self-contained shelter could be built. It would have to be quite deep, sealed off from the surface, and prepared to supply its occupants for at least five years. That presents a number of problems, but I suppose they could be tackled and licked. Yes, it's an interesting problem."

"And what do you suppose such an outfit would cost, Somerville?" Mr. Baxter asked greedily.

Mr. Somerville would have preferred a month to work it out, with estimates from various builders and exact costs on every item, but he knew that Mr. Baxter wanted his questions answered immediately, even if not too accurately. So Mr. Somerville leaned back, closed his eyes, and figured at top speed, while Mr. Baxter preserved an unusual and interested silence. Finally, Mr. Somerville said, "I think it could be done for three million—that's not an accurate figure, of course, but it shouldn't cost a great deal more."

Mr. Baxter's lunch in Cleveland that day was with Harvey Ramson, who was sixty-eight, who had made a cool fifty million out of an aircraft industry he had developed since the war on government orders, who knew everyone in Washington, and who had just returned from a special job in Washington. He called the president and every member of the president's cabinet by their first names, and they called him Harvey. Mr. Baxter stood in a certain awe of Harvey Ramson and his opinions, and therefor managed in the course of the luncheon to ask him whether he thought there would be war with Russia.

"Got to be, sooner or later," Mr. Ramson said. "Got to be a showdown. The whole free world and the American way of life's at stake."

But didn't the H bomb make a difference, Mr. Baxter wanted to know?

"Don't believe they got it, and if they got it, don't believe they know how to get it off the ground. No technology in Russia, no know-how. A land of peasants."

But if they did have it, Mr. Baxter insisted?

"Got to wallop them before they get it off the ground. Massive retaliation—that's the word for it."

But somehow, "massive retaliation" was less than satisfying to Mr. Baxter, and once again, he slept poorly. This time, however, instead of nightmares, he had a dream which he afterward thought of as something of a vision. Not that he ever mentioned this thought to any of his friends, but there it was. He dreamed that he stood on a high peak, with his wife beside him, his two sons and their wives and children, his daughter; and the world lay dead and silent beneath him. Then a voice said, "Go and make it fruitful." A fine voice, and it was a lovely dream. Henry J. Baxter woke up feeling refreshed and at peace for the first time since he had heard about the cursed bomb.

"Clarise," he told his wife at breakfast, "I'm going to build an air-raid shelter, self-contained."

"I think that's very thoughtful of you, Henry," his wife nodded. She had no idea that the shelter would, according to Mr. Somerville, cost about three million dollars.

For the next twenty weeks, Mr. Baxter was absorbed in the building of the shelter. He built it on the grounds of his lake-front estate, which covered three hundred acres, and gave him all the privacy he required. Mr. Somerville himself designed it, and they employed the three brightest young engineers in the plant to expedite its construction.

But about the bright young engineers, Mr. Baxter often felt as he did about the various managers of his plant. They were all right, but it wasn't their plant; and while these bright young engineers were all right, it wasn't their shelter they were building. Mr. Baxter stopped going to the country club and spent long hours compiling

lists of things a large family would need for several years in a shelter.
He was amazed at the endless number of things required to continue
the Baxter family in the style to which it was accustomed—and he
was also amazed at his wife's attitude.

"If you think I'm going to spend five years down in that hole and
do my own housework, Henry," she said firmly, "you've got another
thought coming."

"It's not a hole," Mr. Baxter said coldly. "It's every bit as good
as the one Ike has under the White House, but you can't go adding
rooms to it."

"Yes I can," countered Mrs. Baxter. "Either you install servants'
quarters, or leave me out."

"For a quarter of a million dollars?"

"What?" Mrs. Baxter looked at her husband as if she were seeing
him for the first time. "Henry, just what is this shelter costing us?"

"About three million dollars without the servants' quarters."

"I think you've gone out of your mind," she whispered—which
came as a surprise, for it was the first time he had ever known
Clarise to be concerned about money.

"You won't think so when those H bombs begin to drop."

But what Mrs. Baxter thought when her husband cancelled their
European trip and even intimated that until the bombs began to
fall, there would be no more trips for them, does not bear printing.
For two weeks, she did not speak to him, but it is questionable
whether he realized that, so deeply was he involved with the shelter.
He sat up a whole night with the grocery list. He read five brochures
on vitamin pills before he ordered the twenty thousand that he felt
would be necessary, and he regretted a hundred times that he had
not trained one of his sons to be a physician. He pored over seed
catalogues in order to select the germs that would once again make
the earth fruitful. He called in experts on livestock and experts on
horticulture, and he read the pages of his favorite magazine, *U. S.
News and World Report*, more carefully than ever before seeking
for inside information as to the imminence of war; for now, as the
shelter neared completion, he felt that he was involved in a desperate race with time, and it made him sick at heart to think that they
might start throwing the H bombs before he was ready.

Strangely enough, his hatred of communism, which had at one
time been outstanding, even for an Ohio millionaire, began to cool.
The Russians had provided what was now the prime motive in his

life, and at times he felt rather warmly toward them. He was becoming more and more religious, and he began to believe that in his dream, he had met God face to face. Even that long sought after dinner at the White House, which Harvey Ramson had promised to arrange, paled into insignificance against this.

Meanwhile, his beautiful meadows on the bluff overlooking the lake had been turned into a construction site. Great steam shovels bit deeper and deeper into the ground. Wooden forms rose in the gaping hole, and an endless stream of concrete poured down to provide security for the Baxter family. Tractors lumbered back and forth and steel girders swung on booms. The temporary slack in construction in Northern Ohio was taken up with Mr. Baxter's vision, and hundreds of men brought paychecks home each week and turned them into food for their children and clothes and rent; but of all this Mr. Baxter was superbly unaware. And when finally the form of the massive underground house which could survive even a direct hit of a hydrogen bomb took shape, Mr. Baxter's mood could be compared to one of actual ecstasy. Everyone at the plant, his friends, his associates, his wife—everyone noticed the change in him, the manner in which he held his head, so straight and confident, the way his eyes shone, the way his voice had become, so soft, so knowing.

One September evening, when the shelter was almost complete, as Mr. Baxter stood near the elevator that led down to it, admiring the concrete result of his vision, a quick autumn thunderstorm blew out of the lake. Mr. Baxter ran for shelter, but the rain overtook him before he reached his house. On the garden path to his den, deluged by sheets of water, his foot slipped, and he fell and struck his head a resounding whack on the flagstones. He lay there in the rain for more than an hour, and it was only when he failed to appear for dinner that his wife sent the servants out to look for him. When they found Mr. Baxter, he was quite dead and already cold.

All of his children and grandchildren came in for the funeral, and for the reading of the will. He had told them nothing about the shelter, for he had intended to inform them only after it was complete, and now Clarise thought it better not to mention it at all. She looked very youthful and beautiful in black, and while she bowed to all the conventions of sorrow, everyone remarked on how well she looked. The will allocated the lake place and some five million dollars in securities to Mrs. Baxter, the other interests being divided among the sons and the daughter, and Clarise, who had never been a greedy woman, was quite content with her share.

Clarise waited three months before she left for Europe, and in that time, she did her best to sell the lakeside place; but the air was full of talk about negotiations and banning the H bomb and no one wanted to invest three million dollars in a self-contained shelter. In the south of France, Mrs. Baxter met an Austrian count, whom she married in what her children thought was an indecently short time—and it was remarkable how much attention the count, who had never been a business man, gave to her securities. When he discovered that her lakeside property had been reassessed to a value of four million dollars, he persuaded her to let it go in default for the taxes—and the county simply boarded it up and let the acres of lawn go to weed. The hermatically sealed elevator began to rust, and the twenty thousand vitamin pills lay silently, waiting vainly for someone to gobble them.

Sometimes, Mrs. Baxter had wistful thoughts of her first husband, Henry; but whenever she found herself giving way to feelings of guilt, she imagined five years in the self-contained shelter, and that stiffened her spine. As for her second husband, the Austrian count, with five million dollars to spend, he never gave a second thought to the H bomb.

Only Mr. Somerville was really regretful. He had been sure that science combined with American know-how could lick a direct hit by an H bomb, and sometimes he felt very sad because Henry J. Baxter never really had a chance to test his theories.

The Children

CHAPTER ONE

Up the street, slowly, Ollie swaggered, his head cocked, his hands in pockets bulging with the immies he had won. Because he knew he would win again; he knew he could go on winning until there wasn't another immie left in the world. He selected a round beautiful red glassy, and tossed it away. That was the way Ollie felt.

The world was full of hot sunlight and red brick walls, and the world, stretching from avenue to avenue, was held in by the walls. Maybe that was why Ollie loomed so big, because the world was so small. Big and small, big and small; but, until something larger came, Ollie was king. He knew he was king, and he attempted to walk like a king, brushing back his long yellow hair from his eyes, throwing back his head. Still, it was an easy world to be king of now, dozing and hot, and all sort of vague. Ollie was conscious of that vagueness that came in the middle of the summertime; it made him too lazy, even, to fight. It was easy to be king, and if nobody wanted to fight, you didn't want to fight yourself. What then?

He rattled his immies, and then he noticed a little Jew sitting on the curb. Dimly, as a king, he knew that the little Jew's name was Ishky.

"Hey, yuh stinkin' kike!" Ollie yelled good-naturedly.

"Hey, Ollie."

"Wanna fight?"

"Naw, Ollie."

"Wanna shoot immies? Aincha got none?"

"Yer a shark."

"G'wan, I ain'."

"Y'are."

"Awright, den—gimme yer immies."

"Aw, Ollie," the little Jew began to beg.

"Yuh heard me."

"I'll play yuh."

"Gimme dem," Ollie commanded. Again he brushed back his yellow hair, weaving luxuriously. The sun was hot; it is never so hot as in July, and no matter how many times they wet the streets, it does no good. You can't cool streets when they become hot as the summer sun.

Then Ollie walked away with four more immies. He was eleven years and two months, Ollie was, with yellow hair and blue eyes. He was a king, his eyes twinkled like the blue sky, and he was beautiful.

I didn't hate Ollie, because he was beautiful—not like Ralph the Wop; I just sat there after he had taken my four immies, and after a little while the hot sun made me feel better inside of myself. There was a big hole in my shoe, and there was a hole in my stocking, too, so I could see my large toe, watch it as I moved it about from side to side and then up and down. There was the toe and the street and the sun, and anyway I would have lost the immies sooner or later.

Ollie was lazy and rich; otherwise he might have taken a sock out of the little Jew bastard. But when Ollie was lazy and rich, he became big; it wasn't hard for Ollie to become big.

Now it was the morning, only half-past nine in the morning, and all of the long hot summer day stretched ahead. For Ollie, there was adventure in any one of a thousand possibilities.

Now, almost at the avenue, Ollie could look down the block. It was long—or maybe Ollie was small and the block was not so long. But the block was his, and if he stayed on the block he would be king. He wouldn't be king anywhere else; anywhere else he would have to fight his way, and when you fight, you take your chances on winning or losing. His pockets were full of round beautiful glass immies; the day was young and bright, and the spirit of adventure was hot inside of him.

He stopped to tease a cat. The cat was yellow and white; as soon as it saw Ollie, it arched its back, drew its four feet together, and began to yowl and spit. The cat knew Ollie; Ollie knew the cat.

"C'mere," Ollie said.

The cat lifted a foot, daintily, warningly.

"Pussy—pussss—"

The foot wavered, and then it wavered a moment too long, and Ollie had the cat. By the scruff of its neck he lifted it, swinging it back and forth.

"Dere, liddle yellaw bastard—dere, whaddya goin' t'do now? Whaddya goin' tuh do now I got yuh? Whaddya goin' t'do?"

The cat whimpered pleadingly, clawing feebly with its feet. It was an old cat, without a great deal of spirit; and it knew Ollie. Vaguely, in its cat's way, it knew that Ollie was king. What are you to do with a king, if you are a cat? If you fight back, in the end it doesn't matter, because otherwise the king wouldn't be a king. So what are you to do?

Ollie swung the cat in a great circle, and then he sent it flying through the air. Catlike, it landed on its feet, and again it paid the penalty for being an old cat, for Ollie was upon it, kneeling next to it. Spreading its paws, he turned it over.

"Hey, Ishky!" he screamed.

Ishky looked at him. Ishky had admired the battle with the cat. When it came to cats, there wasn't anyone like Ollie.

"Hey, Ishky, c'mere."

Slowly, warily as the cat, Ishky approached. You could never tell about a king, or what new kind of devilishness he was up to. You had to always watch and watch. That was how life went on, otherwise it would not be endurable at all. Only if you watched, and even then you were caught plenty of times.

"What?"

"C'mere, Ishky—lookit dis cat."

"What?"

"Betcha, it's a she cat, Ishky?"

"Maybe."

"Betcha—betcha I c'n tell if it's a he cat or a she cat."

"Maybe."

"Betcha you can't."

"I dunno."

"G'wan an' putcha finger dere, Ishky. Feel aroun' an' see. G'wan an' do it, Ishky."

"No . . ."

"Whatsa matter? Yuh yella? Whatsa matter witcha anyway? Geesus!"

"I ain't yella, Ollie. Hones', I ain'. Oney it's dirdy."

"Well, a liddle dirt ain' goin' tuh killya."

"You do it, Ollie. I'll hol' duh cat."

"Yuh ain' got guts tuh."

"Well, lemme showya, Ollie."

Ollie glanced up at him, hesitated, then nodded. How beautiful Ollie was, with his yellow hair and his blue eyes. Those two, the most beautiful things in the world, yellow hair and blue eyes. Yellow hair like silk or spun gold;—and Ishky was looking at the yellow hair, and that was why the cat sprang away, and for no other reason than that. The hair is beautiful and fine, and the eyes sparkle like the sky; if the sky is inside of the eyes, could you expect any less than that from Ollie? But the cat got away.

"Oh—Ollie."

"Geesus Christ, yuh liddle Jew bastard!"

"I swear I din' mean tuh do it, Ollie."

"I'm gonna beat duh ass offana yuh."

"I din' mean it, Ollie."

"Put up, or do yuh wan' me tuh giveya lumps?"

"I din' mean it, Ollie."

Ollie got tired of hitting him; after all, he was a king, and what was the use of fighting, when the person you fought with didn't fight back? What was the use? So Ollie left him and wandered around the corner. There was a garbage can there, full to the brim, and smelly. First, Ollie took the cover off. Then he ran at it and kicked it. The can went over, and the garbage spilled into the street. For a little while, Ollie kicked the garbage around, but he tired of that. He stood in the sun, in the garbage, hands in his pockets—

Alert, defiant, laughing inside of himself, Ollie was. Let the land-lord come out, or the janitor. The janitor was a wop, and Ollie hoped he would come out himself. He split an overripe melon with his toe, scattering it onto the hot stoop. Laughing, he showed his white teeth. Let the whole world come out of the house, and it would make no difference to Ollie.

The janitor came out, raging. He was a small man, with long black mustaches, and part of a breakfast egg was still on his cheek.

"Dirdy Irish louse!" he screamed.

"G'wan, yuh dago bitch!"

"Bummer!"

"Piss on yer cheek."

Then Ollie fled, laughing and waving his arms.

I was hurt more because Ollie had hit me than from the pain of the blows. What are blows? Blows pass, and then the pain is gone. And the pain inside of you? Well, that passes, too, I guess. I guess that all things pass, because in the end I don't remember too much. I just remember what is nice.

My name is Ishky, and even that is contempt. But there isn't con-tempt inside of me. Could Ollie dream the way I do about things that might happen, but don't? It is early in the morning, and everything is clean and beautiful and warm, and I am happy to be alive. I am happy even after Ollie hits me, only—

Why didn't I hit back? I thought of doing it. No matter how much Ollie hurts me, if I hit back, it's not so bad. But instead I stand there and do nothing at all, and then I begin to cry. And why is that so?

But I don't know, and, anyway, how long should I think of that when the sun is so bright in the morning? And Ollie is gone. He's gone off the block, which is what I mean when I say that he is gone.

I sit down on the curb again, and I find a little piece of wood with which to disturb the water that runs in the gutter. There is always water running in the gutter, brown and black water, wonderful water. But any water is wonderful. Don't I know that?

CHAPTER TWO

On the block then, and it wasn't so long ago, there was a division in this way. At the top, or east end, there were Americans, real old Americans, and their fathers had been American, and their fathers —nobody knows how far back. They lived in the four houses at the top of the block.

Then there were the Jews, in two houses, two small red houses. They had a certain sense of apartness, because they lived so near to the Americans.

The Italians were all in one brown house, a little shabby brown house, yet there seemed to be more Italians than Americans and Jews together.

The Spaniards were scattered here and there, and the spick gang was nothing at all, because even the Jews could beat them up.

In the middle of the block, in wooden houses, the Irish lived and ruled. They could fight like hell. You were always very careful of the micks, because they could fight like hell. Even the little shanty bastards who had nothing at all, could at least fight like hell.

There were Negroes down the block, and everyone said that it ruined the block to have black folks there, but who could stop the Negroes from coming? You never knew what was what, and then all of a sudden there were a lot of little Negroes on the street. They simply came from nowhere at all, and of course everyone said that it would ruin the block in the end. But they did no harm; they weren't people to go around picking fights.

There was more to the block than that, fences and railings and dark halls, and cellars—ah, what cellars there were, deep ones, and strange ones, and silent ones.

Mostly life was battle, battle from morning to night; it was strange how you went about, just living. But wounds heal quickly, and it is easy to forget. Even when you are hard hurt, you heal quickly.

Sometimes, there is peace. That is how it was this morning nearing ten o'clock, hot and beautiful as only a summer day could be. Low hanging, the sun made shadows with the houses. There were birds pecking their breakfast from the street.

CHAPTER THREE

If only I had a beautiful name, like Arthur or Daniel. But I'm Ishky—and that's all. I knew it then, when she came to the stoop and stood there.

She had a small white dress and a blue ribbon, and she was the most wonderful creature on the block. Her name was Marie, and she was an Italian with long yellow hair. You can only imagine how beautiful she was, because I can't tell you. But she had the kind of eyes that are like flowers.

She was looking for Ollie, not exactly looking for him, but looking at everything on the street, wondering whether, perhaps, Ollie would be some part of it. She was afraid of Ollie—still.

There was nothing on the street now but Ishky and people who were grown. Ishky sat on the edge of the curb, his feet in the gutter, his head in the palm of one hand; with the other hand he stirred the murky water that ran beneath him. To Marie, he seemed aware of nothing at all—unless you would call the water that ran beneath him something. But why was he concentrating upon the water?

Marie looked at the water—plain murky water. And she tossed her head. There was nothing there to look at. Yet Ishky took on a new attraction, simply because he was looking at the water.

Marie stepped gingerly down to the sidewalk. Twice, she skipped; then she crossed the street. Then she walked in a circle about Ishky. Ishky's face burned, but he stirred the water with the same intense concentration.

"Whatcha got dere?" Marie demanded.

"Jus' wader."

"Whaddya doin' wid it?"

"Playin'."

"Whaddya playin'?"

"Jus' playin'."

Marie sat down next to him. She knew he was a Jew. When you were very close to a Jew, you felt kind of funny about it, if you remembered he was a Jew. Anyway, all the Jews were funny, funnier than the micks.

She looked at him. His shirt was dirty, and his shoes were full of holes. His toes stuck out. The Jews were very poor, but she knew they had money hidden away. Everybody said that they had money hidden away, only they never spent it. They kept it, and each night the counted their piles of gold. That was one of the queer things Jews did.

"It's dirdy," she said.

"I know. No good tuh drink."

"C'n I play?"

He turned around to look at her. He had brown eyes, curly hair, and a very thin face. But his face was flushed and red, and his mouth half open. And when she looked at his face, she thought of Ollie, though she didn't know just why.

"Yuh wanna?"

"Whaddya playin'?"

"Jus' playin'. Y'wanna play?"

"Gimme yer stick."

He gave her the stick. She was so beautiful that he would have given her the world, had it been his; and he was happy. He was happy just to sit, lazy, in the sun, with her next to him.

That was all he wanted. He could see how the sunlight sparkled on her hair.

Then she threw the stick away—tossing it out into the gutter.

"Dat ain' no good."

"Yeah, I guess so."

She threw an arch sidewise glance at him. He wasn't so much, but anyway she wasn't afraid of him, like she was of Ollie. Only Ollie wouldn't sit on the curb and do nothing at all. They said that a Jew could just think of being a Jew, and that was enough.

"Whatsit like t'be a Jew?" she wanted to know.

"I dunno."

"Like bein' Christian?"

"Maybe."

"C'mon over duh stoop," she said.

They walked over to the stoop, sitting down there again. Shyly, he reached to her hand, hesitated, and then took it. Warm and small, it rested inside of his, and she glanced at him, raising her upper lip.

"Yuh mustn' do dat."

"Why?"

"It's bad."

"I don' wanna be bad."

Calculatively, she looked at him, smiling just a little, her upper lip still raised over her gums. With a precise motion, she drew her dress down over her knees. She turned away; then she looked at him again.

"It's like lookin' at a nakid lady," she said.

"It ain'."

"Dincha never see one?"

"What?"

"A nakid lady."

Ishky stared at her, at her yellow hair and her wonderful blue eyes.

"Wanna see one?"

Ishky was running across the street. She stared at him, unbelievingly, and then she waved her arms over her head.

"G'wan run, yuh dirdy Jew!"

You see, that was Marie, whom I loved then. Maybe I love her now, since that was not too long ago.

But where is the summer day? Everything is gone—except that I am still Ishky; but everything else is gone.

The beautiful song inside of me went. I ran into the hall, where it was dark and comfortable, and I sat down against one wall. Nobody would think of looking for me there, but who would want to look for me? Through the darkness, I stared at my fingers, counting them. One to ten—they were all there. Why did my fingers make so much difference?

But Marie— If I only could tell her some of the things I know, she would not be the way she is; for Marie is beautiful and perfect and fine. If I could tell her of the secret garden. . . .

I read about the secret garden somewhere, and then I began to look for it. A beautiful garden, where you simply have to be happy. I knew it was somewhere.

Behind our house, there is a yard, surrounded by a high wooden fence. To get into the yard, you go through the cellar, and then up a little flight of wooden steps with an iron railing. You open the cellar door, and you are outside in the sunshine, and in front of you is the fence. And just at the bottom of the fence, a little grass grows. I knew the secret garden was there, though I had never been there.

If I could tell that to Marie—

We could both come and stare at the fence. If you have a secret word, a door in the fence opens, and then you are in the garden. I saw myself walking in the garden with Marie. Of course, there is more sunlight there than anywhere else, and what a picture the sunlight would make of Marie's hair and face! There would be flowers as blue as her eyes and as red as her cheeks. . . .

But that's dreaming—no more than dreaming, because I'm here alone in the hall, hiding from Marie. And what if Marie should come into the hall here, looking for me? What if she should?

Jews were funny. . . .

Marie screamed after him, "G'wan, run, yuh dirdy liddle basted, g'wan an' run away!" And then she stopped abruptly, sat down with her hands in her lap, and then she began to cry. She didn't know why she was crying—except that she satisfied some desire inside of her. But she would have to cry a great deal to satisfy it completely.

Still crying, she rose and walked up the block. She crossed the street, and then, quickly, she stopped crying, rubbed her fists into her eyes. Ollie was coming.

Ollie swaggered down the block, his hands in his pockets. She didn't like Ollie, but how can you help admiring Ollie when he swaggers like that?

"Hey, Marie," he called.

"You lemme alone, you Ollie."

"Aw, Geesus, Marie, I ain' goin' tuh touchya. Whatsa matter witcha, anyway?"

"Yer allus fresh. You lemme alone, y'hear?"

"Awright."

Ollie stopped in front of her, his legs spread, his hands still in his pockets. He smiled slyly at her, his handsome face knowing and sure, and then he took a handful of something out of his pocket. Whatever it was, it sparkled and gleamed in the sunlight.

"Whaddya got?"

"Wouldncha like tuh know?"

"Aw, lemme see, Ollie." She stared eagerly, then threw back her head, laughing. "Jus' immies."

"Beauties."

They were red and yellow and blue, and the more she looked at them, the more she wanted them. Slowly, she reached out her hand.

"Git away."

"Jus' gimme one, Ollie."

"You git away."

"Jus' one."

Ollie seemed to consider. In his role of king, he was not above being benign. First to one side, then to the other, he cocked his head. He swayed back and forth, perched on the balls of his feet. He thrust out his hips, his hands in his pockets.

"Well," he said finally, "whaddya gonna gimme?"

"I ain' got nuttin'."

"Wanna come down duh cellar?"

"Nah."

"I ain' goin' tuh hurtya, hones', Marie."

"Whaddya gonna do?" She was wary and ill at ease. She knew what Ollie would do. She didn't want the immies, but they were an excuse for what Ollie was going to do. If she did it because she wanted the immies, that would make it all right. Then she wouldn't be bad, and she could say at confession that she had simply traded for immies. But not too quickly—

"How many immies?"

"All yuh wan'," Ollie said.

"Well . . ."

"Aw, c'mon."

When I went down in the cellar, on my way to the secret garden, I saw her with Ollie. But I guess no matter how much you are hurt, you heal quickly. But if you are hurt too much—what then?

CHAPTER FOUR

Now you would think, wouldn't you, that because of this, I, Ishky, would never laugh again. I thought so myself then—until I came out into the warm sunshine. How warm the sunshine is in the summertime, and how good! There is no school, nothing but the whole day in front of you to lazy away, and if you want to do one thing or another, nobody will stop you.

A little spick was running up the street, waving his arms, and screaming, "Aily-baily, a bundle of straw, fartin' is agin' the law!"

"Shuddup," I yelled. "Shuddup, yuh dumb liddle spick." I was bigger than he.

Shomake was standing in front of his store. Shomake is as old as I, maybe, and we call him that because his father makes shoes. I don't know what his real name is. Nobody does.

He waved a hand at me. Well, I like Shomake. I waved back.

"Hey, Ishky!"

"Hey, Shomake! Wanna shoot immies?"

"Gotta practice."

Ishky crossed the street, his eyes lighting up. When he came close to the little shoe repair shop, he smelled the warm aroma of spaghetti, cooking in back. Behind the counter, the old man sat with his head bent over, swinging his hammer; he always swung his hammer like that, always.

"Gonna practice now?"

Shomake nodded his head, looking sorrowfully at Ishky out of oversize brown eyes. His face always appeared to be all eyes, and his skin was brown as a nut.

"Yeah."

"I'll wait."

They went into the back room. Out of the sunlight, there was darkness everywhere; the whole block was that way, darkness ringing sunlight. The back room was small, tight; they all lived and cooked and slept there. At the stove, Shomake's mother stood, cooking, and the smells of the spicy cooking made the air in the room so thick that you had an impulse to cut through it with waving arms. Shomake's mother was a black splotch, vaguely indistinct in the manner of grownups. She turned around to smile at them, and

Ishky thought that there was something wonderfully strange about her small white face in the dusk.

She said some words to Shomake in Italian, and Shomake answered back. Then he went into the corner and got out his fiddle. Small, bent over in a little circle, Ishky crouched on the bed, while Shomake pinked the strings of his fiddle.

"Whaddya doin'?"

"Toonin'. Dat makes duh sound right."

"How do yuh know?"

"Jus' listen."

Ishky wondered how he could see his music, it was so dark there. And he was so small and the fiddle was so large. Ishky waited, trembling a little.

The music whispered into the room, and the skin all over Ishky's body rose in little prickles. He flashed a quick glance at Shomake's mother, who now stood by the stove, very straight, swaying just a little. Then he looked at Shomake.

Shomake swayed, too, with the violin. His bow hand quivered, rose, fell, trembled.

And the music came. If there was a song of that day, of all the other days of childhood on that block, might that have been it? In the little room, black and full of smells, the music came. It came and mixed with the smells—and Ishky heard it.

That was long ago, or not so long ago, I guess. If I tell this story in three parts, the first part is of the children; in the other parts, the dreams begin to go.

I look at Shomake's mother, whom everybody calls "mudder wop." That is what they call her. She wears a black skirt and a black blouse, and she never wears anything else. She stands by the stove, and in the dark—which is light enough to show—there is an expression upon her face which I cannot help noticing, even if I don't understand. I see it, and I wonder. I am Ishky, but that will not help me understand what is meant by that expression. How should I know? Still, I am suddenly conscious of my clothes. My shoes are worn through. At the toes, the fingers of my feet poke out. Glancing down, I try to hide that. I try to pull down the toes, to twist them out of sight. But that is no good. Endless things must be hidden, holes in my long black stockings, wisps of hair on my head that need cutting, a loose tooth. I pull at the tooth.

"Oh, Ishky, you little fool, why don't you sit still?"

She stirs the spaghetti, Shomake's mother, with an even, calculated motion, but all the while she is looking at Shomake; and
what does she see that gives her that air of majesty?

That is what I want. If I had it, I would be a king like Ollie.
But I can't get it. I am just Ishky, quivering all over from the music.

Better for him to stop. Should I scream, "Stop you fool!" But
then, what would they think of me? Isn't it funny that I can't sit
for a little while and listen to music?

Spaghetti—spaghetti, and music, and the big wooden spoon goes
round and round, mixing. In the music, there is a beach! I read
about a beach in a book, and it has palms growing upon it. Tropics,
they call it, tropics, tropics, as all the time summertime on the block,
with dark rooms round, and spaghetti.

I watch the bow quiver; it dances. Why can't I do that? If I had
a violin, like Shomake— Just suppose that for a minute I hold
Shomake's fiddle. Will he let me hold it?

Stop—stop—stop, all in time to the music. Won't he ever stop?
Now his mother is a queen in my secret garden. No, just an old
wop lady. But Ollie takes Marie into the cellar to put his finger inside of her. Does Marie like it? Does Ollie like it? Does Ollie like
music?

"Stop, my heart," she cried in Italian.

"Mother mine, what is it?"

"See how the child sobs on the bed! By all the saints you have
hurt him with your music. Here, my child, my little one, what is
there in music that should bring tears? No tears, but gladness. Do
you know that music is the soul singing?"

Ishky curled on the bed, crying bitterly. When Shomake's mother
bent over him, anxiously, he pushed her away, shook his head. Shomake stood with his fiddle. What had he done? In all his heart, there
was no harm meant. Then what had he done?

"Lookit, Ishky, I ain' playin' no more."

"He gotta in duh cellar."

In her excitement, she spoke in Italian, fondling Ishky, caressing
him, and the soothing movement of her hands quieted his tears.

"What are you saying about a cellar, my child? There is nothing
in darkness to hurt you. Is it fear of darkness, here in this room of
twilight? Then quiet your fears."

"I'm awright."

"No, rest, my little one, and forget about the demons inside of you."

"Awright." He didn't know what she was saying, but it was nice to feel her hands smoothing his skin. That, his mother never did. It made him feel like a big cat, curling in the dark, and suddenly he thought of the cat Ollie had swung over his head. Now he was the cat, and he liked the idea of being a cat—just a big cat curling and comfortable in the dark. How long would she stroke him?"

"You like that. Yes, my little one, beatings hurt and soft hands soothe, and we must take the good with the bad. Look, I will sit down beside you. I do not think my cooking will burn." And to her son:

"Play, my heart."

She sat down next to him. How funny she smelled, of cooking and of earth-odors. But he didn't mind the smells. And now the fiddle played again.

I, Ishky, think that if I take Shomake and his fiddle, and we go together, we can climb the fence and find the magic garden. The music makes me think of that. I'm ashamed, because I was such an awful baby.

Now I close my eyes, so that I can think of the garden. If Shomake comes into the garden, and he plays, who knows what will happen?

But if there is no garden? If we go over the fence, and there is nothing there at all? What then?

CHAPTER FIVE

Shomake's mother gives us each a half of a roll, spread thick with butter. The butter is warm and soft and dripping, good on the white Italian bread, and we go out to the store to eat it. We sit on the bench. Behind the counter, Shomake's father works.

He's a strange man. Maybe he's a little crazy; I don't know, but he's a strange man. You see, he never says anything. If he can speak English, nobody knows about it. Nobody even knows whether he can speak in his own tongue, and some say that he is deaf and dumb. But I don't know, and I never could ask Shomake about it.

He sits and mends shoes. He's a big man—even when he's hunched over his awl, you can see how big he is, and how large and powerful his hands are. What hands they are! I think, if one hand were to grasp me about the waist, and squeeze and squeeze, why I, little Ishky, would be broken in two just like that. Each finger is a claw of steel, and the black hairs on the backs of his hands twist and curl like wires. He has a lot of hair, and his body is big and strong, and round as a barrel. But on his head the hair is gray; his face is gray, and his large wondering eyes are gray. That's the sort of a man he is.

But I like to watch him as much as I like to watch animals at the zoo. He hammers and cuts. But doesn't he think? If his wife strokes him all over his body, the way she stroked me, doesn't he think? And what does he think of then?

We eat the bread, slowly, because it's so good, licking some of the butter from the top; and sometimes Shomake's father glances at us out of his big gray eyes. Yet he doesn't seem to see us. How is that?

Even more slowly than I do, Shomake eats his bread, and he doesn't seem to notice his father at all. When his bread is all gone, he stretches his arms, yawning, and with the same motion his father's body quivers.

"Whaddya wanna do, Ishky?"

Ishky looked at him. He might understand, or he might not. Well, nothing lost, anyway.

"Y'know, behin' my house, duh yard?"

"Yeah?"

"Y'know duh fence?"

"Yeah?"

"Well, dere's grass unner it."

Ishky paused to let that sink in. This business of revealing the secret garden, the beauty and the power and the wonder of it, was becoming more than he had anticipated. How, exactly, could he put it to Shomake, so that Shomake would understand? He knew that behind the fence was the secret garden, but would Shomake believe him?

Ishky said, "Yuh know what a gaden is?"

"Yeah, wid flowers."

"Yeah, like dat. It's behin' duh fence in my yard, oney dere ain' nobody knows."

"Dat's funny. Howda you know?"

"I read in a book."

"Whatcha read—about duh fence?"

"About duh gaden, an' I can' climb over duh fence."

Rolling it over in his mind, Shomake nodded. That much was reasonable; for if the fence were high, nobody would know whether there was a garden behind it or not. And written in a book, it could not be anything but true. Shomake thought of the garden;—flowers, surely, and who knew what else? Fairies, perhaps, and any number of other things equally fascinating. He knew the fence, a high wooden fence. If it came to getting over the fence, no doubt they would find a way.

"Maybe," he considered, "dey won' led us in."

"Maybe."

"Is duh garden empty?"

"Maybe."

Then they went out in the street together, blinking like two owls in the strong sunshine. Then Ishky saw Marie and Ollie.

Marie stood near him; Ollie stood on the other side of the street. Marie just stood, staring at the gutter, but Ollie swaggered back and forth, never looking in Marie's direction. Her long hair curled down to her shoulders, and Ishky wondered what they could find in the garden, when here, outside, Marie was so beautiful.

"C'mon," Shomake urged.

"Awright."

But he stood looking at Marie—and he knew, without seeing, that Ollie had stopped swaggering, and was looking at him. And Marie knew that he was looking at her; she glanced up to meet his eyes.

How beautiful her eyes were, softly blue, and liquid as water. Why did he want the secret garden, if not for beauty? Then, briefly, Ishky knew what he was to know on and off for many years, that beauty is the truth of the world. He felt that he became bigger and bigger as he looked at her. Inside of him, the words came with a rush, soft words and beautiful ones. "Marie, you are my heart and my desire. You see, I know. You are the world and the skies, too. I could go and die for you, bravely."

"Whaddya lookin' at?" she wanted to know.

"Nuttin'."

"C'mon, Ishky," Shomake said. "Ollie's comin'."

"Leddim come."

Ishky knew that he was doomed. But if that's the truth, why then it pays to die for the truth; and life was not much after all, just bickering and fighting. He thought, "I love you, Marie, I love you, I love you. Don't you know that I love you, how I love you?"

"Lookit yer ass!"

Ollie came across the street. Aching inside of himself, he didn't want to fight with Ishky any more than he did with Marie. But he couldn't fight with Marie. Male and female do not strike one another. And Ishky wouldn't fight—

"Leava alone, yuh dirdy sheeney," Ollie yelled.

Ollie was taken off balance. Like a small dog gone mad, Ishky sprang at him, clawing and biting and spitting and kicking; and for a moment his tactics succeeded. Ollie went down with Ishky on top of him, and Ishky fastened his teeth in Ollie's small freckled nose.

"Wow—yuh dirdy Jew basted!"

Marie danced about in excitement. No matter who won, it was for her. All the fury and wonder of the battle surged into her little head. She had beauty, and that could turn the world over. Would anything else make Ishky fight with Ollie? Let them fight, let them fight!

Let the world go round—men must fight for women. "Aye—lookit dem!" she yelled to Shomake.

If his violin had been broken, would it have felt what he was feeling? First there was terror inside of him, and he whispered to himself, "Shomake, run, run." But he stood still, and then the terror was replaced with hot fury. What right—what right had Ollie, curse him for a little mick bastard, to do what he was doing to his friend Ishky? He wanted to fight; why didn't he fight? He wanted to pile on top of Ollie; the two of them together could surely whip him. But he didn't. He simply stood there, watching it. And then he began to sob. And then he could stand there no longer, and he ran down the block, sobbing as if the devil himself were behind him.

Marie screamed, "Run, run yuh dirdy wop! Killim, Ishky!" But she saw that Ishky would be beaten as he never was beaten before.

What made me fight with Ollie? Did I think I would win? but I knew that I wouldn't win, and I didn't mind him calling me a dirty sheeney. My God, if I minded things like that, I would be fighting with Ollie all the time, and what would be the use of that?

Now I am sitting on the roof, all bruised and hurt. This is what happened.

I bit Ollie on the nose. When you are fighting with a king, you resort to anything, but I didn't think of biting him until I found my teeth fastened over his nose. Then I found it was a good thing, so long as I didn't let go. No matter how much Ollie hurt me, I had only to bite harder to hurt him as much, or more. I didn't even feel his blows, or think of them very much. I only bit and bit, holding on to Ollie all the while. They were good tactics, while they lasted.

It ended like this. Something took me by the shoulder, heaving me up. As soon as I felt that, I knew that I had to let go, I knew that the battle was over for the time.

Ollie came at me like a raging maniac, but he stopped short, and both of us looked at the thing that was holding me.

She said in Yiddish, "Go and bury your head in muck, little infidel swine!"

My mother was a big woman, a mountain of a woman, and all over as red as a beet. And with her rage, the scarlet color always increased. Now she looked like a beet, and her shape was the shape of a beet, too. She shook me and shook me, until my brains rattled and my eyes popped, and I whimpered from the pain of her shaking me and the hurt of Ollie's blows.

Ollie crouched just short of her, eying her warily. He wasn't afraid—still, he wasn't prepared to do battle with a creature of her size.

"Go," she screamed, "go, heathen, and find yourself a pile of manure!"

"Aw, go take a hot crap," Ollie muttered.

"Go and consort with the devil, son of Edom," she raged, all the while continuing to shake me. "Go, you with the mind and purpose of a fiend! Go from my sight!"

"Dirdy sheeney!"

"Names to call me—filth of the gentile!"

"G'wan, yuh fat louse!"

Lost entirely, she broke into English. "Vat you call me, doity rotter?"

"Yuh stinkin' Jew!"

Free for a moment, I noticed Marie. Marie stood there, absorbed, her hands on her knees. Her yellow hair was all thrown about her head and shoulders, and her mouth was wide with wonder. But even then, in the few seconds, I noticed how beautiful she was. What was the use? I loved Marie. Nothing mattered; nothing could change that. I loved her, and I would never stop loving her, and that was the way it would be until the end of time. Then I ran.

I ran into the hall of our house, and I climbed up to the roof. It was a long way, but I had to be safe; I had to be where my mother would never think of looking for me. Where else could I go but up to the roof? If she found me, she would beat me, beat me long and unmercifully. I had to be safe.

In the hall, it was dark, with just the faint flares of gas to light the way. But out on the roof it was all sunshine with the delicious smell of hot, steaming tar. I blinked, swayed from side to side. How quiet and peaceful it was!

I sit down in a corner, liking the way the soft tar takes hold of my pants, and I lean back against the wall. I am tired and hurt and bleeding in some places; I have just been fighting, and I wonder whether life will ever be anything but battles and fear from one day to another. But it will. Some day I'll grow up, and in that other world, none of these things happen. Somehow, I know that.

As much as I hurt, I don't think about it too long. Have I said before that hurt passes easily? Well, it does. The hot sun bites into my face, and soon I have stopped whimpering. I even smile a little. It was funny in a way, Ollie and my mother screaming at each other.

Now—now you hurt, but soon it's over. When I grow up, I will have lots of money and marry Marie. (I love you, Marie.) Then she'll love me.

And I begin to think of ways I can make Marie love me. There must be any number of ways for someone as clever as I. Maybe I doze a little in the hot sun, it's so good and quiet up on the roof.

And Shomake? And the magic garden? I have forgotten them entirely.

CHAPTER SIX

Now, how is it that I, Ishky, had never thought of this before? Was there something about that morning, that day—that my dreams should all vanish then?

You see, I am on the roof, basking in the sun, healing the hurts I have just gathered in my fight with Ollie. What a fight that was! But I heal quickly, and curling in the sun like a big cat, I am all pleasure and happiness. That's how it is with one, first battle and struggle, and the next moment ease and pleasure. Sometimes at night, with the gas turned very low, my mother sobs bitterly, rocking back and forth. "Oh, such a life," she moans in Yiddish. "Oh, what a life for one to be thrust into! Why and what for? From the pains of labor to the dusk of death there is nothing but pain and horror. What for? What for?"

But I am not like that. Most of the time I am very happy living, and why shouldn't I be, with all the good things in life? So how did this idea occur to me?

He sat on the roof in the sun, a bundle of not-too-good clothes, with his legs curled way up. He was a very small boy, with thin legs and thin hands and large brown eyes and freckles, and he began to think again of the magic garden.

Whenever there was nothing else to think of, he could think of the magic garden. He could think of how it would be only a matter of time until he was large enough to climb over the fence—and then—why, the magic garden would be his. But might it not be too late then? One grew up, and if he were to rock back and forth like his mother, then—?

He made a face at the thought of his mother, she was so fat and ugly. He shouldn't hate her; God would not like that. Up in the sun, maybe behind the sun was God. God knew everything. God would disapprove, if he thought that his mother was ugly. Still, he would never be like his mother.

Downstairs in the yard, it was cool and gray, and the fence that closed in the magic garden cast a long shadow. But there was grass growing from beneath the fence, and that grass gave a faint, fascinating suggestion of what lay in the garden itself.

And now the thought struck him. The roof—what about the roof? But what a little fool he was, never to have thought of that before! Surely, it was plain enough—he had only to look over the back of the roof to see behind the fence, to gaze into the garden. And he had never thought of it before—

"Oh—wunnerful," he whispered. "Dat's what I shoulda done long ago."

Rising to his feet, carefully, cautiously, he began to move, trembling a little, he was that excited.

Stalking like a red Indian, he approached the back of the roof, and he looked over. For a moment, he stared, and then he sank back to the roof, shaking with short, dry sobs.

Because, in the garden, there was nothing but piles of rubbish.

CHAPTER SEVEN

So you see how it was with me, that I was left all alone on the roof, trying to make something out of nothing. I would never be happy again; how could I ever be happy again? How could I be sure that everything in life wouldn't be like this, an illusion that would pass away as soon as you probed into it? Well, the secret garden was gone, Marie was gone; indeed, everything had been taken away from me, and anyway, what was the use of going on?

I heard my mother calling from the window. "Ishky—Ishky, vare are you?"

I tried to bury myself in the hot tar of the roof. So soon, I would have to go down and eat my lunch. I made little balls of the tar, and threw them away from me, watching the way they bounced, and finally stuck to the roof. And then in the middle of my crying, I managed to smile a little—because one of the pellets remained fastened to a clothesline where it had struck, just remained fastened like that. And here I was smiling again. Well, Ishky, you are a little fool, and that's all there is to it.

But I kept on smiling. If the secret garden wasn't behind our yard, then it was somewhere else. Certainly, it was somewhere else.

Someone was coming from the next roof. As soon as he was out of the glare of the sun, I recognized Thomas Edison. I don't know why everyone calls him Thomas Edison, but he is really nothing to be afraid of. He's big and kind of fat—but crazy. Everyone knows that he is crazy, that something is wrong inside of his head. He has a funny dull look on his face, his eyes popping, his mouth open, but I guess that's not his fault, only a part of his being crazy; I guess anyone who is crazy looks a lot like that. Some people say that he is Ollie's brother, but Ollie won't admit it, and with micks you can't be sure who is whose brother. I don't mind him, and sometimes I feel very sorry for him—he not being able to dream and dream, the way I do.

Thomas Edison crossed three roofs, and then he saw Ishky. In the beginning, he hadn't known what drew him to the roofs. But on the roofs were sunlight and cool winds that blew in from the river, and there was freedom of a sort and nobody to laugh at him. He knew that more than anything else he hated to have people laugh at him.

When he saw Ishky, he halted, eying him warily. Ishky was Ishky, whom he remembered; Ishky was too small to beat him up, and if he had to, he could beat Ishky up. But he wouldn't unless he had to. Why should he beat anyone up when the warm sunshine and the cool air from the river made him feel so contented? Putting a leg over the wall between the roofs, he stared at Ishky, who stared back at him with a curious, even intentness.

"Whaddya lookin' at?" Thomas Edison demanded.

"Nuttin'."

"Y'are so."

"No I ain'."

"Whaddya lookin' den?"

"Jus lookin'."

Hoisting himself over the wall, he let himself drop down on Ishky's side; then, hands in pockets, he came swaggering toward Ishky, ready to fight or flee, not quite sure even now which he would prefer.

"Hey, Ishky."

"Hullo."

"Wanna match pennies?"

"Ain' got none."

"Betcha yuh got."

"I swear I ain'," Ishky protested.

"Yer a dirdy liar. Jews allus got money."

"Awright, search me."

Pocket after pocket Ishky turned inside out, to show only crumbs and little specks of dirt, and with each revelation Thomas Edison shook his head in disgust. "See," Ishky said, shaking the crumbs onto the ground. "Dere ain' nuttin' at all, 'cept dirt."

"Yeah."

Thomas Edison sat down next to him, finding comradeship of a sort in the fact that Ishky had told the truth. It was nice to have someone who would tell you the truth, and of whom you weren't afraid.

"I ain' scareda yuh," he told Ishky.

"Yeah."

Ishky rolled another tar ball, throwing it at the clothesline. But it came nowhere near it. Well, that's the way things were.

"Whaddya doin'?"

"Rollin' tar balls."

"Dere good tuh eat."

"Yeah."

They each rolled a tar ball and chewed on it. Ishky liked the way it stuck to his teeth and the warm sticky taste of it. When he spat, his spittle was hot and black.

"Tar's good," he said.

"Yeah."

"Good as gum."

"Yeah."

"Oney yuh don' dare swalla it."

"I swalla it," said Thomas Edison. "I swalla it whenever I wanna. I ain' no dirdy Jew."

"I ain'," Ishky said.

"Y'are so."

"I ain'."

"Yer yella t'do anythin' a Jew wouldn' do. Yer yella tuh say, screw duh dirdy Jews."

"I ain' yella," Ishky said firmly, but he was wavering. These were terrible words, and he wondered how he could sit there so calmly, listening to such terrible words. Up—way up beyond the sun was God; and if the hand of God were to come down and strike him! But since Thomas Edison was wrong inside—didn't that make everything all right?

"Say it."

"Awright, awright—I'm goin' tuh say it, ain' I? Ain' I gonna say it?"

"Yer yella."

"Awright, screw duh dirdy Jews—screw duh dirdy Jews. Dere, yuh tought I wouldn'."

Thomas Edison was impressed. Into even his dim mind this defiance of the great God penetrated. What would happen? But here, nothing was happening.

"Geesus, Ishky," he said.

"I ain' yella."

"I din' say yuh was yella, Ishky."

"Yuh said it."

"Look—cross my heart, I din', Ishky. Look, duh fader, son, an' hully ghust—lookit dat, Ishky."

"Awright."

"You an' me be pals?"

"Awright."

But had I, Ishky, done right? Why had I denied my God?—for that was what it amounted to. But I knew that I was lonely, and even if he wasn't right in his head, it was better for him to like me than not to like me. You know how that is, how you get tired of all the things in life, the fighting and all of that, and how you want things to be easier.

Now I sit with him in the sun and chew on tar balls. I am not telling all these things for no reason at all; one thing leads to another, and I want you to see how that is, how full of these things life is, how you are happy one moment, and the next?—

"Whaddya gonna do, Ishky?"

He wanted to show him. He had thrown off the Jew, even if only for a moment, and he had assumed some sort of splendor that was better than his rags and his thin body. Thomas Edison looked up to him. He might have considered that it was very little to be worshiped by a subject like that; but Ishky did not consider it at all.

"Wanna play?" he inquired.

"Yeah."

"Wanna folla duh leader?"

"Awright."

Ishky led away, bounding over the roof, Thomas Edison following after. Ishky swung on a clothesline, looped his feet, and returned to the roof. He dashed to the edge, straddled it, and gazed at the sidewalk. So far away, with people as big as dolls, no bigger. He wanted to jump. No. Not down there, not down there. But to be big, and let the world look at you, admiring; as if Thomas Edison were the world. Yet why not? But away from the edge—come away from the edge, Ishky, before you tumble over.

"Geesus, Ishky!"

"Tought I was yella, huh?"

"Don' go near duh edge, Ishky."

"Tought I was yella."

He tumbled back onto the roof, back on the roof that was strong and solid and enduring. If he had fallen, he would have gone over and over, but he would have had guts. Turning, he raced to the narrow airshaft.

The airshaft in that sort of tenement was no more than six or seven feet wide, with a low wall binding it in. And all the way down, from top to bottom, clotheslines were strung, back and forth, from the roof to the rubbish below.

(Look at the airshaft, Ishky! There is glory in the meanest ways of life, if only you look for it.)

At the airshaft, he paused, glancing at Thomas Edison who came puffing behind him. How foolish he looked, with his poor round face that held no intelligence at all; but he would know glory—he would have to know glory. What was glory without an audience, anyway? Oh, if only Ollie were here now!

"Y'tough I was yella."

"Whaddya gonna do, Ishky?"

"You ain' got guts t'do what I'll do."

"Yeah, Ishky?"

"Y'tought I was yalla."

"Yeah, Ishky—whaddya gonna do?"

"Gonna jump over duh arishaft."

"Geesus, Ishky."

"Y'gotta folla."

"I can' do it, Ishky."

"Yuh gotta. Or else, yer yella. Yer yella—dat's all."

He prepared to jump. If he fell—but he must not think of falling. He had to jump—all the way over. God—God! But he had given away his God to Thomas Edison.

(Jump then, Ishky—what are you waiting for?)

"Yuh'll get kilt."

He ran back, leaped forward, sprang to the wall and out into space. Only then—he didn't know why, but he knew he wouldn't reach the other side. The airshaft was long and narrow, and miles down, and all those miles he would go tumbling and twisting, to be crushed into nothing at all at the bottom. Why had he done it? What was glory, when life was so beautiful in the sunshine?

His foot just touched the opposite wall; then his body was flung back into the airshaft. Thomas Edison saw, and he wailed and screamed, a thin terrible wailing and screaming; for in his clouded mind he understood death better than anyone else of his age would have.

Ishky hit a clothesline; the line held for a moment, then it broke. He was falling until he hit another. But he could think; he could think of the death that was rushing up from the bottom of the shaft.

Like a rubber ball, his body bounded from one line to another, and each line hit him like a thin whiplash. The walls of the shaft reeled dizzily about him. And at the bottom, the rubbish awaited him, piled a good five feet high.

When I plunged into the rubbish, it seemed that I, Ishky, was not even hurt. I was cut on one cheek, but that is all. Can there be a God in heaven after all? Can I be alive?

I sit up, and look at the broken clotheslines. How can it be? But I am alive; that is all that matters. I've jumped off the roof, and I am alive. I hear Thomas Edison wailing, but what is that, when I am alive, with only a cut cheek?

(Only—get out of here, Ishky. Windows are opening, and you have broken their clotheslines. Get out of here quickly.)

CHAPTER EIGHT

All I know is that I must get away and hide. Suddenly, I have plunged off a roof, and all the peace of a summer day is shattered. Why did I do it? What on earth could ever have prompted Ishky to do a thing like that?

And, strangest of all things, I am alive and not hurt too much.

Thomas Edison is screaming on the roof. (Be quiet, fat fool—it is I who fell off, not you!) And windows are opening. A quick tumble through an open cellar window, and I am out of the airshaft and into the black cellar. But still, I plainly hear the shouts and the screams. I look up slyly. Yes, a woman is leaning out of the window and screaming; what is she screaming about?

It comes to me like this—as if someone is saying: Oh, Ishky, you have done a terrible thing. You have tried to die. In fact, you have died. You are dead. You see, you, Ishky—

Who is dead? If I pinch myself, see how it hurts. But the cellar is so black, especially here in the coal bin where I have crawled. When I hold my hand in front of my face, I can't see it. Then maybe I am dead. Who knows? It is so black here that one cannot be very sure whether he is alive or dead.

What I don't understand and never will be able to understand, is how, so soon after a terrible thing, I am acting as if it had never happened at all. I mean jumping off the roof; for I am not thinking of that any more, except that my face and body hurt a little. I am thinking of how it would be if Marie was here in the cellar with me.

Pretending, I say: "You see, Marie, my dear, that it is really much nicer to be down here with me than with Ollie."

Marie says: "Yes—true. Now I wonder why that should be?"

I say: "I could tell you that, Marie, my dear."

She says: "You are so wonderful, Ishky. How is it I never knew before? Yes, do tell me."

I say: "You see, my darling Marie, I am a person of splendid dreams and fancies, who will be a king, or at least a millionaire some day. And who is Ollie?—"

She says: "Of course, I have always loved you."

I say: "Yes, I know."

She says: "Won't you kiss me, Ishky?"

I say: "Here in the cellar?"

She says: "It doesn't matter—so long as you kiss me, Ishky."

And in the middle of all that, I heard someone screaming, "Ishky—Ishky—Ishky—Gott!"

Can it be my mother's voice? I hear, in Yiddish, "Oh, God of Gods, what have you done with my son? Where is he, my jewel, my precious one, my beloved? What have you done with him, after the halfwit threw him from the roof? Oh, Ishky, my child, where are you?"

"Quiet—quiet, and we will find him."

"To solace me with his broken body. God!"

"Maybe he is not dead."

"My man will destroy me! Where is my jewel?"

And all through this, I am hiding in the coal bin. Should I come out? But my mother will only beat me; I am quite certain that she will beat me. Then what shall I do—hide there in the coal for the rest of my life? But that's quite out of the question.

What then to do, when I can hear her crying, "Where are you, my heart?"

Someone says, "Maybe it was not he who fell off the roof."

And someone else, "I saw the body drop, like a bundle of clothes."

And my mother, "No—he is dead. I know he's dead."

What a little fiend I am to remain here in the coal!

The big red-faced, red-armed, red-eyed woman saw him emerge from the cellar stairs. She was standing in the hall, sobbing, when he came sheepishly and shamefully out of the cellar. Literally, he was black; his face was black, his clothes and his arms were black. He stood at the top of the cellar steps, looking at her.

"Oh, my heart, my love," she cried.

"I fell offana duh roof."

"God has preserved thee!"

"Gonna hit me?"

"No, no, my child."

She folded him into her large red arms, pressing her face against his dirty face, sobbing and shaking against him. His life now was more than the world had ever given her before, like having labor pains all over, and she sat on the steps rocking him back and forth. Had she been cruel? Then she would make up for it in one way or another.

"Thy face is cut . . ."

"Yeah—dat's where I fell."

"Yes, yes, I will make it better, my little one. You will see how thine mother will heal thy face."

New life now for her and her man. How could she have said to him, when he came from his work, that his son was dead?

She took him upstairs, and in the little kitchen, she washed his face and hands. A piece of plaster brought the cut together, and when she could finally smile, she saw his full lips tremble into a smile, too.

"You will never go to the roof again," she said.

"Naw." And then he added, "I'm hungry."

"God forgive me," she said in her rapid Yiddish, "I am starving the breath of my life. What will you have, my child?"

"I dunno."

"Some eggs—some milk and cake and bread?"

"Awright."

Still panting, she went to the stove, and Ishky sighed with relief. He had not been beaten, which only went to show that it never paid to worry. Things came out all right, somehow. But, still, she

was very hot and uncomfortable in her love. A mother like Marie
would be better, like Marie grown up, with yellow hair and blue
eyes. If he only had such a mother—

"Eat, my pride."

"Awright."

"The food is good to one who has come back from the dead?"

"Yeah."

"You are hungry—with all your fear?"

"Yeah."

"Then eat and eat, my little one, until there is not a shred of
food left on your plate."

"Awright."

"Poor, hurt, tiny one."

He gulped his food down. He wanted to be out. He wanted to go
downstairs, to tell Marie what a wonderful thing he had done.

I wonder just how much one thing is related to another. If I had
not fallen from the roof, would I have ever had Marie?

Now I am happy and tired; I have escaped a beating. And outside
the sun is still shining. I have only to gulp down my food to be out
there in the sunshine.

CHAPTER NINE

Marie, tossing her head, flinging her yellow hair from side to
side, paraded back and forth in front of her house. Now and then,
she stopped to regard an outthrust leg, cocking her head from one
side to another, and her movement was full of instinctive coquetry
and grace. Oh, she knew what she was about, and she said to herself
that if Ishky were going to be such a fool—well, she would waste
only a minute or two more upon him.

Ishky sat on his stoop, rolling an immie from one hand to another, watching it flash and sparkle as it twisted through the air.
If Ishky had an accomplishment, it was the ability to concentrate
upon one thing to the exclusion of all else—apparently. And now,
to the rest of the world, it seemed that he was concentrating all his
powers upon the immie. There was nothing else but the immie,
which, for all of him, might be one of the rarest of jewels. Did
anyone think otherwise?

Thomas Edison came toward him cautiously, with a good deal of awe. Thomas Edison rolled his moon face and looked at the immie.

"Hey, Ishky."

Immie from hand to hand—immie from hand to hand.

"Hey, Ishky!"

Marie said to herself, "Huh, anyone could do it. Jumping off a roof! As if there were anything to that!"

"Hey, Ishky."

Ishky thought, "Marie is across the street. Then is she watching me? But who else, if not me? Will she come over here?"

"Hey, Ishky!"

He glanced up. "Whaddya wan?"

"You ain' saw?"

"Naw, I ain' saw."

"Wasya hurt?"

"Gotta liddle cut."

"Geesus!"

"Yeah."

Thomas Edison stood there hesitatingly, and Ishky went on rolling his immie from hand to hand. Out of the corner of his eye, he saw that Marie had stopped her walking. She was staring at him now. Did that mean she would come over?

"C'n I sit by yuh, Ishky?"

"Yeah."

Thomas Edison sat down by him, still staring at the immie. The more he stared, the more magic there appeared to be in the immie; and he hoped Ishky would not chase him away.

And now Marie, facing gingerly toward Ishky, stepped into the gutter. Slowly, she came toward Ishky, ruffling her dress. Ah, how beautiful she was—all everlasting and wonderful beauty. That is what Ishky thought.

"Aw, Ishky!" she cried.

He glanced up at her, glanced down quickly then at his immie, and with that Marie felt herself burning up inside.

"Dirdy liddle louse—sittin' wid a halfwit!" she screamed.

Ishky paid no attention, but Thomas Edison screamed back, "Go screw, youh wop!"

"Lousy mick!"

"Go screw!"

"Stinkin' lousy mick!"

Thomas Edison rose to his feet. He hated girls. They were like roaches and bedbugs, put in the world for no other purpose than that of creating misery, and most of their jabs were directed at him. He knew that he was a halfwit, and most of the time he accepted the fate with a good deal of complacency. Sometimes, he was even proud of it. But girls never made him proud of it.

Now he knew what he would do with her. He would smear her clean dress with mud from the gutter, and he would smear the mud on her face too. And he would laugh while she screamed and clawed.

She stood waiting for him. "Lousy mick!"

"Yuh'd better run."

"Doncha touch me."

Then Ishky put a stop to what might have followed. "Ledda alone," he commanded.

"Geesus, Ishky, lookit duh way she cussedya."

"Ledda alone."

"Awright."

"An' git oudda here."

"Yuh said I could sit by yuh."

"Well, I don' wancha tuh now. G'wan an' git oudda here."

Mournfully, Thomas Edison walked away. Another time he would have threatened battle. But Ishky had jumped off the roof—so what was the use of threatening battle?

And Ishky went on playing with his immie, wondering how far he could go with this new power. Power was everything, power and glory. Now Marie was looking at him. Well, she must know that he had jumped off the roof.

She walked toward him, until she stood just above him, and he could see how she stood there, swinging one leg back and forth. Life went on with power and glory, and the hot sun made him warm and comfortable. If he touched the leg, what would she do?

"Hey, Ishky."

"Hullo," he said.

The leg swung back and forth; it paused, stopped; then it began to swing again.

"I din' mean what I calledya."

"Dincha?"

"Cross my heart, I din', Ishky."

"Howda I know?"

"Look. Ishky, I'm gonna cross my heart. Lookit dat, Ishky. I crosst my heart."

"Awright."

"Y' believe me if I cross my heart, doncha, Ishky?"

"Yeah."

With a dainty but calculated motion, she sat down next to him, tossing her hair. Now he pocketed his immie, looked at her, and for a moment their eyes held. He saw that her eyes were blue as the sky, and he felt a great rush of gladness in his love for her. Time would pass, but he, Ishky, would love her until the end of time.

"Howda jump offana duh roof?" she wanted to know.

"Jus' jumped."

"Jus' like dat?"

"Yeah, jus' like dat."

"My goonnus," she said admiringly.

"Yeah, it wasn' nuttin'."

"It was too. Betcha nobody else coulda done it. It was awful brave."

"Yeah?"

"Betcha Ollie wouldna done it."

"Maybe."

"Anyway, Ollie's jus' talk."

His heart throbbing, he leaned toward her. Did she mean what she said, or was she playing with him?

"Marie?"

"Yeah?"

"Whoya like better, me or Ollie?"

She cocked her head, tossed it, and smiled saucily. She looked at him out of the corners of her eyes, leaning just the least bit toward him; and then, abruptly, she shook her head.

"Who?"

"I dunno."

"Sureya do."

"Yer nicer'n Ollie."

CHAPTER TEN

Now some people will not think that our street is beautiful. Indeed, I know that many times, I, Ishky, have said to myself, "Surely this is the least beautiful spot in the world." I guess you could understand that. East to west, it is nothing but drab walls of wood and brick. The wooden houses are old, and they seem to be falling into decay; the brick houses are not a great deal better.

So you can see how, when it does look beautiful, you feel it. But I don't know; and I guess that when it does look beautiful, it is something inside of you that makes it beautiful.

Inside of me, then. I am Ishky, and it is hot summer, so hot that everything moves slowly; and now more than any other time, I am not much to look at.

If you ask my mother, she will tell you that I am nothing at all. So how is it that I am a king? Now, I am not sure yet, but I think that Ollie is no longer king. And all this was done by jumping from a roof.

The Lord God preserved me, as he preserved Joseph, who was sold as a slave into Egypt. Maybe I will turn out to be like Joseph, because I am quite sure he could have been no more clever than I. I've won Marie.

I can't tell you enough of my love for Marie. It is all squeezed up inside of me, and I have never spoken of it, not even to Marie. But nevertheless, it is a wonderful thing. When I thought of the secret garden, it was always for Marie. And when I do wonderful things, I do them for Marie, who is quite the most beautiful person in the world. If I am great, it is just because of Marie, and for no other reason.

And now the block is beautiful. The sky is as blue and as clear as any sky can ever be. The sun is shining, like a large, end-on, yellow lemon in the sky. The cement is hot, so hot that everything bakes warm and comfortable. And I walk down the street with Marie.

How is it that I notice things about Marie, which I notice in nobody else? How is it that I see every tuft and curl in Marie's yellow hair? How is it that I watch every shadow that passes across her face? Is it only that I love her?

This time I have courage enough to take hold of her hand.

A forlorn figure, Shomake came up the block. He had been fighting with a large colored boy called Blackbelly. This is how it came about.

When Shomake saw the fight, he ran away, and he never knew

whether Ollie had beaten Ishky, or Ishky had beaten Ollie; but his running away hurt more than any fight could have.

He ran down the block, and all the time he was thinking, "I'm yellow—yellow." He wanted to hide, but where can one hide in a bright, sunny street? Half crying, his sobs came bitter and hard, short gasps of dry breath.

Shomake was a gentle boy. He possessed to a large degree the ability to be hurt, but he himself could not hurt. Everything hurt him. Once, when his mother cut her hand badly, he had sobbed and whimpered for hours. And again, when he had seen Thomas Edison being beaten unmercifully by Ollie, he had sprung madly at Ollie, to take his beating along with Thomas Edison. And later he had said to himself:

"If Ollie is his brother, why, why?"

His fiddle was alive, he always thought, and he loved the music better than anything else. But when something happened, it was always music that he could not get away from; and now the hot sun would not let him escape. Ishky was being beaten, and he was running from Ishky, leaving him.

(Coward, you, Shomake, yellow, dirty son of a dago bitch.)

Counterpoint. When his mother had attempted to explain counterpoint, she said, "It is like the two souls of man inside of him, struggling and struggling." And that was love and hate, love and hate. He had to get out of the sun, or the beating in his brain would destroy him.

Down near the bottom of the block there was a dark alley where some colored people lived. Ordinarily, Shomake would not have gone near the alley. Now he couldn't be afraid, and he dashed into it. And there he met Blackbelly.

Blackbelly went around saying that he had killed a white boy. Of course, nobody believed it, but that was what he said. He also said that he wasn't afraid of any white boy on the block, and because of this he had to be mighty careful, running with his gang most of the time. But once when Ollie had caught him without his gang, there had been a terrible fight, which nobody ever forgot. Blackbelly ended the fight by hitting Ollie over the head with a bottle, but that hadn't decided it one way or another. Ollie still insisted that he would get Blackbelly. And Blackbelly said, "Come and get me."

When Shomake saw Blackbelly, he knew he would be beaten. But there was still time to turn and make a run for it.

Shomake stood there in the half-darkness, trembling.

"Whereya goin', dago?"

The music in his head didn't stop. Because he was afraid, Shomake knew that he was a coward. He would turn and run. This place was dark and terrible as hell itself.

"Boy, yer sure scared."

"Not afraid!" Shomake screamed.

"I'll killya!"

"G'wan, kill me den. G'wan an' kill me, yuh dirdy rodden black basted." And with that he threw himself at Blackbelly.

Blackbelly beat him thoroughly. But he couldn't put too much heart into it. This was not fighting. This was slaughter, more or less.

Afterward, Shomake sat on the curb, sobbing to himself. All over, his body ached, but there was more hurt than that in his heart, and he was not able to throw it off the way Ishky had. Why had Christ died, if the world was only this?

The sun, so hot, only made him suffer more. False beauty. He wanted to go home and put his head in his mother's lap, but that would not solve the whole thing. Still, he had to solve it.

Maybe—if he went to Ishky— He sat there sobbing and thinking for a long time. Maybe if he went to Ishky, they could go and look for the magic garden again. Then, for the first time, he smiled a little, remembering the garden the way Ishky had described it. And it was so near—only in the back of Ishky's house.

If you could go into the garden, just like that, couldn't you stay there? And then, maybe, you could stay there all the time.

Awkwardly, he got to his feet, and he began to shamble up the block. There, sure enough, was Ishky, and Marie was with him.

"Hey, Ishky," he called.

Ishky began to swagger. He wondered what Shomake would think, seeing him holding Marie's hand like that.

"Hey, Ishky!"

Marie turned up her nose.

"Wanna play, Ishky?"

"He's a dirdy wop," Marie confided to Ishky.

"Yeah."

"Wanna find duh gaden?"

And then Shomake stood stunned and forlorn; Ishky had swaggered past without ever noticing him.

CHAPTER ELEVEN

Now—the fight between Blackbelly and Ollie. You must understand why this fight was inevitable, and how out of this fight developed the compact gang formation which divided the block into two distinct parts.

The last time they had fought, Blackbelly had mashed Ollie's head with a broken bottle; but if Ollie resented anything about this, it was the fact that the bottle had not come into his hand before it came into Blackbelly's. A broken bottle was legal enough in any fight.

Out of that, Ollie began to vision his gang, a close, well-knit gang to drive the Negroes out of the lower end of the block. Now, Ollie was no fool; more than that, he was a person who thought a great deal. He knew that he hated the Negroes. In the upper part of the block, he was king; but when he walked down the block he took his safety into his hands. He thought of a time when the block would be his, from east to west. It meant beating the Negroes, and that meant organizing a gang. But when it came to organizing, he was strangely helpless.

This is the way the combination between Ishky and Ollie came about—after Ollie had heard of Ishky's feat of leaping from the roof.

What have I done to Shomake now? He used to be my friend, and now? Now I walk past him, and even though I see the expression upon his face, it doesn't affect me.

(Ishky, what do you know of a woman, except to worship her?)

Afterward, I would say to myself, "It is all Marie's fault." Yet how is that possible? I love Marie, and to me she is the perfect woman above all other women. So how can the fault be Marie's?

Now, in spite of what I have done to Shomake, I am quite happy.

"Y'like tuh read, Marie?"
"Sometimes. What's duh gaden?"
"Jus' sumpen I tol' Shomake."
"He's a dumb wop."

"Yeah—y'like 'venture stories?"

"Sometimes. Where's duh gaden?"

"What gaden?"

"Duh one yuh tol' Shomake about."

"I dunno."

"Den whyya talkin' all about a gaden?"

"Jus' fer fun."

She glanced sidewise at him, and then she said, "Is it dark in duh gaden?"

"I dunno."

"Awright—take yer pissy gaden. See if I care."

How is it that I can't tell Marie about the garden? I told Shomake about it, and I don't love him; and I love Marie, so why can't I tell her about the garden? But I can't. Maybe I am afraid that she would laugh at me. I know that I don't want Marie to laugh at me, ever. And it doesn't matter anyway, since there is no garden.

Blackbelly saw them walking down the block. Well, that's what a woman can do to a man. Blackbelly knew Ishky, and he knew that Ishky was not a person to be caught very often in the lower end of the block. Blackbelly waited; then, when they were close to him, he sauntered out into their path.

He stood like a small blob of solid ink in their path. His eyes on the ground, Ishky saw Blackbelly's shadow first, and then he looked up into Blackbelly's round face. Then he felt Marie cringe against him. Then he tried to smile; but he didn't know why. He knew, though, that with Marie next to him, he couldn't run away. A hundred times before, he had been caught the same way; and each time there was a moment in which he whirled and fled away. That was life—sometimes you stood and sometimes you ran, but unless you were an utter fool, you never stood when the odds were this heavy against you.

Now he was a fool. The moment when he had sprung across the airshaft leaped into his mind. Glory—and what was life when it came to glory? He might have said, "Oh, my wonderful Marie, you will see that no sacrifice is too great for you."

And Blackbelly—if he had stood that way on a jungle path a hundred years ago, he would have been more than splendid. He was just splendid now, because he was still too young to know that

a nigger should cringe, and old enough to know that he hated all
whites.

"Whereya goin', white boy?" he drawled.

"You don' own duh ground," Ishky said.

"Yuh dirdy nigger," Marie said.

"G'wan, yuh liddle whore."

Ishky said, "Shuddup!" Inside of him, Ishky felt funny little bubbles of heat. He began to tremble as the rage crept over his small
body. This was doom, but doom and glory came together.

"What's dat?"

Ishky said, "Yuh take dat back?"

This struck Blackbelly as no end funny, and arms akimbo he
began to laugh, rolling back and forth on the balls of his feet.

"Yuh take dat back?"

"Boy-o-boy."

"You lousy stinkin' nigger!" Marie yelled. Then, as Blackbelly
took a step toward her, she ran screaming toward the other end of
the block. Ishky, everything else forgotten, turned around to look
after her.

Then Blackbelly leaped on him. Under the weight of Blackbelly's
hard, round body, Ishky went down. It seemed that the world was
upon him, smothering him. Blackbelly's fists were already pounding
into him.

He tried to fight back, but what was the use? A blow in the face
took most of the fight out of him. He stopped struggling; he lay
still, hurt, only wondering how long Blackbelly would continue to
beat him. Tears welled slowly into his eyes, but he didn't cry.

Blackbelly stood up, staring down at the twisted, small form of
the other boy. It struck something strange inside of him; thus, all
of a sudden, he wished to fight no longer.

"Gittup," he said.

Ishky lay there, his body trembling with dry sobs.

"Gittup, white boy."

"Lemme alone."

"Yuh yella basted."

"Lemme alone."

"Yuh'd better git up, or I'll beat duh ass offana yuh. Yuh'd better
git up."

Then, glancing up, Blackbelly saw Ollie coming; and that same
deep strange thing inside of him told him that Ollie would fight,

that this would be the fight of their lives. He could still run. This was his land Ollie was invading, and there was still time to run. He could call, if he wished to, and he could smother Ollie with dark, eager bodies.

But he did nothing, only waited. This was a battle of kings, and he had no desire to avoid it. He kicked Ishky, and then he forgot about Ishky. He clenched his fists.

CHAPTER TWELVE

Slowly, weighing his chances, Ollie advanced to the battle. Now for Ollie, this was no new thing. Life was, always, eat or be eaten. No law existed beyond the strength of your body, the quickness of your fists. This land he lived in was the land of fang and claw. A man stood in himself; the weak perished and the strong became stronger. And if you were strong enough, you became king. Now he was king.

They were going to fight. In neither's mind was there any doubt about that. Nevertheless, in the way of those who live by fang and claw, they could not advance to the fight immediately. Perhaps their challenges and blustering hearkened back to something deep in the human makeup, that civilization has successfully bred out. The trained killer can strike like a snake. They were children of battle; but they were not trained killers.

Ollie advanced without hate, but he knew how necessary hate was to successful fighting, and, inside of himself, he fanned his rage, thinking of all the vile things that had ever been attributed to Negroes. Wary, perched upon the balls of his feet, his eyes shot about him. Dangerous land this. He tried not to think of that, tried to think only of what he would do to Blackbelly.

"Hey, yuh dirdy nigger," he called.

Blackbelly eyed him from between thick, dark lids. Blackbelly's eyes were slits of yellow and brown. He stood like a brown stump on the sun-baked street.

"Run off, white boy," he said.

"I ain' runnin' from no nigger."

"I'll break yer ass, white boy."

"Jus' try it!"

"Boy—yuh wanna fight?"

"I ain' fightin' no yella niggers!"

"Yer yella."

"Who's yella?" demanded Ollie. Then he glanced down at Ishky, who was now sitting up, drawing himself over to one side. Ishky knew what was coming, and he watched eagerly. And Ollie—here in enemy country, with the fight close upon him, Ollie drew quickly upon some fancied kinship of skin. Or perhaps it was the old instinct of the feudal lord to protect his serf. Anyway, he threw a finger at Ishky.

"Whatcha hittim fer, Blackbelly?"

"Doncha call me Blackbelly."

"I'll call any goddam nigger what I wan'."

"Doncha call me dat agin," Blackbelly warned.

"Whatcha wanna hittim fer?"

"Nunna yer goddam business."

"Whoya cussin'?"

"You."

"Den eat it!"

"Make me."

Ollie leaped at him. Blackbelly crouched, his arms working like pistons, his feet moving slowly and steadily. Blackbelly was the heavier by a good fifteen pounds, but Ollie moved like a cat, leaping in and out, swaying upon the balls of his feet, pounding always at Blackbelly's face. Sometimes, they closed, standing toe to toe, beating each other as well as they could. Then they would leap apart, stare at each other, panting. Ollie's blond skin was splotched and bruised. A thin trickle of blood ran from his nose.

Blackbelly wanted to beat the other down. Closer to earth than Ollie, he could see himself standing as he was through all time, and presently the white boy would be gone. Instinctively, perhaps, he knew that there was nothing lasting about Ollie. He himself was too solid to be destroyed, too solid.

And Ollie fought with red rage in his heart, feeling nothing—unless it was the stretching of time. Minutes appeared to be hours, until it seemed to him that he had been fighting forever. And he would go on fighting forever. Tears streamed down his face, soft curses wrenching themselves from between his clenched lips.

"Goddamit—dat!"

"White basted!"

"Lousy—"

"Yella—"

Ishky was screaming, "Ollie—Ollie, kill duh lousy nigger, killim, Ollie!"

Sharp pains in his hands, lights before his eyes, and battle, and battle. The yellow hair was stained with blood; to Ishky he appeared to be the son of some warrior god.

Then they closed, rolling over and over on the ground, battering, biting, kicking, and clawing. But the strength was going out of their blows, and they were both sobbing with rage and hate. Ollie found Blackbelly's ear, biting deep into it. Blackbelly tore half the shirt from Ollie's back.

Then, hardly knowing why, Ishky began to kick Blackbelly wherever he could. Blackbelly screamed, roared with rage, and Ishky brought his fist squarely into the colored boy's face. For a moment, he loosened his hold on Ollie, and Ollie slammed his head back onto the concrete. Ishky stamped down on his belly.

Blackbelly roared with rage. "I'll killa bot'!" he screamed.

Then Ollie slammed his head onto the concrete again. Ishky drove a shoe into his thigh.

"Goddamm ya!"

"Killim!" Ishky yelled hysterically.

By main strength, Blackbelly struggled to his feet, tore himself loose, and all three stood panting and staring at each other. Then Ollie saw two more colored boys running toward them, their hands full of ashes and bottles.

"Beatit, Ishky!" he cried.

Together, the two of them fled up the street, the colored boys after them. Sobbing and laughing, they ran until they had reached Ollie's house, where they plunged into the hallway. No safety there. On into the cellar, into the coalbin, where, panting and crying, they perched on top of a pile of coal.

"Whatta fight!" Ollie sobbed.

"Geesus!"

"I beatis ass offana him!"

"Sure."

"Geesus—"

"Geesus—"

Ishky gulped to halt his sobs, and then he whispered, "Tink dey'll come down here?"

"Naw."

"Dey dunno where we are?"

"Naw."

Ishky began to laugh, almost hysterically. "Boy-o-boy," he chuckled, "whatta fight dat was! Geesus, I jus' hope dey come down here, wid all dis coal. Geesus, I'd liketa swat dat nigger in duh eye wid a lumpa coal."

Ollie appeared to be lost in thought, absently rubbing the blood from his face with his arm. Through the dusk of the coal bin, he was staring at Ishky—thinking. Perhaps it was there that he first concretely thought of the gang.

"Hey, Ishky," he said.

"What?"

"How dya jump offana duh roof?"

"Oh—jus' like dat."

"Geesus—"

"Yeah."

"Betcha it took a lotta guts."

"I dunno," Ishky said.

"Betcha it did. I wouldn' have duh guts."

"Well, I was scared at first."

"Was ya?"

"Yeah. But now I'd do it agin jus' like dat."

"Yeah?"

"Sure."

Maybe you can understand how I felt, sitting there with Ollie like that. I had forgotten Marie; I had forgotten the garden and dreams, and everything else—because I was happy. Oh, you can hardly understand how happy I was.

I hurt. Oh yes, but what are hurts, when they pass so quickly? And Ollie is my friend. I know that. And if you ask me how I know it, I won't be able to tell you. But I have lived here on the block all the time, and this is the first time Ollie has ever been my friend. Maybe you will think that I hated Ollie, but that is wrong. Who can hate Ollie?

I sit in the coal bin, and I tell Ollie how I leaped from the roof. I can see that it impresses him. Well, we are friends, and who knows what we can't do together. Anyway, it is better than being a friend of Shomake's.

CHAPTER THIRTEEN

If there was hate, was there nothing else in the world? Why had Ishky refused to speak to him? Shomake wandered up the block, lost in a misery that was as deep as the sewers under his feet. He had no friend, no companion, nothing at all; and why live?

He went into the store. Dim and soft and quiet, smelling of the fresh-cut leather, the store always seemed to welcome him. His father did not even look up. How the old man sat there, hammering and hammering! No fears there, nothing but a great confidence in the repairing of shoes. Shomake envied him.

And the back room was even darker than the store, all pungent and smelling of Italian food. The spaghetti lay in soft coils in the pot on the stove. Tiptoeing over, Shomake put his finger into the warm water, tasting a bit. Ah, it was good! He looked for his mother—but she had gone somewhere.

He took out the fiddle, holding it in his arms. Beautiful fiddle, of red and brown wood, gleaming with the soul inside of it. He caressed it, smoothed it over with his fingertips. But he didn't want to play—not now.

He sat in the dark, moving his fingers back and forth, quiet and comfortable. Here—no one would bother him, ever. If he could stay here all the time—

He thought of the garden. Surely some way to get into it; there were ways and ways. If you were to speak anxiously enough, wouldn't a door open in the fence? Perhaps a very small door. Then you could creep through, carefully, and you would be in the garden —for good. Oh, why had Ishky ever told him of the garden? Now he would have no peace, and if the garden were only a story of Ishky's? What then?

Ishky—well, maybe when Ishky was tired of Marie, he would come back. There was no one quite like Ishky.

On his way out of the store, Shomake stopped again to look at his father. What was there about shoes that could make a man aware of nothing else in the world? Once, he had asked his mother, and she said to him, "In the old country—it was different."

He went out of the house, walking slowly up the block toward the avenue. Already, he was forgetting what had happened before, yet he had thought that he would never forget.

Two blocks east there were open fields and lots, and beneath them and away were the misty houses of the city. Shomake went down, climbing slowly, until he came to a field that was full of grass and tall weeds. Before him, the water tower stood up like a narrow giant, and beyond the water tower the elevated trains crawled slowly into their barns.

He lay upon his back, chewing the stems of grass, and he forgot without ever knowing that he was forgetting.

CHAPTER FOURTEEN

As Marie ran away from the fight, she began to sob, and by the time she had reached the security of her stoop, she was crying bitterly. She ran into the hall.

She was afraid of the hall. When she went down into a cellar, for the terrible thrill of bad, she was afraid, but it was nothing like this fear of the hall. The hall was dark-green, lit by one single jet of gas. When she opened the door, the jet leaped, and shadows danced toward her and away. Crying, she crouched just inside of the door. Then she crept toward the stairs, crept up them. When her mother opened the door for her, she fell into her arms, lay there, sobbing and twitching.

Her mother was a thin Italian woman, with dark eyes and dark stringy hair. She spoke no English at all. Now, her eyes closed, the soft and beautiful Italian was a comfort to Marie.

"What is it, my little one?"

"I'm afraid."

"Of what? Of what?"

She took Marie into a front room, where there was more light. She sat with her in an old rocking chair, rocking back and forth and back and forth.

"What is there to be afraid of, my little one?" she asked in her soft Italian.

Marie wept abundantly.

"You have done nothing, my heart, so what is there to be afraid of?"

Marie told her—in broken words.

"In the cellar?"

"Yes."

The Italian woman rocked, back and forth, back and forth, nodding her head stiffly, touching the blonde skin with her fingertips.

Marie whispered, "In the hall—I saw the devil."

"No, no."

"I'll never go back there . . . to the street."

"Don't you know, my little one, how God cares for children? God will punish the barbarian; but the laughter of children is music in His ears. You are innocent."

"I saw the devil."

"No, no. You see, we are in a land of barbarians, my child . . ."

Marie saw that her mother was crying too; she saw more than that. She saw past the line that separated her world from her mother's. And because she knew that she would go down to the cellar again, she wept with her mother.

CHAPTER FIFTEEN

I have told you a lot about the block, and I will tell you some more; but not too much. If I tell you too much, you will not believe; if I call my story The Children, you will raise your brows— because there are no such children in the world. But aren't there? What do you know about children? And what do children know about the other world, where you work—and try to pay your rent? But are the worlds so different? If once all men were what we were then—then have men changed? I don't know. But in the end, after I have told you all about Shomake's fiddle, about what happened to Blackbelly, I will tell you of Ollie, and maybe a little about Thomas Edison.

You will admit that being a friend of Ollie's is better than being Shomake's friend. I don't have to be afraid any more. But that is not all. Oh no, don't for a moment believe that I, Ishky, am that dull. You see, I know Ollie. Can anybody know Ollie better than I do? Ollie is a fighting machine, but he is not at all the kind of a machine Blackbelly is; he is all nerves and emotion. And in my way, without thinking too much, I decide that I will play on that. Now this is how it all came about.

In the dark coal bin, I know Ollie is thinking. I am thinking, too. . . .

"Geesus, whatta fight!"

Ollie says, "Duh whole block's lousy wid niggers."

I agree with Ollie. "Black basteds."

"We oughta have a gang." That's what Ollie says, and I know he's not sure of himself. If he were sure of himself, would he confide in me?

"It oughta be yer gang," I say.

"Dam tootin'."

"Betcha you could lick anybody," I say.

"Dam tootin'."

Now my chance has come, and I go about it very craftily; oh, never fear—I am nobody's fool.

"Yuh gonna lemme in it, Ollie?" I want to know.

"You can' fight."

"I could makeya schemes, Ollie. I read a lotta books."

"Lookit duh way Blackbelly almost kilt yuh."

"Listen, Ollie," I tell him. "You an' me could have duh biggest gang aroun'. We could kick duh shid oudda any block."

"Yeah?"

"Sure, Ollie."

"We gotta git a gang."

"Yeah."

Thomas Edison saw Blackbelly and his gang chase Ollie and Ishky down the cellar. He ran across the street, taking refuge in front of the shoe store until the colored boys had gone. Then he crept into the hallway, down into the cellar, and lay there, listening to Ishky's and Ollie's eager plans. The more they spoke, the more it appealed to him, and finally he could contain himself no longer.

"Hey, Ollie!"

"Geesus, who's dat?"

"Jus' me."

"It's nuts."

"Git oudda here, loony!"

"Aw—Ollie."

"Screw, bughouse."

"Lemme in duh gang, Ollie. Ollie—"

Simultaneously, Ishky and Ollie fell on him, kicking him and beating him up into the hallway. Tearfully, Thomas Edison fell and stumbled up, fled then into the bright sunlight. Still stumbling, nodding his overlarge head from side to side, he made his way down to his house.

The wooden shack where they all lived was always dirty; there were three rooms, in which eight of them lived, Ollie and Thomas Edison, brothers and sisters, mother and father, and the grandmother. Thomas Edison hoped the grandmother would be there, but none of the others.

She sat knitting, a very old woman, a woman so old that she had forgotten the number of her years. She was good for nothing else now—except knitting. All day long she sat knitting.

Thomas Edison crept into the kitchen, blinking like a huge owl, his mouth gaping, the dampness of tears still clinging to his cheeks. He saw his grandmother knitting.

"Hey, Oloman," he muttered. They all called her that, and if it had meant anything once, they didn't know what it meant now.

"Dirt and filth," she rumbled, in her broad brogue, "and dirt and filth. Who has been beating you now, poor addlebrain? There's no mercy in them for the wonder God has put on you."

"Ollie kicked me."

"A swine's son. Wipe away the tears, poor fool."

"Awright, Oloman."

"And sit down by me."

"Yeah, Oloman." He sat down next to her, pressing his face to her skirt; and one of her withered hands left her knitting to drop and caress his hair. And all the time she stared straight ahead of her, to a small window where a broad slab of sunlight bit into the room. What an old woman she was, with a fine wrinkled, ancient face! She said:

"Tell me of it, poor fool."

"Dey kicked me. Whatta sock Ollie gimme, right on duh backa my head. He says, git oudda here, loony."

"Yes, poor fool."

He leaned back, staring up at her with his round face, blinking his eyes. He was straining for thought, for some sort of deep, wondrous thought that he could put into words. But the words came with difficulty.

"Oloman—whattam I loony fer?"

"What?"

"I'm crazy, huh?"

"Poor fool—poor fool, it is God's wish, and nothing else but that. But I cannot explain that to you. Dirt and filth here, but in the old

country it would have been different. You see, God has put His
wonderful touch on you."

"Yeah?"

"You're not understanding me, poor fool."

"What's God's touch?"

"Madness."

"Yeah?"

"He has made you mad for His own purpose, and for that reason
they will torment you—torment you. Dirt and filth."

"Goddam em," he muttered.

"Yes, my child."

"Some day . . . I'll kill Ollie."

"No."

He stared with implicit faith at the old woman's face, while she
nodded and stroked his coarse hair. She nodded, muttered, and told
him stories of a land of mountains and trolls. Madness is God's
gift. Take heed of that then, Thomas Edison. Laugh at Ollie.
Laugh at Ishky.

"My mother was mad," the old woman said.

"Yeah?"

"She roamed the bog, screaming to the birds—"

"Yeah?"

"When they torment you too much, poor fool, come back to me,
and I will give you comfort, such as I know how."

"Yeah, Oloman."

CHAPTER SIXTEEN

When we got out of the cellar, Ollie and I had all our plans
made for forming the gang, and Ollie was all swelled up with it.
We came out onto the stoop, and Ollie strutted back and forth,
sticking out his chest.

"Geesus . . ." he said.

"Yeah, Ollie—oney we gotta git more kids."

"Yeah."

I sat down on the stoop, and I was feeling important myself, believe me, and I began to think of whom we could get. I was full
of ideas about this and that, wondering what I would do in the
first fight. Maybe I would be yellow, and maybe I wouldn't; but,
anyway, nobody would beat me up anymore, not with Ollie on my

side. Ollie was leaning up against one side of the stoop, rubbing a
hand through his yellow hair, when I saw Kipleg.

Kipleg came down the block, half running, half walking. Mornings, Kipleg worked in a grocery, and he had gotten the job because
he looked a lot older than his age. He was big, too, a good deal
bigger than Ollie or Ishky.

Kipleg lived across the street from Ishky. A peculiar thing about
Kipleg—he never went up the stairs to his apartment. He had his
own way of going home.

Now Ollie and Ishky watched him. They wanted to call him, to
tell him all about the gang, but not for anything would they have
attracted his attention until he had gotten into his house. They
watched him eagerly.

He came down the block, hitching up his pants. When he saw
Ollie, he whistled to him; but he didn't stop. His quick walk
lengthened into a run, and then a monkeylike bound placed him
on top of his stoop. Whistling, he crouched there.

"Watchim," Ollie whispered.

"Yeah."

Kipleg leaped for the low ladder that hung from the fire escape,
and the moment he caught it, swinging from it by his hands, his
mother put her head out of the window. Kipleg's mother was a
large woman, with red hair, and most of the time she was drunk.
He had no father; nobody knew anything about his father, whether
he had died, or whether he had gone off somewhere. But his mother
drank, maybe to forget his father. When she wasn't drunk, she took
men into the house. Now she screamed at Kipleg.

"Git offana dere, yuh liddle bum!"

"G'wan," yelled Kipleg.

"Git off, I say!"

Kipleg swung up his feet, caught them in the ladder, and then
hung swaying. Slowly, he raised his body.

"Yuh liddle tramp," his mother screamed, "cantcha come intuh
duh house like a gennleman? Yer duh disgrace of my life."

"Aw, screw," Kipleg said. He began to climb up the ladder, sticking out his chest, and hanging back by his hands. When he had
crossed the fire escape, come to the window, his mother smacked
him soundly. He tried to smack her back, but she caught him by

the pants, and drew him through the window, screaming curses at
him all the time.

Ollie and Ishky stared fascinated, their mouths wide open. And
everyone else on the block stared too, some laughing and delighted.
Through the open window came the sounds of the battle between
Kipleg and his mother.

"Scum! Oh, dat I shoudda had duh pains of labor fer a liddle
tramp like you!"

"Aw, screw, I tol' yuh!"

"Talkin' to yer mudder like dat. Take it!"

"Ohhh, yuh louse!"

"Call me a louse!"

"Lemme go!"

"Dere—dere—dere!"

"Whore!"

"I'll kill ya."

"Lemme go, d'ya hear! Lemmego, yuh lousy ol' basted! Who d'ya
tink yer smackin'?"

Kipleg came out of the window again, this time backwards. He
ran across the fire escape to the ladder, and then turned to look at
his mother, who was in the window again.

"Scum!" she cried.

But now Kipleg was free, and he hung upon the ladder, screaming
at her, and making faces, like a monkey.

"Hey, Kipleg!' Ollie yelled.

Seeing Ollie, he dropped quickly down the ladder, hung a moment, and then dropped to the stoop. Putting his hands in his
pockets, ignoring his mother who still screamed from the window,
he swaggered across the street.

"Hey, Ollie," he said.

"Geesus, yuh got duh ol' lady goin' den," Ollie said admiringly.

"Yeah."

"Geesus," Ishky said, because he had to say something.

"Yeah."

Kipleg sat down on the stoop, glanced at Ishky, and then spat.
"I don' like sheeneys," he said.

"He's awright," Ollie explained.

"He's yella."

"Noeeain'."

Fearfully, Ishky watched, wondering what would be the outcome of this, but Kipleg was in a good mood. Out of his pocket he fished a package of cigarettes, and he offered them first to Ollie and then to Ishky. They all lit up, and they sat upon the edge of the stoop, puffing. It was the first time Ishky had ever tried a cigarette, and he puffed hesitantly. But Ollie and Kipleg inhaled with great calm and delight.

"Good butts," Ollie said, cocking his head to one side, and looking at the cigarette he held in his fingers.

"Yeah," Kipleg agreed.

"Yeah," Ishky said.

"Go ahead—inhale."

"I am," Ishky said.

They leaned back, crossed their legs, and then Ollie told Kipleg about the gang.

"We're gonna beat duh niggers," he explained.

"Yeah, we're gonna kick duh shid oudda dem," Ishky said. "We're gonna git Blackbelly."

"Yeah."

"Y' gotta have some gang fer dat," Kipleg said thoughtfully. "Dey'd git duh niggers from Eight Avenya, an' yuh'd have tuh have some gang fer dat."

"We'll gitta gang," Ollie said.

"Jews, an' wops an' everythin'."

"Yeah—"

That was how the peace came about, the truce that for a short time united all factions against Blackbelly and his followers. Ishky was in it. From the beginning, it had been Ishky's plan, and Ishky knew that he was in it for good. Now they could use the weak, and it made no difference that he could not fight as well as Ollie or Kipleg.

So then, you see how I, Ishky, am in the seventh heaven of delight. Suddenly, I have become a man. What became of all this, I will tell you later, but now you must see how I became a man.

I sit on the stoop, smoking a cigarette with Ollie and Kipleg. Is it the same Ishky who dreamed dreams about a secret garden? Now I can laugh at that. Gardens— Ollie is my friend, and Kipleg is my friend, too, and I am full of hate against Blackbelly and the rest of the lousy niggers. I know what we will do to the niggers.

The cigarette burns and stings. Well, what of that? It is better to be this way, than the way I used to be. I am sure I will never be that way again.

CHAPTER SEVENTEEN

Perhaps you see by now how through all of this there runs the memory of the secret garden. I can't forget it so easily. What is the use of trying to make me, Ishky, over in one day? I am Ishky, who never was much good for anything, except to dream, and here I am one of the leaders of a gang.

And it has all come about in less than one day—that is what makes it so impossible. It is not more than two o'clock in the afternoon now, when we all sit on my stoop, smoking cigarettes, and very proud of it, too. If the gang was born anywhere, it was born there. What then? My mother puts her head out of the window, way out, and sees me there.

"Ishky!"

Kipleg giggles, and Ollie glances sidewise at me. But I pretend not to have heard, I go on smoking my cigarette, though I know well enough what a beating I am in for.

"Ishky, come op!"

"Teller t'go take a——" Kipleg says.

"Yeah," says Ollie.

Where has my manhood gone, all of a sudden? The cigarette has become very limp in my hand, and I cower back against the stoop. What will my mother do to me? I want to throw away the cigarette, which has made me a little sick already, but I haven't enough courage for that. I look at Ollie and at Kipleg, and they are both grinning.

"Come up, Ishky!"

"Teller tuh screw," Ollie says.

"Maybe I oughta find out what she wants," I say, trying to pass it off easily.

"I tolya he was yella," Kipleg says.

"Like hell I am."

My mother is leaning far out of the window, and by now I can see how red her face is getting. If she leans out just a little more, she will fall. Well, maybe it would be best for me to go upstairs—

I rise very slowly, looking at Kipleg, looking at Ollie. In all my

life, there has been no more shameful moment than this. How I
hate my mother! How I hate everything! But, nevertheless, I stamp
out my cigarette. And all the time Ollie and Kipleg are grinning
and grinning.

"Maybe I'll jus' go up fer a minute," I say.

"G'wan—yella."

"I'll be right down."

"G'wan."

What is the use? I have lost out here and everywhere, and when
I get upstairs, my mother will beat me. When I go into the hall,
I am already feeling the blows, and as I walk up the stairs, I shiver.
I want the sunlight back, the warm comfort of the stoop. Crouch-
ing, I make my way up the narrow stairway, up two flights to our
floor. My mother is standing by the door, waiting for me.

Well, there is no wonder like this.

Instead of hitting me, she clasps me in her arms, holds me close
to her, moving her hands softly back and forth over my body. I
cringe, but she is kissing me, and it seems to me that I am falling
deep, deep into her large, soft body. Her red, broad face is close to
mine.

We go into the house, and in Yiddish she says to me, "Oh, my
dear one, your mother was afraid!"

"Nuttin' tuh be afraid of."

"I could see you again—plunging from the roof. Oh, my heart,
will you ever know what you are to your mother?"

"I wanna go down."

"Yes, yes, my heart, I would not keep you out of the fresh air
and the sunshine. Only stay with your mother for just a while. You
hurt her when you consort with gentile swine. Why must you go to
them, my child?"

"Dere awright."

"No—they are heathens and sons of heathens."

Then she takes me into the kitchen, prepares a huge slice of
bread for me, piling jam high upon it, and it all looks too fine for
me to resist. Anyway, it is almost time for me to go for my Hebrew
lessons, so what have I to lose? I sit down in one corner, munching
upon the bread, and licking the jam whenever it is smeared over my
lips. The kitchen is quiet and clean and cool, and presently my
mother goes out, leaving me alone. When I have finished the bread,
I am full and content.

"Go and learn, small heart," my mother calls out from the next room.

Well, I am glad to get out, and I dash through the dark hall to the sunshine, where I stand blinking. But Ollie and Kipleg are gone. Slowly, I walk to the cellar on the next block, where I receive lessons in Hebrew.

Is everything gone from me already? As I go down the stairs, I find that I am dreamy and lazy. In the dim, poorly lit room, there are three or four boys seated at a long table. At one end, the old man sits, beating time with his ruler. Graybeard blinks at me, motioning me to my place, and I read with the others, singsong, and graybeard beats time.

I am sleepy, and as I watch the black letters in front of me, I grow more and more sleepy.

"Ishky!" graybeard snaps. The stick leaps forward, catching my ear, and I bend to my reading.

"Has the heathen put lead in your brain? Read!"

I read and I read. What else can I do, here in a cellar, where I learn a strange tongue? But I try to think of Ollie—of Kipleg—

The boy next to me jabs me with a pin, and I screech. Suddenly all four of us are doubled in laughter, and graybeard is in a rage.

"Swine! Murderers!"

We read, bending close to our books.

And now I am thinking of Marie. How is that? Here, my heart goes out to her, and my love comes back to me, stronger than ever before. Marie, how I want you! But I am just poor Ishky.

"Ishky!"

"Yeah—yeah—"

Yellow hair is gold in the sunshine, and if I hold Marie in my arms, I have everything I want. Would Ollie understand that? Would Kipleg? Would old graybeard?

Marie is a wop. Then it is a sin to think of her in this place— but what a delicious sin! I am warm and happy inside, with the dreams I am making of Marie.

(I love you, I love you, I love you—)

"Ishky, addlebrained fool," graybeard barks.

"Yeah."

"Attention to your reading. Ah, what heathens you have become —all of you."

But I want to be out of here, old graybeard. Don't you understand that? Outside, there is sunshine and life, and what do you know of sunshine and life, holed up here in your cellar? I am Ishky, learning how to live. . . .

Has there ever been a person as happy as I am, when I go out into the sunshine? I leap and jump, and scream at the top of my lungs, and inside of me I feel a warm kinship with everything that is alive.

I skip and run back to the block. New things now. The gang is waiting.

But nobody is there. Anyway, the sunshine is warm and good and comfortable, and I sit down on my stoop. I stretch out my legs, turning my face up to the heat. How happy I am! How content!

CHAPTER EIGHTEEN

Marie shook the sunlight from her hair, and her hair spilled it to the pavement. And if Ishky had been mistaken in all other things, he was not mistaken in her beauty. She was beautiful as the sunlight, and if they two were the only beautiful things upon the block, still it was enough.

In the sunlight she wasn't afraid, only in the dark. She threw her hair from her face, walked back and forth in front of her stoop. She even dared to throw a glance across the street, where Ollie sat with Kipleg, watching her slyly.

"Geesus," Ollie whispered.

"Whatsa matter?"

"Geesus, I gotta feel like a million bucks oudda Marie. I tooka down duh cellar."

"Yer fulla crap."

"Cross my heart. Listen, Kipleg. I says tuh her, wanna come down duh cellar? an' she says, what fer? An' I says, oh—jus' like dat—an' she says, naw, an' I says, come on down duh cellar an' see what I got. So I givea some immies—"

"G'wan."

"Cross my heart!"

"Whatcha do?"

"Felt aroun' unner her dress."

"Dat's all?"

"Geesus—I din' have much time."

"Yuh stink!"

"Well, if I woulda had more time—"

Kipleg said, "Betcha she wouldn' go on down dere witcha agin. Betcha any money she wouldn'—"

"Betcha she would."

"Well, lemme see."

Ollie glanced across the street to Marie; then he glanced back at Kipleg. He looked at Kipleg pleadingly.

"Geesus, Kipleg, how'm I gonna leddya see?"

Kipleg nodded triumphantly. "Dere. I knew yuh was fulla crap."

"Well, yuh ain' gonna call me fulla crap."

"Well, show me."

"How?"

"I'll go down duh cellar. Den you gitta tuh go down duh cellar witcha."

"Awright—"

Kiplek slipped into the hall, and then Ollie sat alone, leaning back with assumed boredom. Sometimes he would glance sidewise at Marie, but most of the time he simply stared at the ground. He wondered how long it would take for Marie to notice him, to cross the street; and somehow he knew that she would cross the street. But he wasn't eager to go down into the cellar now. In one way or another, Kipleg had tricked him into this.

Marie stopped her pacing. There was Ollie, sitting across the street, but hardly noticing her at all. Well, that was a way Ollie had, and she tossed back her head, to show that it meant nothing to her. Now that he had had a fight with Blackbelly, Ollie was probably all swelled up.

Ollie took out some immies, rolling them from one hand to the other. He couldn't get her with that same old immie trick.

"Hey, Marie!"

She tilted her head saucily, then turned her back upon him.

"Awright—"

She glanced at him again, walked over to the curb, and felt at the gutter daintily with one foot. There was no denying that Ollie was nice to look at.

"Wanna see sumpen?"

"Naw." She fled back to the stoop, seating herself there, crossing her legs.

"Awright—"

She hesitated, tilted her head again, and then called, "Whaddya got?"

"Sumpen."

"What?"

"C'mon over an' see."

She rose, took a few steps toward him, turned back, turned again and crossed the street. Ollie sat where he was, indifferent.

"Whaddya got?"

Ollie yawned, stretched his arms. "Got it down du cellar."

"Yeah—I know." She backed away.

"Aw, c'mon—"

"Naw, you Ollie."

"Jus' dis once."

"Naw."

"Well, c'mon intuh duh hall."

She hesitated. The street was empty, warm, deserted; it promised no amusement, and what harm could come to her if she went into the hall with Ollie? It wasn't like the cellar.

They went into the hall, slowly, and once inside Marie shrank apprehensively against Ollie. Here it was dark again, with the flickering flame of the gas jet. Why did she go into the darkness, when she had hated it so?

"Whaddya 'fraid of?" Ollie wanted to know.

"It's so dark here."

"Well, I'm here."

"Yeah."

They sat down in the darkness under the steep, wooden, carpeted stairs, and Ollie put his arm around her. She shrank away, but it seemed to her that the darkness reached out from the other side to grasp her. Then Ollie's hand crept under her dress. She wanted to scream, but she couldn't; she couldn't make any sound at all, and she trembled with fear. Then she attempted to think her fear into anticipation and thrill. Ollie's hand crept farther up beneath her skirt.

"Don'," she whispered.

"Why?"

"I dunno—jus' don'."

"Why?"

"Well—yer hurtin' me."

"I ain'."

"Yuh are."

His hand crept between her warm legs, clamping the flesh and pinching it. Her body became gooseflesh all over, and she trembled violently. She tried to think of her mother, and could only think about how sick she was getting. She closed her eyes, opened them; but all around her was darkness and nothing else. She thought of how it was out on the street, all warm sunlight and warm stone.

"Lemme go," she whispered.

"Geesus," Ollie said, "whaddya 'fraid of? I ain' gonna hurtcha, Marie. Hones, tuh God, I ain'. Look, I'm takin' my hand away. Dere."

"Less go back in duh street," she whimpered.

"Geesus, whatsa matter witcha, anyway?"

"Nuttin'."

"Well, stay here, den."

Marie heard a noise, and her terror increased tenfold. She shrank against Ollie, shrank away from him then, and with a great, enfolding grasp, the blackness reached out for her. She thought of hell and devils and punishment, and she thought of her mother, whimpering now.

"Aw, stop cryin'."

"Awright."

"Geesus, I never saw sucha baby."

"Awright."

A hand was creeping under her dress again, pinching the flesh that was now hard with pimples. Stifling a scream, she grasped Ollie's arm.

"Don'."

"Geesus, I ain' doin' nuttin'!"

"Y'are."

"I ain'—so help me God. Look—dere's my hands."

But under her dress the hand still caressed her. If it wasn't Ollie, what was it? Dumb with fear, she tried to move, but could not. And then, in front of her, Kipleg burst out laughing.

"Yuh dumb basted!" Ollie yelled.

"Whaddya 'fraid of, Marie?"

"Geesus, yer dumb as hell. Watcha wanna spoil duh whole thing fer?"

"Aw, screw."

But now Marie was sobbing violently, thrusting her fists into her mouth, shaking her head back and forth. Actually, she was in a state of hysteria, and Ollie and Kipleg, half laughing, half frightened, fled.

But Marie sat there in the dark, sobbing. Now, perhaps, the creatures of darkness were reaching out for her; let them reach then, let them have her. She sat there, and cried.

How long she sat there, crying, she didn't know; but when the shame had passed, the fear returned. Like a small, frightened animal, she crept out of the dark into the sunshine. And there, on the stoop, was Ishky.

The sun and the light and the day are the time for love. They are the time for dreams and fancies and happiness; and isn't it strange that I, Ishky, am returning to all that? I sit here on the stoop, not too much on my mind, dreaming.

How is it with dreams? How is it with gardens? If there is a magic garden, and not in one place, then surely it is in another. So if I go off with Marie, isn't it quite possible that together we will find the garden? Not ash heaps, but a real garden, with flowers that smell—

And I turn around, and there is Marie looking at me.

"Marie!"

I look at her, and I am sure that my eyes and my face are filled with love. All the love that is inside of Ishky is written there. (Marie, look at me! Do you see the great love that fills my heart?)

But there is an expression upon her face that I have never seen before, and she is trembling all over. I don't know why.

"Marie!"

"Oh—you—"

"Marie!"

Suddenly, screaming with rage, she leaps at me, beats at my face, claws at me, and then runs away, crying bitterly.

Well, I am only Ishky, and if I understand some things, I don't understand everything. I don't understand this. I can only sit on the stoop, looking after her, and wondering.

CHAPTER NINETEEN

You see the way it is with me now; and how am I to account for Marie? I watch her run into her house, and then I shake my head. Some things simply are, and that is all there is to it.

Here are Kipleg and Ollie, and I am instantly on the alert when I see them. I will have to hold on to what honor I have won. They will remind me of my mother. So my small head is full of things, of Marie, and of what to say to Kipleg and Ollie.

Together, grinning at some deep secret they held between them, Kipleg and Ollie came swaggering down the block, arm linked in arm. They saw Ishky, and they made for him.

"Hey, sheeney," Kipleg called good naturedly.

Ollie was still bubbling inside. In the scene with Marie in the hall, there had been deep drama and deeper humor; and for some reason it struck him as woefully funny. He wanted to laugh outright, to tell Ishky what he had done.

"Hullo," Ishky nodded.

"Where's yer mamma?"

"I don' need her," Ishky said indignantly.

"Yeah—"

"Yeah—"

"Yer yella of her."

"I ain'."

"You stink, sheeney."

"Aw, leavim alone," Ollie said.

"Some gang, wid him in it."

"I ain' yella," Ishky said.

"Aincha?"

"Naw."

"Well, why doncha show it, why doncha?"

"Awright."

"Why doncha?"

"Awright. Geesus, gimme a chance, willya?"

"C'mon."

Don't ask me how the idea came to me. I don't know how it came to me. But put yourself in my place, with the need of keeping face in front of Ollie and Kipleg. What would you have done? You see, I want you to know how things had been leading up to this, and later to that other thing, of which I will tell presently. But about this. I must explain to you why I did it, if I can explain. The reason is—I had to hold up my face in front of Ollie and Kipleg. Maybe you don't understand that, but that's the reason.

I thought of Shomake's fiddle. I don't know why I thought of Shomake's fiddle all at once instead of anything else; but maybe it was because I could never forget the wonder of it. Even the secret garden was not as splendid as this beautiful fiddle.

And when I thought of it, I began to sweat all over. It's very funny when you sweat like that—and know you are sweating. In little bubbles, the sweat crept out of my skin, and I felt it run down my cheeks.

(Forget, Ishky—and don't tell them! Ollie doesn't know, and Kipleg doesn't know, so why do you have to tell them anything at all about it?)

How hot the sun is! How hot the ground is, under my feet. My eyes dart up and down the block, and I see the stiff, straight walls of the houses, baking under the sun. I am baking like that, and presently I will be cooked—entirely cooked.

Shomake's fiddle—

"Geesus Christ," Ollie says.

"Awright, awright, yuh jus' wait fer me at duh corner. Jus' wait dere."

"Whaddya gonna do?" Kipleg wants to know.

"You'll see."

So I am about to do it. And why? Because I must impress Kipleg and Ollie. But what harm will come to the fiddle?

Over, across the street in Shomake's store, it is dim and quiet. I steal in softly from the sunlight, wondering whether Shomake is there. If he is there, then the whole business is off. The old man sits behind the counter, hammering and paring leather; he does not even look up. I knew he would not look up, and I steal past him into the dark back room.

Ah, what smells there are in this place of Shomake's, what good Italian smells, what hot, meaty smells! It is quiet, dismal, and from outside, I hear the tap, tap, tap of the hammer. But I haven't forgotten what I came for. I must hurry; back there, Ollie is waiting for me, and Kipleg is waiting.

There, in its case, I see the fiddle. Now I am trembling. I pick it up, hesitate, and then run from the store. But Shomake's father does not even look up, sitting there with his great shaggy gray head bent over his awl.

I have the fiddle case clutched under my arm, and I run up to the corner. Ollie sees me.

"Geesus!" he gasps.

"Geesus," Kipleg says.

And then we all three run like mad. We run east, down the slope to the river, where there are empty lots and trees. But now I am trembling and shivering. What kind of a fool have I been? What will happen to the fiddle now—?

The three of them, Ollie, Ishky, and Kipleg stopped in an empty lot. They made a circle, crouching with their hands on their knees, and they stared at the fiddle case as it lay on the ground between them.

"I'm gonna open it," Kipleg said.

"Like hell yuh are. I'm gonna."

"Lemme," Ishky pleaded.

"Lay off it."

"Awright, lemme now."

"Geesus, yuh dumb sheeney basted!"

Ollie, awing the other two, knelt and opened the case. There inside, rich, warm, shining, and splendid, lay the fiddle. For a moment, all three of them stared fascinated at the rich red-and-brown wood. Then they all grabbed at it.

Ollie had the fiddle, Kipleg the bow. Ishky was struggling with Ollie for the fiddle, when Ollie pushed him in the face, sitting him abruptly upon the ground.

"On yer ass!"

"Lemme play, Ollie," Kipleg screamed, "lemme play!"

"Me first."

"Geesus, Ollie, jus' lemme touch it once. I ain' goin' tuh run away wid it."

"Gimme dat!"

"Geesus, Ollie—"

"Yuh gonna give it t'me?—"

"Awright, awright—"

"Lemme play, willya, Ollie?" Ishky pleaded.

"Gimme a chance, willya?"

Now with fiddle and bow, Ollie struck a pose. He made a mock bow, sweeping his handsome yellow head from side to side. Then he waved the bow through the air, like a wand; then he struck it to the fiddle, the strings screaming like a cat in pain. Making a face, he began to slide the bow back and forth; and then the pained expression upon his face turned to one of deep pleasure.

"Geesus," Kipleg whispered.

"Dere. Maybe yuh tought I couldn' play on duh thing?"

"Lemme," Ishky pleaded.

"Awright, awright. But Kipleg comes next."

"Geesus, who got duh fiddle?"

"Awright—nobody says yuh not gonna play."

Grinning with delight, Ollie swayed from side to side, forcing sound out of the violin. And then Ishky and Kipleg could stand it no longer. Together, they made a grab at the fiddle; all three rolled over the ground, the fiddle clenched between them. For a moment, there was a mass of squirming, screaming bodies; then, one by one, they detached themselves.

The fiddle lay on the ground, crushed and splintered. The strings were all broken, the sides broken, and there was a great hole where someone had put his foot through the middle of it.

Ishky stared at it, stared and stared at the poor wreckage.

"Now look whatcha done," Ollie said.

"Boy, yer dumb as hell," Kipleg exploded. "Whatcha wanna do dat fer?"

Ishky shook his head, staring at them dumbly. "But I din'—"

"Yuh did so."

"We sawim, din' we, Ollie. Geesus, Ishky!"

"No—no—no!"

"Geesus, whaddya so yella about? We ain' gonna snitch onya, are we, Kipleg?"

"Shid, no."

But what difference does that make? There, all broken up on the ground, lay the fiddle. But it couldn't be called a fiddle now, broken as it was.

What have I done? What will I say when they find me out? Then I will have to confess that I stole the fiddle, smashed it to pieces.

"But how c'n I bring it back?" I plead.

"Leddit go."

"Sure. Geesus, Ishky—whaddya 'fraid of, anyway?"

"Aw—nuttin'."

There is no use picking it up, for even I know that such a pile of

broken wood can never be repaired. I let it lie where it is, and
with Ollie and Kipleg I walk back to the block.

They are still laughing and joking between themselves. Well, for
them that's all right; they never heard Shomake play on his fiddle.
But what will I do? What will I do if Shomake asks me about it?
If he asks me where his fiddle is, what will I say?

"Listen, Ishky," Ollie says to me, when we are back on the
block, "from now on, yer in duh gang."

"Yeah," Kipleg says.

"We ain' goin' tuh snitch."

"Yeah."

But all I want now is to get away from them, and I am glad
when they leave me alone on my stoop. Out of all grand dreams,
nothing is left—nothing.

I am Ishky—but I have nothing now.

I sit in a bundle on my stoop, my head in my hands, and I
hardly notice how it is down at the bottom of the block, where the
sun is beginning to lower, where all the houses are taking on a
rosy glow. Evening is coming.

Someone sits down next to me. Glancing sidewise, I see that it is
Thomas Edison. He has some sorrow of his own, and I don't mind
him sitting next to me. It seems to me again, that there is some sort
of a bond between us.

Warm stone—and warm night air. As the day passes, I am alone,
full of wonder and doubt. What are you anyway, Ishky?

Dreams will not come back—

See how the sun sets—

CHAPTER TWENTY

Evening comes, and the sun fades. From where I sit, from the
edge of the house, a long shadow creeps out into the street; and I
know that soon it will be dark.

Everyone has gone except Thomas Edison, and he sits next to
me in silence, his large head drooping forward. He doesn't speak to
me, and I don't speak to him; I don't want to speak. I only want
to sink into my misery, as deep as I can.

And then, my mother puts her head out of the window. "Ishky!"

Why doesn't she leave me alone? Why must I bring my misery
upstairs to her?

"Ishky!"

"Awright."

"Right avay!"

"Awright."

Why am I afraid to go upstairs? Maybe I am afraid to leave Thomas Edison, but I don't know why that should be so.

From the shadows of the shoe repair place across the street, a small shadow detached itself, hesitated, and then moved over the gutter toward Ishky. Ishky watched it, with large sad brown eyes.

"Hey, Ishky!"

"Hullo, Shomake."

"Hullo."

Shomake sat down between Ishky and Thomas Edison. First he tightened the laces on his shoes. Then he stared straight ahead of him.

"Ishky?"

"Yeah?"

"Yuh still saw at me?"

"Naw—I ain' saw. I wasn't never saw atcha, Shomake."

"I thought yuh was."

"Naw—"

They sat in silence again, three small figures, hunched over, wise and young and old as the world. They sat, while the sun sank behind the houses, to bring evening again. The heat was passing. From either end of the block, cool breezes stole. Voices, one by one, broke into the night, but the small figures paid no attention.

"Duh fiddle's gone," Shomake said finally.

Ishky looked at him. Thomas Edison said, "Whyya cryin', Shomake?"

"I ain'."

"Geesus," Ishky whispered.

Shomake got to his feet. He looked at Ishky and then he looked at Thomas Edison, and then he stared down at his feet.

"Well . . ." he began.

"Listen, Shomake," Ishky said eagerly, "we gotta gang, Ollie an' Kipleg an' me. If y'wanna, yuh c'n git intuh it. I'll fix it."

"Yeah?"

"Sure—an' dat'll be a lotta fun."

"Yeah?"

"Sure."

"Awright." He turned hesitantly, and it seemed to Ishky then that he was afraid to go back to the store. Very slowly, Shomake walked to the curb.

"Well—so long, Ishky—"

"So long, Shomake."

"Seeya tumarra."

"Yeah."

"S'long."

"So long."

Shomake faded into the night, strange Shomake—

"Hey, Ishky," Thomas Edison said.

"Yeah?"

"C'n I git intuh duh gang?"

"Yeah—I guess."

"Geesus—"

They sat a while longer. A yellow cat came up to them, mewing, and it leaped into Thomas Edison's arms. He held it close to him, stroking it, whispering to it. Then he dropped it to the sidewalk, and it darted away.

"Well . . ."

Ishky turned around to look at Thomas Edison, who was standing now, his head drooping forward farther than ever.

"Goin' home?"

"Yeah."

"Well—s'long."

"So long."

And I am alone again now. My mother calls, "Ishky! Ishky! Ishky! Come opstes!"

"Awright!"

If she knew, she would leave me alone. I have done an awful thing, and I don't know why. Oh, if there were some reason, any reason, it would not be the way it is. But there is no reason. I took the fiddle, and I destroyed it.

If there is a God in heaven, what will he do to me? Or is this only the beginning? What is happening to me, Ishky?

I want to cry, the way Shomake was crying, but I can't. No, I can't cry.

I get up, and go into the hall. How dark—and dreary—and

gloomy. Am I afraid of a dark hall now? Step by step, I go up. When I open the door, my mother folds her arms around me.

But no rest in that.

CHAPTER TWENTY-ONE

Morning comes, and all things are forgotten—at least for the time. I stretch, yawn, and wonder about the day, about yesterday. All things happened yesterday, the gang, the garden, and the fiddle. Then I turn over, burying my face in the covers. Why must the fiddle come back to me? I want to forget, but what will Shomake say to me?

"Ishky—Ishky!"

Out of bed. I pull my clothes on, glancing anxiously about the room. Small and dirty, but through the window, the sun is shining in. So that makes up for other things.

I guess that I am a fool. Otherwise would I have destroyed Shomake's fiddle? And now, this morning, I want to find Shomake. I don't know what I want to say to him, but I want to talk to him, and maybe that will make it better.

"Ishky!"

"Awright, mama."

I lace my shoes. Even if they are falling to pieces, they will do for another day. Anything will do for today, a day full of sunshine and gladness.

My father has already gone away, but when I come into the kitchen, my mother stands and looks at me. Since I fell off the roof the day before, it seems that my mother cannot see enough of me. There she stands, big, ugly, and smiles at me. Why can't I love my mother as I should?

"Good morning, my heart," she says to me in Yiddish.

"Hullo."

"Is my man ready for his breakfast?"

"Yeah—"

"Come, then."

I bolt my food. Indeed, it seems that I can never be out of the house quickly enough in the morning, when the sun is shining. Before I go, she holds me and kisses me.

"Take care of yourself."

"Yeah."

I go down the stairs, through the dim hall, and then I burst out into the street, stopping, suddenly, rolling myself in the warm sun. Nobody on the block; but who would be there this early? So I sit down on the stoop to bask in the sun.

Everything is fresh and clean that early in the morning. Do you know how that is? After I have sat there a while, I begin to feel full of the sun, and I stretch like a cat. I am sleepy again.

I watch Shomake's store. When he comes out, I will call him over, and tell him about the garden. You see, about this garden: if it is not in one place, then it is in another. The garden is somewhere, and even if I don't quite believe that, I will tell it to Shomake.

For Shomake, the night was long and bitter, and often he woke, to stare into the darkness and whimper. Once, his mother woke, and heard him.

"Peace, my child," she said in her warm Italian.

"I will never play again."

"Now—what nonsense is that? As sure as I live, I will buy you another fiddle. Am I too poor for that?"

"No, I'll never have another fiddle."

"Foolish child, sleep."

And she could hear him tossing and turning and twisting and whimpering.

"Child—child!"

"Yes—I am all right, never fear."

"Are you trying to cheer your mother now? Only sleep, and to-morrow I will have another fiddle for you."

"Yes."

But the night was long, endless, dreary, and out of the darkness figures rose to torment him. Trembling, he crossed himself, drawing the blankets high over his head. Would sleep never come? And when sleep came, it brought dreams. And in his sleep, they took his fiddle from him. As often as he had another fiddle, it vanished.

He saw the gray light creep into the room. "Wonderful light," he thought. Lying quietly, he saw his father rise, dress, go into the shop. Later, his mother called him.

"Ho, heart of hearts, do you see that the morning has come, after all?"

"Yes."

"And you see how foolish the fears of the night are. God takes

care of the night as well as the day." Only, in her heart, she knew
there was no money to buy him another fiddle.

"Mother—"

"Yes, my dear heart?"

"The new fiddle will be like the old one?"

"Yes, yes, my dear heart."

"You will buy it for me? You are not deceiving me, mother mine?"

"Deceiving my child?" His mother laughed, and then she bent
over the stove to hide her face.

"Fiddles cost a lot?"

"Now are you one to worry about that—or is it my worry? Since
when has my proud son taken it into his head to worry about money
matters?"

He looked at her, and he managed to smile. Slowly, the smile
spread over his small face, grew then, and presently they were both
looking at each other, laughing.

"Eat, my child," she smiled.

Outside, the sun calls to all. The sun was so beautiful, that for a
while he sat in the shadowed shop, just looking at it. Then, hesitantly, he opened the door, stepped outside.

The warm breeze crossed him, bathed him inside of it. Spreading
his body, like a newly awakened bird, he walked toward Ishky. He
grinned.

"Hey, Ishky!"

"Hey, Shomake!"

Grinning at each other, they came together, and together they
walked over to the stoop, sat down. They stretched their legs, leaned
back, looked into the sun for an instant, and then blinked their
eyes. They were full of healthy animal pleasure. They stretched
their arms, yawning.

"Whatta day!"

"Yeah."

"Hot."

"Yeah."

Then they heard someone scream, "Kip!"

Kipleg was making his exit through the window of his house,
and with the screams of his mother, the block woke up. Ishky and
Shomake stared eagerly.

"Watchim."

"Yeah."

Kipleg sprang out onto the fire escape, grabbed the ladder, and swung back and forth, like a monkey. His mother leaned out, screaming curses. Then Kipleg dropped to the stoop, to the street, and darted up the block.

"Swine!" his mother screeched after him.

Ishky looked at Shomake, grinned. Their hands crept together. No matter how you took it, life was good.

"Wanna find duh gaden?" Shomake inquired.

"Duh gaden?"

"Yeah."

Ishky pursed up his lips, considered, and then nodded. "But it ain' back dere," he explained, nodding at the house.

"Somere else?"

"Yeah."

They rose, and they began to walk. Down toward the river, they walked, toward the fields and the open lots.

There is no bitterness in my heart, no bitterness in Shomake's heart. If he knew that I had destroyed his fiddle, would it be any different? I don't know, but I know that I must be good to Shomake.

I will make it up to him. You see, we understand each other. We understand about the garden. Maybe there isn't any garden, and I think that we both know that. But nevertheless we go to find it. I am very close to Shomake now.

But no more music—no more music— Carefully I steer him away from the lot where the remains of his broken fiddle lie. I don't want him to see that. Perhaps if he saw it, I would have to tell him the truth.

It is not too long a way to the fields, but now we walk slowly, and it takes us some time. In the first field, we sit down, talk to each other. What do we speak about? Well, must one find things to speak about on a warm summer day?

We chase butterflies until we are out of breath, and then we fling ourselves full length upon the grass. We pull pieces of grass from the ground, draw them through our lips, and suck out the sweet juice. We are very happy.

Then we go on, climbing down the cliffs until we are at the river. The river flows away into a mist where we have never been, and we both think that the river is a very wonderful river. Some day we will go down there. Some day we will go to all places.

Then I break down the last barrier. I tell Shomake of my love for Marie. He listens, and he understands. He tells me about his new fiddle, which he will have soon. Now—isn't the world at our feet?

CHAPTER TWENTY-TWO

Word of the gang came to Blackbelly through many sources. His own gang was a more natural thing; dark skins herded together. And by twelve o'clock that day, when Ishky and Shomake were still down by the river, Blackbelly sat in the yard behind his house with eight or nine colored boys.

The white gang had formed. When Kipleg came back from work, he found Ollie, with four or five more boys. They drifted east, toward the lots, and by the time they reached the slope that led down toward the river, their number had almost doubled.

Now Blackbelly sat in his yard with the colored boys, making their weapons. Preparation was simple. A long sock was filled with ashes and bits of glass; sand gave it weight, and then a knot was tied above the filling. Luxurious in the sun, the colored boys stretched and yawned, grinned. It would be a big fight.

Blackbelly sat apart. Short, broad, solid, they had only to look at him to be filled with a sense of their own strength. Blackbelly knew what he was about.

A short, thin boy, whom they called Fishface, grinned and hefted his stocking. "My," he said, "lookit dat."

"Dem white boys gonna git it."

"Yeah."

"We gonna mash dem up an' cut dere asses offana dem."

"Oh yeah."

"Lookee—lookee."

Blackbelly wondered— Anyway, today was as good a day as any for the fight. Let it come; it had to come. He wasn't afraid. Hell, no, he was far from afraid. Only—

There was more to Blackbelly than to any of the others. He had a broad good head, wide eyes, and an endless expanse of brow. He fought because he had to fight, but sometimes he looked just a little ahead. He sat now, swinging his stocking from hand to hand, saying to himself, "Let it come, let it come."

"Hey—you Blackbelly."

He grinned, and he stood up. The rest stood up with him. Fishface danced from one side of the yard to the other, and a very small colored boy rolled about, hugging his knees. Blackbelly felt himself trembling—not with fear; only he hoped the fight would come soon.

"Goddammem," he muttered.

"Boy—we'll shid all over dem."

Ollie—Ollie, yellow hair and blue eyes, and the swagger that ruled the world. How he hated him! This time it would be Ollie and he, and for Ollie there'd be no way out of it. He looked at his feet, black toes coming out of broken shoes; torn breeches and a torn shirt. There wouldn't be much left of it; but in the same way he'd tear the clothes from Ollie.

Ollie—Ollie, who was king—

"Geesus, c'mon," Fishface said.

"Whatsa matter, Blackbelly?" Cooly asked.

"Yeah?" the very small one said eagerly.

"Awright, awright—"

But Blackbelly stood there, thinking and thinking. Was he afraid then? He threw back his head, and began to laugh; he laughed until his whole body shook with it, until tears rolled down his dark flat cheeks.

"Geesus!"

Then he led the way toward the street, rolling now from side to side with his old swagger.

"Geesus, yeah."

And they followed him, in a close, compact, trusting group. Swinging their stockings, they went up the block, but Ollie's gang had already gone. At the corner, they stopped.

"Whereya goin', Blackbelly?"

"Down tuh duh river."

"Tink dey'll be dere?"

"Sure."

They walked on, slowly, still in their compact battle group. Blackbelly, Fishface, Cooly—

And Blackbelly tried not to think. Down by the river, they would fight, and that was all. Why think? Only—

("Geesus, I'm scared.")

They didn't have to fight, they didn't have to fight. Only bow to Ollie, who was king. Crawl into alleys.

The weighted stockings swung from side to side—

CHAPTER TWENTY-THREE

Then let them fight.

Marie nodded to herself, stood like a small white elf, leaning against her stoop. But after they had gone, after both gangs had gone, the street was strangely empty. Empty and large and full of sun—oh, enough to make her afraid.

Another girl came out of the house, and they sat down on the stoop to play jacks. The ball bounced and the bits of iron slithered back and forth. But Marie kept looking up, always looking up. She wondered why, because she hated Ollie.

She hated them all, Ollie and Ishky and Shomake and Kipleg. Now they would be beaten—

"Marie!" The other girl's name was Ruth.

"I don' wanna play no more."

"Why?"

Marie ran across the street, stopping by Ishky's stoop. Ishky would be better than nothing, but where was he? Carefully she ventured into the hall. Ruth came after her.

"Whaddya goin' in dere fer?"

"Oh, lemme alone."

They went back into the sunshine, stood there. Marie stamped her foot angrily.

"Whatsa matter?"

"Nuttin'."

"Whyya mad?"

"Oh, lemme alone."

Again she crossed the street, ran up the stoop and into her house. In the hall, she shivered; it was so dark. Step by step, she advanced to the stairs. Then she sat down on the stairs. Then, very softly, she began to cry. But she didn't know why she was crying.

She dried her eyes. She went back through the hall into the street. She went into the shoe repair shop. Cautiously, she stole into the back room. Only Shomake's mother was there. The woman smiled at Marie.

"Hello, lovely one," she said in Italian.

"Hello."

"But today is no day for beauty to bloom within."

"There's no one to play with," Marie answered, speaking in the same tongue.

"And am I any better than the poorest company?"

Marie smiled, and Shomake's mother went on with her work. Then, suddenly, Marie blundered into quick, trembling speech, in English.

"Listen, I know who took duh fiddle."

"What?" Shomake's mother turned around, very slowly; she stared at Marie.

"Ishky."

"What? But no—Ishky would do no harm."

"He took it."

Now the woman looked at her carefully, turning from her cleaning to sit down in a broad chair. She drew Marie to her. "Tell me, child—what do you know?"

"Ishky took it, wid Ollie an' Kipleg. Dey smashed it all tuh pieces."

"No, no—tell me in our tongue."

"Ishky an' Ollie—"

Shomake's mother shook her head, her eyes full of pain; she let go of Marie, and Marie turned and fled from the shop. She ran through the hall and up the steps as if a thousand devils were after her. When her mother opened the door, Marie buried her face in her skirt.

"Child—child—"

She lifted Marie in her arms, took her inside, afraid at the way the girl's body trembled.

"Now, tell me."

"Ishky took it, Ishky took it!" she screamed.

CHAPTER TWENTY-FOUR

They took Thomas Edison because they needed all they could get. He promised to fight.

He moved up the block with them, as proud as he had ever been in all his life, swinging his stocking from side to side, and swaggering almost as much as Ollie.

Across the avenue and down toward the river, he imagined the

eyes of all the world to be upon him. It was good, and it was satisfying; but it wearied his mind. And he was not quite certain whether
he wouldn't be afraid. Once, he wanted to go back, but Ollie threatened to break his neck, and then he went on with them.

Then he began to sing. He sang at the top of his voice, swinging
the stocking, kicking up his feet in front of him.

"Shuddup," Ollie said.

"Geesus yeah."

Some of the boys began to laugh, and that angered Ollie. Everyone knew that Thomas Edison was his brother.

"Shuddup!"

"Awright, Ollie."

His head was heavy, and it began to loll from side to side. Instead
of kicking up his feet, he began to stumble. He was tired, but no
one would let him rest. He knew that he had to go on, to prove to
them now that he was not too different from the rest.

Shomake and I played, and time passed. We leaned over the
embankment, where the sewer flows into the river, and threw stones
at things. Sometimes, a bottle would shoot out, and then we would
throw until we had broken it.

Shomake laughed so much that I was certain he had forgotten
about the fiddle. Anyway, I would not remind him. We set out to
find the garden.

I say, "We'll look over duh whole world."

"A magic gaden, ain' it?" Shomake wants to know.

"Yeah."

Shomake thinks a while, and then a wonderful idea occurs to
him. "If it's a magic gaden, den it c'n be anywhere at all."

"Well—"

"Sure, if it's magic."

"Awright."

We go into a broad field, full of high grass, and we pretend to
look between the grass. That sets us laughing, because how could
the garden be in such a place? Then we look beneath a tree.

We come to a fountain, bubbling with clear water, and we both
drink. Shomake splashes the water all over his face, and then we
throw water at each other. We squirt it from our mouths, and after
that we roll in the grass to dry ourselves.

We are muddy and dirty and wet, but what difference does that make? Suddenly, I spring up and tell Shomake to run. I chase him, and then he chases me, and finally, when we end up beneath the tall rocks, we are both sobbing with pleasure and panting for breath.

"Less rest," I say.

So we sit down, tell each other about the garden, describe it as though we had lived in it all our lives. Isn't it strange that we both know so much about this magic garden, when neither of us has been there? Shomake knows that there will be music in the garden, and fiddles, too; but that does not please me so much, as I cannot play a fiddle.

"Phonagraphs," I say.

"Yeah."

"An' cake."

"Yeah."

Marie, too, I think; but I don't tell that to Shomake. Only, I dream a little by myself of how Marie will be in the garden with us.

Now we are rested, and we begin to climb the rocks. Oh, we climb very carefully, because if you slip here, you will be smashed to bits. And halfway up, we rest on a ledge and look at the river.

How beautiful the river is, winding away into the mist like a streak of silver! The world is at our feet, and we are young and happy. Far off, all clouded with mist, lies the city, a thousand tiny houses. The gas tanks break up like gray monsters; the elevated trains crawl like snakes. And over the river, there are bridges and bridges, as far as we can see.

Isn't this a place to forget all things except dreams? Shomake laughs, and I know why he is laughing; he is happy inside of himself. But he is no happier than I am.

We are like two fat bugs in the sun, stretching, drinking in air and warm sunshine. Ollie is forgotten, Kipleg, too. Fights are forgotten. Who will bother us here?

"Less climb," Shomake says.

So we go up the rocks, hand over hand, thrilling to the great distance under us. And when we reach the top, we sit down to rest. Here, on the top, a cool breeze blows from beyond the river. And the river crawls at our feet, like a thin silver snake. Then, turning around, Shomake sees Ollie and his gang.

"Hey, Shomake!"

Ollie led the way, Kipleg beside him, and behind them the rest of the gang trailed out. The long, weighted stockings swung from side to side, and Ollie's yellow hair blew in the breeze and glinted in the sunshine.

"Hey, Ishky!"

Slowly, Ishky and Shomake rose to their feet. Without thinking a great deal, they knew the purpose of the gang. They went forward hesitantly, Ishky leading the way.

"Hey, Ollie, whereya goin'?" he called.

Ollie grinned.

Kipleg said, "We're gonna git Blackbelly."

"Where is he?"

"He'll come down, awright."

"C'mon," Ollie commanded.

Shomake hesitated. The spell of the river seen from the top of the bluff was still upon him, the peace and the lull of the breeze. And as bitterly as he hated anything, he hated fighting. He held back.

"We gotta go eat," Ishky explained.

"Yeah," Shomake said. "I said tuh my mudder I'd be back tuh eat."

"Yeah."

Ollie stood in front of them, legs spread, hands on his hips. His insolent, ready grin still lingered upon his lips. "Geesus," he said. And that was all.

Kipleg said, "All wops an' sheeneys are yella."

"Hell, yeah."

"Yella as shid."

"Yuh stinkin' wop."

"I don' wanna fight," Shomake protested.

"I tol' yuh he was yella."

"Areya comin'?" Ollie wanted to know.

"Yeah."

"Well—" Ishky began.

"Are yuh comin', or ain'ya?" Ollie swung his stocking in a great circle, bringing it close to Shomake's face.

"I ain' done nuttin' tuh you, Ollie."

"Are ya comin'?"

"Geesus, givem dere lumps!"

"Kick duh shid oudda duh yella basteds!"

"Awright," Ishky nodded.

They fell in at the back, with Thomas Edison, who walked with his head hanging down, he was so tired now.

CHAPTER TWENTY-FIVE

Down near the river, near an overhanging rock, they held their council of war, and now Ollie nodded significantly at a rope he wore wound around his middle. They all sat in a circle, Ishky and Shomake too, and very often they glanced up at the bluff, where Blackbelly might be expected to appear. They had left their invitation by moving boldly down to the river. If Blackbelly failed to take it up—

Ollie said, "Jus' lemme get my hands on dat nigger, dat's all."

"Whaddya gonna do, Ollie?"

"Plenny."

Thomas Edison was good and tired, not a little afraid, too, and he began to whimper. He pressed beseechingly against Ishky, and when Ishky shook him off, he looked at Ollie.

Ollie was explaining the science of battle. "Gittem before dey know what's at. Den kick duh nuts offana dem."

"Yeah," Kipleg agreed.

"Don' git yella."

Thomas Edison said, "Ollie—"

"Geesus, whaddya wan' now?"

"Ollie—I wanna go home."

"Geesus, d'ya wan' me tuh kick duh shid oudda yuh?"

"Naw. I wanna go home."

"Whatcha leddim come along fer?"

"Nevermin'. You stay here, duh yuh hear me?"

"Ollie—"

"Yuh heard me."

"Awright."

"Whaddya got in yer stockin', Ollie?" someone asked.

"Ashes. But I'm gonna use my hands."

"Whaddya got duh rope fer?"

"You'll see."

They went to the fountain, then, and they all had a drink. Then they climbed until they were halfway up the bluff, in a small level space. They waited there.

Thomas Edison sat and blubbered, shifting his heavy head from side to side. Deep dread grew upon him, and more than anything else, he longed to be at home with Oloman. He would go to her when it was over, and he would tell her how Ollie had treated him.

"Yeah," he muttered, "yeah, duh dirdy shid."

And Shomake stood to one side, staring at the ground; already he was trembling, not so much with fear as with hate, hate for Ollie and all the rest.

Kipleg lit a cigarette, passing it around.

CHAPTER TWENTY-SIX

When the cigarette came to me, I puffed on it. Maybe you won't understand that, but there is a lot about Ishky that I don't understand myself. I don't want to fight, so why don't I jump up and run away? I don't know. Maybe because the gang was my idea in the first place.

But now I'm afraid. What is Ollie going to do with that rope he has wound around his middle? If I run, I will lose face, and anyway, they can run after me and catch me. Then they would beat me.

I know I hate Blackbelly. Now is my chance to get back at him, to beat him the way he beat me. Only—

I have to tell you things the way they happened. I have to tell you about this fight, and what came after. You see that Shomake and I are in it already. But we didn't want to fight. Is it any wonder that, when I look up and see Blackbelly and his gang, I am frightened?

They come down slowly, bunching together, and we all gather together, too, even Thomas Edison. Ollie steps to the front, because he has more guts than anyone else. I wonder how soon the fight will start.

The sun is still shining, and that is the strangest thing of all. It comes down through the trees, mottling the ground; I see how it splatters Shomake with light and shadow. And below us, off to one side, is the river, lovely and silver as ever. Why do they want to fight? That is what I ask myself now.

Shomake edges close to me, pressing up against me, and I can feel his body trembling. But I am trembling, too. Then, after all, I am nothing but a coward—no more than that. You are yellow, Ishky.

What will I do when the fight starts? Should I run away. But if
I do, Ollie will only get me later.

Where are all my dreams now? Where is the happiness that
existed between Shomake and me when we spoke about the secret
garden?

He saw Ollie's gang, and he realized that they outnumbered him
two to one, or almost. He could turn around and go back, or he
could go on. Ahead, there was defeat or glory, and because Ollie
had made the odds so big his small wide body swelled with rage.
"Hey, yuh Blackbelly nigger!" Ollie yelled.

Fishface said to him, "Geesus, lookit what dey got. Less git oudda
here."

"You yella basted."

"Geesus, Blackbelly, dey'll kick shid oudda us."

"Will dey?"

Blackbelly advanced slowly, swelling all the while with rage and
hate. He swung his stocking around his head. Let them bring on
ten or a dozen or a hundred. Let them.

He climbed down, until he stood face to face with Ollie, and
behind him the rest of the dark boys came. They stood in a small
cluster, waiting for Blackbelly, waiting for Ollie.

Perhaps if Blackbelly noticed one thing more than anything else
then, it was Ollie's splendid beauty. Just a little higher than Blackbelly he stood, but slimmer, his insolent grin playing about his
lips. His blue eyes blinked and sparkled, and his yellow hair tossed
upon his head. He was laughing at Blackbelly. Blackbelly saw
Ollie's beauty. Perhaps he saw other things, too, for he saw the line
of rope wound around Ollie's middle.

His heart beat with anger, with hate. He wanted to claw the
smile off Ollie's face. He longed to be alone with Ollie. There would
be other times when he would be alone with Ollie.

The boys behind edged up to Blackbelly. He was secure, stout
and solid.

"Lookit duh nigger basteds," Kipleg laughed.

"Shuddup!" Blackbelly snapped.

"Whaddya gonna do?" Ollie wanted to know, swinging his stocking.

"Do what we wanna."

"Yeah?"

"Yeah."

"S'pose we ain' gonna leddya?"

"Try an' stop me, white boy."

"Yeah?"

"Yeah."

Blackbelly waved a hand at his gang. "C'mon," he said.

"Whereya goin'?" Ollie demanded.

"Down dere."

"Oh no."

"Doncha try tuh stop us, white boy!"

"G'wan den."

"C'mon—"

Blackbelly took a step, and Ollie sprang at him, catching the swinging stocking upon one shoulder. In a moment, the two gangs were together, punching, swinging stockings, clawing at, tearing at each other. Only Thomas Edison hung back, Ishky and Shomake were launched into it. A colored boy sprang at them, and they fought back, instinctively.

Now, for just a moment, I have forgotten that I am afraid. I remember only that I hate all niggers. This isn't Blackbelly, but what difference does that make?

A stocking hits me on the face, scratches me, but I hardly notice it. Now I don't seem to know anything except that I am fighting. Shomake is crying, swinging awkwardly with his fists. Out of the corner of my eye, I see Ollie and Blackbelly, rolling over and over.

How long will we fight? Already, it seems that we have been fighting forever. Perhaps we will fight forever.

CHAPTER TWENTY-SEVEN

Shall I fight forever? Is this the same Ishky, who is now battling like a wild beast? I have fought before, but there was never such a fight as this. This is kill or be killed, and I am no longer a human being, but a beast.

They don't give up. Time passes, and it seems that hours have gone by, though it cannot possibly be as long as that. Yet they don't give up.

We can't stop fighting. Brown flesh is under me, and then brown flesh is on top of me. We roll on the ground, holding tight to each other, and then we beat at each other's face.

I catch one glimpse of Shomake. Now he is fighting with someone else—Shomake who never fought with anyone before. You must understand that—to understand this madness of ours. We are not fighters, most of us. I am not a fighter, Shomake is not a fighter, yet now we are fighting like wild beasts. You must understand that, and you must understand how completely mad we have gone.

Shomake screams, sobs, and tears at a boy. He is thrown to the ground, where he lies sobbing for a moment, but then he is back on his feet, and fighting again. His small, thin form is filled with fury. What has come over him?

Has the entire world gone mad? But no, that is hardly possible. The sun still shines. In fits and starts I am aware of it, placid blobs of light creeping through the trees. But the sun is nothing to me now. I have suddenly become a creature of battle, and my only purpose in life is to fight, to fight and to fight and to fight.

"Dirdy nigger!" I hear Shomake scream. It is the same Shomake.

The curses pour from his lips in a rapid stream as he fights on. Now two of them have the enemy beneath them, and they are beating him unmercifully. How can the gentle Shomake beat a living being like that?

But I have business of my own, and my hands are full. This boy is smaller than I, and he has lost his stocking, so now things are more evenly matched. Tearing at each other, we roll over and over on the ground. We spit and claw and bite. I am crying, and he is crying, too; and while we fight, we hammer words at each other.

"Jew basted!"

"Lousy dinge!"

"Stinkin' sheeney, I'll cutcha up!"

"I'll tear yer nuts off!"

Basted — louse — shid — bitch — sheeney — nigger — shid — sonuvabitch — shidface—

The world is tossing, spinning. But the world has always gone round. Now I am seeing it. How strange to see the world go round!

"Niggerdinge!"

A face to beat at, a black face under me. There is no strength left in my arms, but nevertheless I continue to hammer away. Why doesn't the face disappear into the earth?

Then I am underneath. The world turns, and fists beat into my face. My fists? Hardly. I am crying, a little insane, I imagine. I spit, growl, catch a finger between my teeth.

I bite with all my strength. Warm, sweet blood wells out, and then the finger is torn away. Is it the same finger thrust into my eye? Screaming with pain, I twist my body, punch and claw at the thing above me.

There is no end and no surcease. Ishky has become a creature of battle. As long as the world is, he will fight.

We roll and roll. Dreadful fear comes into my heart; perhaps we are rolling to the edge of the bluff. If that is so, we will roll off, plunge down on the rocks. I surge away from the other, gain my feet.

And then, for an instant, I have a spreading glimpse of the battle. No, it isn't over; they are still fighting, and I know that they will fight on and on. Shomake is crying. Above all the other noise, I can hear him crying.

Why don't they give up? Why don't the niggers run away? Why don't we run away? Why don't I run away? I am only Ishky, and no fighter, nor is Shomake any more of a fighter than I am. Yet we keep on fighting. How is that?

"Goddammnigger!"

"Whitebitch!"

"Shiddinge!"

Face to face, we stand, throwing blows at each other. But there is no more force in the blows, no strength left in either of us. We know that, and we both cry bitterly. Is it possible that here, in the middle of all this fighting, I feel kinship with him? I don't know. I only know that I must go on fighting.

We fall again, roll over in each other's arms, doing no more damage, only hugging tightly. That is what the fighting has come to. Then, suddenly, I hear Ollie scream in triumph. The enemy tears himself from me, and I start to my feet weakly. But I don't run after him.

Can it be that the fight is over? I am dizzy, weak; I can't stop my tears or the shaking of my body. I sit down on the ground, holding my head in my hands. Let them come at me now. It makes no difference anymore. I am through with fighting; there is nothing at all left in me.

But the fight is over. It must be over. I see Shomake, who is standing by himself, crying, and trying to wipe the tears from his face. How small he looks now, and how beaten!

Most of the niggers are gone now. But Ollie is still fighting with Blackbelly. Then how long has it been? If nearly as long as it seemed to me, how is it that Ollie can remain upon his feet and fight?

All that are left are making a circle about Ollie and Blackbelly. Some were chasing the enemy, but now they are coming back. They are all gathering about Ollie and Blackbelly. I go nearer. Shomake is close to me, trying hard to smile. But how can he smile, when he is crying so hard?

CHAPTER TWENTY-EIGHT

They had gone, one by one, and now only Blackbelly was left. He saw the end. Well, he had expected no more than this.

At first, he and Ollie had been together upon the ground, tearing at each other; now they were on their feet, face to face, exchanging blow for blow. And around them, in a crouching, battered, silent circle, stood the gang, waiting. In his fighting, Blackbelly could see that gang; and if red mists of heat and anger brought things to his mind human beings have long forgotten—then he saw the pack, crouched and ready, while the leaders of the pack fought.

Had it been that way once, when men were young? Did he remember, or did he know nothing beyond his fighting? Ollie would not be beaten. Handsome, insolent, blond, and still laughing through his tears of hate, he fought as he had fought in the beginning, lightly, eagerly. And, in that, Blackbelly realized his defeat. Doggedly he battled on, tired, moving little now, his short heavy legs anchored to the ground. He put his wide head down and fought, while tears streamed down his face.

And the pack waited for the kill.

Ollie saw victory. At any rate, the gang was behind him, waiting for his word. And Blackbelly, alone, wept tears of rage and disappointment.

They circled warily. The fight was telling, and their arms were heavy as lead. Ollie's freckled skin was cut and scratched, and in one place, from his cheek, blood was flowing freely. There was no strength left in his arms.

Then Blackbelly went down. Taking a step backward, he tripped over a rock, and in a moment, the gang was upon him. As they piled on top of him, Ollie stepped back and out of it, shaking his head dazedly.

Blackbelly struggled for a moment under the mass of squirming bodies, and then he lay still. And Ollie stood there, staring.

"Holdim!" Kipleg shouted. "Hol' duh black basted!"

"Gottim."

"Hey, Ollie, whaddya wan' us tuh do?"

"Geesus—"

But he knew it was over, and the fight gone from him at last, he lay still under the pile of bodies. Breathing, his body heaved and groaned, and from between his clenched lips came little moans of pain. But he no longer cried. Now he didn't care. The battle had come, and now the battle was gone, and slowly there filtered into his mind the meaning of defeat.

Hate grew in him like a slow fire, hate so furious that if it had been translated into strength, he could have thrown the pile of bodies from him.

CHAPTER TWENTY-NINE

In the beginning, when the fight started, Thomas Edison was the only one who held back. He crouched alone by a rock, pressing against it, trembling, and from there he saw Ollie and Blackbelly crash. His eyes grew wider as the two gangs spilled into the fight. He pressed his hands to his large face, his mouth hanging open with fear.

But he stayed then; for the sight was fascinating and wonderful and terrible. It was only when the battle surged over toward him that he ran away. Nobody noticed him, nobody remembered him; but he thought that both gangs would be after him. He didn't look back, he was so certain that a mob of screaming boys with murder in their hearts would be speeding after him.

He climbed up and over the rock, and then he stumbled through a clump of heavy thickets. Branches beat at his face, and he fought them aside as if they were living things. He began to climb, until his heart pounded like a triphammer; and then, losing his footing, he rolled back, over and over, like a limp bundle of clothes.

Scratched and bleeding, he brought up against a tree near the bottom of the bluff. There, for just a moment, he lay still; then he stirred, moved his oversize head. He began to whimper like a hurt animal, and he slapped his hands against his face. Holding his eyes tightly shut, he moved his head, as if peering here and there. Then he opened his eyes, stared behind him in terror.

But nobody came—

Groaning, he stood up, and he climbed again. Step by step, he pulled himself along, until he had reached the top of the bluff, where he lay upon his stomach, inert and sobbing.

Then he turned to look. From where he was, the gangs were hidden, but before and beneath him spread the peaceful misty city, the crawling river and the bridges. He stared and stared, and then he smiled. He began to walk, but in a little while he was crying again. His head hurt.

It was a long way back to the block, and he shambled slowly. Often, he looked behind him, and once he said, softly:

"Ollie—I ain' yella."

On the streets, he ran, and when he reached the block it appeared to open its arms to him. How quiet and peaceful and familiar it was, with its two walls of flat houses, with its sun-baked pavement!

His head hurt terribly. One hand, which he looked at continually, was cut and bleeding, but he didn't mind that so much as his head. It seemed to him that his head was swelling and swelling; and soon it would burst. Then what would become of him? The thought brought tears, and they cut more grooves in the dirt that covered his face.

Almost at his house, he imagined Ollie was calling him, like this, "Hey, yuh goddam Thomas Edison loony!" Stopping, he stared behind him; but there was nobody on the street, nobody at all. Then where was Ollie?

"Awright, Ollie," he whispered pleadingly.

He came to his house as an animal comes to its lair, opened the door, and crawled slowly into the dim hall. The darkness was good and restful, like a mother. Then he knew that he wanted Oloman.

"Oloman," he said.

He opened the door, went into the kitchen, where she sat, rocking and knitting—soft rhythm, rocking and knitting. He swayed his head from side to side.

"Oloman," he said.

She turned to look at him, and then she limped to his side, shaking her old, withered head.

"Poor fool—what have they done to you now?"

"My head hurts."

"Aye, and you're cut and bruised, poor fool." She took a wet rag, water, and she began to wash and soothe him, whispering to him all the while.

Ah—there was no one like Oloman, no one at all. He purred and wilted under her hands, stretching himself. But inside his head, it made no difference, and he was still growing and growing.

"Duh head, Oloman."

"Yes, poor fool—only close your eyes, and try not to think. Thinking is not in its way for such as you. Do not think, and rest that large poor head of yours."

"Yeah—yeah—"

"And tell the old woman what happened."

"Ollie, Oloman."

"Aye, the beast! Don't I know him for the beast he is, out of my own blood? Tell me what Ollie did to you, my poor scatterbrain fool."

"He made me fight."

"Eh? How's that? If he was beating you!—"

"I runaway."

"Yes," she nodded. "Yes, poor fool, we must know how to run from them that are stronger. That is the only way there is out of it."

"I fell, den."

"Poor fool, poor fool," she sighed.

She sat down, and he pressed up against her, trying to forget his pain in her comfort, in the warm assurance her presence gave him. She rocked and knitted, while he mumbled to himself, pressing his hands against his head. Then he stumbled to his feet. His head was still swelling and swelling; he knew that it would never stop: in that way, it would go on swelling until it burst. But not in here. He knew that it must not burst in here, where everything was so close and comfortable. It would frighten Oloman.

He walked toward the door, slowly.

"Where to now, poor addlebrain?"

He went out of the door, shaking his head, and outside he stood with his face turned up, soaking the sunshine into himself. He smiled a little. Out here— Let it burst, because it would harm nobody but himself. And he was not afraid of the harm it would do him, not afraid anymore.

With dragging steps, he walked up the block, until he came to the house where Ishky lived. He turned into the hall, and then he began to go up the steps. No more danger from Ollie now; here, Ollie would never think to look for him. But he didn't care about Ollie. Ollie could hurt him no more than his head hurt now.

The steps were long. After a while, it appeared to his dulled mind that he had been climbing forever. This he associated with the climb up the bluff. Once, he had fallen down, and now he would have to be careful not to fall again, very careful; because his head had swelled to such a size that if he fell once more, it would surely burst. Strangely, he smiled just a little bit at the thought of his head bursting. If he pricked it with a pin— He began to laugh, and in his imagination, he saw his head like a monster balloon. Soon, it would float him away. There was nothing quite so funny as the picture of himself hanging under his head, floating.

He came to the top of the stairs, and he stepped out onto the sun-baked roof. Always full of sun, and steaming with hot tar, making the most delightful smell in the world. Tired, he sat down to rest, sprawling his legs out in front of him. He made a tar ball, chewed upon it.

He spat now and again, as his mouth filled with the dark juice. Once, he touched the cut on his hand, winced with the pain, smiled then.

Nothing in all the world was quite so peaceful as this roof with the sun baking it. Birds around him, and overhead the blue sky, but no other life. If his head burst here, it would scatter into the blue sky. He wondered whether he would drop then.

He made a tar ball, threw it; then he made another and threw that. He laughed with quiet joy and satisfaction, because he was happy and alone, because he was in a place Ollie would never think of.

"Ollie," he said, just to test his theory out; and then he cocked his head carefully to one side, waiting for an answer.

"Ollie."

"Geesus, Ollie, whaddya gonna do?"

His mouth dropped, and his gaze wandered all over the roof, but he knew that Ollie was nowhere near him.

Then he rose, walking over to the airshaft. Vividly, he remembered how Ishky had attempted to leap across it the day before.

Then he had been afraid, and rightly. But now his head was

swollen out and out, like a great balloon. He was hanging from his head, in the same way that a basket hangs from a balloon. And if he stepped out over the airshaft, he would float. Perhaps he would float away—all the way to the sky.

At the thought, he laughed with delight. And, awkwardly, he scrambled over the edge of the roof.

He fell close to the house, where there were no clotheslines to impede his flight. He fell upon the rubbish with a sickening crash, and he lay still.

CHAPTER THIRTY

How is it that I hate Blackbelly no more? It came about like this.

We are all in a circle, watching, and he and Ollie are face to face, showering blows upon one another. I am still crying, from my own fight, but under my breath I manage to urge Ollie on.

"Killim! Duh dirdy black basted! Shiddon his face, Ollie! Makeim eatis nuts!"

Blackbelly goes down, and I leap in with the others. Everyone is trying to hit him at the same time, Shomake, all of them; all our hate is concentrated on Blackbelly. The battle between the gangs is over, but Blackbelly is still left. We want to tear him to pieces.

Suddenly, Ollie yells, "Aw, lay offana him!"

One by one, we separate ourselves, until only Kipleg and two more boys are holding Blackbelly. He's bleeding from the nose, and his shirt is torn all to shreds, but he is no longer crying. Sullenly he stands there, staring at us, his yellow eyes roving from one to another, fixing themselves finally upon Ollie, who is laughing at him.

"Well, shidface," Ollie says.

And then—I no longer hate Blackbelly. It is difficult to explain, but all in a moment, my hate has vanished. Inside, I am limp and weak, but I see something.

(I saw that thing for many years. What did Ishky know of hate, of power and glory and beauty? But as the years went, I saw it, again and again. But I don't know whether I ever saw it so clearly as then.)

More than I see it, I feel it. I want to go over to Blackbelly, very close to him, take his hand and explain. You see, I am close to him, the same way I was close to Shomake before the fight.

I clench my teeth. Otherwise, I will cry, and I don't want to cry

now. I look at Shomake and he looks at me, and perhaps we see the
same thing in each other's face. Shomake edges over to me, and his
hand reaches out for my arm.

"Ishky—"

"Yeah?"

"Whatta dey gonna do?"

"I dunno."

"Geesus, whatta fight!"

"Yeah."

"I wanna go home."

"Yeah."

Blackbelly attempts to wrench himself free, but they only laugh
at him. Then he stands there, in silent rage. Then he appears to
swell, inside of himself, and he tries to smile back at Ollie. But he's
not good at smiling.

"Whaddya gonna do wittim, Ollie?" Kipleg wants to know.

"Less cokalize him," someone else suggests.

"Doncha worry," Ollie tells them.

Blackbelly mutters, "Lemme go!"

"Oh yeah."

"Yuh gonna git yer lumps."

"Yuh better lemme go," Blackbelly mutters. "I'm jus' tellin' yuh
dat yuh'd better lemme go."

"I'll piss in yer face, yuh dirty nigger."

"C'mon," Ollie commands. "Jus' bringim along, an' I'll showya
whatta do." They drag Blackbelly with them, and we all follow
Ollie. Shomake says to me:

"Geesus, I'm scared."

"It's awright."

"I wanna go home, Ishky."

"Yuh wan' Ollie tuh giveya duh lumps?"

"Naw—"

"Den come on." . . .

Ollie leads us deeper and deeper into the woods, and most of the
way, we have to drag Blackbelly. I hope they will let him go, even
if he beats me up the first time he sees me on the block. Then we
come to a little glen, so thick with trees and underbrush that only
a mottled pattern of the sun pierces through. Inside, the ground is
moist and wet, and everything about it is deliciously quiet. It is all

so pretty that I can't help but find some happiness in it. I hurt all over; I'm bruised and cut, but I can still see beauty.

At one side, there's a tall rock, a tree growing out of it; at the other side, the bluff bends down to the river; and through the trees, I can just glimpse the river, all silver and fine.

We stop there, and they hold Blackbelly under the rock. And then, for the first time, comprehension dawns upon us. Instinctively, we all know what Ollie is going to do, but no one of us says anything. We are taut, eager, and we wait, gathering close about Blackbelly. I think that we are afraid he will escape at the last moment. We have forgotten everything but the game, the drama, and we watch Ollie like a pack of dogs would watch their master.

Ollie walks back and forth, looking at Blackbelly, the grin flickering all over his lips. He blinks his eyes, and then he puts his hands in his pockets. He walks up to Blackbelly.

"D'ya know what dey do tuh dinges in duh sout'?" he demands.

"Boy, yuh'd better lemme go," Blackbelly says. But I can see that he isn't sure of himself anymore.

"Gimme a butt," Ollie says to Kipleg. He lights the cigarette, taking several careless puffs. Then, holding the cigarette between his lips, he unwinds the rope from his middle. At one end, he makes a slipknot.

We know what Ollie is up to, and we tremble with fear, with anticipation. Will he dare? Or is it all bluff upon his part? Will he back out at the last moment? Is he only attempting to scare Blackbelly, or is he in earnest? It is an even bet, and, inwardly, we each take our side. I think that Ollie is only bluffing, that he will back out at the last minute.

"Gonna lynchim?" Kipleg asks eagerly.

"Maybe—"

"Gonna really lynchim?"

"Maybe—"

"Nuts!"

"Betcha yuh don', Ollie."

Cutting a piece from the end of the rope, Ollie ties Blackbelly's hands. And slowly, the rage on Blackbelly's face changes to fear. He squirms, struggles, and yells frantically. Then the brief spasm is over, and he stands again in silence, glowering at us. I can see that he is going to call Ollie's bluff, that he doesn't believe Ollie has the nerve to go through with it. I can see that he is making up his mind about what he is going to do to Ollie at some future time. And I can see that now Ollie is beginning to hesitate. All along, it was a game, and he never thought of hanging as hanging. But if he stops now, he will lose face. Ollie is a king, and he can't afford to lose face.

Maybe you will ask why I didn't try to stop it. The answer is simple enough. I was afraid.

God, how afraid I am! Suppose it is Ishky, there in Blackbelly's place. What would I do? Shomake presses close to me. He looks into my eyes, and I only shake my head. I don't know.

Some of the others are like that. They are afraid that Ollie will go through with it. Only they are afraid to lose face. Everybody is afraid to lose face. And they are eager, too. Nobody has ever seen anything like this.

Blackbelly stares at Ollie. "Whaddya gonna do?" he whispers.

"Lynchya."

"Boy, yuh'd better watch out, white boy!"

"Gonna do sumpen?"

"I'll killya dead. Jus' lemme go, an' yuh'll see what I'll do."

"S'pose I don' leddya go?"

"I'll git yuh!"

"Yeah—after we lynchya."

"You ain' gonna lynch me."

"No?—"

"Boy, I'm tellin' yuh, lemme go!"

Ollie stares at him, still grinning. But his lips are trembling, and I know that Ollie is afraid. He turns his back, and begins to climb up the rock. We are all staring after him, even Blackbelly.

Shomake begins to cry. He drops back a few steps, holding in his sobs, but I can see how the tears are running down his cheeks. But I don't cry. I stare at Ollie, horribly, horribly fascinated.

The end of the rope is fastened around the base of the tree, and Ollie ties knot after knot. Then he pulls on it, to make sure it won't slip. I can tell that he got this out of a movie or something, maybe a book, because he seems to know exactly what to do. After he has fastened one end to the tree, he takes the end with the loop, puts his arm through it, and shinnies up the tree. He crawls out on a branch, letting the loop dangle through a crotch. It just about reaches to the top of the rock. Then he drops from the tree to the ground.

We stand and stare, there is something so awfully dreadful about that loop. Blackbelly stares, too. Now he's afraid. His mouth trembles, and the tears crawl down his cheeks.

"Lemme go," he says hoarsely.

Ollie is back in front of him, not grinning anymore, and almost as frightened as Blackbelly. But I know he won't back out now. He can't.

"Gonna stringim up?" Kipleg whispers.

"Yeah."

"Maybe—maybe—"

"We'll jus' chokim a liddle," Ollie says.

"Dat's good fer niggers."

"Yeah."

Blackbelly screams, "Lemme go!" He makes a frantic effort to tear himself loose.

We climb the rock, dragging him up with us. Then we put the noose around his neck, drawing it tight. Struggling there, Blackbelly is balanced on the edge of the rock. Then we push him off, scrambling down to the ground.

No sound now. We stare at him. We have forgotten everything but the figure hanging from the rope. No sound at all from us.

His body twists and struggles, his feet beating against the rock. He sways like a great pendulum, and his face swells and swells. His eyes appear to pop from his head.

God, it is terrible! There has never been anything so terrible as this.

But we do nothing, only stand and stare. Then Shomake whimpers like a baby.

And Blackbelly continues to kick, his lips working frantically. Now his kicks are lessening.

A moment more, we stare; then we bolt and run.

Some of us are screaming. We run in every direction. I have forgotten everything, except that I must get away from this place.

I have forgotten Shomake. I scramble down the bluff, whimpering.

CHAPTER THIRTY-ONE

Coming back into the street, Marie saw Thomas Edison go into Ishky's house. Now, it is difficult to say why she followed him— surely not because of any great interest in Thomas Edison. But the halls— She found it impossible to resist the terrible fascination of the halls, long narrow passageways hardly lit by the flickering gas jets.

She crept into the hall, and again it seemed to her that she was stepping into the corridors of hell. In her haste, she ran up the stairs, but when she got to the roof, it was empty. Where had he gone, then?

She heard someone scream from the airshaft. As she approached the airshaft, her fear increased, and then she looked over and saw him.

Her face trembling, she turned away. The woman in the airshaft was still screaming, but on the roof there was peace and sunshine. Marie sank to the tar, afraid—afraid to look down the airshaft again or to go back to the street. A sparrow, pecking at the tar, walked toward her, and she watched the sparrow, her mouth wide open.

Life was curious and fearful—but filled with fascination. The sparrow was fascinated with her, and obscurely it came to Marie that she was fascinated with the entire wondrous business of being alive. Thomas Edison lay in the airshaft, and probably he was dead. What fascination in death, in everything, in Thomas Edison! She looked at the sky, threw back her head and found herself smiling through her fear. Smiling. Why was she smiling? The reaction set in abruptly, and she began to cry. Then she made her way back to the street.

A crowd had gathered all of a sudden in front of the house. Excited, anticipative, they all knew that something had happened, without any one of them knowing what. Here was life, fascination, curiosity. Squeezing through the crowd, Marie watched the cellar door. Then they brought out Thomas Edison.

"Geesus—"

"Whaddedo?"

"How duh hell should I know!"

"Lookout dere!"

(Room, room, room, room, give us room and let us pass, room, room—)

What did he want with room now? What now?

From the roof, a flight of pigeons circled, lifted, dropped to the crowd, and circled again. A bluecoat swaggered down the street.

"Dere's a cop—"

"Geesus!"

(Geesus, Geesus—softly, Geesus Christ!)

And every mother thought it was her own son, and the crowd surged back and forth, almost overwhelming the small body. A woman screamed and continued to scream. Nobody knew who she was.

"Geesus, what duh hell's she screamin' fer?"

"Now, awright, make way dere, an' gimme some room. Geesus Christ now, howdya except me tuh git through? Awright, lady, I know it's lousy, an' whaddya wan' me tuh do? Now git away an' lemme through."

The cop pushed his way to the front, standing almost on top of Marie, who saw that it was Thomas Edison and no other, all broken up. Curiosity and fascination. She shuddered and felt sick—the way the blood dripped down.

"Now—who is he?"

A woman fainted, and they carried her out of the crowd.

"Now dere, stop duh shovin'! Whoisee?"

"I knowim."

"Me too."

The procession made its way down the block, carrying Thomas Edison. But they all knew that he was quite dead. Jumped off the roof, or fell off the roof, or pushed off the roof—what difference did it make, when anyone at all could see that he was better off dead? And what was the use of someone like him going on living with a stupid large head that he could scarcely carry on his shoulders?

Marie followed them, squeezing, thrusting, hoping she would miss nothing of it. All shuddering, thrilling, sick and almost ready to vomit, she knew it was wonderful nevertheless.

"Well, where's he live?"

"Dere."

"Dat's duh house, right dere!"

The law thrust in with the body, all the way into the kitchen, where Oloman sat knitting. And they stood with the body, while the old, old woman stared at them. Then they set the body down on the kitchen table. The old woman only stared.

"Awright, git out! All of yuh—clear out! C'mon, now no trouble!"

The old woman looked at the body. Thomas Edison there. The law hardly knew what to say, and it twisted its cap round and round.

"What happened?" the old woman whispered.

"Fell offana duh roof, I guess."

"Fell off . . ."

"Yer son?"

"No, no—my grandson."

"Well, I'm sorry—"

"Yes—yes—and he's dead, I take it. He's dead, isn't he?"

"Yeah."

"Dead—poor fool. Reaching to the sky . . ."

"Eh, mam?"

She shook her head, holding out her trembling hands. "No—no, you would not understand that. He reached up—up to the sky. Do you see? Now he's dead, poor fool. Or maybe not so much of a fool —if I could say . . ."

"He wasn' right in duh head, lady?"

"Not right—or maybe too right."

"Take it easy, mam."

"Yes." She turned to him, smiling. "Nothing the matter with me. Only—this poor fool." Then she began to cry, easily, softly.

"Easy, mam—"

Outside, the crowd lingered. No reason to go away, when there was high drama within. Marie lingered, too. What would happen? And where was Ollie? Where was Ollie?

She saw Ollie coming down the street, dirty and bloody. He had been fighting—always fighting. She saw how white his face was— white as a sheet. Now what would Ollie do? What would Ollie do now?

The crowd made way for him; nobody spoke. First, he hesitated, and the crowd wondered whether he knew. Or didn't he know? Wouldn't he go in? He went in very slowly.

He went in, and in the kitchen, he saw the policeman. He shivered, started to go back, and then he saw Thomas Edison. Oloman said nothing. Slowly, he approached the table, until he stood next to his brother, weak, feeling sick, feeling that any moment his knees would give beneath him.

"You'll torture him no more," the old lady said.

He went out, and again the crowd made way for him. Marie followed him, as he started up the block.

"Ollie—Ollie!"

He began to run. Reaching the avenue, he ran until it seemed that surely his heart must break. Then, sobbing, he sank against a building. In great gasps, he cried, his chest heaving, his heart swelling up inside of him.

On and on and on, his legs working under him like pistons. The lots were ahead of him, beyond that, the river. Then he remembered.

Blackbelly was dead.

He swerved aside, but he could run no more. On one corner, he sank into a little pile against a building. His mouth dropped open, hot saliva running from between his lips. But there was no rest here —none. He had to go back to the house.

It seemed to him that he could not find the way back to the block. How long had he been walking? When he came to the block again, the sun was low, the afternoon already gone. No crowd in front of his house now. Had it been all a dream?

He came back to the house. Now it was empty, except for Oloman, who sat alone. Where was Thomas Edison? Slipping in, he peered at Oloman. Then she turned around and saw him.

"Come here," she said.

He came, slowly, trembling.

"You see the black sin on your soul?"

"Yeah," he whispered.

Her eyes softened then, and she held out one hand. Then he was in her arms, sobbing out the story. Night fell on them, and Oloman stared ahead of her—her face stony and silent.

CHAPTER THIRTY-TWO

Kipleg went back, hesitatingly, because the fascination was greater than the fear. Trembling, he crept down the slope, felt his way through the underbrush, and came to the place where they had lynched Blackbelly.

All gone now, but Blackbelly was still there, hanging, not swaying now. Kipleg knew that he was dead.

Kipleg stared at him, trembled, wiped the sweat from his face, and continued to stare. It was so peaceful. Now Blackbelly was no longer struggling; his head drooped forward. No challenge now. No hate. No defiance. Only Blackbelly hanging there, while the breeze from above the river moved his clothes.

(He's dead. Kipleg, isn't he dead? I don't know. Oh, my God, I don't—)

But no hate is left. Kipleg stared without hating, curiously, wonderingly. What had made the change? Was it so awful, now Blackbelly was dead? But what did they do to men who killed? What would they do to him?

He crept away, but all the time he kept looking back. He couldn't help but look back.

And all the time he climbed back up the bluff he looked down to where Blackbelly hung. Death hung over him, like a still, dreadful mystery—dreadful as Blackbelly was in his death. It was more than fear.

"Dirdy nigger," he whispered.

But it meant nothing to him now, for death was the great master, and he crawled on up the bluff, leaving the Negro behind him, not hating. He stood up, and the breeze from above the river played over him.

He walked on, always looking behind him, and as he walked, fear reasserted itself. If they came for him, he would hang, like Blackbelly. Death was a grim master.

Ahead, he saw Shomake, all in a heap. Now he wanted company —any company in his misery. He called, "Shomake!"

Shomake turned around, saw him.

"Whaddya cryin' fer?"

"I dunno."

"Geesus, don' be a baby."

"Is he dead?" Shomake whispered.

"I dunno."

"What'll dey do tuh us?"

"Howda I know?"

They sat down together, staring over the river. Shomake wept silently. Then they stood up, as by some unspoken accord.

"Less git oudda here."

"Yeah."

They walked to the block, looking back, always looking back. Shomake was tired, terribly tired. He wanted to be home, to be solidly encased in the darkness of the back room.

Just before they reached the block, they began to run. Kipleg turned off, ran down the avenue, but Shomake dashed for the safety of his store. His father glanced up at him, but Shomake didn't pause. He ran into the back room, plunged onto the bed;

gripping the covers, he lay there, and the close twilight of the place closed over him.

Dark and comfortable here, where they could never come for him. Blackbelly was dead, but the dark mystery wouldn't come in here. Warm smells and good smells, and close comfort. He crawled onto the bed, up to the pillow, and then he forced his face down onto the pillow, wetting it with dirty tears.

When his mother came into the room, she saw him lying there, his clothes torn and covered with long streaks of dirt.

"Child," she said.

Turning over, he looked at her, his eyes filled with such fear as she had never seen before. He had been crying, and the tears had furrowed lines on his face. Now he stared at her as if she were a thing of horror; then he put a hand in front of his face. His lips were trembling.

"Child, what is it?"

"Nothing—nothing."

"What are you afraid of here? Is there anything to be afraid of here? Tell me—"

"Nothing."

"You were fighting—"

"No, no, no—I swear that I wasn't, mother mine. No, I wasn't fighting. No."

"It's all right, child. Perhaps you were only playing. I didn't mean to frighten you. Come—and let me clean your face." But when she put her hands on him, she felt how he was trembling.

"Tell me what's wrong?"

He thought rapidly. He mustn't tell—anything but that. Blackbelly he must never speak of, never. Otherwise, he would hang in the same way—and he was afraid.

"Tell me—"

"My fiddle. I want the fiddle."

"Yes—yes, you'll have it, child. Ishky took it, and he'll bring it back . . ."

"Ishky! He took my fiddle? Ishky took it?" The world was crumbling all around him.

"Yes, yes, but not for any dreadful reason. I tell you he'll bring it back."

"No—he won't."

"Child, stop trembling—look at me!"

But how could he stop, how, with fear and hurt and terror surging all over his body? Blackbelly was hanging there, dead. Only, she didn't know. She would never know.

CHAPTER THIRTY-THREE

The world goes on, around, the river flows and the sun shines. If Blackbelly is dead, Ishky is alive, and others are alive, too. They must go on.

My story is almost over—almost, but not quite. Blackbelly died, hanging from the tree; and from him came death, the strange master. Death comes like night comes, and if you understand, neither are terrible.

But I was afraid—God, how filled with fear I was! Blackbelly's legs, kicking and kicking. It made a picture for me, fastening itself over my eyes. I turned around, plunged down the bluff.

Now, what difference does it make if I plunge to my death? Death, the strange master, has taken me. Blackbelly is dying back there—

I go all the way down the bluff, as quickly as I can, and then I run frantically toward the river. My heart pounds, and all the time I am looking behind me. Somewhere up there, Blackbelly is dead— swinging. Like a branch in the breeze.

The river stops me. What now? I stand upon the edge, swaying, looking down. Sewage and dirt—but water to take me in, and payment there to the strange master.

Do you see? *I killed Blackbelly!*

All over me, inside of me, the words are written. I killed him, right from the beginning, with my heart full of hate. The gang was mine—not Ollie's. I had thought of it; I led Ollie on—

(Turn around, Ishky, and look at the bluff, where Blackbelly swings. Blood is all over you.)

I begin to scream, hard frantic screams that come from far down in my belly, and I throw myself on the wet, brown earth, burying my face in it. Then I roll over, and I see that a man is watching me. What does he think? Does he know? Does he know? But, of course, he knows—

(You killed him.)

"What'll he say—what'll he say?"

I spring to my feet, and run from him. I must run forever, from everyone; and now I keep looking back at the man. No, he isn't following me. But he knows; he knows. They all know. Sooner or later—

I have to walk, I am so tired; I can run no longer. So I walk, and I find that I am saying to myself, "You don't hate him, you don't hate him, you don't hate him."

That is so. In death, hate is gone.

All things have gone now, all my dreams. But the sun still shines; the wind still blows. . . .

"Where duh hell duh yuh tink yer goin'?" the cop says.

(Not to me. Traffic is passing. I stand and look at him, and then I begin to run.)

Run, run—run, run—

(All the music of Shomake's fiddle. I destroyed the fiddle. I destroyed Blackbelly. Death, the strange master, and I have become one—one and together.)

Run, run—run, run—

(That will never stop. Time passes, but time means nothing to me anymore. I must keep on, and on—or they will find me. And when they find me, they will hang me by the neck until I am dead. I will have to tell them.)

"I killed Blackbelly!"

"Yer lost, sonny?"

"I killed Blackbelly!"

"Run along now, sonny."

(That's my torture, standing large and terrible in his dark uniform. Will he follow me? I run again, looking behind me. God help me, what will I do when I can run no longer, when my feet break beneath me?)

Run, run—run, run—

(Shomake is playing his fiddle. What did he ever do to me, that I should take his fiddle from him? I am sorry. I am sorry. Shomake, I swear to God that I am sorry.)

The king sits in the jungle, broad and black,
And under jungle trails I pass, seeking,
Where are you, Blackbelly, noble king?
Three of us then, me and the master death,
And Blackbelly. I killed Blackbelly,
Laughing and laughing and laughing—

(I stop, panting, crying, laughing. Good God, I have to rest. I can't run forever.)

No, run, run—run, run—

Send the drums from the jungle, men are children.

There. Blackbelly is king of all the jungle land.

Beat the drums—play the children's game,

While death, the strange master, comes.

(Where am I? The sun is setting, and all the streets are in shadow, streets I have never seen before. How did I get here?)

Run, run, run—Ishky.

(No, I can't run anymore. But I will be caught out here in the dark—with Blackbelly. Go on!)

Only tell me why, Ishky? Why, Ishky? Tell me why? . . .

I begin to walk home. What a long way I have come—afraid, always afraid! It's no use, because I know what the end will be, when they have me and Ollie and Kipleg—all of us.

I go on walking. The sun is setting, throwing light on the clouds. But there is no promise for me. Only terror—

(Try to think of the magic garden, of Marie, of all the beautiful things—)

No, all gone now. . . .

Why is my mother so glad to see me? Does she know? Does everybody know?

"Eat," she says, "eat, my heart of all hearts. How worried I was! Where were you this lunchtime?"

"Playin'."

"Yes, yes, and fighting—and eating out your mother's heart. Why are you trembling so?"

"Runnin'."

Then she tells me about Thomas Edison, and I know why. Oh, I know well enough. The strange master and I. I can't eat any more. I push the food away.

"You are sick, my child?" she asks in her Yiddish.

"Naw. I don' wanna eat."

I hide in the bedroom, but it all follows me in there. Thomas Edison is dead; Blackbelly is dead. And I did it. I have done it all.

I creep out into the hall, and fear follows me. The strange master is with me. He will always be with me. Slowly, I go down the stairs to the street, praying all the time. If God is good, he will understand.

There is a small, wan figure sitting on my stoop. I sit down next to him. In the deepening darkness, we sit there, together. Our hands creep out, find each other.

"Shomake," I say, "I took duh fiddle."

"Yeah—I know."

"It's all smashed."

"Yeah."

"Yuh ain' saw?"

"Naw—"

Night comes, and a strange peace. The block is still. Does the strange master go with night?

"Shomake?"

"Yeah?"

We look at each other. Our world is gone, but we have found something. We both sigh. Shomake moves closer to me. Across the street, Kipleg is coming home. Very slowly, we begin to grin. . . .

The
Little Folk
from the Hills

THIS THING happened to me in an old, old land, where I had
been riding forever with a tech sergeant, a staff sergeant and two
thousand pounds of United States mail. The train stopped every six
miles or so, and each time there was no real certainty that it would
ever start again. We were at Agra or Lucknow or Patna or some
place like that; it doesn't matter very much, and one town looks
like another in such a land. When we rolled into a town to stay
for an hour or six hours or maybe all night, a bearer in a green
and red and white uniform, with a great piled white turban topped
by a splendid feather, more imposing than a Coldstream Guard on
dress parade, leaped onto the running board outside of our compartment and said, "Tea, sahib?" or "Tray, sahib?"

Whether he said tea or tray depended upon what arrangements
we had made with the same kind of person ten or fifty miles back.
The time of day had nothing to do with it. In that sun-kissed land
which the British had civilized, it was always teatime, in the middle
of the night and at dawn, too, and if the man with the turban said,
"Tea, sahib?" he had the tray on his hand; a juggler, acrobat and
waiter rolled up together, but he never missed, and he always knew
if there was a dirty empty tray in the compartment.

We talked a lot about it, about this amazing piece of organization
in an essentially unorganized land. In the compartment behind us,
two English officers were riding, and I even talked to them about it.
One was a subaltern, as they say, and the other was a colonel.

"Never thought about it," the colonel said. "I don't see why you
chaps should be so disturbed."

"It's like a game," I explained. "When you got nothing else to
talk about."

"You might ask the station commissioner next place we stop."

"That's too easy. Then we got nothing to talk about."

The two Englishmen were very nice and very pleasant. Every now
and then I'd spend a couple of hours in their compartment. They

had a few bottles of Scotch and gin, and they made you feel that nothing made them happier than for you to be drinking their liquor. But they didn't understand our ways or our methods of thought. The older one, for instance, the colonel, had been in India for thirty years, but it never occurred to him to question how, over a system of maybe a thousand towns and villages, they kept track of those tea trays. It impressed us as organization, perhaps the best piece of organization in the entire theater, but they weren't impressed that way by organization.

The tech sergeant and the staff sergeant didn't like the Englishmen and weren't convinced by what I said about their being nice.

"Limeys are nice," the staff sergeant admitted. "They crap on you with niceness."

"Everything nice," the tech sergeant said. "They live nice. They fight a war nice. They cut your throat nice."

"If they're so damned nice, why don't you ask them if this rattler has a schedule?"

"They say shedule," the tech sergeant said.

"I asked them. They think maybe it had a schedule, but not in wartime."

"Like the train from Laredo to Mexico City—you add thirty-two hours to the schedule and then chop it up. But you got to be an Einstein to figure it out."

"Did you ask them about the bloody tea trays?"

"They don't know. They suggested I ask the station commissioner next place we stop."

"Isn't that just like a Limey?" the staff sergeant asked.

"Well, they seem interested now. That's the way they are—it takes a little time for them to get interested in something. I'm going to have tea with them and we're going to talk about it some more."

I had tea with them and was in their compartment when we pulled into the station where it happened. I really liked them because they talked so pleasantly about small things. When they asked you a question they didn't really expect any sort of a serious answer; they knew how to talk about things and make conversation. The colonel said he liked Bengal because the hunting was good, but when he learned that I didn't hunt or care anything about it, he sort of apologized. They never said anything that could hurt your feelings. But in a way it put you at a disadvantage.

If you said that the folk were poor, they agreed. "Bloody poor," and with sympathy, speaking of the people with respect and consideration, not as GI's would have spoken about them. The subaltern, who was twenty or twenty-two, had a blond mustache and pink cheeks, and a gentle sweetness that was never disturbed by anything around him. Not by the filth, the misery, the hunger, the heat, the bodies of famine victims along the right of way being eaten by vultures as we watched; not even in Lucknow, where they had three or four hundred dead British soldiers laid out under an awning, plague victims—such a sweetness was all over him, a part of him, that he was nice to the two sergeants, even though they were enlisted personnel. The tech sergeant, commenting on that, said he was a swish.

"A what?" I had asked.

"A swish—a loop."

"A queen, he means," the staff sergeant said. "A rosebud, a pansy."

"He's a gentleman, that's all."

"And who says a loop can't have nice manners?"

But he wasn't that, I said to myself on this day, just a nice young fellow. We were slowing down from what was our usual lightning-like sixteen miles an hour to come into a station, and the subaltern thought it was Crumar, but said so apologetically with a deprecating smile.

"I try to memorize the stations."

"Too many of them," the colonel said.

I thought that someone must know them, the conductor or somebody. "Or timetables," I said.

"A bloody waste of time," the colonel thought.

And anyway, the stations are all the same. In the north there are deserts and in the south there are rice fields, but always a wooden platform with three tanks of water, one for Hindu soldiers, one for Moslem soldiers and one for British soldiers. Always the food vendors, when there is food, the water vendors, the soft-drink vendors. Always the crowds, the endless stream of people going somewhere or coming from somewhere. Wrapped in white, clean white and dirty white, men in white and women in white, they mill around the stations. They come early; they bring their food; the smell of curry fills the air, and they wait and wait. When the train comes in, they make a rush for it, stuff themselves into the compartments, hang onto the running board. They did it this time, but with a new element, for there were a hundred or so little people, dark and naked, carrying spears and little leather shields, and bows and arrows, too, making a great rush for the train, but a rush that had in it a tired note of hopelessness that you saw at the first glance.

"I'll be damned," the colonel said.

The subaltern smiled gently as the train guards interposed themselves and firmly pushed the little people back.

"Woollies," the colonel said. "And where do you suppose they come from?" He was more moved than the subaltern, who merely remarked, "You would think they'd put some clothes onto them."

"Why?" I asked.

"You know—decent, and all that."

The train guards were neither cruel nor hard; they were simply firm. They pushed the little people away, and the little folk had not much heart in it and gave it up rather easily.

I got out of the compartment and went back to the mail. "In this country," the tech sergeant said, "anything can happen. Jesus God, anything can happen. It could rain balls."

"What do the Limeys say?" the staff sergeant asked.

"They say they shouldn't be undressed."

"So they hocked their clothes. I'm going over to look." We locked up the mail, and the three of us went over together.

"What about the train?" asked the tech sergeant. "How long does she sit here?"

We guessed one and two and three hours, but in any case this was not something you could pass by without seeing. Alongside the station there was a broad field of sun-baked clay and a little parched grass. It was out in the center of this field that the little people had made their encampment and built small stick fires and raised a few hide lean-tos. There they were, a hundred or a hundred and fifty of them, a whole people, a tribe, a village, a folk, as some would say, with their old and their young, their graybeards, their infants and their children.

They were small people; none of the men were more than five feet in height; the women were like large dolls and the children were like small, fragile dolls. The men and women were tired and hopeless looking, but the tiny children were like other children, even laughing just a little. In color they were a deep yellow-brown, and their eyes made you think of Chinese, but they were not Chinese and they were not anything else that had ever been itemized, catalogued or studied. They wore no clothes, except for a shred of G-string on the men and sometimes a bit of leather on the women, yet they had no consciousness or knowledge of nakedness; you could see that. Also, the Stone Age was ahead of them. Their spears were sticks of wood with fire-hardened tips. Their bows were toy bows, and their arrows had neither tips nor feathers. Their shields were pieces of dry, untanned hide, and their cooking pots were molded crudely from clay. They had no footgear whatsoever, but walked barefoot, and there was just a trace of hair on the faces of the men.

I had never seen such people before. Neither had the staff sergeant; neither had the tech sergeant. They were out of the dawn of man; with each other they were gentle and loving and caressing; they fondled each other, they put their arms around each other, they comforted each other. And they were very hungry; their pots were empty, and they were terribly, terribly hungry. Their bones stood out and their flesh had dried away. Even in that hungry land, they were more hungry than just the hungry, and soon they would die because of the hunger.

We walked among them and their large, soft brown eyes followed us. We stopped by a woman with bare, flat, dry breasts, and the tech sergeant pointed to the baby she held in her arms and said, "Jesus God, that kid has been dead a long time. That kid has been dead so long it stinks."

"Who are they?" I wanted to know. "What are they? And where are they from?"

"You stink after four hours in this heat," the staff sergeant said. "Now I've seen everything."

"Sure you've seen everything. Wherever you are, you see everything. You got a broad Arkansas perspective. The first time you seen a necktie, you seen everything."

The tech sergeant went back to the train and got some rations and some candy we had there. We opened the cans and took the paper off the chocolate, but at first the people wouldn't eat. We had to persuade them to eat, and then they gave it to the children, and the men and women wept and chattered in their strange tongue while the children ate. We spoke to some bearers, some station people, and some of the people who were standing around, but no one knew who they were, or what they were, or where they were from.

Then the train whistle blew, which meant that sometime in the neighborhood of five minutes or an hour the train would start. We walked back, and when we got to our compartment, there in front of it were the two British officers talking to a civilian; and the colonel said to me, "Rum lot, aren't they?"

"Who?"

"The woollies."

"Why do you call them woollies?"

"Got to call them something, don't you know," the pink-cheeked subaltern smiled. "No one really knows who they are or what they are. Can't talk their language and they can't talk ours. Damned shame. They're from up in the hills somewhere and they must have had a hard time of it with famine and all that, and I suppose a rumor reached them about a train being something which takes you from one place where there's no food to another place where there is food, so here they are." He added as an afterthought, "They've been trying to board every train for six days now."

The civilian's name was Johnson, and he was the local commissioner or something. The colonel introduced him to me, but not to the two sergeants.

"What are you going to do?" I asked.

"What can one do?" Johnson said. "They can't ride the train without tickets, and if they could, where would they ride to? Food is tight. They're not properly the concern of my district in any case."

Then he walked off with the colonel, toward their compartment in the car behind ours. The subaltern lingered. Embarrassed and apologetic, he said something to the effect of their not lasting very long. "Bloody shame and all that, but they are on their last legs. It solves a problem for the poor beggars."

"What do you mean?" the tech sergeant asked.

"He means, you horse's ass, that they'll starve to death in a few days," the staff sergeant said quietly; and then, just as quietly, but deliberately, he said to the subaltern, "You, my friend, are a dirty second-rate son of a bitch—an upstanding pile of crap, if you follow me."

The boy's pink flushed to red; he stiffened, he stared at the two enlisted men, muttered something, "Oh, I say," or something of that sort, stared at them a moment or two longer, then turned on his heel and walked away. The train began to move, and we ran for our compartment. The tech sergeant seated himself sadly on a mail sack and started to whistle "Don't Fence Me In." The staff sergeant went to the toilet bowl where he kept a cake of ice and a few cans of tomato juice, and proceeded to open one of the cans.

"What in hell did you do that for?" I asked him finally.

"No more tea? No more nice people to talk to?"

"You hate, but you never hate with your brains. That was just a nice dumb kid."

"You want some tomato juice?"

"Sure. I'll pretend it's a Martini."

"What are you so pissed-off about?" the tech sergeant asked me.

"Nothing—nothing, but what a righteous, clean-limbed race of people we are. Oh, my God, how righteous!"

"To hell with him," said the staff sergeant. "He's got no more nice people to talk to."

Coca Cola

THIS AND THAT has been said about Coca Cola, and many hold that it is more and less than a soft drink; and there are parts of the world where they refer without love to a "Coca Cola civilization." Be that as it may, I have my own feelings about the matter, which I sometimes recall as my "Arabian adventure."

Nor am I in any fashion sold on the romance of Arabia, which I hold as one of the less favored spots on earth. In any case, during the month of June, it's hotter than hell, which I know for a fact; for hell is the product of gullible imagination and an Arabian summer actually exists. This I know, for I happened to be in Arabia one June during the Second World War, traveling from Africa to the Far East and satisfying my curiosity meanwhile about what was happening on the Arabian peninsula. Perhaps in the winter season, I would have developed the kind of interest in Arabia that others have shown; as it was, a few days of the heat, sand and indescribable poverty satisfied my curiosity, and I turned my attention to getting out of Arabia.

This was not as easy as it might seem, for apparently nothing in the way of Army Air Transport went directly out of Arabia, but instead to another airstrip. And the handful of miserable GIs at each of these airstrips, living in a perpetual state of intense dehydration, talked not of sex or the war, but of the superior quality, taste and quantity of water at some other airstrip. And in between their rather profound discussions of water, they spent their pay on Coca Cola. It's amazing how much Coca Cola an American in the Arabian desert can consume.

Time passed and it became hotter, and when I landed one day on an airstrip in the central part of the peninsula, staggered into the shade, and read on the thermometer there that the temperature was one hundred and sixty degrees Fahrenheit, I knew that I had enough of Arabia. I inquired for the next plane out.

I was told that in the next forty-eight hour period, only one plane would be taking off, and that one a C46, due in this very afternoon and scheduled to take off as soon as it had refueled and loaded cargo. What sort of cargo it would load at this godforsaken place in the center of a glaring, burning white-salt desert, I neither knew nor cared, just as I neither knew nor cared what the future destination of the C46 might be—secure in the knowledge that wherever that destination was, it was superior to the place I was in now.

There were three hours before the C46 landed, and I spent those three hours dying slowly, drinking rancid yellow water, swallowing salt tablets, and joining this or that officer or enlisted man in a Coca Cola. They all looked at me as the permanent inhabitants of Death Valley—if there are any—must look at tourists in air-conditioned cars, and some of them, as they sat over Coca Cola, wept with envy and self-pity. The only spark of life they evidenced animated them when they boasted about the heat at their station. There was no denying that they had more and fiercer heat than possibly any other place in the world.

"It's also hot at Abadan," I remember remarking, just to make conversation, for Abadan was well known and spoken of wherever there were GIs as the "second hottest place in the world."

"Abadan," they nodded sadly. "It's never really hot in Abadan. We go to Abadan on leave, and when we tell them how hot it is here, they get angry because they think we're running down their place."

It was that way, and when the plane finally landed, I felt like a doomed man miraculously reprieved. I slowly shuffled to the porch of the mess and waited for the crew of the C46, who were approaching across the blazing concrete airstrip. They were three cheerful, healthy-looking children, with mustaches, blue eyes, and broad smiles.

"Can you take out a passenger?" I greeted them.

"Oh, yes, sir," the pilot said. "That is, if you have papers?"

"My papers are OK. You have a passenger."

"Why, that's fine," the pilot said, "and we like passengers. It makes things interesting. It's very dull flying cargo in the desert. Nothing interesting ever happens. You're a war correspondent, aren't you, sir? Well, all sorts of interesting things must happen to you."

"Getting out of here will be the most interesting so far," I nodded.

"Fine—just fine. It will take us a few hours to load cargo, and then we take off. Where are you bound for, sir?"

"Wherever you're bound for," wondering again what kind of cargo went out of this place. However, I soon learned, and it should have been obvious from the first. There was only one possible kind of cargo that could be shipped out of that forsaken airstrip, only one product that had lavish and extravagant consumer use. A line of sweating, staggering GIs began to load the plane with crates of empty Coca Cola bottles.

The C46 was a strange, vast, ugly two-motored plane, a huge, whale-like, drop bellied plane, used principally to carry cargo. I had traveled in them many times and had nothing against them except the knowledge that pilots did not like them and vivid memories of the ear-splitting, nerve-wracking crash when the retractible landing gear was lowered. But since all planes were equally uncertain to me, I was able to feel kindly toward this ship from the skies that had come to prevent my body and soul from frying.

This one, however, had no doors. The C46 in service in that part of the world had large double doors, wide enough to accommodate a jeep or a howitzer, but somewhere along the line this one had dropped the doors. It was a little unorthodox to fly in a plane not too unlike a convertible car, but I was in no mood to complain, and I watched with interest as the little pile of Coca Cola crates within the plane grew. It is remarkable how many Coca Cola bottles you can load into an empty C46, but I found it even more remarkable how many bottles of Coca Cola one airstrip can consume. My interest turned to fascination. Again and again, I was certain that it could not continue, that the mess could disgorge no more Coca Cola and that the C46 could hold no more, but soon I began to realize that the capacity of both was beyond anything I had imagined. For almost three hours, under that blazing sun, a steady, unbroken stream of empty Coca Cola bottles poured into the C46. Hot as it was, I had to watch, and I was gradually overcome by a sense of fate and a wave of fascination as the great-bellied plane filled up with the crates of bottles. Thoughtfully, the crew left a narrow area between the Coca Cola bottles and the wall of the plane; otherwise there would have been no room for the single passenger.

Finally it was done, and the navigator, the smallest member of the crew, and seemingly no more than eighteen years old under his whispy mustache, came to inform me that they were ready for the takeoff. As we walked out to the plane, I asked him where he wanted me to ride.

"Why you just make yourself comfortable anywhere," he an-

swered cheerfully. "We're awful glad to have you with us, because
it's very exciting meeting someone like yourself."

"Anywhere" was a passage of about eighteen inches between the
Coca Cola crates and the wall of the plane, so I chose a spot just
forward from the gaping doors, spread my raincoat on the floor,
and stretched out to await the cool and soothing winds at five
thousand feet. From where I lay, I had a pleasant view, not unlike
one's view from a convertible car, of the space where doors were
supposed to be, and I watched with interest as the airstrip slid
beneath us and as finally we were airborne. In moments, the airstrip
was far behind us, but the cooling breeze I had anticipated failed to
appear. We had climbed to about five or six hundred feet, and
there we were, and it gave one a very uncomfortable feeling. We had
passed over the white, salt-like expanse of flat where the airstrip
was located, and now we were in a region of rolling sand hills,
remarkably high sand hills, for it often seemed that we only cleared
the tops of them by inches. Then the navigator left the control
room and slid back to me along the wall.

"Well, sir," he said cheerfully, "it's funny, but there seems to be
something wrong with the balance."

"The what?"

"The balance. You see, it's how you load a plane. Now these
C46s are marked off for all sorts of army loadings. For example, the
marks here on the wall show you just how to load an armored car
or a jeep or fifty millimeter guns—all sorts of things that you would
be loading with, but of course not Coca Cola."

"No, I imagine not Coca Cola," I repeated.

"Of course, you couldn't expect them to think of everything. We
just had to use our own judgment loading these bottles, and it's
surprising how heavy they are considering that they are empty. We
can't seem to get any altitude at all, and it's obvious that there's
something wrong with the balance. So the pilot wondered whether
you would crawl back to the tail of the plane with me and that
might alter the balance a little, so we could make altitude."

I looked at the open doors and then at the sandhills, and then
I nodded and asked a foolish question about parachutes.

"You don't have one? Well, that's strange, and it's against regu-
lations too, but it wouldn't be much use at this altitude. There
should be an indraft at the doors."

As we crawled back to the tail, I made a mental note to ask him what had happened to the doors, and whether they purposely flew without them or whether they had left them somewhere because a piece of whatever strange cargo they might have been carrying then had extruded; but I never did, and to this day the mystery of the doors remains unsolved. Anyway, we crawled far, far into the tail, where we crouched in the lee of a rising mountain of Coca Cola crates, but apparently the balance was still off, and craning his neck to see, the navigator admitted that we were making no more altitude than before.

"Suppose we both go up to the control room now," he suggested. "It may need weight forward."

We edged our way back to the control room, joining the pilot and the co-pilot; and in spite of the fact that both of them were that type of young men who are apparently incapable of concern about anything, a faint aura of worry was beginning to gather about them. My own feeling was far more than a faint aura.

"Now isn't that something," the pilot said to me.

"Just can't make any altitude," the co-pilot said.

"It's the balance," the navigator said.

I offered my opinion. "It's the damned Coca Cola bottles. No plane was ever made that could carry this many Coca Cola bottles."

"They are empty, sir," the pilot said gently.

"The plane isn't empty. The plane's full."

"Yes, sir. I meant the Coca Cola bottles are empty. We did estimate the load as well as we could."

"It's not the load, it's the balance," the navigator insisted.

"The trouble is," the co-pilot added sadly, "that there is nothing in the C46 manual about Coca Cola bottles. Nothing at all. You just have to guess."

"The trouble is," I put in, "that sooner or later we're going to run into one of those damned sand mountains."

"They're not mountains, sir, just sandhills."

"They look like mountains to me, and if we lose any more altitude, we're going to hit one."

"It does seem worrisome."

"It's going to be more than worrisome if we come down in the desert. It seems to me that we ought to turn around and go back to the airstrip."

"We've thought of that, sir, but we've lost altitude since we went over a ridge back there. I don't think we could get back to that air-strip."

In a way, I was relieved. "Well," I said, "that does it. There's only one thing we can do."

"Yes, sir?"

"Get rid of some of the Coca Cola bottles."

"What?"

"Get rid of them, sir? I don't understand you," said the co-pilot.

"Dump them," I said emphatically. "Pitch them out of the open doors. And keep dumping them until we're light enough to make altitude."

"The Coca Cola bottles, sir?"

"Exactly—that's just what I had in mind, the Coca Cola bottles."

"You don't mean dump them? You don't mean throw them away?"

"That's exactly what I mean."

"Oh, no sir," said the pilot.

"We couldn't do that," said the co-pilot.

"Not with Coca Cola bottles," the navigator said seriously. Anything else, yes. Jeeps, tanks, guns—oh, yes, certainly, if the situation warranted it. But not Coca Cola bottles. I'm afraid you don't understand about Coca Cola, sir."

"You see, Coca Cola," said the pilot, "well, I don't really know how to explain. It takes years in the army to understand what I mean. I know you probably have had a great deal of experience, sir, but in the army it's something else. You don't just throw away Coca Cola bottles."

"Our manifest would be short," the navigator said. "They would ask what happened to the bottles? We would say, we dumped them into the Arabian desert. Oh, no, no, sir. You don't. You just don't."

"I'll take the responsibility myself," I begged them. "Put it all on my shoulders. I'll be responsible to the Coca Cola Company and the army. As a matter of fact, I'll pay for the damn bottles."

"Oh, no sir—you just can't take such a responsibility."

Plunging wildly, I said, "I outrank all of you. Here's my company status. Suppose I order you to."

"Well, sir, I'm afraid not," the pilot said sadly. "You don't really outrank us as a correspondent. I'm afraid you have no right to order us to do so."

"But sooner or later, we're going to hit one of those mountains of sand. Don't you know what it means to come down in the Arabian desert? You know the Arabs don't like Americans, and that's if they find us and we don't die of thirst, and if they find us, you know what kind of things they do."

"Yes, sir, it's a pretty bad situation, isn't it," the pilot agreed. "It's a shame we have to be in such a situation, but I really don't know what to do about it. The only thing we could think of was to call ahead to the next airstrip and tell them we're coming in to reload. That's about eighty miles from here and no bad ridges in between. We have a very good chance of making it, sir."

I appealed to their pride and pointed out what an ignoble way to die this was, crushed like an insect between sand and Coca Cola bottles; I drew vivid pictures of Arab atrocities against Americans, embroidering them with full barracks detail; I spoke of the process of dehydration in that desert heat and of how it feels to die of thirst, or how I thought it would feel to die of thirst from the best accounts I had read.

It was all to no avail, and they were determined to bring in the plane with all bottles accounted for.

The next twenty minutes were not very pleasant, and I suppose it was one of the better moments of my life when the airstrip appeared in the hazy distance. We were very low as we came in—our altitude possibly less than a thousand feet, and it all happened very quickly. Something was missing, something important and decisive in our momentary existence, and what was missing clawed at my nerves, my memory, my whole awareness; and then, as the cold sweat of fear broke out all over me, I realized that the missing factor was that loud, ear-splitting crash one hears when a C46 drops its landing gear. We were coming in without wheels.

I broke into in wild sound, yelling "wheels, undercarriage—" and other associated words as fast and loud as I could, but it was too late. We were already at the landing strip and settling onto the concrete, and suddenly the fat belly of the plane hit the runway, and we made a beautiful landing, tearing out our belly and a good deal of the runway to a symphony of Coca Cola bottles. It was a very good landing; as I heard afterwards, we would hardly have done much better with wheels, except that the bottom part of the plane would have stayed with us, and you couldn't blame the three young men who flew it for forgetting about their landing gear, considering what we had been through. As a matter of fact, no one was injured, and we picked our way through smashed crates and bottles out onto the lovely earth.

I was still in Arabia, and I stood in the sun, watching the ambulance and jeeps converge upon us.

"Well, here we are," the navigator said.

"Here we are," the co-pilot said.

"You know, sir," the pilot said to me, cheerfully, "once you're in, you can land just as well without the wheels as with them."

"It's hard on the plane," said the navigator.

"They probably jammed up with the heat," the co-pilot lied hopefully.

"A shame about all those bottles, but here we are," said the pilot. "Still, those bottles—we won't hear the end of that."

"We're in trouble—real trouble," the navigator sighed. "If only we were carrying ammo instead!"

The Cold,
Cold Box

As always, the annual meeting of the Board of Directors convened at nine o'clock in the morning, on the 10th of December. Nine o'clock in the morning was a sensible and reasonable hour to begin a day's work, and long ago, the 10th of December had been chosen as a guarantee against the seduction of words. Every one of the directors would have to be home for the Christmas holiday—or its equivalent—and therefore the agenda was timed for precisely two weeks and not an hour more.

In the beginning, this had caused many late sessions, sometimes two or three days when the directors met the clock round, with no break for sleep or rest. But in time, as things fell into the proper place and orderly management replaced improvisation, each day's meeting was able to adjourn by four o'clock in the afternoon—and there were even years when the general meeting finished its work a day or two early.

By now, the meeting of the Board of Directors was very matter-of-fact and routine. The big clock on the wall of the charming and spacious meeting room was just sounding nine, its voice low and musical, as the last of the directors found their seats. They nodded pleasantly to each other, and if they were seated close to old friends, they exchanged greetings. They were completely relaxed, neither tense nor uneasy at the thought of the long meeting that lay ahead of them.

There were exactly three hundred of these directors, and they sat in a comfortable circle of many tiers of seats—in a room not unlike a small amphitheatre. Two aisles cut through to a center circle or stage about twenty feet in diameter, and there a podium was placed which allowed the speaker to turn in any direction as he spoke. Since the number of three hundred was an arbitrary one, agreed upon after a good deal of trial and error, and mantained as an excellent working size, half the seats in the meeting room were always empty. There was some talk now and then of redesigning the meeting room, but nobody ever got down to doing it and by now the empty seats were a normal part of the decor.

The membership of the Board was about equally divided between men and women. No one could serve under the age of thirty, but retirement was a matter of personal decision, and a reasonable number of members were over seventy. Two-thirds of them were in their fifties. Since the Board was responsible for an international management, it was only natural that all nations and races should be represented, black men and white men and brown men and yellow men—and all the shadings and gradations in between. Like the United Nations—they were too modest to make such a comparison themselves—they had a number of official languages and a system of simultaneous translation; but as with the United Nations, English was most frequently used.

As a matter of fact, the Chairman of the Board, who had been born in Indo-China, opened this meeting in English, which he spoke very well and with ease, and after he had welcomed them and announced the total attendance—all members present—he said, "At the beginning of our annual meeting—and this is an established procedure, I may say—we deal with a moral and legal point, the question of Mr. Steve Kovac. We undertake this before the reading of the agenda, for we have felt that the question of Mr. Kovac is not a matter of agenda or business, but of conscience. Of our conscience, I must add, and not without humility; for Mr. Kovac is the only secret of this meeting. All else that the Board discusses, votes upon and decides or rejects will be made public, as you know. But of Mr. Steve Kovac, the world knows nothing; and each year in the past, our decision has been that the world should continue to know nothing about Mr. Kovac. Each year in the past, Mr. Kovac has been the object of a cruel and criminal action by the members of this Board. Each year in the past, it has been our decision to repeat this crime."

To these words, most of the members of the Board did not react at all—but here and there young men and women showed their surprise, bewilderment and unease, either by the expression on their faces or by low protestations of disbelief. The members of the Board were not insensitive people.

"This year, as in the past, we make this question of Mr. Kovac our first piece of business—because we cannot go onto our other business until it is decided. As in the past, we will decide whether to engage in a criminal conspiracy or not."

A young woman, a new member of the board, her face flushed

and angry, rose and asked the Chairman if he would yield for a question. He replied that he would.

"Am I to understand that you are serious, Mr. Chairman, or is this some sophomoric prank for the edification of new members?"

"This board is not used to such descriptive terms as sophomoric, as you should know, Mrs. Ramu," he answered mildly. "I am quite serious."

The young woman sat down. She bit her lower lip and stared at her lap. A young man arose.

"Yes, Mr. Steffanson?" the Chairman said pleasantly.

The young man sat down again. The older members were gravely attentive, thoughtful without impatience.

"I do not intend to choke off any discussion, and I will gladly yield to any questions," said the Chairman, "but perhaps a little more about this troublesome matter first. There are two reasons why we consider this problem each year. Firstly, because the kind of crime we have committed in the past is hardly anything to which we should grow indifferent; we need to be reminded; premeditated crime is a deadly threat to basic decency, and God help us if we should ever become complacent! Secondly, each year, there are new members on this board, and it is necessary that they should hear all the facts in the case of Mr. Kovac. This year, we have seven new members. I address myself to them, but not only to them; I include all of my fellow members of this Board."

"Steve Kovac," the Chairman of the Board began, "was born in Pittsburgh in the year 1913. He was one of eleven children, four of whom survived to adulthood. This was not too unusual in those days of poverty, ignorance and primitive medicine.

"John Kovac, Steve Kovac's father, was a steelworker. When Steve Kovac was six years old, there was a long strike—an attempt on the part of the steelworkers to increase their wages. I am sure you are all familiar with the method of the strike, and therefore I will not elaborate.

"During this strike, Steve Kovac's mother died; a year later, John Kovac fell into a vat of molten steel. The mother died of tuberculosis, a disease then incurable. The father's body was dissolved in the molten steel. I mention these things in terms of their very deep and lasting effect on the mind and character of Steve Kovac. Orphaned at the age of seven, he grew up like an animal in the jungle. Placed in a county home for orphan children, he was marked as a bad and intractable boy, beaten daily, deprived of food, punished in every way the ignorance and insensitivity of the authorities could devise. After two years of this, he ran away.

"This is a very brief background to the childhood of a most remarkable man, a man of brilliance, character and determination, a man of high inventive genius and grim determination. Unfortunately, the mind and personality of this man had been scarred and traumatized beyond redemption. A psychiatric analysis of this process has been prepared, and each of you will find a copy in your portfolio. It also itemizes the trials and suffering of Steve Kovac between the ages of nine and twenty—the years during which he fought to survive and to grow to adulthood.

"It also gives a great many details of this time of his life—details I cannot go into. You must understand that while the question before us is related to this background, there are many other features I will deal with."

At this point, the Chairman of the Board paused to take a drink of water and to glance through his notes. The younger members of the Board glanced hurriedly at the psychiatric report; the older members remained contemplative, absorbed in their own thoughts. As many times as they had been through this, somehow it was never dull.

"At the age of twenty," the Chairman resumed, "Steve Kovac was working in a steel mill outside of Pittsburgh. He was friendly then with a man named Emery. This man, Emery, was alone, without family or means of support. A former coal miner, he suffered from a disease of the lungs, common to his trade. All he had in the world was a five-thousand-dollar insurance policy. Steve Kovac agreed to support him, and in return he made Kovac the beneficiary of the insurance policy. In those days, insurance policies were frequently the only means by which a family could survive the death of the breadwinner.

"Four months later, Emery died. Years afterward, it was rumored that Kovac had hastened his death, but there is no evidence for the rumor. The five thousand dollars became the basis for Steve Kovac's subsequent fortune. Twenty-five years later, the net worth of Steve Kovac was almost three billion dollars. As an individual, he was possibly the wealthiest man in the United States of America. He was a tycoon in the steel and aluminum industries, and he controlled chemical plants, copper mines, railroads, oil refineries and dozens of associated industries. He was then forty-six years old. The year was 1959.

"The story of his climb to power and wealth is unique for the generations he lived through. He was a strong, powerful, handsome man—tortured within himself, driven by an insatiable lust to avenge himself, and his father and mother too, for the poverty and suffering of his childhood. Given the traumatic factors of his childhood, his craving for power turned psychopathic and paranoid, and he built this structure of power securely in his own hands. He owned newspapers as well as airlines, television stations and publishing houses, and much more than he owned, he controlled. Thereby, he was able to keep himself out of the public eye. In any year of the fifties, you can find no more than an occasional passing reference to him in the press.

"How an individual achieved this in a time of the public corporation and the 'corporation man' is a singular tale of drive and ambition. Steve Kovac was ambitious, ruthless, merciless and utterly without compassion or pity. His policy was to destroy what stood in his way, if he could; if he could not, he bent it to his will in one way or another. He wrecked lives and fortunes. He framed and entrapped his competitors; he used violence when he had to—when he could not buy or bribe what he wanted. He corrupted individuals and bribed parliaments and bought governments. He erected a structure of power and wealth and control that reached out to every corner of the globe.

"And then, in his forty-sixth year, at the height of his wealth and power, he discovered that he had cancer."

The Chairman of the Board paused to allow the impact of the words to settle and tell. He took another drink of water. He rearranged the papers in front of him.

"At this time," he said, "I propose to read to you a short extract from the diary of Dr. Jacob Frederick. I think that most of you are familiar with the work of Dr. Frederick. In any case, you know that he was elected a member of our Board. Naturally, that was a long time ago. I need only mention that Dr. Frederick was one of the many wise and patient pioneers in the work of cancer research

—not only a great physician, but a great scientist. The first entry I propose to read is dated January 12, 1959."

"I had an unusual visitor today," the Chairman of the Board read, "Steve Kovac, the industrial tycoon. I had heard rumors to the effect of the wealth and power of this man. In himself, he is a striking individual, tall, muscular, handsome with a broad strong face and a great mane of prematurely white hair. He has blue eyes, a ruddy complexion and appears to be in the prime of life and health. Of course, he is not. I examined him thoroughly. There is no hope for the man.

" 'Doctor,' he said to me, 'I want the truth. I know it already. You are not the first physician I have seen. But I also want it from you, plainly and bluntly.'

"I would have told him in any case. He is not the kind of a man you can lie to easily. 'Very well,' I said to him, 'you have cancer. There is no cure for your cancer. You are going to die.'

" 'How long?'

" 'We can't say. Perhaps a year.'

" 'And if I undergo operative procedure?'

" 'That could prolong your life—perhaps a year or two longer if the operation is successful. But it will mean pain and incapacity.'

" 'And there is no cure?' His surface was calm, his voice controlled; he must have labored for years to achieve that kind of surface calm and control; but underneath, I could see a very frightened and desperate man.

" 'None as yet.'

" 'And the quacks and diet men and the rest—they promise cures.'

" 'It's easy to promise,' I said. 'But there isn't any cure.'

" 'Doc,' he said to me, 'I don't want to die and I don't intend to die. I have worked twenty-five years to be where I am now. The tree is planted. I'm going to eat the fruit. I am young and strong—and the best years of my life are ahead of me.'

"When Kovac talked like that, he was convincing, even to me. It is his quality, not simply to demand of life, but to take. He denies the inevitable. But the fact remained.

" 'I can't help you, Mr. Kovac,' I told him.

" 'But you're going to help me,' he said calmly. 'I came to you because you know more about cancer than any man in the world. Or so I am told.'

" 'You have been misinformed,' I said shortly. 'No one man knows more than anyone else. Such knowledge and work is a collective thing.'

" 'I believe in men, not mobs. I believe in you. Therefore, I am ready to pay you a fee of one million dollars if you can make it possible for me to beat this thing and live a full lifespan.' He then reached into his coat for his wallet and took out a certified check for one million dollars. 'It is yours—if I live.'

"I told him to return the following day—that is, tomorrow. And now I have been sitting here for hours, thinking of what one million dollars would mean to my work, my hopes—indeed, through them, to all people. I have been thinking with desperation and with small result. Only one thought occurs to me. It is fantastic, but then Steve Kovac is a fantastic man."

Again, the Chairman of the Board paused and looked inquiringly at some of the younger members. They had been listening with what appeared to be hypnotic concentration. There were no questions and no comments.

"Then I will continue with the diary of Dr. Frederick," the Chairman nodded.

"*January 13*. Steve Kovac returned at 2:00, as we had arranged. He greeted me with a confident smile.

" 'Doc, if you are ready to sell, I am ready to buy.'

" 'And you really believe that you can buy life?'

" 'I can buy anything. It's a question of price.'

" 'Can you buy the future?' I asked him. 'Because that is where the cure for cancer lies. Do you want to buy it?'

" 'I'll buy it because you have decided to sell,' he said flatly. 'I know with whom I am dealing. Make your offer, Dr. Frederick.'

"I made it, as fantastic as it was. I told him about my experiments with the effect of intense cold upon cancer cells. I explained that though, as yet, the experiments had not produced any cure, I had made enormous strides in the intense and speedy application of extreme cold—or, to put it more scientifically, my success in removing heat from living objects. I detailed my experiments—how I had begun with frogs and snakes, freezing them, and then removing the cold and resuming the life process at a later date, how I had experimented with mice, cats, dogs—and most recently, monkeys.

"He followed me and anticipated me. 'How do you restore life?' he wanted to know.

"I don't restore it. The life never dies. In the absence of heat, what might be called the ripening or aging process of life is suspended, but the life remains. Time and motion are closely related; and under intense cold, motion slows and theoretically could cease —all motion, even within the atomic structure. When the motion ceases, time ceases.'

" 'Is it painful?'

" 'As far as I know, it isn't. The transition is too quick.'

" 'I would like to see an experiment myself.'

"I told him that I had in my laboratory a spider monkey that had been frozen seven weeks ago. My assistants could attest to that. He went into the laboratory with me and watched me as we successfully restored the monkey. Seemingly, it was none the worse.

" 'And the mind?' he asked me.

"I shrugged. 'I don't know. I have never attempted it with a human being.'

" 'But you think it would work?'

"I am almost certain that it would work. I would need better and larger equipment. With some money to spend, I can improve the process—well, considerably.'

"He nodded and took the certified check out of his wallet. 'Here is your retainer—apart from what you have to spend. Buy whatever you need, and charge it to me. Spend whatever you have to spend and buy the best. No ceiling, no limit. And when I wake up, after a cure has been discovered, there will be a second million to add to your fee. I am not a generous man, but neither am I niggardly when I buy what I want. When will you be ready, Doctor?'

" 'Considering the prognosis of your disease,' I said, 'we should not delay more than five weeks. I will be ready then. Will you?'

"Steve Kovac nodded. 'I will be ready. There are a good many technical and legal details to work out. I have many and large interests, as you may know, and this is a journey of uncertain duration. I will also take care of your own legal responsibilities.'

"Then he left, and it was done—possibly the strangest agreement ever entered into by a doctor and his patient. I try to think only of one thing—that I now have a million dollars to put into my work and research."

The Chairman of the Board wore pince-nez, and now he paused to wipe them. He cleared his throat, rearranged the papers on the lectern once again, and explained, "You see, the plan was a simple one and a sensible one, too. Since Mr. Kovac's condition could not be cured, here was a means of preserving his life and arresting the disease until science had found a cure. Timidity was never one of Mr. Kovac's qualities. He analyzed the situation, faced it and accepted the only possible escape offered to him. So he went about placing his affairs in such order as to guarantee the success and prosperity of his enterprises while he slept—and also their return to his bidding and ownership when he awoke.

"In brief, he formed a single holding company for all of his many interests. He gathered together a Board of Directors to manage that holding company in his absence, making himself president in absentia, with a substitute Chairman to preside while he was gone. He made a set of qualifying bylaws, that no Chairman could hold office for more than two years, that the Board was to be enlarged each year and a number of other details, each of them aimed at the single goal of retaining all power for himself. And because he was not dead, but merely absent, he created a unique situation, one unprecedented in all the history of finance.

"This holding company was exempted from all the traditional brakes and tolls placed upon previous companies through the mechanism of death. Until Mr. Kovac returned, the holding company was immortal. Naturally, Dr. Frederick was placed upon the Board of Directors. In other words," the Chairman of the Board concluded, "that is how this Board of Directors came into being."

He allowed himself his first smile then. "Are there any questions at this point?" he asked mildly.

A new member from Japan rose and wanted to know why, if this was the case, the whole world should be taught otherwise?

"We thought it best," said the Chairman. "Just as we, on this Board, have great powers for progress and construction, so do we have no inconsiderable powers of concealment and alteration. The people of the United States and the United Kingdom might have accepted the knowledge that Steve Kovac brought this Board of Directors into being, but certainly in the Soviet Union and China, such knowledge might have been most disconcerting and destructive. Remember that once we had established an open trade area in the Soviet Union and had brought three of her leading government people onto our Board of Directors, our situation changed radically. We were enabled then, through a seizure of all fuel supplies on earth, to prevent the imminent outbreak of World War III.

"At that point, neither the extent of our holdings nor the amount of our profits could be further concealed. I say we," the Chairman deferred modestly, "but of course, it was our predecessors who faced these problems. Our cash balance was larger than that of the United States Treasury, our industrial potential greater than that of any major power. Believe me, without planned intent or purpose, this Board of Directors suddenly found itself the dominant force on earth. At that point, it became desperately necessary for us to explain ourselves, who we were and what we represented."

A new member from Australia rose and asked, "How long was that, Mr. Chairman, if I may inquire, after the visit of Mr. Kovac to Dr. Frederick?"

The Chairman nodded. "It was the year Dr. Frederick died—twenty-two years after the treatment began. By then, five types of cancer had already surrendered their secrets to science. But there was not yet any cure for Mr. Kovac's disease."

"And all the time, the treatment had remained secret?"

"All the time," the Chairman nodded.

"You see," he went on, "at that time, the Board felt that the peoples of earth had reached a moment of crisis and decision. A moment, I say, for the power was only momentarily in the hands of this Board. We had no armies, navies or air-fleets—all we had were a major portion of the tools of production. We knew we had not prevented war but simply staved it off. This was a Board of Directors for management, not for power, and any day the installations and plants we owned and controlled could have been torn from our grasp. That was when our very thoughtful and wise predecessors decided to embark on a vast, global propaganda campaign to convince the world that we represented a secret parliament of the wisest and best forces of mankind—that we were in effect a Board of Directors for the complex of mankind.

"And in this we succeeded, for the television stations, the newspapers, the radio networks, the film industry and the theatre—all these were ours. And in that brief, fortunate moment, we launched our attack. We used the weapons of Steve Kovac—let us be honest and admit that. We acted as he would have acted, but out of different motives entirely.

"We bought and bribed and framed. We infiltrated the parliaments of all mankind. We bought the military commanders. We dissolved the armies and navies in the name of super-weapons, and then we destroyed the super-weapons in the name of mankind. Where leaders could not be bought or bribed, we brought them into our Board. And above all, we bought control—control of every manufacturing, farming or mining unit of any consequence upon the face of the earth.

"It took the Board of Directors twenty-nine years more to accomplish this; and at the end of that twenty-nine years, our earth was a single complex of production for use and happiness—and if I may say so, for mankind. A semblance of national structure remained, but it was even then as ritualistic and limited as any commonwealth among the old states of the United States. Wars, armies, navies, atom bombs—all of these were only ugly memories. The era of reason and sanity began, the era of production for use and life under the single legal code of man. Thus, we have become creatures of law, equal under the law, and abiding by the law. This Board of Directors was never a government, nor is it now. It is what it purposes to be, a group management for the holding company. Only today, the holding company and the means of mankind are inseparable. Thereby, our very great responsibility, which of course you understand. . . ."

The Chairman of the Board wiped his face and took a few more sips of water. A new member from the United States rose and said, "But, Mr. Chairman, the cure for all types of cancer was discovered sixty-two years ago."

"So it was," the Chairman agreed.

"Then, Steve Kovac—" The new member paused. She was a beautiful, sensitive woman in her middle thirties, a physicist of note and also an accomplished musician.

"You see, my dear," the Chairman said, lapsing into a most informal mode of address, pardonable only because of his years and dignity, "it faced us. When we make a law for mankind and submit to it, we must honor it. Sixty-two years ago, Steve Kovac owned the world and all its wealth and industry, a dictator beyond the dream of any dictator, a tyrant above all tyrants, a king and emperor to dwarf all other kings and emperors—"

As he spoke, two of the older members left the meeting room. Minutes later, they returned, wheeling into the room and up to the podium a rectangular object, five feet high, seven feet long and three feet wide, the whole of it covered with a white cloth. They left it there and returned to their seats.

"—yes, and he owned the world. Think of it—for the first time in history, a just peace governed the nations of mankind. Cities were being rebuilt, deserts turned into gardens, jungles cleared, poverty and crime a thing of the past. Man was standing erect, flexing his muscles, reaching out to the planets and the stars—and all of this belonged to a single savage, merciless, despotic paranoid, Steve Kovac. Then, as now, my dear associates, this Board of Directors was faced with the problem of the man to whom we owed our existence, the man who all unwittingly unified mankind and ushered in the new age of man—yes, the man who gave us the right and authority to hold and manage, the man whose property we manage. Then as now, we were faced with Steve Kovac!"

Almost theatrical in his conclusion and gestures, the Chairman stepped down from the podium and with one motion swept the cloth aside. The entire Board fixed their eyes on the cabinet where, under a glass cover, in a cold beyond all concept of cold, a man lay sleeping in what was neither life nor death, but a subjective pause in the passage of time. He was a handsome man, big and broad, ruddy of face and with a fine mane of white hair. He seemed to sleep lightly, expectantly, confidently—as if he were dreaming hungrily but pleasantly of what he would awaken to.

"Steve Kovac," the Chairman said. "So he sleeps, from year to year, no difference, no changes. So he appeared to our predecessors sixty-two years ago, when they first had the means to cure him and the obligation to awaken him. They committed the first of sixty-two crimes; they took no action in the face of a promise, a duty, a legality and an almost sacred obligation. Can we understand them? Can we forgive them? Can we forgive the Board of Directors that voted this same decision again and again? Above all, can we forgive ourselves if we stain our honor, break the law, and ignore our own inheritance of an obligation?

"I am not here to argue the question. It is never argued. The facts are presented, and then we vote. Therefore, will all those in favor of awakening Mr. Kovac raise their right hands?"

The Chairman waited. Long moments became minutes, but no hands were raised. The two older members covered the cold, cold box and wheeled it out. The Chairman of the Board took a sip of water and announced, "We will now have the reading of the agenda."

The
Large Ant

THERE HAVE been all kinds of notions and guesses as to how it would end. One held that sooner or later there would be too many people; another that we would do each other in, and the atom bomb made that a very good likelihood. All sorts of notions, except the simple fact that we were what we were. We could find a way to feed any number of people and perhaps even a way to avoid wiping each other out with the bomb; those things we are very good at, but we have never been any good at changing ourselves or the way we behave.

I know. I am not a bad man or a cruel man; quite to the contrary, I am an ordinary, humane person, and I love my wife and my children and I get along with my neighbors. I am like a great many other men, and do the things they would do and just as thoughtlessly. There it is in a nutshell.

I am also a writer, and I told Lieberman, the curator, and Fitzgerald, the government man, that I would like to write down the story. They shrugged their shoulders. "Go ahead," they said, "because it won't make one bit of difference."

"You don't think it would alarm people?"

"How can it alarm anyone when nobody will believe it?"

"If I could have a photograph or two."

"Oh, no," they said then. "No photographs."

"What kind of sense does that make?" I asked them. "You are willing to let me write the story—why not the photographs so that people could believe me?"

"They still won't believe you. They will just say you faked the photographs, but no one will believe you. It will make for more confusion, and if we have a chance of getting out of this, confusion won't help."

"What will help?"

They weren't ready to say that, because they didn't know. So here is what happened to me, in a very straightforward and ordinary manner.

Every summer, some time in August, four good friends of mine and I go for a week's fishing on the St. Regis chain of lakes in the Adirondacks. We rent the same shack each summer; we drift around in canoes and sometimes we catch a few bass. The fishing isn't very good, but we play cards well together, and we cook out and generally relax. This summer past, I had some things to do that couldn't be put off. I arrived three days late, and the weather was so warm and even and beguiling that I decided to stay on by myself for a day or two after the others left. There was a small flat lawn in front of the shack, and I made up my mind to spend at least three or four hours at short putts. That was how I happened to have the putting iron next to my bed.

The first day I was alone, I opened a can of beans and a can of beer for my supper. Then I lay down in my bed with *Life on the Mississippi*, a pack of cigarettes and an eight-ounce chocolate bar. There was nothing I had to do, no telephone, no demands and no newspapers. At that moment, I was about as contented as any man can be in these nervous times.

It was still light outside, and enough light came in through the window above my head for me to read by. I was just reaching for a fresh cigarette, when I looked up and saw it on the foot of my bed. The edge of my hand was touching the golf club, and with a single motion I swept the club over and down, struck it a savage and accurate blow and killed it. That was what I referred to before. Whatever kind of a man I am, I react as a man does. I think that any man, black, white or yellow, in China, Africa or Russia, would have done the same thing.

First I found that I was sweating all over, and then I knew I was going to be sick. I went outside to vomit, recalling that this hadn't happened to me since 1943, on my way to Europe on a tub of a Liberty ship. Then I felt better and was able to go back into the shack and look at it. It was quite dead, but I had already made up my mind that I was not going to sleep alone in this shack.

I couldn't bear to touch it with my bare hands. With a piece of brown paper, I picked it up and dropped it into my fishing creel. That, I put into the trunk of my car, along with what luggage I carried. Then I closed the door of the shack, got into my car and drove back to New York. I stopped once along the road, just before I reached the Thruway, to nap in the car for a little over an hour. It was almost dawn when I reached the city, and I had shaved, had a hot bath and changed my clothes before my wife awoke.

During breakfast, I explained that I was never much of a hand at the solitary business, and since she knew that, and since driving alone all night was by no means an extraordinary procedure for me, she didn't press me with any questions. I had two eggs, coffee and a cigarette. Then I went into my study, lit another cigarette, and contemplated my fishing creel, which sat upon my desk.

My wife looked in, saw the creel, remarked that it had too ripe a smell, and asked me to remove it to the basement.

"I'm going to dress," she said. The kids were still at camp. "I have a date with Ann for lunch—I had no idea you were coming back. Shall I break it?"

"No, please don't. I can find things to do that have to be done."

Then I sat and smoked some more, and finally I called the Museum, and asked who the curator of insects was. They told me his name was Bertram Lieberman, and I asked to talk to him. He had a pleasant voice. I told him that my name was Morgan, and that I was a writer, and he politely indicated that he had seen my name and read something that I had written. That is formal procedure when a writer introduces himself to a thoughtful person.

I asked Lieberman if I could see him, and he said that he had a busy morning ahead of him. Could it be tomorrow?

"I am afraid it has to be now," I said firmly.

"Oh? Some information you require."

"No. I have a specimen for you."

"Oh?" The "oh" was a cultivated, neutral interval. It asked and answered and said nothing. You have to teach at least five semesters at a college to develop that particular "oh."

"Yes. I think you will be interested."

"An insect?" he asked mildly.

"I think so."

"Oh? Large?"

"Quite large," I told him.

"Eleven o'clock? Can you be here then? On the main floor, to the right, as you enter."

"I'll be there," I said.

"One thing—dead?"

"Yes, it's dead."

"Oh?" again. "I'll be happy to see you at eleven o'clock, Mr. Morgan."

My wife was dressed now. She opened the door to my study and said firmly, "Do get rid of that fishing creel. It smells."

"Yes, darling. I'll get rid of it."

"I should think you'd want to take a nap after driving all night."

"Funny, but I'm not sleepy," I said. "I think I'll drop around to the Museum."

My wife said that was what she liked about me, that I never tired of places like museums, police courts and third-rate night clubs.

Anyway, aside from a racetrack, a museum is the most interesting and unexpected place in the world. It was unexpected to have two other men waiting for me, along with Mr. Lieberman, in his office. Lieberman was a skinny, sharp-faced man of about sixty. The government man, Fitzgerald, was small, dark-eyed and wore gold-rimmed glasses. He was very alert, but he never told me what part of the government he represented. He just said "we," and it meant the government. Hopper, the third man, was comfortable-looking, pudgy, and genial. He was a United States senator with an interest in entomology, although before this morning I would have taken better than even money that such a thing not only wasn't, but could not be.

The room was large and square and plainly furnished, with shelves and cupboards on all walls.

We shook hands, and then Lieberman asked me, nodding at the creel, "Is that it?"

"That's it."

"May I?"

"Go ahead," I told him. "It's nothing that I want to stuff for the parlor. I'm making you a gift of it."

"Thank you, Mr. Morgan," he said, and then he opened the creel and looked inside. Then he straightened up, and the two other men looked at him inquiringly.

He nodded. "Yes."

The senator closed his eyes for a long moment. Fitzgerald took off his glasses and wiped them industriously. Lieberman spread a piece of plastic on his desk, and then lifted the thing out of my creel and laid it on the plastic. The two men didn't move. They just sat where they were and looked at it.

"What do you think it is, Mr. Morgan?" Lieberman asked me.

"I thought that was your department."

"Yes, of course. I only wanted your impression."

"An ant. That's my impression. It's the first time I saw an ant fourteen, fifteen inches long. I hope it's the last."

"An understandable wish," Lieberman nodded.

Fitzgerald said to me, "May I asked how you killed it, Mr. Morgan?"

"With an iron. A golf club, I mean. I was doing a little fishing with some friends up at St. Regis in the Adirondacks, and I brought the iron for my short shots. They're the worst part of my game, and when my friends left, I intended to stay on at our shack and do four or five hours of short putts. You see—"

"There's no need to explain," Hopper smiled, a trace of sadness on his face. "Some of our very best golfers have the same trouble."

"I was lying in bed, reading, and I saw it at the foot of my bed. I had the club—"

"I understand," Fitzgerald nodded.

"You avoid looking at it," Hopper said.

"It turns my stomach."

"Yes—yes, I suppose so."

Lieberman said, "Would you mind telling us why you killed it, Mr. Morgan."

"Why?"

"Yes—why?"

"I don't understand you," I said. "I don't know what you're driving at."

"Sit down, please, Mr. Morgan," Hopper nodded. "Try to relax. I'm sure this has been very trying."

"I still haven't slept. I want a chance to dream before I say how trying."

"We are not trying to upset you, Mr. Morgan," Lieberman said. "We do feel, however, that certain aspects of this are very important. That is why I am asking you why you killed it. You must have had a reason. Did it seem about to attack you?"

"No."

"Or make any sudden motion toward you?"

"No. It was just there."

"Then why?"

"This is to no purpose," Fitzgerald put in. "We know why he killed it."

"Do you?" I nodded. "You're clearer on the subject than I am."

"The answer is very simple, Mr. Morgan. You killed it because you are a human being."

"Oh?" I borrowed that from Lieberman.

"Yes. Do you understand?"

"No, I don't."

"Then why did you kill it?" Hopper put in.

"I saw it," I answered slowly, "and somehow I knew that I must kill it. I didn't think or decide. I just grabbed the iron and hit it."

"Precisely," Fitzgerald said.

"You were afraid?" Hopper asked.

"I was scared to death. I still am, to tell the truth."

Lieberman said, "You are an intelligent man, Mr. Morgan. Let me show you something." He then opened the doors of one of the wall cupboards, and there stood eight jars of formaldehyde and in each jar a specimen like mine—and in each case mutilated by the violence of its death. I said nothing. I just stared.

Lieberman closed the cupboard doors. "All in five days," he shrugged.

"A new race of ants," I whispered stupidly.

"No. They're not ants. Come here!" He motioned me to the desk and the other two joined me. Lieberman took a set of dissecting instruments out of his drawer, used one to turn the thing over, and then pointed to the underpart of what would be the thorax in an insect.

"That looks like part of him, doesn't it, Mr. Morgan?"

"Yes, it does."

Using two of the tools, he found a fissure and pried the bottom apart. It came open like the belly of a bomber; it was a pocket, a pouch, a receptacle that the thing wore, and in it were four beautiful little tools or instruments or weapons, each about an inch and a half long. They were beautiful the way any object of functional purpose and loving creation is beautiful—the way the creature itself would have been beautiful, had it not been an insect and myself a man. Using tweezers, Lieberman took each instrument out of the brackets that held it, offering each to me. And I took each one, felt it, examined it, and then put it down.

I had to look at the ant now, and I realized that I had not truly looked at it before. We don't look carefully at a thing that is horrible or repugnant to us. You can't look at anything through a screen of hatred. But now the hatred and the fear were diluted, and as I looked, I realized it was not an ant although like an ant. It was nothing that I had ever seen or dreamed of.

All three men were watching me, and suddenly I was on the defensive. "I didn't know! What do you expect when you see an insect that size?"

Lieberman nodded.

"What in the name of God is it?"

From his desk, Lieberman produced a bottle and four small glasses. He poured it and we drank it neat. I would not have expected him to keep good Scotch in his desk.

"We don't know," Hopper said. "We don't know what it is."

Lieberman pointed to the broken skull, from which a white substance oozed. "Brain material—a great deal of it."

"It could be a very intelligent creature," Hopper nodded.

Lieberman said, "It is an insect in developmental structure. We know very little about intelligence in our insects. It's not the same as what we call intelligence. It's a collective phenomenon—as if you were to think of the component parts of our bodies. Each part is alive, but the intelligence is a result of the whole. If that same pattern were to extend to creatures like this one—"

I broke the silence. They were content to stand there and stare at it.

"Suppose it were?"

"What?"

"The kind of collective intelligence you were talking about."

"Oh? Well, I couldn't say. It would be something beyond our wildest dreams. To us—well, what we are to an ordinary ant."

"I don't believe that," I said shortly, and Fitzgerald, the government man, told me quietly,

"Neither do we. We guess. We comfort ourselves, too."

"If it's that intelligent, why didn't it use one of those weapons on me?"

"Would that be a mark of intelligence?" Hopper asked mildly.

"Perhaps none of these is a weapon," Lieberman said.

"Don't you know? Didn't the others carry instruments?"

"They did," Fitzgerald said shortly.

"Why? What were they?"

"We don't know," Lieberman said.

"But you can find out. We have scientists, engineers—good God, this is an age of fantastic instruments. Have them taken apart!"

"We have."

"Then what have you found out?"

"Nothing."

"Do you mean to tell me," I said, "that you can find out nothing about these instruments—what they are, how they work, what their purpose is?"

"Exactly," Hopper nodded. "Nothing, Mr. Morgan. They are meaningless to the finest engineers and technicians in the United States. You know the old story—suppose you gave a radio to Aristotle? What would he do with it? Where would he find power? And what would he receive with no one to send? It is not that these instruments are complex. They are actually very simple. We simply have no idea of what they can or should do."

"But there must be a weapon of some kind."

"Why?" Lieberman demanded. "Look at yourself, Mr. Morgan—a cultured and intelligent man, yet you cannot conceive of a mentality that does not include weapons as a prime necessity. Yet a weapon is an unusual thing, Mr. Morgan. An instrument of murder. We don't think that way, because the weapon has become the symbol of the world we inhabit. Is that civilized, Mr. Morgan? Or are the weapon and civilization in the ultimate sense incompatible? Can you imagine a mentality to which the concept of murder is impossible—or let me say absent. We see everything through our own subjectivity. Why shouldn't some other—this creature, for example—see the process of mentation out of his subjectivity. So he approaches a creature of our world—and he is slain. Why? What explanation? Tell me, Mr. Morgan, what conceivable explanation could we offer a wholly rational creature for this," pointing to the thing on his desk. "I am asking you the question most seriously. What explanation?"

"An accident?" I muttered.

"And the eight jars in my cupboard? Eight accidents?"

"I think, Dr. Lieberman," Fitzgerald said, "that you can go a little too far in that direction."

"Yes, you would think so. It's a part of your own background. Mine is as a scientist. As a scientist, I try to be rational when I can. The creation of a structure of good and evil, or what we call morality and ethics, is a function of intelligence—and unquestionably the ultimate evil may be the destruction of conscious intelligence. That is why, so long ago, we at least recognized the injunction, 'Thou shalt not kill!' even if we never gave more than lip service to it. But to a collective intelligence, such as that of which this might be a part, the concept of murder would be monstrous beyond the power of thought."

I sat down and lit a cigarette. My hands were trembling. Hopper apologized. "We have been rather rough with you, Mr. Morgan. But over the past days, eight other people have done just what you did. We are caught in the trap of being what we are."

"But tell me—where do these things come from?"

"It almost doesn't matter where they come from," Hopper said hopelessly. "Perhaps from another planet—perhaps from inside this one—or the moon or Mars. That doesn't matter. Fitzgerald thinks they come from a smaller planet, because their movements are apparently slow on earth. But Dr. Lieberman thinks that they move slowly because they have not discovered the need to move quickly. Meanwhile, they have the problem of murder and what to do with it. Heaven knows how many of them have died in other places— Africa, Asia, Europe."

"Then why don't you publicize this? Put a stop to it before it's too late!"

"We've thought of that," Fitzgerald nodded. "What then—panic, hysteria, charges that this is the result of the atom bomb? We can't change. We are what we are."

"They may go away," I said.

"Yes, they may," Lieberman nodded. "But if they are without the curse of murder, they may also be without the curse of fear. They may be social in the highest sense. What does society do with a murderer?"

"There are societies that put him to death—and there are other societies that recognize his sickness and lock him away, where he can kill no more," Hopper said. "Of course, when a whole world is on trial, that's another matter. We have atom bombs now and other things, and we are reaching out to the stars—"

"I'm inclined to think that they'll run," Fitzgerald put in. "They may just have that curse of fear, Doctor."

"They may," Lieberman admitted. "I hope so."

But the more I think so, the more it seems to me that fear and hatred are the two sides of the same coin. I keep trying to think back, to recreate the moment when I saw it standing at the foot of my bed in the fishing shack. I keep trying to drag out of my memory a clear picture of what it looked like, whether behind that chitinous face and the two gently waving antennae there was any evidence of fear and anger. But the clearer the memory becomes, the more I seem to recall a certain wonderful dignity and repose. Not fear and not anger.

And more and more, as I go about my work, I get the feeling of what Hopper called "a world on trial." I have no sense of anger myself. Like a criminal who can no longer live with himself, I am content to be judged.

Freedom Road

FOREWORD

By W. E. B. DuBois

To err is human; but a human error easily slips into three crimes: the initial mistake becomes deliberate wrong; attempt is then made to cure this wrong by force rather than reason; finally the whole story is so explained and distorted as to preserve no lesson for posterity, and thus history seldom guides us aright.

This is illustrated by the history of slavery in America. It was no unexpected mistake for a new continent in the 18th century to use slave labor. It became a crime, however, in the 19th century to build new commerce and industry on the African slave trade and make black slavery the foundation of the Sugar Empire and the Cotton Kingdom. This cancer of American economy might have been cured peacably by reason and religion, but stubborn men preferred murder and war. When emancipation was the inevitable result of the Civil War between the slave states and the free, but one decent and logical path faced the nation and that was to educate the freed men for full citizenship in the land which they had helped to build and to free.

This an aroused philanthropy led by Sumner, Stevens and Douglass, and helped by some churches, tried to do. This was so frustrated by stubborn slave-holders that all that could be accomplished was immediate enfranchisement of the freed men by permission of greedy Northern merchants, without giving the Negroes education, land or tools. Despite this, the Negro vote gave the South manhood suffrage, free public schools, the beginning of land sub-division, and a new social legislation.

Thereupon the nation permitted a sordid bargain between northern industry and southern reaction: the former slaveholders offered to submit to northern commercial supremacy, provided they were allowed to return the Negroes to slavery in all but name. This agreement was sealed by the *Bargain of 1876*, and disfranchisement and color caste followed, held back only by the persistent struggle of the Negro and a few white friends.

Then the third crime ensued: today history almost without exception teaches that slavery was a mistake which benefited the

Negro; that white America, from the highest motives, freed the
slaves; that fanatics tried to push the freedman too fast and beyond
his ability, resulting in such threats to civilization that the blacks
had to be put back into their places, first by violence, and finally
by law. That as a result the American Negro today is as happy and
prosperous as he deserves, even if he is not treated as equal to the
whites.

This is what white America for the most part believes today and
tells the world; and this distortion of history and apology for crime
is what Howard Fast sought to begin to counteract in 1944, in his
novel on Reconstruction, *Freedom Road*. His story is fiction, but
his basic historical accuracy is indisputable; its psychological insight is profound; and thousands of readers can testify to its literary
charm. That many more may read this book, a new edition is now
being issued; and I am glad to commend it to all people who want
to know the Truth and be free.

PART ONE. THE VOTING

A PROLOGUE

The war was done—the long and bloody struggle that was, at
the time, the greatest people's war the world had ever known—and
the men in blue marched home. The men in gray, stunned and
hurt, looked about at their land, and saw what war does.

At Appomattox Court House, General Lee laid down his arms,
and then it was all finished. And in the warm southland, there were
four million black men who were free. A hard-won freedom, a
precious thing. A free man counts tomorrow and yesterday, and
both of them are his; hunger and there's no master to feed you,
but walk with long steps and no master says go slowly. Two hundred thousand of these black men were soldiers of the republic
when the struggle finished, and many of them went home with guns
in their hands.

Gideon Jackson was one of them. Tall and strong and tired, a
gun in his hand and a faded blue uniform on his back, he came
home to the Carolina soil and the Carwell Plantation. The big
white house stood much as he remembered it, not damaged by the
war, but the gardens and fields were weeds and jungle, and the

Carwells had gone away—none knew where. The freedmen, as they returned, took up their lives in the old slave quarters, together with those who had never gone away. And as the months passed, more and more of the freedmen returned to the Carwell Plantation, from the cold northland where they had gone to find freedom, from the ranks of the Union Army, and from their hiding places in the piney woods and the lonesome swamps. They took up their lives with the deep wonder that they were free.

1. HOW GIDEON JACKSON CAME HOME
FROM THE VOTING

The crows woke Rachel early this cool November morning, and lying in bed, the old cloth pulled up around her neck, Jenny making a warm spot against her breast, she listened to their singing. They sang from far off, caw, caw, caw, a sad sound, but not unpleasant to someone who had heard it long as Rachel, every morning sun up; a good day or bad, it was all the same to the crows.

Against her breast, the warm spot of the girl stirred, and Rachel whispered, "Lie easy, my child, gentle and easy and listen to them old crows, just listen."

But the day begins—you can't stop it. The straw bag was warm and crunchy, and there Rachel would like to stay, but when the sun suddenly broke the mist, it shot the whole cabin through with light, from where the door sagged and in between all the warped boards. Jeff stretched and kicked his heels against the floor. Jenny, pressed against Rachel, came wide awake, pulled away, and cold slippered over the warm spot where she had lain. Marcus made noises, whooee, whooee, and Jeff poked him, and then they rolled over on the floor, scuffling.

All the sounds that made the morning Rachel knew with her eyes closed. Why did human beings wake so sudden and so raucous, she had asked herself a hundred times? She clung to darkness a moment more, and then came to her feet brusque and pacifying:

"Jeff, you shut!"

He had his legs twisted around Marcus's belly. He was fifteen but built like Gideon; the boy was a giant before he even knew what made a man, six feet tall and chocolate brown, more her color than the prune-skin shining black of Gideon, but handsome and long-faced the way Gideon was, born to make a sinful life for women.

Marcus at twelve was skinny and small, and Rachel snapped at Jeff:
"Let go there with your legs, you big fool!"

Jenny was seven. She ran out of the door, first thing, like that
every morning, a creature seeking light. The dog met her, barking
his fool head off.

Jeff stood up and Marcus pounded him, a woodpecker pecking at
a big oak tree. Jeff was easygoing, like Gideon that way, but without the iron inside of him that made Gideon something; Jeff was
slow to anger and then the anger came like fire, but Gideon's anger
was always inside of him.

"Get out, you both," she told them. "Get on out of here, get out."

She was laughing already. Small herself, it was a constant wonder
to her that these masses of dark flesh were hers, out from between
her legs, out of a little bundle tied onto her with a cord. Well, she
had a big man; and these were Gideon's children, she thought with
pride. She stirred about the cabin. It was full of sunlight now,
the door swung back. Jeff came in with kindling, his head dripping
wet from the rain-water barrel. She went out to the barrel herself,
doused head and hands, and called to Jenny:

"Come and get your wetting, come on now!"

Jenny hated water. Five times she had to be called before Rachel
caught her and dipped her woolly head into the water, and then
screaming as if a little cold water could kill her. When Rachel
came back into the cabin, Jeff had the fire burning. She took her
wooden bowl and mixed the meal, while Jeff blew the fire up to hot
coals. The dog lay in front of the fire—leave that to him on a cold,
sharp November morning.

At the time of its greatest glory, almost a decade ago now, the
Carwell Plantation covered twenty-two thousand acres of good
South Carolina soil. A hundred miles inland from the coast, it lay
in that gently rolling country that makes a broad belt of demarca-
tion between the flat tidewater and the high uplands. When cotton
was king there, a bale and a half was gathered from the acre, and
when the bolls opened, there was a sea of white as far as the eye
could reach.

The big plantation house dominated the scene. Four stories,
twenty-two rooms, the portico columned like a Greek temple, it
stood on a tall hill, almost in the geographical center of the plantation. A line of willows made a fine driveway. Live oaks made a

protective wall. If you stood at the slave quarters, half a mile away, and looked up at the big house, its likeness to a temple was increased; and when the white clouds scudded across the sky behind it, it made one of the prettiest sights in that part of the country.

That was in the old times. In this year of 1867, there had been no cotton planting at Carwell. It was said that Dudley Carwell was living in Charleston, but nobody really knew. It was also said that the two Carwell boys had been killed in the war. Debt and unpaid taxes had thrown the plantation into that curious state of suspension that had overtaken so many of the great southern manors. It was said that the government owned it now, and it was also said that every former Carwell slave would be given forty acres of land and a mule. That sort of talk ran like fire, but nobody could put his finger on exactly what was to be done. Several times, white folks had driven out from Columbia, poked around, and gone away.

Meanwhile, the freed slaves lived there. A good many of them had stayed on all through the war, putting in crop after crop and caring for the place. Others, like Gideon, had gone off and joined the Union Army. Still others had run away and hidden themselves. But even when emancipation came, most of them stayed, not so much because they feared the dire punishment set out for runaways as that they had no place in particular to go. This was their home, their land, their country—it had always been so.

For a generation, the Carwells had for the most part lived in Charleston, leaving the plantation to overseers. After the third year of the war, Dudley Carwell visited the place only once, and when he left he closed up the house and took the house servants with him. The last overseer went away in sixty-five, and from there on the slaves were left alone. They no longer planted cotton; that was a cash crop, and they had neither the need nor understanding for cash crops. They put in corn and rice in the lowland part of the plantation. They grew greens in the gardens; they had pigs and chickens, and that way they lived.

They were more fortunate than most freedmen. Three times columns of regulars came by and picked the place clean, but they managed to get through those times of hunger. The bitter, defeated troops had only killed four of their number; that was not as bad as what happened in most places where freedmen lived.

And now, from far away, the thing called Congress had given the

order for freedmen to go and vote. It was a time of wonder in the
land, you may be sure.

Marcus was the first to see Gideon coming back from the voting,
and afterwards he remembered that. He and Axel Christ and a few
other boys were playing up toward the plantation house; when they
got well up on the hillside, they could see two miles of the road
stretching out into the sunny, dusty distance. The road was a door
into nowhere. Some said, follow it long enough and you'd come to
Columbia, but that was hearsay and the world was full of hearsay.
To Marcus and his friends, the road just went off—and why should
it have to go anywhere?

Four days before, Gideon and Brother Peter had called together
all the men over twenty-one years. A lot of it was a matter of
estimation, for how can most men know certainly whether he is
twenty, or twenty-one or twenty-two or what? Age isn't a dead
reckoning, but something to be set in broader figures. Brother
Peter had to search his memory and separate all the multiple small
black births, and finally through all the noise and talk, he separated
out the cows from the calfs, as he put it. Twenty-seven men in all
to go off for the voting.

"Now how about this here voting?" They turned to Gideon for
answers.

Marcus recognized it was natural that they should turn to Gideon
for questions. Death and God—well, they'd ask Brother Peter, but
most everything else, planting and sickness and the rest they'd pile
onto Gideon.

And now they were coming back from the voting. Two miles
away and down the dusty road, Marcus saw a group of men, walking
together and walking slowly for the companionship. Marcus ran
screaming down the hillside, "They're a coming! Whooee!"

The other boys piled after him. They set up a screeching that
could be heard a mile off, and everyone came tumbling out of the
cabins to see what was up. Rachel thought murder had been done,
and she had to slap Marcus twice to get some sense into his talk.

"Who's a coming?"

"Pa."

"Gideon?" sister Mary asked, and someone else added, "Lord be
praised," expressing the sentiments of most. This was a mystery
thing, this voting, it was ominous. All the men went off, and there

was a lonesome waiting on the plantation with the menfolk gone, the more so since nobody really knew what the voting was. The women stayed closer than ever before, and from hour to hour the speculation on what a voting was grew wilder.

Now everyone shaded their eyes and looked down the road. Sure enough, the men were coming back—moving slowly, what with all the miles they had walked, but coming back. Everyone who could count counted, and it seemed that all the men were there. Rachel could recognize Gideon already, his big body bulking so large.

Gideon was a quantity of man, built like a bull, heavy in the shoulders, narrow in the waist, lean in the legs; that kind of man, the saying went, would be bull-like, with brains in his hands, but Gideon was not a man for sayings or proverbs. He was himself, and there was a reason why people turned to him; it was true that he moved slowly, both his body and his brain, but if he had a need to, he could move fast. When he had an idea, he turned it over and over, but when he had it at last, it was his.

He came first, and Rachel made him out; that slow, bent walk meant the miles were behind him. He carried his rifle at trail, the way he had learned in the army. He carried a sack on his shoulders, and in that would be something for the children. Alongside of him walked Brother Peter, tall and skinny and unarmed, the way a man of God should be. Then the two Jefferson brothers, both with rifles. Hannibal Washington, the little one. James, Andrew, Ferdinand, Alexander, Harold, Baxter, Trooper—those were men still without family names. By and by, a thought would come to them and they'd take names; but a family name was a thing to ponder on, and most men weren't easily satisfied.

Now Jeff was off, loping down the road to meet the men, a crowd of boys and girls and women following him. Rachel stayed; she held onto Marcus's collar and got him to help her draw cold water out of the well, so that Gideon could quench his thirst. She didn't have to run down to Gideon like a fool child; they understood each other better than that.

It was hot for a late November afternoon. When Gideon and the men plodded in among the cabins, the sweat was running down their dark faces, washing shiny ribbons in the dust.

There was a reward for Rachel for knowing their need, the way they gulped down the clear cold well water, and then held out the wooden mugs for more and more. Everyone had some question to ask, and they came fast and furious as rain:

"What's this voting?"

"How come you don't bring nothing back? Where this voting is?"

"You done bought the voting?"

"Bought and paid for it?"

"How many them voting you find along down by the white folks?"

"How big them are?"

"How many?"

Until Brother Peter declared desperately, "Brethren, sisteren and children, a little peace, a little quiet, and we all will give out them answers."

The men had kissed their wives and children. Gideon had taken Rachel in his arms and kissed her knowingly and gently. They had sweet candy, some of them, and were already handing it around. They opened their sacks; for Jenny, Gideon had a rose made of red gingham, a beautiful thing that was just like real with a perfume smell on it. The talk made a racket, but no one was telling about the voting. The dogs scampered around like mad, because dog-like they felt a need for a large share of affection. Finally, Brother Peter spread his arms and asked for quiet. A sort of quiet, he managed to get; the men squatted on their heels; the children sat and lay on the grass; the women sat down too or stood close together with arms entwined.

"Brother Gideon will tell you," Brother Peter said. "This here voting's like a wedding or Christmas sermon, matter for all. Government puts out a strong right arm, like the angel Gabriel, and says, declare yourself. We done that. Along with maybe five hundred other niggers and white folk, Government says, choose out a delegate. We done that. We pick Gideon."

Gideon stood up slowly, the people watching him with uncertainty. Rachel knew he was frightened; she knew every mood and impulse of Gideon. What did it mean that he was chosen out? What was a delegate?

"We gone and voted," Gideon said. He had a mellow voice, but it came slowly now because he was turning things over and setting them right.

"Voting—" Gideon said.

Gideon remembered how it was only a few days ago when they came into the town for the voting. There was, in their own group, a certain doubt as to just what voting meant; both Gideon and Brother Peter had tried to explain it as a wilful determination of their own destiny. They were free men and they had a voice; when there was a matter in question concerning their lives, they used that voice, and that was voting. But all these things were abstracts, and abstracts bewildered them. They would wait and see just how it turned out.

When they came into town, Gideon thought to himself, every nigger and white man in the world is here. Packed down the main street, packed on the portico of the columned courthouse, packed here and there and everywhere—and all of them talking at the top of their lungs about the voting. Half of them armed, white men and black men with guns in their hands. There was a company of Union troops detailed to keep order. Gideon thanked God for that; there were too many guns, he thought, too many hotheads.

Too many niggers who thought that voting was forty acres and a mule to take home with them, too many who thought voting would make them rich—too many who stared baffled and angry at their empty hands after they had cast the vote.

Now Gideon tried to tell the listeners how it was when his turn came, the dirty, bruised interior of the old courthouse, the registrars sitting around the long table with their huge open books, the stars and stripes prominently displayed behind them, the half-dozen soldiers standing guard, the voting booths and the ballot boxes. How he was given a sheet of paper upon which it said, "For a Constitutional Convention," and under that, "Against a Constitutional Convention," and under that, "Vote one by placing an x in the box indicated." All day long Yankees and Negroes had been talking in the street about how every black man ought to vote for the Convention. That was not hard to realize; the Convention would make a new world, or so they said. As Gideon stared at the paper, a registrar said in tired, bored tones:

"For the Convention or against it. Make your mark. Go into the booth, then fold your ballot."

Another registrar read off, "In the Js, Gideon Jackson." The men at the table ruffled through the pages of their books, and one said:

"Sign here, or make your mark."

Gideon took the pen and wrote painfully and crookedly, "Gideon

Jackson," trembling and frightened, but thanking God that he had learned how to write his name and would not have to humiliate himself by making his mark. Then he took his ballot into the booth and tried to read it through before he marked it. He would have said he could read a little, but such words as "Constitutional Convention" might have been Sanskrit. He made the mark where it said "For"; that at least he could read, but his shame was something he'd remember a long while afterwards. He told the listeners now:

"We come like children, ignorant and unknowing. Brother Peter, he pray to God we done right."

"Hallelujah," a few of them said softly.

"A Yankee man, he talk to us," Gideon went on. "He break us down like flocks of sheep, and there was maybe five hundred of us standing unknowing and ignorant. 'Pick a delegate,' he say to us. Then he hand out more ballots. One nigger speak and then another nigger—then a white man speak. Brother Peter, he speak up and say, 'Gideon's the man!'"

Gideon couldn't say anymore than that. Everyone understood now how it had come about that Gideon was a delegate, and they felt such pride as they had never known before. As imperfectly as they understood it, they still felt the pride. Brother Peter took over now and told how Gideon would go to Charleston and join in the Convention. Rachel wept. Gideon stared at the ground and scuffed the grass with his feet. Marcus and Jeff threw out their chests; they would be too uppity to condescend for a week to come.

"God be praised," Brother Peter said.

They answered, "Hallelujah."

Then they broke up into little groups; each had his own wonderful story to tell.

Tonight, Rachel had Gideon back with her again; they lay on the straw pallet and listened to the regular breathing of the children; they listened to the frogs croaking in the pond and the nightbirds twittering.

"Cry no more," Gideon begged her.

"Afraid."

"What for you afraid?"

"You go away, and I get me uneasy."

"And I'm back now."

"And you go on off to Charleston," Rachel said, speaking of a legendary place in another world.

"And I come back," Gideon said gently. "Why for a woman should cry in a time of rejoicing? This is the best time there ever was for a black man. This is the hallelujah time, honey child. Nestle close. This here's the sun rising. I'm full of fright, but it ain't fright for my woman and babes."

"What for you're full of fright?"

"I'm a black nigger fool," Gideon said miserably. "I'm a black nigger man. What is there I know—can't read, can't write but my name."

"Brother Peter's no fool."

"How's that?"

"He comes up and says, here's a man to be your delegate. Why you think them niggers pick you?"

"Don't know."

Rachel wept softly and happily. She was prone to tears when there was a good time and good things happening. She told her husband, "Gideon, Gideon honey, you recollect the time when you set off to join the Yankee soldiers? You say to me, when I cry my heart out, here's the way a man has to do, he does it. This ain't no different, Gideon."

"How's that?"

She put her lips close to his ear and hummed, "Nigger in the field picking cotton, picking cotton, thinking about the gal he loves—"

And to that, Gideon fell asleep, to that and tumbled memories, and hope and fear.

2. HOW GIDEON JACKSON AND BROTHER PETER TALKED TOGETHER

At breakfast the following morning, the whole family sat together; and Gideon thought with pride that there were few men who had all this, a wife like Rachel, two strong sons, and a pretty little daughter like Jenny. The boys were wild and headstrong, but so had he been in his time; and on his back were the scars of more than a hundred lashes to show just how headstrong he had been.

They had started in on the hot corn pone covered with a gravy of molasses, when Brother Peter put his head through the open doorway and said, "Morning, brother, morning, sister, morning, children."

They didn't have to urge him too much to have him join them at the table. The whole cabin was full of the smell of hot corn baking, and it made a man wet his lips before he even tasted the food. He was lavish in his praise. And after that, he had sugar sweets in his pockets for the children. Rachel always warmed specially to a man who talked up her food; too many of God's men were sour as a vinegar apple.

After the meal, Brother Peter asked Jeff, "Son, could you manage Gideon's chores?"

"I guess," Jeff nodded.

Gideon and Brother Peter walked over to the corncrib and sat down with their backs against the slats, their legs stretched out on the ground. It was a sunny place, and the cool morning wind blew up from the valley. The dog came and laid alongside of them. They pulled sticks of grass and chewed on them.

"When you plan to leave, Gideon?" Brother Peter asked.

"For Charleston?"

"Uh-huh."

When a long moment went by without Gideon answering, Brother Peter said, "Why for you afraid?"

"How come you think I'm frighted?"

"Uh-huh. Look a here, Gideon, you and me, we know each other long time back. Come the Lord's time, you be thirty-six years old. How come I remember that clear? When your mammy had her time come, she lay down on her back with you inside her and screamed, oh Jesus little child, my time's come. Fourteen, I was then. Your daddy say, Peter, run up tell the boss man Sophie's dying. I run up, and old Jim Blake—him the overseer then—say he never remember a nigger woman not dying when it comes her time. Get a doctor? Oh, no. Old mammy Anna, the midwife, she fight the devil three days, then you're born but your mammy's dead. Then old Jim Blake whips the hide off me and swears to God to Mister Carwell I never done told him. So I got a memory of you being born. I got a memory of days we work them hot cotton fields. I got a memory of how we talk, what for a nigger live? When you say, I'll take my life go down to sweet sleep. I'm the nigger, praise God, makes you see the terrible sin. Who you come to when you want to go off fighting with the Yankee men?"

"Come to you," Gideon nodded.

"Say, take care Rachel, take care three little babes. I done that."

"Uh-huh."

"Now you rear up like a mule when I say you afraid."

"Tell me to go down Charleston Town," Gideon muttered. "Nigger can't read, can't write, can't hardly spell his name, you tell me, go down to Charleston Town to Convention. Go down to city full of white houses like that there big house, full of white folks making fun at a damn fool nigger man."

Tracing a pattern on the sand in front of him, Brother Peter asked gently, "How you come to Charleston first time, Gideon?"

"Come in with the Yankee men," Gideon recalled. "Come in with the blue uniform and gun in my hand and ten thousand along side of me, singing a hallelujah song—"

"You wasn't afraid. You is just afraid to go in alone, no blue uniform, no gun in your hand, no hallelujah song, just the hand of the law saying to black nigger man, my child, you is free."

Gideon didn't answer, and Brother Peter said softly, "The Book say of Moses he was frightened man, but God say, lead my people—"

"I ain't Moses."

"People need a leader, Gideon. I say to myself up at voting place, law say, a nigger man's free, law say, vote, law say, nigger man come out of slavery—make a life. Nigger can't read, can't write, can't think even. Slave got the whip or sold down the river for thinking. Slave got three hundred lashes for learning to read. Nigger's like an old hound dog pushed out of house and set to get his own food. I say to myself, who's going to lead these people? Walk big or talk big, they all frightened. Who's going to lead them?"

"Why you pick me?" Gideon demanded. "Why not you?"

"People picked you," Brother Peter said. "Going to be that way from now on." Brother Peter leaned over and put his boney hand on Gideon's knee, "Look a here, Brother Gideon—say you can't read. Ain't nobody born with reading power. You learn that. You learn to read, you learn to write. Me, I got a little writing knowledge, maybe fifteen, twenty words. Well, I write them down and you study them for a start—"

Gideon shook his head helplessly.

"Take a matter of talking," Brother Peter said. "Words match up, white folks call that grammar. Man with a head on his shoul-

ders, he talks the words right, old nigger like me, he don't. How you
going to get that?"

"God knows," Gideon said.

"God, he knows. I know too. You going to listen. You going to
listen to white man talk. You going to listen every minute of day.
You going to learn yourself. Come a time, maybe, you be able to
read a book. Ain't nothing you can't find in books—gospel truth
there."

"A man puts his mind to raising a crop," Gideon said. "That's a
day's work. Then how come a man's going to fill his head with
learning?"

"Cross that bridge when we come to it. Meanwhile, Jeff's able to
do chores. Got a fine boy in Marcus. Got the blessings of Jesus all
down the line. Going to be a new world, Gideon. Going to be a
bright new world." He smiled and motioned to the huddle of win-
dowless slave cabins. "Shake this off." He folded his long, thin arms
and bowed his head. "Praise God."

Gideon said, "How you figure this here Convention?"

"Makes out the laws. Constitution's like a Bible book. Can't have
a world with niggers running around like wild hogs. White folks
hate the nigger—nigger fears the white folks. That ain't the good
way."

"How I going to know a good law from a bad law?"

"How you know a good man from a bad man? How you know a
good woman from a sinful one?"

"I got a measure to go by."

"Well, you got a measure here," Brother Peter said. "How come
you got no reading, no writing. Well, never was a school for niggers—never was a school for poor whites either. There's a start.
Make a law for schooling, that's a good law. Here's this Carwell
place, maybe twenty thousand acres. Who it belong to? Belong to
Mr. Carwell? To Government? To niggers, white folk? Nigger
wants land—so does white folk. Well, there's enough for all, plenty
for all, but how it going to be divided?"

"How I know that?"

"Patient, Gideon, slow and easy."

"How come you don't go to be a delegate?" Gideon asked.

"How come people don't go and ballot me? Got a way of knowing, Gideon. I'm an old nigger man, just as smart as I'll ever be.

Someday, you look at me, Gideon, you say to yourself, how come I ever take comfort from that old nigger man? That old ignorant nigger man."

"I never say that."

"God bless you, maybe you don't, Gideon. But you like a little babe. All ready. Just fill you up, like bucket drawing water from the well. Just wait and see."

Gideon shook his head. "How I wish I believe that—"

"Don't matter, you believe it, you don't believe it, Gideon. All a same, that happen. Like a bucket drawing up cool, clean water."

"Supposing they just laugh and mock this nigger?"

"Sure they going to laugh, Gideon, son. How come we laugh when some poor swamp nigger come out, say where master is? You free, we tell him, and that nigger don't know no more what's free than hound dog. Natural for us to laugh at poor devil. But you going to take laughing, take scorn. First time they give you delegate pay like Yankee man said, maybe dollar a day, you take that dollar buy a book. Maybe you hunger like starving man, but you take that book, buy candle to read by, and you figure out them words."

Gideon nodded. The more Brother Peter spoke, the more terrified Gideon became about the prospect of a Convention at Charleston, but at the same time there was that sickening, wonderful thrill he had felt when he ran off to join the Union Army.

"What kind of book first?"

"Suppose a preaching man ought to say Bible. But Bible ain't easy, Gideon, tie you up in snarls. Get yourself learning book first, spelling book. Then maybe book of sums. Come that time, you know yourself what kind of book you want next."

"Uh-huh," Gideon agreed.

"Ain't all to be found in books," Brother Peter observed, feeling the time had come when he could plant a reservation.

"How that?"

"Ain't no books wrote unless there's something happened. This here thing of a nigger man being free never happen before. Maybe nothing like this since Moses led the Children out a Egypt. Moses, he don't have book, he turn up face to God. He say, what the good thing to do?"

"How I going to know that?"

"Gideon, fill your heart with love. Fill your heart with understanding."

"I is prone to anger," Gideon admitted.

"And who ain't? Born in sin, we is, brother. Gideon, who you think smartest man in world?"

"Live or dead?" Gideon said thoughtfully.

"One or another."

"Old Abe, I reckon."

"Uh-huh. How come old Abe he got to know all that? How come old Abe, he say to nigger man through the land, you is free?"

"Guess he see that's right."

"Maybe so, Gideon. Maybe more so, he got a heart full of love and mercy. Come right out of the piney woods, they say old Abe was, just no different from you. But got a heart big like that there plantation house."

"Got a big heart, all right," Gideon admitted.

"Now, take a matter of judgment, Gideon. Come two men and bear a witness. One fine, get-up, big-city man, he say, old wind ain't blowing. Other man, dirty, hungry, he say wind blow fine. You got to judge, wind blow or don't blow. How you going to judge?"

"Put up my own hand and see if the wind blows—"

"Uh-huh. Or ask folk, maybe ten, twelve folk. Don't take no man's witness just cause he struts like peacock or talks smooth and fine. Now, Gideon, you going to feel hard about white folk—got the whip lash on your back, got the heart hardened. That just means suffering and misery. Come from here on—color of a man's skin don't matter. There's good men and bad men, black and white."

"I see that," Gideon nodded.

"Ain't no more than that, I guess," Brother Peter reflected. "God's blessing. Let Him walk by your side, Gideon."

"Amen," Gideon said.

3. HOW GIDEON JACKSON WENT TO CHARLESTON AND THE ADVENTURES THAT BEFELL HIM ON THE WAY

As the days went past and nothing happened, Gideon's election to the Convention became of less importance, and sometimes for two or three days he would not think of it at all. Actually, what proof had he that he was the delegate? At first, immediately after Brother Peter had made his long speech at the voting, it had seemed that all the men in their section had been for Gideon; afterwards, no one said that they had voted against Gideon, and he and Brother Peter just naturally concluded that he had been the delegate. But the voting was by secret ballot; they were told that when the ballots were counted, the delegates would be notified and receive the proper credentials. But here it was, two weeks later. Wavering between fear and hope, Gideon often asked himself how long it took a good counter to count up to five or six hundred. Of late, he simply shunted the matter off. No Yankee men in their right senses would call on fool niggers to be delegates.

There were things enough to keep him busy now, with winter coming on. In the summer, living was easy and life was good; men had to be prodded into worrying about the cold weather coming. For a whole week, Gideon had the men cutting wood in the tract they called The Lower Section. In the old days, when the place had an overseer, the wood was just cut back from the cleared section, nothing spared, and a stubble of two foot stumps left to rot through the years. Gideon had been thinking about that, and this year he proposed that they dig at the roots and fell the trees from below ground level.

"Double the work," they said. "What for?"

"Easier to take out the tree with the stump than the stump without the tree," Gideon said.

"Who going to want to take out the stump?"

"That we don't know," Gideon said. "Don't know who the land belong to, but maybe it belong to you and me some day."

"We worry about that when that time come."

They might have argued the question half the day, had not Gideon seized upon an inspiration and suggested that they have a vote. Even as he said it, he was not sure it would work, not certain of the application of so miraculous a principle to a work-a-day occupation like cutting wood. But the idea caught hold, and in the dead silence that followed his suggestion, Gideon applied the yes and no method. Even though the men had voted for the Convention, the mechanics of the thing was new and revolutionary. They had to thrash out the matter of whether a man could vote yes or no only or both yes and no. But in the end, the principle was applied and it worked, and Gideon's proposal for taking out the trees by the roots won with a considerable majority.

Again, when Trooper, big and strong as an ox, protested that he was sawing three times the wood he'd ever use, while a little man like Hannibal Washington didn't contribute half his share of the work. Gideon fell back on the vote. Only this time, a new innovation appeared, for the men laid down their tools and discussed the whole matter of cooperation. In the overseer days, working together had become second nature to them; only now, as they actively awoke to the fact that they were free, did they actually question it. Why shouldn't each man work for himself? If freedom didn't mean that, what did it mean?

The innovation, suggested by Brother Peter, consisted of an appraisal of the many sides of a question, before it was put to a vote. Hannibal Washington, his small, lined face tight with anger, said to Trooper:

"Looka here now, you go off cut your wood single. I say it won't be no account against equal share this wood we cut together. What for then you come to mock at me, you big hunk of black crow meat?"

Trooper raised his ax. Gideon and others held them apart, and Brother Peter cried, "Shame for men to go as spill blood over something like this!"

For an hour they talked themselves hoarse, and this time the vote won by only a slim margin. Afterwards, Gideon said to Brother Peter:

"We ain't going to be trouble free."

"What man is?"

"Anyway, my head aches—men to scrap and cry like children."

"Gideon, they don't know, work together, work apart. They like children now. How come you expect big things, a nigger's one summer, two summers away from slavery. Time moves slow."

But time brought trouble. The voting was like a bright, sharp sunrise, but afterwards nothing happened, life went on as before. Gideon noticed how often now the people peered through the windows of the big plantation house. It was full of beautiful things, and there was too much talk about those things. In that, there was a certain resentment against Gideon; for, a year past, the disbanded South Carolina troops had come through, broken into the big house, taken what they wanted, and scattered other things about. Gideon, it had been, who ordered the things replaced and the house boarded up once more. When they asked him, "What for?" he said, "They ain't no things of ours." "How they different from the clothes we wear, the houses we sleep in?" "The one is needful, the other ain't," Gideon answered.

And now he found Marcus with a silver spoon that could have come from nowhere but the big house.

How then?—Marcus had broken into the house. A big rambling house with a hundred entrances and exits, and breaking into it wasn't a difficult thing; but for the first time Gideon felt uncertainty about how to handle his children. Reflecting, it seemed to him that he had known just what to do with a child until now; now he had an immense and frightful sense of his own ignorance. Each night he sat in front of the fire with the list of words Brother Peter had written. Duz, ant, man, wumen, gel, yu, shurnuf, nigru, wide, and so forth and so on, a mountain of fact to confound him and terrify him. Right and wrong became malleable matters instead of great constants, and instead of punishing Marcus firmly, he said to him, uncertainly:

"How you come in that big house, Marcus?"

"Ain't been there."

So Marcus lied. "This is a good boy," Gideon reflected. The puzzles and problems were becoming numberless.

"Where you get that spoon?" Gideon demanded.

"Found it."

"You don't find that spoon, Marcus. You better tell me the truth."

"Found it."

"Then where you find it?"

He caught Marcus unprepared, and the tale came out piece by piece. They had gotten into the house through the kitchen cellar. Other boys had taken things, silk, silver, hidden them. Gideon couldn't whip Marcus; he had never taken a hand to any of his children—his people didn't. Leave the whipping to the white folks; he knew what a whip on his back felt like. He called a meeting of the people, and had Marcus up in front of them, and there, each word like a knife into the boy, he told what had happened. Brother Stephan demanded:

"How long that big house going to stand there, Brother Gideon?"

"Come doomsday, if it got to."

"Nigger live in a dirty little shack, but that damn big house, no one live in it."

"Come doomsday," Gideon said stubbornly.

And that night, Rachel took it to him, sobbingly, "How come you ever done that to the boy, Gideon?"

"Done what I had to do."

"Laying it into him like that in front everybody."

"He done an evil thing."

"Seem like nothing but evil come out of the voting."

"What—?"

"Take you off to Charleston, set the niggers grunting and growling, don't do nothing, don't settle nothing."

Gideon pretended he had fallen asleep. Rachel stopped talking and he heard her crying quietly.

At fifteen, Jeff was chafing and pulling at his bonds. He was headstrong and healthy as a wild beast. To him, Gideon was an old one, Brother Peter was an old one; they drew the world around his neck and tightened it like a noose. He was imprisoned, and he wanted to break the bonds and be free. In this little community, where no one could read or write with any facility, where there was never a newspaper, time became the elastic, primitive thing it had been many thousands of years before. Not even a clock; the sun swung overhead, a big, orange timepiece, and the slow parade of the seasons made an easy calendar. Jeff was fifteen now, and his memory of the time before the war was blurred and uncertain. The constant talk about the difference between freedom and slavery made little impression upon him; as it was, he had been born in chaos, and all his young boyhood had been chaos.

Now he was a young giant, and still just a boy. It made him sick when the men marched away to the voting and he was left behind. Every road sang a song to him, and he felt that some day he would go off down one of them and never come back. Sometimes, Gideon sensed the subdued violence in the boy. For that reason, he let him go off hunting alone, into the swampy lowlands. Jeff could rove the swamps for hours, singing wordless, wild songs. Hunting quelled his impatience as nothing else could. When he came to a cold pool, trodden around, no one had to tell him that here the deer drank. He could lie there, ten hours at a stretch, patient and restful, waiting for a wild horned buck, or a fierce swamp boar. In those long and silent hours, he would dream formlessly and endlessly.

In his dreams were the cities he had never seen, fairylands formed from the words of the men. In his dreams was Father Abraham, shapeless like a God, singing hallelujah songs. Sometimes, in his dreams, there was a poignant longing, utterly formless, that stretched his heart like rubber.

Once, in the swamp, he had met two white men; this he hadn't told Gideon. They were soldier men, the old gray uniforms torn and stained. They looked at Jeff and swore at him, and when their guns came up, he leaped behind a tree. The two guns went off, and echoed like a battle in the swamp. If they had gotten him, it would have been just another nigger dead, face down in the water, gradually absorbed by the mud and slimy leaves and then forgotten. If anything marked young manhood for Jeff, it was this, for as they ran off through the swamp, he could have shot either of them; yet he didn't—just watched them curiously, quite unafraid, plumbing the mystery of why they should have desired to kill him so immediately and coldly. He never told anyone of that.

This was the first time a letter had come to the Carwell place since the overseer had gone. It was weeks after the voting, and therefore no one made a connection between the two remarkable events. Early one afternoon, a buggy drove up the Columbia Pike, and old Cap Holstien, the postmaster, dismounted in that slow, lazy manner he accentuated in his dealings with the freedmen. All during the war, Cap Holstien had held his job as postmaster, first under the Rebels and then under the Yankees and then under the Rebels and then under the Yankees again.

It wasn't that Cap Holstien was a loyal man; he was a tobacco-chewing, tobacco-spitting, profane enemy of the Constitution, which he cursed from dawn to sunset, nor had he ever saluted the flag. But he was the only man who knew where everyone was through all the chaos of the war and the post-war period; he was the only one who knew who was living and who was dead, who had stayed at home and who had gone off to Charleston, Columbia, Atlanta—or the north. And he was the only man who knew most of the several thousand freed slaves in the countryside. So the military kept him on as postmaster, in spite of the fact that he cursed them out each day and swore that he'd live to see the time when he'd kill a Republican with his own two hands. Now he drove up to the Carwell place and yelled:

"Hey, you nigra black bastards!"

It was a fact that he wasn't afraid of anything that walked. The

people, men, women, boys and girls came running. They gathered
around him, and he spat tobacco juice in the dust, rubbed his hands,
and took out of his pocket a long brown envelope. He squinted at
it and then demanded:

"Which one you thieving coons is Gideon Jackson?"

Gideon had been smiling at the little old man. There was something he liked about Cap, just what he didn't know, something
summed up by Brother Peter's comment, "There's a man'll sore
need praying." Gideon stepped forward, and Cap, who knew him,
looked him up and down and asked:

"Gideon Jackson?"

"Uh-huh."

"Sign here."

"Yes, sir."

Holstien held out the stub of a pencil. "Can you write? If not,
just make a nigger mark right there."

"I can write," Gideon said. His name anyway. The people hardly
gave him room to breath as he shaped it out under Cap's watchful
eye. He had never performed the public practice of writing like this
before, and the people commented in soft tones upon his skill. Then
the old man got back in his buggy, swung it around, and whipped
his mule back along the way he had come.

Gideon turned the brown envelope slowly. In the upper left hand
corner, there was printed:

> If not delivered in ten days return to
> General E. R. S. Canby, U.S.M.O.F.
> Columbia, S.C. S.M.D.

Most of that, he could read, although he didn't know what the
long string of initials stood for. Brother Peter, looking over his
shoulder, said:

"General Canby, he the new Yankee man, come to look after
things. That there S.C., that mean South Carolina, S.M.D., maybe
that mean second military district, like that time they come to tell
us go to the voting. The Lord knows what them other letters
means."

In the opposite corner it said:

> Official Business
> Penalty for use to avoid payment of postage $100.00

Neither Brother Peter nor anyone else in the packed group around Gideon could make any sense of that. In the center of the envelope was the address:

Gideon Jackson, esquire,
Carwell Plantation,
Carwell, S.C. S.M.D.

Brother Peter read Gideon's name aloud, but paused at *esquire*. He had never seen the word before, had no idea of its meaning and could not pronounce it. He tried, silently, making motions with his lips. Hannibal Washington, who could read a few words, had a try at it too. So did Marion Jefferson, who had learned to read a few words while in the Union Army—but that completed the literacy of the group, and after that they simply stared at the letter in silence. Finally, Gideon said:

"How you figure that word, Brother Peter?"

Brother Peter shook his head, and Hannibal Washington volunteered, "Could be that like mister or colonel or something."

"Then how come it ain't afore Gideon's name? How come it traipses after it?"

Silence again, until Brother Peter said, "Open her up, Gideon."

Slowly, Gideon opened the envelope. It was full of papers. Around all the others, there was a letter, addressed to Gideon in the same fashion as the envelope. It said:

This will notify you that you have been elected delegate from the Carwell-Sinkerton district, South Carolina, to the State Constitutional Convention, to convene at Charleston S.C. S.M.D. on the Fourteenth of January, 1868. Here inclosed are your instructions and credentials. Major Allen James, at Charleston, has been notified of your election and acceptance, and will receive your credentials. The Government of the United States trusts that you will honorably and conscientiously fulfill your duties, and the Congress of the United States asks that you will truthfully and faithfully play your part in the reconstruction of the State of South Carolina.

signed,
General E. R. S. Canby
U.S.M.O.F. S.M.D.

That was what the letter said, but hours went by before they could discern even a part of the meaning. Now, on top of everything else, Gideon's election became, to him, a grotesque, a caricature of a thing that made a mockery of all their fine, new-won freedom. Black, black ignorance covered all, black as his skin, black as the night. It was a trick, like the dreams he had almost every night of the free days, dreams during which he felt the whip on his shoulders, dreams during which he labored in the hot cotton field, dreams so real that he had to crawl out of bed and go to the door and see with his own eyes that the fields were not planted with cotton. Now his waking was a dream. He longed to run away and hide.

And Brother Peter and Hannibal Washington labored over the letter. The people lost interest and the sun set. They went into Gideon's cabin and sat with the papers held in the firelight. Hannibal Washington said:

"We might fetch them to town and let the Yankee man make them out?"

Gideon roared a furious "No!" that brought looks of surprise from everyone. Marcus and Jeff had never seen their father like this, and they sat silent; but for Jeff, this was the beginning of something. He saw three strong men, three men whom the community looked up to, solid and God-fearing, knowing the secret of a good crop, of butchering a cow, a calf or a pig, of many other things, held frustrated and impotent by a scrap of paper. There was strength in that paper. Jeff's way of thinking was in vivid imagery, and now he saw the printed word in its power, in its calm purpose and intention. He knew he would learn to read, and for the first time he felt superior to Gideon.

Also for the first time, he felt a certain contempt for Gideon—a feeling that he, in Gideon's place, would not have been so enraged and baffled because he lacked the skill to read. Rachel sensed this; she was strung to the emotions of these men like a finely-tuned harp, and she was the most disturbed of any. The night before, she had given a copper coin she had been treasuring to old Mammy Christy, and the old woman made her a luck fetish, a little image that was hidden in the cabin now. If Gideon knew, he would be somberly angry; he hated that sort of thing and stolidly defied bad luck whenever he had an opportunity to; and Brother Peter called such things un-Christian, heathen-like.

In time, the three men unraveled the letter, more or less completely. Words like *reconstruction* and *conscientiously* they could only guess at, and other words they interpreted wrongly, but the gist of it was theirs. Gideon had to go to Charleston; that they knew. The vague shape of a Convention extended into the remote future; it might be a permanent thing, it might not. Gideon was given over; he was one of them no longer. The other papers and cards in the envelope they examined only cursorily; those things Gideon would take with him, and eventually the meaning would emerge.

Gideon asked about the date. A cold wind blew through the cracks in the cabin wall. Could it be January fourteeth already? But Brother Peter thought of the postmark on the envelope:

"Right here, it say January 2."

"Take a long time to walk to Charleston," Hannibal Washington sighed. In a way, the little man envied Gideon.

"Can't go like this," Gideon said, frowning at his ragged cotton trousers, his old blue army shirt, and his ancient army boots.

"Wouldn't be fitting," Brother Peter agreed. "Got my black frock coat. Got a torn sleeve, Rachel can mend. Maybe a little tight, but you can get it on, Gideon."

"Ferdinand's got a pair of pretty pants."

"Get that old stovepipe hat Trooper's been keeping in his cabin. Mighty fine hat, little crushed—but mighty fine hat."

"Gideon, honey, I can wash the shirt and mend it," Rachel said.

Hannibal Washington said generously, "Got that old watch Yankee man give me in the army, Gideon—" It was his most precious possession. Gideon felt a wonderful warmth for these people who loved him so. "You take it, Gideon," Hannibal Washington said. "Got no works and can't keep time, but a mighty nice watch to wear."

"Got to have a hand-kerchief," Brother Peter decided. "Not a nigger sweating kerchief, but one to keep up in breast pocket, the way white folks does. Got a fine piece of red and white calico Rachel can sew into shape."

That was how it came about that Gideon Jackson set off on his long walk to Charleston Town. Two days later, in the bright and early morning, he had left the Carwell place some miles behind him —and now he strode along the dusty road, the stovepipe hat tilted precariously, singing in his rich bass voice the old marching tune of his regiment:

> "There ain't no grass grows under my feet,
>   On freedom road,

There ain't no grass grows under my feet,
On freedom road,
Old John Brown, grand-daddy,
We're coming,
We're coming,
Down freedom road."

A defiant song. Worth a man's life to sing that song on a South Carolina road, but that was the way Gideon felt right now. He had more than a hundred miles to walk to Charleston, a hundred miles of the open road, and he was a walking man. Now the die was cast, and he felt curiously happy and light, like a boy going off to fish in a forbidden stream. Later the old doubts and anxieties would come back; but how could an old slave man feel anything but excited joy at the prospect of such a long walk?

There was some talk before Gideon left as to whether he should take a musket with him; for all of the danger, he agreed with Brother Peter that it would be the wrong way to come to a Convention, gun in hand.

"Come with peace and love in your heart—and in your hands too," Brother Peter said.

Anyway, he had in his breast pocket the credentials of the United States Government; who would dare to molest him? "Official Business," it said on the brown envelope. Funny, the way his heart and his hopes went up and down, frightened one moment, happy and excited the next. As he strode along, a package of corn bread and cold pork under his arm, singing his song, a cold wind blowing through the piney woods on either side the road, he thought of what would come from this Convention. Strangely, the more he turned it over in his mind, the more clearly he saw the conception of a new state and a new life emerging from the Convention; enough to make a man frightened, and enough to make him proud.

Ahead of him, the pines thinned out. There was the shack and a clearing of some ten acres. Abner Lait's freehold; at least, they still called it a freehold, although Abner Lait had been tenant to the Carwells and so had his father. Lait was a tall, boney, red-headed white man, slow-spoken, regarding the world suspiciously and uncertainly. Hard times were wrapped around him; before the war, he had barely scraped a living out of the land; when he had a good crop, the Carwells took it; when he had a bad one, they put him deeper in debt. When the war came, he went off with Dudley Carwell's regiment. After three and a half years and four wounds and more battles than he wanted to remember, he was taken prisoner, and spent the time between then and the end of the war in a Yankee prison camp. Somehow, while he was gone, his wife and his four children had existed; how, he didn't know—nor did she care to remember. Now he was back, and he had put in two crops. Things were bad, but not as bad as they had been. At least, the Carwells had forgotten him; he raised corn and some pigs and chickens; at least, bellies were reasonably full.

Abner Lait hated black men in the formal way of hatred he had always known, a thing expected. He hated the planters with reason and precision. Between him and Gideon, there was a respectful animosity. As Gideon came along the road now, Abner stood at his fence line, leaning on a spade.

"Morning, Mr. Lait," Gideon said.

"Now that's a hell of a song for a nigger to be singing."

"When my feet walk the road, there's a song in my mouth," Gideon smiled. "When I marched with the Yankee men, that was the song we sing."

"God damn you to hell," Abner said lazily. It was not a morning to nurse anger. Peter and Jimmy, his two tow-headed boys came shyly up to the fence. "I do wish I might of found you in my sights when you was with them damn Yanks," Abner added. "I would of filled you fuller with holes than that there black coat you wearing. How come you all trussed up like a monkey, Gideon?"

"Off to Charleston to the Convention."

"Convention! God damn, if that don't beat it all."

"Got elected at the voting."

Abner whistled and said, "What do you think of that. Nigger at a Convention at Charleston. Reckon they'll damn well lynch you before you open your mouth, Gideon."

"Maybe so," Gideon nodded. "But I got government writing right here in my pocket. You been at the voting?"

"I been, but I don't vote for no nigger."

They stood a while longer, and one of the boys found enough courage to sidle up to Gideon, who stroked his yellow hair gently. Then Gideon said goodby and set off down the road again. Abner Lait stared after him and murmured:

"Off to Charleston. Jesus God, see a nigger walk off to Charleston to sit in a Convention!"

Gideon walked on until the sun was high overhead. Then he stopped by the wayside, built a little fire of brushwood, ate some cornbread and meat, and then lay and rested for about half an hour. It was warmer now than before. The birds sang merrily, and the sound of a brook nearby told Gideon that he would be able to quench his thirst. He was quite happy.

As nightfall came on, Gideon looked about for a place to sleep. If necessary, he would build a fire in the pines and lie down on a soft bed of brown needles; there were worse places than that to spend a night. But to Gideon it seemed a dreary waste of the evening hours not to hear a human voice or a little laughter; he wasn't one for loneliness. He was tired from the day's walking, and he had come a long way, perhaps twenty-five or thirty miles. He had passed through a town and put it miles behind him. He had walked on a causeway through a cypress swamp, and ahead of him were the flat tidewater lands. The gentle haze of evening had come into the sky, and there was a cold bite in the air.

So when Gideon saw a cabin on a flat, a ribbon of blue smoke fluttering from the chimney, and three chocolate-colored children playing in the sand at the doorway, he felt relief. As he crossed the field, the man of the house came out to meet him, a Negro of sixty-five or seventy, but strong and healthy-looking and smiling.

"Now I bid you good evening," he said.

"And the same to you," Gideon nodded, reflecting how much the same children were everywhere, shy and curious and warmly-excited by the presence of any stranger.

"And what can I do for you?" the old man asked.

"Name's Gideon Jackson, sir. I come down the pike from up a ways, Carwell Plantation—off and down the road to Charleston. I'd mighty appreciate a corner your shed there to spend the night. Ain't like I'm just a footloose nigger asking for bread, got my victuals here in a bundle. Got government papers here in my pocket." The old man was smiling. Gideon stopped, gulped, and swallowed what he was going to say about the Convention at Charleston. The old man said:

"Any stranger is welcome to a place by my fire and a bite of food. The shed is for animals. We can't offer you a bed, but a blanket by the fire, if that will do you. And I ask no man for credentials, sir. My name is James Allenby."

"Thank you kindly, Mr. Allenby," Gideon said, the old man's

smile putting him more at ease. Allenby led the way into the shack, an ancient bundle of sticks that might have once been a freehold farm, since it had windows and shutters, a feature lacking in most slave cabins. A girl crouched by the fire, stirring something in a pot; as they entered, she rose, tall, round of limb, brown-skinned, strikingly handsome, her head high and poised, as if she were balancing an urn atop of it. Her eyes were large and lustrous; Gideon realized that even in the dusk; but there was something strange about her eyes, something in the way they never fixed upon his face. Allenby took her by the hand and said:

"My child, we have a guest for the evening. His name is Gideon Jackson. He is journeying through to Charleston, and I have asked him to spend the night with us. He is a good and a gentle man, I think."

Something in what the old man said, in the way the girl continued to stare past him, gave Gideon the clue he had been seeking. The realization that she was blind terrified him for a moment, and he sought reassurance in the children, hanging onto her skirts now, in the good smell coming out of the pot, in the clean if miserable interior of the cabin. Perhaps she was the old man's daughter, certainly not the mother of the children; she was too young for that. He could not ask for explanations now. She said, "I bid you welcome, sir," and then went back to the fire. Gideon sat down on a chair of pine branches, and Allenby set the table with tin dishes and spoons. Night fell outside. Gideon had a way with children; they warmed to him, and soon one was in his arms, the other two bent over his knees.

"They like songs," the old man said.

Gideon sang, "Brother rabbit, he live in the old bramble patch, sky's his roof, he don't want no thatch . . ."

Gideon had finished telling his story, the voting, his being chosen as a delegate; it was late, and the fire was a bed of coals. Ellen Jones, the girl, had climbed the ladder to her bed under the eaves. One of the children slept up there with her; the two boys, Ham and Japet, shared a pallet, and now they were asleep. The old man sat by the fire with Gideon.

"So now you're off to Charleston," the old man said. "The dawn comes after such a long time. How I envy you, Gideon Jackson—

God help me, how I envy you. But it's right the way it is—for the young and the strong and the hopeful. For men like you—"

"For all of us," Gideon said.

"Yes?—perhaps. How old do you think I am, Gideon?"

"Maybe sixty-five—"

"Seventy-seven, Gideon. I fought in the 1812 war against the British. Yes, we were allowed to fight then—for this country's freedom. No, I'm not bitter. Then they thought slavery would die its own death. That was before cotton became a great cash crop. Slaves were a liability then, for the most part. They even educated me, turned me into a tutor; they didn't understand then that education was like a disease, that if you educated a man he was no good for slavery and that he would spread his freedom-sickness to others."

"Eat my heart out for a little learning," Gideon said.

"Learning and freedom—patience, Gideon. They come together. Don't I know? When that old British war was over, the master found I was teaching the other slaves to read and write. How could I do that? he wanted to know. How could I not do it? So he sold me down the river. Like a pattern, Gideon. Wherever I was, there was the same hunger for a little learning, to read a passage in the Bible, to spell a word or two, to write a letter to someone they love and who was now gone away. So they sold me, whipped me, threatened me. Can you cure a disease that way? I have read Voltaire, Paine, Jefferson, yes, and Shakespeare. You never heard his name, Gideon, or his golden voice; but you will—you will. Could I be quiet?"

Gideon shook his head dumbly.

"I had three wives, Gideon, and I loved them all—and each time I was sold away from them. I had children, too, but I know where none of them are, Gideon. Four times, I escaped—and each time I was found and brought back, whipped, but permitted to remain alive because I was wealth; a steer is worth something dead, but our flesh was worth nothing unless there was life in it. I don't talk about these things often, Gideon; I tell them to you because it is of utmost importance that you should remember our past, what our people have suffered. In you, Gideon, there is gentleness and strength and fire, too, I can see. You will become a great leader of our people, but you will be worth less than nothing if you ever forget. Now you have been wondering about this blind girl and the three children. I'll tell you—"

"Ain't no call for you to tell me 'less you want to," Gideon said.

"That's why I tell you, Gideon, because I want to. The three children are strays. This poor southland of ours is full of orphans and strays, lost children, black calves who never knew father or mother, cattle abandoned when the cattle market was destroyed. I was in slavery in Alabama when the war began. And when freedom came, I made my way north and east; not to go to the Yankee country—I love this southland—but the deep south I can never love. It lashed me too hard. I thought there might be some place in the Carolinas or in Virginia where a teacher would be needed. And on the way, I picked up the children. How? It happened, Gideon—it would happen to you. I found the girl, too. Ellen is sixteen. Her father was a free Negro in Atlanta, a doctor. That's another story; he's dead; let him rest. After Sherman had gone away, some terrible things happened. I blame no one. Some rebel soldiers—and there are evil men as well as good in every army—killed the girl's father, in her sight, spitted him with their bayonets and cut his eyes out. You see, he had helped the Yankees. I tell you this, Gideon, not to make hatred but understanding. You go to Charleston to make a constitution, a new state, a new world, a new life; then understand how simple people can do devilish things—because they know no better. After they had killed her father, they attacked her. Then she became blind. I don't know about such things, whether a shock can cause blindness or whether she had a sickness in her eyes. But when I found her, she had lost her senses, even the knowledge of who she was; she lived in the woods like a wild animal, and she was as timid as a wild animal. But for some reason, she trusted me, and I added her to my little company." He paused; Gideon was staring at the coals, his hands clenching and unclenching. "Gideon," the old man said softly.

"Sir?"

"Gideon, when you put those government credentials in your pocket, you stopped being a man and became a servant. A man, Gideon, can indulge his hate. He can want to kill and destroy, as you want to at this moment. A servant cannot; he must work for his master. Your people, Gideon, are your master. Now listen to me, and I'll tell you the rest."

"I'm listening," Gideon said.

"I found this shack. God knows where its tenant is—killed in the war, I guess. There are a thousand such lonely shacks in this southland of ours. For two years, I lived here. I raise a small crop, enough for us. I have a few chickens. A litter of wild pigs gave us some livestock. Since we are here, no one has molested us. Ellen is almost normal now—but blind. It's not a bad life for me, to have four young souls to teach. I hired out to work in the village; I am a middling good carpenter, shoemaker, tinker or letter writer, and I made a few pennies at each trade, enough to buy some clothes and some books—"

He left off there and for a long time Gideon said nothing. Then, "and when you die?"

"I've thought of that," Allenby answered. "There is my fear and unhappiness."

"Or suppose you sicken? Or suppose sheriff come along, say, get to blazes out a this shack."

"I've thought of that too, Gideon."

"Now look a here," Gideon said, a note of excitement in his voice. "Man like you, he's a knowing man. Maybe you old—seventy-seven, that's a far along age. But you're brown and tough, like an old nut. Maybe you die tomorrow, old man don't know what God's got in store, maybe you live ten, fifteen year."

"What are you driving at, Gideon?"

"Got a thought. Here's me, black man made free, skinning his heels down the road to Charleston town, proud like a peacock to be a delegate in a Convention. But can't read, can't write, just wrapped in ignorance. Here's maybe four million black men in this southland, just whimpering for a little bit of learning. Got freedom a mile high, like a gracious sweet song, but where that all get a man who bows his head with ignorance? You teach three little ones, that's good. Up at the Carwell place, I got my people—just like you, feeling about, just like every other nigger in this land, don't know what's theirs, don't know what ain't theirs, don't know if land is theirs or old slave shack is theirs. How they ever going to know that when there ain't man on the place can read or write sufficient?"

Gideon paused, swallowed, and then marked his words with a long forefinger. "You go up there—fetch along your little ones. Tell them Gideon, he send you. Talk to Brother Peter, he's our preaching man, tell him you'll teach them, give them learning. They'll take care of you good—"

Allenby shook his head. "I thought so once, Gideon. I'm too old.

I'm frightened—I'm content here. There's a Freedman's Bureau that takes care of such things—"

"You wait till doomsday, you wait for Freedman's folks," Gideon said. "What for you frightened? Go along up this road—ask anyone where you find Carwell place. Better some morning those little ones wake up, find you dead, no one to lay you out, no one to shave your beard, no one to shroud you and build a pine coffin? Who going to do it, that poor blind girl?"

Still the old man objected, and Gideon went at him, mercilessly, until at last, when the fire had almost died away, he nodded and said, yes, he would go. He sat in the faint gleam bent over, his head forward, as if he was trying to search the darkness for some assurance. And then he asked:

"Does it seem like a dream to you sometimes, Gideon, this business of freedom?"

"Ain't no dream," Gideon muttered. "I marched along with the Yankee men, made a piece of this with my own two hands. Ain't no dream."

On the next day, many things happened, causing Gideon to reflect, as he had before, that a few hours on the open road can be like a month in the bucolic pace of a country farm. He helped start a stubborn mule for a boy, and rode for two miles in his cart. He spent fifteen minutes talking to an old woman, who was bringing a basket of eggs to the village to sell, and as far as their ways coincided, he carried her basket. A white woman offered him lunch for splitting her cord-wood, and her husband came around from the milking shed and said he had never seen a nigger could make cord-wood fly like that. It was a fine lunch the white woman set out for him, and Gideon, thinking discretion the better part of valor, said never a word about the Convention. Later in the day, he passed by a plantation; there were the black men in the fields with a white overseer, digging a drainage ditch in the hard ground. "Working for wages?" Gideon called. They answered never a word and the overseer yelled, "Get on to hell, you black bastard!"

Late that afternoon, a rainstorm gathered, and Gideon crawled into a haystack while the pelting shower lasted. A cow had already taken shelter there, and Gideon lay against her warm side, humming to himself:

"Gather in the calves, all the little white calves,
    Gather in the calves, oh, mammy."

But that sort of treatment did his black frock coat no good.
Gideon picked the pieces of straw off him, but the stovepipe hat
was too far on its way to perdition to be saved. The crown fell off,
and Gideon debated with himself the question of whether or not
to wear it, topless as it was. He sensed that a stovepipe hat without
a crown was a redundancy, but he could not bear to just throw it
away. Saving it, he traded it later to an old colored man for two
juicy apples.

He slept that night under the stars, with a bed of pine boughs
between himself and the damp ground. It was not too comfortable,
but now his heart was high and the wonder of his mission had taken
hold of him.

The next day, Gideon walked through the low country of the
coast, and on the fourth day, he saw the roofs of Charleston in front
of him.

4. HOW GIDEON JACKSON LABORED WITH
BOTH HIS HANDS AND HIS HEAD

The feeling of panic that came over Gideon Jackson once he was
in Charleston could not be reasoned away. It was terror of the deep-
est and most threatening unknown, the white man. It was a memory
of childhood Gideon called onto the veranda of the big house:—
"Here, boy," flung at him perhaps thirty years ago. Men and
women sat on the veranda then, the men in boots and close-fitting
breeches and fine coats, and the women's dresses remembered only
as beauty. Whoever this woman was, she had mud on her shoe. A
man said, "Boy, come here!" Shivering with fright, he wiped the
mud off her shoe, and the man flung him a silver coin. He remembered scrambling for it as it rolled in the mud, clenching it in his
hand, and then facing them questioningly as they all roared with
laughter. He was a small black animal, and he knew it then, and
even as a six-year-old child the terror was complete, awful, aching
loneliness; hope that should be a part of every living thing was
denied him. The white man, thereafter, was in a sense a locked
gate, and though he had come very close to that gate since, he had
never actually opened it.

Now he had his hand on the gate. Not as it was the last time he came to Charleston, marching shoulder to shoulder with others, a gun on his shoulder; but alone now, and frightened.

Gideon walked through the city. He had no money and no food, and he had not the courage to present himself to the officer of the Convention. He was hungry and tired, and he realized now how shabby and ludicrous his clothes were. Even his checked handkerchief hanging from his breast pocket did not cheer him.

Why, he asked himself, had he ever left home? Why had he allowed Brother Peter to lure him into this trap? Of course, he couldn't present himself to the Convention. What then? Go home? Suppose he went home and they asked him about the Convention— what would he say then? What could he say? Lie? To his own people, to Brother Peter, to Rachel? Face Jeff, who would look at him very coolly and know? And how did he know but that there was some severe punishment for delegates elected to the Convention who did not attend? Suppose he just disappeared? But what kind of a fool notion was that? Leave Rachel, his children, his people—like being sold down the river in the old days? Had he lost his mind?

His feet took him on. He had wandered through the muddy lanes where the Negroes lived, shacks hastily constructed in the time since the war had ended, a few more imposing houses abandoned by the whites. He heard a woman's voice call, "Look at that big buck! Where you going, man?" He didn't know where he was going. He walked through the old part of the city, the fine white houses with their Grecian porticos, the palmettos, the wrought-iron gates and balconies. No kind looks here, no kind word flung at him, a city withdrawn into itself to suffer the terrible indignity of a Convention made by such men as Gideon Jackson—and that Gideon felt, like a quivering wall of frustrated hate.

Once, as evening approached, Gideon glanced up at a handsome building, and there, over the doorway he saw the word, CONVENTION, in great block letters—and painfully he put together the rest of the message, learning that here was the place where the Convention would sit. In front of the building were a guard of a dozen Yankees, leaning lazily on their rifles and chewing tobacco, and nearby were numerous little groups of Negroes and whites, talking and gesticulating and sometimes raising their voices to shout fine words. Gideon noticed with a wave of shame how well some

of the men were dressed, one with pearl-gray trousers, a checked
coat, and a beautiful green cravat, another in high black boots and
white trousers, and still another in plaid from head to foot; such
clothes as Gideon would never dream of owning; nor did it cheer
him to see that there were a good many dressed no better than himself and some worse, in the shapeless, honest clothes of the field,
with no cravats and no hats.

He walked on, down Meeting Street to the Battery, and then over
to East Battery. At this time, Charleston, which had suffered so
grievously during the war, was in the process of becoming an important port again. There were ships in the harbor, and in the docks
at East Bay Street, there was a line of masts like the broken edge of
an old comb. It was almost sunset now, and as Gideon walked along
the Battery the water shimmered and boiled with red and golden
color; old Fort Sumter, hazy out in the harbor, assumed a fairy-like
pink shell, and all along the Battery the gulls swooped and screamed.

But all of this served only to deepen Gideon's despondency; he
was hungry and cold, he had no money nor any place to sleep. On
East Bay Street, there was a yard with cotton bales piled high; three
of them made a sort of a cave, and into this Gideon crawled. He
could not even sing or hum a song to lift his spirits now. He lay
there, awake and miserable for hours and hours before he fell
asleep.

Early the next morning, Gideon fell in with a group of black
stevedores. He was walking past the dock where they sat and waited
for a ship to be warped in, and they picked on his frock coat:

"Now look a there, boy, you a preaching man?"

"He's a deacon, no mistake."

"Look at that coat, must have rolled in cotton!"

Their booming, half-mocking comments had no effect on Gideon;
silent and miserable, he stood there and watched them munch a
breakfast of cornbread, home-squeezed cheese and onions; and indeed his despair was so obvious and complete that presently they
stopped their taunts, and one of them said:

"Have a piece of bread, deacon?"

Gideon shook his head.

"Working?"

Again, Gideon shook his head.

"White boss taking all hands for fifty cents a day."

Gideon nodded; a man worked or he starved; for many things he might be unfit, but he had two strong hands and a back like a bull, fit for lugging a bale, if for nothing else. As things went, fifty cents a day was a good deal of money. Why not?

So all that day he was able to forget, the sweat running down his face, his muscles tensing, bulging, straining until some of the Negroes shouted with respect:

"He's a buck man from way down the river!" "He's a cotton-toting man!"

He had put aside his coat, but the government papers he would not part with. He put them in his pants pocket, and there was a certain comfort in feeling them, stiff and crackling.

For the moment, the future had ceased to exist, and Gideon felt a deep and needful sense of relief. They offered him food at noon, but out of his sense of pride, he refused it. When the day had finished, he was tired and hungry as a bear, but at the same time possessed of fifty cents. With Joe and Harko, two of the stevedores, he went to a place near Cumberland Street where an old colored woman cooked rice and prawns and Jerusalem artichokes, all in one savory mess. For ten cents, she piled a dish high with the stuff and threw in two corn sticks for good measure. Gideon ate his fill. It was a good thing to have money with which to buy food, a full belly, a warm feeling. Joe had a woman, sinful and willing, and he asked Gideon whether he would come; but Gideon shook his head, jolted back suddenly to reality, remembering Rachel, remembering how he and Brother Peter had talked together, wondering where this strange and hopeless road he had embarked on would take him.

Sometime during the course of this evening Gideon recognized the fact of his fear, and the simplicity and naturalness of his going to Major Allen James and presenting his credentials. Long afterwards, he would try to remember how the change came in him, whether it was one thing or another that had done it; whether it was his buying a newspaper for five cents and the pride with which he held it under his arm; whether it was the house where he found a bed, the residence of Mr. Jacob Carter; whether it was one or another of the things that had happened to him that evening.

Jacob Carter was a cobbler, a free Negro before and during the war, an industrious and respectable colored man who had saved pennies for years to buy his freedom. He had a little four-room house on the edge of Charleston, and he put a sign out, "Delegates to the Convention boarded." The man who sold Gideon the newspaper told him about that and how to find the place; he called Gideon "sir," perhaps only because he had bought a newspaper, but whatever the reason with good effects upon Gideon's sunken spirits.

It was dark when Gideon came to the Carter house. He knocked at the door. It opened a crack, letting out a yellow shaft of light, and a woman's face stared at him suspiciously.

"What you want?"

"Please, ma'am," Gideon said. "I'm looking for a place to sleep— seen the sign out. Ain't this the Carter place?"

"That's right. Who you?"

Then a man appeared behind her, opening the door a little wider, looking less suspiciously at Gideon.

"Name's Gideon Jackson, sir. Delegate."

"Delegate?"

"Uh-huh." Gideon was wretchedly conscious of his clothes. "Old clothes," he mumbled. "Ain't had time to buy city things. Come from up country."

Carter smiled and said, "Come in."

Perhaps it was Gideon's meeting with the Carters, the first city folk whose home he had ever entered that erased his fear. They gave him a small but clean room, a bed with a cotton mattress, the first he had ever slept on, and a real kerosene lamp. All this and two meals a day for two dollars a week. When he pointed out that his work at the Convention might not net him two dollars a week, they smiled at his naivete and assured him that the Government would not think of paying a delegate less than five dollars a week, and might even pay them ten.

The Carters had no children and were past middle age; through all the terror of the war years and the two post-war years when the ruthless black codes were in force, they had fought desperately, and in a sense courageously, to sustain the small dignity of their position as free Negroes and homeowners. Yet where other free Negroes had the greatest of contempt for the illiterate, up-country blacks who were delegates, the Carters, in their simplicity, treated people like Gideon much as they would treat their own friends.

That night, in his own room with the yellow light of the lamp to make things bright and clear, Gideon struggled through the newspaper. He had seen newspapers before, but this was the first time he had ever set himself to reading one. The type was small, which made it difficult, forcing him to read even more slowly than was his habit, putting a finger under each word until he had analyzed it and either understood it or guessed at its meaning. Out of most of what he read, he could gain no continuity of thought; there were too many words he did not understand, too many long, blank spaces. Yet he labored through an editorial on the Convention, a mocking thing that compared the Negroes to monkeys, calling the coming assembly a circus, a zoo, a gathering of apes. He found himself fascinated by a story of a ship that had been wrecked, and in a disconnected way he unravelled a statement of Negro outrages throughout the state, all the while wondering why he himself had not seen or heard of any such outrages.

Finally, too tired to keep his eyes open, he took off his clothes and crawled into the soft and comfortable bed. It had metal springs, and experimentally Gideon jounced up and down on them; it was like floating on air. He fell asleep thanking God for all his good fortune and creating a dream world where he and Rachel slept every night on such a bed.

And the next day, without thinking too long or too hard about it, without being too frightened, Gideon presented himself to Major James. Mrs. Carter had cleaned his coat, sewn up the tears, and pressed it. Jacob Carter had put a patch on Gideon's left shoe, where a toe was coming through, and had covered both boots with black grease. Gently as he could, Carter suggested that the checked handkerchief would be more at home in Gideon's pants pocket than hanging from his breast pocket, and after much persuasion talked Gideon into wearing one of his white Sunday shirts. Carter had two of these which he had treasured for years and worn only on the Sabbath, but both he and his wife were charmed with Gideon, and as old people will do, had taken him to their hearts as if he were a young boy.

They brought a basin of hot water into Gideon's room, and Carter sat and listened while Gideon scrubbed off a week's dirt and related patches of his life, to make Carter more at home with him. In return, Carter talked of Charleston, of the Negroes and whites, of the peculiar, ominous tension that had hung over the town since the Convention was announced.

"Seems like they is two nigger delegates for each white," Carter
said. "White ones for the most part what they call Scalawags along
here, Union men. Making up to a dark time. Seems like there ain't
been nothing but dark time a long while now. Maybe you noticed
how they's Yankee soldiers everywhere?"

"I noticed."

"Me, I don't take to Yankee soldiers, not one bit," Carter said.

"Why for?"

"Well, you tell me, Gideon, what business they got down here?
I say, let them go back to their own land."

"Wouldn't be no free men, excepting for the Yankee soldiers,"
Gideon said quietly. "Wouldn't be no Convention."

Carter didn't argue the point. Gideon didn't think that Carter
went very deeply into anything, but the little cobbler's generosity
was complete and unselfish. He was a good churchman, and two
thirds of his conversation concerned the church.

Gideon was presentable when he left their house, black coat,
white shirt, somewhat tight on him but serviceable nevertheless,
black tie. When people turned to glance at him, for his height, his
breadth of shoulder, and his clean, large features, he was certain
they were admiring the shirt and the black string tie.

Major James was a harried man. Not only was the Constitutional
Convention shaping up as a sprawling, unorganized affair; but
Charleston was becoming more and more suggestive of a barrel of
gunpowder with a lighted fuse.

Major James was attuned to signs and indications; with reason,
for in the course of the long and bitter war he had seen some half
dozen southern cities occupied by Yankee troops. He knew that a
city is a live organism with a heart and a temper, black and sullen
moods as well as light and gay ones. A city was dangerous or not
dangerous, according to the way it reacted; and like a man who is
all on the surface, hot and loud and frequent in anger, a city that
bubbled and boiled with fury would not have disconcerted Major
Allen James so much as this quiet and ominous Charleston. Too
many shutters were bolted; too many of the leading people of the
town had not left their homes in days—even weeks. And those who
came out of their homes for business or for some other reason,
walked the street quickly, looked straight ahead of them, and said
much too little.

All of which was not a good thing, in Major James' lights. Too much could go on behind those bolted shutters. How many guns were there in Charleston? How many loaded pistols? His superior, Colonel Fenton Grace, said unimaginatively, "Let it come, and when it comes we'll put it down, and then we'll know where we stand, and anyway you drink too much and think too much." Which was the answer a military man would give, one who did not, as Major James did, covet a peaceful convention and transition from the military to the civil, and perhaps a promotion and a six-month leave. Major James did not like the south; it was enemy territory. He trusted neither the whites nor the blacks, nor did he understand either group too well. He had no love for "niggers," whom he held at fault for the war; he had no love for Bourbon whites, whom he hated instinctively, out of his Ohio middle-class upbringing; and as for the plain, impoverished southern whites—well, they were the men who had killed his comrades—the god damned rebels.

But as the members of the Convention gathered, came to him and presented their credentials, his hope for a successful outcome waned. What a crew they were! What an ungodly, ignorant, filthy, vulgar crew they were! What sort of an idiotic, mad circus was this that the Yankee radicals, the Sumners and the Stevens and the rest, had imposed upon the south! Field hands that had walked a hundred, two hundred miles, too stupid to know that railroads ran and that as delegates they were entitled to ride the railroads; demobilized Negro soldiers who considered themselves on his level because once they had worn the Union blue and held a gun in their hand; men who couldn't read or write; long-limbed, illiterate white mountaineers who had supported the Union because they hated the slaveholders; black schoolteachers who because they could read and add sums considered themselves scholars;—indeed, was it any wonder that Charleston boiled with suppressed rage?

Major James began to see that there was some justice in the rebel contention that a Negro was a savage with the mind of a child, and his feeling was borne out when a huge Negro in a black frock coat, a white shirt so small that it had begun to split at the seams, and ancient patched pants, presented himself as the delegate from the Carwell-Sinkerton district. The Negro's name was Gideon Jackson; he had walked into Charleston. He could write his name and not much more. Could he read? A little, a proud possessor of perhaps a hundred words of literacy. Did he understand his duties as a delegate? Duties? Well, putting it a little different, did he realize the significance of the Convention?

Significance? No—of course, he didn't even realize the meaning of the word. One had to walk down a step-ladder to a single syllable language—that this was the reconstruction of a state, to begin with the drafting of a new Constitution; one couldn't; it was impossible. Desperately, James went to Colonel Grace and demanded:

"Sir, do we have to seat that kind?"

"If he was legally elected."

"He has his papers. They all are, if we call this a legal election."

Colonel Grace said frigidly, "I don't question the election. Please remember, sir, that these Negroes were loyal to us in our hour of gravest need." There was no love lost between the two men; Grace had gone into the service willingly and proudly; he came of abolitionist people.

"I warn you, sir, this city will not see a convention of field hands rule over them."

"I tell you, sir," Colonel Grace said quietly, "that this city will damn well do as our Government orders."

"They're proud people."

"The kind of pride that puts a half a million men in their graves," the colonel said.

So Major James went back and countersigned Gideon's right to sit in the Constitutional Convention of the state of South Carolina.

As Gideon was leaving the Military Adjustment Offices, he was stopped by a well-dressed, light-complexioned colored man who introduced himself as Francis L. Cardozo. He said:

"You're a member of the Convention?"

"Uh huh."

"Mind if I walk along with you?"

"Don't know as I mind that," Gideon said uncertainly, troubled somewhat by the ease with which this well-dressed, well-mannered stranger had insinuated himself. They started off down the street, Gideon glancing sidewise at the other again and again, until finally Cardozo, with a slight nod of his head, asked, "And what is your name, sir, if I may inquire?"

"Gideon Jackson."

Cardozo said that he was also a member of the Convention, from the district of Charleston, and would Gideon care to meet with some of the other members? They would be at Cardozo's home that afternoon at about three o'clock, to talk about matters pertaining to the Convention. Had Gideon met any of the delegates?

"Guess I ain't," Gideon said.

"Well, of course you will, once the Convention convenes. This, however, may make some things clear. These are good people, I assure you, Mr. Jackson."

"I'd mighty well like to come," Gideon said.

"Do come then, and I'll write down the address for you."

He wrote it down on a card, which he gave to Gideon. They shook hands, and then Gideon walked away with the salutation ringing in his ears, Mr. Jackson, the nice rounded sound of it and the increasing wonder of it. Like Church singing to glory were all the things that happened to him; and here only a little while ago he was afraid to present his papers. Tomorrow a day, the Convention would begin. The hammering, unnatural pace of Gideon's heart was almost a constant factor now; he walked briskly through the streets, telling himself, "There's a sunshine brightness in the world. Jesus Christ walks. I was born a slave and a slave until maybe yesterday. My little ones, they was born slaves. Look at now—just look at now!"

A white man, walking down the street, facing Gideon and on a line with him, came toward him with the compact assurance that Gideon would give way. Gideon was inside himself, and the world didn't exist. They would have met head on, but at the last moment, the man swerved aside, lashing at Gideon with the cane he carried, catching him full across the back; and Gideon, plucked back to reality by the blow, stood there, surprised, tense, shamed, the welt on his back burning, rage growing inside him; rage and shame and the desire to spring after the white man, but a sense of something that held him back and talked to him until the white man had turned a corner and was out of sight.

Gideon walked on, and the world returned to a place that still needed patching here and there, not perfect yet, Gideon asking himself, "Why for did he had to do that?"

In Gideon's pocket was still twenty-five cents. Money went a long way; money was not like rice or potatoes, crops of the ground that went into a rigid calculation, so much eaten each day and finally the supply exhausted; there was a flexibility to money—one could use it for this or that, or one could not use it at all. The brisk, cool

weather had given him an appetite, and he stopped at a stand in
the covered market where they were selling rice and onions, five
cents for a steaming plate. Then he bought another newspaper,
went down to the docks and sat on a bale of cotton, spread the
paper, the sting in his back almost gone now, the wonder of print
reoccurring and in a certain sense erotic, making his skin tighten
and prickle with excitement as he read.

"Georgia reports give promise of a more *stabilizing*—" a word his
mind underlined for the future, a mystery he moved his lips over,
"Stab—stalabl—no, stay-billy—" And as his eyes shifted, "Cotton
futures on the New York market—" What was a *future*? The word
"market" he could comprehend, a place where they sold things, a
homely word; but what sort of a market was this in New York
where cotton became cotton futures? His eyes ached and he became
drowsy; he dozed a little there in the warming afternoon, coming
awake every so often and looking at the newspaper again. Stray
words caught his eyes. "Black savages from the Congo—" The stevedores were shouting and singing as they toted their great loads. Was
the Congo in Carolina or Georgia? Savages was a familiar word;
make a nigger out to be a red, wild Indian. Out in the bay a full-
rigged ship tacked back and forth, and all the gulls raced after it.
Gideon looked up at the sun and estimated that it was close to three
o'clock.

He came to Cardozo's house with his paper folded neatly under
his arm, and bowed correctly as he was introduced to Mr. Nash,
Mr. Wright, and Mr. Delany, middle-aged Negroes of Charleston,
each of them raising a brow at Gideon's clothes, at his soft, slurred
back-country slave speech. Gideon was impressed; these were educated men, well-dressed in dark clothes. He was beginning to understand that certain circles preferred dark clothes to the bright, gay
colors some of the delegates wore. Mr. Nash said:

"I presume, Mr. Jackson, you come with some instruction from
your constituents?"

"We recognize the need of a formulated program," Mr. Delany
added.

"I don't know," Gideon muttered.

There was a more gentle understanding in Cardozo. "This is
high-falutin' talk, Mr. Jackson," he smiled. "Becoming a legislator,
a man leaves half his brain in his pants pocket and tries to operate
with an unused half he never knew he possessed."

Gideon nodded, making up his mind to keep his mouth shut and listen. Mr. Wright expressed complete hopelessness about the future. He said to Cardozo:

"But when you come down to it, Francis, there are at least thirty delegates who can neither read nor write!"

Gideon was glad he had the folded newspaper under his arm. What did they think of him, and why had they asked him here?

"So much the better," Cardozo nodded.

"But make sense, please!"

"I'm inclined to agree with Francis," Nash said. "The literate people of this world have worked no wonders."

"That, of course, is sophistry. We're faced with the problem of field-hands participating in the making of a Constitution. Not to mention the anger this is raising among the white population, we're faced with the very real question of the field-hands themselves. What will they do?"

"They can be managed."

Cardozo said lightly, "Do you feel that you can be managed, Mr. Jackson?"

"Sir?" Gideon had the feeling that he was being the butt of something; the bewilderment was changing into anger.

"But don't be angry, Mr. Jackson," Cardozo said. "You were a slave."

"I was."

"A field-hand?"

"That's right."

"How do you see this business of a Constitution? I mean that seriously. What will you want in a Constitution you have a part in making?"

Gideon looked at them, the heavy-set Nash, the slim, almost courtly Cardozo, Wright, round and suave, like a well-fed house servant. And the room they sat in, a room that to Gideon seemed elegant almost beyond belief, upholstered chairs, a stuffed squirrel, even a rug on the floor, and three crayon pictures on the walls. How does a black man come by all this? Where did he fit into it? And the other delegates who had plodded across the state in their shapeless cotton-field boots?

"Don't be offended, Mr. Jackson," Cardozo persisted.

Gideon nodded. "I ain't high. I guess you want an answer. Talk about a man can't read, can't write, just an old nigger come walking out of the cotton fields, that's me. What I want from Constitution? Maybe it ain't what you folks want—want learning, want it for all, black and white. Want a freedom that's sure as an iron fencepost. Want no man should push me off the street. Want a little farm where a nigger can put in a crop and take out a crop all his days. That's what I want."

Then there was a silence, and Gideon felt embarrassed, provocative and high and mighty without reason, a man who said a lot, none of it making sense. A little later, the others made their good-byes, but when Gideon rose to go, Cardozo plucked at his sleeve and begged him to wait a moment. And when the others had left, said to Gideon:

"Have some tea, please, and we can talk. It wasn't so clever of me bringing you into this, was it?"

"That's all right," Gideon nodded, wanting to go, but too unsure of himself to know how to go about his leave-taking. Cardozo's wife came in then, a small, pretty brown woman. Gideon loomed over her like a giant.

"Are they all as big as that in the hills?" she asked, in the way of making conversation, and Gideon, quick to take offense at anything now, answered, "I ain't from the hills, ma'am, but from the middle country."

Cardozo said, "Won't you stay? There's a lot for us to talk about." Gideon nodded.

"Then look at it this way," Cardozo said. "Here were a few of us who have been free Negroes, maybe not as close to our people as we should have been. Just a few of us, against the four million slaves. But the books were opened to us, and we learned a little; but believe me, in a way we were more slaves than you. Now there comes a situation so strange, so open in its implications, that the world cannot fully realize it. The Union government, backed with a military machine it built during the war, says to the people of the south, white and black, build a new life. From the beginning. A new Constitution, new laws, a new society. The white planters rebel against this, but they are the defeated. Yet they stay away from the voting, and as a result here in this state black men, slaves only yesterday, choose their own people and send them to the Convention. Do you know, Gideon, that we, the blacks, are in the majority, that seventy-six out of one hundred and twenty-four elected delegates are Negroes? That over fifty of these are former slaves? This is the year eighteen sixty-eight; how long have we been out of bondage? The Children of Israel wandered in the wilderness for forty years."

After a moment, Gideon murmured, "I don't quote Scripture when I'm afraid. I'm a God-fearing man, but when the fright was strongest inside of me, I took a gun in my hands and fought for my freedom."

"And what will these field-hands do in the courts of law?"

"What they do? They ain't no black savages, like newspaper say. They got a wife and child and love in their heart. They say what is good for me, for woman, for the child, and they vote that in. They got a hunger for learning, and they vote for that. They know about slavery, and they vote for freedom. They ain't going to be uppity; you lead them by the hand, and by God, they come. But you don't take no lash to their back no more. They know how it taste to be free man."

Thoughtfully, Cardozo said, "That'll take courage from me, Gideon."

"Took courage from me to come to this Convention."

"I suppose so. Tell me something about yourself, Gideon."

The telling came slow and stumblingly from Gideon; it was nightfall when he had finished. He felt dry and used up. But before he left, Cardozo gave him two books, one *Geldon's Basic Speller* and the other *Usage of the English Language* by Fitzroy and James. They were the first real books Gideon ever had; he held them gently in his big hands, as if they were made of eggshell. Plucking a name from his memory, he asked:

"You got the Shakespeare book?"

For a moment, Cardozo hesitated; then, without smiling, he went to his little shelf of books, took *Othello*, and handed it to Gideon.

"Thank you," Gideon said.

And Cardozo nodded, and after Gideon had left, said to his wife, "If I had laughed—if I had! God help me, I almost laughed! What animals we are!"

Gideon asked Carter to tell him something about Cardozo. In a way, a purely social way, that Gideon could not as yet comprehend, Carter was impressed by the fact that Gideon had been to Cardozo's home.

"He's part Jew," Carter said. "That's how he come by the name. He's a proud nigger."

Gideon, who had never seen a Jew before, said, "Looks the same like any black man."

"But uppity," Carter said.

Carter said that Gideon could use the lamp, and then, at the end of the month, by which time surely the delegates would have drawn some wages, pay him for the oil burned. Gideon lay half the night with the speller, writing out the words on the margins of the newspaper, saying the words aloud and trying to hear whether or not they sounded strange. His incessant mumbling brought Carter to the door.

"Ailing?" Carter asked.

"Learning," Gideon apologized.

The speller was a marvelous book, but it fell down on the meaning of words—and Gideon wondered if there was any book that could tell a man what a word meant. He thumbed through the book on usage; a paragraph which caught his eye said:

"While contractions as a whole are to be frowned upon, 'ain't' is certainly the most vulgar. It is an indication of class, as well as a sign of whether or not a person desires to be taken for a gentleman. A gentleman will avoid contractions when possible, and will never, under any circumstances, use 'ain't.' The ambiguity of this contraction twice condemns it, for a person of culture will not use a word which might mean 'is not' or 'am not' or 'are not.' A person of culture will be as precise in his speech as in his thought and his personal habits."

Gideon determined to avoid "ain't" like a plague; the more he read out of usage, the more his fears grew, the more awesome and terrible the matter of learning became. He turned to *Othello* with some small shred of hope, and that was blasted as he read:

IAGO: I am about it; but indeed my invention
comes from my pate as birdlime does from frize . . .

And he fell asleep finally, his head aching, his despair as complete as ever it had been.

Cardozo lay awake longer than Gideon. Like a gap in his life, like a gap in human history, in the whole aching, crawling stream

of human life was that space left on his shelf after he had removed
the three books. How did he come to Gideon Jackson? Who was
this huge, slow-moving, slow-spoken black man who had come out
of the Carolina back country, out of slavery, out of darkness, and
why did he make Cardozo feel so small? What was the measure of
a man? He, Cardozo, had been born free; in his memories there was
an education at the University of Glasgow; there were garden parties
outside of London. There was a great meeting where he had
addressed three thousand Englishmen, and had been accorded honor
and respect. He had crossed oceans and been in homes of the great.

He had been a minister in New Haven, and Abolitionists had met
in his house and spun their plots. There was in his veins white
blood and black, Negro and Indian, Jew and Gentile spun together.
Even the white men of Charleston accorded him respect. He, Cardozo, was closer to a Pringle than Gideon Jackson was to him.

Yet he recognized in Gideon Jackson the salvation, if there was
to be any in this dark confusion; the huge, illiterate black man was
looking at sunshine which Cardozo did not see. Cardozo, who could
not sleep because his fears were so many, his ambitions so hopeless,
lay awake and envied a freed slave.

In the way of things, coming finally however long that coming
seems, the Convention came, and Gideon Jackson sat among the
delegates. It seemed to him that for this moment, time stood still.
Thirty-six years he had lived, born a squalling black brat and killing
his mother in the birth, cattle from the day he walked, to be
pinched and tested and priced—and now he sat among men who
were making a world. Still. Quiet. Motionless. The world stood on
end. Gideon with his hands clasped in his lap, his knees pressed together, hearing each separate thump of his heart, hardly daring to
breathe; well, it was not so easy to breathe, the way the hall was
packed, opposing rows of chairs on staged steps, bank after bank of
black and white faces, men in country clothes, in city clothes, in
fancy clothes and drab clothes, men in stiff black frock coats and
men in old army jackets, old men and young men, men born slave
and men born free, scalawags and carpet-baggers and tall, blond
sunburned Unionists from the mountains, men who had marched
with the Rebels sitting knee to knee with those who had marched
with the Yankees; no, it was not at all easy to breathe.

And as if that was not enough, the Charleston people had finally come forth from their homes and pressed in to see the circus, to see the "ring-tailed monkeys," and the "black baboons." The press was there too, not only local reporters, but scornful writers from Georgia and Louisiana and Alabama and other southern states, prepared to put the blight once and for all on this insanity, New York reporters, sophisticated, and trying to sort out of the mess just those bits of unique local color the big city readers would properly appreciate; there were reporters from Boston, old Abolitionist editorial writers from New England, and of course the Washington people with a special ear for all that might set the Capital buzzing. Add to that the Yankee soldiers who ringed the hall and you had every single human soul the place would hold.

But for all the apprehension, the anticipation and excitement, the first day of the session went off quietly and in an orderly fashion. A roll was called; Gideon sat sick and terrified until his name came, but after he had spoken "Here!" and the chairman passed on to the next name, it seemed like nothing at all that his voice should be heard by all these people.

After the roll-call, ex-Governor Orr of South Carolina rose to address the Convention. He was there by special invitation, a gesture by the delegates that they were going to work within the body of the public, not outside it. The hall became very still, and Gideon leaned forward that he might not miss a word that was said. He was pleased at first; Orr spoke of the dire need for education on the part of the former slaves. But then, in no uncertain terms, he declared that they did not represent the intelligence of the state, not the wealth, not even the potential. It was a dream that they should talk, as they were talking, of complete suffrage.

Much of this Gideon did not understand. He raged at himself that half-spoken, half-suggested ideas should pass him by, that the meaning of every third or fourth word should escape him. Was Orr laughing at them? Despising them? Attacking them?

There was not a great deal of applause when Orr finished. But there was order. An agenda for the following day was then arranged, after which the Convention was declared adjourned until the next morning.

Gideon listened to a group of delegates who had gathered on the street and were talking hotly. They were country people, heavy-set, muscular field-hands with the shoulders that told of years behind the plough. One of them, an elderly man, black as tar, long-faced and keen-eyed, was saying:

"Education, that we ain't got—who got it in this here state? Whole counties without schools. Boss man, he don't mind that, bring a teacher into his house, send his little ones to Europe. But that ain't what Orr calls intelligence; that learning. How long we been at this—two years freedom, one day Convention. I say, why that man wants to tear us down?"

A tall white man, raw-boned, his speech the slow and stumbling talk of the mountains, elbowed into the crowd and said, "Plenty of reason, uncle."

"How come?"

"Uncle, why don't you niggers open your eyes? This equality thing ain't going to hold water unless you put your shoulders under it. Sure they'll talk you down; they'll talk me down. You're a nigger; I'm white trash. White trash elected me and niggers elected you, and maybe there was a few of your kind in my vote and a few of my kind in yours. I'm no nigger lover, but I like the kind of thinking that makes two and two add up to four. That kind of thinking tells me what we can do if we keep our senses; but it don't tell me they're going to stop calling us animals."

"What you going to do about it, white man?" someone asked.

"Keep my head. Come out of this convention with schools and the right to vote. I know what my enemies are going to say."

"You let them say it?"

"That's right. Then I speak my piece."

"How about land? What good are schools and voting, if you ain't got the means to take out a crop?"

"Land," the white man said, chewing at the word. "Brother, ask them for land and they're going to lick you right down the line. No land's going to come out of this Convention; if we want land, we're going to work and sweat and buy it."

"Ain't we worked that land for maybe a hundred years? Ain't we put in the crop and take it out? Then they go try to smash up the country. Who got a better right to the land?"

"It ain't a question of right, uncle, it's a question of property. I don't shoot for the stars, I aim for the brow of the next hill—"

The argument went on, getting hotter and hotter. When Gideon saw the white man detach himself, he walked along with him and plucked at the other's sleeve.

"Mister?"

The white man paused, looked at Gideon out of a pair of very cool blue eyes, and made as to walk on. Gideon sensed something of the struggle inside the other, a southerner born and bred in the south, hating a slave system that made him a landless scavenger, but hating Negroes too because of the economics that forced him into their class, his white skin the only badge of respect left.

"Please, sir, I'd like to talk to you," Gideon said. "My name's Gideon Jackson."

"Mine's Anderson Clay," the white man nodded grudgingly, walking on then, Gideon alongside of him.

"I don't mean to presume," Gideon said. "It ain't—it not I want to poke uppity, but I hear what you say about the land. That mighty important to me, that my people have land. You figure they won't give us none?"

"They damnwell won't."

"How we going to live?"

"Nigger, that's one for you to figure out."

Walking along in silence for a while, Gideon said finally, "Maybe we can talk this around again?"

"Maybe."

"I'm proud to know you," Gideon said.

Writing to his wife a few days later, writing the first letter he had ever created, feeling the wonder of each word he put down, Gideon said:

"Dear wife Rachel,
I think for you all the time. I make a picture of you to myself. You are pretty I think all the time. Like when I was with Yankee men in war I feel sad for being away from you. I learn me writing and reading from books and I am delegate in convention to make good law. My pay is very much 3 dollar every day I save most. Before I sleep I see you and children every night and god be good to you I pray. I write so good only with book but learn. I talk at convention once about pay I was so afraid. That is called debate. Be good to Jams Alenb if he come to you god bless you I write again soon.

That was the letter Gideon wrote, hours of labor far into the night, each word checked and copied carefully into the copy book he had bought. It gave him a warm sense of nearness to Rachel, to the people he had left at the plantation. How would they feel when they learned that he had already taken part in a debate on the Convention floor? Not that it was an important matter, nor had he meant to speak; but somehow—exactly how he couldn't recall—he was on his feet and talking. It was the session wherein they took up the question of pay for delegates:

Leading the discussion, a Mr. Langly said that twelve dollars a day would be a round figure. "Certainly, the delegates to this Convention are deserving of that!" The reporters present scribbled furiously. Wright, a Negro, took the floor and said that ten dollars ought to be sufficient. "It will satisfy the basic dignity requisite to a legislator." The gallery hooted and the speaker pounded for order. Parker, a white man, upped the pay to eleven dollars, a fantastic sum to ninety percent of the Convention, men who by and large had always worked with their hands, slaves some of them, tenant farmers some of them, men who had not seen the sparkle of silver in years. Three scalawag delegates joined with two carpet-baggers in earnest seconding when Mr. Leslie, a black delegate, gained the floor and cried:

"I am willing to receive three dollars a day for my services. I want to go on the record for that, as a black man. I think that is all my services are worth. I ask you delegates, if you were called on to pay a similar body of men out of your pockets, how much would you be willing to pay? Wouldn't a dollar fifty be enough? What is this business of eight or nine or ten dollars a day? It looks like fraud!"

A Mr. Melrose spoke through the scattered applause. "—the damned insult of suggesting one dollar and fifty cents a day to the members of this Convention!"

That was when Gideon gained the floor and was recognized, forgetting himself in this incredible contradiction, his deep, rich voice filling the hall.

"I hear all this talk, ten dollars a day, eleven! I read the newspaper calling us robbers, then I'm mad, angry. We ain't robbers—but how come this—" At that point, the enormity of what he had done occurred to him; he felt himself grow hot and cold, and the next words came falteringly, "I come to Charleston—just a few years ago in Yankee army—what pay I got there?—twenty cents a day, maybe, but I fight for freedom. I was a slave, no pay, never. I come along to Charleston before Convention, got to eat, got to work. Then I go down on water and tote a bale for fifty cents a day, and

good pay. How come I worth ten dollars now?" Somehow, his terror
had passed; more assured, he said, "Maybe like other man say, it's
dignity. Then three dollar are sure enough for dignity. Makes a
difference between delegate and dockhand, even if that difference is
not real. But I is not worth ten dollars every day."

That was how Gideon spoke for the first time in the Convention
hall, carrying a motion.

5. HOW GIDEON JACKSON WAS A GUEST OF HONOR AT A GREAT AFFAIR

As the days during which the Convention was in session became
weeks, and the weeks months, Gideon lost the feeling of fear and
strangeness he had brought with him to the first sitting. As with
other incidents in his life, what had been unnatural became natural,
and what had been strange became commonplace. The qualitative
change within himself was not completely conscious; there was no
point where he paused, observed himself, and saw that he was not
the same man he had been a little while ago. The doing of a thing
made him practiced in it. Brother Peter had once told him to listen
when men spoke, since speech was one of the many things by which
men were judged—and for thirty and fifty and ninety days he sat
in the Convention Hall and listened. And sometimes he spoke—
and it did not seem too curious to him that each time he spoke men
listened a little more intently.

Things bore fruit. The three books in his little room at the
Carters increased to a dozen and then two dozen. Each night, as
soon as he had finished dinner, he went in there, closed the door,
and spread his books on the little table under the lamp. He rarely
worked less than three hours, sometimes five, sometimes all night
through—as was the case when he first opened *Uncle Tom's Cabin*.
It was his first novel, and when one of the members of the Convention, a colored man called DeLarge, offered it to him, Gideon
objected that he had no time for story books.

"This," DeLarge said, "is one of the factors that made it possible
for you to be here, at the Convention."

"A book?"

"When old Abe Lincoln met Mrs. Stowe, who wrote this book,
he said to her, 'Is this the little lady who plunged a great nation
into war?'"

Smiling, Gideon said, "I reckon maybe one or two other things contributed."

"But take the book and read it."

Gideon took the book home, but it was weeks before he came around to reading it; then a world opened up, and the Carters pleaded with him that unless he slept he would surely break down. There were parts of the book he copied—keys to matters that had puzzled and disturbed him and which were now apparently plain, such as the following passage:

"Now, an aristocrat, you know, the world over, has no human sympathies, beyond a certain line in society. In England the line is in one place, in Burmah in another, and in America in another; but the aristocrat of these countries never goes over it. What would be hardship and distress and injustice in his own class, is a cool matter of course in another one. My father's dividing line was that of color. *Among his equals*, never was a man more just and generous; but he considered the Negro, through all possible gradations of color, as an intermediate link between man and animals, and graded all his ideas of justice and generosity on this hypothesis . . ."

And this piece.

"Alfred, who is as determined a despot as ever walked, does not pretend to this kind of defense; no, he stands, high and haughty, on that good old respectable ground, *the right of the strongest;* and he says, and I think quite sensibly, that the American planter is 'only doing in another form what the English aristocracy and capitalists are doing by the lower classes'; that is I take it, *appropriating* them, body and bone, soul and spirit, to their use and convenience. He defends both—and I think at least, *consistently.* He says there can be no high civilization without enslavement of the masses, either nominal or real. There must, he says, be a lower class, given up to physical toil and confined to an animal nature; and a higher one thereby acquires leisure and wealth for a more expanded intelligence and improvement, and becomes the directing soul of the lower. So he reasons, because as I said, he is born an aristocrat; so I don't believe, because I was born a democrat."

That, Gideon copied and studied, and when he saw DeLarge again, said, "I've been reading the book."

"And learning?"

"I always learn a little," Gideon smiled. "Tell me, was the book printed in England too?"

"Yes, and translated into German, Russian, Hungarian, French, Spanish and a dozen more tongues. In Europe, working men call it their Bible."

"A book about a black slave?"

"Or just slaves, Gideon."

The work told; for the first time in his life, Gideon's eyes ached. He had lost weight, become leaner, and more tired than he had ever been with his two hands on a plough or marching thirty miles a day in the army. Heretofore, all his life, it had seemed to him that there would be time for everything, days coming and going as the sun rose and set, the slow, bucolic rhythm of the cotton fields, things that had always been, the piney wastes, the dark swamps, the slow and mournful melody of the work songs; but here was a world of flux that would not wait; each day counted, each hour. A dictionary he bought had fifty thousand words in it, and words were the tools he worked with now. Knowledge was never-ending, and always he had the despairing realization that he was only scratching the surface. A whole week given to learning addition and subtraction, basic multiplication; a whole night spent wakefully on a single-page speech he would deliver the next day on the subject of education. The presumption of it—the presumption of Gideon Jackson rising in the hall and stating:

"I have heard, these past days, my fellow delegates argue about education which is enforced, like a law. I have heard gentlemen say that it was beyond reason or the right thing to hope to enforce education. I disagree. Maybe people would go naked if it wasn't law that they must wear clothes. They must wear clothes because it is law, and they become soon used to it. I think that in five or ten years soon people would become used to the fact that they must go to school if they want to or not. Why it was that slave owners would sell a slave so soon they found he could read or write? I tell you only because ignorant people can be slaves. Democracy and Equality cannot understand themselves to men and women who have no knowledge to learn about these things. No people can be free without learning about it."

A whole night to write that little bit; and afterwards a feeling of how completely inadequate it had been, badly phrased, not saying the things he had hoped to say and wanted to say. Yet for all of that, Cardozo came to him and wanted to know:

"Where have you been hiding, Gideon?"

"Hiding?"

"I mean you disappear after each session."

"I study," Gideon said.

"Every night?"

"Every night."

"No rest, no play," Cardozo said thoughtfully. "You meet no one, do you? That isn't the best thing either."

"I come to the sessions."

"Yes—but I want you to meet some people, white as well as black. It's important that you should know white people, know what they are thinking, saying, doing. We are going to have to work closer and closer with the white folks, Gideon."

"I guess so," Gideon nodded.

"Will you come and dine with us tomorrow?"

"Dine?" Gideon hesitated, but Cardozo pressed him, "Please come, do come."

"All right."

"But that wasn't what I wanted to speak about. I was impressed with what you said about compulsory education. It's something I'm extremely interested in, and I think if we fail in that point, we fail in the whole of the Constitution. It goes to committee next week. Will you serve on the committee?"

Gideon stared at Cardozo, but there was no trace of humor in the man's eyes. Gideon agreed.

"I'm glad," Cardozo said.

Some time before this, Gideon had decided that he must have a suit of clothes. For all of Mrs. Carter's patching, the trousers he wore were in a process of deterioration that would soon end in ruin. Hardly a day went by when the frock coat, which had been too small for him all along, did not split at one seam or the other. For two dollars, Jacob Carter had made Gideon a fine pair of shoes, but the suit situation was definitely at a crisis. Mrs. Carter said that it was a shame for him, a delegate, to come to the Convention day after day in those old rags.

"Clothes," Gideon said, "cost money. I got better ways to spend it."

"Clothes go along with the man who's inside them," Mrs. Carter said. So Gideon took the bit in his teeth and went to old Uncle

Baddy, who had a shack behind the Henry place on Rutledge Avenue. The Henry place was a huge, white Georgian town house and Uncle Baddy had been one of the Henry slaves during and before the war—for as long as anyone could remember. He was seventy-five, possibly eighty years old; the Henrys had trained him as a tailor, and for two generations he had sat on the table in his shack, legs crossed, stitching away at ballroom dresses, brocade gowns, and gentlemen's suits of fine brown and gray and black worsted and broadcloth. When emancipation came, he just stayed in the same place; the Henrys let him have the shack for the family sewing he did, and of late he had been doing a little cutting and sewing for hire.

Carter sent Gideon there. The old man looked Gideon up and down, blinked his eyes, and said, "Ain't no end to you, sure enough. How I'm going to find cloth enough to cover a nigger your size?"

"Don't have to be much of a suit," Gideon said. "Just so long as I can wear it."

"What you mean, ain't much of a suit? Made suits for the Henrys these forty, fifty year. Don't go telling me how to make a suit."

Gideon apologized, and two weeks later the suit was finished, the price ten dollars for a fine set of beautifully-tailored black broadcloth clothes. Gideon wrote to Rachel:

"Dear wife Rachel,
I had to buy a suit of clothes, for my old ones were done and gone. It cost ten dollars, mostly for the cloth, and so much money I know it is a shame but everything is a lot of money here in Charleston. I am happy to hear that things are quiet and good with you and Mister James Allenby is learning the children and happy. It was sad for me to hear from Mister Allenby's letter about the murder of four Negro people in Sinkerton by lawless men who hate us and use terror but such badness will stop when the Constitution is framed and a Civil Government makes our pretty Carolina a good land. I meet good men and I think it will all be good but be patient. Kiss the children for me God bless you and them."

He put a dollar bill in the letter; he did that each day, and each day he managed to write something to Rachel. And Gideon wore the new suit to dinner at the Cardozos.

Dinner at the Cardozos then, in 1868, was in the manner of a pause in history, even as the whole incident of the Convention was in the way of being a pause, a gap, a hole scooped in the developing stream of America by Union bayonets. Charleston, the beautiful, fairylike, palmetto-fringed city, the crown and glory of the south, lay exhausted. The war had torn the guts out of the town. There was hardly one of the great white Georgian houses that had not felt its portion of death and economic ruin. The mighty fortunes that built this cluster of white and wonderful houses, unequaled anywhere in America, were founded upon one thing, the broad back of the black slave. Not only was labor, the source of all wealth, tied up in the slaves, but the slaves themselves had been capital, the most important capital the south owned, in a sense primitive machine tools, bought and bred and sold, and in their fluid state the bottom rock of southern economy. Then, in the course of a ruinous war, a war that wrecked the monetary system of the south, blockaded its ports, Charleston among them, and sent armies marching and counter-marching across its lands for four years, the slaves were liberated: liberated by an edict signed by the great, tired man in the White House, a liberation enforced by the strength and guns of the Union Army.

In the immediate post-war period, the south lay stunned and sick. Two hundred thousand black slaves had taken up the arms and uniform of the north and fought in the last fierce struggle for their freedom. The southern armies had dissolved; the southern leaders sat back in exhaustion, staring wonderingly at the dissolution—a house of sugar which upon being thoroughly saturated suddenly collapses. And the plantation kings, the men behind the war, the men who had engineered it, made it, and plunged their hands elbow-deep in blood that their great empires of cotton, rice and sugar and tobacco might endure, saw the impossible happen, the slaves emancipated, millions and millions and millions of dollars of capital they once owned taken from them and overnight dissolved into thin air.

Perhaps never before in human history had a whole class, a ruling class of a nation been so stunningly and quickly deprived of its property. The first reaction of the planters was silence, a sick and bewildered silence during which time they contemplated the ruin that had been accomplished. They could not rebel, because they possessed no means of rebellion; they could not plan because they had never envisioned a future without slaves. Some of them had counterbalanced their wealth of slaves with large loans, and when the collateral of slavery disappeared, their empires went with it.

Great plantations stood empty and abandoned, or worked in a desultory way by the Negroes who stayed upon the soil because they had no place in particular to go; other plantations were put up to auction, sold for debt or taxes. Fields lay fallow; cotton planting dwindled and in many sections disappeared.

When the first paralyzing shock passed, the planters bestirred themselves. This farce of Emancipation, they thought, would not be played through; the slaves could be kept slaves; a nigger was a nigger; that was the beginning, it would also be the end; what went on in Washington was one thing, practical needs of the south were another. With almost hysterical haste, they set about inaugurating a set of laws called "Black Codes." Laws that returned the Negro legally to precisely the position he was in before the war; it was simple at first. There was a president in the White House who played along with them, who generously supported the terror they were establishing. They smiled to each other, "Tennessee Johnson is useful," despising the man and using him at one and the same time. Once more, the planters saw a future, the same future they had always seen, propped on the backs of four million black slaves.

And then their house of cards fell down. A bitter, wrathful, revolutionary Congress that had fought one of the most terrible wars known to mankind, decided that the blood spilt should not be in vain. In their anger, they almost impeached the president; they sent troops into the south and smashed the incipient terror. They legally nullified the rebellious states, established military districts, and called upon the whole population to vote for delegates to state Conventions, Conventions which would frame new state constitutions and create a new democracy in the south, one in which the black man and the white man stood side by side, building together.

In South Carolina, the black population outnumbered the white. Under this second stunning blow, the planters could see only one course of action, one device—to show their contempt by remaining away from the polls. Let the illiterate niggers and white trash vote, and the result would destroy this incredible and monstrous plan of Congress. The result, much as they had planned, gave the Negroes an overwhelming majority of delegates to the Convention; yet where the result went askew was that instead of making a circus, the black and white Convention was slowly, painfully but certainly nevertheless, beginning to operate as a sound legislative body. A constitution was emerging.

And in Charleston, while that happened, the white aristocrats locked their doors, barred their shutters, and waited. Yankee bayonets in the street made them impotent for the time. There was no future and no past in this moment. In the deep strange hole that had been violently scooped in the stream of history, something was happening. In that hole a dinner was given at Francis Cardozo's house; in that hole, Gideon Jackson dressed himself in his new suit of black broadcloth.

And the planters waited.

The curious part of this dinner was the way in which it led to the other, the great affair at which Gideon was the guest of honor; for one of the guests at the Cardozo home this night was Stephan Holms, delegate to the Convention and former slave owner. Technically Holms was a Scalawag, the term for a southern white who collaborated with the freed slaves and the Yankees; actually, he was not of them. The Scalawags were poor whites for the most part; Holms had been and still was wealthy. Singularly, he had defied the rule that planters should sit back and have no part of this incredible revolution; he was elected to the Convention on the votes of his former slaves; he sat in the Convention as a spectator. He watched and listened; he said nothing. He was courteous to white and colored alike, and he became an enigma that Cardozo determined to solve.

On the surface, he had no secrets. He was the last male of a good South Carolina family; a brother and a son had died in the war. Holms had been a Major, had fought with Jackson and Lee, and had gained neither distinction nor fame. It was known that he disapproved of the war, that he thought the Secession unutterably stupid and hopeless from the very beginning. He had once owned a plantation on the Congaree River not far from Columbia, but he now lived with his mother in their Charleston house, and it was taken for granted that the country place had been lost, either through debt or taxes; in any case, he did not speak of it.

He was handsome, in a pale, self-effacing manner; stomach-trouble jaundiced his skin, gave it a yellow tinge; he was dark, long-faced, with a full head of hair, taller than the average, delicate in his movements, consciously a gentleman, quiet in his speech. He had singled out Cardozo, talked with him several times, indicated an interest in education and land, and graciously accepted Cardozo's uncertain invitation to dinner.

It was an invitation and an acceptance that troubled Cardozo. When white men dined with black in the city of Charleston, the world stood on end and shivered, and that was a part of what Cardozo felt as he introduced Gideon Jackson, former slave to Stephan Holms, former slave-holder. And Holms said:

"I am honored to meet you, Mr. Jackson," pleasantly and quietly, as if this were the most everyday thing, looking at Gideon appraisingly. Gideon was a matter for appraisal, tailored well, his great chest and shoulders set off by the black coat, a plain white shirt and a black string tie. His woolly hair was cropped close to his head; clean-shaven with big features to hold the flesh, but leaner than he had ever been before—recalling to Holms that once such a man on the auction block would have created a near-riot, the bidding mounting in dizzy spirals, the auctioneer screaming, "My friends and gentlemen, you who know and value breed, here's a bull stallion such as you never laid eyes on before!"

"I am pleased to meet you, sir," Gideon said.

Dr. Randolph, a small, quick-speaking, brown-skinned man, also a delegate, was the fourth for dinner; he was more nervous than Gideon, more nervous than Cardozo at the presence of Holms; he stuttered as his speech spilled out. Mrs. Cardozo was the only woman at the table, and she tried to put people at their ease; Holms joined with her, and they were gracious back and forth. Gideon asked himself, bewildered, "What is the man? Why and how and who?" It was the first time in his life he ever took the hand of a man of Holms' class, first time he had ever spoken to one, man to man, first time he had ever sat down to eat with a white man. Obviously, it was not the case with Cardozo, but wasn't it with Randolph? Randolph was frightened. Gideon stared behind his hostess to the buffet, where a stuffed partridge stood under a bell of glass. There was patterned wallpaper and prints on the walls. Cardozo knew the world, but Gideon could not help but be aware how carefully he was treading with Holms, saying, "Education, sir, you see, is a necessity."

"A necessity?" Holms asked. Holms neutralized himself completely, never stating but always asking, his constant withdrawal being a most effective blandishment.

"Simply by a statement of the fact. Four million illiterate slaves are possible. Four million illiterate free Negroes are obviously impossible."

"That's a curious way to look at it," Holms admitted. "What do you think, Mr. Jackson?"

"I think education is like a gun," Gideon said.

"Like a gun?"

Cardozo frowned and Randolph played with his fork. "Go on, please," Holms smiled.

In Holms' smile, there was something Gideon reached for and almost found, a balance of qualitative changes, part in himself, part in Holms, a play of forces. Bluntly, he stopped the process of attempting to understand Stephan Holms; he would not understand Holms, ever. "Like a gun," Gideon said. "Maybe better. Take a man who got a gun, you want to enslave him, you got to take that gun away. You got to take your chances, maybe he kill you, maybe he don't. But you got to take the gun away. Why?"

"Isn't it obvious?"

"It ain't obvious," Gideon said slowly. He groped for the words he wanted, struggled with his thoughts, his hands gripping the edge of the table. "A man who's got no gun is a slave or not a slave; that depends on many things. A man with a gun is not a slave, depending on one thing, his gun. Before he come like other men, you got to take away gun. Now with education—that you cannot take away from a man who has learned, and I believe a man who has learned truly cannot be a slave. In one way, it like a gun, in other way, it is better than the gun."

"I wouldn't put it quite that way," Cardozo smiled.

"Of course you wouldn't," Holms said easily. "Nevertheless, Mr. Jackson's analysis is most interesting, since he looks at education in terms of two things, freedom versus slavery. I think that is understandable. You were a slave, weren't you, Mr. Jackson?"

"I was."

"But slavery has been abolished."

Gideon nodded slowly.

"But you think it will return?" Holms asked gently.

"It could return," Gideon said, happening to glance at Mrs. Cardozo at that moment, seeing in her eyes complete, animal-like terror . . .

The dinner broke up early, but it led to something else. A week

later, coming out of the Convention, Holms stopped Gideon and
said:

"I am having some people at my home, Mr. Jackson. Would you
come?"

Gideon hesitated, and Holms said winningly, "I want you to
come, I assure you. After all, if we are to work together—"

Gideon agreed to come.

The Convention made progress. Out of the initial confusion,
slowly, measure after measure appeared, small things at first, then
larger things. The small things made agreement possible. Duelling
was abolished. Imprisonment for debt was abolished by a large
majority. The very naivete of the majority of the delegates gave
them a fresh and curious approach to legislation; there was behind
them no awesome, imposing tower of law, mores, habits, customs and
deceptions; the insoluble became obvious, and very often the obvious became insoluble. So when these men approached the relationship of women to men in society, they broke walls that had stood
for ages. A white swamp delegate said:

"Four years I fought the Yankees, and all that time my wife
carried the house. Fed the kids, clothed them, broke ground, put in
a crop, took it out. Now I ask these gentlemen, do they propose to
give me the vote and deny it to my wife?"

Gideon took the floor and said, "I took my wife in slavery. We
married in secret because my master did not approve marriage for
slaves. We was equal beasts in his eyes. We was equal in the work
we did; we was equal when we nearly fainted in the cotton fields.
Sure enough, we suffered equal. Then I say, my wife is equal to me
in the eyes of this Convention."

They came as close to universal suffrage as man had come yet,
and only the realization of the radical nature of the measure kept
it from being passed, a fear that they might abuse the power given
to them by a Congress in far-off Washington. However, out of their
argument came the first divorce law in the history of South Carolina, a sane and simple divorce law that sent the southern newspapers to screaming that the black savages had already given the
land over to infamy and degradation. Out of their argument came
a law which said that the property of a wife could not be sold to
pay her husband's debts—and that too was a beginning in South
Carolina. Out of their argument came a long and curiously sane

debate on the whole matter of suffrage, a debate that led Gideon to read the Constitution of the United States over and over, until he almost knew it by heart. He fought, along with others, for absolute equality of black and white at the polls—a forceful prevention of discrimination. And the motion won.

It was March already, and spring was coming to the land. The sky over Charleston was bluer than anywhere else in the world. The gulls swooped and shrieked over the bay and the rain fell fine as mist and cleared and left the sky brighter. A delegate offered from the floor that this should be known as the "Glory Year," but his motion was laughingly rejected. Yet men knew that this was a year like no other year, and a reporter of the New York *Herald* wrote:

"Here in Charleston is being enacted the most incredible, hopeful, and yet unbelievable experiment in all the history of mankind."

Charles Cavour, an aged colored delegate was attacked and badly beaten by three former soldiers, but the threatened explosion in Charleston did not come. The palmettos sent forth green shoots, and Gideon, enjoying the fine sea breeze, stood on the Battery and watched the ships cross the bay with white sails spread. He had found a book called *Leaves of Grass*, and in it were these lines:

> Earth! you seem to look for something at my hands,
> Say, old top-knot, what do you want?

"What do you want" echoed back and forth in his head; he wanted the whole world, and it was here at hand. Even the stevedores, singing as they went about their work, knew that this was a hallelujah year. Gideon was not alone in his study now; eight of the delegates had joined in a class which met three times a week at Cardozo's home to study American history and economics, and two of the members of that class were white. And Gideon, leaving the Convention one day, had been joined by Anderson Clay, who said:

"Wait a minute there, Jackson!"

Gideon paused, and then they walked along together, Clay even taller than Gideon, his blond hair loose and long and bright as brass in the sunlight.

"What I'm thinking these days," Clay said bluntly, "is that you're going to work with us, not against us."

"How's that?"

"I've eaten more crow sitting in a houseful of niggers these past weeks than anytime before in my life. I figured in the beginning I could just as well go home, live in a nigger land, and maybe raise some hell about it."

"You shouldn't feel that way," Gideon said softly.

"All right. I'm beginning to think maybe a black man and a white man can live together—I don't know. Do you want to talk about it?"

"I'd like to talk about it," Gideon said.

For some time, they walked in silence, neither able fully to break a wall that was so high and old between them. They walked through the narrow Charleston streets and under the whitewashed walls that split the world off from the houses, through the rich splashes of sunshine, and finally Clay said:

"What do you do when a new world comes? You make a piece of it, or you smash it. And I don't like the folks who are getting ready to do the smashing."

Gideon slept little these days; work on the committee for education drew him closer to Cardozo, nor did Gideon resent the fact that the sharp, cultured Negro was using him as a sounding board. The one was a product of education, the other a person who having just tasted it was already drunk upon it. Together, they set their shoulders for a single object, in a sense the basis for the whole new state Constitution—universal compulsory education. They had good support; they had opposition, on the other hand, that pleaded with them:

"Compromise—conciliate! You cannot force education on a whole population of illiterates."

"Why?"

"They won't stand for it."

"Then we make it law."

"Where will you find field-hands if you educate a population to be lawyers?"

"Not all men are lawyers, even in New England where literacy is so high. An educated man can work as well in the field as an uneducated man."

"The whites won't go to school with the colored."

"Then we'll build separate schools for those who want them. But all children, black and white, must go to school."

"This is insanity. There has never been such a law before in this country."

"Then we will begin. It has to begin somewhere."

"And can Carolina niggers do what the smartest folk in the world haven't done?"

"We can try."

Finally, the committee brought their bill to the floor, and for hours the debate raged hotly and stridently. Gideon noticed that they found support where they had least expected it, from white southern delegates, the poor white trash that the newspapers raged at even more fiercely than they condemned the Negroes, the despised Scalawags, the tall, lean, slow-spoken, straw-haired men elected by that shadow-race of the poor and landless, men from the swamps and the lonely piney woods. Anderson Clay, who rose and yelled, "Damn it, yes! If the only way is schools where black and white go together, then sure enough, I'm for schools! If I can sit in a Convention hall with niggers, then my son can sit in a schoolhouse with them!"

And Clair Boone, from the Pee Dee Swamp, "I fought in this war. I fought three years before I got enough learning to read a newspaper, or a book. Two brothers of mine, they're dead—for what? A war to keep a few damned slave operators in power! We didn't know, by God, we couldn't! Damn it, I say educate—educate and to hell with the consequences! We sit here, the elected representatives of the people of this state, and we chew our fingernails about the consequences of every word we say."

Gideon spoke shortly. "No man stays free," he said. "I know a little history, and the little I know makes it a fight for freedom, all along. There's one big gun for freedom—education. I say, arm ourselves."

Summing up the following day, Cardozo said, "It was argued by some yesterday with some considerable weight that we should do everything in our power to incorporate in the Constitution all possible measures that will conciliate those opposed to us. No one would go further in conciliating others than I would; but we should be most careful of what we do to conciliate. In the first place, there is an element that is opposed to us no matter what we do, which will never be conciliated. It is not that they are opposed so much to the Constitution we may frame, but they are opposed to us sitting in the Convention. Their objection is of so fundamental a nature, that any attempt to frame a Constitution to please them would be abortive. Next, there are those who ask us to frame a Constitution to please our enemies, promising us that if we do, they will come over to us. Then, there is a third class who honestly question our capacity to frame a Constitution. I respect them, and believe that if we can do justice to them, laying our Constitution on a sure foundation of republican government and liberal principles, the intelligence of that class will be conciliated.

"Before I proceed to discuss the question, I want to divest it of all the false issue of the imaginary consequences that some gentlemen have illogically thought would result from the adoption of this section with the word 'compulsory.' They say that it compels the attendance of both white and colored children in the same schools. There is nothing of the kind in the section. It simply says that all children should be educated; but how, it is left with the parents to decide. It is left to the parent to say whether the child should be sent to a public or private school. There can be separate schools for white and colored. It is left so that if any colored child wishes to go to a white school, it shall have the privilege of doing so. I have no doubt that in most localities colored people will prefer separate schools, particularly until some of the present prejudice against their race is removed."

Looking around the hall, Gideon noticed the rows of intent faces, black and white making a pattern, faces such as had not filled a legislative gallery since so long ago when the farmers and the artisans met to vote in a revolution, faces that unconsciously nodded to Cardozo's words. Warmth and strength and brotherhood; Gideon felt like laying his head on his arms and crying; he thought to himself, a black man is like a lost child, he has no country or piece of soil he can call his own: but they were making a land now; the speaker's platform was draped in red, white and blue, and behind it were two big flags of the Union. Gideon stared at them and heard Randolph, in his wavering voice, say:

"We, the undersigned, people of South Carolina, in Convention assembled, do hereby recommend that the Bureau of Refugees, Freedmen and Abandoned Lands be continued until the restoration of civil authority; that then a Bureau of Education be established, in order that an efficient system of schools be established . . ."

Nearby Gideon, an old black man sat and wept, nodding his head to a slow and ancient rhythm as applause filled the hall, as newspaper men dashed for the exits to write stories such as the one that appeared in the next day's *Observer:*

THE INCREDIBLE MOVE OF RECKLESS BLACKS

Yesterday, abandoning all scruples, the circus that calls itself a Convention set in motion a proposition that will complete the ruin and bankruptcy of this state. Black and white children of all classes are to be herded together in the same schools. Southern womanhood is to be degraded and debauched even before the teen age is past, and honest citizens will be starved and ruined to support a corrupt school structure . . .

And so forth and so on, stuff that Gideon was used to now, that he had come to expect as the result of each day's session, as the structure of the Constitution became more and more plain, as the judicial system was reformed, judges to be elected instead of appointed as all discriminations of race and color were abolished, as free speech was guarded and enforced, as a motion was passed to petition the Government to buy and subdivide great land holdings. The last was a great uncertainty; that the Federal Government would destroy the plantation system was more than could be expected, yet the proposition was adopted out of principle . . .

It seemed now an eternity ago that Gideon had first come to the Carters. Sitting at their dinner table, painting the future for these two old people, he became in their eyes sufficient reason why they might boast to their friends that Gideon Jackson, the delegate, lived with them.

Stephan Holms told his mother, "At dinner, tomorrow night, there will be a nigger."

And she, thinking he referred to the servants, said, "Naturally, Stephan."

"I don't think you understood me, my dear. At the dinner table, I mean—a guest of mine."

She began, "I wish you wouldn't, Stephan. You say things—"

"I'm serious, mother. Understand me, I invited a nigger to dinner tomorrow, as the guest of honor, you might say."

She sat down in a chair and stared at him, and he, looking over her head and through the window, studied the vague outline of Fort Sumter. Looking at him, she realized that he had gone into himself; she might argue with him for a while, but in the end, he would have his way. His strength was complete, beyond her understanding, intellectual, and to a degree very frightening. If people said this or that of Stephan, approved him or disapproved of him, she could say in his defense, and always did, "You don't understand, my dear. Stephan does things—"

Martha Holms was close to sixty, tired; she was ready to accept the fact that part of a world had disappeared in the great blood bath and cling to what was left; Stephan would not accept the fact that any had been irretrievably lost nor would he cling to what was left. When he told her, "My dear, I am going into the Convention because the only way to fight this monstrous thing that has happened is to understand it, and the only way to understand it is to become a part of it," she attempted to understand but could not. Nor could she now when Stephan told her.

"Mother, it is necessary for me to have a nigger at dinner. Please take it for granted that if I say it is necessary, it is."

"But why? What earthly reason—?"

"Several earthly reasons, very sound ones. I would gladly explain to you—"

"Stephan, I can't."

"But you can, and you will."

"Stephan, if you must make a clown of yourself, a Scalawag and a buffoon, can't you at least respect my feelings?"

"My dear," Holms said, "there is no one whose feelings I respect more highly."

"And what will people say?"

"They will say nothing. Colonel Fenton will be here, Mrs. Fenton, Santel, Robert and Jane Dupre, Carwell and General Ganfret and his wife."

"And they know a nigger will be at dinner?"

"They know."

"And who is this person, if I may ask, Stephan?"

"A former slave of Carwell's," Holms said. "His name is Gideon Jackson—"

In the end, the wall reared up against Gideon, the wall of childhood, youth, young manhood, the wall of a thousand memories when these people bred Negroes like cattle, and he would not have gone had not Cardozo said:

"Go, Gideon. It's important that you go. Holms asked you for one of three reasons; firstly, because he may sincerely wish to work with and understand us, and that I doubt. He's a clever man and an old slave holder. Secondly, because he desires to make a fool of you, and that too I doubt. I don't think that you will be easily made a fool of, and I don't think Holms is childish enough to indulge in that sort of thing. The third reason, and the only reason I can put credit in is that, suspecting some mysterious Negro plot, Holms wishes to get at it, get at what he may think goes on behind his back. If that is the case, certainly you have nothing to hide."

Gideon had nothing to hide but his fears, all the old, ancient fears that rose like a sick feeling in his stomach. A man can tell himself this and that, freedom has come and black men and white men are working together to create a new world, the old chains are broken, slavery is only a bitter memory—all that a man can tell himself, yet fears and memories are burned like brands on the skin, beatings, flight, old songs, let my people go, let my people go, scorn and hatred—

He walked slowly along the Battery, came finally to the proud white house that fronted on the Bay, rang the bell next to the gate, shivered at the clang it made, and was let in by an old Negro servant who eyed him curiously but had evidently been warned beforehand. He went up the walk and mounted the stairs to the veranda, his legs so weak that they would hardly hold him, and then the door of the house was held open to him and he entered.

It was the first time that Gideon had ever been in such a house, a house like this, lit, alive, hostile, and beautiful beyond words. As a child, he had been in and out of the kitchen wing of the Carwell house, never in the main rooms; later, as a man, he had walked through the Carwell house, empty, dead. This house was not empty, not dead. Light blazed from lamps and candles, dazzling him. The woodwork in the hallway was snow white, the furniture twisting in all the gracious curves of a generation before. The stairway spiraled up into misty distance; the drawing room beyond yawned like a devil's mouth. He felt sick, hopeless, and his feelings were not bettered much by Holms' warm and pleasant greeting. "So glad you came, Jackson."

Gideon nodded; he couldn't speak. Holms led him into the brightly lit drawing room, and Gideon had an impression of people carved from ice in all this warmth, the women in their fine gowns, the men in black and snowy white for dinner, glitter and dazzle from the great chandelier, rich mahogany furniture that made Cardozo's furniture pathetically poor by contrast, silver and glass. One by one, Holms introduced the people there to Gideon, but no one rose and no one offered their hand, and when Gideon faced Dudley Carwell, who had once been his master, the white man gave no sign of recognition—which was reasonable enough, since Gideon had been a field-hand and no more. They had been talking when Gideon entered, and they went on talking after the introductions were over, leaving Gideon to Holms, who, smiling thinly, said:

"Forgive them, Jackson. Sometimes our so-called courtesy does not rise to the occasion. What will you drink?"

Black servants moved through the room like shadows; in fact, for Gideon everything was blurred and nightmarish, nothing that afterwards made a clear, cohesive picture in his memory. He shook his head now. Nothing. Nothing at all? Nothing. He stood as still as stone, his skin prickling all over, conscious of the way the servants' eyes moved sidewise to glance at him. He was an animal trapped; he was a runaway slave brought to bay; he was a man roped to a stake and beaten there—and worst of all, bitterest of all, most terrible of all, he was afraid.

And it seemed like an eternity to him before they finally went in to dinner.

He had seen how people eat; his people at the plantation ate one way; the Carters ate in another way; the Cardozos in still a third way: but none of it was like this, nowhere the array of plates and silver so large and confusing. It was hard for him to hold a fork or spoon the way they held it; he was clumsy; he dropped things; he had to wait and watch them, and they knew he was watching. Why had he ever allowed himself to be trapped like this? Thirty times thirty he had been a fool; his thoughts raced like squirrels in a cage; what did Holms mean? What was all this? Why? What did it profit Holms?

Presently, he realized that they were talking to him, and after a fashion he was answering. Holms forced the conversation; Holms was driving at something—something that Gideon could not put his hands on. Gideon's head cleared; now he was angry, seeing these people for the first time in his thirty-six years, listening to them for the first time. They spoke words, and the words were the same words he used. He drove words back at them. He listened carefully, and what they said was not too clever; all in an instant, he had to

fling a century over his head and come whirling through a read-
justment that left him reeling. Anderson Clay, the poor white,
could think more coldly to the marrow of a thing than they could;
they thought they were baiting him, but his deep voice answered
slowly; he wouldn't permit himself to be baited. Holms was his
equal, but not the others, Holms smiling slightly as Colonel Fenton
said:

"I imagine, Jackson, that you find lawmaking a diversion. As a
change from other things?"

"It's more profitable than picking cotton," Gideon answered.
"We are paid three dollars a day."

"More than many an honest man lays hands on these days."

"What can a nigra do with that much money?" Jane Dupre wondered. She was slim and blond and fragile, and her husband
frowned as she spoke. The extra consonant was a concession to
Gideon's social place at the table.

"He could spend it on clothes and food," Gideon said. "But
mostly he just drinks it up."

He seemed simple enough, and they too were uncertain as to
what all this meant. If anything, their position was more difficult
than his, for they realized that Holms was enjoying the situation.
Afterwards, Jane Dupre said that she almost retched at the table,
watching that black eat, using his fork like a shovel.

General Ganfret said, "I would presume, Jackson, that education
might be accepted as a prerequisite for legislation. Don't you find
it difficult at the Convention?"

"I find it hard," Gideon agreed.

"The more so since I understand you were one of Carwell's field-
hands only a few years ago."

"I was," Gideon smiled.

Santel, a man of fifty, owner of one of the largest plantations in
the state, long-faced, hard, small-eyed, remarked that Gideon had
come up in the world. Gideon said, yes, he thought so, but the world
was changing. For the worse, someone said.

"That," Gideon nodded, "depends on how you look at it."

"You do read," one of the women remarked.

"I learned to read a little when I was in the army."

"When you were in the army?" the general asked.

"I was with the Yankee troops that marched into Charleston—you
remember the colored brigades?"

There was a fuse lit in the room, a barrel of gunpowder sitting under it. Holms chuckled, but the general and most of the others sat frozen; Gideon likened them to ice again, the old strain running through his mind, nought ain't nothing, three's a figure, all for the white boss, none for the nigger: he realized this couldn't go on; something would explode. Mrs. Holms excused herself and left the table. The sound of her tears followed her from the room; Holms, who had followed her, returned and said, "Forgive my mother—she is slightly indisposed."

The general retreated into grim silence; Fenton, to break the general unhappiness, said to Gideon, "You bear a fine southern name, Jackson. But I understand that niggers take their master's name."

"Some do," Gideon said. "I went without a family name until they made me a sergeant in the army. Yankee captain tells me, you got to have a name, Gideon, got to have a family name. Who owned you?" Gideon paused, nodded at Carwell, half-believing that at that moment, were it not for the women present, they would have killed him. "I tell him," Gideon continued, "that man who own me for a slave, his name I never take. What about Jackson—"

Gideon did not finish his story. Carwell rose and said. "Get out of here, you black swine!"

As Gideon walked home, he felt strangely light-hearted. How many mysteries there were that had evaporated into nothing! How many fears there had been that were groundless! All the world was part of a great unknown until you examined it. The dark and silvery bay, so ghost-like now, would become a placid sheet of sunlit water tomorrow. The chains that bound his people would never be forged again; there was no place for those chains in the sunlight. The rule of the many by the few, the darkest, heaviest evil man had borne in all man's memory, could be pricked like a water-filled bladder, and the content would ooze out the same way. Gideon sang softly, "When Israel was in Egypt land—let my people go—oppressed so hard she could not stand—let my people go!"

At the Holms house, the women had retired and the men were left at the table, with their cigars, the general saying, "This, Holms, is unforgivable."

"Hardly."

"You said you had a reason," Santel put in, his voice hard and cold. "You said there was reason enough, Stephan, for us to sit at dinner with a nigger. You've always had your reasons—and we've humored you. You were dark and mysterious when you went into the Convention, licking enough niggers' asses to put you there, and you said you had a reason for that. I, for one, am sick to death of your god damned reasons."

"Reason," Holms said lightly, "is nevertheless at a premium. There was little enough of it tonight, and if I may say so, that nigger made fools of all of you."

From the general, "I think you've said enough, Stephan."

"I don't," Colonel Fenton put in. "Whatever you think of Stephan he's right in this case. The nigger made fools of us. Accept that, gentlemen."

"I'll accept an explanation from Stephan, or—"

Holms broke in, "For Christ's sake, Dupre, you're not going to challenge me to a duel! That would be too much. Are we infants? Babes? Idiotic fools? I asked you gentlemen here tonight because I considered you, in one fashion or another, persons of character. Permit me to retain a few of my illusions—"

"Holms!"

"All right! Let me do the talking for a while! I staged a circus here tonight, granted. I took that nigger and I put him and you into an impossible situation. Granted. I guessed what would follow; but I did not think that you would be so completely demoralized by the presence of a single nigger sitting across the table from you. Let us analyze the situation—I begged you, as a favor to me, a favor that was of extreme importance to each and every one of us, to spend a social evening with a black member of this Constitutional Convention. I made it a social evening, because only in that way could I make my point; I did not tell you the point in advance because the point did not exist at that stage. Am I not clear? Then bear with me a little longer.

"What is your attitude, the attitude of the whole class to which I belong? Faced with the federal order of reconstruction, you refused to accept it. You sulked—yes, all over the south, men of our kind sulked, refused to register, to vote, to campaign. You called the niggers and the white trash savages and said that this whole thing would overnight dissolve of its own accord. Did you believe that, gentlemen? Did you really believe that? Have you, after fighting this damned bloody war, so infantile a conception of power? Have you been watching the progress of this Convention? Watching it, I mean, not reading about it in our stupidly partisan newspapers?"

"Isn't this enough—" Dupre began and Colonel Fenton cut him short with a savage, "Shut up, Dupre! Go on, Stephan." Dupre, spluttering, bewildered, looked from face to face. Holms bit off the end of a fresh cigar, lit it with a candle from the table, poured himself a splash of brandy, and continued:

"What is our situation at this point, gentlemen? Do you remember our world, the world that existed for us only eight years ago? That isn't so long; I was twenty-six then, I am thirty-four now, still young—young enough to have a taste for life, gentlemen, as I think you all have. I remember our world then—and what is our situation at this point? One thing we all have in common, we were or are plantation owners; we are the base, the rock upon which this south of ours exists. Another thing we have in common—we all face the same destiny, ruin, complete, unequivocal ruin. I have lost a plantation which has been in our family one hundred and thirty years. Dupre has lost his, so has Carwell—debt, taxes, war, emancipation. The others cling to what is left. When we went into this senseless war, I predicted the outcome—and fools accused me of being disloyal. Disloyal! Do we have to lie to ourselves? Can I be disloyal to what has made me, to what I am, blood and body? I say to you earnestly, gentlemen, we have to understand this situation in which we find ourselves. There is our only salvation."

The general, trailing smoke from his cigar, said, "Stephan, do you propose that we go into this circus of baboons?"

And Santel added, "How? We've tried to buy the niggers, wheedle them, threaten them—they remember only one thing, we owned them."

"Why did you bring that nigger here tonight?" Fenton asked.

"That, gentlemen, is the key to it. I object to the general's terminology—circus of baboons. When we think that way, gentlemen, we defeat ourselves. This Convention is not a circus of baboons, it is a gathering of determined and intelligent men who, for the most part, are honest according to their own lights."

"You're talking nonsense," the general objected.

"Am I? Have you been to one session?"

"I read the papers."

"And the papers lie! Believe me, I have been at almost every session—and the papers lie! I brought that nigger here for only one reason; two or three years ago, he was completely illiterate. A few years before that, he was Carwell's slave. Did you see him tonight? Was he a baboon? What is the potential of these black people we've bought and sold for two hundred years? We don't know, gentlemen, and we don't dare to guess. Will such men as this Gideon Jackson easily give up what they have? And they are not alone; they are learning to work with the white trash we despised until we needed them to fight a war. And these whites who fought the war for us are beginning to think. Gentlemen; when you gave the Convention over to these niggers and these whites, you made the second greatest blunder in these times; the first was the war itself. You said that the Convention would fall to pieces, it did not; it has been sitting for more than ninety days and it has framed a Constitution. You said that the nation would rise indignantly and crush this monster; the nation has not risen indignantly; instead, Yankee reporters are spreading the truth about this Convention all over the country. When we inaugurated our stupid reign of terror after the war, our fanciful Black Codes, we thought that we were bold enough and strong enough to snatch victory from a nation that just defeated us in battle; we used that fool Johnson, thinking that the people would follow him, and instead Congress crushed him. Now the niggers are winning the sympathy we sacrificed, and that too, gentlemen, is our fault."

Dupre said, "You don't have a high opinion of us, Holms."

"Frankly, I don't. In a sense, I have a higher opinion of that nigger I brought here."

"And I haven't—"

Fenton said, "For Christ's sake, Dupre!" And to Holms, "What do you propose, Stephan? Stop moralizing. We saw the nigger and you made your point. Now what do you propose?"

"All right," Holms nodded. "You saw the nigger—you must accept him for what he is, a representative example of the potential of four million people here in the south."

"Very well, go on!"

"Let's look at this Convention—and what it's done. Firstly, education; it has made it universal and compulsory throughout the state. Which means that niggers and white trash will be fighting us on equal terms—"

"They'll still be niggers and white trash!"

"God help me, can't I get you to look at reality? One generation of such education, and we'll be a vague memory—I assure you. Now another point, the Convention has moved and petitioned for a sub-division of the land, a breaking down of the plantations to small farms. Combine that with education, and you have the death-knell of the plantation. The Convention has legalized equality of race and color everywhere—contemplate that, gentlemen. The Conven-tion has assured us that black men will sit with white men on juries, that black judges will sit on the bench; let that soak in, my friends. The Convention has safeguarded the ballot—and there goes what-ever legalized dream of power you might have had. And last of all, gentlemen, the Convention has consistently made its appeal to black and white together; in every law, in every edict, every proposal, the poor white has been bracketed with the nigger. Does that awake a response, gentlemen?"

A long moment of silence was broken by the general, who said, "They can't carry it through, Holms. It'll break down. The finances of this state will not carry it. At the elections—"

"At the elections, they will move into the Government, just as they moved into the Convention."

"And where do we stand, Stephan?" Carwell asked.

"Precisely nowhere."

"Why not play their game?"

"And offer the voters what? Twenty cents a day wages? A return to slavery? No small farms? Ignorance?"

"There are ways."

"Yes, but not that way. We've had power; we lost it; we propose to regain it: that is all, simply. You saw that nigger here tonight. Can you wheedle him, coddle him, deceive him?"

"No—" Fenton said thoughtfully. "But you could hang him."

The general observed, "We tried terror and failed, Stephan. You pointed that out."

"Yes, we failed—because it was stupid terror, and because terror with only terror as the end is predestined to fail. We pitted mobs against Yankee bayonets; we indulged in adolescent outrages, prod-ding ex-soldiers to bludgeon and lynch and steal. And we had no plan, no goal—and this most of all, no organization."

Fenton lit a fresh cigar. One of the women opened the door and asked, "Are you going to sit here forever?" A colored servant came in with whisky, and Holms said to him, "When you go, I want no one else to interrupt us." The ash on Stephan's cigar was long; he touched it with his finger and it fell to the cloth; then he blew it away.

"An organization," he said, "a plan, and a destination."

Fenton said, "You've thought of the Klan, Stephan."

"Yes, I've given some thought to that. Their record in the two years or so they've existed doesn't make for brilliance or cohesion, but at least there is an organization. And rather than split our forces and organize counter to them, we would be wiser to take what they have and work with it. If we decide to, it must be done quickly, before they destroy their usefulness."

"They are officered by army people," the general said.

"That's a point—and it will help. Dupre here is already a member of the Klan; he can help us on that score. This business of white nightshirts and burning crosses is tomfoolery, but it has its use. The weasel type, the timid, the frightened—they become bolder when they hide their faces."

"I don't like that kind of talk."

"Don't you, Dupre? Do *you* intend to put a white napkin on your head and go scampering through the night? No—this is a tool, let's understand that. And to operate it, we'll need men, thousands. Where will they come from? Some army men, not too many; whatever you say about our troops, they had courage, yes, and honor, the kind of honor we talk about; they won't take kindly to nightshirts, terror, hanging, murdering."

"I don't like the way you put that, Stephan," the general said.

"How else shall I put it? We can tell ourselves the truth, can't we? But there'll be men enough, the scum that we used for overseers, the trash that bought and sold slaves and bred them, the kind who were men with bullwhip and filth without one, the kind who have only one virtue, a white skin. Gentlemen, we'll play a symphony on that white skin, we'll make it a badge of honor. We'll put a premium on that white skin. We'll dredge the sewers and the swamps for candidates, and we'll give them their white skin—and in return, gentlemen, they will give us back what we lost through this insane war, yes, all of it."

"But how, Stephan?" Fenton wanted to know. "When we tried before—"

"Yes, but this time, we know. We start slowly—organization and nothing but organization to begin. We enter the Klan, we subsidize it, gentlemen, yes, with what little we have left, we subsidize it.

While the occupation troops are here, we do nothing—that is, nothing they could counter. A few acts, a nigger put in his place, a rape scare, a lynching—those will come about naturally; and when they come, the Klan can ride. As a matter of advertisement, you might say, romantic hooded figures dashing through the night; but only as a matter of advertisement. We wait; we organize; we do nothing premature. Concurrent with that, those of us who can enter politics, not as an opposition, but as men who wish to work with the reconstructionists. I propose to do that; others must join me. We move step by step, and we wait—"

"And how long do we wait?" the general demanded.

"I don't know—certainly two or three years, possibly five. But we wait until we are certain of success, until a reconstructed south becomes a matter of importance in national politics, until every Yankee soldier is withdrawn. And while we wait, we are not idle. We suffer, not hysterically, but patiently and manfully—and we let the North know the extent of our sufferings. We do not scream stupidly, but rather declare with dignity that we have been wronged, and when we have said it enough, we will be believed. We win sympathizers and adherents in the North, where there are thousands who have always envied us, envied those very things they fought against, our plantation system, our slaves, our pomp, our way of life—envied these to an extent which will not be covered by their false and flimsy moral scruples. Yes, and more than that—the nigger was pitied, the slave, the bondman; but what will become of that pity when we show the world that he is the oppressor, the black savages are taking all that is worthy, human, good, decent from gentlemen, from ladies?"

"As they are," the general said softly.

"Very well. We win adherents. We cultivate northern capital. The center of manufacture is shifting from England to the North; they will be screaming for cotton; we will give them some, but not enough. But we cultivate them, we invite their industry South, and we give them a stake in our future, a stake that will matter once they forget the moralistic frenzy that drove them to war, once they begin to realize that their war was unjust, that we were a freedom-loving people who fought to retain our American freedom."

"As we were," the general said.

"And then, when that time comes, whether in two years or five years, we strike—with force, force and terror; because force and terror are the only two things that can decide the issue. But by then, we will have achieved our goal; the North will not know, and what little they hear, they will not believe. The Klan will be an army by then, and the Klan will smash this thing that has arisen, smash it so completely that it will never again rear its head. Gentlemen, the nigger will be a slave, again, as he has been, as he is destined to be. Yes, he will fight—but he will not be organized for terror, for force, and we will be. Some white men will fight on his side; most, I assure you, will not; fear and the badge of a white skin will take care of that. And gentlemen, when that time comes, we will win!"

As he spoke, Stephan Holms showed fire and passion, a dynamic strength that impressed even the general, perhaps the least sensitive person there. But when he had finished, the flare died; the passion resolved into the pale and composed figure of civilization complete. He lit another cigar, and when the others had talked enough about his plan, pro and con, he suggested, "Shall we join the ladies now?"

6. HOW GIDEON JACKSON WENT HOME
TO HIS PEOPLE

Now it was finished, a constitution made, laws one after another set down, a definition of freedom, life, liberty and the pursuit of happiness as presented by the people of a state of this Union, the United States of America. It was the spring of the year 1868, a bright, fresh new year, a new era, as the chaplain said:

"Lord God of mercy, understanding, forgiveness, we ask thy blessing for our efforts. Our mistakes were not willful, but rather because we are mortal men, subject to the evils, the sins, the transgressions that all mortal men make . . ."

Then the whole Convention stood and sang, their voices rich and proud, "My country, 'tis of thee, sweet land of liberty, of thee I sing!"

"What are your plans?" Cardozo asked Gideon.

"To go home."

"It's been a long time, hasn't it?"

"Too long," Gideon smiled. "Funny thing about black folk, Francis, they got a homesick heart. Back in the bad old times, sell a nigger down the river, and that was worse than if you killed him. I got a hunger to go home."

"And then what?"

"I been thinking," Gideon said reflectively. "My people, they know the soil, they know how to coax up a little cotton, a little corn, and not much more. Where they live now, it's the old Carwell plantation—but that won't last forever. I been to the land office, tracing the place; Carwell lost it for debt, then the debtors for taxes. One of these fine days, it's going to be knocked down from the auction block, and where will my people be then?"

"Where so many colored folk are, landless, footloose, starving. That's a problem, Gideon, the biggest problem we face."

"Maybe I can do something about it, not much, but at least show my people how they can buy a little land. Even that I'm not certain of; there might be a way, there might not. I don't know—at least I can go home and try."

"Which might help a few, Gideon, but wouldn't solve the problem in any real way."

"I know."

"Gideon, have you ever thought of politics?"

"How's that?"

Cardozo, smiling somewhat uncertainly, recalled to Gideon the first time they had met. "I began to realize then," he said, "that I would have to put my trust in people like you."

"Why people like me?"

"Because this whole state, in fact this whole southland, except for a tiny minority who oppose us, has only one future, to pull itself up by its bootstraps. You've done it, so have hundreds of others. We don't agree, Gideon; we're an ocean apart on many things; you're a man of violence, for all of your gentleness, and I don't think that way. But there's much in you that I lack, much of great strength, great value. How will you use that?"

"If it's there," Gideon smiled. "It may be, and maybe it ain't; I sure enough don't know. I want to think about it; I want to learn. I'm an ignorant man, Francis; if I had known, three months ago, how ignorant, I would have given up then."

"Gideon, before you decide to go back, just think a little. In a few days, the Republican delegates from this state are going to meet. I'm one of them. Think of that, Gideon; Abe Lincoln's party is going to come in here, and it's going to carry the state; we know that, we've seen the results in the Convention vote. It means a state legislature, a whole governmental structure, congressmen, senators, everything from the bottom up. You've been in at the beginning of this, Gideon, a piece, no matter how small, of our Constitution came from your hands. Well, you have a chance to follow it, to implement the laws—"

"How's that?" Gideon said slowly.

"Some of us want you to sit in the State Senate, to be a candidate—"

Gideon shook his head.

"Why not?"

"It wouldn't work," Gideon said.

"Are you afraid?"

"I'm not afraid anymore," Gideon smiled. "It just wouldn't work —I know what I am. Maybe in a year or five years, not now. I'm not fit, Francis."

"You're fitter than most of the men who'll go in."

"Maybe," Gideon shrugged.

"You'll think about it?"

"No. I'm going home."

"And if I said you were wrong, Gideon?"

"I have to do what I think best."

"It's no use to argue with you is it?" Cardozo realized.

"No use, I'm afraid."

"I'm sorry," Cardozo said, sincerely.

He and Gideon shook hands, and Cardozo said, after a moment, "Knowing you, Gideon, was a good thing to happen to me."

"How is that, sir?"

"Maybe I'll be able to go home sometime."

When the time came for Gideon to go, Mrs. Carter wept frankly and unashamedly, held Gideon in her arms and kissed him on the mouth. "If you come back to Charleston, you stay with us, Gideon." They fussed over him, made up a box of things to eat; there was a pair of shoes Carter had made for Rachel, black shoes, high and button-up. Gideon wanted to pay him. "This is just a little gift thing, Gideon, son." Another gift was a Bible. "For comfort," Carter said. "You're a good boy, Gideon, but turn your face to God." Gideon had a sense of how desolate they would be after he left. They made a big and festive meal, fried chicken, fried prawns, hot cornbread, pots of greens, and their neighbors came in until the little house was packed full. Gideon hadn't known it was like this; they all wanted to shake his hands, and there were more tears than

at a burying: for Gideon, in a sense, the Convention and the Constitution had existed alone, not in relation to people, weeping and
laughter and pride . . .

He spent an hour with Anderson Clay, who said to him, "Gideon,
I'm not like some who are crazy with joy and hallelujahs. This is
a beginning. Suppose it smashes; then we begin again. There'll
always be some of us here and there; we'll know each other."

"We'll know each other," Gideon nodded, holding the hand of
the tall, lean, red-faced man.

But already things were moving out past him and beyond him.
He had stepped away, but the little world he had occupied these
past fifteen weeks was in a flux of change and excitement. For all
his eagerness to see his people, he was lonely as he packed his books,
a good-sized pile of them now, as he filled a small carpet bag with
his clothes. He had his ticket on the railroad already; no, he was
not walking back to Carwell. To a degree he envied that black man
who, with long strides, had walked a hundred miles and more from
the back country to Charleston town.

And had nothing changed at Carwell? The old colored man who
drove him the last twenty miles in a mule-hitched ancient surrey
was completely unaware of the Convention, of the earth shaking at
Charleston, of all the great events that Gideon had been a part of.
"Convention, I ain't heard—" And as he told Gideon the news of
the countryside all about, it was the same news as ever, births,
deaths, bucolic tides of peace and violent outrages to erupt like
little, hidden volcanoes. "Missy Buller's boy done ambling to town,
just ambling, and five white folk take hold of him, beat him with
sticks and then hang him up on the cottonwood tree." "What did
he do?" "Ain't done nothing, so far I know, just ambling." The old
man told Gideon that the railroad was coming through, over by the
big swamp, and that they were going to build an embanked causeway clear through the swamp. "Taking on men, they is. Dollar a
day." "A dollar a day for colored men?" Gideon wanted to know.
"Dollar a day. Yankee men building this here road." And how was
it at Carwell, Gideon asked him. He said he didn't get up to Carwell
much, not this past year. "What do you hear?" "What all you expect
to happen, younger?" the old man said testily. "What for you all so
impatience? You just wait and see. Ain't no kingdom come, tell you
that. Old cow calves and old nigger woman gets a belly. What else

you expect?" So Gideon held it inside of him and heard how the weather had been, six weeks back and week by week; now it was spring and lovely, and the crops were in the ground. The crows flew along, caw-cawing, as they always had, and there was a man out hunting, his shotgun in the crook of his arm, his setter dog splashing through the meadow grass in front of him.

And then, in late afternoon, the shadows long and tired, Gideon was back at Carwell, the great and stately plantation house showing first on its high perch, caught in the rays of the sun, shadowed white on one side, pink and golden on the other. The mule was tired and stepped slowly. "Come a long ways," the old man complained. "Going to drive back in the almighty dark."

As always, it was the children who came running first, screaming at the top of their lungs, children springing out from everywhere, like a meadow of quail flushed; Marcus was among them; Gideon hadn't remembered him as so tall. Jeff was manly and far behind, walking and not running, a dignity there. And finally, Gideon was standing with Rachel in his arms, his eyes wet, and ashamed of that in front of his children.

Rachel had him back now; for her, too, time had become a flexible thing, like an instrument of rubber that can be pulled taut and far apart, or allowed to relax and tie itself together into a tight and small knot. These three months were an eternity; and Rachel had known, in her own way of knowing, that the same Gideon would not be coming back.

Her fears were formless, changing, shadow-things; their substance was the unknown, which began over the brow of the hill on the horizon and extended on to include all of the world. The beginning and the end of everything was Carwell, because she had not known any other place. Her mother, brought down from Virginia and auctioned on the block at Charleston, had a suckling babe in her arms that added forty-two dollars to her price; that was Rachel, with a memory that began at Carwell and included no other place. Even the war, which eddied all over the South, never laid its stamp very hard on this place. Once a young man, with red cheeks, blue eyes and golden-brown whiskers, dressed in a dirty blue uniform and riding a tired black horse, led a long column of tired men in blue uniforms over the lawns of Carwell—those were her first Yankees, the young man calling out to her, "Lassie, when've you seen your last reb?"

She could hardly understand his nasal, clipped New England speech; Marcus hid behind her skirts, and the dreadful thought occurred to her that they might take Marcus, sell him down the river or something, so she ran away: and when she came back, the Yankee men were gone. As time passed, there were other Yankees, rebel troops too, the surf of the war washing first at one side of Carwell, then at the other. In one part of that surf, Gideon and Hannibal Washington and others disappeared—going off to take up the Yankee gun and fight for their freedom. The maw of the great and mysterious and yawning outside world swallowed them, and Rachel left with two children had to find faith in their return. But Gideon was vast and certain as the rising and setting of the sun; if the other women wept, Rachel kept her eyes dry and told herself, "Gideon say he come back." That might make for faith, but it didn't quiet her fears. If she lost Gideon, the whole world ceased to be. Other women weren't like that; take sinfulness—some women might give their body in a sinful way; understanding that and even the desires and loneliness that prompted it, Rachel would sometimes project a situation where she was unfaithful to Gideon, and the whole vague shape of that situation would make her smile; for she was Gideon, Gideon was she. Even as their marriage had been, going in the night to Brother Peter for the secret ceremony, whereas so many men and women simply gave their bodies to each other, knowing that for them marriage was for a day, a month, a year, not a bond before God but a flickering happiness before they were sold, traded, debauched. Yet she and Gideon married and swore an oath to each other.

She had been happy in a way that made an expression, "Like Rachel." If a lark sang well, it sang like Rachel. She knew her man; God was smiling when he gave her Gideon; she knew that. When he went away, it increased her suffering, but that too was a part of having Gideon which she recognized and understood. Her understanding was different from Gideon's: as a child, she accepted with the other children the fact that the moving branches of the trees made the wind; when Gideon pointed out that it was quite the other way, she accepted that because Gideon said so. Gideon had to know why, always; for him nothing existed without a reason: but inside of her the warm tides of her blood made for reason enough.

The deep, strong feelings inside of her could know things, and sometimes the knowledge was strangely exact. She did not have to know about Charleston, the Convention, the new world created, to realize that the man who went away would not be the man who returned. "Let my people go," had meant to her having Gideon, having her children always; yet she sensed the sunlit horizons the phrase held for her husband. The first letters Gideon ever wrote came to her from Charleston, and at the beginning they had to be read to her, by Brother Peter, by James Allenby. The shame of that made her learn to read, sitting at night with the other men and women, crowded into a little cabin, while Allenby taught them as he taught the children in the daytime; but she learned slowly; her head ached. Gideon was moving away, farther and farther . . .

And then he came back and held her in his arms again, and she knew better than ever before the meaning of the phrase, "Freedom is a hard won thing."

The day after Gideon came back was Sunday, and Brother Peter held meeting on the lawn in the sunshine. In their strong voices, the people sang, "Take me by the hand, oh Lord, take me by the hand." Brother Peter opened the Book and read from Isaiah: "Behold, the Lord God will come with a strong hand, and his arm shall rule for him: behold, his reward is with him and his work before him. He shall feed his flock like a shepherd: he shall gather his lambs with his arm, and carry them in his bosom, and shall gently lead those that are with young." "Amen," the people nodded. The children shifted and twisted, and pulled each other's hair and clucked at the dogs. Gideon sat with Rachel, Jeff, Marcus and Jenny; but Rachel would not let him be on the grass in his fine Charleston clothes and had spread a piece of cloth underneath him —they were all so proud of the way he looked. "Say ye Amen," the people nodded. Jeff's eyes went again and again to where Ellen Jones, the blind girl, sat with old Mr. Allenby, and Gideon, noticing it, frowned. Marion Jefferson's little girl began to cry, and he leaned over her, "Hush you, hush you now." "Hallelujah," the people nodded, rocking back and forth. Brother Peter said:

"I will make no sermon today on account of Brother Gideon is here with us again, praise God. The good God seen fit to give us our freedom, he hear our prayer; he seen fit to reward us here with the blessing of the land, rich as milk and honey, when other black folk, they don't eat, they don't have a place to lay the head. The good Lord God seen fit to give us a voting and been along with Brother Gideon far off there in Charleston Town. How that was? Brother Gideon he sat there in Convention Hall with the high and mighty folk—the good Lord exalted him like he done with young King David, praise God!"

"Amen," the people said.

"Brother Gideon he come back, he going to talk to us in place my usual sermon. He going to tell us how that was. Stand up, Brother Gideon. Come up here where the whole congregation can face you."

So Gideon spoke to them. As plainly as he could, he told them all that had happened, how he walked to Charleston, his fears, how he had worked as a stevedore, how he had come to live with the Carters, and how finally he had taken his seat in the Convention. For the first time, he was able to make plain to them just what the voting had meant, what lay behind the whole policy of reconstruction as ordained by the Congress and how the process of reconstruction would proceed, now that a new State Constitution had been created. One by one, he outlined the measures included in the Constitution, explaining them, but making clear what a great gap lay between a measure written into the Constitution and the practical application of that measure. The Constitution said there would be universal education in the State of South Carolina, but money would have to be found, teachers trained, school buildings erected—and until that time they must learn in whatever way was possible. He pointed out that a measure abolishing racial discrimination did not do away with it; that would take years and years.

"And what about us, us people here?" Gideon said. "How do we fit in with the future? Well, I done gone and poked around and found out something. Dudley Carwell lost this here place to another man, who let it go for taxes. That means, sooner or later it come up on the auction block and knock down to the highest bidder. That time come, out we go, less we do something first. I don't know what we going to do; I thought about it—give it a lot of thought, and whatever we do, we need money. Where we going to get that money, I don't know yet. But it ain't no reason for despair. Reason for despair is dead and gone; it's a bright new time we can see in front of us, bright new time coming up."

There was not the same haste here, the same press of time that Gideon had felt in Charleston. The sun set and the sun rose; his fine clothes put away, he wore his old jeans and his old shirt. A sick sow trying to give birth to a litter kept him all night in the barn. Contrasts were not so startling now, and the slaves shacks that had seemed so dreadful on his return gradually became what they were before, an old and familiar sight.

Nights, he read by candle-light, mostly aloud. Marcus, Jeff, Jenny and Rachel sat and listened. Often, Allenby would come in with Ellen Jones, sometimes Brother Peter, sometimes some of the others. He read them from Whitman and Emerson, the ringing last words of old John Brown, the poems of John Greenleaf Whittier. Poetry caught their imagination, and Gideon read well; they rocked with the rhythm and softly clapped their hands. Jeff would watch him as he read, and Gideon thought that sometime soon he would talk with the boy and discover what was behind the dark eyes and the stolid black face. Marcus took life easily, impressing Allenby by his agility at learning. This, altogether, was a pause, an interval, a time when Gideon found himself disturbed by a growing impatience. Brother Peter said to him, "Recall you, Gideon, I say you would fill up, like drawing cold, clean water out of the well."

"I remember," Gideon nodded.

"You done go off to Charleston where the Lord exalted you—you come back and feel no bond with your people."

"That isn't true," Gideon said.

"Turn your face from God, Gideon, and God turns his from you." Brother Peter added thoughtfully, somewhat sorrowfully, "You done that, Gideon—"

"No—no, that's not it, more than that. I looked at things, Brother Peter, in the only way I can, in the way of my understanding. I seen men in bondage, and not God broke the bonds but men. I seen bad men and I seen indifferent men take up guns in a good cause, because good men had their way, and out of the blood and the suffering there came something."

"And salvation, Gideon?"

"Maybe I can only see salvation my way, in the truth of something, in schools, in good laws, in good houses instead of these shacks we live in—"

And Rachel, at night, would whisper to him desperately, "Gideon?"

"What is it?"

"Tell me you loving me, Gideon."

"Who else am I going to love?"

"Then what happen, Gideon, the change come over you, talk different, act different—what going to come of you and me?"

"Nothing, darling, nothing."

"Soon enough, you going off, you going off, Gideon—"

"No."

"Mouth say one thing, heart say another."

"No, no," Gideon reassured her.

And Cap Holstein brought a letter from Cardozo, which said, "Have you thought about it, Gideon? You can't vegetate there while the earth is shaking."

One late afternoon, they sat down with their backs to the corn-crib, their feet stretched out, as in the old days, Gideon, Brother Peter, Hannibal Washington, Allenby, Andrew and Ferdinand who had both taken the name of Lincoln, chewing on pieces of straw, kicking at the dust—

"Look like rain."

"Maybe it do, just a wee bit."

"Old dirt can use a little rain."

"Old dirt can."

"Coming up from the west."

"Coming up mighty strong."

Gideon said, "I almost wish you'd put in a few acres of cotton."

"Be happy if I never see a cotton boll break again."

"A sorrow crop."

"It's the crop of this land," Gideon said. "It's a cash crop, and we need cash."

"You keep saying that," Allenby observed.

"Yes—nothing's ours. Not the land, not even the shacks we live in. Nothing. Until now, everything was confused, no one to straighten out the records, no one to ask, what are them niggers doing there? Comes the first election, we're going to have civil administration, and then there won't be an acre unaccounted for."

"Who's going to put us off the land, Gideon?"

"Whoever buys it."

"Ain't a white man going to work the land alone. Man'll need niggers."

"Yes, he'll need niggers, work it on shares the way white folks did before the war. Put every acre in cotton, and have the nigger come a begging for a little piece of fatback to feed his children. Like Brother Peter say, this is a land of milk and honey now. But why? Because we put the land into corn, into feed, because we do without cash. Just a little candle to read a book by cost cash, just a lesson book for the children cost cash."

"Gideon, won't the Government buy land for the niggers?" Hannibal Washington asked.

"Maybe—but suppose the Government does that. Government's a thousand folk moving slow. Might be a year or two years or not at all. Government might say, here's a piece of land down Georgia way, move over to it. That ain't good. Here we lived; here is our place, right here. We got to have this land."

"How?"

"Buy it," Gideon said. "Work and get money, and buy the land."

Allenby said, "That would take a lot of money, Gideon."

"Sure, but things can be started. Banks lend money—yes, even to niggers if they see something sound, see our intention, see a little cash of our own. Railroad's putting a causeway through the swamp, asking for men at a dollar a day, nigger and white. Suppose we go down, work six or eight weeks on the railroad—"

"And the crops?"

"Come back and take out the crops."

There was a long silence until Brother Peter said, "It's a sad thing, Gideon, to take the men away from the women."

But Hannibal Washington said, "Gideon's right."

"We'll have a meeting," Gideon told them.

But for the women it was a sad thing. Washing in the brook, they looked at Rachel, who pounded and scrubbed her clothes in silence. Change was a troublesome thing, and from now on there would be change, which though it was a part of freedom was a troublesome thing. All right to be like the children, who splashed naked in the water, shouting and laughing and screaming, feeling no shame; but they weren't like children. The swamp was heavy with malaria and men would sicken and die; the swamp was a bewitched place. Rachel pounded and wrung the clothes in silence, when she saw Jenny fall, cried, "Jenny, Jenny, come on out," and then said nothing when the other women looked at her so strangely . . .

And Allenby asked Gideon, "Are you going to take Jeff with you?"

"Yes—he's strong as a man."

"I wouldn't, Gideon."

"Why?"

They were in the part of the barn Allenby used as a schoolhouse, his desk a feed-box, light pouring down in broad shaft from the open loft. There was a pile of cheap paper, sharpened sticks of charcoal, a sense of children that Gideon could not define, hunger and longing in the air even though the children had gone. Gideon had been at one of the lessons and watched the old man's incredible patience. "They are like little animals," he had said then. "Of course, what did you expect? But they learn." Their eagerness was apparent enough, and Allenby was a good teacher, patient.

"Why?" Gideon asked him, wondering that he had never gotten around to that talk he intended to have with Jeff.

"That's hard to say. Perhaps because he's like a fire. Do you know what goes on inside of him, Gideon?"

Embarrassed, Gideon did not answer.

"He can read and write already. He's like a sponge, soaking things in. He's trying to soak the whole world in—so quickly that it makes me afraid. He knows what he wants to do, Gideon; he wants to be a doctor."

"How do you know?"

"He told me."

"He never told me," Gideon said.

"Did you ever ask him?"

Gideon shook his head, and Allenby went on, "Did you ever look at yourself and ask things, Gideon? Do you remember the man walking down the road to Charleston? That wasn't so long ago, but you're not he. Do you ever ask yourself what's happening to you, what's happening to all of us, this world we live in? When you sat in the Convention and planned the change, did it ever occur to you that the change would be like birth agonies?"

"What about Jeff?" Gideon said slowly.

"What about him? He's your son. Take him into the swamp and he'll earn a dollar a day, and I'm not saying that would be wrong. But we have to make a beginning; there are no schools here yet, but he could go to a school in the north; there are schools there, in Massachusetts, that will take a colored boy, educate him, train him—"

"I don't know how," Gideon said bewilderedly.

"You have friends in Charleston. This Cardozo could tell you."

"Just send him away?" Gideon said.

Jeff took her into the piney woods; he told her about the many things, small and large, that surrounded her. "There's a hop toad crossing over in front your feet." The setting sun he told her about, "Coming like an old rose through them branches." She could feel the wind herself, "Like someone's hand," she said to him. At first her fears were wrapped all around her, and it was only by some miracle, knowing why and how instinctively, that Jeff gently broke through; she lived in a deep, dark cave and there was no color, no light in there. Jeff never made a move, a step, or spoke a word to frighten this blind girl who was, for him, the most beautiful creature that had ever existed. He took her into the meadows and let her feel the texture of the meadow flowers, the meadow grass, and once he crushed a wild strawberry in her hand. Allenby lived in a shack the men fixed up for him, and he didn't mind if Jeff came there and read from his books to Ellen while she did the work in the house. From old Uncle Sexton, who had died the year before, Jeff had the swamp tales, the birds and the beasts and the reptiles who spoke to each other, living their own wonderous lives; those too he told Ellen Jones. Rachel knew he was in love and understood his lumbering tenderness, so like Gideon's, whacking Marcus across the knuckles when he laughed at Jeff. Yet it made her sad, a blind girl; a blind girl had to be cared for; a blind girl was a burden on a man, no matter how you looked at it, and here was Jeff already almost as old as Gideon had been when he married her. A man needs a woman and a woman a man, but an equal thing, like the two halves of a scale pulling together.

Allenby told her, "It will be all right Rachel, believe me."

Through the woods, half a mile from where the south field ended, there was an acre of space that had been lumbered out, and lay open and stump-filled in the hot sun. The buzzards came there, perched on the rotting stumps and nodded at one another, and coiled garden snakes sunned themselves there. There Jeff took Ellen; there was a place on the hot sand where they could sit with their backs against a fallen tree, and there they were wonderfully alone. For hours Jeff could sit and make the world with words for the girl who couldn't see, a cloud winding across the sky, a bluejay, and in time his own dreams built up into pictures for her.

Slowly, slowly and gently, something happened to her; part of it was being in a community of friendly, warm people, the sound of voices all day, children laughing and people calling to each other across a distance; part of it was Jeff, who said to her one time, "I love you sweetly, Ellen." Another time, when he took her in his arms, she said to him, "Don't hurt me, Jeff, please." And he began to realize what life was and had been to this girl. This was strange and special; he had to know and there was no one to ask—and the other boys his age were hiding in the shrubbery of the creek to watch the girls when they bathed, or running after them and dragging them down to the grass—

"What will you do?" she asked him once.

"Whatever I want to do, I feel that way."

"But what?"

"Like your father," he said; he was the first one able to talk to her about her father.

"A doctor?" she said. He said, "That's right." His thoughts made pictures; the doctor in the village was a profane, whisky-drinking man with a tobacco-stained beard; once, when one of the women lay dying, he had heard folks talking wildly and aimlessly about doctors. He thought of talking to Gideon; his father would know, yet he couldn't talk with Gideon about that, for all that he worshipped his father. He asked Allenby:

"A doctor—what is it just?"

"A man who heals sick people."

"Sure enough?" There was a poor old woman who lived in the brush a few miles off, practiced a sort of voodoo, made charms and sold them. "Like that?" he wanted to know.

"Not like that, with science, with a knowledge of what makes men sick."

"What make them sick?"

So, that way, it had begun, and now, leading Ellen by the hand into the pines, he told her, "They going to send me off."

"Send you off? Where?"

"North, maybe. Study and be a doctor."

That was incredible; she asked him, pleadingly, who would be here when he left, and he was able to see how the darkness would close in. It was as if the thought had not occurred to him before. "I love you," he said. "You, I love, only you."

"But you want to go?"

"I want to go," he said, miserable. "Come someday, I'll come back, sure enough, I swear I come back . . ."

Gideon told Rachel only after he had received an answer from Cardozo. Cardozo said, yes, it could be arranged. Jeff should come to him in Charleston; he would write to Frederick Douglass and some other friends of his in the north. Twenty-five dollars would be enough for a time, and Cardozo would arrange for Jeff to go by sea to Boston. Then Gideon told Rachel.

"How far this place, Boston?"

"A thousand miles, I guess," Gideon said. "But do you understand what it means, Rachel, a son of ours, a child born in slavery, going to Boston to study doctoring?"

Rachel nodded.

"Don't you think I wanted him with me?" Gideon demanded.

Again, Rachel nodded. Gideon took her in his arms, "Look, baby, little baby, going to be proud of that son, going to be almighty proud of him, going to see him walking with long, glory steps."

"I know," Rachel said.

The Yankee boss, a tall, bearded man, leather-booted, mud-stained in his dank clothes, just out of a malarial bout, said to Gideon, "You talking for these men?" "That's right." "How many?" "Twenty-two," said Gideon. "Shovel, ax and pick. One dollar a day. Seven days a week—sunup to sundown. We pay on Tuesdays." "That's right," Gideon nodded. The boss said, nodding at the pay shack, "Have them sign or make their mark."

Gideon, Trooper, and Ferdinand Lincoln were with the cutting gang. They went into the six- and eight-inch second growth, standing knee-deep in mud and water, and all day long their double-bladed axes cracked and gouged at the wood. For most of the black men who made up the gangs, their work on the railroad was the first free labor they had ever performed. When the Yankee company set up employment offices in the nearby towns to recruit gangs for construction, the local merchants shook their heads and decided, "A waste of time. Nigger won't work without a whip at his back or a master to own him." It was scandalous, they said, to pay niggers a dollar a day; spoil them and ruin them—who ever heard of such a wage? The Yankee gang bosses and engineers shrugged their shoulders and went on with the hiring. "Anyway," the local people said, "you cain't put a causeway through that swamp, and serve the goddam Yankees right." But strangely enough, the causeway was going through. When the crisscross corduroy of logs and branches sank out of sight, the engineers filled with gravel and started over. When the rains came and made the swamp a tar-like sea of mud and glue, men stood in the ooze waist deep and sank their logs by feel. When the mosquitoes bred and malaria sent the shivering, fever-ridden men out to be hospitalized, the hiring signs went up again. The first casual enthusiasm that the countryside had indulged in when they heard that the railroad was breaking south soon passed; to the former plantation owners, overseers and slave drivers, there was something ominous, foreign and inevitable about this New England formed, New England owned company that was driving a railroad through in the same heedless, incredible manner that Sherman had driven through to the sea.

But for the black men, it was something else. For the first time, Gideon had an inkling of the relationship of labor to the whole of life and civilization. As slaves, he and his people had worked, year in and year out, having nothing, gaining nothing, the way the mule or the ox works. Now the railroad had advertised for a product they wanted to buy; the product was labor; Gideon and his people came and sold their labor for a dollar a day, and out of their labor was coming a conception and a dream, a causeway, shining steel rails, a train screaming in the night. They would go away free men, men with some money, and they in turn would buy. And they would leave behind them what their strength and sweat had built.

Whether or not this right of way could have been built with slave labor, Gideon didn't know; he did know that slaves had never worked like this, even with the lash crossing their backs. His gang cut and trimmed logs for the corduroy. Facing, two men would attack a tree, one low, one high, eight cuts on the young second growth, and then, boomed out and echoing, "Timber, timber!" The slopping crash of the log as it hit the water, the trimming down the line, blow for blow, and then eight men lifting and tossing it onto the mule sledge. The men worked bare to the waist, their black bodies gleaming, muscles rippling. First they sang the old slave work songs; but that was no good; rhythms didn't fit, the pace had changed, and this was no lament. So first without words, the new songs came; they had to sing, and the first words were the simplest threads of thought—"Old wood don't like my ax, old wood don't like my ax—" the words came and the music came . . .

Gideon had grown soft. With the night, his whole body ached, and he had no desire, no thought except to throw himself down on the stiff barracks cot and sleep. Sleep and work and food, and that was all; and he began to ask himself, "Where is learning, rest, books, anything at all but work in a life like this?" The step from slavery bridged a whole era in civilization, but did men stop here?

The food was stew three times a day, meat, potatoes, rice, good enough if unvarying in its sameness. The men stood in line and it was ladled onto tin dishes, the only breaks in a fourteen-hour day. The men slept in long, wooden barracks, hastily thrown up, and old army tents. Kelly, boss of number four gang, told Chief Engineer Rhead, "Give me ten gangs like mine and I'll build you a road to hell." And Rhead, who had been with the engineers during the war, answered, "Hold your water, and you'll find the equivalent right here." Malaria came in one of its recurrent waves, and Rhead's words were borne out; the swamp turned into a pest-ridden oven; day and night the mosquito swarms twisted and hummed. George Rider, one of Gideon's people, came down with the fever, and in four days he was dead. Hannibal Washington and Brother Peter went home with the body, so that the women might see the burying and weep and take some comfort from that. No matter how it was, you paid the price. Gideon went into the gravelling gang, and then he shaved hickory for ties. And one night they heard the scream of a whistle as the work train poked forward. The swamp water sank; the mud dried and cracked; the heat increased but in spite of that conditions were better for work. An apron of gravel and crushed rock dressed up the crisscross corduroy, and steel rails laid a path for the work train. Gideon's head ached fom attempting an understanding of this; Hannibal Washington asked him once:

"Gideon, up north, do white folk work like this?"

"Maybe some do."

"No rest, no play, no time with a woman?"

"Maybe."

"You figure it's right, Gideon?"

"I don't know—maybe I'll find out."

The thing happened while the men were gone. Trooper had a daughter called Jessie, who was fourteen years old, and it happened to her. She could reconstruct the tale only brokenly, incoherently, how she had wandered out onto the old tobacco road, just walking along and daydreaming to herself, when two white men came along driving a mule cart. They had yelled at her, "Hey, you—you come here." She ran across the fields and they chased her. She ran into a patch of bramble, fell, and they pulled her out of there, tore off her clothes, and raped her. They talked about killing her or not killing her, but finally let her go, and she ran home naked and half insane with fear.

When Trooper heard about it, he went half mad himself; his main reaction was violent, he wanted to kill. He said sure as hell itself, he would kill a white man. Gideon and Brother Peter reasoned with him and pleaded with him, "You going to get yourself hanged, sure as God." "Then I will." "What good that going to do?" "Do some good." Gideon said finally, with cold anger, "You're talking like a fool—you'll not do that. Seven weeks we worked in that swamp—what for? Ask yourself what for, Trooper? A man died of malaria and they took him back and buried him. We never lay back and saw the blue sky, never saw a woman, what for, ask yourself that?"

"What for?" Trooper said dully.

"For a new life, damn you, understand that!"

"Sure enough, you talk big, Gideon. Talk mighty big and loud. Go off to Charleston, high and mighty. Eat the fat of the land. Sit with fancy nigger and white folk—"

"You fool! I went to Charleston because I was forced to go to Charleston—I went afraid, small, because there was so much to be feared. There still is, yes—" He put his arm around Trooper and said, "Look a here, man. This is a terrible thing that happened, a sad and terrible thing, a little girl with a wound cut deep into her. But that wound going to heal, Trooper; wounds heal. She'll forget. Give a what-for and a how-come to our own; you got a wife, you got other children. We come back from the swamp work with near a thousand dollars—hear me, Trooper, near a thousand dollars, never was that much money together in the world for a nigger. Enough money to get drunk on, enough money to go a whoring on; sinful things to be bought high and wide and handsome for that money, calico dresses, sweet candy, Lord knows, I could go on, Trooper. That's a temptation, but I spoke to the men and they say, All right, Gideon, put that money away, buy the land. Why for they do that, these old ignorant nigger slave men? Why they got such a hope, such a trust in the future?"

Trooper shook his head miserably.

"Let me tell you why. Future shapes up, slow, like tomorrow, like when that old sun goes down and a man can't sleep. Then he say to himself, never be tomorrow, never come another sunrise, going to be night forever and ever, just twisting and turning and counting all that long, lonesome time when he can't sleep. Well, that time's almost gone; tomorrow's going to be here real soon, sure enough. All the old, evil bad things, they fade out slowly, a nigger is lynched, a poor little nigger girl is mistreated. But they fade out."

Reading to Rachel, Gideon described the school where Jeff was studying. It seemed astonishing to him that the round, careful script should be the only projection of his son; he tried to bridge the gap for himself, more so for Rachel and Jenny and Marcus. When Jenny and Marcus asked to know precisely where Massachusetts was, Gideon could only tell them it was a long distance, a great distance. It was a place where Yankees lived. "Only Yankees?" "Only Yankees, I guess." Gideon said, "Here he tells about the town, listen: 'Worcester is pretty and with many people, a city such a place is called. At first it is frightening but you soon are used to be living here in a city.' "

"Like Charleston?" Marcus asked, though he had only the haziest notion of what Charleston could be like. "Yes, like Charleston, I guess," Gideon replied uncertainly, reading then:

" 'There are fourteen students here at the Presbyterian Free Academy, all of them colored boys like me only most of them orphans who have no mother and father not like me. The Reverend Charles Smith and the Reverend Claude Southwick who is a Unitarian not a Presbyterian teaches us Reading, Writing, Sums, Latin, History and Geography—' "

"What is a Unitarian?"

Gideon didn't know; but he could tell them what geography was and that Latin was a language spoken hundreds of years ago by people who lived in another country. "Do they talk it now?" Gideon wasn't sure, nor could he say whether they planned to send Jeff to that country. He read:

" 'We learn and sleep in a room behind the manse called the annex. The ladys committee do our meals and they have clothes for us to wear. These are clean and good clothes that were worn only a short time. We do work in return. We mow grass, wash windows

and do sweeping and keeping the church clean which we get 10
cents a week for spending. I am lonely for you but happy here.
Ellen tell her I miss her too . . .' "

Rachel wiped her eyes, but Marcus and Jenny lived life in the
north with Jeff, arguing the fascinating points he brought up.
"You see," Gideon said, "how good this is for him—" Gideon could
walk with Jeff's dreams. In letters, he became closer to Jeff than he
ever had been in life; in one of them, he said, "Read the books
Charles Dickens writes. They will teach you much of brotherhood
and of good and bad men."

Before beginning his negotiations over the land, Gideon went to
see Abner Lait. Walking down the road to Abner's place one morning he leaned on the gate and waited for the white man to notice
him. Mrs. Lait came to the door of the house, glanced at Gideon
and then went back inside. Jimmy scuffled up and informed Gideon
that Abner was feeding the hogs.

"What's your name, nigger?" the boy said.

"Gideon Jackson."

"I seen you before."

"That's right," Gideon nodded. "I guess maybe you remember
how I came along here last fall."

"Uh-huh."

"How old are you, boy?" Gideon asked.

"Ten summer."

"Got any schooling?"

The boy grinned and shook his head. "Don't want any neither."

Abner came around from the hog pen and nodded at Gideon.
"Morning."

"Morning, Mr. Abner," Gideon said. "Got a mighty nice corn
stand, I see. Got a few acres of cotton, too. That's going to be a paying crop, a good, solid cash crop, come this year."

"If I get the picking done," Abner said.

"You will."

"Well, that's mighty nice of you to be that optimistic," Abner
said. "Maybe you'd like to come down and help?"

"Maybe I would."

Abner hitched his pants, spat, and rubbed his hands up and down
his pants seat. "Hear you been working on the railroad, Gideon,"
he observed. Peter came up now and Abner's little six-year-old girl,

hanging onto her father's belt and staring at Gideon from a circle of red hair.

"That's right."

"Seems a sure enough come down for an uppity nigger who sat on the Convention."

"Maybe it is, maybe it's not, depending on how you look at it," Gideon smiled.

"Seems like the niggers are going to run the state."

"I wouldn't say that, Mr. Abner."

"You wouldn't?"

Gideon said, "Might I come on in, Mr. Abner? I'm sure enough dry and I'd appreciate a glass of cold water."

"I'll get it," Peter cried, and ran for the well.

"Come in," Abner said shortly, and led the way over to a broad shade tree. He squatted and Gideon let down beside him. Peter brought a tin cup of water, and Gideon drank gratefully. "Got a fine well," he nodded. Abner said, "It stays cool. I keep it shaded." "Nothing like fine cool water." Abner's wife came out on the porch again, stared at them for a moment, and then went inside. Gideon said, "Good times don't come so often you can turn a cold shoulder on them."

"Just how you figure it."

"I figure this is going to be a better time than before the war," Gideon answered, slowly. "Maybe it's going to be hard hoeing for plantation people, but the small farmer'll have a chance. Never did have a chance before."

"Uh-huh."

"Still and all," Gideon said, plucking a stem of dry grass and chewing on it thoughtfully, "good times are one thing, fool's heaven's another." Abner remained silent; he cast an eye at the sun, as if estimating the time Gideon had stayed already. His hound dog came up, sniffed at Gideon, and then stretched out. The children drifted away. Abner's wife called from the house, "Peter—you come here, you!"

"Look at it this way," Gideon said. "Bygones are bygones, but there ain't no man here the war didn't make it almighty hard and sorrowful for. Women at home worked and suffered and hoped; you and me, we came back, rolled up our sleeves, and say, make something out of all this grief. Got a little seed, got an animal or two. Put in some feed and greens. Sure enough, that's a mighty big

ploughing you did for one man, corn and cotton; just about broke
your back over it, I reckon. Well, you got a crop in, crop for a man
to be proud of. But who owns that land you're ploughing, Mr.
Abner?"

"Who owns it?" Abner stared at Gideon. "Damned if I know—
damned if I care. Belonged to Dudley Carwell one time, seems he
lost it to Ferguson White. They say White's moved over to Texas."

"That's right. The land's gone for taxes, every foot and acre
Carwell owned."

"All right, let it go. God knows, I ain't got cash for taxes."

"This is the point," Gideon said quietly. "The Carwell place is
going to be sold at auction in Columbia sometime during October.
I got that from the Federal Commissioner. It will probably go in
thousand acre lots, not in smaller parcels. When it goes, where are
we going to be, Mr. Abner—where're you going to be?"

"Right where I am," Abner said stolidly. "Ain't no goddamn
Yankee going to tell me to get off of here, ain't no goddamn nigger-
owner going to tell me that. I fought this war through—and what
in hell did I get from it? No sir. I'm sitting right here on my ass,
and ain't nobody going to tell me to move!"

"Begging your pardon, Mr. Abner, just look at what you're saying. Nobody going to tell you to get off, that's fine, but that's not
practical. Sheriff come along, what are you going to do? Fight the
law? You going to fight a plantation man with law and order behind him? How can you do that?"

"I don't need a nigger to tell me how."

"All right, but wait a minute, Mr. Abner. How you feel about
niggers, that's your business and don't come into the argument nohow. But let me say, what ever you feel, nigger is not your enemy."

Abner told Gideon coldly, "You can damnwell get to hell out of
here."

"Sure I can," Gideon said, his mouth tightening. "I can get out
of here. Carwell place is knocked down on the auction block, and
then you going to hate the whole world, but what are you going to
do? I'll tell you something, Mr. Abner, whether you want to hear
it or not. Me and my people went down to work in that swamp to
get money to buy land. A man without land in this here country is
no better than a slave, and it don't make much difference, Mr.
Abner, if a slave's a nigger or a white man. We got near a thousand
dollars now, and if we can get a banker to give us a draft against a

mortgage, we can go in there and bid for a few thousand acre lots. Mighty nice feeling that would be, going in there and bidding for your own piece of land."

Abner Lait rocked slowly on his haunches, stared at the ground, and traced curious patterns with his fingers. Minutes went by, the white man saying nothing, just staring at his large, angular hands, at the orange-colored hairs that stood out from the skin, curling like stiff wire, at the scar across his wrist that a Yankee bayonet had made. Watching him, Gideon tried to understand something of the struggle he was having with himself, with a lifetime of heartbreaking contradictions: whom did he hate? what had he fought? for what? A man isn't the same after years of killing, marching, and trying to keep from being killed. A man can come back and get behind his plough again and feed his pigs again, but he isn't the same.

"I got no money," Abner said finally, tiredly, the edge gone from his voice. "Four dollars, sixty cents inside the house, Gideon. That's all."

"You don't need money," Gideon told him. "Takers is what I want, families. Money we got is enough to make things go, or else they'll never go. On this here Carwell place there's twenty-seven colored families and seven white—all of them living on the old acreage, all of them going to get off or be share tenants when the land is sold. Suppose we say eighty, ninety acres of land to a family, more or less, just depending. That includes a piece of scrub for burning, a piece of pasture, a piece of ploughland. Three thousand-acre lots would make out for us, give every man his piece."

"Why do you want me?" Abner asked. "What've I ever done for you? I ain't no nigger lover or goddamn Scalawag that you got to come here licking my ass."

"That's right," Gideon agreed.

"How come, then?"

"All right," Gideon said. "Look at it this way—this here South of ours got four million niggers, eight million white folk. Right here in South Carolina, the black man's got a little edge in population. Things ain't ever going to be again the way they was; the war killed the old way. Out of the Convention and the elections is coming a new life for this southland. What's that going to be, Mr. Abner, that new life? Don't look like much from here, same rotten old shacks folks lived in before the war, same bad feeling, same hate, same dark ignorance. Where's that new life? Well, it don't happen, can't just happen of its own wishing; nothing does. Everything's made. Got a railroad causeway through the swamp because men went in there and worked—talking didn't do it. Well, same thing here. This is a good land, this country here, a sweet land, full of milk and honey if you work it right. Ain't cold, like in the Yankee country, ain't full of sickness, like down in the river country. Got good people in it too, good white folks, good black folks—"

"Until the goddamn Yankees ruined it," Abner said.

"Did they now? War's a sad thing, sad and wasteful. You took up a gun, I took up a gun, and in a way of speaking you and me fought against each other. Why for? Sure the Yankees come in here, freed the niggers and maybe half the plantation owners see themselves ruined. But how many plantations are there? Just look around you—everywhere the eyes rest, there's the same old Carwell place. Me, I'm a free man instead of just a nigger slave; you got the same as before the war, maybe better. Never had no hope of owning your own piece before the war. Every inch of good land was part of some plantation—poor white could have some swamp or patch of pines to raise a crop. The Yankees left us the land, and maybe a little more hope than before."

Abner stirred the dirt with his fingers. "Go on," he said.

"All right. What's this future going to be except what we make it? And it won't be no good unless we make it for black and white the same. Ain't no end of hate here unless the future belongs to both of us. We're stronger to buy the land if you come in, if Max Bromly comes in, if the Carson brothers come in, if Fred McHugh comes in."

"They won't."

"Maybe they will, Mr. Abner. This here world's changing. Now we got a little school up among my people. No reason why your children shouldn't come to school there. Some day, Government'll come in and build a real fine school hereabouts. Nothing stopping your children going to school with mine excepting one's white, the other's black."

Abner shook his head.

"That's something to think about, Mr. Abner. Takes time, I'll admit that. But there's no reason you shouldn't come in on this land thing."

"I don't need no goddamn nigger charity," Abner said stubbornly.

"It ain't no charity to strengthen my hand. If I come to the banker and say white folks are in this with me, then I got a so much stronger hand."

"Maybe so." After a moment, Abner said, "How do you know they'll sell us the land?"

"I spoke to the Yankee land agent. He says it'll be a fair auction, gone off to the highest bidder."

"Suppose you're lying?"

"Suppose I am," Gideon said, and then they looked at each other, and for the first time Abner smiled.

"Who's going to do the buying?"

"My people want me to talk for them. That's not set. We could discuss the matter."

"I'd settle on you."

"Then you'll come in with us?" Gideon asked.

"I'll come in."

"I'd be pleased and proud, Mr. Abner," Gideon said, "to shake hands with you on that."

Abner Lait shook hands with a Negro for the first time in his life.

After two hours of talk with the Carson brothers, they came in and gave Gideon sixty-five dollars to add to the fund. Max Bromly shook his head to all Gideon's arguments; he'd have nothing to do with niggers, and that was the end of it. Fred McHugh came in, and so did his brother-in-law, Jake Sutter. It took three days and pleading enough with Gideon's own people. "What for we need white folks?" they demanded. The money was theirs. Hadn't one of them died in the swamp?

Gideon told them. He repeated it over and over. At least half of them were on his side to begin, and finally the rest were persuaded. Gideon was triumphant, vibrantly triumphant for the first time in months. Now, holding Rachel in his arms, it was like old times, so long ago.

And then, four mornings after Gideon had been to see him, Abner Lait came walking up the hill with his two boys. He told Gideon, "I talked it over with Helen, and she thinks they ought to have some spelling."

The boys twisted, squealed and kicked. Abner clouted them and said they'd damnwell mind, or he'd know why. His own shame at coming this way to niggers was something he had to stand up to, and Gideon, recognizing that, made it as easy as possible. He said, "Thank you, Mr. Abner. This is a beginning."

Abner nodded, stood around a while without saying anything, and then turned and left.

7. HOW GIDEON JACKSON JOURNEYED FAR AFIELD AND HOW HE MADE BOTH A BARGAIN AND A CHOICE

Carl Robbins, vice president of the First National Bank of Columbia, shook his head and told Gideon, no, he was not interested. Hardly. No, completely uninterested, smiling slightly to convey his opinion of such an affair. He had a heavy bald head, Mr. Robbins, sandy fringes of hair, tiny blue eyes, a roll of flesh in the back of his neck that seemed to support his skull. He said to Gideon, patiently:

"You see, Jackson, things are not done so simply; if they were, we should have chaos. You come to me with a thousand dollars, tell me that you represent some motley lot of niggers and white trash, squatters on the Carwell place, and suggest that I give you a draft on this bank to buy with at the public auction. That is completely fantastic."

"Not just a draft," Gideon argued. "The same sum you advance will be a mortgage—"

"Come now, Jackson," Robbins interrupted. "Be sensible. These are bad times; one hesitates about taking any mortgages, much less a mortgage on land that doesn't exist. What kind of security are a few footloose niggers?"

"Please, sir, Mr. Robbins," Gideon said, "we are not footloose. We have been on the land, this land, all our lives, most of us, worked it, took out three crops on our own. If you would only come over and see the Carwell place you would think differently, I am sure."

"I'm not used to having niggers tell me how to think," Robbins said.

"Mr. Robbins, sir, I didn't mean that. I am acting in good faith and honestly, believe me, sir. Our only hope is to own a few acres of land."

"I don't see that at all," Mr. Robbins said impatiently, looking at his watch, and nodding at the guard who was standing a little distance away, outside of the enclosure. "If you show good faith and a desire to work, whoever buys the land will keep you on to work it. As a matter of fact, I don't approve of niggers owning land; spoils them. I'm sorry, Jackson, but I'm a busy man—" And at that moment the guard came, took Gideon's arm, and led him out.

Rachel said to him, "It'll be all right, Gideon, mind me—sure enough it'll come out all right," and Gideon heard her with part of his mind, wondering how many of his people thought that way, always today and not tomorrow, the bone and marrow of slavery not being a thing that is shed overnight, like chains. He had come back miserable and beaten, and Rachel was only glad to have him home. He began, almost fiercely, "Don't you see—" but broke off when Rachel said, "It'll come out all right, you setting your mind to it, Gideon honey."

Then he began to smile, looking at her, the roundness of her, the woman of her, the flat cheeks, the small turned-up nose, the skin with just enough sheen on it to catch the light of the fire, the note in her voice as she asked, "What for you laughing at me, Gideon?"

"Not laughing, honey child," and thinking to himself how strange were links and reasons and the simple way of life becoming so incredibly complex—the fact of this woman here, his wife, whom he loved so warmly and completely at this moment, the fact of her in relation to a poor black man snatched from the African coast once so long ago, the fact of her in relation to Jeff, to himself—to a continuing, pulsating stream that made up humanfolk, climbing and reaching, joyous and tired . . .

"What you thinking, Gideon?" she said. Jenny climbed into his arms. Marcus lay in front of the fire. Rachel said, "Time you got bedded, Jenny."

Gideon asked Jenny, "What for now, pigeon?"

"Brother Fox." "Old Brother Fox—I told you all I know, honest to May," Gideon said. Jenny wanted to know, "How come he never have to do with Brother Tortoise." "Mind as he did," Gideon said. "Brother Fox being mighty smart, smartest old man in the piney woods, he wouldn't consider Brother Tortoise. Old Tortoise got a shell so thick no one ever credit him with smartness—" Rachel watched Gideon, half listening to the story, as Marcus listened with half an ear, an old tale being that way, not asking too much attention, but being good for the sure and specific qualities it always contained. There was a knock at the door and Rachel let James Allenby in. He sat down and said nothing until Gideon finished the story, it being a flexible thing he adjusted to Jenny's falling asleep. The child clung to his neck as he set her down on the pallet. Marcus dozed by the fire, a comfortable, half-grown animal. Allenby said finally, after commenting on the weather outside and on how fine Rachel looked:

"What happened in Columbia was to be expected, Gideon."

"I suppose so."

"Have you considered what to do now?"

"Charleston, I guess."

"They won't be more receptive."

Gideon said, "There's Boston, New York, Philadelphia—"

"Onto the other side of nowhere," Rachel thought, and Allenby reflected, "You'll have that land, won't you, Gideon?"

"I'll try."

"I think you will, Gideon," the old man said. "In the way of things, after you spent that night with me in my cabin, I was sure you would go your way fully. What's going to stop you, Gideon? I think nothing. Only don't do the thing for doing it; power's no good as of itself. Keep coming home."

"How do you mean that?"

Allenby shrugged and smiled. "I'm an old man talking, Gideon, and maybe I talk too much. If you go up north and see Yankees, remember this—they aren't cut of a cloth. Some of them hate a black man worse than any southerner, and to those people we are alien, strange creatures with black skins. Even to southern folk who hate us, we are never alien, but as much a part of this land as the piney woods and the cotton and tobacco. Also, you will meet Yankees, a few, who have turned themselves into something strange and wonderful; they will sit at a table with you and take your hand and the color of your skin will no longer matter. Trust those people, Gideon; accept them for what they are. For two generations they fought to make us free because they believed in the brotherhood of man; don't credit the lies that you will hear about them."

Gideon nodded; the old man leaned over, put a hand on Gideon's knee, and said, "Don't be too proud to take, Gideon. If there were none who took and none who gave, we would be like savages. You will go for more important things, but if some books should come your way, some paper, some slates and chalk—we need them so much, Gideon."

"I'll remember," Gideon said.

Gideon's learning continued. In Columbia he found a copy of Blackstone's *Commentaries on the Laws of England*. Old and battered, he bought it for sixty cents. Anderson Clay sent him a dog-eared edition of Paine's *Rights of Man*, a book which for all its vagueness, for all its being out of context with Gideon's knowledge and experience, became for him a constant wonder, a pool of astonishment that never dried up. Allenby had some poems of Poe which he gave to Gideon, but Gideon reading them was troubled and confused. "No one is alive," he said. He was happier with Emerson, and Allenby said, "If you could meet him, Gideon—"

It was in early fall that Gideon came back to Charleston, came back to the Carters, who welcomed him so gladly, and then walked into the house of Francis Cardozo, who took his hand, smiling rather strangely, and said, "So you're back again, Gideon."

"I'm back."

"A little older and a little wiser?"

"Some of each," Gideon agreed. In Cardozo's parlor he sat stiffly, his hands between his knees. He had a glass of wine and a few sweet cakes; the room seemed smaller than he remembered it, Cardozo seemed smaller too. Gideon talked slowly and carefully, and Cardozo said nothing until Gideon came to the incident of the Columbia banker.

"Were you surprised, Gideon?"

"No, I wasn't too surprised. I half expected that to happen."

"And probably," Cardozo reflected, "the same thing would happen here. You know, Gideon, according to his lights, Robbins was not too unfair. What can you present? A few dollars of cash, your own word, the supposed backing of a few penniless colored and poor white families and a very vague and dream-like future."

"All futures are dreams," Gideon said.

"More or less, I'll grant that. But can't you see, Gideon, that this problem of land exists everywhere in the south, that it's the single great problem upon which our future rests. How is it solved? A year ago this past March, Thaddeus Stevens introduced his Land-Division bill into Congress. What was his proposal? To take the great rebel plantations, break them down, and give each freedman forty acres and fifty dollars for a homestead. Wait a moment, I want to read you precisely what Stevens himself said on the subject—" Cardozo went to his desk, shuffled among some papers, and then turned back to Gideon and read:

"This plan would, no doubt, work a radical reorganization in Southern institutions, habits and manners. It is intended to revolutionize their principles and feelings. This may startle feeble minds and shake weak nerves. So do all great improvements in the political and moral world. The Southern States have been despotisms, not governments of the people. It is impossible that any practical equality of rights can exist where a few thousand men monopolize the whole landed property. How can republican institutions, free schools, free churches, free social intercourse, exist in a mingled community of nabobs and serfs, of the owners of twenty-thousand-acre manors with lordly palaces, and the occupants of narrow huts?"

Cardozo crossed back to Gideon now and spread his hands, "All right, there it is. As Stevens puts it, we, with our Convention and our new Constitution created a contradiction, for unless there is a free basis for all our fine proposals, what good are they? And that basis means free, land-owning farmers instead of landless serfs and peons."

"And what do you propose?" Gideon demanded. "I, at least, have a plan for a few of these people, a practical plan that can be made to work."

"And I have a plan for twelve million of them," Cardozo smiled, leaning back against a chair, his hands behind him. "When Thaddeus Stevens died last month, we lost a great, good fighter and friend. But he pointed out the way—make it plain to the people, enforce their power to vote, educate them, give them honest representatives, and legally in the halls of this state's legislature and this country's Congress, fight for legal, universal land division."

"And meanwhile the people suffer," Gideon said.

"Meanwhile, they suffer. That's right. We alleviate their suffering all we can, but in the large overall picture of the thing, there is not much we can do."

"Still and all," Gideon said, "I intend to buy land. If I can't find the money here, I'll find it in Boston, or in New York."

For a while, Cardozo just looked at Gideon, bending back over the chair; then he sat down; then he said, "I'll make a bargain with

you, Gideon. I know Isaac Went, a Boston banker, an old abolitionist, and a man who doesn't put a silk thread on every dollar he
lets go of. I'll give you a letter to him, and, I think, a letter that
will carry some weight. I'll also give you a letter to Frederick Douglass, who might be able to help you with this if other things fail.
In return, I want your promise that you'll stand for the state legislature at the next election."

"Suppose I let you know tomorrow," Gideon said.

"All right. Come for dinner tomorrow."

The next day, Gideon saw two Charleston bankers; one of them
was Colonel Fenton, whom he had met at the dinner Stephen
Holms gave. When he saw Cardozo again, Gideon expected the
question:

"What happened?"

"What you thought would happen," Gideon said, smiling a little.

"At least maintain the nigger reputation for mirth. He's happy
poor and he's happy rich."

"I'm doing that," Gideon said sourly. "I'm not unhappy."

"And about the legislature?"

"If anyone wants me," Gideon agreed, "I'll go in. I'll try not to
realize what I was a year ago or five years ago," and then added,
"Considering what I've read of laws and lawmaking, I can't do
very much worse."

"I'm glad, Gideon," Cardozo said.

"And I ain't—you see, I still talk like a swamp nigger. If I can,
I'd like to leave for the north mighty soon—tomorrow?"

"I suppose you could, tomorrow."

The train that carried Gideon Jackson through the night, north
from Washington, D. C., roared into a new world. That was in the
exact sense of the word. All that had happened to him until now, in
his thirty-seven years of life, storm and eruption, had been within
the world he knew, the southland that had borne him, bred him
and fed him, whipped him and gouged and cut at him; yet that land
was one and the same; he knew that land, the erosion, the darkness
and ignorance, the wasted soil and life, the great feudal homes
looming over the sub-strata of white peons and black slaves. And
knowing that, there had been a warmth and goodness wherever he
went in the south, a sameness. In this new world, there was no sameness; Washington, the city of giant white palaces and muddy streets,

was like nothing he had ever experienced; now he sat in a railroad car among white people who read their newspaper, spoke to one another, and neither minded nor cared that a black man was among them. In early fall, it was cold here. When it rained, the rain whipped angrily and savagely. When people spoke, they talked in hard, clipped, hurrying tones.

"Grant, that's a general, not a statesman." "And what, mister, is wrong with a general being president." "I don't like it." "No, maybe you'd like another term of Johnson?" "Don't put words in my mouth, mister, I do my own thinking." "Not much of it." "Wheat—wheat's at sixty-two." "Is that your *Herald*, mister? Mind if I read it?" "I got two sons in Chicago, believe me, they're doing all right."

Gideon dozed off to the sound of those voices. Later, he woke when a conductor came through, blinking off the smelly kerosene lamps. The plush seat was hard and uncomfortable; the train stopped every few miles, jolting, starting again. People sat down next to him, then rose and left the train, a white man, a white woman, a young girl . . . And the next day, there were the Jersey flats, the sprawling, ugly city of Newark, and finally a disgorging at Jersey City with New York just across the river. On the ferry, Gideon gripped the rail and stared; boats on the river like dry sticks on a pond, ferries, steamers laying their lush black smoke on the river, like charcoal marks on shiny white paper, sailing craft of all sizes, angry little tugs, strings of barges, and across the river the mass of houses—just pluck out a handful, and there was Charleston, another handful and there Columbia, not the queen of cities but a great, nursing mother. This was what Whitman meant; this was the meat and blood of countless thousands.

Staring, Gideon thought of the dogged, slogging, uninspired Yankee armies that had pushed their way into the south, cut to pieces a hundred times and closing their ranks each time, clumsily, foolishly, painfully learning the art of war, and finally rocking and splitting the whole southland with their battle hymn of freedom. This was it, these small, colorless folk who crowded the ferry, the crowds on the streets, hurrying, minding their own business, the jumble, confusion, rush, roar, clatter, the goods piled high on the wharves, the dirty streets, the strings of pushcarts and sidewalk stands, the carriages, carts, wagons, vans pushing past each other in the streets, the pall of smoke over the red brick buildings, the clatter of tongues. The nations were here, and no one minded or noticed the tall black man. Gideon had two and a half hours between trains; he walked from the river to the financial district; he passed through acres of hastily erected tenements. The day was as blisteringly hot as the day before had been unnaturally cool; this was weather to keep pace with the city, the blustering, cocky, dirty, miserable, confident metropolis that was already becoming one of the wonders of the world. It rained and it cleared; the streets ran with water and dirt where they were paved and became sluices of mud where they were not. Olive-skinned children sailed bits of wood in the gutters; other children sold newspapers, running and shrieking along the sidewalks. Gideon tried to understand; this was the city where a hundred Negroes were murdered in insane mob rage. This was also the city where working men, by the thousands, laid down their tools, gave their own money to buy uniforms and guns, and knowing nothing of war, nothing of death and slaughter, marched hundreds of miles to the south so that black men might be free. This was the city that had spawned regiment after regiment, year after year, to fight in the war—yet here too were the worst draft riots, the worst anti-war riots that the country had ever known. Gideon looked, wondered, and saw too much . . .

Boston was more simple, more what he was used to in the way of a city. The quiet bay street where Isaac Went lived might have been a street in Charleston; there were green trees shading it. The houses were old, and being old, unaggressive; under the clean white paint, the woodwork was cracked and worm-eaten. In response to Gideon's uncertain tap with the knocker, a starched maid came to the door and said politely, who would he see? Mr. Isaac Went, if he might. "Won't you come in, please, sir," the maid said, a blue-eyed girl with corn-colored hair and Vermont in her voice.

His hat in his hands, Gideon entered the house. Just beyond the door was a small vestibule, two facing oval-framed mahogany mirrors, four prim mahogany chairs and two small black tables, covered with Chinese lacquer and design. Walnut doors, opened by the maid, disclosed a fine old staircase that divided the parlor from the dining room. The rooms were large, but low-ceilinged, in contrast to the great, high ceilings of the south. Here was, Gideon saw, as clear an evidence of wealth as in Stephan Holms' house; yet there was a division, a split; he was expected here, for all that they had not known of his coming. The maid said to him:

"Won't you sit down, please, sir, and I'll tell Mr. Went you're here—what did you say your name was?"

"Gideon Jackson."

"Just Mr. Gideon Jackson?"

"With a letter from Mr. Francis Cardozo?"

"Uh-huh," the maid said. "Just sit down." Her politeness was blunt, taking him for granted. She made no effort to put him at ease, yet he was more at ease than ever before in the house of a white man. He glanced around the room, noticed the two large, comfortable wing chairs that flanked the fireplace, rejected them, took a step toward the couch that backed on the other wall, caught himself, tested a broad-bottomed Chippendale chair, and then rose quickly to his feet as he heard footsteps. It was about five o'clock in the afternoon now, and he wondered whether he had been right to call at such an hour. He stood stiffly and awkwardly as Isaac Went came into the room.

Isaac Went was a small man; standing against Gideon, the top of his bald head would just touch Gideon's string tie. He had a sandy little mustache, a thin mouth and a pointed chin. Now he wore a smoking jacket over black pants, silk slippers, and a stiff white collar with a black tie. His walk was nervous; birdlike, striking toward Gideon, he thrust out his hand and said:

"What is your name? Jackson? Gideon Jackson? The girl said you have a letter from somebody, couldn't remember who. It's a wonder she remembers her head's on her shoulders."

"The letter, sir, is from Francis Cardozo," Gideon said.

"Cardozo? You from the south?"

"South Carolina," Gideon said.

"Well, what is Cardozo doing? Making a bigwig out of himself in politics? Where's the letter?"

Gideon gave it to him. Tearing it open, he read it quickly, and then looked at Gideon again. "Cardozo thinks a lot of you," he said. "Why don't you sit down? Do you want a drink?" He nodded toward one of the wing chairs, meanwhile taking a decanter and two glasses. Gideon sat down. "This is sherry," Went said. "Do you like sherry?"

Gideon nodded.

"Yes or no," Went shrugged. "Most black people don't give two

damns about liquor, you know. Never had a chance to get a taste
for it. That's all it is, a taste; I used to drink whisky, now sherry. I
still miss the whisky, I'm not in good health. Will you have a
cigar?"

Gideon shook his head.

"All right. You don't mind if I smoke? No—I don't give a damn
if you do mind. When my wife was alive, I saved these damn things
for after dinner." He took out a long, black cigar and lit it, stretched
out in the wing chair, and blew smoke at the mantle. "It says
here—" he referred to the letter—"that you sat in the Convention.
You must tell me about that. I couldn't make anything out of the
newspaper stories. First tell me about this land scheme of yours—
no, save that for dinner. I want Doc Emery to hear that, he'll be
here, he's just stupid enough to swing the balance. Tell me about
the Convention now—"

Gideon told him. With the little man, Gideon was on flat, unruffled ground. Went spat, argued, disagreed, lost his temper and
yelled at Gideon; but always as one man to another. Gideon was
not a black man; for the first time in his life, whether with colored
people or white people, Gideon completely forgot the color of his
skin; for the first time in his life he was talking to a man who by a
long and studied psychological process, a period of training that
must have begun in his earliest childhood, had conditioned himself
to racial democracy in clean and simple terms. For Went, subjec-
tively, Gideon was a man; he could not think otherwise, willingly
or unwillingly, anymore than the average American could think in
Latin. When he yelled at him, in relation to the land question in
debate at the Convention:

"You were a fool, Jackson, you and all the rest! Stevens was alive
then; did you consult him? Did you ask for support from Washington? No, all by yourself you were going to remake civilization!
That's Cardozo! That's all your narrow, cultured imbeciles! Well,
you missed a historic opportunity! You could have destroyed the
plantations then and there—you didn't—"

When he yelled at Gideon that way, he was screaming at his
equal, not at a black man, not at a white man, no courtesy here, no
barriers. Later, he gave Gideon a hint as to the background of this,
telling him, "I come of Abolitionist people, Mr. Jackson. Maybe
I'm not the best product they've produced. I sat on my behind when
others were in there, fighting and dying. But I did a little; my money

was useful. Did you know that old Osawatomie Brown sat right there where you're sitting, pleading for money, for guns, for powder, for men—yes, he was going to march through the south to glory and sweep away slavery like the wrath of the Lord. And I gave him money and guns. That seems like a thousand years ago, doesn't it, when men spoke so glibly of doing away with that rotten disease? And then we bled ourselves dry for four years. Right there, old Brown sat, with his beard, his eyes burning—would you like to hear his words? I remember his words—'The Lord God has not deserted us, Mr. Went,' he said. 'But we, Mr. Went, we pitiful, small, frightened, crawling creatures have deserted the Lord God of Hosts, the God of our fathers who led the children of Israel from the land of Egypt.' Those were his words as nearly as I can remember them, Jackson. He was sitting where you are sitting; Emerson was sitting here; I was standing. Waldo looked at me and I looked at him. You understand, Jackson, that old John Brown was a great man, a great and misunderstood man. The old man could give people the power of belief. I am not a believer; I pride myself on my atheism even more than Doc Emery prides himself on his; but right here, at that time, with old Osawatomie talking, I believed. God was at my right hand, my great-grandfather's God, the grand and terrible old man of a God who came over to this land with the Pilgrims. Have I offended you, Mr. Jackson? I don't know if you're a believer. So many black people are—"

"You haven't offended me," Gideon said slowly.

They talked a while longer; then Went suggested that both he and Gideon lie down for a while before dinner. "I have the habit—I'm getting old. You, you're a young man, Jackson, but you might enjoy a nap." Gideon pointed out that as yet he had no place to stay in Boston, that Went might suggest a hotel for colored people. "Of course you'll stay here," Went said. Gideon objected weakly, but Went brushed his objections aside. "Douglass stays with me," he said. "It ought to be damn well good enough for you." Then the maid came and led Gideon upstairs to his room.

"The effect," Gideon said, "of the two years right after the war was to wake us up. The bad black codes were made to drive us straight back to slavery. You see, the planters felt they could just push away the Union victory, and they were almost right. But it won't happen a second time. We made a good and an honest alliance with the poor whites; we're united now, and we got our eyes open. We got the power, and we mean to hold onto it."

There were three of them at the dinner table, Isaac Went, the banker; Dr. Norman Emery, who had made a name for himself and Boston with his pioneering in the field of abdominal surgery; and Gideon. Emery was a tall, lean, dark-eyed man; he wore a pointed beard and pince-nez on a black ribbon; his appearance was deceptive, aloof, disinterested; by blood and marriage he was related to the Lowells, the Emersons, the Lodges. He had an incisive mind, a knife-like subtle humor with which he cut at Went constantly. As Gideon noticed soon enough, he was a humane man, though parsimonious and watchful of his humanity. Between him and Went, both widowers, there was a warm yet wary bond. Now Emery asked Gideon:

"But by what means, Mr. Jackson, do you intend to hold onto the power?"

"In three ways," Gideon said. "First, by the ballot. There on every count we got the planters beat, twenty votes to every one they can find. Second, we are going to educate. All we need is ten years and in that time we raise up a whole generation of educated children. That, Dr. Emery is going to be our biggest gun. The planters taught us that way back, when they made it a crime for a slave to want education, even to learn himself. Third way is the land, like I said, like I told you. We're a planting people down there, all of us; we ain't—have not got the mills you got here. Folk live off the soil; man with a plough in his hands has bread and shortening in his mouth. When we get the land, when we parcel it out, when we set up a nation of free farmers down there, like you got here, then we stand on our own feet and talk loud and sure. Once that land's our own, we are not going to give it up, never."

"All right," Went said. "Granted your utopian conception of a new south, granted all your fine dreams of schools. Do you want a tot of brandy, Emery?"

"I told you it's bad for your heart. I'm sick of telling you that."

"All right. I have little enough heart. Granted all you say, Jackson, it adds up to a legalistic projection of the future. Business is another matter. If you were to come to me asking for charity, I might help you, I might not, depending on many things. Understand, I'm not a soft-hearted man, not a sentimentalist."

Emery said, "I think he realizes that, Isaac."

"But you come with a fantastic scheme. Your people earned a little money; with that money you intend to undertake a staggering land venture, a venture that would require at least fifteen dollars of mortgage money for every dollar you propose to invest. And what have I to go by, a handful of former slaves, a few poor whites, men who were recently members of the rebel army, and some good intentions. You ask me to invest money in an unknown quantity and quality. Is that reasonable, Jackson? I put it up to you." He lit a cigar; Emery leaned back and watched Gideon, smiling a little. Hopelessness made a hot, heavy load inside of Gideon; he had come this far; he had spent part of the money. A dollar was something you broke your heart for. A man died for a dollar. A railroad ticket cost so many dollars. How far he had gone by now—and how much farther could he go? Was Cardozo right, completely? Was all progress born out of suffering, endless suffering, a mighty burden carried by the poor for ever and ever?

"Maybe it is not reasonable," Gideon said. "I know very little, nothing, I guess, about business. But I know cotton and I know rice. All my life I seen the cotton plant grow, seen the bolls burst, seen the black man out in the field doing the picking. Show me a cotton seed, and I'll tell you quality. Show me rice and I'll tell you where it growed, highland or lowland. I know that, believe me. I know something else; here you Yankees got a way of making cotton cloth. All over this New England of yours, the mills are building. How you going to spin that cotton if no one's growing the bolls? Want the planters to grow it? That'll take time; they'll have to break us before they grow cotton the old way. And what's the price going to be with a few planters controlling it? You ask what security you got from my people—just this. This is a cotton-hungry land, a cotton-hungry world. There ain't been a real good cotton crop in four years now. It's a seller's market. Give my people the land; let them set an example; let them show Carolina it can be done, the way the black man showed it with rice on the sea islands before the Government turned its back on them and took away the land, the same land they seized fighting rebels who wanted to destroy this Union. If you do it, if you not afraid, then others not afraid. Give us five years of our own land, and we'll break our backs putting in the cotton; we'll break our backs picking it. We'll pay you off, every cent and with a profit. You ever seen niggers work? If you been down the south in the old slave days, then you seen how niggers could work with a lash on their back. Well, I tell you this, I tell you a free nigger on his own land can work twice as hard. I know. Believe me, Mr. Went, I don't come asking for charity. I ain't too proud. Old teacher, learning the children down among my people, he said to me, Gideon, don't be proud. The children need books, paper, if they give, take and don't be proud. But this is different; this is not charity. I pledge you that, with all my word of honor."

Gideon finished; he had never spoken so heatedly before to white men, never at such length; embarrassed and uneasy, he sat and stared at the tablecloth. Dr. Emery studied his fingernails. The long while of silence was punctuated by the ticking of the tall grandfather clock in the corner. Then Went tapped the ash from his cigar and said:

"How big is this Carwell place, Jackson?"

"Twenty-two thousand acres and some little more."

Emery whistled. Went nodded slowly. "You don't know," he said. "If you know, you forget. This whole god damned war is forgotten."

"In the old country," Emery remarked, "that would be a dukedom, a nice-sized dukedom."

"What kind of land?"

"At least half is good acreage," Gideon answered. "The rest is brushwood, piney woods, some pasturage and a piece of swamp."

"There's a house on it, isn't there?"

"The big plantation house. The Carwells lived in it only on and off; mostly they lived in Charleston."

"Do you think anyone would buy the house, buy it as a serviceable plantation house?"

Gideon shook his head. "It's too big—planters who hold their land are just holding on. I don't guess there's that much free money in the state."

"Do you know the evaluation on the place, land and house and all?"

"The Federal agent put the prewar valuation, less slaves, at four hundred and fifty thousand dollars. At auction, they reckon it to bring five dollars an acre. They're going to break it into twenty-two thousand-acre sections, and some will go for more and some for less."

"You say you have some thirty-odd families. Three thousand acres is a good deal. I've known Massachusetts men to run a good farm with twenty or thirty acres and put money in the bank to boot. And this isn't the best soil in the world."

"That's right, sir," Gideon agreed. "We got good soil. But the sections'll be only about half working land. Men'll clear, but that's slow work. Then we do different kind of farming from you folks up here. You got dairy land here; aside from the corn and greens we eat, aside from a hog or two, we got to raise a cash crop. You can't make money out of cotton unless you put in fifteen, twenty acres."

"How would you market it?"

"Buy an old gin, old baler, plenty of them. The railroad's coming through, and there'll be loading with a ten-mile haul."

"Got mules?"

"Got a few. We can buy more."

Went turned to Emery and asked, "What do you think, doc?"

"I've seen you lose your money on worse things."

"Will you go in for a third?"

"I'm not a banker," Emery smiled.

"You have more money than I—and you can't take it with you when you go."

"But it's nice having now."

"Will you go in for a third if I guarantee?"

"If you guarantee, why do you want my third?"

"I want companionship," Went said resignedly. "This is the most damnfool thing I ever indulged in."

"You can't take it with you either," Emery said.

"That's right. Look, Jackson, you're costing me just three times what old Osawatomie did—and I don't know if you're half the man he was. All right; I'll give you a draft for fifteen thousand dollars. Don't thank me. Tell us something about yourself for a change, now that's done."

Went was more things than one man. After Emery left, he sat until far into the morning talking with Gideon; he smoked his long black cigars, he drank too much brandy. Huddled in his dressing gown, the little man told Gideon:

"I'm sixty-seven years old, son, and alone. So I look back most of the time. When I was your age, Gideon, there were still soldiers of the revolution alive; we were a vigorous breed here in New England then. Think about that. We came here with the word of God and the law of God, a staff in our hands and unsmiling lips, and we scratched a living from this inhospitable and rocky land.

And we did great things, Gideon; in our meeting houses, democracy became a thing that lived and breathed. The old prophets walked with us, and in the revolution our farmers and fishermen fought with a living, just God peering over their shoulders. That's all forgotten now, isn't it? I'll die soon, Emery soon, Waldo growing old, Thoreau a recluse, Whittier hidden away, Longfellow drooling inanities—where is all our glory? This Brooklyn man, Whitman, roars like a savage, but loud and clear enough; there are others while we begin to sit and contemplate our navels. We have just a little spark left, Gideon; old Thad Stevens was right when he left New England and went to Pennsylvania. But don't forget that while we lived we did great things. It was our song, 'Mine eyes have seen the glory of the coming of the Lord.' Well, come upstairs with me—"

Gideon followed him; Went walked slowly and tiredly, pausing on the landing to catch his breath. They went into a boy's room, and Gideon saw that it had been a long time unused. There were stacks of books, notebooks, a mineral collection, two stuffed owls, a pencil drawing of a young girl, a pair of lacrosse sticks, Indian moccasins, a cleverly carved schooner model. Went said:

"He died in the Wilderness, Gideon, on the second day of the battle. Afterwards, I spoke to his captain and he told me about it. The boy was wounded three times, twice in one arm, once in the head, and he stayed in the battle. Gideon, maybe five hundred times I've sat downstairs in front of the fire, trying to understand, trying to reach the boy, put myself inside of him, and see why he should stay in a battle, cut all to pieces, bleeding, dying on his feet. Gideon, you're a young man, but you've got something inside you. You'll be a leader of your people; Gideon, understand us, don't cut yourself off from us—whatever happens."

"Whatever happens," Gideon nodded.

"All right. Now I'm going to have these books crated, everything here crated. His toys and childhood books are in the attic, you can have those too—"

"I don't feel right about taking—," Gideon began.

"That's nonsense. I haven't been in here for a year. I keep my part of the boy inside of me, I don't need this trash. You can make some use of it, and that's as it should be. If I'm in for fifteen thousand dollars, I'll be in for twenty slates and a bin of chalk. Just tell me where to have it sent, and I'll take care of the rest."

Gideon tried to thank him, but it was not easy. Falling asleep in the ancient four-poster bed, the roof eaves cutting down over his head to a moonlit window, Gideon thought long and wonderingly of the many things that had happened, the many faces men may have, notwithstanding the color of their skins, and the many directions in which they went. The hallelujah song was not something that roared up; it came quietly and slowly. In logical and scientific analysis, all things were answerable but one, that being why at least a few men should find their only happiness and sustenance in a dream of brotherhood.

The next day, before going on to Worcester to see Jeff, Gideon paid a visit to Dr. Emery's dispensary. There, the suave and polished gentleman had vanished; a white-gowned, efficient scientist with two young assistants were waiting on a room and corridor packed full of patients. This was a part of Boston that reminded Gideon of New York, shacks, crumbling houses, dirty streets, poverty, poor Irish and poor Poles and poor Italians. Emery's dispensary was an old house, repaired, painted a clean cream throughout. Gideon sat in the examination room and watched the doctor. A boy with a sunken chest and misshapen bones—

"You see this, Jackson?" The boy naked, eight years old, standing there with his arms crossed, shivering. "We don't know what it is; I have a dozen cases every week, only among the poor. I have my own name for it—Maleficio Paupertatis, sufficiently descriptive."

He ran his hand over the boy's skin. "All right, son, put on your clothes. You see, Jackson, the ills of society have their different faces. We fought and died to free your people while our own cesspool was bred right here. It is not pretty, is it, when we who call ourselves civilized cannot provide free medicine, no, cannot even provide a little adequate research so that we may understand this black art called medicine. Here, in this rich land, people sicken and die of starvation, of the lack of fresh air, sunlight. Charity, which is what I dispense, Jackson, is a nauseous, fungus growth, and sometimes I think my illustrious neighbors here in this town are right when they keep their pockets sewn tight."

Afterwards, Emery asked Gideon about Jeff. "You're sure he wants to be a doctor?"

"How sure can a boy of sixteen be?" Gideon said. "He's a smart boy, I don't say that just because he's my son."

"Well, to get an education in this country is practically impossible. Our medical schools do not admit that a black man can either be sick or heal the sick. In time, when you've created your utopia down there in Carolina, I presume you'll take care of that. However, that's still in the future. If he passes the examination, he can be admitted to the university at Edinburgh in Scotland."

"Scotland?" Gideon shook his head uncertainly. "That's a long way, isn't it?"

"A good long way. Fortunately, in the old countries, they have not yet realized that a black skin makes a man subhuman."

"I don't know," Gideon said. "He's just a boy—send him off all that distance by himself. Maybe a year—"

"At least three years," Emery nodded, watching curiously the expression of pain on the Negro's face. Gideon, falteringly seeking a way out, said, "Not like I couldn't see what's best, but Rachel, his mother—"

"Then I would suggest," Emery shrugged, "that you give up the notion of his being a doctor."

"That's what he wanted," Gideon said.

"It will cost some money."

Gideon said, "Come back south, I plan to stand in the elections, go to the legislature." He hesitated. "When I sat in the convention, pay was three dollars a day. I could save maybe a dollar and fifty cents of that—would it be enough?"

Emery turned away. "It would be enough," he replied quietly. He walked over to a window and stared out, then turned back to Gideon. "Look, Jackson, where is that boy of yours now?"

"At the Presbyterian school at Worcester."

"I know the place—he'll learn to read and write and not much more. How long has he been there?"

"Four months."

"Let him stay there for six. You say he's sixteen. He can come here in two months, and I'll teach him more in a year than they could in ten. Mind you, he'll have to earn his keep; I can use a boy to sweep out, wash the lab, clean the instruments and vessels. I'm not a half baked Abolitionist like Went. If the boy is bright enough, if he shows any aptitude at all, if he's willing to work, I can train him sufficiently in two years for him to pass the Edinburgh examination. If he isn't—"

Seated in the study of Reverend Charles Smith, in Worcester, Gideon repeated what Dr. Emery had said. Smith, a timid, gentle, uncertain man, said, yes, Jeff was a good boy, very good, very earnest, gave them no trouble; but Gideon should understand that education was a slow process, a tedious process; Gideon should remember that only a short time ago the boy could not read or write. It was true that he showed great imitative ability, that he absorbed things quickly, but medicine was a profession that required scholarship of the highest degree. Wasn't it presumptuous of Emery to say that in two years he could prepare the boy for Edinburgh? Gideon didn't know. And should one conclude that medicine was the only way in which a young man could serve his people? What of the pulpit? There was a spiritual side to the boy that might almost be recognized as a sign.

"It's not that I am ungrateful for all you have done," Gideon said. Could he tell Smith what it would do to him, to Rachel not to see Jeff for five years? Did white people understand what a child meant to a black man? "But I want the boy to do what he has to do."

"Naturally, insofar as a boy knows."

"I'll talk to him," Gideon said.

Jeff was taller than Gideon remembered him as being, taller and more like his father. Now they had been strangers for a while, they could see the resemblance in one another more easily. Gideon found himself able to talk; he had not been able to talk to Jeff before. Now, this afternoon, they walked together. Jeff knew many people in the town, and he would introduce Gideon with pride. "This is my father." Gideon was used to change in people; he lived in a world of change; he could estimate the change in Jeff without being too puzzled by it.

They left the town and walked down a country road. The maples were red; the fields were parceled out, neat and square, and the land seemed to be old and thoughtful, the red barns, the clean white houses, the rock-speckled pastures.

"You like it here?" Gideon asked.

Jeff said, yes, he liked it here. Not just that the people were good to him; it went deeper than that. The people weren't saints; some of them called him a dirty nigger. A large number of people in town hated black men and always had. But all in all, the feeling was so different here than in the south.

Gideon nodded. That he could understand, although for him it would have been exile to live here. In a way he couldn't describe, this was a cold land.

"I study hard," Jeff said.

"That's good." And then, a while later, Gideon asked him, "Have you thought much about what you want to do—afterward?"

"I still want to be a doctor," Jeff said.

They came over the brow of a hill, and the sun was setting beneath them. A farmer was nudging his cows out of pasture, his dog yapping excitedly.

"We'd better turn back," Gideon said.

They walked slowly and Jeff tried to put things into words. Gideon stayed silent. "We're new people," Jeff said. "You know what I mean?" Gideon nodded. "I mean, white boy does what he wants to or what's set out for him; he don't have to reckon careful with service—"

Again, Gideon nodded.

"I get to thinking," Jeff went on, "here I am up here, how come? Marcus, Carry Lincoln, all the others, they don't come up here. In a way, I got special luck. So I figure it to be some service, something I go back with and say, See here, I got all this, I bring it back. Man's sick, I can make him better, maybe."

Gideon said, "Reverend Smith, he'd like you to be a preacher. That could be likened to a service."

"Maybe," Jeff agreed. "But Brother Peter, he's a mighty fine preacher, I think. Preaching ain't a science. Reverend Smith, he's a good man, a fine man, but that's not for me."

Gideon told him about Emery, about the dispensary, about Emery's offer and how a colored man might become a doctor at the University of Edinburgh. Jeff listened, tight, eager, anxious. Gideon painted both sides of the picture. Emery might change his mind. Two years might not be long enough to educate Jeff, and Emery might grow weary of the whole thing.

"Two years'll be enough," Jeff said. "I swear it will, I'll do any work he wants me to—just work myself down, anything. I'll sweep and clean that place of his out so fine it'll shine like gold, sure enough, father, I swear I will. It ain't no trouble for me. They say I'm the strongest boy here in town. Old Mr. Jarvis' cart was in the ditch, I lifted it out all myself, sure enough. That white doctor

won't wear me down; I'll work all day long for him, he just lets me
come there. I'll learn, too."

They walked on; already, Gideon was wondering how he'd tell
Rachel. He wanted to put his arm around Jeff and hold him close
and warm, but he couldn't. He felt a great and unreasonable pride.
He felt—if only he could sit down with Jeff, talk out all the things
there were to talk about, tell him all he might tell him. Jeff said,
suddenly:

"You'll let me do it, won't you, please?"

"I'll let you do it," Gideon agreed.

It was almost dark now, and they hurried back to the manse. Jeff
was buoyant, exuberant; Gideon had to take long strides to keep
by his side.

Before Gideon left, he said to his son, "Jeff, boy, you and me,
both of us coming out of the dark old days and remembering, we
got an idea about distance being a lonely thing, calculating how far
a man can walk in a day. But that's not right; a few days, Jeff, and
you're here or down there in Carolina. If you want me to come to
you, I'll come—you want to go home, just don't fear, write to me
and I'll send you money to go home."

He gave Jeff the few presents he had for him. They shook hands—
and then Gideon kissed his son, the first time in years.

When Gideon came home to Carwell, a man who had accomplished a great deal, the impossible in one sense, this was the first
thing he heard about. They told him about it even as he was saying
his hellos, lifting Jenny up in his arms, and then seeing beyond her
the few blackened sticks that were left of the barns, and among the
homes two gaunt chimneys that were left of shacks. They were silent
and unsmiling and troubled, and Rachel clung to him.

"Where's Marcus?" he cried.

But Marcus was all right, crowding through to him. "Well, what
is it?" he demanded. "When did it happen? How?" He had that
strange, almost mystical sensation of death, and he looked around
to see whether a face was missing. Marion Jefferson's arm was band-
aged. Hannibal Washington's wife, Ada, held her new baby, born
while he was gone in her arms. Life and death went on together.

"Well, what happened?" he demanded.

Then Andrew Sherman's wife, Lucy, began to cry, Andrew calm-
ing her, petting her, "There, Lucy, now—" and Gideon realized

that her son Jackey, nine years old, such a pride to her for his light brown skin, his unearthly beauty that was a product of the blood of two of South Carolina's "best families," was gone. He looked at Brother Peter who said quietly, "The Lord givith, the Lord takith away."

"How was it?" Gideon asked.

Brother Peter told him; sometimes, the others filled in. One saw one part of it; others saw another part of it. It happened four days after he had gone—something they had heard about but never seen before in the vicinity of Carwell. About nine o'clock in the evening, they were coming from the vespers, which Brother Peter had held in his barn, there being a chill in the air. That night, his text had been from *Psalms,* 100, he couldn't forget, "Make a joyful noise unto the Lord, all ye lands. Serve the Lord with gladness." They came out of the barn and didn't go home immediately, but stood around in little clusters for a while, as people do after church services. Then they saw it, on the hillock beyond the west pastures, a giant burning cross, something that flared into light all in a moment, one of the women screaming out and attracting the attention of the others.

Others of the women screamed and some of the children became sick with terror. Yes, Gideon could understand that, there being nothing but the soft peace of sunset first and then the grim sudden outline of the burning cross. Yet the men managed to calm the women and children soon enough. Brother Peter said, very matter of factly, that the sign of the holy cross, whether in blood or fire, could work evil to no man. Some of them took comfort from that; others, having heard of a thing called the Ku Klux Klan, tightened their lips but kept their knowledge inside their heads. The people stood around until the cross had burned itself out, and then went home to their houses, many of them still considerably upset.

"Then," Hannibal Washington told Gideon, "I figured that something to look about, crosses don't burn in air without someone to light them up, no sir. Seem there something mighty strange, and I tell Trooper, you and me, we going to look at that piece of hill."

Taking their rifles, he and Trooper circled the pasture and cut up in back of the hill. No one was there, but as they had expected, there was a charred cross made of two pieces of blackjack pine. A strong smell of kerosene filled the air and there were wisps of hay on the ground. It was not difficult for them to surmise what had happened. Someone had set up the cross, bound it up and down with hay, soaked it with kerosene, and then set flame to it. It was the sort of childish, terroristic, imbecilic thing they had heard rumors of; and being that, it puzzled and disturbed them more than any real menace would have.

When they came back, the men were waiting up for them. Hannibal Washington reported what they had found. Allenby said, "We haven't had our share of the scum and trash of the south here at Carwell." About that time, Abner Lait arrived with the Carson brothers, Frank and Leslie, all of them armed, calling out, "Hello— hello, there," as they came through the darkness. They had seen the cross from their places and had come over to find out just what it was about.

"Probably ain't nothing," Hannibal Washington said.

"Or maybe that Klan. Or maybe some fool folks here in the neighborhood."

"Don't know that any folks round about here would do a damn-fool thing like that," Abner Lait said. After that, there was much talk and much discussion about what should be done. Actually, there was nothing to be done. They wanted to know whether Gideon could see that, telling him the tale. What could be done in the face of such nonsense? Someone suggested a guard, and someone else, quite rightly, said that they were law-abiding folk living in a civilized land. They couldn't be setting guards every night

"You can see that, Gideon?" Brother Peter said uncertainly now.

"You were right," Gideon nodded. "What happened then?"

Well, they went to bed, later than usual, but finally all of them slept. When the thing happened, it must have been long after midnight. Each had the same story to tell now, of being awakened by the thunder of hoofs. Some of the women, screaming, woke out of nightmares; some of the men, frightened, stayed in bed. Hannibal Washington, Andrew Sherman, Ferdinand Lincoln, and Trooper had all left loaded rifles near their beds, and when they heard the hoofs they seized the guns and ran outside. So did Brother Peter, Allenby, and a dozen more of the men, but none of those were armed. All of them reported the same sequence of events—mounted men in white shrouds, twelve of them, armed, although they did not notice that at first. At least half of the men carried pitch-soaked torches, and by the time the men emerged the old, dry barn was already on fire, the hay hissing and giving out long tongues of flame. The cows and the mules were screaming with terror. Trooper admitted to firing first; he said that when he heard the mules screaming, he shot at one of the white-shrouded men without thinking, but he was certain, and so were the others, that he hit nothing—he had just fired in red anger. At that point, perhaps because of the shot, the white-shrouded men wheeled their horses, tossed the torches they had left at the shacks, fired a volley of shots at the people, and rode off.

"You must understand, Gideon," Allenby said now, "the sort of cowardly scum they were. The one shot sent them away. With all their white shirts, their dirty night raiding, their burning crosses, they were afraid once they knew we were armed. They scampered off like rabbits, and it wasn't until a while later that we noticed Jackey Sherman stretched out in the dark with a bullet between his eyes. One of the wild shots they fired—we were trying to put out the fire, save the stock, and the child didn't make a sound, he couldn't, poor thing."

Lucy Sherman began to sob again. Brother Peter told Gideon what was left to tell. The dead child took the heart out of their fire fighting; they saved the stock, but the barns and two of the shacks burned to the ground. The fire brought Abner Lait, Fred McHugh, his son, Jake Sutter, and the Carson brothers. Hannibal told how Abner Lait looked at the dead child and cursed the way they had never heard a man curse before. "You see, Gideon," he explained, "that take away what we been thinking, God help us, we been thinking any white men, maybe them. Then they come and we know it ain't them. Can't bring back child's life, but that help."

"And what have you done about it?" Gideon demanded, his voice so even and bitter that it seemed like another man speaking.

Allenby said, "What was there to do, Gideon? The next day, Abner Lait took his mule and rode off to town. We heard afterwards that he demanded something from the sheriff—and the sheriff just laughed at him. You know a man called Jason Hugar, he used to run slaves in the old days?"

"I know him."

"Well, Abner heard talk that he was the local Klan leader. Abner accused him, and they say he called Abner a dirty nigger lover. They had a fight, and the story goes that Abner half killed him. There was a mob, and Abner pulled his gun and said, yes, who would be first? Charley Kent, who was in Abner's company in the war stood by him, and then Abner got on his mule and came back. The next day, Hannibal hitched up the cart, and we both went to Columbia and spoke to Major Shelton there."

"And what did Shelton say?"

"He said that measures would be taken. That's an expression, Gideon—measures will be taken."

In Columbia, Major Shelton said the same to Gideon, "You can rest assured that proper measures are being taken." Shelton was a tall, hard, narrow-eyed man, nine years out of West Point, young enough to feel resentful of a fate that kept him here in the south, miles from anywhere, a police command that earned him bitterness from the people he respected and sympathy only from those he despised.

"What are those proper measures?" Gideon demanded.

"Military measures which I am neither inclined nor obliged to discuss with you. Your complaint was filed; action is being taken."

"And meanwhile, a dead child stays dead, and it ends there."

"No, of course it doesn't end there," Shelton said impatiently. "Don't try to put words in my mouth, Mr. Jackson. As I understand the case, it was purely accidental that the child was killed. Nevertheless, we are doing all we can to apprehend the criminals."

"Accidental!" Gideon said. "Accidental that those white-robed bandits burned the cross, raided our village, set the barns on fire, barns which are not ours, Major Shelton, but at that moment the property of the Government of the United States. What kind of an accident was that?"

"I'm sorry—"

"Mighty sorry, I guess. Have you looked into Klan organization hereabout? Investigated and questioned men like Jason Hugar? Have you done that?"

"Don't shout at me, Jackson? I'm not going to run in circles for every nigger who comes in here, screaming for protection!"

Gideon said evenly, "Look, sir. I am not losing my temper, I will not. I am not asking for anything, I talk about our right. Congress of this here country provided military protection for this district until civil law established. Either you provide that protection, or we will. I fought in the war too; I was master sergeant with the Black Fifty-Fourth Massachusetts—no, we was not a ditch-digging, wall-building nigger work battalion; we was free niggers and escaped slaves from this state and we fought nine separate battles, and eight of every ten men in our regiment was a casualty. Do you remember how we attacked Fort Wagner, leaving on the works four hundred dead from our regiment and our Colonel Shaw among them, and the rebels cut up his body and threw him in a mass grave with the niggers, because he, a white gentleman, a saintly white gentleman led a regiment of niggers? And do you remember our song—if you fought in this state, you heard men sing, *The gates of heaven opened wide for Colonel Shaw.* I don't like to talk about them things; they gone and in the past, the bad past. But I say, if you don't provide that protection, we will provide it ourselves."

His voice hard, Major Shelton said, "I will put down any disturbance, whether originated by whites or blacks."

"And we will protect ourselves," Gideon said.

Afterwards, back at Carwell, Gideon called a meeting of all the men, black and white together, and told them:

"You know what came of my trip to the north. Isaac Went, a Boston banker, gave me a draft of fifteen thousand dollars on him. We are going to buy the land—and we are going to keep the land. This evil thing rising up here will oppose us. I propose that we stand for our rights, that we organize our own militia, that we drill once each week until the need for that goes."

There was a good deal of discussion. Frank Carson said, matter-of-factly, that he did not like the idea of drilling under a nigger. He had ridden with Stuart, and he was uneasy about this whole business. Gideon proposed Fred McHugh, who had been a non-commissioned officer through the war, as drill-master. It was voted, and he accepted. In turn, he chose Hannibal Washington and Abner Lait to help him. Allenby questioned the legality of the matter, but Gideon pointed out that they were merely exercising their Constitutional right to bear arms; that they had borne arms, all of them since the war, and that their organized drilling would merely serve notice to night-shirted gangs that they were not fair picking. To a degree, he was right, for after that a long time passed before the Klan again rode in the vicinity of Carwell.

Ellen Jones, the blind girl, asked Gideon about Jeff, and Gideon told her how it would be, the time with Dr. Emery, the chance that Jeff would go to Edinburgh. Edinburgh, across the world and at the beginning of nowhere. Gideon realized now that the girl loved Jeff;

why was he shut to so many things? She said, "Maybe five years," and there was a tone in her voice that made an end of everything. "Maybe," Gideon agreed, and then tried to make it as gentle for her as he could, but thinking to himself all the time, why did Jeff let it go on? He thought so much and often of Jeff now, when he saw the way the other boys skylarked with the girls, when he saw Marcus shooting up like a reed.

Ellen would come and sit with Rachel. They had a lot to talk about. Rachel had said little to Gideon about Jeff. "It is best for him, no doubting it," Gideon had said. Then Rachel accepted that. Sometimes Gideon would take hold of himself, realized that a tide of things was carrying him farther and farther from Rachel, and try to be extra gentle, extra sweet, show her many little attentions. She would say, "Gideon, Gideon, don't pay no worry to me."

"I love you, Rachel honey."

But he even said it differently now; the change in him was with his speech, his bearing, his thoughts, his actions. When Rachel realized that some of the other women were talking about her and Gideon, she made more of a point than ever of Gideon's accomplishments. She could tell the other women that there was no one in the world like Gideon, fan their jealousy, their admiration or envy; but she couldn't tell it to herself in the same terms. She would wake at night and lie stiff and still by Gideon's side for hours, Once, something told him she was up, and he asked her:

"What is it, honey child?"

"Nothing."

"Then sleep."

After a while, she said, "Jeff's gone. God, I want another baby."

"We got two fine boys and a girl," Gideon said.

"I want a baby. I'm empty inside."

"Just like the good God plans it," Gideon whispered. "Child comes or it doesn't—you can't help that."

"You don't believe in God," Rachel said.

"Honey—honey."

"Child comes to them that have love."

Gideon said, "I love you, baby, believe me, with all my heart."

"Jeff's gone," Rachel said miserably. "He gone, that's all."

It was decided that Abner Lait, Gideon, and James Allenby would appear at the auction to buy the land. The men delegated to Gideon their power of attorney, and Daniel Greene, a Yankee lawyer who had recently set up in Columbia procured Gideon a tracing of the land holding. During all the time that was left, they went over the tracing, dividing it and subdividing it. They had no clear idea about how the government surveyors would apportion the land into thousand-acre lots, but they tried to provide for all eventualities. For a whole week, Gideon, together with Abner and Frank Carson, roamed over the twenty-two thousand acres of Carwell land. They found places they had not known the existence of. Frank Carson pointed out that in one spot, where the creek dropped a full seven feet, a waterwheel could be cheaply built and they could grind their own hominy. They found a fine stand of sycamore, high and leafy, a good place for living. When Abner Lait, pointing to a seven-hundred-acre stretch of swamp, said that was something they would do well to stay away from, Gideon asked closer investigation. The swamp trees were second growth and would make easy clearing; the ground was black muck, wonderfully fertile, oozing decay. "Two fine crops of rice a year," Gideon said. "No man'll ever starve if he has a piece of rice paddy." Gideon, full of dreams now, showed how a causeway through the swamp would bring them within four miles of the railroad. Frank Carson, straining the muck through his fingers, grinned and said, "Going to build me a fine house, right up there on the sycamore hillock. Set in rice and get me a clean cash crop instead of that goddamn cotton. Goddamn, I never seen a man to get no happiness out of cotton." "I'll plant cotton," Gideon said. "This is going to be a hungry country for cotton. I'm going to watch the bolls break and say, they're my own." "Never seen lowland without malaria," Abner said.

They went on; they walked through miles of piney woods. They emerged on hillocks, with land sweeping below them like a never-ending ocean. Frank Carson, regarding it strangely, said in a quiet voice, "I seen the land before, but never like this. I'm seeing it the way my granddaddy must have done, just coming out here slow and easy, a gun over one shoulder and a fry over the other."

That way, in the time that was left, they saw all the land they could pace over. The crops were being harvested; it was a good year that was ebbing out in this fall of 1868. The yellow ears of corn were stacked in the temporary cribs that had been built; a rough shed housed their fodder and stock. There was a market for the cotton the white men put in, and one night the people heard the shrill whistle of the first through freight train.

On the twenty-second of October, Gideon, Abner Lait, and James Allenby stabled their cart in Columbia and joined the crowd for the big public auction. Daniel Greene, who had been hired to handle their bids, waved to Gideon as he darted in and out of the crowd; he wore a checked suit, a white straw hat, and a fat black cigar poked from a corner of his mouth. "See you, Jackson, see you!" His pockets were full of tracings and titles.

People had come in from all over the state for the auction. Recently, it had rained, and the muddy streets of the state capital were crowded with carts, carriages, and saddle-horses. The auctioneer's pulpit had been set up on the steps of the Capitol, a huge, half-completed stone pile that stood on a hilltop and overlooked the countryside for miles in every direction. On improvised billboards, maps of the tax-forfeited holdings were posted, with the section-cuttings marked out in bright crayon lines. In the packed crowds around them were people of every description, Charleston gentlemen, Negro fieldhands, Yankee speculators, up-country farmers, plantation owners from as far as New Orleans and Texas; there were representatives of Morgan and representatives of the Unitarian Church, and there were representatives of two English land companies. One hundred and sixteen thousand acres were going on sale.

Gideon, his sleeve plucked, turned and looked in the level, slightly-smiling eyes of Stephan Holms. Casual, at his ease, gently polite, Holms was gracious as Gideon introduced Abner Lait and James Allenby.

"Here to buy, Gideon?" Holms asked him.

"That's right."

"Then we're both on the same mission. I'm representing Dudley Carwell, Colonel Fenton, and to a degree, myself."

"Are you interested in the Carwell place?" Gideon asked, as off-handedly as he could.

"Possibly—or any other piece as good. Dudley doesn't want the house, it always has been a white elephant. I heard you were negotiating a loan in Charleston?"

"I made the loan in Boston," Gideon said.

"Did you? Well, let's try not to bid against one another—enough strangers for that. Wasn't it your folks, Gideon, that had some trouble recently with—"

"With the Klan," Gideon said.

"Scum and damn white trash," Holms said. "Glad to have met you, Gideon—and you, sir, and you."

When he had walked on, Lait remarked, "That kind I know, Gideon. Was he an officer?"

"I think so."

"A mighty fine man. How many niggers did he have in the old days? I reckon he'd put a knife in his mother's back."

A little while later, the auction started, and from there on, for Gideon and his two friends as well as for most of the others in the crowd, all was hopeless confusion, two auctioneers spelling each other, screaming out, "Block four, Chipden, twenty-two, north and south, two dollars government minimum, eight hundred, two dollars, two dollars, two dollars, going, going, up to three, three dollars ten cents, I got fifteen cents, fifteen cents—" Greene breathless, his cigar bent and lifeless, found Gideon and said, "Look at this tracing! I got the section breakdown, twenty-three blocks, slightly less than a thousand acres each! The house goes separate with two hundred acres! Government minimum is dollar an acre!"

Gideon, Lait, and Allenby pulled out of the crowd and peered at the tracing. "Pick three," Greene said, "and then successive alternates through the rest."

"How do you mean?"

"Well, the best land first. I mark that A1." They pointed out the three most desirable sections. "Now from there on, in case we lose out at first—" Gideon and Abner, weighing pros and cons quickly, numbered the remaining twenty blocks. "Top price five dollars?"

"Five dollars," Gideon nodded. "But get it cheaper if you can."

"The best," Greene nodded, plunging back into the crowd. The voice of the auctioneer droned on. From all over, men shouted their bids. Land agents fought their way to the platform. The bidding had started at nine o'clock in the morning; by noon, it was still going on, and the Carwell place had not yet come up. Then, at two o'clock, the first Carwell section was put on the block. Gideon saw Greene close to the pulpit, shouting his bids, but Gideon could not keep pace with what was going on. But by five, it was over; the lawyer, exhausted, crumpled but a triumphant grin on his face, pushed out of the crowd, "Got them!"

"Which ones?"

"Two of them A1." The lawyer spread the battered tracing on the board walk, knelt down, Gideon, Abner, and Allenby grouped over him. "These two, four dollars straight." Lait whooped with joy, leaping up and down, slapping his thighs. "God damn, God damn, Gideon! Look at that! That's the hill with the sycamores! That's them flats, meaty, like a gal's ass!" Gideon got down on his knees next to Greene, grinning happily. "Where's the third?"

"Your number four alternate—funny, the bidding on that went up to five. You sure you know these places?"

"Hell, yes, we know them!" Abner said. "All right—that's good piece, damn good piece."

"Seven thousand three hundred for the first two pieces—that's a bargain, Gideon, a damn good bargain, that's giving away the land. Four thousand, seven hundred and fifty dollars for number three. You got land there. Near three thousand acres—"

They came home triumphantly, Old James Allenby driving the mules, Gideon and Abner singing drunkenly, "Green grow the lilacs, so wet with the dew, I'm lonely, my darling, and thinking of you." Abner had invested two dollars in a jug of corn, and he and Gideon had polished it down over the whole long ride from Columbia. Gideon wasn't a good drinker; he drank rarely and gingerly. Three quarters of the jug had gone into Abner, the rest into Gideon, and they had achieved the same state of glory. Gideon roared out to the people, "We are tomorrow, we are, sure enough!" Allenby told the story of what had happened. Rachel, laughing at Gideon, put him to bed; he dragged her down with him, while she protested, "Gideon, have some shame." But it was like old times, Gideon laughing and singing out in his deep bass voice, until at last he fell asleep.

The next day, Brother Peter held a special meeting. As he told Gideon, "Forget the Lord God, brother, be not humble but brazen and loud, then sure enough the Lord God he going to forget you." And his voice more gentle, "Gideon, you going to lead the people, then you got a dispensation, and you got to know that. Know it humbly, Gideon. When you do good, you do good on account the people put their trust in you. Long time back, I put my trust in you. Don't disappoint me, Gideon. You a knowing man, climbing high up a ladder. Look down, Gideon, just look down."

"I'm sorry," Gideon said. "Believe me, Brother Peter, I'm sorry."

"Sure, Gideon, you sorry, you got a big heart. But hear me, Gideon, look inside yourself and find God. Find God and give him your trust."

"Your way is your way," Gideon said softly. "Mine is mine. Brother Peter, there's no man in this world I reverence more than you, believe me."

"I got to believe you, Gideon," Brother Peter said softly. At the meeting, he said, "My text is from Numbers, We came into the land whither Thou sentest us, and surely it flowed with milk and honey; and this is the fruit of it." He preached his sermon slowly and pointedly; in a place of the landless, they had land. Theirs was the mercy and a sign too, far wherever a black man bought a piece of land, a thousand eyes would be upon him. "Use it well," Brother Peter said.

After the meeting, the dividing of the land began. It had to be done immediately if they were to move from here, take over their pieces, and build some sort of shelter against the winter. Gideon had thought it would be difficult, but not so difficult as this, men fighting, arguing, protesting, weighing each one's piece against the others', jealous, name-calling, the white hunching together against the black, the black instinctively putting shoulder to shoulder against the white, until at last Gideon roared:

"Stop it—damn you all for fools! We've come this far already and now you're ready to cut each other's throats. We going to pick one man, vote for him, and let him portion out the land. Now who's it going to be?"

They wanted Gideon, but he refused. They nominated Allenby and Brother Peter, and in the voting, Brother Peter won by three votes. Trooper asked him, "Who's going to pick your land?" and Brother Peter answered, "Whatever's left—it don't matter." Then they looked at each other shamefacedly, grinning sheepishly. It went better after that.

In the way of things, it was natural and easy that this should be the time for voting again and that they should not contemplate the thousand matters that had wrought a change in them. A year ago, they had walked in to the voting with their guns, but things were different now. The land had changed; the people had changed; the future overtook them, and they were part of it now. They went into town together early on the first Tuesday in November, black men and white men together. There was a nip of coming winter in the air. Dead leaves scurried across the dusty road. The black men were going to vote Republican, solid, but Abner Lait said that when all was said and done, he thought he'd vote Democrat. His daddy had; his granddaddy had; he didn't like to upset a thing like that. Yet all of them, together, walked into town for the voting.

PART TWO. THE FIGHTING

8. HOW GIDEON JACKSON WENT TO SEE A TIRED MAN

Gideon took out his watch and looked at it. It was twenty minutes to three, and he had been waiting since two o'clock. He had hoped to have his appointment and be at the station by five-sixteen, to meet Jeff, who was coming down from New York. Well, likely enough, he would still make the station in time to meet Jeff. Actually, he had very little to say here and now, and what he said, he was sure, would not be to too much effect.

Outside, on this bleak February day, it was snowing, Washington snow, large wet flakes that folded against the window panes and then dissolved into globs of cold moisture that wriggled down the glass. Gideon relaxed into the leather chair and folded his hands in his lap. At this moment, he felt, he would like to sleep, a long, long sleep such as he had not known for many months—just to sleep and be free of thinking for a time, and then to wake up, fresh and eager. But how eager could a man be at forty-five? Gideon shook his head and smiled and began to think about Jeff; it was better to think of Jeff than to think about other things; Jeff was reality. Jeff would swing off the train and come striding toward him. Or would he? Perhaps he would just stand, uncertainly, and look at Gideon, and perhaps there would be nothing at all between them. But that was impossible. Seven years do not make such a difference. But seven years in Edinburgh, seven years during which a frightened black boy becomes a doctor of medicine; seven such years are something to be considered.

Gideon, recalling that day when Dr. Emery put the matter up to him, smiled wryly. What had Emery been thinking? What, indeed, had he said to Dr. Emery? Something about money—did it cost much money? That was so long ago—eight years? Nine years? He would have liked to have known Emery better, to have known Went better; now they were both of them dead. He recreated the picture of himself standing in the dispensary, talking with Emery, watching the shivering, naked rickets-stricken child, and that way memory after memory came back, until the flow of pictures was dissolved by the striking of a tall grandfather clock in the corner, one, two, three. He must have been sleeping. The secretary, standing in front of him, said:

"The president will see you now, Mr. Jackson."

Gideon rose, blinked his eyes, and followed the secretary to the office. Grant was sitting behind his desk, hunched, tired, red-eyed, a man defeated and lost and regarding the long, empty years before him without hope and without pleasure. He nodded and said:

"Sit down, Gideon," and then told his secretary, "I don't want to be interrupted."

"If Senator Gordon—"

"Tell him to go to hell! I won't talk to him, do you understand? I don't want to be interrupted!" The door closed behind the secretary. The president said to Gideon, "Do you want a cigar? No—I forgot, you don't smoke. You don't mind if I do?" He bit off the end of his cigar, struck a match, puffed long and deeply. Gideon watched him, but the president avoided his look. Age had come suddenly and ruthlessly on Ulysses Simpson Grant; his eyes were sunken, his beard streaked with gray. Even his smoking was in short, jagged, nervous motions. When he spoke, he barked at Gideon:

"I know what you're going to say."

"Then why did you let me come here and say it?" Gideon asked gently.

"Why?" Grant looked at him with sudden bewilderment, and Gideon felt a complete and understanding pity for this beaten, helpless man, this man who was understood by so few, loved by so few, used by so many, hated by so many, despised by so many, this man who by fate and circumstance had been elevated to a remote and hopeless glory.

"Why come here?" Grant said dully.

"Because you are still president of these United States," Gideon answered carefully. "Because you are my friend and I am yours—"

"So I have friends?"

"And because," Gideon went on, "when all is said and done, this is your country and you love it as few men I know do. You love it in a way that I understand, in a manner that is beyond the conception of the cheating, lying, small men who have done their best to wreck it. Do you remember Everett Hale's story, *The Man Without a Country*? Do you remember how Philip Nolan came to love and understand his native land?"

Grant smiled ruefully. "Are you going to preach me a sermon, Gideon?"

"No—I'm going to talk to you about this land. I'm going to talk because it's the last chance I'll have to talk to a president of the United States. I've tried for two weeks to see you—"

"I was busy, Gideon."

"You were busy, Mr. President," Gideon said. "That is all, you were busy. God help us, we have so many pat phrases, busy, occupied, a thousand things to do. Why aren't our enemies busy? Why?"

"I've heard all that," Grant said coldly.

"And you don't want to hear it again. At this time, you'd like me to go. Well, perhaps I can put it differently. Leaving aside what the newspapers have said and what the histories will say of the eight years during which you were president, what is the truth?"

"Say it—I was used!" Grant growled.

"I won't say that. My God, Mr. President, this is—well it's our country; let's use the schoolboy phrases, nothing else will do now. This is our native land. We fought for this. We lived for this, what men died at Gettysburg for. We don't exist apart from it, or from each other. It is all bound together, making one. What is a country?" Gideon hesitated, then went on, "What is the United States of America? Is it a dream, an ideal, a piece of paper called the Constitution, a coalition? Promoters? Grafters? Robber barons? Is it Morgan or Jay Gould or Senator Gordon? Or is it a man standing out in the street and looking at the White House?" Now Gideon spoke more haltingly, "Is it the Episcopal Church or the Congregational Church? Is it a prayer or a fool's fancy or fifty million men? Is it Congress? All the years I sat in Congress I thought of that, watching small men or great men, listening to fools like Peterson and heroes like Sumner. Or is it you and me, and bound into us, and inseparable from us—because what we are is America, what we have, what we've done, what we have dreamed!"

Grant's cigar had gone out. Clenched between his stubby fingers, it made a focus for his eyes. Slowly, automatically, he shook his head. "I'm through, Gideon."

"You're president."

"For a few more days—"

"For long enough to hit them!"

Grant said wearily, "But I don't know, Gideon. I'm tired. I'm finished. I want to go home and rest. I've been dragged through sewers. I want to go home and forget."

"You won't forget," Gideon said.

"Maybe. I'm no Solomon; I'm no God of judgment. I didn't ask for this. I won battles because I wasn't afraid to pay the price. Did that make me a president? Did that fit me to play their dirty, rotten game of politics?"

"There are still battles," Gideon said.

"When you don't know the enemy? When you don't know who fights on your own side?"

"And when Hayes slides into that chair where you're sitting, his legs knee-deep in blood, will you rest easy?"

"God damn it, Gideon, where are your facts? Hayes is a Republican; so am I; so are you. He was legally elected president. I am sick of the calamity howlers. Life will go on; so will this country—"

"All right," Gideon said, and rose.

"Are you going?"

"Yes."

"What were you going to say?"

"Why bother? It won't matter."

"God damn you, say it!" Grant growled. "Say it and get it done!"

"Do you want to hear it?"

"Stop being a prima donna and say it."

"All right," Gideon nodded. "There was a deal."

"Where is your proof?"

"I have the proof, sir," Gideon said quietly. "Will you listen to me for a while?"

"I've been listening." Grant lit his cigar. Gideon sat down again. The clock on Grant's desk showed a quarter of four. "I'll start a while back," Gideon began. Outside, it still snowed, fat, lazy white flakes that melted on the window panes. It was growing dark in the president's office. The single lamp on his desk threw a circle of yellow light, and as the darkness increased his face became more tired, more indistinguishable. The smoke from his cigar drifted into the light, twisting, turning, running up the chimney of the lamp.

"You remember the South Carolina Convention?" Gideon said. "That was nine years ago."

"I remember."

"In a way of speaking, that began the reconstruction. I served on the Convention. Two years later, I served a term in the State Senate, and five years ago I came to Congress. In the light of that, I think I can speak with some knowledge of what happened. The word *reconstruction*, which they use for all that happened in the south since 1868, is too pat. It is meaningless. It was not essentially a problem of reconstruction, not even a problem of readmission of the rebel states into the Union. All this I have said in the House; I have said it over and over, these five years past. I am saying it now, I suppose, for the record—for I think that this is the last time for a long while to come that a Negro representative of his people will sit in the office of the president of the United States."

Grant knocked the ashes off his cigar; now his face was lost in the shadow.

"What is reconstruction? What has it been? What has it meant? Why has it been destroyed? I ask you because you're the only man in the country who can bring it back to life—and doing so, save this country untold suffering and misery in the future."

"Go on, Gideon," Grant said.

"Reconstruction was the beginning of the new and the death of the old. The plantation slave system, a feudal thing, abhorrent to the nature of this country, only a few years ago set out to rule and conquer this nation. It had to be destroyed or it would destroy democracy. It was destroyed, and in the course of that destruction my people were freed. Do you want me to go on?"

"Go on," Grant said.

"Very well. Out of that terrible war came reconstruction—essentially a test for democracy, a test of whether freed Negroes and freed whites—for the poor white was as much a slave before the war as the black—could live and work and build together. I say that test was taken and proven, that democracy worked in the south—with all its faults, its blunders, its boasting extravagances, its fools and loud-mouths—with all that, it worked! For the first time in the history of this nation, black men and white men together built a democracy in the south. You have the proof, the schools, the farms, the just courts, a whole literate, eager generation. But this was not done easily and never done completely; the planters organized their army, white-shirted scum by the thousands. They haven't given up. You yourself, Mr. President, said that only the presence of Union troops in the south preserves order. I tell you, the day Rutherford

B. Hayes takes office, those troops will be withdrawn—and the Klan will strike. In one form or another, it will strike everywhere, and there will be terror such as this land never knew, murder and destruction and burning and looting, until every vestige of that democracy we built is destroyed. We will be put back a hundred years, and for generations to come men will suffer and die—"

Grant's voice came wearily, as from a great distance. "Even if I accepted what you say, Gideon, and I don't accept it, what is the alternative? To keep troops in the south forever?"

"Not forever. But for ten years more—to give us a chance to bring to manhood a whole new generation, black men and white men who have learned to work together, to stand together. Then no force on earth will take away from us what we have built."

"I don't accept that, Gideon. I don't accept your accusation of Hayes. I don't accept your fanciful notion of the power of the Klan. This is 1877."

"You wanted proof," Gideon said. "I have the proof." He took some papers out of his pocket, spread them on the desk in the lamp-light. "Here are the statistics of the election. The popular vote for Tilden is 4,300,000, and Hayes' popular vote is 4,036,000. That is the first lie; I say that half a million Negroes and whites in the south who voted the Republican ticket had their votes destroyed, miscounted, tampered with. No, I can't prove that; I'll prove other things later. Actually, it does not matter; these two men, Tilden and Hayes, are both corrupt, sad commentaries on what our presidency has sunk to. They are Tweedlededum and Tweedledee, cut out of the same cloth."

"So far," Grant said, "you are making groundless accusations. I won't listen to much more of that, Gideon."

"You said you would listen. I'll give you the proof; first let me establish my facts. Even our Congress, which fears democracy and the people more than anything on earth, will let me establish my facts when I rise to speak. I'll be quick with it. My boy, whom I haven't seen for a long while, is coming in on the five-sixteen train from New York; I assure you I'll be through before then."

The room was quite dark now outside of the circle of yellow light. "Go on," Grant said.

"We come to the electoral votes, 184 Tilden, the Democrat, for Hayes, the Republican 166 undisputed votes. With one more vote, Tilden could be president, but Hayes claimed South Carolina,

Louisiana and Florida, enough to give him the 185 that would make him president. And Hayes was right—those votes belonged to him; as I said, they were tampered with, destroyed. What was the situation? A Democratic House, a Republican Senate, one to give the election to Tilden, the other to Hayes, and the whole country screaming of the second Civil War, of a southern march on Washington. Mr. President, did you believe that? Did you believe there was a difference between these two corrupt men?"

Grant said, "God damn you, Gideon, I've listened to enough!"

"I come to the proof now, Mr. President. Let me give you the proof, and then I'll go. I think we are both through. As you said, you have only a few days to be president, and I have not too much time either."

"Go on," Grant muttered.

"Yes—evidently our southern Democrats knew that the two men were of a stripe. They threw Tilden aside; he would be too much trouble; they had risked a civil war once and they had failed; they were not prepared to risk it again. They made their deal with Hayes. He could have South Carolina, Florida, Louisiana—and to make the deal certain, Oregon, too. In return, he would give them a very small and inconsequential thing, control of South Carolina and Louisiana, and withdrawal of Union troops from the south. Such a small matter to stand between a man and the presidency, between the Republican party, Lincoln's party and power! Here is the proof, a record made by two of Mr. Hayes' friends, Stanley Matthews and Charles Foster. It gives the gist of certain talks they had with Senator John B. Gordon of Georgia and the Kentucky Congressman, Mr. J. Young Brown. This is an exact copy, made and brought to me by a colored servant of Mr. Foster; I will swear to that. I'll read it:

* " 'Referring to the conversation we had with you yesterday in which Governor Hayes' policy as to the status of certain southern states was discussed, we desire to say that we can assure you in the strongest possible manner of our great desire to have him adopt such a policy as will give the people of the States of South Carolina and Louisiana the right to control their own affairs in their own way, subject only to the Constitution of the United States and the laws made in pursuance thereof, and to say further that from an

* This document may be found in Williams' *Life of Rutherford B. Hayes*, Vol. I, p. 533.

acquaintance with and knowledge of Governor Hayes and his views, we have the most complete confidence that such will be the policy of his administration.'

"There it is, Mr. President."

A long silence then; and finally Grant asked tonelessly, "Why don't you bring it before the House?"

"Because I haven't the original, because while I am prepared to swear on a stack of Bibles that this is the truth, I cannot bring evidence; I cannot set the word of a poor old colored servant against that of the president elect of the United States. If I were to stand up in the House and say to them what I just said to you, ten of our cultured Bourbon members would be screaming that this damned, insolent, lying nigger be lynched."

"Why should I believe you?"

"Because the whole future of this country is at stake. Because when we fought our revolution, when we fought our civil war, we were moving down a proud and shining road, what my people call a hallelujah road. We were moving with all the good men who lived behind us, and we had our faces turned to God. Do you hear me, Mr. President? Now we're going to leave that road; from here on, we turn our face to darkness. For how long, Mr. President? How many shall have to die before we can call this a government of the people, by them and for them?"

"It's not as bad as that—" Grant began.

"But it is!"

Grant stood up, lifting himself from his chair with both hands, leaning over into the lamplight, staring at Gideon, and then pushing away from the table and striding angrily across the room.

"That's all?" Gideon asked.

"What can I do?" Grant demanded, whirling on him. "Even if your insane, fairy-tale of a story were true, what in God's name could I do?"

"Everything. You're still president. Give this to the people. Hold a press conference tomorrow; there are papers with guts enough to print this. Let Hayes prove the accusation false. Throw this whole rotten thing open and let the people look at it. They'll know what to do. We're not a bad people, here in America; we're not an ignorant people. We've moved the world before; we've done bad things, but we've done more good things. Go before Congress and demand the truth—"

Grant shook his head. "Gideon—"

"Are you afraid?" Gideon cried. "What have you to lose? Those who remember the days when you led them to victory, they'll support you. And the others—" Gideon's voice trailed away.

He gathered up the papers and put them in his pocket. "All right. I'll go now."

After Gideon had left, long after, Grant sat at his desk, face sunk in his hands, staring at the closed door.

It was late when Gideon got to the station. The train had already pulled in. On the station platform, he saw Jeff, a tall young man, broad, like a mirror of himself, standing between two carpet-bags with his hands in his pockets. It was not a question of memory, not a question of change; the two of them looked at each other and knew each other, and though each was many years older, each was more like the other. They approached and shook hands. Gideon swallowed; Jeff smiled slowly, letting one hand grasp his father's arm.

"You're bigger than I remember," he said.

"And you too," Gideon nodded.

"You recognized me."

"Yes, I'm glad you're back, Jeff."

"I'm glad to be back," Jeff said. Gideon bent for the bags. "I'll carry them," Jeff said.

"One apiece."

"All right," Jeff smiled, looking curiously at Gideon, measuring him from top to bottom, casually, but in such a way as to make Gideon feel that he was being appraised. They stood shoulder to shoulder, two large men, moving slowly, uncertainly, each trying after this long time to adjust his movements, his thoughts, his desires to the other. They walked down the length of the platform, through the station, and Jeff said, with a sense of guilt and omission, "How is mother?" "Fine," Gideon said. "We all get older." "You look no older," Jeff said. Gideon had a cab waiting for them; they climbed into it, filling the tight space with their long-limbed bodies. Snow flurried around like a white fisherman's net. "I thought of Washington as a warm place," Jeff said. "I've never been here before—" "No, you haven't," Gideon realized, thinking of all the years this sprawling, boastful city on the Potomac had been a part of his

life. The horse set off with an easy clack, clack of shod hoofs. "I've
had a small house here these past two years," Gideon said.

"Mother—"

"She tried it last year," Gideon said. "I think she's happier at
Carwell."

"You still call it that, Carwell?"

"Carwell?" Gideon seemed a little puzzled. "Yes, we never thought
of calling it anything else. Have you room?" The bags were tight
against their knees.

"It's quite comfortable," Jeff said.

"You must be hungry?"

"I am, a little."

"We'll have dinner at home, just the two of us. I didn't ask anyone else."

Jeff wondered why his father said that.

The house Gideon had was a small, white-frame five-room building. A withered old Negro woman kept it clean and prepared his
meals. Gideon called her Mother Joan. "Mother Joan," he said,
"This is my son, Jeff." "That's a fine big boy, Mr. Jackson. You a
proud man." "Mighty proud," Gideon said. They had a simple dinner, hot bean soup, and then chops, greens, and buttered grits.
"These are the first grits in how long—?" Jeff smiled.

"You wouldn't have them in Scotland," Gideon remembered. Of
course, he couldn't expect it all to come flooding out at once, the
moment the two of them met; it would come bit by bit, as they
broke down all the things between them. Seven years was a long
time; they even spoke differently, Jeff's speech harder than Gideon's,
with a curious foreign sound.

Jeff said, "I worked for a year with Dr. Kendrick. He had a grant
dispensary at the mines. It was good experience—bad accidents,
crushed arms or legs, burns, lacerations, and the household things
too—croup, mumps, little things that are so difficult to get onto."

"White people?"

"I was the only Negro in the county. That makes a difference."

"There was no feeling?"

"Not the way it is here. I was a curiosity. They're not a complicated people, and their fears and suspicions were basic things. You
could put your finger on them and clear them away."

They went into Gideon's study, a small, book-filled room that he also used as an office. They sat with their feet stretched out to the glowing coal grate, and they talked of many things. It was easier now; Jeff was able to say:

"You know, I'm terribly proud."

"Of what?"

"Your being in Congress. I don't know how to say it, but that's a wonderful thing."

Gideon's eyes were thoughtful. "It's a matter of circumstance. People are made. The things were present to make me into this or that, and those things operated."

Jeff asked him about the election, and slowly at first, and then with more passion, Gideon told him, traced the whole sequence of events in the last eight years, told how he had gone today to see the president. "And I've failed," Gideon said.

"Are you sure? Can a thing come to an end that way, suddenly, the way a bomb explodes? Do things happen that way?"

"Not suddenly," Gideon said. "This has been going on for a long time. More than eight years ago, the Klan raided our people at Carwell. That was a clumsy thing, a frightened thing. They burned the barns and killed one little boy. But they were beginning then, as far back as that. From the very first, they planned to destroy us. The war was hardly over before the same people who made it set about planning for the next war, a different one this time, armies that ride in the night, underground organization, intimidation, threats, terror. Now their preparation has been completed; they're ready."

"I can't believe it."

"If I could only think that I was wrong," Gideon said. "But I'm not wrong—"

"What are you going to do?"

"I don't know yet; I want to think about it. In any case, I'm going home. I want to be with them." Jeff nodded. "That's right for me, I think," Gideon pointed out. "But what is right for me is not necessarily right for you. Do you see, Jeff?"

"What are you driving at?"

"I'll be leaving in the next few days," Gideon said. "I don't want you to go back with me. There is no reason for you to come with me. If things are all right in the spring—"

"What on earth are you talking about?" Jeff wanted to know.

Gideon shook his head. "Easy, Jeff. Now you listen to me. There was a time when you'd listen to me." He stood up for a moment, rubbed his long fingered hands together, leaned toward his son, and then sat back in his chair abruptly. He sat there silent, staring ahead of him, the glow from the fire picking out highlights on his long, high-ridged face. Jeff looked at him, noticing how the large, full mouth was set, how weary and red-rimmed the deep-sunk eyes were. The man was older, older than forty-five years, older than logic and reason. The broad shoulders that Jeff had so often seen as a child, bared to the hot sun, sweat-covered, immensely powerful, bound over as they were with layer upon layer of flat, hard muscle, were now bent and slack. The short, kinky hair that covered his head like a tight cap, was streaked through with grey. Jeff didn't know him; Jeff had never known him; a boy of fifteen is malleable clay. Nine years had stretched Jeff but broken nothing; he had learned, grown, expanded, been hurt and healed his hurt; he had found a God in science, and under a microscope a man's skin is not of a color but of many cells, wonderfully placed together. All the world was reason. A man called Darwin had cleared away the haze that covered the uncounted ages beyond man. A broken leg was set in such and such a fashion, whether the skin that enveloped it was black or white. In a lonely cabin on the moors, he had delivered a child of a white woman, slapped it, and watched it scream with the wonderful agony of birth. The world was an understandable place, a planet twisting through nothingness, gently enveloped with a protective skin of atmosphere. Men were evil because they did not know, but a man who dedicated his life to knowing, in the scientific nature of the world, could have no fears. That was how it had been with him; but what had been with his father? He remembered the tall field-hand who set off for Charleston, a delegate walking to a convention, a crushed stovepipe hat on his head, a bright checked handkerchief hanging out of his pocket. Another man had come back, but what sort of twisting agony had made that second man? And what convulsions within Gideon Jackson made the third man, the fourth man?—the man of whom Dr. Emery had said, "That is greatness in the essential of the word, Jeff, remember. There are no scientific definitions. When you come to the end of logic, think about him." Jeff thought about him now, the man who sat in the State Senate of South Carolina, the man who served in the Congress of the United States and in answer to a Georgia representative made that statement that every child in the country knew:

"Yes, as the gentleman from Georgia says, I was a slave only a

short while past. And today, as a free man, I answer him in the
Congress of this nation. That, gentlemen, is the American testament, my American testament. I need not indulge in patriotic
sentiments. The fact that I stand here defines the country I serve
better than any words a man could speak or write."

That statement Jeff saw reprinted in Scottish magazines; a member of parliament spoke it in Commons; over that statement, a fierce
debate raged in the French Chamber for three hours; and in Ger-
many, Hungary and Russia, underground revolutionary groups of
workingmen had translated that statement, printed and circulated
thousands of copies of it.

Now, looking at Gideon, Jeff felt a complex of pity, of pride and
longing, a desire to come close to this man, his father, to understand
him and be understood by him; yet a sense of himself as an individual, a man beyond Gideon, ahead of Gideon.

"I'll listen to you," he said. "Whatever I have to do, I'll still listen
to you."

"I'm going back," Gideon explained, speaking slowly, softly, "because I belong there. The nature of all I am, Jeff, son, all I have
been, is in my people. I come from them; I have my strength from
them. It took me a long time to learn that; I have a gift; I could
learn, I could talk, I could soak in things, but there was nothing
in me that wasn't a part of them. I want to go back to them because
that will give me the greatest happiness, and the nature of a man,
Jeff, is to seek his happiness, whether in the small things he does or
in the large ones.

"With you, it is different. You have been away for a long time.
You have been schooled and trained, and today you are a doctor.
A doctor is like a fine book; it has a use outside of the toil and
effort that went into creating it. I have no use outside of the things
that went into me; you have. No matter how bad things are, when
the need comes, my people will find other Gideon Jacksons. With
you, it is different. I can talk to you as a man; that makes me proud
and happy. When I told President Grant today that I thought this
was the last time in many years a black man would talk to the president, I was saying something I believed. I also believe there will be
few black men trained as you are in the years to come. Stay here;
you can live in this house. There will be enough broken bodies to
heal. It would be waste if you came back with me."

When Gideon finished talking, they sat in silence for several minutes. Jeff knocked out his pipe, filled it again, took a coal from the fire with the tongs and dropped it onto the soft, fragrant tobacco. Gideon poured some wine. Looking about the room finally, Jeff said, "This is a nice room, a warm room. I should like to read some of the books."

Gideon nodded.

"I always think of reading books tomorrow, when there's time. Somehow, there's never time today."

"There's time," Gideon said.

"Tell me," Jeff asked him. "If it happens, the way you think it might happen, would you fight?"

"I don't know," Gideon said.

"Marcus wrote me that when someone is sick, you call old Doc Leed. Sometimes he comes, sometimes he doesn't."

"Mostly, he comes."

"He won't come anymore now," Jeff said. "If what you tell me is true, he won't come anymore now." Jeff rose and walked to the window, wiping away the moisture that had gathered inside the pane. "It's still snowing," he remarked. "It's funny, being away so long, I never learned to love any other place. Did Allenby ever show you any of the letters I sent to him, to read to Ellen?"

Gideon shook his head. "The old man died last month. I thought you knew."

"I didn't know," Jeff said. "I'm going back with you, father."

In the last few things Gideon did in Washington, there was a sort of compromise between an attitude of leaving for good and a half-formed hope that he might be back for the spring session. He would find himself thinking that Jeff was right, that a world simply could not explode like a bombshell. He left the house as it was, telling Mother Joan to keep things in order. He attended a meeting of the Ways and Means Committee, and found himself hotly engaged in the discussion of a law pertaining to railroad land grants. Well, a man was so constituted; he went ahead with habitual things; he dressed and ate and shaved and slept. And one day, soon after Jeff came home, he was told by his secretary that Senator Stephan Holms would like to see him.

"You may tell Senator Holms," Gideon said, "that I am completely engaged. I have only a few days before I leave Washington, and I am making no appointments."

The secretary came back and said that Senator Holms was quite insistent.

"All right," Gideon nodded. "Let him come in." Holms entered; Gideon made no effort to rise, no offer of his hand. Smiling, Holms smoothed the nap of his hat, took off his coat carefully, set his stick and gloves on a corner of Gideon's desk, and seated himself.

"What do you want?" Gideon said.

"I wanted to see you, Gideon, because we are both civilized human beings, because on that basis we can discuss things, because in a world full of fools, idiots, small men, and little minds, you and I can certainly discuss the truth, recognize it, and make our peace with it without passion."

"You believe that, don't you?" Gideon asked, watching the slim, delicate man who sat so completely at his ease, so immaculate in his clothes, so unruffled in his demeanor, the smooth, shiny, faintly-yellow skin untouched by the years, the ascetic face both an enigma and an invitation, reacting to Gideon's every mood and word. Certainly, this was a product of civilization; after a fashion, too, this was a truthful man, a strangely truthful and direct man in a strangely untruthful and indirect world. Yet at this moment, Gideon felt for him a loathing such as he had never felt for a living being, loathing, disgust, hatred; Gideon Jackson, who in all his life, as a slave and as a free man, had reacted from hatred, who had tried to understand what makes one man good and another bad, what makes one man gentle and another hard, who with a whip on his back had tried to feel and comprehend reason, logic and truth, who had fought and killed without hating what he was fighting and killing; this man, Gideon Jackson, would have quickly and surely killed Stephan Holms and felt no regret for it. And now, Gideon repeated, "You believe that, don't you?"

"I believe it, Gideon," Holms said quietly. And added with complete sincerity, "I assure you, Gideon, that I am one of the few people of my class who does not draw back in horror from the color of a man's skin. You see, I am essentially a reasonable and logical human being: so are you. We recognize that certain shibboleths have been set up. I can afford to smile at them, at the brainless, empty idiots—my friends, I admit—who look upon all creatures of your race, and so many of mine, as being inferior. God knows, I recognize their caliber. But my lot is with them, Gideon, partially by birth, partially by choice. Let us face the facts; my people lost a great deal by the war, not only power—which is no small thing in itself—but material things that result from power, a way of life. I wanted those things back, and I fought for them sensibly."

"And now you have them."

"To a degree," Holm admitted. "There are still matters to be arranged, but to a degree we have succeeded. I need not pretend; you know why Rutherford Hayes is our next president, and you know that he is at least gentleman enough to keep his word. At any rate, the Republican party has made its peace with us, and certain things will be done."

"You are a truthful and a reasonable man," Gideon said, staring at Holms with real curiosity. "You pride yourself on that, don't you?"

"After a fashion, yes."

"And you didn't come here to gloat. You are much too civilized for that."

"Much too civilized, Gideon. Too civilized to be impressed by a black man's irony. And you, I think, are too civilized to throw me out of here."

"I want to hear what you have to say," Gideon answered quietly.

"I thought you would. Let's dispense with innuendoes. I admire you, Gideon. I watched you during the Convention, during the years that followed; there was an amazing development. You are a man of great ability and profound talent. You have a mind. The mere fact that a former slave, whose speech was back-country gibberish, should be the cultured man I speak with now, is in itself incredible. I have listened to you in Congress, often with admiration. Your delivery, which has that rare combination of being both rational and emotional, is most effective in moving men."

"You are flattering," Gideon said. "Go on."

"I think that if you had the original of that amazing and stupid document you showed to President Grant, you might have gone to Congress with it and changed history. Or perhaps not. Our party has a majority in the House, and it is doubtful whether one man in one act can appreciably change history."

"So you know about that too. At least, you are thorough."

"We have had to be thorough, Gideon. We were the conquered. Our country was an occupied country—"

"You think of it as your country?"

"Essentially, yes. The country of a few select men, men who are fit to rule. You should recognize that, Gideon. Neither the degenerate white trash that we have used in the Klan, nor the debased and childlike nigger field-hand is capable of rule. You are an exception. I am an exception. That is why I appeal to you, both with sincerity and logic. There are other ways, but how much simpler it would be if you were with us, if some of your colleagues joined us. The nigger will follow you; he has before; he will continue to. In the long run, our way is best. I dislike force and I dislike violence, believe me; I will use them if necessary, but how much better it would be to achieve our ends without resorting to wholesale violence. A land where prosperity and order is combined for the good of all, where the man in the field has enough to eat and can sleep without worry as to his next day's bread."

"And you propose this to me?" Gideon asked incredulously.

"Will you accept?"

"That I should lead my people back to slavery?"

"If you would put it that way."

"You are incredible," Gideon said softly. "I should have recognized that the first time, when I went to your house. But I looked upon you as human. I looked upon all men as human. I failed to realize that a disease could enter a man's mind, a disease beyond cure. I didn't understand that some men are sick, and with their sickness they could contaminate the earth. We all make mistakes, don't we? I think that was the greatest mistake that the men on my side made. When the earth ran with blood during the war, they thought that the evil had been stamped out. But the blood of the sick, the diseased, the debased beyond reason—that blood never ran at all, only the blood of good men, men who had been led and lied to. We let your kind live—"

Gideon had not seen Senator Holms angry before, a tightening of the lips, a few vertical lines on the high, smooth brow. Senator Holms rose, put on his coat and hat, picked up his gloves and stick from the desk.

"I take it that is your answer," he said.

"You may take it as such," Gideon agreed.

Gideon and Jeff took the three o'clock train for the South the following day. There was not much that Gideon took with him, a small bag and a briefcase which contained his old copy of Whitman's poems, a signed photograph of Charles Sumner, which had been given to him just before that man's death, and a notebook. He intended to write a report of the whole Hayes-Tilden affair, and he thought he might start it on the train, to pass the hours away.

With Jeff, he walked down the platform, the length of the train. "The last car," he said.

"Why?"

"You don't know, do you?" Gideon realized, looking at his son. "You remember, I told you it did not come like a bomb bursting. You see, it's been going on."

They came to the last car, an old and venerable veteran of the road. The windows were dirty; two of them had been replaced by boarding. Over the door, a sign said simply, "Colored." Jeff read it and turned on his father.

"No—no, it's impossible! It's rotten, do you hear me, rotten! You—a member of Congress—"

"Get in, Jeff," Gideon said. "This isn't a new thing. It grows in popularity. One gets accustomed."

They got in and sat together on the old wooden bench. Other colored people filed in. And in time, the train started. Gideon said: "After all, it's only for a while. Soon we'll be back at Carwell."

9. HOW GIDEON JACKSON AND HIS SON CAME ONCE MORE TO CARWELL

Marcus was waiting for them at the station, and to Jeff, this was a stranger, actually and completely, this slim, handsome Negro boy, lighter-skinned than any other Jackson, reaching only to Gideon's shoulder, but well-proportioned, small in the hips, broad at the shoulders, moving so easily, so gracefully that Jeff's first thought was of a wild animal, unafraid, possessed of itself, and completely integrated. Dressed in blue jeans and a brown leather jacket, he stood casually by a one horse chaise, grinned at Gideon, waved a hand, and then engaged in a frankly curious study of his brother.

"Hello, son," Gideon said, and then began to toss the bags into the freight box. There was a way between them, a warm regard that Jeff recognized in the offhand manner they shook hands.

"Picked a fine day to come back," Marcus remarked, and then, "Hello, Jeff. Don't know me, do you?"

"You've grown," Jeff admitted. He put his bags in with Gideon's. Then he shook hands with his brother; then they stood there, facing each other, Marcus grinning a little. Gideon came around the chaise, watching the two of them, feeling the wonderful achievement of having them both with him, together like that, the massive, earnest pile of Jeff facing the grinning, handsome boy. "I'll drive," Gideon said. "Get in." "Dr. Jackson?" Marcus smiled. Jeff said, "That's right. My God, how old are you?"

"You've forgotten that too—twenty."

"Twenty," Jeff repeated.

"Get in," Gideon said. Marcus told Jeff, "You first, doctor," bowing and extending a hand. "All right," Gideon told them. The three crowded onto the single seat, and Jeff put an arm around Marcus. "How was Scotland?" "Lonely," Jeff said. Marcus said aloofly, "You talk like a foreigner; you back to stay now?" "Maybe." "You'll find it changed," Marcus said. "We haven't sat still."

Gideon listened to them; it was good to be in the old chaise with his sons, to have the reins in his hand, and to be guiding the little black mare down the road. It was a fine, clear March day, not too cool, not too warm, the sort of a day just before the spring that can be more wonderful in South Carolina than anywhere else in the world. The mare was a five-year-old that he had bought two summers before, a small, alert animal with a smooth trot. He liked to drive; all during the long winter months in Washington, he had been thinking of this, of sitting behind the mare, listening to the steady thud of its hoofs. When they turned off the dirt road onto a corduroy causeway through a neck of cypress swamp, he told Jeff proudly:

"We built this four years ago. It cuts the distance to the railroad in half."

"We built other things," Marcus remarked, unable to keep a smug note of satisfaction out of his voice. Jeff had been away; he had done the things Marcus wanted to do. Gideon glanced sidewise at them. "Jeff's home to stay," he said.

"Is he? He'll find it mighty lonely at Carwell."

Gideon told Jeff how they had built the causeway. Most of them had worked on the railroad right of way, and knew the mechanics behind the principle. They had laid out the line of the road themselves, straight as an arrow, without an engineer, a mile and a half of it. "When I mentioned it in the house," Gideon said, "the only comment came from one of my colleagues, who wanted to know how we came by the right to build on government property."

Marcus looked at his father. Jeff sang softly, "My daddy went a hunting, Lord, Lord, Lord, my daddy went a hunting, Lord, Lord, Lord . . ."

"You remember that?"

"I remember a good deal," Jeff said.

Jenny was grown, a woman, her full breasts high under her smock; Jeff held her and his mother in his arms. "You're so big, so big." "I'm no bigger," Jeff smiled. Rachel wept with complete happiness; she had grown old more markedly than Gideon; she kept touching Jeff's face, running her hand across his woolly hair.

Gideon and Marcus stood apart from them. Marcus said to his father, "I read in the papers—"

"Yes."

"How was it? Does it mean—?"

"I'm not sure what it means," Gideon said. "We'll talk about it later."

Marcus said, "They don't know us if they think, up there in Washington, that they can wipe us off with the stroke of a pen."

"We'll talk about it later."

"They don't know us," Marcus said.

They led Jeff around and showed him things. Suddenly, everything had become new again. They showed him the house, a simple frame structure of five rooms, painted white outside. The chimney was red brick. "Kiln brick," Jenny said. Rachel showed the kitchen; they had tin pans, bright and shiny, a whole set of them in graduated sizes hanging from the wall; there was an iron spider. And more wonderful than anything, there was an inside pump. Rachel pumped fresh, cold well water. "Here, just you try it, Jeff." He had to try it, drink a glass and say what fine water it was. Jeff said, "Are the other places like this, the other people? I mean, you being a Congressman—"

"A person's house is like himself, different in one man than in another. We haven't had to complain. This is a good land for a man who loves it and understands it." Jeff wanted to know what became of the old slave cabins, and Gideon said they were still there, untenanted. "No one lives there now?" "No one," Gideon said. "No one bought the house, no one wanted it." There was a note in his voice that made Jeff look at him curiously. Marcus said that afterwards, if the doctor had time, they could walk over to the big house.

Rachel was torn between a desire to serve the hot bread and chicken she had prepared and show Jeff the rest of the house. She would say nothing about the real beds with metal springs; he would have to see them for himself. She led him into the bedrooms.

"Where does Ellen live?" he asked.

"With Brother Peter. All of Allenby's children with Brother Peter."

"Was it bad for her when the old man died?"

"She came here," Marcus said. "She wanted to be here."

"But she went back?"

"Yes, she went back."

"She knew I was coming?"

"Yes, she knew. All the people know. They'll come later."

Rachel spread her hands on the bed and pushed up and down. "Soft and sweet, like a baby in a cradle. Feel here, Jeff." He pressed on the mattress. "Just set on it." He sat down, smiling at her. "Go ahead, go ahead and move up and down, up and down." He jounced up and down, then rose and put his arms around Rachel. She couldn't resist the kitchen now, whirled him through the other bedroom and then into and out of the parlor, a small room packed close with overstuffed Victorian furniture, a table, and Gideon's books. Then they sat at the kitchen table and Jeff told her how wonderful the bread was. "There ain't no corn bread in Scotland?" Jeff answered, no, none, none anywhere in that whole land. To please Rachel, he ate more than he could hold, just ate and ate, and then she began to cry again, looking at him and touching his hands. "All right, mother, now everything's all right." But she kept on crying.

Gideon and Marcus went out to the porch. "She shouldn't take on so," Gideon said uneasily. The need, the aching hunger in Rachel had never been so apparent as now. "I'll unhitch the mare," Marcus said.

"He'll want to go to Ellen."

"Will he?"

"I guess he will."

"Well, they're going to come over here, all of them, they are. He can just as well wait here. I'll unhitch the mare."

Gideon nodded. Marcus led the horse away, and Gideon stood on the porch, leaning against one of the posts, somewhat sad, somewhat lonely. This should be a beginning; instead it was an end. He shook his head savagely; only a fool would think that way. Washington was one thing, unhealthy, full of small, hungry, frustrated, ambitious men; this was something else, this was his home. Washington was not America; this, multiplied over a million times, was—this small frame house, the homely furniture that filled it, the live oaks and the locusts that covered it over and shaded it from the sun, the sweeping hillsides, the fields where cotton and corn and tobacco would grow soon, the plough that Marcus had left out there, a few hundred yards from the house, tilted, the stiff, wet March soil clinging to its blade—all this was his, his own. This he had fought for, slaved for, worked for, planned for; a man is not parted from the ground that has tasted his blood, his free footsteps. A man has his feet in the soil, and there he stands.

Marcus went into the house, and told Jeff, "She's coming now," nodding over his shoulder. Jeff went outside alone. Brother Peter came walking through the slanting shadows toward the house, holding Ellen's arm. Brother Peter had grown a beard since Jeff last saw him; close to sixty years, his thin, tall figure had a patriarchal dignity. The beard was white, and he walked with a limp. Gideon said that he had been ailing. When an old field slave passed forty-five, he was hardly ever much good for anything; rheumatism crept into all his bones; malarial fever wracked him, and an enlarged heart recorded the endless hours of toil behind him. But the girl by his side was as she had always been, as Jeff remembered her, more mature, rounder, more full in body, but much as Jeff remembered her, the head held high, the glossy black hair braided behind her shoulders.

Jeff walked toward them, and Brother Peter and the girl stopped. Jeff saw the old man bend toward her and say something. Then the girl stood without moving. Brother Peter smiled at Jeff and said:

"Welcome home, my son."

Jeff halted a few paces from them. Ellen's face was turned toward him. Then he went over to her and took her hand and said, "Hello, Ellen. Do you remember?" She nodded, just slightly.

"I'll go up to the house and pay my respects to Brother Gideon," Brother Peter said. "And you two just come along when it pleases you."

Jeff nodded. The old man walked away. Jeff remained there, holding her hand, and she didn't move, standing straight and still. She wore a green calico frock, a blue cape thrown over her shoulders, black stockings and black shoes. And finally she said, "Jeff, do I look the same—do I look the way you wanted me to look?"

"Just that way."

"No difference, Jeff?"

"There's always a difference. But you look the way I wanted you to look."

"I'm older, Jeff."

"We're both of us older."

He took her arm and they began to walk. Jeff led her along the slope, toward the field Marcus had been ploughing. As it was in the old times, he told her how the sun was setting. He was full of Carwell, choking with it, feeling all the sensuous rush of discovery that comes with a return to youth. The smoky, mist-filled, fog-corroded Scottish skies were already part of an only dimly-recalled past; here the sky was a glaze of March blue, streaked with the sunset colors of gold and orange and pink. Here the land was warm and lush and soft; he and his kind were not made for rocky, treeless hillsides. He had finally come home, and as with Gideon, that in itself was sustenance and comfort. He told Ellen how the sky was, but not how it had been in Scotland. He bent over the plough and crushed the strong-smelling dirt in his hands, and then pressed it against hers. "How far is Scotland?" she wanted to know, and he told her that it was at least four thousand miles from here. But that was distance beyond her conception, just distance and distance, gathering on without end. "It's good you're back. But you're different now, Jeff. You're a man. You're a doctor. My father was a doctor. Did you know, Jeff?"

"Of course I knew."

They climbed the hillside toward the house, stopping to rest where Marcus had built a bench. The house stood like a small, squat box in the gathering dusk above them. People were coming; the sound of voices drifted down. There was a steady thud-thud of horses' hoofs on the other cheek of the hill, on the little road that led to the house. Someone up there called:

"Jeff—oh, where are you?"

"They're calling us," Ellen said.

"We'll go up in a little while."

They sat there, and it grew dark. A dog barked and barked. Jeff said finally, "Have you thought that you would marry me when I came back?"

"Do you want to marry me?"

"I want to," Jeff said.

"A blind woman."

"Some day," Jeff said, "I'll learn how to give you back your eyes."

"They're calling us," she told him.

He took her hand and led her up to the house.

Everyone at Carwell had come. Horses and mules were hobbled all the length of the barnyard. The women had brought their children, new children whom Jeff had never seen before. The house was full; the porch was full. People crowded around him, the older people, flinging more questions at him than he could answer. The young men, who were children when he had gone away, stood apart. The girls stared at him. The women cried with Rachel. It surprised Jeff to see how many white folks there were, the casual, easy way they mingled with the Negroes. Some of them he knew, the lanky, red-headed Abner Lait, squat, small-eyed Frank Carson; others, he didn't know. There were young men his age, tow-headed sunburnt boys who watched him curiously but without malice. The new schoolmaster was there, a Rhode Island Yankee called Benjamin Winthrope. He said, "The benefit to the community of having you here, Dr. Jackson, is inestimable. I presume you'll stay." "I hope to," Jeff nodded. There was a white man, a worn, small man, Fred Mc-Hugh by name, who said to Jeff, "The way my woman's ailing—you couldn't come along and see her?" "I could, tomorrow," Jeff agreed. McHugh said, "There's a pain in her belly like a snake eating her." "I'll come," Jeff said.

Marcus had an accordion. He sat on the edge of the porch, playing, "My mammy chased me home to Atlanta, to Atlanta, to Atlanta." The young people around him kept time, beating their feet on the ground, clapping their hands. Gideon opened three jugs of corn, and everybody had to drink. Rachel and the women stood over the stove with frying pans and pots. The strong sound of voices singing ran over the dark fields, "My mammy chased me home to Atlanta—"

Brother Peter said to Gideon, "We have our rewards, we taste of happiness." And some of the people standing by nodded, "Amen."

Jeff said to Marcus the next day, "Come along."

"Some men can play, others got to work."

"There's time for work."

"Go with him," Gideon said. "I'll pick up your plough." He was back in his old and shapeless shoes, jeans, a brown shirt. "Go with him," Gideon said. Marcus harnessed the mare, and they drove the chaise to the schoolhouse. It was a single-room, white-painted frame building with a short steeple on the farther end, and that way served the dual purpose of meeting house and school. Some thirty boys and girls of varying ages sat in the pews; Winthrope's was the complex problem of teaching all subjects for all ages and preserving order at the same time. A harried man, he was flustered and flattered that Jeff had come so soon. The visit broke down discipline, and he alternated between imposing order on the class and explaining his methods to Jeff. One age group would study while he gave oral instruction to another.

"It's difficult," he admitted. "Two teachers and two rooms would be so much better. I've found, however, that certain things break down. If I speak on literature for the oldest, it does not harm the youngest to listen."

"Naturally not," Jeff admitted.

"Of course, I am comparatively new here. Old Mr. Allenby, who preceded me, had his own methods. They were not the most modern, you understand."

"Still, when I remember that even a schoolhouse was once a dream . . ."

They drove on. Jeff said, "I want to stop at McHugh's house. You know where that is?"

"I know. Because his wife's sick?"

"He wants me to look at her."

"So we have a doctor now."

"Worse things could happen," Jeff said.

"Maybe so."

Jeff looked at him, but Marcus said nothing more. McHugh's place was in sight of the old plantation house, a small building, but set off with care. He had planted shrubs around it, an unusual thing in that section. He lived with his wife, a good deal alone, mixing hardly with anyone; he had no children. When Jeff came in and saw the neglect, he asked McHugh, "How long has she been sick?"

"Ailing on and off a year now. She stays to bed now. Last night she didn't scream none, just moaning and whimpering. He led Jeff into the bedroom, where a colorless, thin woman of forty lay. "This is Gideon's boy, Jeff. He's a doctor man from studying in the old country. He's a fine boy, Sally. He going to look at you, please, Sally."

She said nothing, just lay there, staring at the ceiling. "Would you go out?" Jeff asked McHugh. After he left, the woman didn't move. Jeff said, "Please, ma'am, I'm a doctor. Maybe I can help you."

"If you can, you can."

Jeff touched her abdomen, and she twisted and groaned with pain. When he came out, McHugh was waiting for him. "Did you have Dr. Leed up from town?"

"I had him."

"What did he say?"

"He say she's going to die," McHugh muttered.

"Did he know what it was?"

"Can't ask Doc Leed no questions," McHugh said. "He don't take to Carwell folks. He say she going to die, that's all."

Marcus, standing there, asked, "Do you know what it is, Jeff?"

"I think I know. I think it's what they call typhlitis—that's an inflammation of a part of the intestines, a small, finger-like projection. Often, for some reason we don't understand, an inflammation sets in, and if uncontrolled, becomes gangrenous. At a certain stage, it responds to ice treatments. At this stage, it doesn't."

"You mean she's going to die?" McHugh asked.

Jeff nodded.

"You can't do nothing? Jesus Christ, you can't do nothing?"

Jeff said, "I remember, when I was with Dr. Emery, I saw a surgeon cut out the part. The patient recovered. That surgeon operated. I never saw another operation of the sort. In Edinburgh, they admitted it fatal."

"Could you operate?" Marcus asked.

"I don't know—"

"Well, God damn it, you can try, can't you? If she's going to die anyway!"

"I don't know how," Jeff said. "You can't try something when you don't know how."

"Why not?"

Jeff stared at Marcus. McHugh was watching them both, his upper

lip trembling. He said, "Look a here, Jeff. I know Gideon—way
back. I know Gideon. Time was, they said to me, God damn you,
McHugh, stay away from that nigger. You know how it was, send
me a note with blood on it, stay away from that nigger. Then
Gideon come to me and talk about buying the land; I go along with
him. I go along with him every time. I go off to Aiken to be a vote
watcher, after they tar and feather a white man for voting niggers.
You ask Gideon? Just ask him if I held back. Just ask him how I
told that son of a bitch Jason Hugar—"

"All right," Jeff nodded. "If I leave her alone, she hasn't more
than a few days to live, and she'd be in pain all the time, terrible
pain. Marcus, drive back to the house. Bring my small bag; bring
some clean sheets and towels. Tell mother to come back with you.
Have you any corn whisky?" he asked McHugh. The man nodded.
"All right, go in and ease her and begin to feed her whisky, just a
little at a time; try not to make her sick; don't give her enough to
make her drunk, no more than half a cupful all told. Wait a minute, put a fire in your stove first and set some water to boil. Who
does she trust, among the women?"

Pale, frightened, McHugh said, "Helen Lait."

"Fetch her, Marcus. Can she stand up? Do you understand what
I'm going to do, McHugh? I'm going to cut open your wife's stomach and cut out that diseased portion. It's going to hurt her. It's
going to be a bad thing to watch. And I have to do it right away."

McHugh nodded.

"I want your permission. I want you to say that you're willing."

"I'm willing," McHugh whispered.

"Understand—this is something I never did before. I don't even
know how to do it. If I make a mistake, your wife is going to die.
Even if I do it right, the gangrene may set in and she may die.
That's a risk you take in any operation, and here, with these primitive facilities, it's worse."

"I'm willing," McHugh said.

Gideon was on the porch, waiting, when Jeff came back to the
house. It was almost sunrise. Jeff said tiredly, "Didn't you sleep?"

"No—I had a lot to think about. Is she still alive?"

Jeff nodded. "She's sleeping now, quietly. She's all right, I think
—no, I know it. She's all right."

"Try to get some sleep yourself."

Jeff smiled and shook his head. He sat down on the edge of the
porch, next to Gideon. The world grew lighter. Presently, the first
edge of the sun showed. A cock crowed somewhere. Softly, Jeff said,
"My God, when I think about it—when I think that only two
men in the whole world have done it before. When I think of how
simple it is, once you know. When I think that I did it here, with
nothing, do you understand, with nothing."

"I've been thinking that," Gideon said.

"Do you know how many people die every year with typhlitis?
Thousands, perhaps. A country doctor calls it acute indigestion, or
poisoning, or a tumor. But it's typhlitis—"

Gideon nodded, put a hand on Jeff's shoulder.

"You didn't want me to come here."

"I didn't want you to come," Gideon admitted. "I had reason,
Jeff."

"There are no reasons," Jeff said. "Do you know that when I was
just a boy, I used to envy you. You were possessed; you were building a new world. Well, I don't envy you now; I think I know you.
I'm going to go on building, here—I'm going to build—"

"Try to get some sleep."

"I can't sleep now," Jeff smiled. "My God, how can I sleep now?"

A week later, Jeff and Ellen were married. All of Carwell packed
the little schoolhouse. Brother Peter, in his new black deacon coat,
said, "Do you, Jeff Jackson, take this woman—?" Gideon watched,
thinking how strangely, how surely and slowly time moved. He felt
old; in a sense, he felt used up. He stood with his arm around
Rachel, and he listened to Brother Peter's voice, that voice which
had been with him all his life, that sure, confident, resonant
voice . . . .

Jeff had picked for his home a small plot of land near the schoolhouse, a piece that was owned by the people in community. They
had set this section aside for a school and a cemetery, and as Jeff
said lightly, it might well do for him to be near both. Gideon
arranged for the building; they were old hands at it by now. The
timber was their own, two by fours, sweet-smelling pine siding,
three-quarter inch plank for the flooring, dovetail oak to do the
inside properly. All of it was cut at the mill and carted over. Hannibal Washington, a fine bricklayer, set in the hearths and chimneys.
Jeff spent hours drawing plans: a sunlit examination room, a space

for two beds, a large section that would someday be an operating room. He said to Gideon, finally, "It comes out the largest house at Carwell."

"Which is fitting," Gideon agreed.

"Where will the money come from?"

"I have enough money for that, I think," Gideon smiled.

"I can't take any more from you. I've been taking all these years."

"I wouldn't worry about it, Jeff. You'll want equipment, won't you, furniture, beds? Other things?"

"They cost a lot."

"We'll manage. I suppose you could find some of it in Columbia, but I think we'd do better in Charleston. We'll go there soon." He had other reasons for wanting to go to Charleston, but he thought it would be nice if the two of them, he and Jeff, could go together. For the time being, Jeff and Ellen lived with Gideon. There was a deep trust and close communion between Ellen and Rachel, something Gideon did not share. Once Jeff said to his father, "Do you hold it against me, my marrying Ellen?"

"A man should marry the woman he loves," Gideon replied. And he tried to tell that to himself, to make himself believe that along with many other things. As he realized later, much of the world he lived in that March of 1877 was a fool's world; for Gideon Jackson to believe that the sun stood still and that time stood still was strange: stranger even than that was the fact that he had so much real happiness in those few weeks, happiness marred by many small things—but real happiness. For the first time in almost a decade, Gideon laid aside his books; he didn't want to read, to study, to think. Giving Jeff his parlor-study to take care of the increasing number of patients, he spent the whole of every day working with Marcus.

For people so far apart, so different in basic matters, he and Marcus understood each other well. Marcus lacked the driving pain that was a part of Gideon and Jeff; for them there was the whole of the puzzling world, for Marcus the world was constrained and understandable, and in a sense more complete. Marcus was a sinner; Brother Peter admitted that sadly yet comprehendingly; Marcus loved the fact of women, body, breast and thigh, without shame yet without lust—and animal health and freedom filled him like a cup brimming over with life liquid. Small and slim as he was, he could outwork Gideon; he drank with the white men, the way they

drank, matching Leslie Carson's son, Joe, drink for drink, down a
half-gallon jug of raw corn. He loved to dance. His accordion made
the old music new; all the old swamp songs, the tired, pleading songs
of slavery, he played, but under his fingers they became something
new. He gave them new rhythms, new life—

He worshipped Gideon. He knew cotton, but Gideon knew it
better; he knew the soil and bowed to Gideon there. They worked
at the forge in the barn and put a new tire on a cartwheel. Stripped
to the waist, Gideon drove his hammer like a smith. Forty-five
years hadn't taken the strength out of his arms, and as the hammer
came down again and again, it filled the world with its sound.
"Mark it," the boy sang, turning the iron, "mark it, mark it, mark
it!" And Gideon piled on, sweat streaming down his face. They
shifted all the remaining fodder into a new bin, working together in
smooth rhythm with their forks, singing together, "I got a crick in
my back, I'm old and tired." They cleared swamp growth for planting, swinging two-edged axes in short, stinging blows, and came
tramping back to the house, laughing with pleasure, filthy but delighted with themselves. Jeff told Gideon, "At your age, that isn't
the wisest thing—"

"At my age," Gideon smiled.

"It's not as if you did it all the time. When you live a sedentary
life most of the year—"

Gideon and Marcus took a day off hunting, Gideon with a rifle in
hope of raising a deer, Marcus with a shotgun, saying he would be
satisfied with rabbits. They whistled their two speckled pointers,
filled their pockets with bread, and set off across the fields one cold,
crisp morning. They sang their own song, softly and happily,
"Daddy went a hunting, Lord, Lord, Lord, yes, Daddy went a
hunting, Lord, Lord, Lord . . ." The dogs fanned out and cut back
and forth across the meadows. The two men didn't talk much;
somehow, it never mattered that Gideon and Marcus had so little to
say to each other; they fitted.

It was almost nightfall when they came home. Not hide nor hair
of a deer had Gideon seen, but Marcus's pouch held a brace of fat
rabbits. He took them to the barn to skin and dress them and give
the dogs their reward of the gizzards; Gideon went to the house.
Jeff was waiting for him, his face like a piece of granite, his eyes
hard, the way Gideon had never seen them before. He led his father

into the parlor; Abner Lait sat there, his big red hands tight on his knees.

"What is it?" Gideon wanted to know.

Abner Lait looked at him strangely, and Gideon said, "For God's sake, what happened?" Jeff motioned him into the bedroom; Rachel sat there, her face blank of expression. A man on the bed moaned a little, twisted a little; his whole body was wrapped in bandages. "McHugh," Gideon whispered. Jeff said, "That's right."

Gideon went to the bed and said, "Fred—hello, Fred." McHugh lay there as before, twisting a little, moaning a little. Gideon took his hand, "Fred—it's Gideon."

Back in the parlor, they were joined by Marcus. "He was whipped?" Gideon asked.

"You could say it that way, whipped."

"His wife?"

"She's dead," Abner Lait said quietly. "Those sons of bitches murdered her. Those filthy bastards took her out of her bed and killed her."

"Who?" Gideon whispered.

Jeff told him as much as they could get from the tortured, half insane McHugh. Six men in the white robes of the Klan had come to his house last night. They dragged him and his wife from bed, in spite of his pleading that his wife was sick, that it would kill her. They dragged them into the barn, tied their crossed wrists to a rafter, and whipped them.

"I don't think his wife suffered much," Jeff said. "I think she fainted almost immediately. The wound opened, and she died. But Fred had to hang there and watch her, until almost three o'clock when we found them."

"Will he live?" Gideon said.

Smiling strangely, Jeff answered, "That's an academic question. He's out of his mind and his arms are no good. He'll never be able to work again."

Abner Lait said, "You know what I want to do, Gideon. I'd like to know what you're going to do."

"It's time you told them, isn't it?" Jeff said.

"I didn't see any use in telling them."

"It's time you told them, I think," Jeff said.

"All right, tomorrow," Gideon nodded. "We'll have a meeting tomorrow."

Jeff was waiting for Marcus on the porch. He caught him by the arm and stopped him. "Marcus."

"Yes?"

"What are you holding against me?" Jeff asked.

"Holding against you? I ain't holding a thing against you."

"Do we go on like this?"

"We're going on all right," Marcus said.

"What have I done?" Jeff said.

"It's nothing you done."

"Is it because I've been away and you stayed here? Is that it?"

"No—"

"What then?"

"Nothing," Marcus said. "How many times I got to tell you that? Nothing."

"All right—don't be angry."

"I ain't angry."

"You remember, when we were children, it was different."

"Everything's different for children."

"You think that, don't you?"

Marcus kept silent.

"You think that, don't you?"

Still, Marcus kept silent.

"Do you know what's coming? Did he tell you what's coming? What he thinks is coming?"

"I didn't ask him, he didn't tell me," Marcus said.

"He thinks it's the end of all this—did you know that?"

Marcus nodded.

"What are you going to do?"

"He knows what to do," Marcus replied.

The men filled the schoolhouse, black men and white men in their work clothes, blue jeans and blue overalls, heavy leather shoes, brown and red shirts. With the white men, the sun line ended at the neck and wrists; the skin was wind-blown and sun-tanned. The black men ranged in color from plum to ivory. Counting Winthrope, the school teacher, counting the eighteen- and nineteen-year-olds, there were more than fifty men in the room. One was a doctor, one was a preacher, one was a schoolteacher, one was a congressman; the main trade of the rest was farming. Principally, they grew cotton, but they grew tobacco too, some rice, corn; they held cattle and hogs and horses. They made up a community called Carwell, and what they made had not existed a decade before, nor did it have its exact counterpart anywhere outside of the south. War, ruin, death, emancipation, and peonage had thrown them together; they had built from nothing in the strictest sense of the word, and they could look about them and say that this or that or everything had come from their hands. They had created everything among them, schools, houses, mills, ideas, because there had been nothing before. All the long centuries between feudalism and democracy, they had crossed over in one long step.

As Gideon Jackson stood before them now, looking at them, weighing them, remembering faces, remembering the different lives each man there had lived, he thought of that. Jeff wanted to build —and Gideon had a sudden despairing vision of how men could build. He said to the people:

"All of you know me. I have talked to you before."

They knew him; they had voted for him; they had driven their wagons twenty miles in every direction, telling people that a vote for Gideon Jackson meant something.

"You know what happened to Fred McHugh. We buried his wife this morning. In our little graveyard, outside of here, four people lie who have died through violence, who have been murdered at Carwell in the past eight years. That is a terrible thing. To take a human life in any cause is a terrible thing. But men become beasts when they murder to impose terror on free men. You know why Fred McHugh was whipped, why his wife was tortured to death— only for one reason, to tell the white men here at Carwell that they can no longer live together or work together with black men.

"Why is that so important? Why is it so necessary here that the white man should learn to hate the Negro, to despise him, to humiliate him, and that the Negro in turn should learn to fear the white man, avoid him, mistrust him? Is it because the two, the black and the white, are incompatible, that they cannot work or live together? But Carwell, a thousand Carwells all through the southland have proven differently. Is it because the blood will mix, the white being debauched by the black, as the Klan has screamed all through the South? But we have lived here for almost a decade, and that has not happened. Our children have sat in this schoolhouse together, and that has not happened. Then what is the reason? What is this great sin that we have committed here at Carwell, that black men and white men have committed everywhere in the South when they put their good right arms together? It is important for us to know, not only the black people here, but for the white people.

"I don't want to frighten you, my friends. God knows, I had reason enough to be frightened in Washington, but when I came back to Carwell, all seemed different. It reassured me; this is my home; these people are my friends. They knew me when I was a slave, when I ran away from Dudley Carwell, my master, when I came back, as so many of you came back, to a great domain which had lost its master, its overseers, its whips and its compulsions. I looked around me, and here was reason, here were the good things of life; so I said to myself, all the evil things I dreamed of cannot be, not here, not where we have built. I lived for a little while in my fool's paradise.

"That is gone, my friends. I want to tell you the truth now, I want you to understand why Fred McHugh lies in my house, his arms twisted from their sockets and useless to him, his wife dead, his mind gone. I want to tell you why, when my son and I came down here from Washington, we were forced to ride in a separate car marked, 'Colored.' I want to tell you why, all over the South, from Texas to Virginia, cries of suffering fill the air. And most of all, I want you to know why, from here on, the white man will be set against the black like a dog against a sheep; why, if they succeed, it will be a dream that there had ever been such a place as Carwell.

"How is it that no one here at Carwell belongs to the Klan? How is it that all over the South honest, hardworking farmers till their land and do not belong to the Klan? Who belongs to the Klan, if it is, as our newspapers tell us, the honest protest of an indignant and suffering and prostrate South? Where does it come from? Who organized it? If it wishes to save the South from the savage nigger, why does it strike down two white men for every black man, why did it come here to Carwell and kill Fred McHugh's sick wife?

"It took me a long time to realize what the Klan is, how it operates, why it was organized. I know now, just as you know. The Klan has only one purpose, to destroy democracy in the South, to kill off the independent farmer, to split, in so doing, the black man from the white man. The black man will become a peon, not too different from the slave he was before the war. And because he is that, a slave in effect if not in fact, the white man will be drawn down with him. A few will become great and mighty, as before the war. But only a few. For the rest of us, poverty, hunger, hatred—such hatred as will become a sickness for this nation.

"That is the sin Fred McHugh committed at Carwell. He was tortured so that Abner Lait, Jake Sutter, Frank Carson, Leslie Carson, Will Boone—every white man here would take heed and play his correct part in the day of reckoning. That is up to you; there is a way out that is no way out. Join the Klan, cooperate with the Klan, don't resist—and destroy yourselves. You know those men, the dirty, diseased, degenerate louts who were the slave runners, the overseers, the whip men, the hangers on, the toughs, the gamblers, the cheats, the sheriffs, the men who became brave with a gun in their hands but not brave enough to be seen at the front, not brave enough to die, the way thousands of southern men died because they loved their land. I don't have to describe them; when they dragged Sally McHugh out of her bed, hanged her up by her hands, and whipped her to death, they described themselves. They are the scum, the dregs of this land. For every one of them, there are a hundred decent, good men in this South; but the scum are organized; the decent, good men are not. They have money; they have hirelings to plead their cause at Washington; they have rich planters to lead them and direct them. We have none of those things—and I, for one, say thank God.

"What are we to do? I know what my friend Abner Lait wanted to do, to take his gun and kill Jason Hugar. That's not the way. To lose our heads, to murder the way they murder—that's not the way."

"Then what is the way, Gideon?" Abner Lait shouted. "Why don't you tell us what happened at Washington?"

"I'll tell you. At Washington, we were sold. We were sold by the Republican Party, my party, Abe Lincoln's party—and the price was the presidency. The planters paid that price. In return, when Hayes takes office, the troops will be withdrawn, from Columbia, from Charleston—from everywhere. The Klan will become the law—"

"Then you admit it!"

"I admit it. I told you I would give you the truth. But what are we going to do? Lose our heads? Murder? Rip ourselves to pieces? Do their work for them before they're ready to do it themselves? Is that what you want?" Gideon paused and stared at them. "Is that what you want?" he repeated. "If that's what you want, I'm no use here—I'll go."

There was a long moment of silence, and then Frank Carson said, "Go on, Gideon, tell us what you think."

"All right. Remember that we're still strong. Here in this room are fifty of us; we have arms; we have ammunition; we have drilled together and worked together. I think we can defend ourselves if we don't lose our heads. On the other hand, defense will not help us; to lose gloriously will not help us. We have to organize with others; all over the South are thousands like us. I've arranged to go to Charleston and meet with Francis Cardozo and other Negro leaders. Anderson Clay and Arnold Murphy, white leaders, will be there. Perhaps together, we can find some way of forestalling them. I'm not promising you anything; I'm not hopeful. I don't know— But let me try. After that, there will be time for other things. Let me try; let Jason Hugar live; it won't change things to kill him. If you'll give me a chance—"

The men sat there, and then a few heads nodded. "All right," Abner Lait said softly. "Try."

Ellen couldn't sleep; all night long she heard, through the wall, the soft, animal-like moans of Fred McHugh. It was the body and the sound and the memory of terror; she remembered the things she didn't want to remember; she remembered hiding in the woods; she remembered death and screaming. She lay there shivering and listening until, unable to stand it any more, she woke Jeff. He said, "What is it, what is it, darling?"

"I'm afraid."

"There's nothing to be afraid of."

"I'm afraid—" His body shaped itself under her hands, his strong, narrow thighs, his great barrel of a chest, the slabs of loose, relaxed muscle that lay all over him, his neck, his chin, eyes, mouth. In the night, in the darkness, he and she were the same; she clung to him, whispering, "Jeff, Jeff, Jeff."

"You see I'm here, Ellen. I'll always be here."

But she couldn't stop being afraid; she lay there, listening to the moans of the hurt man, short, sharp moans that came through his sleep. Suddenly, the full deeps of darkness encompassed her; a well of darkness that people moved into and went out of, all those shadowy figures, Allenby and the others, coming and going. She clung to Jeff with all her strength, but it was no use.

Cardozo said to Gideon, "I'm not denying the essential truth of your conclusions; I deny the dramatic form in which you present them."

"I'm not concerned with abstracts, but with the form itself. It's with the form I have to live."

Anderson Clay said, "There, I go along with Gideon."

Eight of them, five colored men and three white, sat together in Cardozo's parlor. Four of them were from South Carolina, one from Georgia, two from Louisiana, and one from Florida. They had been talking for almost three hours now, and had come to no conclusion. Some of them were militant, others were frightened; at least half of them seized upon the momentary opportunity of taking refuge in words. They talked in circles; they recounted their achievements, what they had won, gained, done—until Gideon snapped at them:

"That's over now, I tell you. That's in the past, finished. It has no meaning for today."

"But the record, dozens of Negroes and poor whites in the House, in the Senate, in the state governments, governors too—"

"I tell you it's done," Gideon said.

"By virtue of what?" Cardozo asked calmly, his judicial, quiet voice making reason where there was no reason. "Nobody, Gideon— and you know this—respects you more highly than I do. But aren't your conclusions empirical, to give them the most credit?"

"Because a man has been lynched here, tortured there, threatened, because Senator Holms confided in me, I must not anticipate results? Is that what you infer? Am I an alarmist?"

"To a degree, yes."

"Yet you, Francis, were state treasurer a year ago, and today you are not. What were the forces that operated? If I say that I will not be permitted to sit in the House again, must that be tested? Can I see no farther than my nose? If that were so, Francis, I would be a slave today, and four million other black men would be slaves."

Capra, a small, aging colored man, one time representative from Florida, interposed, "Nobody, Gideon, is denying your personal integrity."

"I don't give two damns about my personal integrity!"

"But Gideon, you tell us that the Republican Party sold the reconstruction for the election. We are the party; our lives have been dedicated to the party; the party fought for us, gave us our freedom. You have no proof. You say that the troops will be withdrawn from the South in ten days—but you have no proof. You say that there will be terror, that all we have built will be destroyed. Where is your proof?"

"It is being destroyed," Gideon said tiredly. "Look around you. No niggers on this train, no niggers on the bench, white only, white only—no niggers in this school; we built the school, but no niggers now, no niggers on this jury, the lawyer for the defense objects. Last year the Judge was a black man, a poor white—today a planter or a planter's lackey supports the lawyer's objection. A nigger is on trial, but no niggers on the jury."

"I concede that," Cardozo nodded. "Essentially, we have been forced to compromise—"

"Is that compromise?" Anderson Clay smiled. "Do you compromise with the air you breathe, Francis? With the food you eat? These things are the blood and bone and muscle of our lives! You can't compromise with a son of a bitch who wants your blood!"

"You talk as a white man. Ask a black man—"

"God damn it, I'm sick of hearing that! Whatever we have we've gotten because black men and white men stood together. Gideon's right, think the way you do and we go down separately—we go down to hell."

Ables, who three years ago was a secretary of state, asked Gideon, "But why, precisely, should the Party have sold us, as you put it? For what end?"

"Because we've served our purpose, we've broken the planters' backs. In the last eight years, this has become an industrial nation, the greatest industrial machine on earth. The north has the west and the southwest; even here in the South mills are beginning to open. Let the planters have their serfs back—the North is safe."

"And the people's party—"

"There is no people's party today," Clay growled.

Cardozo answered wearily, "Still, what you ask cannot be done, Gideon. To reinaugurate the Negro and poor white militia after it has been abolished—how? In defiance of the law?"

"The people are the law."

"That, Gideon, is a more primitive conception than I would expect from you. The people are the law only through due process."

"A process that wrote into the Constitution the right of the people to bear arms, to have a militia!"

"We could carry the matter to the Supreme Court, that would take months. You suggest a convention to unite every pro-reconstruction force in the South—that, indeed, Gideon, would produce violence."

"I see. If we raise a voice in our defense, we promote violence."

"Yes."

Gideon said, "And if there should be violence regardless? As, indeed, there has been."

Abels shook his head. "What's the use, Jackson? We have been over this and over this, again and again."

"Do you all feel that way?" Gideon asked. He was used up now; you got to the end of a thing, and that was the end. "Is that the end, gentlemen? Well—it is one thing to have every newspaper in the country scream its lies, the golden cuspidors we spit into, the millions that go to walling our legislative hall with mirrors and gilt, the thousands in graft we have squeezed from a defenseless land, the way we have debauched southern manhood and womanhood, the carpet-baggers, the evil, money-mad Yankees who pull the strings—all that I read in my newspaper. That is one thing, gentlemen. It is another thing to sit here and have you tell me that we must not raise our voices in defense, that we must not try to bring unity to this twice damned southland of ours. I love my country, gentlemen; I didn't want to talk like this—but I have to. I love this country because it is my own, because it has been good to me, because it gave me dignity, courage, hope. Am I alone in that, gentlemen?"

They sat silent; some of them stared at the floor; some of them watched Gideon uncertainly. Anderson Clay smiled a little.

"Then you all agree with Mr. Abels?"

Still silence.

"And the curious part is," Gideon said quietly, "that even those things which you cling to will be forgotten. The black men who sat in the House, in the Senate; they will be forgotten, the black men who built schools and justice—all of it, my friends. We will not be men any more. They will grind us down until we lose our humanity, until we hate the white men as truly as they hate us. They will make of us a tortured, debased people, unlike any other people on earth.

And how long, my friends, before we see a little sunlight again? How long? Ask yourselves that."

Gideon asked Anderson Clay to come with him and meet Jeff. They walked together through the sunlit, still, white-walled streets of Charleston. It was such a spring day as Gideon remembered from long ago, here in this same city. The palmettos wore the clean green of the new season high on their spreading tops. The birds sang and flashed their bright plumage. The sky was a gentle blue, traced through with streaks of mist. The things that Gideon had seen on and off for so many years were familiar, and the familiarity gave the lie to his gloom. The city was so staid, so beautiful, so gently civilized that it made its reassurance without protest or pressure, but simply and matter of factly.

Anderson Clay said, "I thought I'd like to live here some day."

"It's a nice place to live."

Clay said, after a while, "You know, in a way, Gideon, you were wrong and they were right. They'll live on, but you—" "They'll live on and they'll change slowly," Gideon answered thoughtfully. "Each year a little more pressure, a little more of this and that taken away. They won't know. Is that best?"

"I don't say if it's best."

"But you thought it was hopeless, from the beginning?"

"You see, Gideon, we didn't know. We started from nothing, groping around in the dark. We had only one idea, to build— schools, courts, hospitals, roads, people too. Maybe you could say that all of us, your people, mine, went a little insane when they saw there was freedom stretching ahead, maybe forever. All they thought was to build. The others wanted to destroy, and they organized for that. Ten days isn't long enough for us to organize, Gideon—a year isn't long enough."

"Then what?"

"Well, we'll fight," Clay shrugged. "We'll fight because we've fought before, because we're trained to fight. But they've taken that into consideration. We'll be fighting alone."

Jeff was waiting for them by the Battery. Gideon said, "My son, Dr. Jackson. Jeff, this is Anderson Clay, a good old friend of mine." Jeff shook hands with the tall white man.

"I hear you've come to Charleston, doctor, to buy supplies."

"We're building a hospital at Carwell, a small one."

Clay said, "I intend to come to Carwell next year."

"You've said that for nine years," Gideon smiled. "Each year, it's next year."

"That's right. Next year, Gideon." They crossed to the waterfront and walked along slowly. Clay and Jeff talked about Scotland, about medicine, about the lack of any sort of adequate hospital facilities in the state. "Give us time, son," Clay said.

"Some of those great old plantation houses, like the Carwell place," Jeff said. "They just stand, empty, useless—that's what a hospital should be, in the country, big, clean."

Gideon looked at Anderson Clay.

"A statesman could do worse things," Jeff said.

"He could," Clay nodded. "I hear you were just married. Congratulations."

"Thank you," Jeff said. And after a moment, "It's strange, I don't know what came of your meeting—I don't know that I care a great deal. You see, we're going on. A man who sells his soul to live in the White House can't change that."

They walked slowly. The setting sun gave the water of the bay a turning sheen of color. The gulls dropped down to the water and rose triumphantly. A small sign on the rail, unobtrusive, said, "White only." A steamer, trailing its smoke, was being piloted into the harbor. A laughing group of boys lay on the deck of a sailing gig on close tack. A carriage clattered down the street, and two children, in a grassy, iron-railed enclosure across the street, skipped rope.

At Carwell, for the first time in so many years, suddenly and desolately for Gideon, things stood still. Brother Peter, coming over to his house the day after Gideon returned, saw him sitting on the edge of the porch, elbows on knees, chin in hands. "Like that for hours," Marcus said, "low—" Gideon answered, "Evening, Brother Peter."

Brother Peter said, "Tired, Gideon?"

"Uh-huh."

Brother Peter sat down beside him, first spreading the skirts of his black deacon coat. He leaned his cane, which he had been using of late, on the porch next to him, and he set down his high black hat alongside of it. Then, sighing, he stretched his legs and remarked, "A long walk. Ain't as spry as I used to be."

"No."

"Not near as spry, Gideon."

Gideon didn't answer. Rachel came out on the porch, and Brother Peter started to rise. "No, you just sit there. Mighty glad to see you."

"Thank you, sister."

"Stay for supper?"

"Now, I don't mind if I do, thanking you kindly," Brother Peter said. Rachel glanced at Gideon, who had not turned around, and Brother Peter shook his head. Rachel stood a moment and then went back into the house. Brother Peter sat down on the edge of the porch again. "Fine woman, Sister Rachel. A pleasure to eat her food, a pleasure to sit at her table. There's something I sure miss, you up there in Washington, Gideon."

"Yes."

Brother Peter went on, after a moment, "Do you good to talk, Gideon—do any man good to talk. Let the bile out from inside him, believe me. Was it that bad in Charleston, that awful bad?"

"Just about."

"How come then, Gideon? How awful bad is something? The good Lord gives and the good Lord takes away, measure for measure. You got no faith, Gideon."

Smiling a little, Gideon said, "I wish it were faith."

"How come then? Man comes in this world just a naked little babe, goes out naked. There's the judgment and the proof, Gideon. I ain't talking about God—long time ago I give up you ever being a believer. You got a mighty store of strength, Gideon, but maybe it would have been more, you just had faith. All right, then I talk to you about men. Just leave God aside, Gideon, He don't mind that, just leave him aside and talk about men. You believe in men, Gideon?"

"Believe in men?"

"That's right, Gideon."

Gideon looked at the old man thoughtfully. Brother Peter brushed a speck of dust off his tall black hat. It was a gift from his congregation; four years, day in and day out now he had worn it, excepting rain, and it looked as good and new as ever.

"I think I believe in men," Gideon said. "I don't know—"

"How come you don't know that? Maybe man got a load of sin

on his shoulder, but how come nigger's a slave one day, free man the next?"

"And a slave again," Gideon said.

"You think that? Suppose we all die off, Gideon, everyone here-abouts. You don't think there's a little speck of something left on, little speck more than there was before. You think there ain't no hallelujah songs going to go on ringing?"

Gideon said nothing; the evening wore on, the sun sank. Marcus came up, glanced at them, and entered the house. Finally, Gideon said, "Supper soon, Brother Peter."

"Sure enough. Tell you, I got a good appetite too for an old gentleman my age. Walking does that. You just go in and I'll join you, brother."

Gideon rose and went into the house. Jeff had just finished wash-ing his hands at the kitchen pump. Rachel said, "Going to have Brother Peter for supper, Gideon."

"I know."

Jeff left the kitchen. Rachel turned to Gideon, looked at him for a moment, and then went over to him.

"Gideon?"

"Yes."

Rachel went over and touched his shirt, ran her hand down his arm. "I can stand near anything, Gideon," she said softly. "But I can't stand to see you with misery. I been less and less use, but I can't stand to see you with misery."

Gideon took her in his arms and the pressure drove the breath from her. He held her to him in a bearlike, desperate grasp, and her words came jaggedly, "Can't stand it, Gideon, can't—"

"Rachel, Rachel, baby."

"You going to smile, Gideon?"

He smiled at her, and she lay against him, inertly, her fingers plucking at his shirt.

The next morning, as Gideon stood with Jeff and Ellen, watch-ing Hannibal Washington lay the bricks for the chimney of the new house, Abner Lait stopped on his way in from town. Dropping his reins, he climbed out of his wagon and joined Gideon.

"Where'd you learn to slap that mortar?" he asked Hannibal Washington.

"Learned from my pappy—he gone and built them seven stacks up there at the big house."

"Don't tell?"

"Sure enough," Hannibal Washington said. "That a long time ago, though."

"When'd they build that old house?"

"Fifty years ago, sure enough."

"Seems like it been there forever," Abner said, plucking at Gideon's sleeve. Gideon walked over behind the wagon with him, and the white man said, "I just come from town, Gideon. Seems you were right, President made his deal with that damned old son of a bitch, Wade Hampton. The troops at Columbia got their marching orders—come April tenth, they're going to entrain for the North."

"Who said that?"

"Well, look a here at this newspaper," Abner told him, reaching into the wagon, pulling out a newspaper, and pointing to the headline: SOUTH WINS SECOND EMANCIPATION. "There it is, the whole story. The town's full of talk. Jason Hugar's strutting around in an army uniform, going to march in the victory parade at Columbia. You said make no trouble; well, I made no trouble, just watched that son of a bitch, Hugar. Where'd he fight? I been on a hell of a lot of fields, but never saw no man called Hugar."

Gideon was reading the story, scanning the lines quickly and nervously—"in amiable agreement with the governor, President Hayes set his signature to an order which finally establishes democracy and home rule in the south. The last Federal troops will be withdrawn on the tenth of April—"

"It's going to be a picnic," Abner Lait muttered.

"What?"

"You know, Gideon, my grandpappy should have gone west. Old Dan Boone come down here and just beg him to go over into Kentuck. Hell no, my smart grandpappy said. Jesus God, I wish he'd gone—I wish he'd gone into Kentuck and into Illinois and right across the whole God damned country and out of here. I wish he'd gone out of here to that blue Pacific Ocean, I wish—"

"Shut up," Gideon said, nodding at where Ellen stood. Hannibal Washington and Jeff were looking at them.

"What are you going to do, Gideon?"

"Today's the sixth, isn't it? We've got four days. I'm going to Columbia. I don't know what I'll do there; I'll try to do something."

When Gideon finished writing out the telegram in the Western
Union office, on Sumter Street in Columbia, he handed it across the
counter to the clerk. The clerk was a pimply-faced boy of nineteen.
"Read it back to me, please," Gideon said. The boy looked at him
and made no move.

"I said, read it, please."

The boy read:

"RUTHERFORD B HAYES
THE WHITE HOUSE
WASHINGTON DC

MR PRESIDENT I BESEECH YOU TO DELAY YOUR ACTION
WITHDRAWING FEDERAL TROOPS FROM COLUMBIA
STOP ABOLITION OF NEGRO AND POOR WHITE MILITIA
LEAVES PRO RECONSTRUCTION FORCES DEPENDENT
ON FEDERAL PROTECTION STOP FEAR RIOTING AND
TERROR STOP LOYAL REBUBLICANS HERE CANNOT
COMPREHEND ABANDONMENT OF ALL UNION ELE-
MENTS IN SOUTH WE PLEAD YOUR HELP AND SYM-
PATHY
                    GIDEON JACKSON
          REPRESENTATIVE FOR SOUTH CAROLINA"

"How much is it?" Gideon asked.

The boy hesitated, then said, "Ten dollars."

Gideon looked at him a moment, paid him and left. The boy
walked back to the operator and boasted, "Never seen a nigger yet
knew what a telegram cost."

"God damn you if I don't have you fired for that! How much he
give you?"

"Ten."

"Well, you going to split, God damn well. Give it here." The boy
handed over the telegram and the operator glanced at it. He
whistled and read it more carefully. "Who gave you this?"

"Some big nigger."

"Well, look. You take this over to Judge Clayton. Tell him I
want to know if I should send it. And keep your big mouth shut!"

In about twenty minutes, the boy was back. "The judge kept the
telegram and give me a dollar."

"You split!"

"The judge said we'd better damnwell keep shut, or he'd know
the reason why."

From the telegraph office, Gideon went to see Colonel J. L. Williams, in command of the Federal troops. The colonel was a busy man that day; it was an hour and a half before Gideon was shown in. Then he said, "Representative, I'm sorry. Every one in the South wants to talk to me today."

"I know," Gideon nodded. "I don't know how different my case is. Here is a copy of a telegram I sent to the president. An answer may come in a day or in ten days—until it comes, I beg of you not to let all your troops entrain."

The colonel read the telegram and then shook his head. "My orders—"

"I know you have orders, Colonel," Gideon said. "I'm not asking a personal favor. This is a matter of life and death to a great many people."

"I can't," the colonel said. "I'm sorry."

"Do you know what will follow when your troops leave?"

"Whatever I may think will follow," the colonel said, "I have to obey my orders. If you took this up with General Hampton, in command of the district—"

"That would be useless," Gideon said. "He would not. I know what orders mean. I've been in the army, Colonel."

"It's no use."

"Don't you see that the president cannot ignore the telegram."

"I could be court martialed."

"I have some influence in Washington."

"I can't do it," the colonel said, raising his voice. "Believe me, sir, however much I might want to, I can't do it. Don't you think I have eyes to see? I'm a soldier, I'm not a politician!"

For a moment, Gideon stood there, tense, sick, terrified; then he nodded. "I'm sorry."

"So am I," the colonel said.

Then Gideon left.

He remained in Columbia until the tenth of the month, making frequent visits to the telegraph office. On the ninth, he sent a second wire. On the tenth, he watched the troops march to the waiting train, and then he went back to Carwell.

On the afternoon of the fifteenth of April, the people of Carwell heard a woman shrieking. Her loud, shrill screams echoed across the place, bringing people running from many directions. A terror-stricken boy, pushing through the woods, whimpered, "The horse came back, he came back." The people followed this boy, Juddy Hale, to his father's farm. His father, Zeke Hale, was a stolid colored man, a quiet family man who farmed well and turned over a larger net cash cotton profit than almost anyone on the place. There they found Franny Hale, his wife, screaming loudly and insanely. There they found a wagon with a horse harnessed to it, and when they saw what was inside it, they turned away.

They pieced the story together. Zeke Hale had gone to town to buy some new shoes and a present for his boy, who had just turned ten. Evidently, he had been driving back slowly and enjoying the fine spring afternoon. Anyway, he was a man who liked to walk his horse whenever possible, especially if the weather showed any signs of turning hot.

At some point, on the way back from town, someone had stepped up to the slow-moving wagon and fired both barrels of a shotgun at Zeke Hale's head. The noise of the gun had caused the horse to bolt forward, pitching Zeke back into the wagon. The horse had run all the way back to the place, and Franny Hale had looked into the wagon and seen what a shotgun fired at close range can do to a man.

They buried Zeke Hale, and after that, for the first time in nine years, the men who lived at Carwell went to their work with guns slung over their shoulders.

10. HOW GIDEON JACKSON FOUGHT THE GOOD FIGHT

It was the morning of the eighteenth of April, 1877, at Carwell. The mist lay in the valleys and ran like white milk through the cypress groves. Four pointers, out hunting most of the night, loped wearily home through the pines. The high-pitched call of the roosters met them, and crows winged overhead crying, caw, caw, caw to the dawning. Then men at the various farms, milking and doing the other pre-dawn chores, thought all the thoughts that had always, from time out of memory, been a part of such morning work, would it be a fair day or a muggy day, would Nelly try to kick the bucket over, she always tried, would that fool dog across the valley get tired of his hollow belling, how fine and simple and good the voice of the crows is, just the same and just as nostalgically pleasing morning after morning, would there be bacon or fried chicken with the grits this morning, would the sick calf go on vomiting like that, would the rheumatism down near the small of the back start acting up again—none of these thoughts very complicated, none of them very important, yet none of them entirely unimportant. The sun rose over the brow of a hill, and light came with a sudden and glorious rush. In hilly country, the light splashes on one side of a slope while the other stays in shadow. The mists in the valleys churn and vanish, except where they cling to the watery bottom of a swamp hole. The snakes, copperhead, blacks, and others crawled gratefully toward the warmth; the fat terrapins came out into the sunlight. The rabbits crawled deep into the bramble patches, and the squirrels raced up and down the fine old hickories. The deer moved away to the thickets to bed down and rest.

Morning at Carwell, after the chores were done, found the men sitting down to breakfast, hot cakes, pan bread, molasses, white, cold butter with little drops of water standing stiff on the surface, bacon, grits, eggs, sometimes fried chicken or fried fresh fish, buttermilk heavy with clods of turning, milk, fried potatoes, yellow cornmeal mush cut in slices from the pan where it had set since the night before, fried in the bacon grease—all of those foods in some combination were breakfast at Carwell, and not too much for men who had already worked two or three hours. The schoolbell called for the children; they took shortcuts, no roads for them. They were filled with life at eight o'clock, pushing ankle deep through the ploughing, whooping to each other, shouting as they raced up a hillside, chucking cones at each other as they cut through a neck of piney woods. Their incredible, violent, unpredictable energy made each day a rather awesome adventure for Benjamin Winthrope. He tugged the schoolbell to give himself courage, and philosophized that anyone could teach well-behaved, gentle students. He thought of Frank Carson's daughter, sixteen years old, staring at him boldly all day with those round, clear-blue eyes of hers, and he thought of all the things that went on inside of himself. The Congregational Educational Service that had dispatched him to Carwell spoke of it as God's work, and after only a few months here he could understand why God had relegated the duty. He took comfort in his few prize students, Hannibal Washington's son, Jamie, Abner Lait's daughter, two or three more. Today, he would introduce the upper levels to Emerson. "Emerson," he repeated to himself, standing in front of the school, listening to the children's shouting, and letting his eyes roam over the sundrenched fields and woods. "Emerson," he told himself firmly.

At the breakfast table, talking to Marcus, Gideon thought vagrantly of how adaptable the human mechanism is, how easily the bizarre can become the normal, and how complete is the adjustment to almost any condition. He was saying to Marcus:

"I would add an acre of tobacco, not cotton," talking like that, matter of factly, with the two rifles leaning against the door jamb, waiting for the men to leave.

"This ain't tobacco country."

"Still," Gideon said, "we grow a good leaf. Not as fine as Piedmont or Virginia, I admit that, but it's marketable. These new things they call cigarettes are going to increase smoking."

"It's bad for soil."

"So is cotton. You sicken your soil in either case unless you rotate or leave the fields fallow. I've been preaching that for years."

Rachel said, "If it was my doing, I'd plant corn."

"We're not stock farmers."

"Got to go on doing what your grandpappy did?"

"I want to go for buying this afternoon," Jenny said.

"To town?"

"Uh-huh."

Marcus shook his head.

"Why?"

"There'll be some folks going in later on in the week," Gideon told her.

"This is a fine day."

"You stay here," Marcus told her.

"Well I don't take orders from you. I don't have to stay anywhere for you telling me."

"You stay here!"

Jenny began to sob. Ellen, who had been sitting next to her, fondled her hand. Gideon rose, then Marcus. As he started from the room, Gideon glanced toward the rifles, hesitated, then picked one up and went out with it.

At ten o'clock, Jeff was at the home of Marion Jefferson. His wife, Louise, had broken out with boils all over her hands; they were nothing serious, but they were painful and itchy and kept her awake nights. Jeff told her how to mix a soothing paste, and then he lingered on the porch to pass the time of the day with Marion. As a boy, Jeff had been one of Marion's favorites; now, as a doctor, he was like a God in Marion's eyes. As they stood there, talking about one thing and another, Trooper came running across from his place. He stopped, panting, took a deep swallow, and said:

"Jeff, I just seen Jason Hugar and Sheriff Bentley headed for your pappy's place. I been standing on the rise, and sure as God I couldn't miss the sheriff's gig. The other man's Jason Hugar, I swear."

"Well, it's nothing to be alarmed about," Jeff told him.

"Maybe it is, maybe it ain't," Marion said. "Just suppose we ride up there in your chaise." He went inside the house for his rifle. His wife, frightened, asked, "What is it? What you going to do?"

"It ain't a thing, not near," he smiled. "Just the sheriff riding over to Gideon's. We going up there to make sure."

"Don't make no trouble, Marion. We had enough of trouble."

"We sure enough did," he told her quietly. "This ain't going to be no trouble, not at all. All the same, I guess you better walk over and tell Abner Lait the sheriff's up at Gideon's."

Cutting a tall pine out by its roots, digging around it, and then chopping at the fat, moist tendrils, had employed Gideon and Marcus since they left the breakfast table. It was good work for the cool morning; it let a man give himself to the ax, taking his anger out in the best way, on inanimate objects that in no way resented it. When the pine fell, they would leave it lie all through the spring and summer, and when the leaves were turning it would be fine and crisp for cutting, ready to be marked off into four-foot logs that burned like paper. Now it had begun to totter, its long stem vibrating ever so slightly, when Marcus spied the sheriff's little gig, wheeling up from the swamp and taking the climb to the Jackson house. He dropped his ax and pointed.

"The sheriff?" Gideon asked.

"Looks enough like his gig. I'm going up to see."

Gideon nodded; they picked up their guns and walked quickly toward the house. When the shoulder of the hill hid them from the road, they broke into a run, and, panting, reached the house just a moment or two after the gig got there. Jason Hugar and the sheriff sat together, their sleeves rolled up, both of them wearing leather vests, each of them with a double barreled shotgun across his knees. Rachel was on the porch, tense, worried, breathing a sigh of relief when she saw Gideon and Marcus.

"Morning, sheriff," Gideon said. Jenny and Ellen came out on the porch and stood behind Rachel. Fracus, their spotted pointer, made a fool of himself over Marcus until he saw that he was neither noticed nor wanted, and then he lay down and watched. Marcus stood with his gun hanging through the crook of his arm, tight, bent, and only Rachel there knew that he was like a charge of gunpowder, stable yet ready to explode. Nodding at Gideon's rifle, the sheriff said:

"Going hunting, Gideon?"

"Maybe so!" Marcus snapped. "And when you talk to my father, call him mister, understand?"

"Mister," Jason Hugar drawled. "Mister."

"That's right."

"All right, mister," Hugar smiled.

"What can I do for you, sheriff?" Gideon asked softly.

"There you are," Bentley nodded. "For my money, you're a reasonable man, Gideon, and my God, if that ain't a virtue these days, I don't know what is. No use losing our heads. I got a job to do and come up here on a small matter of business—and find you menacing the law with guns. Jesus Christ, Gideon, that ain't a way for niggers, it leads to trouble—"

Marcus said, "Shut your God damned mouth!"

"Now look, son," Hugar said. "Now look, you nigger bastard," his finger curled across both triggers of the shotgun. "If you make one move with that bird gun of yours, I'm going to rip the God damn guts out of you—"

Rachel cried out, half a whimper; Gideon gripped Marcus' shoulder so that the boy felt the fingers sink in, like iron claws. "Just take it easy, Mr. Hugar," Gideon said. "There's no cause for trouble. Sheriff Bentley knows that; he knows we're law-abiding folk and never give him any cause for trouble. If we're carrying guns, it's not out of disrespect for the law; it's because a neighbor of ours was murdered just a few days ago."

"Tell you something, Gideon," Bentley said. "When a nigger gets too high, it makes trouble. The way you folks have it, that nigger was just driving along the road when someone up and shot him.

My God, that don't make sense, Gideon, it don't make one bit of sense. How in hell's name do I know what he was up to? Give a nigger one inch and he'll take the shirt off your back."

"That's why we're here," Hugar agreed.

"Why are you here?" Gideon demanded.

"God damn you, we'll ask the questions!"

"Now take it easy, Jason," the sheriff said evenly. "Gideon's got a right to ask questions; we're on his property; that's a legal matter of law. But we got a right to ask questions too. We want to settle what we're here for quiet and peaceable. Yesterday afternoon, Gideon, three niggers come up to the back door of Clark Hasting's house. Clark's in the store; Sally and the little girl are there at home. Just as nice as pie, one of the niggers says, please, Miss Sally, we're a hungering, you got a little bite to spare. Well, you never known Clark to turn a nigger away, and Sally goes to fetch something, never thinking. Meanwhile, Clark's girl, nine years old, stands there, watching the niggers—"

At that point, Jeff, Trooper and Marion Jefferson came riding up in the chaise. Gideon was heartened when he saw them. Marion and Jeff got out; Trooper sat in the chaise, gripping his Spencer, the same one he had carried in the war, and said, in his slow, deep voice, "Take your finger off the trigger of that shotgun, Hugar."

The man's face reddened; a vein swelled out, a vertical band across his brow; his whole square body tightened.

"Take it off quick," Trooper said.

Bentley whispered, "Don't be a damn fool and do as he says." Abner Lait came riding up on his plough-horse, a shotgun over his shoulder. "Do as he says," Bentley told him.

Hugar's fingers unhooked themselves.

"Put that there gun at your feet," Trooper said. "You, too, sheriff."

"You can't talk—"

"At your feet," Trooper nodded.

They put the guns at their feet. Abner Lait joined the group around the gig. Frank Carson's wagon turned the corner of the road, up from the swamp. Hugar said:

"We got to remember some things, Lait."

"I got something to remember."

"The sheriff was telling us," Gideon said, "just why he's here."

Gideon repeated what the sheriff had said. "Go on, sir," Gideon told him. "We want to hear the rest."

Frank Carson joined them. Bentley, watching them narrowly, continued, "The little girl stands there, watching them, and one of the niggers goes for her, rips her dress off. She began to scream, and Sally came running. One of the other niggers hits Sally. Sally crawls for a cabinet where Clark keeps his revolver, and then the niggers take to their heels."

"And how does that concern us?" Gideon asked.

"The niggers were recognized, and they all of them came from up here, at Carwell."

At first, there was dead silence. Then Abner Lait laughed. Then Jeff began, "Of all the insane—" "Keep quiet," Gideon said. "I'll do the talking."

And he asked Bentley, "What do you want?"

"We want them three niggers, Gideon."

"On what charge?"

"Assault and attempted rape."

"Who are these men you charge?" Gideon asked.

"Hannibal Washington, Andrew Sherman, and another nigger Sally says she seen in the store with Carwell niggers, but don't remember the name."

"All right," Gideon said. "We won't talk about your story; it doesn't concern me. But neither of the two men has been over to town for a week. All day yesterday, Hannibal Washington worked over by the schoolhouse, laying bricks. Andrew Sherman is ploughing and has twenty witnesses. These men will bear me out. So there are your charges, sheriff. No one from Carwell was in town yesterday."

"We ain't taking nigger witness," Hugar said.

Gideon's mouth tightened. Abner Lait walked over to the gig, "I'm not a nigger, Hugar. Look close."

"We ain't taking your witness either."

"A long time ago I made up my mind to kill you, you dirty son of a bitch," Abner said quietly.

Bentley said, "That talk won't get us nowhere. We don't want trouble, Gideon."

"We don't want trouble either."

"But we aim to take those men back. They're going to get fair witness and fair trial."

"You have fair witness here," Gideon said.

"I'm going to make an arrest. Are you going to obstruct me?"

"Put it that way if you want to," Gideon nodded.

"I'm putting it that way. We came here peaceable on business of law and order. You surround us and offer us armed resistance. That's a God damned serious thing, Gideon."

"You're going back without those men," Gideon said. "If you want it, sheriff, you can have it. I say you're lying. I say no sane man could believe that cock and bull story you told. I say that."

"I hear you," the sheriff nodded. "I can hear a nigger five miles off. I can smell one. I'm going to have those men, Gideon, if I got to deputize every man in the county."

"Or outside the county," Gideon nodded. "Or every rotten scoundrel Hugar can lay hands on. Meanwhile, get out of Carwell, Bentley. You're standing on our land. Get to hell off it!"

The men stood in a close group, watching the gig as it drove back along the road. For a while there was silence. Then Abner Lait began to curse, softly, fluently, completely. Jeff said, "I wonder if you should have talked to him like that?"

"It don't matter," Frank Carson shrugged. "This was a long time coming and it ain't nothing a man says is going to change it."

"Every day I woke up this week, it was going to be like this," Gideon reflected. "A whole week, and every day you think about it. Every day, and then one morning it comes."

Standing around, subdued, quiet, not quite understanding why they had been dispossessed in the midst of a school day, the children watched the men enter the schoolhouse. A few of the older boys pushed in along with the men; they were not stopped. Half the men who sat down in the pews carried weapons of one sort or another; all of them moved slowly, the way men do when they can make no conciliation between their thoughts, their actions, and their hopes. Benjamin Winthrope stood at one side of the hall and watched them; he was both disturbed and frightened. He was a young man, Williams, '73; he came of a very average, religious New England family that traced their descent from the old governor, although they spelled their name differently; and coming from that sort of a family, complete within itself, the love he felt for his own humankind was more abstract than actual. It had taken a great strength of will, a constant struggle with himself to remain here among these—to him—strange, quiet, yet violent people. Now, watching them, he saw as well as they did that all was over. His job was done; he would go to the station and take a train, today, if possible.

Brother Peter opened the meeting by saying, "Brethren, we are gathered here today in fear and anger. God help us to choose the right way—and if we go and choose that way, God give us strength to bear with it. You going to talk, Gideon?"

Rising from where he sat, toward the back, Gideon answered, "This isn't a matter just for me alone. I can talk no better than anyone else. I know no more of what we should do than my neighbor does. The people can talk for themselves."

The heads turned to look at Gideon. He seemed older now than he ever had before. Hannibal Washington spoke up, "Maybe it's better you should talk for the people, Gideon. A man comes from us or he don't; you come from us, Gideon. You never gone away. You got your faults, God knows, but you walk low and humble, Gideon, God knows. Go on and talk."

"There isn't much to talk about," Gideon said. "You all know what happened. You know why, too. You know that if they take three of our people away and hang them, it would be only a beginning."

Andrew Sherman said tiredly, "I don't want to make no trouble for all, Gideon. Ain't we had enough trouble? Maybe they ain't going to do something so bad as hanging. Suppose I go in there to town and they look at me, and they say, no, that ain't the same nigger? How they going to say I'm the nigger did those things? I never been off the place yesterday or all the week before."

"They'll hang you," Abner Lait said. "Just as sure as God, they'll hang you."

"They'll hang you," Gideon agreed. "I'll make no decisions from here on, the decisions are up to you. After that, if you want me to lead, I will. But you decide. That story—well, they had to tell some story; they had to have some method that resembled legality. After all, it is only eight days they've had the power. Eight days are not enough time for them to shed all we've built in eight years."

"Well, what do we do, Gideon?" Frank Carson demanded.

"That's for you to decide. I think they'll be back tonight—if not tonight, tomorrow, but they'll be back, not two of them, but a good many more. Then they'll start the business of smashing us, and after a little while they won't feel any need for legal methods. As to what you can do, there are several things. You can stay in your homes and be murdered by twos and threes—not all of you, some may escape. You can run away, and there'll be a plantation some-where you can hire on, for fatback and grits and a place to sleep, and if you keep your mouths shut, you can live that way. For the white men, it's a little different; perhaps they can join Jason Hugar, although I don't know if he'll have them—I guess it's not too different for the white men. Or else, you can stay together and fight!"

Jeff cried, "This is still the United States of America! There is still law and there are still courts! My God, sir, do we have to destroy ourselves?"

"We don't have to," Gideon said. "I gave the other alternatives. I'm making no choices. For eight days there has been no law but the law of violence; the courts are not ours—and only because this is America do we have the strength to fight! Destruction? I don't know—when old Osawatomie Brown went into Harper's Ferry with nineteen men, he had less strength and less hope than we have, but he shook this nation—he woke it up, he made men see. I don't propose to fight to die; I want to fight to live. I want to fight so that this whole country will see what is happening here."

"There must be another way," Jeff said.

"What other way?"

"If you went back to Washington?"

"I tried there and I failed," Gideon said.

"If you tried again?"

"I would fail again, and it would be too late. Tomorrow will be too late."

Will Boone said, softly and lazily, "Suppose we reckon to fight, Gideon. I like to stand up for mine; that's a good way as I see things. But how? We ain't an army—three and half thousand acres, you take in all the places. That's a little thin, a little spread."

"I've thought of that," Gideon agreed. "God knows, I've been thinking of little else. If we fight, it means putting the women and children where they're safe, where they can be safe for a long while, long enough for this to get out, for this to burn. There's a place like that, big enough, easy to defend, nearby—I mean the old Carwell House. It stands on a hill, it commands the countryside—

"I've said enough," Gideon finished. "Decide for yourselves."

An hour later, they had decided; out of their strength and their weakness, their fear and anger, their hurt and pain and memory of their toil had come this, Abner Lait speaking after the welter of voices had quieted:

"We'll fight, Gideon. Do you stay with us?"

"If you want me?" Gideon said.

"We want you."

Gideon looked around the hall, and then he nodded. His steps dragged as he walked up to the front of the room. Brother Peter watched him, the old man's eyes full of pain. Gideon, glancing at his watch, said, "It is almost three o'clock now. Whatever we are going to do we should do before dark. I don't know if they'll come back tonight, perhaps not for several days. I suggest this—that we take our families up to the big house, that we take food and blankets. We can leave them there with a guard during the day while we work our places. At least, we'll know they're safe. We'll use the school bell for an alarm, but I would not use the schoolhouse—"

He turned to Benjamin Winthrope. "I don't know how you feel about this, Mr. Winthrope. Certainly this is not your concern. We shall have to discontinue the school for the time being."

Winthrope, rubbing his hands uneasily, answered, "I'm not an advocate of violence, Mr. Jackson. I don't approve of what you are doing, but it's not my affair. But you can't have the children run wild, all of them together in one place—"

"There's nothing else we can do."

Winthrope, resignedly, said, "I'll stay for a while until things are orderly. They're never orderly in the beginning."

"If you want to stay, we'd be thankful." He turned to the people, "Take whatever powder and shot you have up to the house. I would say take cornmeal, smoked meat—whatever you can move conveniently."

They left the schoolhouse the way they had come in, slowly, not talking much; each man gathered his children to himself as he walked or rode back to his house. Coming out, Trooper stopped Gideon and said:

"I ain't leaving my place."

"Why?"

The huge black man, standing inches higher than Gideon, inches broader, a great, slow mass of a man, shook his head. "I ain't leaving, Gideon."

"That's up to you," Gideon said.

Word by word, Trooper let it out. "I ain't like you, Gideon. When I'm a slave, that lash come down harder on me than anyone else, you big black bastard, you stupid black bastard, you god damn black bastard. All the time that. Mr. Dudley Carwell buy me at auction in Orleans. Pay a higher price any other man bring. Work me harder too. Work me morning, noon and night. Never see happy sunrise, never see happy nighttime; when there's whipping, old overseer say, whip that black bastard for example, won't hurt him none."

He pulled off his shirt. "Look at that back, Gideon!" Brother Peter and a few others had stopped to listen; they looked at the back that had whip scars all over it, like a moulded relief map.

"I ain't going off my place, Gideon. Me and my woman, we break our damn backs turning over that dirt. Got a piece of dirt's all my own. Got no master, got no overseer. Sometimes, I feel like kneeling me down and kissing that there earth, sure enough. Got a house my own; sit down there and woman brings me food. Ain't no slave shacks, ain't no punishment cell—just my own house. I'm going to stay there, Gideon. Ain't nobody going to move me out of there."

"And your children?" Brother Peter asked.

"They going to stay. Ain't no harm going to come to them."

Eight years ago, Gideon would have stormed and pleaded; now he said, "All right, Trooper. If that's what you want, all right."

During all the long afternoon of that day, April eighteenth, the people of Carwell moved from their farms to the plantation house. Women filled wagons with bedding, pots, food, a few small, treasured household things, a calendar, a book or a Bible, a sewing basket, a plaster of Paris figure, a bright Currier and Ives print. There was not much talk now about this thing, which they had talked about so much for weeks. Even the children, though filled with excitement by this one earth-shaking event in their simple, slow-moving lives, were more than ordinarily hushed. Tempers were short. Men found themselves exploding over small and unimportant matters, a tool misplaced, a child underfoot; women became furious over nothing: while the great and single fact was accepted without comment, without tears. A family, loaded down in its wagon, drove slowly toward the hill, and waved at another family coming from another direction. One by one, the wagons converged on the house.

When they were all there, the old, white, porticoed building gleamed all pink and golden in the setting sun.

Gideon took a few books, not many. Jeff took his instruments and some of the medicines he had bought in Charleston. They laid out the bedding on the big hay wagon, making poor Fred McHugh as comfortable as they could. They took all their arms, Gideon's army Spencer, Marcus' cavalry carbine, two shotguns, and a heavy, long-barreled Colt revolver that Gideon had bought in Washington the year before. They took Rachel's best pans and most of their household linen. Rachel had wanted to leave that behind, it was such fine white stuff; for years Gideon had been buying it, a little at a time, knowing how much she loved the feel of smooth white sheets and pillow cases: but Jeff said, "Take it all," offering no explanation.

Abner Lait said to Jimmy, his nineteen-year-old son, "What do you think? These ain't the times they were ten years ago. I'm stringing with Gideon because it's kind of become a habit. You don't have to."

A year before Gideon had helped Abner to buy an extra hundred-acre piece for Jimmy to move onto when he married. Now the boy reminded him.

"I know that. It's no skin off your back."

"I'll go along with you."

Abner nodded and laid an arm across the boy's shoulder. That was a rare show of affection. The boy shrugged it off and went into the house to help his mother.

Brother Peter and the Allenby boys were among the first to arrive at the big house. The course of years had not changed the outside too much, weathered it some, peeled off some of the paint. From a distance, the building had its old dignity and beauty, almost unimpaired; but when you came closer you saw that the windows were broken, the weeds grown higher, the doors hanging from their hinges. All of the furnishings had been sold at auction, but emptiness could not entirely displace the former grandeur. The big central staircase, with its mahogany banisters and oaken treads was if anything more impressive in the emptiness. The old hand-blocked wallpaper hung in leaves and shreds, but its color remained. The wonderfully carved walnut dados seemed waiting, patiently, to be backed once more with cabinets, chairs, and sofas, and here and there the fine hardwood floors showed through the years' accumulation of dirt, dead leaves, and refuse brought in by the children who had played in the empty rooms.

Being encumbered by few possessions, Brother Peter had been able to make the change quickly. The three boys, who had been living with him since old Mr. Allenby died, came with him, and soon they were at work with brooms, cleaning the place. After a while, others joined them. The accumulated debris of a dozen years isn't quickly disposed of, but by the time the families were arriving in any numbers, a sort of neatness prevailed in the big house. Gideon took charge of the incoming folk. While there were more than twenty rooms, it would still mean a communal sort of life. The men would sleep in what had formerly been the main reception room. Keeping the families together as much as possible, he divided the women and small children among the many bedrooms. In some cases, such as that of Jake Sutter, where there was a grandmother, a wife, a sister and three daughters, he gave the family a room for itself. An overflow of the men would sleep in the dining room along with the teen-age boys; in the daytime, the room would be used for meals and as a schoolhouse. The food was put in the kitchen annex, and Gideon appointed a committee of women to apportion it and supervise the cooking. Another group of women set about cleaning the place. Men put paper patches over the broken windows, and Hannibal Washington and two others climbed down into the cistern and set about making it usable. Since the cistern was enclosed by the two back wings of the house, only a step from the kitchen door, Gideon saw no reason why it shouldn't be used to store all the water they needed, instead of relying on barrels in the house. It was clean by the time the sun set, and Hannibal Washington set a crew of boys to filling it from the well. Meanwhile, Gideon sent half a dozen wagons back for cordwood.

Some of the people, those who had small children, had brought cows with enough fodder to last them at least a few days. Since the Carwell barns and stables had been burned down long ago, Gideon put the cows and horses in the space between the wings, and made a fence for them out of the wagons.

It was amazing what had been accomplished by nightfall, and the very fact of that accomplishment cheered the people immensely. Except for Winthrope, there were no strangers here; those of the people who had not known each other from birth had at least been

intimate for many years. Habits and mannerisms that would have
been peculiar and annoying to others were not so to them. There
was a novelty that buoyed them up in this being together, in sharing
each other's problems, in being able to sit talking much later into
the night than had been their habit. The old chandeliers had not
been removed from the Carwell house; Gideon was wasteful of
candles this night; he had two dozen put in each of the main chandeliers, and the bright glow that came sparkling through the cut
glass gave a merry and cheerful atmosphere to the place.

Gideon broke down the men into committees. Ten would be
sufficient to stay by the house, which meant, including the older
boys, that a man need only give one day a week to this. They could
not go very far into the future; if they did, it threw a pall of depression over them; they were content with tomorrow or the next day.
A committee would see to the horses, another would be a sort of
judicial board in the house itself. Things might go well tonight, but
after a while this living together would get on people's nerves, and
there would be squabbles and disputes to settle. There was much,
too, that the children could do, a thousand small tasks which would
keep them out of mischief.

Out of boxes and boards, Gideon had made himself a sort of
table. Many of the people had brought chairs, a simple and needful
thing for elementary comfort. When the confusion of the first meal
cooked and served together in the house had passed, Gideon sat himself down to write a series of telegrams. He would send one to the
editor of the New York *Herald*; Bennett had dispatched reporters
through hell and high water before to get stories not half so good
as the one that might presently unfold at Carwell. Another telegram
to the president, another to the secretary of state, another to Frederick Douglass, the old and venerable Negro leader. One to Cardozo,
describing the impending situation and make a last plea for unity
and common action by every decent force in the South. In the message to Cardozo, he said, "I beg of you, Francis, to remember that
we are not alone, that thousands of good and just men in the South,
both black and white, can be inspired and united by the fact that
here at Carwell, people have refused to accept tyranny and terror
as the inevitable course of things." He sent a telegram to Ralph
Waldo Emerson, that the old man lift his voice once more in the
cause of justice. As each was written, he passed it among the men

to read and comment on. And when he had finally finished, he took Marcus aside and told him:

"I want you to do this, son. It's important."

Marcus nodded.

"Go all the way to Columbia. I want you to go tonight, and you can be there when the Western Union office opens in the morning. Take the mare; Abner will let you use his saddle. Whatever happens, Marcus, boy, see that the wires are sent. Then get back here."

"I'll get back here," Marcus said.

Gideon walked outside with him before he left. Marcus wore high boots; he had the big Colt revolver in his jacket pocket with the telegrams. He had said his offhand goodbys, supremely assured of his own ability to do a thing. Now he was alive and eager with excitement; it was a fine moonlit night, a fine night for a ride to Columbia. The little mare could run like the wind; nothing would stop him, nothing could catch him, and in a few hours people all over the land would know what was happening at Carwell. Gideon watched him with pride; this was his son, this clean-limbed young man, unafraid, alive, proud—this was a testimony for what had been. The time to come would take care of itself. "You're not afraid?" he asked Marcus, and the boy just smiled. Jeff came out as he was mounting. "Good luck," Jeff said, squeezing the boy's thigh, smiling at him.

"Thank you, doctor " Marcus grinned, the same elusive note, part of sarcasm, part of respect in his voice. "I'll bring you back a box of pills." Then he was off, walking his horse down the hillside, past the decaying ruins that had been the slave cabins.

Shortly after that, Gideon lay down on his pallet in the reception room. It was strange to be lying there with the hoarse breathing and the restless movements of many men all around him. The silvery moonlight, streaming in through the tall windows, gave an added dream quality to the place. It took Gideon back to the time, so long ago now, when he had been in the army, stretching out for some tired bivouac, a long way from Carwell, a long way from young and lovely Rachel, a long way from the children he had left behind —because a time comes when a man does what he must. Thinking that way, of one thing and another that had happened long ago, Gideon fell asleep—to be awakened, how much later he did not know, by the sound of many shots echoing across the valley. Shots that went on intermittently until there was silence again.

Katie, Trooper's wife, would say nothing to him; she loved him and yet she feared him. He was bigger and stronger than any man at Carwell, yet he could be gentle as a woman; he could be moved to tears or to hot anger with equal ease. Katie put up with that; she had a good life with her man; she was small and plain, but Trooper was good to her, never sinned with other women, provided well, and had never raised a hand to her or the children. It was true that he had his ways; when he set his mind on something, that was that, and you could forget about it right there. When he said, no, he wasn't going to take a surname as everyone else was; Trooper was a name, a good enough name; it had always been his name; it would continue to be his name; when he said that, you just had to take it, and it was no use to argue with him. When he said he was going to stay, Katie accepted the fact. She told her two little girls, "We going to stay right here." Though her heart sank as she saw the families coming by on their way up to the plantation house, what could she do? And as night fell, and Trooper's little cabin appeared to sink into a well of lonesomeness, Katie became more and more terror-stricken, though she hid her feelings from her husband.

She didn't sleep at all that night. She lay awake and listening beside Trooper's inert body; he slept; he feared nothing. This was his, who could take it away? She lay there thinking of all the forces that would rear up, and as she lay there, as the minutes and hours passed by, she heard something.

She woke Trooper. "Listen!"

"What that?"

He listened and he heard the quick, even thud of hoofbeats. He climbed out of bed, pulled on his pants, located his Spencer in the moonlight that streamed into the room, and started out, barefooted.

"Where you going?" Katie whispered.

"Outside. You stay here!"

He went out and stood in front of the little house, gripping the rifle. Remembering that he had no cartridges, he went back and filled a pocket with them. The children stirred, and Trooper bent over them and soothed them. Katie watched him but said nothing. He went out of the house again and stood in the moonlight, listening, a giant of a man, bare from the waist up, the heavy, bulging muscles rippling with his every movement.

He heard the hoofbeats stop. He heard them pick up again from the direction of Gideon's house, and then grow softer as the pines swallowed the road. Then the road came over a bluff, bathed in moonlight, and there Trooper saw a body of men appear, at least thirty men bunched close together, all of them wearing white sheets and the pointed hoods of the Klan. He drew in his breath, cursed softly, but did not move. Then the road dipped out of sight again, and the hoofbeats stopped. That would be at Hannibal Washington's house. They were close enough now so that Trooper could hear the faint noise of their voices. The hoofbeats picked up again —his house was the next on the road. Trooper braced himself, feet apart, his chest swelling slightly.

In a little while, he saw them on the mottled, tree-shadowed road. His dog began to bark, a fine setter that charged fearlessly and stupidly into the mass of horses. They came on warily and slowly, walking their horses, and then dropping even that pace when they saw Trooper. They saw him like a strange, inhuman column of shiny black. They saw his waist high, level rifle. For a long moment, they paused, and then they came on, very slowly.

"What you want?" he asked, his deep voice rumbling with hate and anger. Katie came to the doorway; she saw the hooded men and began to sob hysterically.

A man in the lead said, "We want Hannibal Washington, Andrew Sherman, and you."

"You see me," Trooper said.

"Put down that gun!"

"You see me," Trooper repeated, his voice booming with hate now, like a resonant bass drum. "You on my land! God damn you sons of bitches, get off my land!"

The setter, taking the note from his master's voice, began to bark furiously, ripping at one of the horses. The horse reared. Someone said, "Quiet that god damn hound!" A revolver cracked, and the dog rolled over on its back, twisting from side to side. Trooper, his face contorted with rage, snapped up his rifle and fired. One of the hooded men became loose in his saddle, wavered, and then slipped to the ground, hanging by one foot from his stirrup. The horses stamped nervously. A half a dozen rifles cracked at once. The bullets were like hammers on Trooper's flesh, but he began to walk forward. The blood, in little rivulets, ran down Trooper's massive chest. His wife was screaming hysterically now. Someone yelled:

"Shoot the bastard!"

A rifle cracked again and Trooper staggered. The horses were

milling around him now. He swung his rifle; the upraised arm to
ward it off cracked like a dry twig. Trooper swung his rifle again,
and the stock splintered on the man's collarbone, driving the broken
bone deep into his chest. It was difficult to fire at him now without
the danger of hitting each other. Trooper dragged a third man from
his rearing horse, and shook the screaming wretch as a dog shakes
a rat. Another man slipped off his horse, jammed a shotgun muzzle
against Trooper's back, and fired. The giant body stiffened, then
collapsed like an empty sack. The man he had just dragged from
his horse lay on the ground, moaning with pain. The man with the
broken arm and collarbone began to scream suddenly, wild, inhuman screams. They kept shooting into Trooper's inert body.
They were all dismounting now. Katie ran from the house, trying
to get to her husband. They caught her and tore off her thin night-
dress. They got her down on the ground, clawing at her legs to
pull them apart. Somehow, she twisted loose, and one of the hooded
men, whimpering with excitement, brought down his rifle butt
across her head. Her skull gave; suddenly, she was dead, her limbs
without meaning or direction. A man yelled:

"You god damn crazy son of a bitch!"

They stood there, staring at the dead, naked body that had become so quickly and completely useless. They gathered around the
man with the broken collarbone. The one Trooper had shot was
dead. This one was dying; they stood there, watching him die,
watching the blood well in a thick stream from a severed vein.

They turned toward the house; everything was so quiet now. One
of them went to the barn and returned with a pitchfork full of hay,
which he tossed into the open doorway. Someone else struck a
match. They kept feeding hay to the blaze, and presently the whole
front of the house was burning.

Then the children began to scream. Their fear, trapped inside of
them until now, broke forth in the terrified wailing of those who
fear without being able to know or understand the origins of their
fear. The men stood around uneasily.

"Kids in there," someone said.

Someone else remarked, "Too damned many nigger kids anyway."

"Well, where in hell are these black bastards?"

"You ask me, they're all up at the old Carwell house."

The man who had spoken first said, "Harry, you ride back to
town and ask Bentley where in hell's name is the bunch from Cal-

houn County? He was going to have two hundred men up here tonight. Well, where in hell are they?" And then he added, as an afterthought, "Tell him Matty Clark and Hep Lawson are dead."

Then he turned back to watch the burning house.

All of the men in the reception room were awakened by the shots. They crowded up to the windows to look across the moonlit hillside that seemed still to echo and re-echo with the sound. They ran with their rifles out onto the broad veranda, peering through the hazy and beautiful moonlit night. Women called down from upstairs, "What is it? What is it?" The children were awake and chattering excitedly.

A few of the men circled around the house, but found nothing.

Gideon's first thought had been of Marcus, but it was three o'clock in the morning now and he knew that Marcus was miles away. Standing out on the porch now, he said to Abner Lait, "Where do you think it came from?"

"Sounded like down in the valley where Trooper has his place."

They remembered Trooper now, and the men looked at one another. "Jesus God," Frank Carson said softly. Pointing, Hannibal Washington cried, "Look a there!"

There was a ruddiness in the night that grew and grew. It seemed to be a barn-fire at first, and then a tongue of flame licked up and they knew that something bigger than a stack of wood was burning. The glow reached up into the sky, until someone gave voice to what they had all been thinking,

"Trooper's house."

"His two kids—"

They started off the veranda with a rush, but Gideon called them back. "Don't lose your heads! For God's sake, don't lose your head! Stay here! Hannibal, could you slip down there and see what happened?"

Hannibal Washington nodded and darted away, a small, deft shadow of a man that disappeared in the moonlight. There was silence after he left, only some of the men watching Gideon.

"We stay together from here on," Gideon said. "You wanted me to lead you, then take my orders or find someone else."

"All right, Gideon," Abner said gently.

"James, Andrew, Ezra, each of you take one side of this place, stand out about thirty yards from the house and sing out if you hear or see anything."

The three men moved off. Some of the women came out onto the veranda and whispered to the men; they were sent back; they were told to get the children back to sleep. But there was no more sleep for anyone at Carwell that night. As time passed and nothing happened, the men broke into little groups, discussing and speculating on their situation in hoarse whispers. Some of them sat down on the broad steps of the house, and others leaned against the Doric columns that ranged up so majestically into the night. All of them kept scanning the hillside where Hannibal Washington had disappeared, and presently, about an hour after he had left, they saw a man moving.

"Hannibal?"

He came up panting, wet from head to foot with dew; he had to get his breath first, before he could tell them all he had seen.

"Where's the children?"

He shook his head. "Burned, I guess." He said, "I crawled as near as I could—I seen the bodies just as clear. I heard them talking."

"What did you hear?" Gideon asked dully.

"They're waiting for about two hundred men coming from over in Calhoun County. The Klan branch south of here, maybe Georgia folk, I guess, are supposed to send some men up. They know we're here at the house."

A seventeen-year-old boy began to vomit; he hung over the veranda, retching constantly in a convulsive, aching rhythm. The glow was dying now, but a few of the men were straining their eyes in another direction. There, above the dark trees, a new spot of rosy red appeared; as it swelled, the men turned, one by one, to look at Abner Lait. He stood on the porch, his big red fists clenched, biting his lower lip until a trickle of blood ran down his chin. Then, though his long, sunburned face did not move, he began to cry, the tears welling out over his lean cheeks. He spoke in a whisper:

"The bastards—all I had, all I ever wanted to have, God damn them bastards, God damn them—a man works, builds, plans, dreams, God damn them—"

Hannibal Washington said, "Gideon, why don't we stop them before they burn every house on the place?"

"That's why they're burning the houses," Gideon nodded. "They want us to come out of here."

"I'm going down there," Abner Lait said.

"You're not. We let Trooper stay, and he's lying there dead now and his wife next to him."

"I'm going, Gideon."

Gideon's voice was level and cold. "You're not—"

There was something now. Ezra Golden sang out; they could hear the dull hoofbeats of many horses at a walk, and then through the haze loomed the ghostly outlines of the hooded men. They halted at a hundred and fifty yards, a mass of white-cloaked riders, more than twenty now, many more.

"Hello there!"

"What do you want?" Gideon called out. "Who are you?" The words floated through the night, rising, falling.

"You damn well know who we are, Jackson! We want those men!"

"It's no use to answer," Gideon said. "It's no use."

"We're coming up to get them, Jackson! We're going to get them or burn every house on the place!"

Gideon said sharply, "Spread out around the house! Keep down in the weeds! Don't fire until they're at fifty yards!" The men spread out, crouching down in the dry spring stems and shrubs. Those on the veranda lay at full length. Gideon, Abner and Brother Peter stood next to one of the columns. Gideon glanced at Abner; he was sighting on his rifle, a long, old, but accurate Sharps percussion gun. He stood as motionless as a rock, yet the tears still ran across his cheeks. "God forgive us," Brother Peter said, "God forgive us." Gideon lifted his Spencer and sighted; how long was it since he had looked across those sights at a man? In all the world there was nothing so insane, so unreasonable as killing; yet that was what made the ultimate right or wrong. The white line surged forward, a quick trot at first and then slower. At one hundred yards, Abner Lait's long rifle flashed and a man slumped from his horse. The men in white began to fire. At seventy-five yards, there was a crackle of answering shots from around the house, in spite of Gideon's warning. Another man fell from his horse; another screamed in pain. The white line stopped, hesitated, and then galloped away, fading into the moonlight.

The men from the veranda came forward slowly. Two of the

hooded figures lay in the grass; two of the men from Carwell bent and removed their hoods. Both men were dead, strangers; no one at Carwell had ever seen their faces before.

In that first attack, no one at Carwell was hurt, but whatever small elation the people might have felt at that disappeared as the glow of new fires showed in the sky. One after another, houses and barns became pyres, each signalling the location of another man's ruin, another man's despair, another's agony. The women and children huddled together and watched. The sun rose, and still the houses burned, sending twisting flags of grey smoke upward.

The women cooked breakfast, and the people ate, but there was little talk and no laughter. Gideon's only consoling thought was that by now Marcus had sent off the telegrams.

Marcus had walked his horse down and taken a shortcut through the Carwell pastures, where in the old days the fine-bred saddle horses were kept. That way, he avoided the new road and the swamp causeway entirely, coming out on the main pike. The little mare picked up a smooth and distance-eating trot; she could keep that up for hours. The moonlit road was empty, on such a night as this, with the cool wind flowing past, a man could race to hell and back again. About eight miles from Carwell, at a time when he had pulled in his horse to rest her, Marcus heard the sound of many men riding. He dismounted, drawing the mare off the road into a clump of pine, whispering to her and stroking her soft nose. As they stood there, a group of mounted men came into view, about twenty in the white hoods of the Klan. Marcus waited until they were well out of sight and hearing; then he mounted and rode on again.

He was disturbed at first about the night riders. Obviously, they were bound for Carwell, and he wondered whether he shouldn't cut back, running the mare the way she was able to run, and warn the people. But then he reasoned that twenty men would be hardly enough to raid the big house, that his father would be on the alert, and that if he turned back he stood a good chance of being cornered and shot down. With that in mind, he pushed his horse on, leaning forward in the saddle, half dozing sometimes with the rush of the wind and the quick, gliding trot of the mare. The road slipped by underneath, and the hours passed. Young enough to forget quickly the situation at Carwell in the pleasure of his own mission, Marcus talked to the mare happily, "You wonderful horse, you sure enough beautiful little horse, you got a heart like a cannon blasting, you got a heart like a big sun rising—"

As the night sky turned gray with dawn, Marcus pulled the horse in to a walk. A while farther on, he turned off the road into a little meadow. The mare was breathing hard; they both needed rest. He was very tired now. Hitching the reins around his wrist, he lay down, only for a moment, only to catch his breath; certainly he couldn't really sleep here on the hard, damp ground. He closed his eyes for what seemed to be only a moment, and was awakened by the tugging of the reins. The hot sun was up now, and as he pushed himself up from the ground the mare came over and lowered her head for his caress. Glancing at his watch, he saw that it was past eight, that he had slept for an hour. He mounted and pushed on, and by a little after ten he rode into Columbia.

People glanced at him curiously as he rode through the outer residential streets. There was an air about the town, a mood, a warning. He went straight to the Western Union office, hitched his horse onto the rail outside and entered. The nap had not refreshed him a great deal; he was tired; he wanted to get his job done, get out of town, find a shaded place in a piney grove somewhere, and sleep. The pimple-faced boy was not there now, just the operator, a sullen, dark man of forty. He stared at Marcus for a moment before he got up and came to the counter.

"What do you want, boy?"

Marcus had the telegrams out in front of him. "Send all of these, please."

Just glancing at the sheets of paper, the operator said, "That's a lot of money, boy."

Marcus took out five ten dollar bills and laid them on the counter.

"That's a hell of a lot of money for a nigger to have."

Gideon had told Marcus, "Send the telegrams, I trust you." Now Marcus said, as ingratiatingly as he could, "I'm sending them for Representative Jackson. He gave me the money."

"Did he?"

Marcus said, "Please, mister, I tell you he did."

The operator began to read through the telegrams. Then he looked keenly at Marcus, at his dusty, mud-streaked clothes, then past him at the mare. Marcus put his hand in his jacket pocket, closing his fingers around the Colt. The operator read some more of the telegrams. Then he picked the lot up and said:

"All right, boy. I'll send them." He reached for the fifty dollars.

"Send them now, while I'm here," Marcus said.

An edge came into the man's voice. "Now look, boy—this sending telegrams takes time, a lot of time. I don't like to have niggers tell me how to do my business. You get out of here and don't worry about those telegrams."

"I paid you. Send them now," Marcus said.

"Get out!"

Marcus drew the Colt and let it lie on the counter, the muzzle a few inches from the man's stomach, his own body shielding the gun from anyone who might pass the shop or enter, his finger curled around the trigger. "Send them now," Marcus said. "Just sit down at your key and start sending."

The operator paled a little. His lower lip began to twitch. He started to say, haltingly, "Boy, this is a hell of a—"

"Start sending," Marcus said. "Don't try to make any trouble. I'll know what you're sending."

Keeping his eyes on Marcus, the operator walked over to his desk and sat down. He spread the telegrams and touched the key; then the key began it click, "attention central attention central Sumter street station columbia reporting nigger holdup in station wire railroad operator inform police attention—"

The operator kept sending the signal, over and over. He pretended that he had finished the first telegram, crumpled it into a basket, started on the second. The pimply-faced boy entered the store. Marcus glanced at him, motioned with the revolver, "Get behind there, over against the wall." The boy stood against the wall, mouth open, speechless. The operator's key clicked, "attention central i must keep sending—" He finished the third telegram and crumpled it into the basket. A middle-aged business man entered the station. Marcus motioned with the revolver and he took his place alongside the boy. The operator dropped the fourth telegram into the basket. The key clicked on. The fifth and sixth telegram followed.

"That's all," the operator said hoarsely.

"Stay where you are," Marcus told them. He backed out. "Just stay where you are. Just don't move." He backed through the door into the street, still holding the revolver; then he heard the crack of a rifle, and together with the noise there was a smashing pain in his left arm, a red-hot hammer blow that left it hanging broken and useless. The pain was like nothing he had ever known; somehow, he kept on his feet, but he dropped the revolver. He staggered over to the mare, unhitched her, and tried to crawl into the saddle. Two men with rifles were running down the street. One of them stopped to take aim. This time the searing brand was in Marcus' thigh. Four more armed men darted around the opposite corner. People were running from every direction.

Marcus clawed onto the saddle. He got a leg over, telling the mare, "Run, baby, run." He lay across the saddle, and the mare started down the street with her smooth, gliding trot. Now the armed men stopped and began to shoot as if they were on a range. Rifle after rifle cracked, and the bullets ripped through Marcus. One caught the mare, and she stumbled and fell, pitching Marcus onto the earth. Neighing wildly, the mare gained her feet and raced off. The men approached Marcus slowly, still shooting, pausing every few steps to jam cartridges into their guns. Finally, they realized that he was dead. They walked close then, and one of them turned the boy over with his boot.

After the first breakfast at the plantation house, Gideon took Benjamin Winthrope aside and said, "Do you feel that you still want to stay here? They might let you go through."

"I've been thinking of that all night," Winthrope nodded. He was unshaven and haggard. "I'll stay, if you want me to. I can help you, I think."

"Thank you. I hope to God you don't regret it."

"I've given it some consideration," Winthrope said. "I try not to do things I'll later regret."

"If you could take the children upstairs and organize some sort of lessons?" Gideon said. "Brother Peter will help you. You know, it will be hard for them, cooped up here in the house all day. This sort of thing is terrible for children; they can't understand why. If you could, in very simple terms of course, make them understand why we are here and what we are doing, it would be a fine thing."

"I'll do my best," Winthrope said.

"Don't frighten them. Hold out hope to them. I think we have reason to hope."

Winthrope nodded and went to speak with Brother Peter. Most of the women were gathered in the dining room now. Gideon spoke to them, telling them simply and directly what their situation was.

"This is nothing we could have avoided," he said. "We must stand together. Trooper went his own way, and you know the result. Our only hope is to come through this together, to rebuild together, to make something enduring and fine that will be worth the price we are paying. I am full of hope. We are in a good place here. We have food for many days, plenty of water, medicine, and a doctor. Mr. Winthrope has agreed to remain with us and teach the children. I think that is very important; I think that lessons will go on and should go on, regardless of what happens. In a sense, we are a whole community here in this big house, and our great problem is whether we, the many families that we are, can live together for this time, however long or short, and solve the problems that arise. I think we can. In the past, we have met larger ones than face us now, and we have solved them together. We have here in the house more than two colored people for each white; I don't think that will be an obstacle. We have learned to live and work together, to respect each other. All that we have done has been based on the premise that in this state, where black and white live together, we must work together and build together. The men outside deny that fact. They have burned our houses to prove that they represent the right and justice. We have other ways to prove the justice of our contentions. We do not believe in terror, in murder, in destruction. We shall fight only in defense of our lives and our lands, and we will set an example to this nation of an orderly and disciplined and freedom-loving people.

"We made plans yesterday to go on working our land. For the time being, that is impossible. No one is to leave the house without permission. The men will have their tasks; in addition to seeing that the cistern is kept full, that the stock is cared for, and that there is sufficient firewood, they will guard this place. The administration of the house itself will be left to you, the women. You will apportion the food and be responsible for it. You will care for the sick and wounded, if there are wounded. You will do all the other many things that are part of running a house.

"Lastly, I beg of you not to despair. It may seem to us that we are alone here. We are not alone. We are part of this country and of all the many good people who make this nation. They will not abandon us."

All morning Gideon and others watched the small figures of men moving, in and out of the woods at the far edge of the fields. They remained out of rifle shot; they seemed to move aimlessly, without plan or order. A few still wore the white robes and hooded caps, but most had laid them aside. After last night, and from what they could see now, they estimated that there were at least two hundred and fifty men around the Carwell place. Today, at about eleven o'clock, those were joined by about fifty more men who came riding up the road from the south. Many of the newcomers rode around the house, looking curiously up at the hill where it stood.

The men and older boys had been divided into six groups, eight men in each group. The groups had captains, and each had a four hour sentry stand, two men to a side of the house. Gideon was in over-all command, under him Abner Lait and Hannibal Washington. Each group captain was a veteran soldier. Leslie Carson, who had been a trumpeter during the war and still had his battered army bugle was appointed to blow a short call for alarm. In the back of the house, between the wings, the wagons were tipped over on their faces, wheels in the air, to form a more effective barricade. A space was left to lead the stock in and out.

Gideon and Abner were standing on the veranda at about noon, when they noticed the man coming up the hill. He was on foot, and he carried a white pillowslip tied to a stick. About a hundred yards off, he halted and shouted:

"Hello there, Jackson! Can I come up?"

"It's Bentley," Abner Lait said.

Gideon told him, "Come along!"

A good many men and some of the women came out of the house; they made a compact group at one side of the veranda, staring at Bentley, their faces sullenly curious, as if arson and murder had given a new character to this man, something they had to understand. Bentley came up to the steps and sat down, bending one knee and folding an arm about it. There was no doubt about his courage; these were people whose houses he had burned, whose neighbors he had killed, but he had come up here alone and unarmed. He said to Gideon:

"Let's talk sense, plain and simple. We don't have to start a war, Gideon. I come up here to arrest a few men, and just look what's gone and happened."

"I know what's happened," Gideon said.

"All right, suppose you hand over those men."

"And then?" Gideon asked.

"Then we leave you alone," Bentley said.

"And then we go back to our homes, is that it? Or do we live in the fields like beasts? Or do we get out of Carwell?"

"Now look, Gideon," Bentley said easily, "you got no call to talk like that. You killed two men last night. I could have every last soul here at Carwell indicted. I'm willing to call that an accident. I'm willing to take those men and go away."

"And you needed three hundred to arrest them?"

Bentley made a deprecatory gesture. "The Klan is one thing, Gideon. I'm no Klansman, you know that. Jason Hugar's got his own row to hoe. You find a little excitement and the boys want to come along, and maybe they lose their heads a little. All right, that's done."

"And Trooper's two children were burned to death," Gideon said grimly.

"That was an accident. The boys lost their heads."

Will Boone, standing back on the veranda, said loud and clearly, "It's no use to talk. Why don't we shoot the son of a bitch, Gideon?"

Bentley just glanced at Boone. "I'll remember that, Will," he nodded.

"I'll tell you what I think," Gideon said. "I think you're alive at this moment, Bentley, because we are civilized and law abiding people. I think you knew that. It's a quality of your kind to have an instinctive if primitive understanding of what constitutes civilization. Do you follow me?"

"I follow you," Bentley said, smiling thinly.

"I want you to understand me. Do you know the rights of citizens of this state and this country, Bentley? I know them quite well; I helped to frame the Constitution of this state. You will not arrest any person in this house. On the other hand, we shall hold you and every one of your gang out there accountable. We shall hold you accountable for the murder of Trooper and his wife, for a piece of savagery that outdid most of your Klan's deeds, the burning of two small children alive. We shall hold you accountable for the sense-less, insane arson you have committed on the homes of a whole vil-lage of people. We shall hold you accountable for the death of Mrs. McHugh, for the assault and torture of Fred McHugh, for the mur-der of Zeke Hale, for the murder of Annie Fisher—for all the whippings and tortures and murders you have committed at Carwell. For all those things we hold you and your gang accountable, Bentley. We have been patient; we have been building a large and important thing, and we would not be turned from our course. We are going to continue building that thing. We are going to put an end, not only to you, but to all that you and your friends represent. That's what I have to say, and I speak for my people. Go back and tell that to your friends. Tell them that we will kill any man who approaches within rifle shot of this house. Tell them all of that."

"That's all you have to say, Jackson?" Bentley asked.

"That's all."

"Very well." The sheriff rose, dusted his pants, let his glance sweep across the faces of the people on the veranda, lingering on those that were white. Then he walked back down the hill.

Toward evening of that day, the first real attack came. Some two hundred of the Klansmen, unencumbered by their white robes now, began to crawl up the western face of the hill. They arranged the assault with care, choosing a time when the blazing red sun of evening lay low on the horizon, bathing the house with light and at the same time blinding those who defended it. Gideon told off three companies to take that side of the house, the side with the wings. They lay behind the wagons and at windows. The remaining eighteen men covered the other three sides. They set their rifles and shaded their eyes as best they could. Upstairs, the women and children were ordered to lie on the floor. The Klansmen came on slowly, trying not to show themselves, taking advantage of every clump of weeds, every hummock.

"I wonder how many of them heroes was at Gettysburg?" Frank Carson remarked, recalling how lines of men, in close order and unafraid, had walked into a blazing hell.

At three hundred yards, Hannibal Washington, squinting along his Spencer, wetting the sights with his thumb, tried the first long shot. "Missed," he nodded. The Klansmen began to fire now. Their shots found the earth, or almost spent, smacked into the wagons and the house. Marion Jefferson, who had been lying rigid over a long, old squirrel gun, fired and hit something. A man screamed with pain out there. Others fired, slowly and carefully. At one hundred yards, the Klansmen rose and attempted a charge. The sun was low now, too low, its force spent, its melon-pink silhouetting the charg-

ing, yelling men. The whole rear of the house, between the two
wings, blazed with rifle-fire. Within twenty yards, the rush of the
Klansmen broke and dissolved; at least a dozen of them fell. The
rest tumbled back down the hillside, a few limping, a few crawling.

"Hold fire!" Gideon shouted. "No more!"

The silence was painful now. Behind the barricade, someone
moaned with pain, and someone else called for Jeff. The space
between the wings was in deep shadow. A man pressed a hand over
an arm that was spurting blood. The one who was moaning, Lacy
Douglass, had a smashed collarbone. Jeff, tying a tourniquet on the
arm, ordered, "Don't touch him. Let him lie as he is." The men were
standing, seeing what damage had been wrought, staring down the
hillside. Marion Jefferson lay where he was, tight over his squirrel
gun. When Will Boone touched his shoulder, he rolled over. He
had a hole between his eyes. A few of the men gathered around,
standing quietly and looking at him. Out on the dusky hillside, a
voice began to cry out spasmodically. Jeff, glancing up from the
man whose shoulder had been broken, asked, "Why don't you do
something? There's a wounded man out there." No one moved.
Then Will Boone took off his jacket and covered Marion Jefferson's
face. Gideon touched Hannibal Washington and said, "Take someone out there and bring in that man."

Hannibal took a step, then hesitated. "Let him lay," Abner Lait
said.

"Go ahead," Gideon told them quietly.

Jeff had prepared a room as a hospital in advance. He had fitted
it out with the best lamps available and had pressed Eva Carson
and Hanna Washington into service as nurses. Now, with the lamps
held close over him, he probed in the leg of the Klansman for a
bullet. The man had been shot in two places, there and in the
stomach; there was just a chance that he would live. Jeff found the
lead slug and withdrew it. The man had a small red face and watery
blue eyes, and what he was trying to say to Jeff was not too intelligi-
ble.

"Where are you from?" Jeff asked him. "What's your name?"

"Screven," he mumbled. "Screven, Screven—" But whether he
meant that was his name or the name of a county in Georgia, Jeff
didn't know.

Lacy Douglass was in torment, but there was nothing Jeff could do for him. The break was compounded; if he escaped blood-poisoning, he would have to lie recumbent and in one position for weeks. The other man had suffered only a flesh wound, and aside from the loss of some blood was not seriously injured.

As Jeff worked over the wounded men, he felt an increasing bitterness, an increasing frustration. This was Gideon's way, but it was insane. What came out of men fighting; what else but waste and death and ruin?

They laid Marion Jefferson out in one of the small rooms in back of the house, and there his wife and sister and children and old mother came to weep and lament. All through the house the people could hear their weeping. There, too, Brother Peter came to comfort them. He said to them the old words, "The Lord giveth, the Lord taketh away. Blessed be the name of the Lord."

But he could not answer why. His flock was not like the flock of other preachers; he had seen these people through all the stages of life, birth and childhood and youth and young manhood and maturity, and now he was seeing them in death, not death as it should come, gently, easily, naturally, a man or a woman giving out the soul-breath and lying down, but death that was smashing and terrible in its violence. He didn't understand. He had told Gideon once, "You like a little babe. All ready. Just fill you up, like bucket drawing water from the well. Just wait and see." That was what he had told Gideon once. But now he didn't know. Gideon had become hard and strange and certain in his course; when Gideon came here into this room and looked down at the dead man, not a muscle of his face had moved. He just stood there for about five minutes, staring at Marion Jefferson, and then he nodded and walked out. No word to Louise for her sorrow; no word to Brother Peter, no word to the children . . .

Gideon, Hannibal Washington, and Abner Lait stood on the veranda, talking about the things that had happened and the things that would happen, the things that had been done and the things that should be done. This was another night of moonlight, another night when the meadows and fields around the big house lay bathed in silver radiance. Down below them, just past the trees, they could see where the Klansmen had built fires. The fires ringed the house, but there were wide, dark spaces in between. All this early evening, Gideon had been thinking of Marcus. If everything had gone well, the boy should be back soon, unless he had stopped somewhere to sleep. He would not have much difficulty slipping past the Klansmen. Marcus was like a supple animal in the woods. Even if he had to leave the mare, he would easily come through to the house. But it would be more like him to dash through them and race up the slope. Gideon had warned the sentries. It made the inside of him go cold and sick and empty, just to think of anything happening to Marcus. He could never explain to anyone, not even to Rachel, how it was with him and Marcus, flesh of flesh, blood of blood; the most complete happiness he had ever known was to be with the boy, to hunt with him, to work with him, to sit and listen to the squalling of his accordion. With Jeff, it was different. He knew how different it was with Jeff.

Now Abner Lait was saying, "One dead ain't hopeless, Gideon, not against fourteen of them."

"One dead is the man of a family," Gideon said.

"It don't look like they'll attack again."

Hannibal Washington observed, "They stupid, but mark me, they going to learn. They frightened. They ain't got no guts to come into the place again, but maybe they bring up more men. They bring up six, seven hundred men, they find a way to do something, I swear."

"We were wrong on some matters," Gideon said. "It would be better if our men were upstairs, firing down. They couldn't take advantage of hummocks then. The women will be safer downstairs."

"I been figuring our shot," Hannibal said.

"I know."

Neither of them asked about Marcus, but Abner Lait said, "I stand a chance of getting through to Columbia, Gideon."

"We'll wait."

Abner Lait said, "I'm going to tell the men about the shot. Jesus God, they don't got to shoot unless they damn well see something to shoot at. Tonight they just shot off their guns like a pack of kids at a Fourth of July celebration.

"I want the dead buried tonight," Gideon said.

"Marion?"

"The others. I don't want the children to see it in the morning." And after a while, Gideon asked, "How many rounds have we, all told?"

"Ain't figuring shotgun shells?"

"For the rifles."

"About two thousand."

Gideon said, "Marcus will be back tonight, I know."

Later, Rachel came out on the porch where he was standing alone, and whispered, "Gideon?"

"Yes?"

She came over to him and pressed against his side. "Let me stay here, Gideon." He put his arm around her.

"Marcus will be back soon," he said.

"Why you sent him, Gideon?"

"Because I trust him the way I trust myself."

They stood there for a while, and then she asked, "Which way he come if he be coming, Gideon?"

"I don't know—whatever way is best."

"You think he'll come, Gideon?"

"I think so," he said.

"Whatever you say, Gideon. You say so, that way it comes."

He turned her around to him and said, "Rachel, honey, I love you."

She reached up to touch his face.

"Believe me, whatever happens, I always loved you. I became something I never wanted to become. The people needed someone, and I became what they needed, and when I became that, I turned into something strange to you. I couldn't help it; maybe if I were a better man, a stronger man—"

"You're a good man, Gideon," she whispered.

"I'm a makeshift. Maybe it's the strength of the people that they could take a thing like me and teach me what to do—and then I don't know. I don't know which way is best. Some day, there will be men who know, who understand why a thing like that out there should happen, who can work together, and plan, and build things that won't be burned down—"

"Gideon, child, honeychild," she told him, as she had in the old days.

Later on, she fell asleep, lying there in his arms on the porch. Gideon dozed a little, on and off. He was stiff when Hannibal Washington awakened him and said:

"It's come dawn, Gideon."

Then, like a cold, stabbing pain in his heart, it came to Gideon that Marcus would not return.

On that day, the second day, the Klansmen drew their line close. There were at least five or six hundred of them now, and they seemed to be better disciplined. They crawled within rifle range, dug holes in the ground, and kept up an intermittent, sniping fire. Two mules and a cow in the space behind the wagons were hit and had to be killed, but beyond that, not much damage was done. The women and children were brought down to the large reception hall, and the walls were buttressed with mattresses and planks. Gideon gave orders that no one should reply to the firing except Will Boone and Hannibal Washington, the two best shots. They climbed to the roof and lay there side by side, wetting their sights, hanging for as long as five minutes over a target, and then squeezing their triggers with infinite patience and care. Will Boone kept talking about his great-granddaddy, his great-granddaddy could bark a squirrel at a hundred yards, his great-granddaddy could do this and that, until finally, out of patience, Hannibal Washington demanded:

"Just who in hell is this great-granddaddy of yours?"

"Why you poor, dumb nigger, who in hell would he be with the name I got?"

But their sniping drew the concentrated attention of the Klansmen. Two or three hundred guns were turned on the roof-top. The bullets ripped through the base of the railing, sending splinters into their faces; about ten minutes of that before Hannibal Washington, sighing just a little, relaxed over his Spencer. Will Boone nudged him; then the white man began to curse, softly, steadily, firing while the rifle grew hot under his fingers. But in a little while his firing stopped too.

They buried their dead in the little compound where the cattle and horses and mules were. Curiously, no one cried now; the people watched with dry faces that were strangely old and hard; even the faces of the children were old. Brother Peter read from Psalms, "In my distress, I cried out unto the Lord, and he heard me." Gideon, watching, listening, tried to remember a time when there had been no Hannibal Washington, no small, gnome-like colored man, black as coal, gentle, wise, courageous, a man of great and incredible dignity, a man who could turn his hand to any trade, a man who was a repository for the misfortunes and complaints and problems of all the community. Now he lay in the warm Carolina earth, side by side with a white man whose great-grandfather had been Daniel Boone.

All through the night, the firing continued, but at dawn it stopped. In the silence, the people ate their breakfast. In the silence, Benjamin Winthrope read the children *The Legend of Sleepy Hollow*. In the silence, Jeff stood over the little, red-faced Klansman and watched him die, never knowing his name, where he came from, or what strange pressures had driven him here.

In the silence, Bentley walked toward the house with a white flag, and called out, "Can I come up?"

There was no answer. He advanced slowly and stopped about fifty yards away, shouting out what he had to say. The Carwell folk had a doctor, Jeff Jackson. Old Doc Leed was drunk as a lord and had been for a week. They, the Klansmen, had wounded. They had a man whose leg was broken and swollen. The leg had to come off or the man would die. Would Jeff Jackson come down and treat their wounded? He had their word he would be allowed to return.

Abner Lait stared at Gideon, and Gideon, smiling bitterly said, "You see, they understand us. They know us better than we know them."

Bentley walked away. Jeff came out on the veranda. "Did you hear that?" Gideon asked. Jeff nodded. Abner Lait said, "Let their God-damned wounded die."

Frank Carson said, "I swear to God, the next time that son of a bitch walks up here, I'm going to plug him."

"I'm going down there," Jeff said.

Gideon grasped his arm, swung him around, and cried, "You poor damn fool! My own son, too! Can't I make you understand this? Can't I make you understand that we're not dealing with civilized men, that we're not dealing with an enemy as you comprehend an enemy? Those men down there want to destroy us! They're not human as we think of human folk! Their word means nothing! Good and bad, in their eyes, does not exist! You cannot reason with them; they've corrupted reason! It's because we've misjudged them, because we were such fools as to consider them bound by the rules that bind men, because we laid before them, on a silver platter, decency, right, and justice, that we're here today. That's why they

are winning! That's why all over this southland of ours, good, decent men and women are cowed, divided, confused!"

"I'm going down there," Jeff said. "I took an oath, an oath to
heal, an oath to put together the things men break—"

"No," Gideon said. "I've lost one son. But at least he understood.
He knew what we fight."

"You'll have to kill me to keep me here," Jeff said quietly.

"So help me God—" Gideon began, and Abner Lait said, "Let
him go, Gideon."

Jeff finished the amputation and they took away the moaning,
half-conscious man. As Jeff wiped his hands, he said to the clump
of curious men who had been watching:

"He'll need rest now. Nature has to take its course. When the
dead tissue sloughs away, the sutures will come off easily. You test
them by pulling gently, very gently, for it's painful. When the
sutures come off, the basic healing is done. Any doctor can follow
up the treatment—unless poisoning sets in. That's the main danger."

He was tired; a plank in a field under the hot sun is not a place
to operate. He had treated a dozen wounded men. He was tired.
"I'll go now," he said.

"Sir!"

He was bending over his bag, closing it; he glanced up at the man
who had spoken, a broad-shouldered, sunburnt man whose hand
rested on the butt of a revolver.

"I said I'll go now."

"Sir."

Jason Hugar, standing beside Sheriff Bentley, said, "You're a doctor, Jackson. That's something that happened. When a nigger becomes a doctor, it's the sort of God damned thing that makes this
trouble we're having."

Jeff stared at him for a moment, then snapped shut his bag,
picked it up, and started to walk away. The broad-shouldered man
placed himself in Jeff's path.

"Sir," he said.

"What do you want?" Jeff asked.

"I want you to act as a God damned nigger should! Say *sir* when
you talk to your betters!"

Jeff looked at the man, half in curiosity, half in wonder. A part of him was fear, a part was horror; but more than that was a logical curiosity that operated in spite of himself, a desire to rationalize this man in front of him with what Gideon had said, with the whole insane pattern of what was happening at Carwell.

"You want me to say *sir*, is that it?"

"That's it."

"Sir," Jeff nodded, and added, "If you'll permit me to go, sir?"

Bentley laughed. Jason Hugar said, "You're not going, Jackson."

"What do you mean?"

"You're not going back, that's all."

Bentley interposed, "Tomorrow there won't be any need for you up there, Jackson. Better stay here."

Jeff watched them; still, fear was only a part of curiosity. The impossible did not occur in a scientific method. There was always a reason, always a cause. "I came here," he said, "because I felt it my duty to aid the hurt and the sick. Do you understand that? I came here because you asked me to come. As a doctor, I could not refuse. Can you, in all reason, demand that I stay here?"

The broad-shouldered man said, "*Sir*, you God damned nigger son of a bitch!"

Jeff shook his head. "I'm going." He pushed past the broad-shouldered man. That was all he knew, a memory that ceased to be a memory, an exploding crash that ceased as it came. He lay on the ground, his bag under him, and the broad-shouldered man said:

"That God damn nigger."

Rachel and Jenny sat with Ellen, but there was nothing they could say to her. Her blindness took in the whole world now; there was no edge to the darkness.

That night, Abner Lait told Gideon, "You know about Marcus."

"I know."

"Maybe he never sent the telegrams."

"Maybe he didn't," Gideon said. There comes a limit to hurt and a limit to pain.

"Somebody has to send them," Abner said evenly. "How in hell is anyone going to know that we're here? How in hell is anyone on this whole damned earth going to know what's happening here? Do we know what's happening anywhere else? They've sealed off this place; they've sealed it tigher than hell itself. Maybe everything in the South is sealed off that way. Maybe no one knows."

"Maybe," Gideon said.

"Write those telegrams again. I'll take them to Columbia and send them."

"And if they won't send them?"

"Then I'll take them clear to Washington."

"All right," Gideon said. "If you see it that way, all right."

Abner took the best horse, a fine large bay that had belonged to Hannibal Washington. To do the thing on foot would be hopeless; the only way was to ride through them; it could be done.

It might have been done, but they shot down the horse half a mile from the house, and Abner Lait lay under it with a broken leg. They took him out, held him upright for Jason Hugar to tell him:

"There's a special way for nigger lovers. Fred McHugh had a taste of it."

"Go to hell," Abner told him.

Abner Lait didn't speak again. They hanged him up by his hands and whipped him all through the night. Jason Hugar took a turn at the lash. "I'll make the son of a bitch talk," he said. But Abner Lait kept his lips closed. All through the following day, they let him hang there; but he was no longer conscious, no longer aware that his strength was part of the strength of many, no longer aware of the good fight that he had fought, of the good world of which he had seen a small piece, of the good comrades he had known.

Gideon watched them drag the howitzer into place the next day. It was emplaced a third of a mile away, and at first he had not known what it was. But the very fact that they had not fired on the house for almost twenty-four hours led him to expect something unusual. This was one of many possibilities. Frank Carson said:

"They must have got that from an arsenal somewhere."

"We're that important," Gideon said bitterly. There was nothing more beyond this. He was strangely calm as he told Benjamin Winthrope, "Take them all down to the cellar, all of them." You tried to put off the end; you continued to fight. You continued to hope; that was a process. Through all the terror, you realized that there was something beyond this, beyond the inevitable end; it gave you a link with others, with all the small, brave, frightened men who had held up their heads when the end was inevitable.

"It will be all right," Benjamin Winthrope said. "We'll sing. I'll keep them cheerful." He still wore his metal-rimmed spectacles.

"Thank you," Gideon said.

He stood on the veranda with Frank Carson, with Leslie Carson, with Ferdinand Lincoln, watching them try to find the range.

"They're no gunners," Leslie Carson said contemptuously.

The first shell burst a good hundred yards past the house and to one side. Four more shells burst wide of the house. Gideon called the men inside. They crouched behind the mattresses and planks, taking hopelessly long range shots at the gunners, careless of ammunition now, shooting because they had to strike back some way, had to resist. The first shell to strike the house burst on the floor above, showering them with plaster.

"Put up a white flag," Gideon cried. "Put it up, and we'll try to get the women and children out of here!"

Jake Sutter went out on the veranda with a white sheet. He stood there, waving it back and forth, while the Klansmen watched him and changed the angle of the howitzer, ever so slightly. The next shell burst square on the veranda, where he had been standing.

Brother Peter stood among the people, among the women and the young girls, the children and the boys who had just come into their troublesome and wonderful adolescence, among the girls whose fresh, firm new breasts stood like ripe apples under their frocks, among the grandmothers and the infants, among the suckling babes and the children who were just learning to mouth the mystery of words. He said to them, unafraid, "The Lord is my rock and my salvation, whom then shall I fear?"

The first shell burst overhead. Mr. Winthrope put his arms around the shoulders of a black boy and a little girl whose hair was like cornsilk.

"Of whom then shall I be afraid?" Brother Peter asked.

The people said, "Amen."

"The Lord is the strength of my life . . ."

Gideon's last memory was of the beginning, of how a people had been slaves, of how they had been bought and sold like cattle, of how their own condition had debased those other people whose skin was not black but who also worked with their hands, of how in this land there was little to hope for, of how in spite of that the people hoped.

Gideon Jackson's last memory as the shell struck, as the shell burst and caused his memory to cease being, was of the strength of these people in his land, the black and the white, the strength that had taken them through a long war, that had enabled them to build, out of the ruin, a promise for the future, a promise that was, in a sense, more wonderful than any the world had ever known. Of that strength, the strange yet simple ingredients were the people, his son, Marcus, his son, Jeff, his wife, Rachel, his daughter, Jenny, the old man who was called Brother Peter, the tall, red-headed white man, Abner Lait, the small and wizened black man, Hannibal Washington—there were so many of them, so many shades and colors, some strong, some weak, some wise, some foolish; yet together they made the whole of the thing that was the last memory of Gideon Jackson, the thing indefinable and unconquerable.

The men around the Carwell house, the men who hid their faces from the sun with white hoods, watched the old place burn. The wood was dry, and once the flame had started, nothing on earth could have put it out. All day long the house burned, and by night-fall, nothing was left except the seven tall chimneys that Hannibal Washington's father had built.

AN AFTERWORD

You may ask, and with justice, is there any truth in this tale? And if there is, why has it not been told before?

As to the first question, all the essentials of this story are true. There was not one Carwell in the south at that period, but a thousand, both larger and smaller. All that I have told about as being done at Carwell was duplicated in many other places. White men and black men lived together, worked together, and built together, much as I have described here. In many, many places, they died to-gether, in defense of what they had built. There are enough sources for the person who cares to check on these facts. On the Ku Klux Conspiracy, there is the testimony taken by the Joint Select Com-mittee to inquire into the condition of affairs in the late insurrec-tionary states, thirteen volumes of incredible material. There is the report of the Senate Committee detailed to inquire into the Mississippi elections of 1875, two volumes. There is Carl Schurz's report to Congress on Conditions in South Carolina, Georgia, etc. There is Hollowell's *Negro as a Soldier in the War of Rebellion.* There is *South Carolina During Reconstruction,* by Simkins and Woody. And that is only a beginning; there are the newspapers of the time; there are the Congressional debates: There are editorials, from both northern and southern papers, that showed complete awareness of the wholesale slaughter and destruction that was going on.

As for Gideon Jackson, he is a combination of several Negro statesmen of the time. All the things attributed to him were shared in good part by one or several of these men.

Carwell is an invented name. The people of Carwell, given names for this book, are taken from people who actually lived. Many of the other characters are real persons; some have been given fictional names.

The answer to the second question, why this has not been widely told before, is not complicated. When the eight-year period of Negro and white freedom and cooperation in the south was destroyed, it was destroyed completely. Not only were material things wiped out and people slain, but the very memory was expunged.

Powerful forces did not hold it to be a good thing for the American people to know that once there had been such an experiment— and that the experiment had worked. That the Negro had been given the right to exist in this nation as a free man, a man who stood on equal ground with his neighbor, that he had been given the right to work out his own destiny in conjunction with the southern poor whites, and that in an eight-year period of working out that destiny he had created a fine, a just, and a truly democratic civilization.

Spoil
the Child

THE FIRST morning Pa was gone, I tried to ride one of the mules. I didn't think that would hurt, because the mules were unharnessed anyway. But Maude told Ma, and Ma licked me. Ma was in the wagon, and she wouldn't have seen. I told Maude I'd remember.

Pa left about six in the morning while Ma still slept. "Goin' after meat?" I asked him. He had his rifle.

He nodded.

"Kin I go?"

"Stay with Ma, sonny," he said. "She ain't well."

"You said I could hunt—"

"You stay with Ma, sonny."

Maude got up a few minutes after that. I could see Pa like a black dot out on the prairie. I pointed to him.

I said, "That's Pa out there huntin'."

Maude was combing her hair, not paying a lot of attention to me. Then I tried to ride the mule. Pa would never let me ride his horse. It was only half-broken, cost four hundred dollars. Ma was always saying we could have lived a year on what that horse cost.

Maude woke Ma. My mother was a tall, thin woman, tired-looking. She wasn't well. I could see that she wasn't well.

"Dave, get off that mule," she said. "Where's Pa?"

"Went out to hunt."

"Come here. Can't ever get it into your head to behave." I went over, and she slapped my face. "Don't bother them mules. When'll he be back? We can't stay here."

"He didn't say."

"Get some chips for a fire," Ma told me. "My land, I never seen such a lazy, shiftless boy." But she didn't say it the way she always did, as if she would want to bite my head off. She seemed too tired really to care.

I guess Ma licked me every day. She said I was bad—a lot worse than you'd expect from a boy of twelve. You didn't expect them to be bad that young.

"You learn to leave the mules alone," Maude called.

"You shut up," I told her. Maude was fifteen, and pretty. She had light hair, and a thin, delicate face. Ma said that someday Maude would be a lady. She didn't expect much from me. She said I would be like Pa.

I walked away from the wagon, looking for chips. By now, Pa was out of sight, and where he had gone the prairie was just a roll of yellow and brown, a thread of cloud above it. It frightened me to be alone on the prairie. Pa laughed at it, and called it a big meadow. But it frightened me.

We had been on the prairie for a week now. Pa said in another few weeks we'd reach Fort Lee, due west. He said that if he had cattle stock, he'd settle down right on the prairie. This way, he'd cross the mountains, grow fruit, maybe, in California. Ma never believed much he said.

I went back to the wagon and started a fire. Ma had gone inside, and Maude sat on the driver's seat.

"You might gimme a hand," I told Maude.

"I don't see you overworking," Maude said.

"You better learn to shut up."

From inside the wagon, Ma yelled, "You hold you tongue, Dave, or I'll wallop you!"

"You're a little beast," Maude said.

"You wait," I told her.

I went to the keg, drew some water, and set it up to boil. I could tell by the sound that there wasn't a lot of water left in the keg. Pa had said we'd reach water soon.

When I came back to the fire, I glanced up at the sky. It was an immense bowl of hot blue, bare except for a single buzzard that turned slowly, like a fish swimming. I guess I forgot. I kept looking up at the buzzard.

Ma climbed down from the wagon slowly. "You're the same as your Pa," she said. "Lazy an' bad." Her face was tight-drawn. For the past few weeks she had hardly smiled, and now it seemed that she wouldn't smile again.

"And fresh," Maude said.

I put the water on the fire, not saying anything.

"Spare the rod and spoil the child," Ma said.

Then her face twisted in pain, and she leaned against the wagon. "Well, don't stand there," she told me. "Water the mules."

I went to the keg. I knew there wasn't enough water for the

mules. I hoped Pa would come back soon; I had a funny, awful fear of what would happen if he didn't come back soon. I kept glancing out at the prairie.

Pa had an itch in his feet. Ma said I would grow up the same way—having an itch in my feet. She was always sorry that she had married a man with an itch in his feet. Sometimes she said that the war had done it, that after the war between the North and the South, men were either broken or had to keep moving, like Pa. Always west.

We lived in Columbus. Then we moved to St. Louis; then to Topeka. Pa couldn't stop, and Ma got more and more worn out. She said that a wild land was no place to raise children. It was hard on Ma, all right. Pa didn't do much, except when we were moving west, and then he would be like a different person. Ma never complained to him. She licked me instead.

I gave the mules enough water to cover the bottoms of their pails.

Ma came over and said, "That's not enough water."

"There ain't a damn sight more."

"Don't swear!" Ma exclaimed. She clapped a hand across my head.

"He's always swearing," Maude said. "Thinks he's grown up."

Ma stared at me a moment, dully; then she went over and prepared breakfast. It was gruel and hardtack.

"Fresh meat would be good," Ma said. She looked over the prairie, maybe looking for Pa. I knew how much she cared for Pa. She would talk a lot about itching feet, but that didn't matter.

After breakfast, I gave the mules some oats, and Maude cleaned up the dishes. I kept glancing at Maude, and she knew what I meant. She didn't care, until Ma went back into the wagon. It hurt me to look at Ma.

"He'll be back soon, I guess," Ma said. Then she climbed into the wagon. It was a big sixteen-foot wagon, the kind they called freighters, with a hooped top, covered with dirty brown canvas.

Maude said, "You leave me alone."

"I'll leave you alone now," I told Maude. "I gotta leave you alone now. Maybe you know what's the matter with Ma?"

"That's none of your business," Maude said.

"It's my business, all right."

"You're just a kid."

I went to the back of the wagon and pulled out Pa's carbine. It was the one he had used during the war, a short cavalry gun.

Ma saw me; she lay inside, and I could hear her breathing hard. She said, "What're you up to now? Pa back?"

"Not yet."

"Well, you tell me soon as he gets back. And don't get into any mischief."

"All right."

In front of the wagon, I sat down on a feed box, and cleaned the gun with an old rag. Maude watched me. Finally, she said, "I'm gonna tell Ma you're fooling with Pa's gun."

"You keep your mouth shut."

Ma groaned softly then, and we both turned around and looked at the wagon. I felt little shivers crawl up and down my spine. Where was Pa? He should have been back already. I put down the gun and walked around the wagon. In a circle, the prairie rose and fell, like a sea of whispering yellow grass. There was nothing there, no living thing.

Maude was crying. "Why don't Pa come back?" she said.

I didn't answer her. I guess it occurred to me for the first time that Pa might not come back. I felt like crying. I felt like getting into a corner and crying. I hadn't felt so small for a long time. It would be a comfort to have Ma lick me now. You get licked, and you know you're a kid and don't have to worry about anything else.

I said to Maude, "Go inside the wagon and stay with Ma."

"Don't you order me around."

"All right," I said. I turned my back on her. I didn't hold much with girls when they're that age.

Then Maude went inside the wagon. I heard her crying, and I heard Ma say, "You stop that crying right now."

I loaded the carbine. I untethered one of the mules, climbed onto it, and set out across the prairie in the direction Pa had taken. I didn't know just what I'd do, but I knew it was time Pa came back.

It wasn't easy, riding the mule just with harness straps. Mules have a funny gait. And we didn't go very fast. I was glad Ma and Maude were in the wagon, otherwise Ma would probably lick the pants off me.

In about a half-hour, the wagon was just a tiny black dot. It might have been anything. I kept glancing at the sun to remember the direction I had taken. Then a swell hid the wagon. I kept on going. I knew that if I stopped, even for a little while, I'd cry my head off.

I saw a coyote. He stood like a dog and watched me. An antelope hopped close, and I might have shot at him. But I couldn't bring myself to fire a rifle there. It would have done something to me.

I found Pa. I guess I had been riding for about an hour when I saw him, over to one side. A buzzard flapped up, and I felt my throat tighten until I thought it would choke me. I didn't want to go over to him. I got down from the mule, and I walked over slowly. But I didn't want to; something made me.

He was dead, all right. Maybe it was Indians and maybe it wasn't; I didn't know. He was shot four times, and his gun was gone.

The buzzard wouldn't go away; I shot the buzzard. I didn't cry. The carbine kicked back and made my shoulder ache. I was thinking about how Pa always called me an undersized, freckled little runt. He said I wouldn't grow up. Maybe that's why I didn't cry.

I went away a little distance and sat down. I didn't look at Pa. I tried to remember where we were, what Pa had told me about going west. When I thought of Ma, I had a sense of awful fear. Suppose it happened now.

The mule walked over and nuzzled my shoulder. I was glad the mule was there then. If he wasn't, I don't know what I would have done.

Pa had to be buried. I knew that men had to be buried, but I couldn't do it. The prairie was hard, baked mud. I went back to Pa and stood over him; I guess that was the hardest thing I had ever done in my life. I straightened his clothes. I pulled off his boots. Men in the West were always talking about dying with their boots on. I didn't know what it meant, one way or another, but I thought Pa would be pleased if he didn't have his boots on.

Then I climbed up on the mule and started back for the wagon. I tried not to think that I was twelve years old. If you get to thinking about that, then you're no good at all. When I got back, Ma would lick me plenty.

The mule must have found its way back, because I didn't pay much attention to that. I let the reins loose, holding onto the harness straps, and I kept swallowing. Then I saw the wagon.

I thought, "I can't tell Ma now—maybe later." Nobody had ever told me about a thing like that, but I knew it wouldn't do to tell Ma now. I guess I only felt it instinctively, but I knew that the importance wasn't in Pa any more. All that was important was life, and life was just a fleck of dust in the prairie. It was like a nightmare to think of the distance of the prairie, and how we were alone.

I rode up to the wagon, and Maude and Ma were both standing next to it. I could tell from Ma's face how worried she had been about me.

"There he is!" Maude screamed.

Ma said, "I guess there ain't nothing a body can do with you, Dave. Get off that mule."

I slipped off, tethered the mule. My whole body was twisted up with the strain of keeping what I had seen off my face. I came over to Ma.

"Where you been?" she demanded.

"Hunting."

"I reckon there's nothing else for a little loafer like you. Spare the rod and spoil the child. Come here."

I went over and bent down, and she walloped me a bit, not too hard. She wasn't very strong then, I guess. I cried, but I wasn't crying because of the licking. I had had worse lickings than that and never opened my mouth. But it seemed to break the tension inside of me, and I had to cry. I went over and sat down with my back against one of the wagon wheels.

Maude walked past me and said, "I guess that learned you."

I just looked at her, without answering. I took out my jackknife and began to pare at one of the wagon boards. Then my eyes traveled to the water keg.

I got up and went around to Ma. She was still standing there, staring off across the prairie in the direction Pa had gone.

Without turning, she said to me, "Seen anything of your Pa?"

"No."

The sun was westward now, a splotch of red that blazed the whole prairie into a fire. I could get a little of how Ma felt; I could see the loneliness.

"Get a fire going," she said. "He ought to have enough sense to come back early. Stop that whimpering. God help a woman when a man has itching feet."

I gathered chips and started the fire. When I took water from the keg for mush, the keg was just about empty. I didn't mention that to Ma. She went about preparing supper slowly, awkwardly, and Maude watched her, frightened.

Ma kept glancing toward the west.

"Be dark soon," I said.

"Guess Pa'll be here any minute," Ma said dully. I could tell that she didn't believe that.

"I guess so," I nodded.

We ate without speaking much. Ma didn't eat a great deal. As soon as we had finished, she went into the wagon.

Maude was saying, "I don't see how I can clean dishes without water. You fetch some water, Dave."

"There ain't no water," I said.

Maude stared at me, her eyes wide and frightened. She had heard stories, just the same as I had, about travelers who ran out of water. She opened her mouth to say something.

"What about Ma?" I asked her quietly, nodding at the wagon.

"Why don't Pa come back?"

"Ain't no sense thinking about Pa if he ain't here. What about Ma? I guess it won't be long."

She shook her head.

"You don't need to be scared," I muttered. "It won't do no good to be scared. I reckon the worst part of this trip is over."

"Where's Pa?" she whispered. "What happened?"

"How do I know what happened? You girls make me sick. I never seen anything to beat you girls."

I got up and went over to the water keg. I shook it, hoping, without having any reason to hope. I knew it was just about empty. We had plenty of food—dried meat and meal and dried beans— enough to last a month, I guess. But Ma would need water.

Maude was crying.

"Why don't you go to bed?" I told her.

"Don't order me around."

"Well, you go to bed," I said. "Go in and sleep with Ma. I'll stay out here."

"You're not big enough to stay out here alone," Maude said, but I knew she was afraid to stay inside the wagon with Ma. I knew how she felt, and I didn't blame her for the way she felt, she was such a kid, with Ma petting her all the time. We couldn't talk it over between ourselves, and that would have made it a lot better. But we couldn't.

"I'm plenty big enough," I said.

Inside the wagon Ma groaned, and out on the prairie a coyote was barking. There's nothing like a coyote barking to make your insides crawl. I was all shivers, and I could see that Maude wanted to stay close to me. But that wouldn't have made it any better.

"Get in the wagon, damn you!" I cried. I was glad Ma couldn't hear me swear. Ma would lick me good and plenty when I swore like that.

Surprised, Maude stared at me. Then, without a word, she went into the wagon.

I stood there, outside, for a while. It had grown quite dark. In the sky there was a faint reflected light of the sun, but it was quite dark. I walked over to the wagon and picked up one of the mule blankets. It was a warm night, summertime; I decided to put the blanket under the wagon and lie down on it.

I heard Maude saying her prayers in the wagon, but no sound from Ma. I couldn't say my prayers. Usually, Ma saw to it that I did, but tonight I couldn't say a word aloud. I tried, opening my mouth, but no words came out. I thought them, as much as I could. I tried not to think about Pa. Spreading the blanket, I lay down on it, holding the carbine close to me. It seemed a part of Pa and all that was left; I hugged it.

I couldn't sleep. I tried for a long time, but I couldn't sleep. It was quite dark now, with no moon in the sky. The mules were moving restlessly; probably because they wanted water.

I think I dozed a little. When I opened my eyes again, the moon was just coming up, yellow and bloated. I felt chilled thoroughly. Bit by bit, what had happened during the day came back, and now it was all more real than it had been in the daytime. While I lay there, thinking about it, I heard horses' hoofs; at first not noticing them, and only becoming aware of them when the horses bulked out of the night, two men riding slowly.

They were in the moonlight, and I was hidden in the shadow of the wagon. They didn't see me. They stopped just about a dozen yards from the wagon, sitting on their horses and eyeing the mules. The mules moved restlessly.

When I realized they were Indians I couldn't move, just lay there and watched them. They were naked to the waist, with their hair in two stiff braids to their shoulders. They both carried rifles.

I thought of Pa. I thought of screaming to wake Maude and Ma.
I thought, "If they shot Pa—"

They were cutting loose the mules.

I felt for the carbine, twisted around, so I lay on my belly. One
of the men had dismounted and was coming toward the wagon.
He held his gun in one hand and had drawn a knife with the other.
I sighted the center of his breast and fired.

I remember how the sound blasted out the silence of the prairie.
In the wagon, someone screamed. The Indian stopped, seemed to
stare at me, swayed a bit, and crumpled to the ground. I remember
the sharp pain in my shoulder from the blow of the recoil.

The mounted man's horse had wheeled about. He pulled it back,
and fired at me. The shot threw sand in my face. I had a few
cartridges and caps in my pocket, and I tried frantically to reload.
The cartridges slipped through my fingers.

Then the Indian was gone. He had taken the other horse with
him, and I heard their hoofs thundering across the prairie. I
dropped the carbine. My shoulder ached terribly. Inside the wagon,
Maude was whimpering, my mother groaning.

I climbed from under the wagon. The Indian lay on his back, his
face hard and twisted. I stood there, looking at him.

Maude climbed down out of the wagon. "What is it?" she cried.
Then she saw the Indian and screamed.

"All right—I shot him."

She stood there, holding her hand to her mouth.

"You get back in the wagon. I guess he killed Pa, all right. Don't
tell that to Ma."

She shook her head. Ma was groaning. "I can't go back," Maude
said.

"Why?"

And then I knew. I should have known from the way Ma was
groaning. I went up to Maude and slapped her face. She didn't
seem to feel it. I slapped her again.

"Get in there with Ma."

"I can't—it's dark."

"Get in there!" I yelled.

We had lanterns on the outside of the wagon. I took one and
lit it. I wasn't trembling so much now. I gave the lantern to Maude,
who was still standing the way she had been before.

"Go inside," I said.

Maude climbed into the wagon, taking the lantern with her. Then I cried. I crouched under the wagon, clutching the carbine and crying.

Finally, I went over to the Indian. I forced myself to do that. He lay half across the rifle he had carried. I pulled it out, and it was my father's rifle, all right.

I don't know how long I stood there holding the rifle. Then I put it under the seat, along with the carbine. I didn't want to look at the wagon.

I walked over to the mules. It was hard to harness them. When it was done, I ached all over, and my shoulder was swollen where the carbine had rested.

I climbed to the driver's seat. The curtains were down, and I couldn't see into the wagon, but the light still burned. Taking down Pa's whip, I let it go onto the mules' backs. I had seen Pa do that and sometimes he let me try. The whip was fourteen feet long and I couldn't do much with it, but I got the mules moving. They had to keep moving. We had to find water.

At night, under the moon, the prairie was black and silver at the same time. Somehow, it didn't frighten me, the way it had during the day. I sat there thinking, I guess, of nothing at all, only awfully aware of the change inside me.

We drove on like that. I kept the mules at a slow pace, so the freighter wouldn't roll much. I was very tired, and after a while I didn't use the whip at all.

Then Maude came out of the wagon, sat down next to me. She looked at me and I looked at her, but she didn't say anything. She pressed close to me.

I whistled at the mules.

Inside the wagon something was whimpering. It made me tremble to hear that.

"Reckon we'll find water soon," I told Maude.

She nodded mechanically. Her head kept nodding and I dozed, myself. I guess I kept dozing through the night, fell asleep toward morning.

Maude woke me. The wagon had stopped, and the sun was an hour up. The mules had stopped on the bank of a slow, brown stream, lined with cottonwoods as far as I could see.

Maude was pointing at the water.

"Don't you start crying now," I said, rubbing my eyes.

"I won't," Maude nodded.

Ma called me, not very loud, "Dave, come here."

I climbed inside the wagon. Ma was lying on the bed, her arm curled around something. I peered at it.

"Do you know?" she said.

"I reckon I do. I reckon it's a boy. Girls ain't much use."

Ma was crying—not much; her eyes were just wetting themselves slowly.

"Where are we?" Ma asked me.

"We been traveling through the night. There's a river out there. I guess we don't need to worry about water."

"All night—Pa back?"

I said slowly, "I killed an Indian last night, Ma. He had Pa's gun."

Then she just stared at me, and I stood there, shifting from one foot to another, wanting to run away. But I stood there. It must have been about five minutes, and she didn't say anything at all. The baby was whimpering.

Then she said, "You harnessed the mules?"

"Uh-huh. Maude didn't help me—"

Ma said, "You don't tease Maude. You don't tease Maude, or I'll take a stick to you. I never seen a boy like you for teasing."

"Uh-huh," I nodded.

"Just like your Pa," Ma whispered. "It don't pay to have a man whose heels are always itching—it don't pay."

"No use cryin'," I said.

Ma said, "What are we going to do?"

"Go on west. Ain't hard now to go a few hundred miles more. Reckon it won't be hard. Pa said—"

Ma was staring at me, her mouth trembling. I hadn't ever seen her look just like that before. I wanted to put my head down on her breast, hide it there.

I couldn't do that. I said, "Pa told me. We'll go west."

Then I went outside. I sat down on the wagon seat, looking at the river. I heard the baby making noises.

I said to Maude, "A man feels funny—with a kid."